A SHIVER OF LIGHT

www.transworldbooks.co.uk

A SHIVER OF LIGHT

LAURELL K. HAMILTON

BANTAM PRESS

LONDON · TORONTO · SYDNEY · AUCKLAND · JOHANNESBURG

TRANSWORLD PUBLISHERS
61–63 Uxbridge Road, London W5 5SA
A Random House Group Company
www.transworldbooks.co.uk

First published in Great Britain
in 2014 by Bantam Press
an imprint of Transworld Publishers

A CIP catalogue record for this book
is available from the British Library.

ISBNs 9780593067468 (cased)
9780593067475 (tpb)

Addresses for Random House Group Ltd companies outside the UK
can be found at: www.randomhouse.co.uk
The Random House Group Ltd Reg. No. 954009

The Random House Group Limited supports the Forest Stewardship Council®
(FSC®), the leading international forest-certification organisation. Our books
carrying the FSC label are printed on FSC®-certified paper. FSC is the only
forest-certification scheme supported by the leading environmental organisations,
including Greenpeace. Our paper procurement policy can be found at
www.randomhouse.co.uk/environment

Typeset in Minion Pro
Printed and bound in Great Britain by
CPI Group (UK) Ltd, Croydon, CR0 4YY

2 4 6 8 10 9 7 5 3 1

To the fans who let me know
how much they missed Merry and her men.

You finally get to read the next part of the story.

ACKNOWLEDGMENTS

To my husband, Jonathon, partner, friend, lover, who stands by my side and behind the throne. Thank you for holding my coat. To Genevieve, who is both our beautiful maiden and able to grab her own sword and charge into battle. To Shawn, who stood at the battlements when the night was dark and the dragon was fierce. Dragon stew, at last! To Spike, who has entered the fray and proved himself stalwart and true. To Jess, who joined the team this book. To Will, who helped with research on the last book—so nice when friends have expertise that I need. To Pilar, my sister, so glad we're both happy, at last. Welcome to the family, Fran! To Missy, who keeps reminding me of things I've forgotten. To Sherry, Teresa, and Mary, who never give up trying to organize a houseful of artists. And to our dogs, Keiko, Mordor, and Sasquatch, who stayed at my side through all the long nights and early mornings, faithful to me, and their treat drawer.

I feel like one
Who treads alone
Some banquet-hall deserted,
Whose lights are fled,
Whose garlands dead,
And all but he departed!
Thus, in the stilly night,
Ere slumber's chain has bound me,
Sad memory brings the light
Of other days around me.

—THOMAS MOORE

CHAPTER

ONE

woke in the desert, far from home, and knew it was a dream, and that it was also real. I was dreaming, but where I stood was real and whatever happened here tonight, that would be real, too. Stars covered the sky as if electricity had never been invented, so that starlight was enough for me to see my way down the dirt road, with its bomb craters making it almost impossible for anything to drive down it. IEDs had blown the road to hell, partly to kill the soldiers in the armored vehicles that had triggered the bombs, but also to make the road impassable by anyone who came after them. I stood shivering in the cold desert wind, wishing I were wearing something besides the thin silk nightgown that strained over my very pregnant belly. I was only days away from giving birth to twins, and my body was mostly baby now. I moved slowly down the road and found the dirt cool underneath my bare feet. There was a small hut close to the road, and whatever had called me from my bed in Los Angeles was there. How did I know that? Goddess told me, not in words, but in that quiet voice that's almost always in our heads. Goddess and God talk to us all the time, but we are usually being too loud to hear them; in these dreams that "quiet voice" was easier to hear.

I knew my body was still asleep thousands of miles from here, and I'd never been hurt in any of the dream journeys, but I felt the rocks slide under my feet, and as pregnant as I was, my balance wasn't good. I had a moment to wonder what would happen if I fell, but I kept walking toward the hut, because I'd learned that until I'd helped the person calling me, the dream would remain, and I would remain in it.

It was my dream, but it would be someone else's nightmare reality. I was never called unless it was a matter of life and death. Someone who had saved my life, risking their own, and been healed by my hands was nearby and in need; that was always the way it was, who it was. They prayed and I appeared, but only if I was asleep, only in my dreams, so far. I had no idea if some night I would vanish in my real life to be called to someone's side while I was still awake. I hoped not. The dreams were disturbing enough; if it spread to my waking life, I wasn't sure what I'd do.

Soldiers prayed, and collected nails that had been used as shrapnel against me, and rubbed them with blood, and fit them onto leather thongs that they had made, and wore them as others wore a cross. The nails had come from my body, as had the blood, but magic had healed me. The Goddess had given me the ability to heal that night, and the soldiers who had taken the nails and worn them had started healing by touch, as well, in the far-off war. Sometimes their need was great enough to bring me to help them find a way out of an ambush, or shelter from a mountain blizzard.

I am Princess Meredith NicEssus, Princess of Flesh and Blood; I am faerie and only part human, but I am not a goddess, and I didn't like these midnight rambles. I liked helping people, but as I'd gotten more and more pregnant I had worried about the babies, and the men I loved had worried about it, but all they could do was watch over my body until I woke.

Still, the Goddess had work for me, and that was that, so I walked carefully over the smooth dirt and the rough stones, and felt the call, my call, as if I were truly some kind of deity able to answer prayers. Really I thought I might be more like a human saint; there were tales of saints being able to translocate through time and space. I'd done some reading on them, especially the Celtic ones, and there were some really odd stories. Quite a few saints had been Celtic deities that the human Church had adopted. The early Church had preferred to make friends of the local deities, rather than make war; it was so much easier to convert people when they could keep their local saint's day celebrations.

Some saints had appeared in people's dreams, or to lead people to safety, or even to fight in battles, when other witnesses knew they were asleep or wounded. None of the old stories talked about a pregnant faerie princess, but then the Church usually sanitized all the old tales.

The wind spilled my hair around my face in a mass of blinding red curls, though the color must have been more brown than scarlet in the starlit night. I could see nothing but the spill of my own hair for a moment, but when the wind cleared there was a figure in the doorway of the hut.

I didn't recognize her at first, and then the very darkness of her skin let me know that underneath the desert camouflage it was Hayes. She was the only female African American among my soldiers.

I went to her smiling, and she smiled back, as she began to slide down the edge of the doorsill. I wanted to be next to her, and I just was, without having to walk the distance. Dream rules worked sometimes in these journeys; sometimes they didn't.

I knelt beside her, having to grip the doorway to get to my knees. I was heavy enough with child that it was debatable whether I could stand again, but I had to touch Hayes, see what was wrong.

Her hand fell away from her neck and I caught the dull glint of the nail she'd been holding on to with its leather thong necklace. It was my symbol. I took her hand in mine and it was slick with blood. They had to touch the nail with blood to call me; that had been true every time.

"Hayes," I said.

"Meredith, I prayed and here you are. Wow, you're huge. Must really be twins like the news said?"

"It is. Where are you hurt?" I asked.

She patted her side with her other hand. Her armored vest was there, but it was wet, and even as I searched for the wound fresh blood welled out. I knew it was fresh because it was warmer than the stuff that had cooled in the night air.

"It's deep," she said, voice pained, as I tried to find the wound through her clothes and gear.

"What happened?" I asked. I wasn't sure that talking was good for her, but having something to think about while I found the wound and figured out what to do about it was better than just thinking about the fact that she seemed to be bleeding to death. Wasn't it? I'd been answering prayers for only a few months and I still felt out of my depth. I trusted Goddess to know what She was doing, but me, I wasn't so sure about me.

I prayed as I found the wound. It was almost as wide as my palm, and blood was welling out of it. Something that held a lot of blood had been punctured. I'd had human anatomy in college, but for the life of me, or for the life of Hayes, I couldn't seem to think what organ was on this side of the body. I didn't know what had been damaged, but I knew she was going to die if I couldn't help her.

"We were just supposed to take some supplies up to a school, but they ambushed us. The cutest little boy stabbed me, because I hesitated. I couldn't kill a child, or thought I couldn't, but they killed Dickerson, and Breck, and Sunshine, and then he tried to kill me, and suddenly he wasn't a child anymore, he was just another murdering bastard." She started to cry, and that made her groan with pain.

I prayed for guidance. I was trying to hold pressure on the wound, but without a medical kit, or the Goddess granting me the ability to heal with my hands, I couldn't save her. And then I realized that she, Hayes, had healed other wounded with her hands, because she'd told me so when she was on leave last time; had that only been two months ago?

"Heal yourself, Hayes," I said.

She shook her head. "I killed that little boy, Meredith. I killed him. I killed him, and I can't forgive myself. We killed the men before everyone but me died, but the boy . . . he couldn't have been more than ten. My little brother's age. Jesus, Meredith, how could I kill a kid?"

"He tried to kill you, Hayes, and if you don't heal yourself, he will have killed you."

"Maybe I deserve to die."

"No, Hayes, no you don't." I kept pressure on the wound to try to slow the blood loss while I helped her forgive herself, because I knew now that was why I was there.

She cried harder, and that made the wound hurt more and gush hot around my hands. She slipped lower in the doorway. She was going to bleed to death in front of me.

"Goddess, please, help me to help her."

I smelled roses and I knew the Goddess was with me, and then I felt/saw/knew that she would be standing over us. To me she was a cloaked figure, because Goddess comes to us all in different ways, or all ways.

Hayes looked up and said, "Grandma, what you doing here?"

"You let this woman heal you, Angela May Hayes. Don't you fight her."

"You don't know what I did, Grandma."

"I heard, but Angela, if a boy is old enough to pick up a weapon and kill you, then he's not a child anymore, he's a soldier just like you are, and you did what you had to do."

"He was Jeffrey's age."

"Your brother would never hurt anyone."

"Jeffrey was a baby when you died, how do you know?"

I felt the smile like the sun coming through clouds after a storm. You couldn't help but smile when the Goddess smiled. "I keep watch over my babies. I saw you graduate from college. I'm so proud of my angel, and I need you to live, Angela. I need you to go back home and help your mama and Jeffrey and all the rest, do you hear me, Angela?"

"I hear you, Grandma."

"You have to get better; you'll be my angel for real one of these days, but not tonight. You heal and go home to our family."

"Yes, Grandma," she said.

The blood slowed and then stopped pouring out. I hadn't done anything, but Angela Hayes had, and the Goddess had, and Hayes's grandmother had.

"I think I'm better," Hayes said, and grabbed my hand with hers. "Thank you, Meredith, thank you for bringing my grandma to talk to me."

"The Goddess brought your grandmother," I said.

"But you brought the Goddess."

I held her hand tight and said, "The Goddess is always there for you; you don't need me to find Her."

Hayes smiled and then frowned. "I see lights."

I glanced down the road and saw a line of armored vehicles of all kinds coming over the hill, their lights cutting the thick starlight so that the night seemed both more black and less at the same time.

"They talk about a red-haired Madonna that appears when people need her. No one seems to know it's you but us." I knew she meant the other soldiers.

"It's better that way," I said.

She gripped my hand tight. "Then you better go before the trucks get closer."

I touched her face and realized I still had her blood on my hands, so I left the bloody imprints of my fingertips on her skin. "Be well, be safe, come home soon," I said.

She smiled, and this time it was bright and real. "I will, Meredith, I will."

The dream broke while I was still holding her hand. I woke in my bed in Los Angeles with the fathers of my babies on either side of me. My hands and nightgown were covered in blood, and it wasn't mine.

CHAPTER

TWO

You'd think, after a goddess had sent me halfway around the world to save a life and brought me back to my own bed, that my life would be full of magic, and it was, but it was also full of normal things. That's what no one tells you: that even when Deity takes a hand in your life, and you answer their call, your ordinary life doesn't go away. I was still pregnant and it had not been a trouble-free pregnancy. If you are following Deity's plan for you, it isn't always the easy path; sometimes it's the hard one. So why follow? Because to do any less is to betray your own abilities and gifts, and the faith that Deity has in you. Who would do that willingly?

Ultrasound pictures are grainy, black and white and gray, and really not all that clear, but it's a way to get the earliest picture of your unborn child. We had quite a little album of the blurry images at thirty-four weeks into the pregnancy, but the latest one . . . it was the money shot, because it showed something the other ones hadn't: We were having triplets.

The twins, as we'd begun to call them, were still floating in front of the picture, but it was as if they were petals of a flower finally opening up enough to show a third baby, shadowy and much less distinct, but very there. The third baby was visibly smaller than the other two, which wasn't uncommon, Dr. Heelis, my main obstetrician, assured us.

We were all sitting in the conference room at the hospital now, because Dr. Heelis had been joined by Dr. Lee, Dr. Kelly, and Dr. Rodriguez. They each had their specialties in gynecology and delivering babies, or something else needed as a precaution. I hadn't gained most of the extra medical specialists since they spotted the third baby; they'd been my team almost from the beginning of my pregnancy, because I was Princess Meredith NicEssus—legal name Meredith Gentry, because *Princess* looks so pretentious on a driver's license. Dr. Kelly was the new face, but then what was a new doctor compared to a whole new baby?

I was the only faerie princess to be born on American soil, but not for much longer. One of the babies was a girl. My daughter would be Princess Gwenwyfar. We were still negotiating on the rest of her names, since we wouldn't know until DNA testing who her father was; I'd narrowed it down to six.

All six of them sat on either side of the long oval conference table, strung out like strong, handsome beads on the string of my love.

Doyle, Darkness, sat on my left. He was everything his name promised: tall, handsome, and so dark he was black. Not the way people's skin was black, but like a dog's skin and hair could be so black that it had blue and purple highlights in the sun. In the dimmer light of the conference room his skin was just unrelieved blackness, as if the darkest night had been carved into flesh and made real. His ankle-length hair was back in its usual braid so that his pointed ears with their edging of silver earrings showed. If he'd hidden the ears no one would have known he wasn't pure-blooded Unseelie sidhe, but he made sure the one sign that he wasn't pure sidhe showed most of the time in public. I'd never asked him why, but it was a constant slap in the face to every other sidhe who could hide their mixed heritage. He'd stood at the side of the Queen of Air and Darkness for over a thousand years with his less than pure genetics, flaunting them, and the glittering throng had feared him, because he had been the queen's assassin and captain of her guards. No one lived that Doyle was sent to kill. Now he was my Darkness, the Princess's Darkness, but he wasn't my assassin. He was my bodyguard, and he'd guarded my body well enough that I was pregnant with his child. That was some good guarding.

Frost, the Killing Frost, sat on my right. His skin was as white as mine, as though the luster of pearls had been made flesh, but whereas I was five feet even, Frost was six feet of muscle, broad shoulders, long legs, and just one of the most beautiful men in all of faerie. He wore only the upper part of his hair back, leaving the rest of it to fall around his body like a silver veil through which you could glimpse his gray suit, black shirt, and silver tie with black fleur-de-lis done small on the silver. The barrette that held the thickest of his hair back so that if there was a fight it would be out of his eyes was carved bone. It was very old, and he would never tell me what kind of animal it had been carved from. There was always the implication that it had been something that I would have considered a person.

Frost had been Doyle's second-in-command for centuries, and that hadn't changed, but now they were both my lovers, and potential fathers of the babies I carried. The three of us had found love, that true love that they write songs and poems about, but this fairy tale didn't have a happily-ever-after ending, not yet. As I sat there with my hands folded over the round tightness of my belly, I was scared. Scared in the way that women had been for centuries. Would the babies be all right? Would I be all right? Triplets? Really? Really? I didn't know how to feel about it yet, it was too new. I'd been happy about twins, but triplets—how much more complicated had the pregnancy and our lives just become?

I prayed to the Goddess for safety, wisdom, and just a calm center from which to listen to the doctors and the plan. I smelled roses, and I knew she'd heard me, and I knew it was a good sign. I hoped it was a good sign. I knew that sometimes bad things happened for good reasons, but I really, really wanted this to be one of the good things, period, with no caveats.

Doyle squeezed my hand, and a moment later Frost did the same. The men I loved more than anyone in the world were with me; it would be all right. The other men that I loved, but maybe not quite so much, were looking at the doctors and glancing at me, trying to be reassuring and not show that they were worried, too.

Galen was failing to hide his worry, but his face had always been a mirror for his heart. His pale skin had a faint green cast to it to complement the darker green of his short curls. He still had one long, thin braid, which was all that was left of his once-knee-length hair. A cream T-shirt made of silk embraced the lean muscles of his chest and upper body, an apple-green suit jacket that was his only concession to dressing up. The rest of his outfit was jeans, pale blue with holes worn through, giving tantalizing glimpses of bare flesh as he moved. The jeans were tucked seamlessly into brown tooled cowboy boots, which were new, and not his choice. We all represented the high court of faerie and we had to dress accordingly when we were likely to be photographed, and any trip to the hospital had the paparazzi out in droves.

The last of our happy, but tense, sextet of men were Rhys, Mistral, and Sholto. Rhys was mostly shades of white and cream from the waist-length white curls to the cream-colored suit and pale leather loafers hidden underneath the table. His open-necked dress shirt was pale blue and brought out the tricolored blue iris of one eye; the other eye was lost behind a pale blue satiny eye patch. It brought out the wonderful blues of his remaining eye but didn't hide the trailing scars that came from that empty eye socket. Goblins had taken his eye centuries before I was born. At five-six he was woefully short for a purebred sidhe, but still taller than my own humble five feet even. I was the shortest royal in either court.

Sholto was all long, straight white-blond hair in a curtain that almost obscured his black suit and white shirt with its high, round collar so no tie was needed. It wasn't this year's style, but he was King Sholto, Lord of That Which Passes Between, ruler of the sluagh, the dark host of the Unseelie Court, and he didn't really worry about this year's fashions. He wore what he liked, and it usually looked scrumptious on him, or scary, depending on the effect he wanted. The black made his tri-yellow-gold irises very bright, very beautiful, and very alien.

Mistral was the last of my would-be fathers. He was the tallest by a few inches, broadest of shoulders by a fraction, just a very big man, but the bulk of muscle and centuries of warrior training didn't help him be okay inside a man-made building with too much metal and technology for his fey sensibilities. Lesser fey have more trouble with such things, and Mistral was dealing the least well of any of my lovers with this extended stay in the human world. It showed in the hollow look around his eyes, their color that swimming yellow-green that the sky gets just before a tornado sweeps down from the sky and destroys everything in its path. He'd been a storm god once, and his eyes still reflected his moods as if the sky were still his to command. Centuries ago the true sky would have reflected his anxiety. His own black suit made his gray hair look almost charcoal dark, as it fell around his shoulders and swept below the table edge. He wore a white dress shirt half unbuttoned, tucked into his pants, but fanned open to reveal a hand-stitched linen under- shirt. The linen was from his old wardrobe. He'd found that wearing something that felt "normal" against his skin helped him deal better with all this frightening newness.

I sat there surrounded by some of the most beautiful men in all of faerie, feeling like a small, less than beautiful jewel in their midst, but it's hard to feel glamorous when you're eight months pregnant with triplets. I hadn't seen my feet in weeks. My back ached as if someone were trying to saw me in half about a third of the way up. It was the worst my back had hurt, as if now that my body knew it was carrying triplets it didn't have to pretend to be brave anymore.

"How could all the tests and ultrasounds have missed a third baby?" Galen asked.

Dr. Heelis, tall, with white hair cut short, smiled his best professional smile at us. He had to be sixty, but he looked about a decade younger with his handsome square-jawed face and clear gray eyes behind their silver-framed glasses.

"I won't make excuses, except that two large babies in a small space just hid the third. It happens sometimes when you have more than twins."

"Is that why there was that echo with the heartbeats a few weeks ago?" I asked. I shifted in my chair, but there was no true way to be comfortable. If my back had just hurt a little less, or the pressure had let up, I'd have felt better.

"It would seem so," he said.

"So all those tests that Merry and the babies had to go through were because you couldn't figure out there was a third baby?" Galen asked.

"We thought there was a heart issue with the twins, and it is possible that what we were picking up was the third baby's heartbeat."

"How did you miss this?" I asked, finally. Heelis had built up months of confidence, and now I doubted it all. Or maybe it was just the pain? I shut my eyes for a moment; it felt like someone was sawing my back in half and trying to push the pieces apart at the same time.

"Are you all right, Princess?" asked Dr. Lee, the only woman on the team.

I nodded. "My back hurts from all the weight. I'm tired of being pregnant."

"It's normal," she said, smiling. Her face was square and always pleasant somehow. Heelis exuded confidence, but Lee was calm, like the eye of the storm. I liked her for it, but then probably all her patients did.

"Multiple births are always a physical challenge, but for someone as petite as you, Princess Meredith, it can be more uncomfortable. We will do everything to make you as comfortable as possible."

"How about if Dr. Kelly just tells us why he's here?" My voice rose a little as if I were fighting not to yell at someone, and maybe I was. I just hurt, and I was just so tired of it all. One of the babies moved, rolling in their sleep, or maybe playing, I didn't know, but it was still an odd sensation for something to move inside me that wasn't me. It wasn't a bad feeling, but it was . . . odd.

Dr. Kelly was having trouble concentrating because he could see that Mistral's eyes were streaming with storm clouds, and a slight movement of wind, as if his irises were a tiny television set forever to the Weather Channel.

"Would Dr. Kelly be able to concentrate on his job if Mistral put his sunglasses on?" Galen asked.

Dr. Kelly startled, and said, "I'm so sorry, I was staring, I . . . I just . . . I'm terribly sorry."

Doyle said one word in his deep, thick voice: "Mistral."

Mistral fished a pair of expensive sunglasses out of his pocket and slid them on. They were silver, metal frames with mirrored lenses that reflected everything like a silver mirror. They looked incredibly sexy on him, but for right now, more importantly they hid his distracting eyes.

"Better?" Mistral asked.

"I do apologize, Prince . . . Lord . . . Duke Mistral, I just . . . I'm new to the team and . . ."

Mistral had surprised me by having a title of duke in his own right. We'd been told to trot out our titles for humans, so we had, but it threw the Americans who weren't used to titles.

"It's okay, Kelly," Dr. Heelis said, "it took all of us a few visits to adjust to the . . . view."

"Not to be rude, but why do we need yet another doctor?" Doyle asked.

Dr. Heelis folded his arms on the table, his hands very still; I'd come to recognize it as part of his "it will be all right, I'm here to reassure you" pose. It usually meant something was wrong, or might be wrong. So far the pregnancy had been remarkably problem free for twins, but we'd had several meetings where Heelis had reassured us as things happened that could have been scary but turned out not to be. Some potential problems that he'd wanted us to know about had fixed themselves with a combination of modern medicine and luck, or maybe it had something to do with me being descended from five different fertility deities. It meant I'd been able to carry twins with much less difficulty than most women, but it was also probably the reason we were now looking at triplets. That was really a little more fertility than I'd wanted.

"When I informed the other members of our team that Princess Meredith was having triplets, they all agreed that Dr. Kelly would be a good addition to our pool of knowledge."

"Why?" Sholto asked, and he seldom spoke in these meetings.

They all turned and looked at him, and then most looked away, except for Heelis, who managed to hold the weight of everyone's gaze without flinching; there was more than one reason he was in charge.

"King Sholto."

Sholto gave a nod to acknowledge his title, and as a sign for Heelis to proceed, which he did.

"First, I know that you were all hoping for a vaginal birth, and we were willing to try with twins, but triplets means it's a cesarean birth."

I must have looked unhappy, because Heelis looked at me. "I am sorry, I know you felt quite strongly about avoiding surgery, but with triplets we just can't risk it, Princess; I am sorry."

"I figured as much when we saw the third baby," I said. I leaned forward in my chair trying to find a more comfortable position, but there really wasn't one. Doyle changed hands so he could still hold my hand and also rub my back. Frost mirrored him and they rubbed my back as if they were hands from the same man instead of two different ones. They'd been best friends and battle buddies for hundreds of years; it meant they seemed aware of each other physically without having to look. It meant they could rub my aching back without bumping into each other's hands, and when the doctors lifted the moratorium on sex, they'd be able to prove that they mirrored each other there, too, again. The last insult had been the "no sex" rule starting a few months ago.

I held on to their hands tighter; it helped distract me from how uncomfortable I was. I wasn't sure why the idea of a cesarean birth bothered me, but it did.

"You do understand that too much could go wrong as the babies all crowd toward the birth canal," Heelis said.

I nodded.

"Whatever will keep Merry and the babies from harm is what we want," Frost said.

The doctor smiled at him. He liked Frost and Galen best for long eye contact, probably because their eyes were the closest to human-normal, gray and green.

"Of course, that's what everyone here wants." He did that reassuring smile that he must have practiced in the mirror, because it was a good one. It filled his own eyes with warmth, and just seemed to exude calm.

"But my question remains unanswered," Doyle said. "Why is Dr. Kelly here?"

"He has the most experience with birth delay of multiples."

"What is birth delay?" I asked.

"With a cesarean birth we might have the option of delivering the first two babies but leaving the third, smaller one in utero for a week or two. It's not a given, but often smaller size means certain systems might not be as developed, and this would give more time for the baby to grow in the perfect self-sustaining environment of the womb."

I just blinked at him for a few seconds. "Are you actually telling me that the triplets might have different birthdays by weeks?"

He nodded, still smiling.

"And if we can't delay the third baby's birth, what then?"

"Then we'll deal with whatever issues may arise."

"You mean we'll deal with whatever is wrong with the babies, especially the smaller . . . triplet."

"We don't like the word *wrong*, Princess, you know that."

I started to cry. I don't know why, but for some reason the thought of having two babies delivered and leaving the third inside me to cook a little bit longer just seemed wrong, and . . . I wanted it over with; I just wanted our babies to be all right and to be on the outside of me. I was tired of being pregnant. I couldn't see my feet. I couldn't tie my own shoes. I couldn't fit behind the wheel of a car to drive myself anywhere. I felt helpless and bloated like a tiny beached whale, and I just wanted it over. Even though nothing had actually gone wrong, the doctors had still warned us about every awful possibility, so that my life had become a list of nightmares that never happened while the babies grew inside me. I was beginning to think I'd had too many good doctors and too much high tech, because there were always more tests, even though in the end all the tests told us was what wasn't wrong. Or maybe they'd missed something and it was all going to go wrong. They'd missed a whole third baby; how could I trust any of them anymore? All the months of confidence building and trust in my doctors was in ruins. I was having triplets. The nursery was done, but we had only two cribs, two of everything. We weren't ready for triplets. I wasn't ready.

I was screaming quietly into Doyle's shoulder while everyone ran around trying to calm the crazy pregnant woman when my water broke.

THREE

His name was Alastair, and he fit in my arms as if he'd been carved from a missing piece of my heart. He blinked up at me with huge liquid blue eyes set like shining sapphires in the pale, luminescent skin of his face. His hair was thick and black, and one tiny, slightly pointed ear was as black as his hair. The curled tip was almost lost in the midnight straightness of his hair. The other ear was like a carved seashell, shining mother-of-pearl set in the velvet of his hair.

All the exhaustion, all the pain, the panic of finding that Gwenwyfar was too far into the birth canal for a c-section, and her brother, Alastair, came so close behind her there was no time, and it was all lost on the wonder of tracing that tiny ear down through Alastair's hair to find that the black of the one ear trailed down onto the side of his neck, like a spot on the side of a puppy's ear.

Doyle was still in his surgical scrubs, pink against his shining black skin. He traced the side of Alastair's neck and said, "Do you mind?"

It took me a moment to understand the question, and then I blinked up at him, like I was waking from a dream. "You mean the spot?"

I smiled up at him, and whatever he saw made him smile back. "He's beautiful, Doyle; our son is beautiful."

I got to see what very few had ever seen: The Darkness cried as he turned our tiny son gently in my arms so that he could show me a black star-shaped mark on his tiny back. It was a five-pointed star, almost perfect, taking up the middle of his back.

Alastair made a protesting sound, and I turned him back so I could see his face. The moment he had eye contact again, he quieted and just studied my face with those solemn blue eyes.

"Alastair," I said, softly. "Star, our star."

Doyle kissed me softly, and then kissed his son's forehead. Alastair frowned at him.

"I think he's already competing for Mommy's attention," Galen said from the other side of the bed. He had Gwenwyfar wrapped in a blanket, but she was already pushing at it with all the strength of her small legs and arms.

"She doesn't like being swaddled," Rhys said, and took her from Galen's so-careful arms, and began to unwrap her from the careful swaddling the nurses had done.

"I'm afraid I'll drop her," Galen said.

"You'll get better with practice," Rhys said, and he grinned down at me and helped slide Gwenwyfar into my other arm, but with a baby in each arm I couldn't touch them, look at them like works of art that you wanted to see every inch of, explore, and memorize.

They both stared up at me so seriously. Gwenwyfar was bigger just at a glance, and one pound made a big difference in newborns, but she was longer, too.

"So you were the little troublemaker who couldn't wait to get out," I said, softly.

She blinked deep blue eyes up at me, and there were already darker blue lines in her eyes; in a few days we'd see what her tricolored irises would look like. Right now they were baby blue, but if she took after Rhys maybe it would be three shades of blue? Her hair was a mass of white curls. I wanted to touch her hair, feel the texture of it again, but I was out of hands.

Dr. Heelis was still squatted between my legs, stitching me up. It had all happened too fast. I was numb, not from drugs, but just from abuse of the area. I felt the tugging of what he was doing, but the baby took all my attention—babies.

Gwenwyfar flailed a small fist as if trying to reach my hair, though I knew it was too early for that, but something caught the light on that small arm like gold, or quicksilver.

"What is that on her arm?" I asked.

Rhys lifted her arm out of the blankets and let her wrap one tiny fist around his fingertip, and as he moved her arm we saw a trace of almost metallic lace. It was forked lightning traced like the most delicate gold and silver wire across her arm, almost from shoulder to wrist.

"Mistral, you need to see your daughter," Rhys said.

Mistral had huddled at the edge of the room through everything, terrified and overwhelmed the way some men are, and suffering in the presence of too much technology.

"There is no way to know who belongs to who," he said.

"Come see," Rhys said.

"Come, Mistral, master of storms, and see our daughter," I said.

Doyle kissed me again and lifted Alastair up to make room for me to hold our daughter. She kept Rhys's finger in a tight grip, so Mistral came to the other side of the bed. He looked scared, his big hands clasped together as if he were afraid to touch anything, but when he looked down and saw the lightning pattern on her skin he grinned, and then he laughed a loud, happy chortle of a sound that I'd never heard from him before.

He used one big finger to trace that birthmark of power, and where he touched Gwenwyfar tiny static bolts danced and jumped. She cried, whether because it hurt or scared her I didn't know, but it made him jerk back and look uncertain.

"Hold your daughter, Mistral," I said.

"She didn't like me touching her."

"She'll need to start controlling it; might as well start now, and who better to teach her." Rhys handed Gwenwyfar to Mistral while he was still protesting.

Without a baby to distract me, I was suddenly aware that I was getting more stitches than I'd ever had in my life, in a part of my body where I'd never wanted any stitches.

"How is Bryluen?" I asked, and I looked to the incubator where our smallest baby lay. There were too many doctors, too many nurses huddled around her. I had concentrated on the two babies I had; I'd known that there was a third baby only an hour before it all started, but somehow seeing her, so tiny, with her curly red hair, body almost as red as her hair, as my hair, I wanted to hold her, needed to touch her.

Dr. Lee came with her black hair peeking out of her scrubs, but her face was too serious. "She's five pounds; that's a good weight, but she seems weeks younger than the other two developmentally."

"What does that mean?" Doyle asked.

"She's going need to stay on oxygen for a few days and be fed fluids. She won't be able to go home with the others."

"Can I hold her?" I asked, but I was scared now.

"You can, but don't be alarmed by the tubes and things, okay?" Dr. Lee smiled, and it was totally unconvincing. She was worried. I didn't like that one of the best baby docs in the country was worried.

They wheeled her over, and five pounds might be a good weight, but comparing it to the six and seven that Alastair and Gwenwyfar had made her look tiny. Her arms were like little sticks too delicate to be real. The tubes did look alarming, and the IV in her little leg didn't look like birth, it looked more like death. The aura that blazed around the other two babies was dim in this tiny spark of a baby.

Frost stood on the other side of the tiny incubator with tears shining unshed in his gray eyes. We'd had no third name, so he'd wanted Rose, after a long-lost love and a long-lost daughter. *Bryluen* was Cornish for "rose." It had seemed perfect for our tiny red-haired daughter, but now I watched the fate of those earlier lost roses in Frost's face and it tightened my chest, and made me afraid.

Doyle took my hand in his, and asked, "Dr. Lee, is it just her size that makes you believe she's developmentally behind the other two?"

"No, it's her test scores. She's just not as engaged as the other babies are, very much as if she's simply a few weeks behind them. We'll use the technology to make up for what she didn't get inside you."

"And she'll be all right then?" I asked.

Dr. Lee's face fought between cheerfully blank and something less pleasant. "You know how this works, Princess; I can't say that with absolute certainty."

"Doctors never guarantee things, do they?" I asked.

"Modern doctors do not," Doyle said.

"But then modern doctors aren't likely to be executed for saying they can cure the princess and then failing," Rhys said. He came with a smile to help cheer the gloomy bunch of us. Galen was normally cheerful, but not about our little Rose; Frost was usually the gloomiest man in my life, and Doyle was a serious person. I'd just given birth to triplets. I was allowed to be worried.

Dr. Lee looked at him as if she didn't find his joke funny at all. "Excuse me?"

He grinned at her. "Trying to lighten my partners' moods; they are determined to think the worst."

"Look at her," Galen said, motioning at the tiny, tiny infant.

"Remember what my specialty is," Rhys said. "She doesn't shine as bright as the others, but neither does she have a shade around her. She is not dying. I would see it."

Doyle's hand tightened on mine, and he said, "Swear it, by the Darkness That Eats All Things."

Rhys looked very serious then. "Let me swear it on the love I bear Merry, our children, and the men in this room, the men and women who are waiting for news at the home we have all built. Let me swear on the first true happiness I have known in lo these long, dark centuries, our little Rose will not die here like this; she will grow strong and crawl fast enough to frustrate her brother."

"You see this in the future truly?" Frost asked.

"Yes," Rhys said.

"I don't understand anything you're talking about, but did you threaten our lives if the baby doesn't live?" Dr. Lee asked.

"No," Rhys said. "I just wanted to remind my family here that modern medicine can do wonders that even magic could not do once, and to have faith. The bad old days are past; let us enjoy the new good days."

Doyle and I both held our hands out to Rhys, and he came to take them both. He laid a kiss on mine, then did the same to Doyle. "My queen, my liege, my lover, my friend, let us rejoice and chase despair away from this day, as we chased it from each other this year past."

Galen went around and hugged Rhys from the back, which turned Rhys laughing to hug him back. It made us all laugh a little, and then the nurses were putting the tiniest of babies in my arms. She was so light, birdlike, and dreamlike. It reminded me of holding one of the demi-fey, those of faerie that look like butterflies and moths, but who feel more like the hollow bones of birds when they land and walk upon you.

Bryluen had tubes coming out of her nose trailing to her oxygen, and an IV in her tiny leg, like the one in my arm. Even with Rhys's reassurance, she looked injured. She was loosely wrapped in one of the thin blankets, and everywhere her skin touched mine she burned as if with fever.

Bryluen started to cry, a high-pitched, thin, and piteous sound that only the very youngest infants make. I knew something was wrong just by her cry. I couldn't explain it, but something the doctors were doing wasn't the right thing for this one.

"Doyle, help me unwrap this blanket. She doesn't like it."

He didn't question it, just helped me unwrap Bryluen, and it was as we lifted her gently that my hand crossed her bare back and found something unexpected. I raised her against my shoulder, one hand firm to support her head, and the other her lower body, so that I could see what my hands had felt.

Scales graced almost the entire back of her body, trailing down into the tiny diaper. They weren't the rainbow scales of a snake like Kitto had on his back, but more like the wide, delicate scales on a butterfly or moth wing, except these were impossibly large, bigger than any natural butterfly on the planet.

Doyle traced one big, dark finger down the brilliant pink-and-seashell shine of the scales that trailed like a cape from her thin shoulders to sweep down her miniature waist and be lost underneath the diaper.

"They're wings," he whispered.

Frost was on the other side of the bed, leaning over to draw his own large hand gently down Bryluen's back. "Wings more real than Nicca's. They are raised above her skin, not like a tattoo."

Galen leaned in to touch the miracle of shining proto-wings. "They don't look like any insect I've ever seen," he whispered.

Mistral came close with Gwenwyfar held in his arms as if she'd always been there. Frost moved up beside them, touching a hand to Gwenwyfar's white curls and gazing down at Bryluen. "I have not seen dragon wings on our demi-fey since I was not the Killing Frost, but only little Jackul Frosti."

Sholto came closer and said, "They look almost like the wings of a baby nightflyer, but light and jewel-bright instead of dark and leathery."

It was when I brushed her tight red curls near her forehead and found the buds of antennae that I understood. "Get the plastic out of her, now!" I held her out to the doctor.

"Without extra oxygen and feeding tubes she will not survive."

"Do you see the wings and the antenna buds? She's part demi-fey, part sluagh, a part of faerie that doesn't do well around metal and man-made things. If you keep putting artificial things into her, she will die."

"You mean she's allergic to man-made plastics?"

"Yes," I said, not wanting to waste time to explain the unexplainable.

Dr. Lee didn't argue but took Bryluen, and she and the nurses began to strip out everything they'd put in. The baby cried piteously as soon as they took her from me, and it made my heart ache to hear it. The other two babies started to cry as if in sympathy.

Rhys picked Alastair up from the nurse and seemed to know just how to hold him so that the baby just watched everything with dark solemn eyes, as if he understood more than he could say yet. Gwenwyfar just tried to yell loudest no matter what Mistral did.

"You never mentioned a family allergy this severe," Dr. Heelis said, and he looked angry.

"Give her to me, please; it's important that she just touch natural things," I said.

I think they were sending for different things to use on Bryluen and gave her back to me simply as a delay while they rushed around. They gave her back to me nude, because the diaper was man-made, too. I held my tiny naked daughter and could feel that the wings went almost all the way down the back of her body, and they were raised above her skin, part of her, not just a design.

I didn't think I had any demi-fey in my genetics, but I knew that the demi-fey could die in the city, fade and just die from too much metal, too much plastic, too much garbage. I gave her the only thing I knew was absolutely natural. I turned her so that tiny rosebud of a mouth could nurse.

"She's too small," one of the nurses said, "she'll never latch on enough to feed."

Bryluen did look impossibly small against my swollen breast, but she latched on tight enough for me to almost say *Ow*, but it was a good sign. I felt her begin to feed and it was the most amazing sensation. I watched her delicate throat, almost bird thin, swallow convulsively over and over as if she couldn't get enough. My other breast began to leak in sympathy.

Mistral handed Gwenwyfar to me, though it took him, Frost, and me to get our other girl into the twin football hold that I'd been practicing for months in preparation for twins. I realized as the two girls settled in to nurse that I needed an extra breast. I had triplets; there was no hold for triplets.

As if on cue, Alastair began to cry, wanting his share. I had no idea what to do about it, but as I felt Bryluen drink hungrily, strongly at my breast, I was too relieved to worry that much. Gwenwyfar and he could take turns until Bryluen caught up. A nurse handed Rhys a bottle, and just like he'd practiced in class, he fed our son. Alastair didn't seem to mind that he was sucking on something plastic and man-made. All three babies sank into a happy, satisfied silence, and looking around at the men in my life I knew we might need at least two more fathers to round out my men. I'd had sex with one demi-fey and one snake goblin while I was already pregnant with the twins, so I thought I didn't need protection. I was already pregnant, as safe as a girl could be, but as I felt the first tiny flexing of those wings on Bryluen's back, I knew that I needed two more men to come see their daughter.

I was descended from a handful of fertility deities, but I guess I really hadn't understood what that meant. I mean, there was fertile and then there was being able to get pregnant while you were already pregnant. I started to laugh, and the laughter turned into happy tears. One of my daughters had wings; maybe she would be able to fly?

CHAPTER

FOUR

They say you have no sense of smell when you dream, but I woke to the scent of roses and had a moment of wondering why the dim hospital room smelled like wild roses in the noon warmth of a summer meadow. The room was almost in darkness except for night lights underneath a shelf and one near the only inner door, which led to a bathroom. But I saw a pale, fluffy cloud across the room from where I lay in the bed. Galen was asleep in a chair underneath the cloud, which wasn't a cloud at all, but the massed blossoms of a small fruit tree that had grown behind his chair. I'd seen temporary plants grow like this from too much magic in a place, but to my knowledge we hadn't done magic. Maybe I'd missed something while I slept, or maybe surprise triplets were magic enough. Galen had one hand inside the plastic crib beside him. I couldn't tell in the dim light which of the bigger twins lay inside the blanket, but Galen's hand was resting on the tiny form, as if even in his sleep he had reached out to our child.

It made me smile. Galen might not be the best warrior of my men, and he was a terrible politician, but it didn't surprise me at all that he would be good at this part.

The sound of movement beside me made me turn and find another plastic crib on its tall wheeled legs beside me. There was a woven basket with little handles for carrying inside the plastic so that Bryluen wouldn't touch the man-made things that seemed to hurt her. There were wings softly flexing inside the blanket with her, more than just Royal and his sister Penny, who had come to visit his daughter, and her niece.

I smelled roses even more strongly and looked up to find that there were rose vines growing above my bed, like a living canopy of thorns and pale flowers, starlike in the darkness. I smelled the sweetness of apple blossoms now, and knew what kind of tree grew across the room.

I wondered what the nurses thought of the new decorations. There were moths fluttering in the flowers above me, and I could see the movement of them in the blossoms across the room now, but I knew they only looked like moths. Dozens of demi-fey fluttered in the new garden, but they weren't just sipping nectar and pollen, they were guarding, and they were attracted to this new magic like an ordinary moth drawn to a light.

I glanced to the far side of the room and found Rhys on the couch, asleep on his back with Gwenwyfar across his chest. Her white curls looked so very like his in the dim light. One of her small fists was wrapped around his finger, as if they held each other even in their sleep.

Sholto sat artfully slumping in a chair with his back to the room's only window. He'd changed clothes since last I'd seen him, because his clothes were dark enough that they blended in with the darkness, leaving his long hair to gleam like a pale yellow curtain around the darkness of the rest of him. His eyes were pale, but I wouldn't have wanted to guess at their color in this light. Nothing human had yellow eyes like his; they were just some pale color, but not as pale as his white, white skin, which gleamed like Rhys's and the baby's hair in the near-blackness of the room.

The wall behind him moved. I had to narrow my vision and concentrate to see that it wasn't the wall that was moving, but that there was a solid sheet of nightflyers hanging on the wall like giant bats, though even bats wouldn't be able to hang flat against a smooth modern wall, but then bats didn't have tentacles with suction on them and the nightflyers did. Their fleshy bodies framed the window and clung halfway across the ceiling. Once they'd chased me like the nightmares they appeared to be, but now the nightmares were on my side, and I knew that while they were in the room almost nothing in this world, or the next, dared to attack us.

A tentacle much bigger than anything the flyers could boast waved at the window behind them all. That let me know that more of the sluagh was on guard outside our room. We had powerful enemies, but we hadn't needed this much overt protection since we escaped from faerie and came back to California to have the babies.

I had to fight to keep my voice soft, not wanting to wake anyone, but needing to ask, "What's wrong?"

Sholto blinked at me, and there was a shine to his eyes as if they'd caught what little light there was in a way that human eyes did not reflect. He sat up a little straighter, and I could see the gleam of jewels against the black of his shirt. The necklace covered most of his upper chest. It was a piece that even the Hollywood elite wouldn't have worn. They were jewels meant for a king, which he was, King of the Sluagh. I'd seen him wear the piece in the high courts of faerie when he was reminding other nobles that he wasn't just another lordling, or even princeling. Short of wearing his crown he was declaring himself king; the question was, why? Or rather, why now?

My heart sped at the sight of the jewels, because he might bring the sluagh out to warn enemies not to try us, but to dress as a king. . . . It was a very short list of situations he would do that for.

He smiled almost too faintly for me to see it in the dimness. He spoke quietly, too, the way you do around sleeping people. "Why should anything be wrong, Merry?"

"It shouldn't, but it is," I said.

"We are your bodyguards, sweet Merry; becoming fathers does not change that. I merely watch over your slumber, and that of our children, and my fellow fathers."

"You are wearing court clothes and kingly jewels, something I've only seen you do in the high courts of faerie. You don't waste such finery on the human world, or on me."

"When you are recovered and the doctors free you of restrictions, I would gladly wear all this to your bed."

I glanced up at the clinging nightflyers, which he was totally ignoring, as if I couldn't see them.

"You do know that I see the nightflyers, right?"

He grinned then, and shook his head. "I am not trying to hide them from you."

"Could you, if you wished?"

He seemed to think about it, and then said, "I believe so."

"Could you hide them from the queen herself?"

"I do not want to hide them from her," he said.

I smiled then. "So that is why the show of force. The queen has threatened us."

He sighed, frowned, and fidgeted in his chair, which he didn't do often. "I was told not to worry you."

"Who by?" I asked.

"Doyle—you know it was him, or I wouldn't have tried so hard to obey him. He is technically the captain of your guard, and when in the Unseelie Court my captain."

"You are the Lord of That Which Passes Between in the Unseelie Court, but you sit here now as King Sholto, ruler of the darkest part of the Unseelie host. What did our queen do, or say, to warrant this show of force, Sholto?"

"Doyle will be unhappy with me if I tell you."

"Just Doyle?" I asked.

He smiled again. "No, not just Doyle, but I am not worried about Frost."

"You think you could take my Killing Frost in a duel, but not my Darkness," I said.

"Yes," Sholto said. It was interesting that he didn't try to equivocate or salve his ego. It was just a statement of fact; he feared Doyle's prowess in battle, but not Frost's. "But your using their more fearsome nicknames is also a show of force, my dear Merry."

"Why do you say, 'my dear Merry,' as if it's not true?"

"Because I am no longer certain that any of the babies are mine."

I frowned at him. "Goddess showed me that you were one of the fathers."

"Yes, but She did not show me, and I see none of my father's bloodline in any of the triplets."

His father had been a nightflyer like those that clung in alien layers to the wall and ceiling of the room. He wasn't the product of rape, either, but of a highborn sidhe woman wanting a night of perverted pleasure. To be willing to sleep with the monsters of the sluagh was one of the few things that even the Unseelie Court saw as perverse. As Doyle had been the Queen's Darkness for centuries, and Frost her Killing Frost, so she had nicknamed Sholto her Perverse Creature, but where I could call the other two men by those pet names, I could not do the same for Sholto. He had hated being called her Perverse Creature and feared that someday as Doyle was simply her Darkness, so he would become her Creature, or just Creature.

Sholto looked as handsome and perfect as any of my sidhe lovers, but once he had not. Once, from about midchest to just above a truly beautiful groin, had been a nest of tentacles identical to those on the underside of the nightflyers that clustered around him. Magic and the return of the blessings of Goddess and Her Consort, the Gods that had long withheld their favors from the sidhe, who had been worshipped as deities themselves, had given Sholto the gift of being able to turn the tentacles to a tattoo. Before that he had been able to hide them visually with glamour, that magic that faerie used to trick the eye of mortals, but it had been an illusion, a trick, and the first time I'd touched him with the mass of tentacles touching me, I hadn't been able to work past it for sex. Now Goddess had given him the body that the rest of him promised, and I'd learned that all those extra bits had pleasures of their own that no more humanlike body could give. I went to his bed joyfully now, and he valued that I loved all of him physically with no squeamishness. I was the only other sidhe lover he'd ever had, because the rest of the courts feared him as proof that the noble blood was wearing thin and we would all be monsters someday, as they feared my mortal blood as proof that their immortality would be the next to vanish.

"I think you're overly sensitive about your father's genetics, and you might want to ask yourself if your new ability to make your wonderful extras into a true tattoo might affect the children, too."

His face grew serious as he thought about my words. He was a serious man as a general rule, and thought about, or even overthought, most things.

"You may be right, but I don't seem to feel the connection to the babes that others of your lovers feel."

"Have you held any of the babies?" I asked.

"All of them," he said. "I felt nothing except that I was afraid I would drop them. They are so small."

Galen's voice came thick with sleep, and soft as if he were whispering to not wake the babe beside him. "I was afraid I'd drop them, too, but I worked through it. Once I got over feeling like I didn't know what I was doing, it was wonderful."

"I did not find it so," Sholto said.

"You didn't stay and take care of them, the way most of us did. I think because they didn't come out of our bodies, fathers have to work harder at feeling connected."

Galen sucked at court politics, and at a lot of stuff that the other men in my life were good at, but most of the men wouldn't have had that insight. It was a good insight.

"I hadn't thought about how hard it might be for all of you to feel connected to the babies," I said.

Galen smiled. "You've felt connected to them for months, but then you have been holding them more intimately than we ever can."

Sholto asked, "Are you saying that you did not feel connected to the babes at first either?"

"Not like I do after having held them, cuddled them, and helped give bottles. There was a moment when Alastair looked up at me with those dark eyes, so like Doyle's eyes, but that was okay, he was suddenly my son, too."

Rhys's voice came even and quiet. I think he was trying not to wake the baby sleeping on his chest. "I had the same moment with Gwenwyfar. She's obviously Mistral's daughter, but now she's mine, too."

"Wait," I said. "I thought we decided to call her Gwennie, when I went to sleep."

"She liked Gwenwyfar better," Rhys said, matter-of-factly.

"Gwennie wouldn't stop fussing, but the moment Rhys called her Gwenwyfar she stopped," Galen said.

I frowned at him. "She's too young to know the difference."

He smiled and gave a small shrug. "She made a tiny bit of lightning when Mistral first touched her, Merry. Is her preferring a name any less amazing than that?"

I couldn't argue with his point, but I wanted to.

"Gwenwyfar has your hair," Sholto said. "None of them have anything of mine."

"We don't know that yet," I said.

"They're too new," Galen said. "Give them a few weeks to find out what they are, who they are."

Sholto shook his head. "I had thought about having an heir to my throne. I have been a good enough king that the host might allow our kingship to become heredity, as well as choice of the people, but not if none of them are descended from the host."

I hadn't thought about the fact that we had more than one throne to sit someone on, and suddenly Sholto's worries about his father's genetics didn't seem so silly.

"You're saying that it was your extra bits that helped make the sluagh comfortable making you their king," I said.

"Yes," he said. "They will not take a completely sidhe king or queen."

"Bryluen is not completely sidhe," Galen said.

"She is demi-fey, and perhaps goblin, but those wings are nothing that flies with my people."

I wondered if he'd meant to make the modern Americanism *It doesn't fly with me*, but I thought it more likely he'd meant it literally.

"Galen is right, Sholto. The babies haven't been here a whole day yet; they'll change how they look and who they look like as they get older."

"They won't change that much," Sholto said.

"You might be surprised how much babies change as they get older," Rhys said.

"That's right," Galen said. "You've had children before."

"Yes," Rhys said. Gwenwyfar moved restlessly on his chest, and he rubbed her back, laid a soft kiss on her curls. It was all done almost automatically. I knew that it had to have been centuries since he'd had other children—did parenting skills stay with you forever once you'd learned them? Or was Rhys just more of a natural father than I'd expected? I wanted to ask him but wasn't certain how to ask it without implying that I hadn't expected him to be this good with the babies.

Doyle had felt instantly bonded with Alastair, but he hadn't helped feed and take care of him as much as Galen had. Maybe it was what Galen had said: He hadn't felt bonded, so he'd worked at it. Doyle had, so he didn't have to work at it. Or maybe Doyle was just too busy trying to keep the Queen of Air and Darkness from doing something bad to be a baby-daddy right now.

"Did the queen threaten us, or the babies?" I asked.

The men shifted uneasily—Galen looking at the floor, not meeting their eyes; Rhys kissing the baby again and again purposefully not looking at the other men. Sholto glanced at both of them and then back at me. His face was very serious, arrogant, unreadable, which let me know that whatever the queen had done was frightening, or would at the very least upset me.

My heartbeat was in my throat now, and I was frightened. What could the queen have said, or done, to make them not want to tell me? I probably didn't want to know. I just wanted to enjoy being a new mom and watch the men I loved be fathers, and just enjoy the moment, but my relatives had been ruining the happy moments of my life for as long as I could remember. Why should this be any different?

"One of you talk to me," I said. My voice was only a little breathy. I gave myself a point for sounding so much calmer than I felt.

It was Royal who rose into the air on black-and-gray moth wings, with a bull's-eye spot on the lower wings of scarlet and yellow. His tiny silken loincloth was red, to echo the red in his wings and make you see it more. His wings beat much faster than those of any actual moth, more like the buzzing wings of a dragonfly or bee. Royal was ten inches tall, bigger than any real moth, so he needed wings that were bigger and moved as no moth or butterfly could. He had short curly black hair with delicate antennae coming out of those curls. Bryluen's hair color was mine, but the antennae were his. But I hadn't had sex with him until after I was supposed to already be pregnant with the twins. Unless there was some unknown demi-fey genetics in my background, or one of the other men's, then she had to be partly Royal's child, but how? I'd accepted it calmly in the moment of wonderment of holding Bryluen, but now I was thinking, not feeling, and it made no sense.

I'd invited Royal and the other demi-fey to the hospital in a fit of postdelivery endorphins and baby intoxication, but now I was sobering up and logic had never been a friend to faerie. We weren't about logic; in fact, most of faerie defied logic and science. We were impossible; that was sort of the point of fairyland.

I was the first of my kind to go to a modern college in the United States, and my degree was in biology. It was like I'd been driven temporarily mad and now sanity had returned, and I didn't understand why I'd been so happily sure about Royal and about Kitto. Poor Kitto was out shopping for all the things we needed to turn our twins' nursery into one for triplets. He'd been so happy, and Bryluen could be his, because he'd been my lover longer than Royal, but . . . she had wings and antennae, so it had to be demi-fey blood, didn't it?

One minute Royal looked like the picture from some child's storybook and the next he stood beside the bed as tall as I was, taller than Kitto, who was only four feet tall, the smallest of my lovers. The moth wings that had been a blur of color when he needed to fly were like some fantastic cape at his back, except this cape flexed and moved with his breath, his thoughts, emotions. Wings could be like the tail on a dog, giving away involuntary things.

He stood unselfconsciously nude, because the little bit of silk he'd worn hadn't survived the shape change. It wasn't like the Incredible Hulk's pants that always magically stayed on; when Royal shifted size, his clothes either shredded or became a mound of cloth for his smaller self to fight free of.

"I will tell you what the queen said."

"Merry looks pale, as if she already knows all our news," Sholto said.

"Are you all right?" Galen asked. He stood up and stopped touching Alastair, who waved tiny fists in the air almost immediately, as if only Galen's touch had kept him still. Maybe he was a cuddly baby and liked skin contact, or maybe it was magic like the tree and the roses?

"I don't know," I said.

"What's wrong, Merry?" Rhys asked. He was sitting up, rubbing Gwenwyfar's back as she rested against his chest. She was moving fitfully even with the touching.

I didn't want to say it in front of Royal. I wanted time to think and to be able to discuss it with the other men. I needed time to think.

"Royal, tell me what my aunt has done to frighten everyone."

"She wants to see her great-nieces and nephew," he said.

"She wants to visit the hospital?"

"She does."

I pictured my aunt, the Queen of Air and Darkness, tall, sidhe slender, with her long, straight black hair tangling around her legs, dressed in her signature black, her eyes circles of black and shades of gray with black lines encircling every color so that it always looked as if she'd outlined the iris with eyeliner. It was always a startling and frightening effect, or maybe that last part was just me? Maybe if she hadn't tried to drown me when I was six, or torment me casually on so many occasions, I would have simply thought her eyes were striking. Perhaps, if I hadn't seen her covered in the blood of her torture victims, or had so many of them flee to us here in California looking for a sort of political asylum with the wounds of her creativity still unhealed in their flesh, I would have thought her beautiful, but I knew too much about my aunt to ever see her as anything but frightening. "Is she still torturing her court nobles on mad whims?" I asked.

"Last we checked," Rhys said.

"Then she's too crazy to be trusted among humans, or near our babies."

"We agree," Rhys said. He was rocking Gwenwyfar, gently, but she was moving more. I thought she was working up to a cry, but I was wrong. It was Bryluen who let out a high, thin wail more like the sound that a small animal makes than a baby; just the cry alone said how tiny she was, and how newborn. My body responded to it with milk seeping out of my breasts and soaking through the nursing bra and the gown I was wearing. Well, at least something was working the way it was meant to. I reached for my smallest daughter. I wasn't sure who her father or fathers were, but I knew she was mine. That was one of the nice things about being the woman: You never had to guess how many kids were yours. Men . . . did they ever really know before genetic testing existed?

CHAPTER

FIVE

I seemed to have enough milk for all three babies but was short a breast, so whichever baby wasn't feeding cried, which made the others fussy. The nurses brought bottles and were thoroughly scandalized that Royal was naked. They brought him a set of surgical scrubs to wear when he was big, after we explained the problem. Rhys took Gwenwyfar to Sholto in his chair with the nightflyers shifting restlessly around him.

"No," Sholto said, holding his hands up as if to keep the baby at bay.

"Yes," Rhys said, and put the baby in the other man's arms so that he had to hold her, or risk having her fall. Sholto held her as if she were made of glass and would break, but he did hold her.

"Hold the bottle like this," Rhys said.

Bryluen and Alastair were content, feeding deeply, and that near-magical endorphin rush came over me so that it was comforting to me to feed them and make them feel comfortable. I wondered if cows felt that way around milking machines, or just around their calves.

Gwenwyfar started to cry, and it was high and told some part of my brain I hadn't even known was there that she was little, but that part of me also knew instinctively that she wasn't as little as Bryluen. How did just the sound of their cries tell me that?

"You're too tense," Rhys said. "She's picking it up."

"See, she doesn't like me."

Galen sighed and came beside my bed. "May I take our boy? He's more easygoing than Gwenwyfar."

"You can tell that already?" I asked.

"Oh, yeah," he said, and there was something about the expression on his face that made me wonder.

"What did I miss while I slept, besides my aunt wanting to visit?"

"We all got to know the babies," Galen said with a smile.

I had a little trouble getting Alastair to let go of his nice, warm meal—me—and he fussed as Galen picked him up, but he didn't cry.

Gwenwyfar was crying full-out. Rhys picked her up and he and Galen passed each other as Gwenwyfar came to feed beside her sister, and Alastair got to be bottle-fed by Sholto.

Gwenwyfar settled onto my other breast across from her sister with a little sigh of contentment. Did babies really come into the world knowing that much of who they were and what they wanted? Gwenwyfar already had a strong preference for Mommy, as opposed to the bottle.

I realized that the room was quiet, full of contented noises, which meant Alastair was taking his bottle. I looked across the room to where Rhys and Galen had both been working with Sholto to help him bottle-feed. Sholto had a little smile on his face, and he had relaxed, so that Alastair fit in the crook of his arm and the bottle was at a good angle. The baby was drinking hard and steady, his tiny curled fist on one side of the bottle as if he were already trying to help hold it. I knew that part was accidental, but it was still amazing to me. I guess everyone thinks their babies are wonderful and precocious.

"Alastair takes the bottle easier," Galen said.

Sholto glanced up. "You had trouble feeding the girl, too?"

"I got her to take the bottle, but she doesn't like it as well, and she let me know that." He turned and grinned back at the bed and his reluctant daughter.

Rhys said, "She has strong preferences, our Gwenwyfar."

"Already?" I asked.

"Some babies come like that," Rhys said with a smile.

I stared down at my two daughters, and I just liked the phrase *my two daughters*, and smiled. I could feel that the smile was silly and almost an "in love" type of smile. I had expected to love the babies, but I hadn't expected to feel like this. I was still sore and aching in places that had never hurt before, but it was okay, and long moments like this made me forget that anything hurt. There is power and magic in love, all kinds of love.

Royal came to the other side of the bed by Bryluen. He was wearing an oversized hospital gown turned so the open back let his wings be free, and a pair of surgical scrub pants. It made him look even daintier than he was, and somehow less like he belonged.

"May I feed one of the babies?"

"Of course," I said.

Rhys was already moving across the room, with the last bottle that the nurses had brought. He didn't apologize but let Royal settle onto the edge of the chair that Galen had used. Royal couldn't sit back too far, because of his wings. I wondered if people with wings got backaches from always having to sit without a back support.

Bryluen didn't look so small in Royal's arms. There was a fit there; was it just that the sizes matched better, or was it the happy smile as he gazed down at the baby?

"She's looking right at me," Royal said in a voice that held wonder.

"She keeps her eyes open more than the other two," Rhys said.

I wasn't sure about the other men, but Rhys and Galen had spent my nap learning the ins and outs of our children. I liked that a lot.

I fitted my bra back over one breast and looked down at Gwenwyfar. "So, you're already demanding what you want?"

The baby didn't even open her eyes, just continued to feed happily. I held her closer and leaned over so I could lay a kiss on her white curls. The top of her head smelled amazing, clean and like baby lotion, even though I was almost certain no one had put lotion on her. Did baby lotion smell like newborn babies, or was that just my imagination?

"They smell so good," Royal said; he'd bent over Bryluen's hair just as I had over Gwenwyfar.

"They do," I said.

I caught movement out of the corner of my eye and saw that Sholto had bent over Alastair. "The smell is clean and somehow calming." He sounded surprised.

"Have you never held a baby before?" Rhys asked.

"Not one that was this . . . human," he said.

"You know these aren't antenna buds," Royal said; he was rubbing his cheek against Bryluen's hair, apparently, over the little black beginnings of her antennae.

"What are they then?" I asked.

"Something harder. I think they're tiny horns," he said.

"Did you say horns?" Sholto asked.

"I think they are," Royal said, "but I'm certain they aren't antennae."

Sholto looked down at the baby in his arms. He smiled down and said, half to the baby and half to Galen, "I hate to disturb you, but can someone else finish feeding him?"

"Happy to," Galen said. He took Alastair out of Sholto's arms like he'd done it forever. I wondered if he'd sit in Sholto's chair, but he didn't. Galen moved to the couch to finish giving Alastair his bottle. Would the nightflyers have cared if Galen had sat where their king had sat, or would it have made Galen uncomfortable to be surrounded by them? Most of the sidhe, of both courts, were afraid of the sluagh. We were meant to be, otherwise they weren't a threat, and they so were that.

Sholto walked over to Royal. He offered, "Do you want to feed her?"

"No," Sholto said, and knelt beside them. His hair pooled around his legs so that he was lost in a cloak of it, except for the black of his boots. I couldn't see what he was doing, but Rhys was watching him closely.

"I think they are horns," Sholto said.

I could see his shoulders moving even through the mask of his hair. He exclaimed, "Blood and fire, it can't be!"

I hugged Gwenwyfar tighter and asked, "It can't be what?"

Sholto turned, still on his knees, so that I got a just a glimpse of that handsome face framed by all that hair. "The wings do not feel like butterfly scales, or moth."

"They're like butterfly wings fresh out of a chrysalis, before blood pumps them into full shape," I said.

"They may look like pink and crystal gossamer, but they feel leathery, more like bat, or reptile," Sholto said.

I frowned. "I don't understand."

He smiled, and it was that rare one that made his face look younger, as if it were a glimpse of what he might have been like if his life had not made him so hard.

"Horns and leathery wings are sluagh, Merry."

In my head I thought, *Goblins have horns*, but I didn't say it out loud. The horns and wings could be his genetics; we really didn't know. If his throne hadn't been potentially on the line, it wouldn't have mattered, but to rule the sluagh you had to be part sluagh, just as to rule the Unseelie and Seelie courts you had to be descended from their bloodline. Every court in faerie was like that; you had to be the type of fey to rule that type of fey. Since I'd thought we'd given up all plans for any of our children to be on any throne, I hadn't worried about it.

Sholto's throne was not normally an inherited one. You were elected to it, chosen by the people. It was the only rulership in all of our lands that was democratic. I hadn't known he would look down at our babies and begin to dream of a royal bloodline for his people. Funny, what fatherhood means to different men.

"If it's sluagh, then it can't be demi-fey," Royal said, and he looked sad.

"We have a geneticist who's going to be testing the babies. We won't really know without that," I said.

The men all did another of those looks, almost looking at each other, and avoiding my eyes.

I hugged Gwenwyfar to me, for my comfort this time. "What were those looks about? You told me my aunt wants to see the babies and we're guarding them and the hospital, because she's still insane and too dangerous to come, but that look just now says there's more you haven't told me."

"Have you always been able to read us this easily, or have you grown more observant?" Sholto asked.

"I love you all in my way; a woman pays attention to the men she loves."

"You love us," Rhys said, "but you're not in love with all of us."

"I said what I meant, Rhys."

He nodded. "It was diplomatically worded." His tone was mild, but his face unhappy.

"Rhys," Galen said.

The two men exchanged a long look, both their faces serious. Rhys looked away first. "You're right, you are so right."

Since Galen hadn't said anything out loud, I wasn't sure what he was so right about. It was as if the men had had a conversation that I hadn't heard and were still saying bits of it. I could ask, or . . .

"I'm sorry that you're unhappy with me, but you aren't going to distract me from my question. What else has gone wrong, besides my aunt?"

"Some of us love you more than you love us; it's an old topic," Rhys said.

"Stop changing the subject, and trying to distract me with emotional issues we've already discussed. It must be something bad for you to bring this back up again, Rhys," I said.

He nodded, and sighed. "Bad enough."

Sholto stood up, brushing the knees of his pants automatically. "I'm not in love with Merry, nor do I expect her to be with me. We care for each other, which is more than you usually get out of a royal marriage."

"Then you tell me what the three of you, four of you, are keeping from me," I said.

Galen held Alastair closer, much as I had with Gwenwyfar. "It's the other side of your family."

"The other side, you mean the Seelie Court?"

He nodded, resting his cheek against the top of the baby's thick black hair.

Sholto came to stand beside the bed and laid a hand over my arm and half cradled Gwenwyfar, because his hand was that big in comparison to the baby. "Your uncle, the King of the Seelie Court, is trying to get permission to see the babies, also."

I stared up at him. "My aunt wants to see the potential heirs to Unseelie thrones and her beloved brother's grandchildren. I understand that, and if she weren't a sexual sadist and serial killer we'd allow it, but what in the name of all that is holy makes Taranis think he has the right to see our children?"

Rhys came nearer the bed. "He's still claiming that one or all of them are his, Merry."

I shook my head. "I was pregnant when he raped me. They are not his."

"But you were only weeks pregnant, not showing at all. He's maintaining that you were with child only after he . . . was with you," Rhys said, but I didn't like the long hesitation before he finished his sentence.

"What is he really saying, Rhys?"

"He's made it a 'he said, she said' sort of thing."

"We knew he'd deny the rape, but we have forensic evidence that he did it. The rape kit came back . . ." I couldn't even say it. Taranis, the King of Light and Illusion, ruler of the Seelie Court, the golden court of faerie, was my uncle. Technically he was my great-uncle, brother of my grandfather, but since the sidhe do not age, he didn't look like a grandfather.

"He's saying that it was consensual, but we all knew he would."

"He's probably come to believe his own lie," I said.

"Taranis will not believe that you refused him in favor of the monsters of the Unseelie Court," Sholto said.

"He's the monster," I said.

Sholto smiled, and bent and laid a gentle kiss on my forehead. "That you mean that, when speaking to me, means a great deal to me, our Merry."

I looked at his face as he stood back upright. "He raped me while I was unconscious, Sholto, and he's my uncle. That was monstrous."

"I'm sorry, Merry, but one of the reasons that Taranis is making a case is that you don't remember. He's saying that you consented and then passed out, but he didn't realize you were unconscious until it was too late," Rhys said.

"Too late to stop? Too late to not have sex with his own niece? Too late for what, Rhys?" I was almost yelling.

Gwenwyfar stopped nursing and started to fuss, as if she hadn't liked me yelling. I spoke in a calmer voice, but I couldn't control how I felt. "Rhys, you said 'make a case'; is he actually trying to get legal visitation with the babies?"

"He was, but our lawyers countered, and now Taranis is pushing for genetic testing of the babies. He's so sure that one or all of them will be his, I think he believes his own delusion now."

"He's always believed his own magic more than he should," Sholto said.

"Once his illusions could become real," Rhys said.

"That was a very long time ago."

"If the genetic tests come back negative for him, then I think his days as King of the Seelie Court are over," Rhys said.

"If we can prove that he knew he was infertile a hundred years ago but didn't step down from the throne, they may execute him," Galen said, and there was a hardness in his voice that I'd never heard before.

I looked past the other men to my green knight. "You want them to kill him, don't you?"

"Don't you?" he asked, and his green eyes held a bleak rage that was so not like him, but truth was truth.

"Yes," I said.

"Good," Galen said, and that one word wasn't good at all. The tone was very bad, very sure of its anger.

"If the ruler of court is infertile, then it condemns the entire court to be childless; no true king would stay on the throne under those circumstances," Rhys said.

"Or queen," Galen said.

We all looked at him.

"That's why she agreed to step down if Merry had a child, because she'd tried all the modern fertility treatments and was still childless."

"She had a son," I said, softly. Holding my own child in my arms made it seem like I should add out loud that I'd killed that only son. He'd been trying to kill me and the men I loved, but I'd still killed him, and his death seemed to have driven the last of her sanity away.

"Cel was hundreds of years old, and her only child. She knew she was infertile long before," Galen said, and again there was a hardness to him that I had never heard or seen in him. People think that becoming a parent will make you soft, more sentimental, and maybe it does for some, but for him it seemed to have helped him find a new strength. I'd wanted him stronger, but I hadn't understood that perhaps with the extra strength, some softness might be lost, that with every gain, there might be a loss.

I studied his face, and the other men were doing the same thing. We were all looking at my gentle knight and realizing that maybe he wasn't that anymore. There were other men in my life that I counted on to be harsh and protective; until that moment I hadn't realized that I'd counted on Galen for softer things. My eyes felt hot, my throat tight; was I going to cry? Not about the rape and the legal mess, but about losing Galen's softness? Or maybe I was going to cry about it all, about both, about all three, or maybe baby hormones made you more emotional, or maybe, just maybe, I would cry because Galen wouldn't anymore.

Doyle came back in while I was still crying, which led to him asking what happened and the other men admitting they'd told me.

"The last orders I gave were for Merry not to be upset."

"First, we are all fathers of her children," Rhys said, "so as our captain you can order us, but as just another of Merry's sweethearts you need to give us all room to decide the parameters of our relationship with her and our children."

"Are you saying you deliberately went against my orders?" Doyle stalked farther into the room toward Rhys.

"I'm not stupid," I said. "I could tell something was wrong and I demanded to know what it was."

Doyle didn't look back at me but continued to loom over Rhys. Galen still had Alastair in his arms as he moved toward the other men.

"Merry is our princess and crowned by Goddess as our queen; she outranks her own captain of the guard," Galen said.

Doyle's head turned, ever so slightly, neck and shoulders so tight it looked painful. His deep voice held anger like it was all he could do to contain it. "Are you saying that none of you will obey my orders?"

"Of course we will," Galen said, "but Merry is supposed to lead not just us, but all our people. How can we ignore her when she demands something from us?"

Sholto got up from where he was kneeling by Bryluen. He left her in Royal's arms. The demi-fey looked frightened and didn't try to hide it. Sholto joined the other sidhe in the middle of the room.

"If you were the only king that Goddess and faerie had crowned for Merry, then we would obey you, Darkness, but you are one of many kings."

Doyle turned to face the other man. "I have not forgotten that she was crowned to be queen to your king, Sholto."

Sholto raised his arm and pushed back the sleeve just enough to show the beginnings of the tattoo that he and I shared. It had been real rose vines that night, and had pierced both our arms, entwining like the rope, or thread, that was used for a regular handfasting, but this "rope" had set thorns into our flesh and wedded our hands together more completely than any mere ceremony could have, and the marks of those vines and roses were painted on our arms.

"We were handfasted by Goddess and faerie," Sholto said.

"And I have no such mark; you have pointed that out more than once over these months," Doyle said.

That was news to me. Sholto was the only man to whom Goddess had personally handfasted me, but She had crowned Doyle and me as King and Queen of the Unseelie Court.

"Maybe the reason Goddess bound Merry to you was that you were the only one who is king in his own right," Galen said.

The two men looked at him, as if he'd interrupted a longstanding disagreement. It isn't always wise to get in the middle of two people who are fighting.

Galen smiled at them and shifted the baby in his arms, just enough to remind them the baby was there. I didn't think the movement was accidental; Galen understood that the baby was a free pass from any violence. He was right, but I hoped he didn't push the idea too far, because he wouldn't be holding a baby forever, and both Sholto and Doyle had long memories.

"Merry had to become your queen; the rest of us had to become her kings."

"Why should that matter?" Sholto said.

"Merry had to marry you to become your queen; for the rest of us, we had to father a child to become Merry's kings, or princes. I think for the Unseelie Court, the Goddess and Consort already chose the king."

"I gave up my crown to save Frost," Doyle said.

"Barinthus still hasn't forgiven you, or Merry, for that," Galen said, with a smile.

"He is a Kingmaker, or a Queenmaker," Sholto said. "The two of you gave up what Barinthus had worked for decades to accomplish."

"He dreamed of putting my father on the throne, not me, and certainly not Doyle," I said.

"True," Sholto said.

"Very true," Doyle said.

"I don't believe we would all have lived to see the babies born," Rhys said.

"Too many enemies still left in the darkling court," Doyle agreed.

"Or perhaps the Goddess and God would have protected you," Royal said.

We all looked at the delicate figure still tucked into the chair with a baby who might, or might not, be his daughter.

"What do you mean?" I asked.

"If the Goddess and God crowned the two of you, maybe they would have worked to keep you safe on the throne?"

I thought about it. "Are you saying we needed to have faith, little one?" Doyle asked.

"You still talk as if the power of the Goddess has not returned to bless us all with Her Grace, but she has moved among us these last months even here outside faerie, in the far Western Lands."

I said, "The Goddess told me that if the fey weren't willing to accept Her blessings, then I should take them out among the humans and see if they appreciated them more."

"Humans are always impressed with magic," Sholto said.

"But it's not magic," I said. "It's miracles."

"Aren't miracles just a type of magic?" he asked.

I thought about that, and finally said, "I'm not sure, perhaps."

"What did the queen say when you told her not to come?" I asked.

Doyle met my eyes, but his face was unreadable, as closed and mysterious as he had ever been, but now I understood what the look meant. He was hiding something from me, protecting me, he thought. I saw it as not sharing information that I needed.

"What makes you think I have spoken to the queen?"

"Who else had a chance of persuading her to stay away but the Queen's Darkness?"

"I am no longer her Darkness, but yours."

"Then tell me what she said, and what she wants."

"She wants to see her brother's grandchildren."

"You've told me that she's still torturing random people at court," I said.

"She was the most composed I have seen her since this last madness gripped her."

"And how composed was that?" Rhys asked, and by tone and expression he showed that he didn't believe it would be composed enough.

"She seemed her old self, before Cel's death and our giving up the throne drove her mad."

"You still believe that she was trying to be so insane that some of her court would kill her?"

"I believe that for this space of time she sought death, or didn't care whether she lived or died," Doyle said.

I thought about the broken, bloody bodies of the people that had been brought to us or escaped to find refuge with us. The queen had not tried to hunt down any of the refugees of her court, even though it was well known that her nobles had come to seek asylum with us.

"If positions had been reversed, she would have sent me to kill you months ago," Doyle said.

I nodded, hugging Gwenwyfar a little closer, feeling her deeply asleep in my arms. It helped me stay calm and say, "She would have said, 'Where is my Darkness? Bring me my Darkness,' and you would have come like a shadow and ended my life."

"I would have done the same if you had asked, Meredith."

"I know that, but I would not risk you back in the Unseelie Court by yourself, Doyle."

"If anyone could assassinate the queen and live to tell about it, it is Doyle," Sholto said.

"If anyone could do it, he could, I know that."

"Then why have we hesitated?"

"Because the word *if* is in every conversation we have about this, and I'm not willing to risk Doyle on an *if.*"

"You love him and the Killing Frost more than a queen should love anyone," Sholto said.

"Do you say that from experience, King Sholto?" I asked.

"You do not love me as you love Doyle, or Frost. We all know that they are your most beloved, so I am not betraying you if I say that I am not in love with you either."

"Don't you love the babies more than duty, or crown?" Galen asked. I'm not sure I would have asked, not out loud.

Sholto turned and looked at him, so I couldn't see the expression he gave the other man, but I was almost certain it was his arrogant face. The one that made him look model handsome and was his version of a blank face.

"I would give my life to keep them safe, but I do not know if I value them above duty to my people and my kingdom. My throne and crown they could have, but not if it cost my people their independence or their lives. I hope I never have to choose between the children and the duty that I owe my people."

"You are the best king that faerie has had in a very long time," Doyle said.

"You don't hold duty above the lives of our children, do you, Doyle?" I asked.

He turned and smiled at me. "No, Merry, of course not; they are more precious to me than any crown, but then I already proved that I prefer love to a throne. If I would give up being King of the Unseelie Court for love of our Frost, then I would do no less for our children."

And that was the answer I wanted, that no duty or sense of honor outweighed the love to these small new lives. I laid my cheek against the soft curls, breathed in the sweet scent of our daughter, and asked, "Who has persuaded the king to stay inside faerie?"

"The lawyers and the police," Rhys said.

"Human lawyers and human police? How have they persuaded the King of Light and Illusion to do anything?"

"Human law confined him to faerie after he attacked us and the lawyers with us."

"He hadn't left the Seelie Court in years," I said. "It was no hardship for him."

"There's also a court order keeping him five hundred feet away from you and all your lovers and an injunction preventing him from contacting us directly, even by magic."

"That was a fun one to get a judge to sign off on," I said.

"We have set new precedents for human law and magic," Rhys agreed.

"He attacked a room full of some of the most powerful attorneys in California; it helped our case."

"Human police will not be able to arrest him," I said.

"There will be no arresting him, Merry. If Taranis escapes faerie and comes for you, or the babies, he will die."

"He'll slaughter the humans," I said.

"He's not bulletproof," Galen said.

"Human police aren't trained to kill first, but second, and that will be all the time he needs to kill them," I said.

"Soldiers are trained to kill, not save, and that is what is needed," Doyle said.

"Is there still a National Guard unit outside the faerie mounds in Illinois?" I asked.

"You know there is," he said.

"I don't want them dying for me, Doyle."

"They won't die for you, or us, but as I understand it in defense of their country and constitution."

"And what does fighting a king of the sidhe have to do with defending the constitution?"

Rhys said, "Merry, if Taranis could be king of this country, he would be, and he would rule with the same arrogance and cruel carelessness that he has displayed toward the Seelie Court."

"There is no danger of him ruling this country, and you know that."

"I do, but he still needs killing."

"Because he raped me?" I asked, and studied his face as I said it. It had taken me months to say the words that casually.

Rhys nodded. "Oh, for that, definitely for that."

"Definitely," Doyle said.

"Yes," Galen said.

"If it would not cause war between the sluagh and the Seelie Court, yes."

"I am too weak to ever harm anyone so powerful, but if I could kill him for what he did to you, I would," Royal said.

The demi-fey that were still fluttering tiny and fragile-looking among the roses and blossoms in the room rose in a cloud of wings and said in small voices, "Command us, Merry, and we will do what you need."

"Are you saying you would kill Taranis for me?"

"Yes." They said it in unison like birds chirping a word all at once.

"Rid me of this inconvenient man, really?"

"Yes," they sang again.

"No, I would not send so many of the demi-fey to their death. I do not want vengeance so badly that I would sacrifice all of you."

"And that is why we would do it for you," Royal said.

I shook my head. "No, no more deaths of those I value. I've lost too many people and seen too much blood spilled because of the madness of kings and queens."

"Then what do you want us to do about him?" Rhys asked.

"I don't know; if he loses his head and tries to come near me or the babies again, then we kill him. I won't let him hurt me again, and I won't let him near our children."

"We kill him then," Doyle said.

"If we can," Rhys said.

"Oh, we can kill him," Galen said, as if it were a matter of fact and not a nearly impossible feat.

"How can you be so sure?" Rhys asked.

Galen's face wore that new harsher expression as he hugged our son. "Because if he comes for Merry and we don't kill him, he'll hurt her again, and we won't allow that."

"So we'll kill him, because we have to," Rhys said.

Galen nodded. "Yes."

The men all looked at each other and then at me, and I saw the beginnings of a determination that could only end in one way. Taranis, King of Light and Illusion, was going to have to die.

CHAPTER

SEVEN

The triplets were in the nursery with Doyle, Frost, and a handful of other guards watching over them while the nurses and doctors did last-minute things in preparation for going home. Galen, Rhys, and I were in the room trying to figure out how we were going to get everything else home. Flowers and other gifts had come from friends, but most of it was from strangers. The fact that Princess Meredith had had her babies had made the news, and America was thrilled to have their faerie princess have triplets! I appreciated the thought, but we were a little overwhelmed by their generosity.

"We'll need a van just to cart all the flowers and presents home," Rhys said. He stood in the middle of the room with his hands on hips, surveying all the bouquets, balloons, stuffed animals, potted plants, and gift baskets of food that filled most of the room. We'd started turning away some of the well-meaning gifts, because we needed to leave room for us and the medical personnel to use the room. The hospital had been much happier with the florist shop invasion than with the plants that were still growing in the room. The blooming apple tree curled above all of it. The treetop was pushed against the ceiling as if still trying to grow taller, as if it had come up against the sky and been surprised to find it solid and unforgiving. The nurses had asked if the tree was permanent, and I'd given the only answer I had: I didn't know.

They were even less happy with the wild roses around the bed because they had thorns. Two nurses and a doctor had pricked themselves on the thorny vines.

"We've already given away a lot of it to other patients," Galen said.

"Most of the stuffed toys should go to the children's ward," I said. I turned too fast to motion at the toys and had to stop and try a less dramatic turn. I felt good, but if I moved a certain way I could feel the stitches and the abuse my body had suffered to get our little trio on the outside. I was just happy to be in real clothes again. The sundress was designer maternity, one of the many gifts we'd had over the months that came with the words, "Just tell people what you're wearing and it's free." Since we were supporting a small army of fey on not-large-enough salaries, we'd taken most of the gifts. The ones that didn't come with contracts to sign, those we'd let our entertainment lawyers to look over.

We'd been offered a reality show. Did we want cameras following us around everywhere? No. Did we need the money? Yes. Which was why the entertainment lawyers were going over the contracts, but we had to decide today. The producers wanted it to begin with the babies coming home, so that meant that the film crew needed to either come to the hospital to start filming, or film us as we brought the babies into the house. We needed the money, but what would my relatives do on camera?

As if he'd read my mind, Rhys said, "I think the reality show is a bad idea, have I said that yet?"

"You mentioned it," I said, still staring at the stuffed animals, some of which were nearly three feet tall. What would newborn babies do with such a thing? We'd leave them for older children who would love them and needed them more than our tiny ones. Bryluen, Gwenwyfar, and Alastair weren't able to reach for things yet, let alone manage a forest of giant toys. The world was big enough to them right now without that.

"I agree with Rhys, but I know that Merry feels it's wrong to expect Maeve to keep supporting all of us."

"It's an old tradition that when the ruler visited his nobles they were expected to entertain him, or her, and all their traveling court," Rhys said. He picked up one of the potted plants and shook his head. I think he was thinking what I was thinking: We couldn't possibly take all the plants home. It would be a full-time job just to water them all. Though some of the tiny winged demi-fey had picked a few of them to cuddle into; those we'd bring home.

"I've read that Henry the Eighth used that tradition to bankrupt rivals, or nobles he was trying to control," I said.

"People make jokes about fat Henry, but he was a very good politician and understood the power of being king."

"He abused that power," I said.

"He did, but they all did. It's hard to resist absolute power, Merry."

"Is that from personal experience?" Galen asked.

Rhys looked at him, and then down at the piles of gifts. "Being a deity with worshippers does tend to make a person a little high-handed, but I learned my lesson."

"What lesson is that?" I asked, and came up to wrap my arm through his so that I could rest my cheek against his shoulder.

He turned his head enough to smile at me, and said, "That just because people call you a god doesn't make you one."

A tiny and very female voice said, "You were the great god Cromm Cruach, and your followers healed all hurts."

We looked at one of the winged demi-fey; it was Penny, Royal's twin sister. She'd been fluttering among the flowers but now rose so she'd be head height for us. She had her brother's short black curls, pale skin, and black almond-shaped eyes, but her face was even more delicate, her body a little smaller. She was wearing a gauzy red-and-black dress that looked very nice with her wings.

Rhys looked at her, face not happy. "That makes you very old indeed, little one, much older than I thought."

"I had no wings then, because our Princess Merry had not worked her wild magic and made us able to fly. We wingless ones among the demi-fey went even more unnoticed than the rest; at least they were color and beauty, but those of us who had not been so blessed only watched from the grass and the roots of things. It gives a perspective that I might not have had if I'd been on the wing back then."

"What perspective is that?" Rhys asked.

"To know that everyone starts on the ground. Trees, flowers, people, even the mighty sidhe must stand upon the dirt in order to move forward."

"If you have a point, make it," he said.

"You have no illusions about what and who you are now; you can make a life that is real, not some fantasy, but something true and good, just as a tree that puts down deep roots can withstand storms, but one with shallow roots is knocked over by the first strong wind. You have become deep-rooted, Rhys, and that is not a bad thing."

He smiled then, nodding and squeezing my arm where I touched him. "Thank you, Penny, I think I understand. Once I built myself on power that was given to me by the Goddess and Her Consort, but I forgot that it wasn't my power, so when we lost the grace of the Gods, I was lost, but whatever I am now it's real and it's me, and no one can take that from me."

"Yes," she said, hovering near Rhys's face, her wings beating so quickly that the edge of his curls blew softly in the wind of her flight.

"Did I seem like I needed a pep talk to you?" Rhys asked.

"There is often an air of melancholy about you."

I glanced from the tiny fey to Rhys and wondered, would I have thought that? Was that true? He joked a lot and made light comments, but . . . behind all of it, Penny was right. I found it interesting that she had paid that much attention to him. I thought of several motives for a female to pay that much attention to a man—did Penny have a crush on Rhys? Or was she just that wise and observant of all of us, of everything? If the first was true, then I doubted Rhys would realize it, and if the second was true, then hearing her thoughts on other things might be interesting.

"Penny, do you think we should do the reality show?" I asked.

She dipped down, which was a flying demi-fey's way of stumbling. I'd surprised her.

"It is not my place to say."

"I've asked your opinion," I said.

She cocked her head to one side, then moved in the air so she was more in front of my face than Rhys's. "Why ask my opinion, my lady?"

"It will affect you, as it will affect everyone who lives with us, so I am interested in what you think."

She gave me a very serious, searching look. I saw the intelligence in that tiny face that I hadn't seen before; she was as bright as her brother, but maybe a better thinker, deeper anyway.

"Very well. The queen is always very careful to look good in front of the human media, so if you did the reality show, then cameras might keep us all safe from her."

"The queen is insane, she can't help herself," Galen said.

Penny looked at him, then back to me. "If that were true, then she would have lost her control at a press conference decades ago, but she never has; if she can control herself to that degree then she is not truly insane, she is simply cruel. Never mistake someone who cannot control their murderous impulses from someone who simply has no one to tell them, 'Stop, behave yourself.' I find that most cruel people, no matter how awful their actions, once faced with punishment, or someone stronger, behave. Mean is not crazy, it is merely mean."

I thought about what Penny had said, really thought about it. "She's right. My aunt has never lost control of herself in front of the media. If she were truly serial killer crazy, she'd have lost it at least once, but she never has, not that I remember." I looked at Rhys and then at Galen.

They looked at each other, and then back at me. "Well, I'll be damned," Rhys said.

"Penny is right, isn't she?" Galen asked.

I nodded. "I think she is."

"The king also has never lost control in front of the media."

"He attacked our human lawyers and us once before he kidnapped me," I said.

"But there was no media to record it, Princess Merry. It is still a matter of witnesses, but no video or pictures."

"I think that the king was honestly insane during that attack," Rhys said. "His guard had to physically jump him, bury him under their bodies to keep him from continuing the attack."

I shivered and cuddled into Rhys. Taranis had almost killed Doyle in that attack, and my Darkness was not an easy kill.

"If that is true, then a television show may not protect us from the king."

One of the other demi-fey flew upward on tiny white wings with little black spots on them. She was even tinier than Penny's Barbie doll size, as if she were trying harder to ape the butterfly she resembled. It was a Cabbage White, an American butterfly, which meant she'd likely been born here.

Her voice was high and musical, as if a trilling bird's song could be words. "My sister is still in the Seelie Court. She told me that the king was enraged that you had slipped his seduction magic. He'd never had a woman except for the queen of the Unseelie Court escape from his spells."

"Which is why he came for me later," I said, softly.

The little faerie flew closer and laid a hand no bigger than the nail of my little finger on my hand. "But even then his magic did not work; he had to hit you with brute force like any human. He knows now that his magic does not work on you."

"Did your sister hear him say that?" Rhys asked.

She nodded so hard that her pale blond curls bobbed.

"We think the king will not try magic again," Penny said.

"We, you mean the demi-fey?" I said.

"I do," she said.

The little one patted my finger, as I might have patted someone's shoulder. "We are all sorry that he hurt you, Princess Merry."

"That is much appreciated," I said.

The little one flew up higher, her butterfly wings a blur of white as she hovered, but also showing agitation, nerves.

"Tell her, Pansy," Penny said.

"Many speak in front of us as if we are dogs and can neither understand nor report to others," Pansy said.

I nodded. "You are some of the best spies in all of faerie because of it."

She smiled. "The king has decided that it was his magic you found objectionable, and he plans to try to woo you as a regular man might."

"What does that mean?" I asked.

"It might mean that he would behave for the cameras as nicely as the queen," Penny said.

"How long have you known this bit of information?" Rhys asked.

"Pansy only heard from her sister recently, and the gossip came up. Her sister did not realize the importance of it, or the use we might make of the information."

I found the "we" interesting. Penny didn't mean just demi-fey, but us, her, me, all of us fey living at the estate in Holmby Hills. It was rare for one type of fey to include themselves with others not of their kind. But then I'd accepted any fey who came into exile with us, or were already here in California in an exile older than my own. With a few exceptions, everyone was welcome.

There was a knock at the door, and the guard opened the door and peeked in, saying, "The ambassador is back."

I sighed, and said, "Send him in."

Peter Benz walked through the door smiling, his handsome face set in easy lines, his hand already out to shake. His dark blond hair was cut short and neat; his suit was tailored to his five-foot, eight-inch frame so he looked taller, and it showed off that he exercised and ate carefully enough that he was in shape. He was vain enough that he'd paid for his suit to fit, rather than hide his body. The last ambassador had been vain, too, and Taranis had played on that vanity for all he was worth.

I didn't really want to play that game, but I wanted this ambassador to be one who worked for both courts, not just the Seelie, so I made myself smile and walk toward that extended hand.

His even white teeth spread in a Hollywood-worthy smile. Mr. Benz was an ambassador now, but he had the feel of someone who had much bigger goals for his future. Ambition wasn't a bad thing; it could make a person very good at his job.

His handshake was firm, but not too firm. He also didn't have an issue with my hand being small; so many men either engulfed my hand in theirs or barely touched my hand as if afraid they'd crush it.

"Princess Meredith, thank you for seeing me again."

"Mr. Benz, you are the new ambassador to my people; why wouldn't I receive you?"

He raised a well-groomed eyebrow at that, but turned with a smile to shake first Galen's hand and then Rhys's. The cloud of flying demi-fey he didn't really look at; he treated them as if they were the insects they resembled. I would have said, *How very human*, but even among the sidhe, we forgot to count them, or many did.

I glanced at Penny and Pansy as they hovered in the air. They met my look with one of their own; they'd noticed his lack of notice, too. The demi-fey would be wonderful spies on human politicians. To my knowledge no one in faerie was doing that, but it was a thought, a potentially useful one. I filed it away for later, much later. We had a long way to go before spying on human politics was a priority for me.

"I know you must be eager to go home."

I looked at him. "Define *home*," I said.

He smiled again and made a little push-away gesture with his manicured hands. "You've made it very clear that Ms. Reed's mansion is your home for now."

"While my uncle is confined to faerie, I think I will not be safe there."

The smile faded. "I am sorrier than I can say about all the problems you and King Taranis are having."

"Did you know that once upon a time the king could hear any conversation that mentioned his name?" Rhys said.

Benz gave him a skeptical but pleasant look. "I was told that hadn't been true in a very long time, Mr. Rhys."

"No, but then he hadn't been able to use his hand of light through a mirror being used as a magical Skype interview in centuries either."

"We also believe he's reacquired the ability to use the mirrors as a door that he can step through, or pull someone else through," I said.

Again, that eyebrow rose. "Really?"

"Yes," I said, "really."

"No one saw him step through a mirror or pull someone else into one during the unfortunate events in your lawyers' chambers," Benz said.

"But we did see herbs touch the surface of the mirror, and they floated as if on water tension," I said.

"When a mirror runs like water, or even semiliquid, it usually means that the person on the other side can step through," Rhys said.

"Does it really?" This time Benz looked more interested than skeptical.

We both nodded. Galen was sort of ignoring us all as he continued to sort the things we were taking from those we were donating. Oddly, Galen was probably best suited to have charmed the ambassador; it was actual ability for him, a type of glamour magic, which was why we'd decided he would leave the talking to us. We didn't want to be accused of trying to magically influence the new ambassador after what had happened to the last one.

Benz said, "I am learning so much about faerie and its magic. Thank you for being my teachers."

"We are some of your teachers, but not all," I said.

He gave a little self-deprecating head gesture, almost an aw-shucks head bob, like a bashful movement. I wondered if it was the last remnant of an old gesture. Had our so-secure Benz been shy once?

"That is true; I am to be ambassador to all the courts of faerie, not just your lovely part of it, Princess Meredith."

"Have you spoken to all the courts of faerie, then?" I asked.

He nodded, flashing that brilliant smile that would probably look amazing on camera.

"How did you like King Kurag?" I asked.

He looked puzzled, the smile slipping. "King Kurag, you mean the goblin king?"

"Yes, Kurag, the goblin king."

"I haven't actually spoken to him."

"What about Queen Niceven of the demi-fey?"

"Um, no, I have spoken with King . . . the king of the Seelie Court, and your aunt, the Queen of Air and Darkness."

Leaving off Taranis's name because we'd just said something about it was good, but leaving off both their names, just in case, meant he'd made the logical leap. If one sidhe ruler of faerie could hear when his name was spoken, then maybe the other one could, too. I liked him better for being a quick study. Quick and smart was good.

"You have spoken with King Sholto, because we were here for that talk," I said.

He looked uncertain, but only for a second, and then his face was back to smiling and pleasant. "I spoke to him as your royal consort and father of your children, but not specifically as king in his own right."

"Then you plan to be ambassador to the Unseelie and Seelie courts of the sidhe, and not really ambassador to all the courts of faerie," I said.

He fought that puzzled look away and said, "My duties, as described by Washington, are to the sidhe, both Unseelie and Seelie."

"So the other courts are to be ignored?"

"They are smaller courts within the two larger ones, or that's what I was told; was I misinformed?"

I debated, and finally because we aren't allowed to lie, I said, "Yes, and no."

"Please enlighten me; what do you mean by that, Princess?"

"The goblins, sluagh, and Queen Niceven's demi-fey are part of the Unseelie Court. The ruler of the Seelie Court's demi-fey is no longer an official royal, but a duchess."

His smile flashed back to full brightness. "Then I deal with the high king and high queen of faerie as I was told."

I nodded. "It's the way most people in and out of faerie do it."

He cocked his head to one side and studied me for a moment. "And how else might a person deal with the rulers of faerie?"

"I deal with the kings and queens of faerie as leaders with rights and merits of their own."

"Do you encourage me to deal directly with the goblins and the sluagh?"

I laughed a surprised burst of sound.

"Isn't that what you're hinting at, that you want me to treat them as equal to the sidhe courts?"

"Not equal to, but important, but Goddess, please do not try dealing with the goblins by yourself. I would not want to be responsible for the diplomatic disaster that might follow."

He frowned, just a little, as if he were fighting not to frown harder. "I am very good at my job, Princess Meredith; I think I could avoid offending anyone."

"It's not your offending the goblins I'm concerned with, Mr. Benz. I'm more afraid that they might injure you if there was a cultural misunderstanding."

"What kind of cultural misunderstanding?" he asked.

"The goblins revere only strength and power, Mr. Benz. A human without magic or the martial arts training of a Chuck Norris would find himself treated badly."

"Maybe that's why the humans stopped dealing with the goblins directly," Rhys said.

I glanced at him. "You may be right."

"I don't understand," Benz said.

"I would like you to appreciate more of faerie than just our two courts, but culturally we are the closest to human, and the safest for you, so perhaps you should just ignore me for now. If I ever feel safe to return to faerie, perhaps you can accompany me on a visit to some of the lesser courts."

Rhys patted him on the shoulder. "We'd keep you safe."

"Surely they wouldn't harm a representative of the United States government."

We all laughed then, even Galen, and the demi-fey's laughter was like the sweet ringing of chimes, or tiny bells. The sound alone made Benz smile. The demi-fey have some of the most powerful glamour and illusion ability left in all of faerie. It made them so much more dangerous than they looked.

Benz frowned again, looking puzzled, and smoothed his hands down the front of his suit. It was almost as if he knew that something had just affected him in a more than normal way, but he wasn't sure what it had been. I was betting the ambassador was carrying some kind of charm against our magic. He'd need it.

"It is the last country on the planet that would allow your people to immigrate," Benz said.

"That is true, but the goblins would not see it as harming you, but as your proving unworthy to deal with them as a representative of the government."

"Are you saying that an ambassador to the goblin court would have to be a soldier?"

"Unless you're willing to shoot someone when you step through the door, no, not a soldier," I said.

"What then?" he asked.

"A human witch or wizard, though it's a more patriarchal society, so a wizard would be better."

"A wizard with military training would be your best bet," Rhys said. He came closer to the ambassador and raised the eye patch that was covering the smooth scars of his empty eye socket. "The goblins took my eye, Ambassador Benz, and I'm a lot harder to injure than a human."

Benz did a long blink but didn't flinch, which earned him another point. I wondered what he'd think if he saw the goblins. They prided themselves on extra limbs and eyes, so that females that looked like humanoid spiders were the height of beauty among the goblins. For that matter, he hadn't seen Sholto with his extra tentacles visible. Benz was going to have a lot more chances to practice not flinching.

"Are you saying the goblins would attack me?"

I stepped in. "No, it is perfectly possible to visit and negotiate with the goblins in safety, but it requires an understanding of their culture that is rare even among the sidhe. I know of no human who has ever been that successfully intimate with the goblin court."

Rhys snugged his eye patch back into place. "I've learned that my injury came through a lack of cultural understanding." His voice was only a little bitter. He lost his eye hundreds of years ago, but I'd explained the misunderstanding to him only about a year ago. He'd hated the goblins and blamed them for it for a very long time, and had only a short time to get used to the idea that his injury was as much his fault as that of the goblin who took his eye.

"My goal is to be a true ambassador to both of the high courts of faerie, both Unseelie and Seelie, but no one in our government has spoken to me of the goblins, or even of Lord Sholto in his role as king."

"Perhaps if your post as ambassador goes very well, we could escort you through the other courts at some point," I said.

"I would be most grateful for the education in your wider culture," he said, with a very nice smile. Even his brown eyes were shining with pleasure. I still felt we'd presented him with something he wasn't prepared for, but he covered it better than most envoys, human or faerie.

I smiled, and turned carefully away in my designer sundress, not sure I could equal his pleasant falseness. He really was very good.

"Now, Princess Meredith, I had my own security wait outside the room with yours, since those inside the room are fathers and royal consorts, and security stays out. I've acted in accordance with your wishes this time."

"Thank you, Ambassador," I said with a smile.

"But I also have additional diplomatic security for you."

"We discussed this, Ambassador; they are not needed."

"Not meaning any insult to your bodyguards, but you were allegedly kidnapped by the king while under their care."

"We've explained that I told them all to leave me alone, and they had to obey my orders."

"But don't they still have to obey your orders, Princess?"

"We've all agreed that Merry is never to be left alone without guards, and the same is true of the children," Rhys said.

"Even if she orders you to do so?" Benz asked.

Rhys and Galen both nodded. "She will never be left alone again," Galen said, and his voice held that new seriousness. I knew he meant it, and he was well trained as a fighter, but he didn't have the skill level of Rhys, or Doyle, or Frost. I wasn't sure if it was just the difference in years of practice, or if it had been a willingness to do deadly harm. The other men had been in real wars and had learned what it meant to kill and be killed. Galen had never had that; he'd had very few "real" fights. Honestly, I'd always thought that it wasn't just lack of battle hardness, but that his personality, the very gentleness that I loved him for, prevented him from being the warrior he could have been. Now I was no longer sure of Galen, or of many things.

He came to me then, took my hand in his, and smiled down at me, his green eyes filling with that warmth they'd always held. "You look sad, my Merry. I would do anything to chase that look from your eyes."

How could I tell him that it was his new resolution that made me sad? I couldn't; we were all being changed by the events of the last year. We were parents now, and that would change us more.

"Kiss me, my green knight, and it will wipe the sadness from my eyes."

I was rewarded with that brilliant smile of his, the one that had been making my heart skip a beat since I was fourteen, and then he leaned over, bending that six feet of muscle down to lay his mouth upon mine. The kiss was chaste by our standards, but the ambassador finally cleared his throat.

I had to break away from the kiss and explain, "Throat clearing is a human way of expressing awkwardness, or impatience with something sexual, or romantic."

Galen glanced at the ambassador. "That wasn't sexual by court standards, not by Unseelie standards anyway."

"I've been told that sexuality is freer among the sidhe," he said.

"If you try the throat-clearing routine with my aunt, the queen, either it will prompt her to say something scathing, or she will be more vigorous at whatever is bothering you."

"It was not the kiss, but the fact that I think you are changing the subject from the princess having extra security from our government, that made me want to interrupt. I think of myself as fairly bohemian."

"Bohemian," Rhys said, "that's not a term I've heard in a while."

Benz looked at him, and there was intelligence in all the charm, which was good; he'd need it. "Is it the wrong word to use?"

"No, but to thrive at the Unseelie Court, you'll need to be a little bit more than bohemian."

"What would you suggest?"

"Profligate, perverse, but perhaps not." Rhys looked at Galen and me.

"You've thought of something," Galen said.

"I was just thinking that the queen never allows the human media to see her at her most flagrant. I was wondering if a human ambassador to our court might have a . . . calming effect." His eye was full of humor at the very mildness of his word choice. If Queen Andais had to behave for human sensibilities, then torture as dinner entertainment might be over. It was always mild torture, by her standards, and it wasn't common, but her love of true torture might have to be more controlled if Benz was visiting our court—if she could control herself and hadn't gone so far into her own madness that nothing would help her regain herself. That was actually the question that stood in the way of her visiting the babies. Was she truly mad or just aiming her grief at her own court because she could? If she had to find other outlets for her grief, I wondered if I could talk her into grief counseling. She'd gone to human fertility specialists; maybe she'd do therapy.

Rhys came to join Galen, adding his arms to the other man's so he had an arm around both my waist and Galen's. "Now it's you who've thought of something interesting, our Merry."

I nodded. "We'll discuss it later."

"When I'm not here to listen in," Benz said.

I glanced at him. "Yes," I said.

He laughed then, and said, "You know that most humans would have denied it, just to be polite."

"It's too close to a lie, and a lie that you would know was one. Why should I bother?"

"Ah, Princess Meredith, I think I am going find being ambassador to you a very interesting, even educational, experience."

"Which means it could be good, or bad," I said.

He nodded. "I don't know which it will be myself, yet."

"Be careful, Ambassador Benz," Rhys said, "or we'll make you too honest to be a diplomat out among the humans."

He looked surprised then, before he could stop himself, and then he laughed out loud, head back. It was the most unprotected and real expression I'd seen from him.

"Oh, Lord Rhys, a diplomat who cannot lie would be useless indeed out among the humans, but for a time I think a little brutal honesty might be a nice change. Now, about adding some diplomatic security agents to the princess's detail . . ."

We let him talk, and I hoped that the "brutal honesty" wouldn't be too brutal on Ambassador Peter Benz, or on us, for that matter. I couldn't trust my aunt, Queen Andais, to be safe and sane around our babies, but I also wasn't entirely sure we could keep telling her no. How do you tell someone who has been the ultimate power of life and death for more than two thousand years that she can't come visit her great-nieces and nephew? That was always the trouble with dealing with the immortal; they were so used to getting their way.

CHAPTER

EIGHT

Detective Lucy Tate was tall, dark haired, and dressed in the female version of the plainclothes detective pantsuit, black with a white dress shirt this time. It seemed only color varied for the detectives of the homicide bureau. When Lucy had first come through the door I'd thought she had a murder she wanted a fey perspective on, but she'd had a trio of small teddy bears in her hands, and I was pretty certain that made it a friendly visit, not business. I'd been half right.

"Merry, it's reasonable for the local police to be worried that Maeve Reed's estate isn't safe. The bastard kidnapped you from there."

"I can't go into a safe house with the babies," I said. The room was almost empty now. Most of the flowers had gone to other people in the hospital, as had most of the toys. We'd kept flowers and presents from actual friends, or people whose gifts it would be impolitic not to keep, and just that had filled up a second SUV, leaving room only for a driver. Lucy's bears, two pink and one blue, had been newborn safe, and were tucked into the things we were keeping.

Doyle said, "This isn't a homicide issue, Detective; why are you here?"

"She's a friend, Doyle," I said.

"She is, but they sent her because they thought a friend could persuade you where the others had failed, isn't that right, Detective Tate?"

He looked at her with that black-on-black gaze; his face was unreadable, blank so that it was almost threatening in its absolute neutrality. The way a wild animal will look at you: It doesn't want to hurt you, but if you crowd it, it will defend itself. If you don't crowd it, then you can depart in peace, but the warning is there. Back off, or things will go badly.

Lucy reacted to it by taking a half step back, one foot in front of the other in a stance that let her move if she needed to. I doubted she was even fully aware of what she'd done, but the cop in her had seen the implied threat and reacted accordingly. Doyle wouldn't attack and she wouldn't do anything to push that neutrality, but it was still unsettling to watch my friend and my love face off. I didn't want unsettling, I wanted settled. I wanted to just be happy with the babies and the loves of my life, but my family was going to make sure this milestone was as traumatic as they'd made every other important event in my life. My father had protected me from them as much as he could, but once he died it had just been me trying to survive. I was tired of this shit, so tired of it.

"I'm not going into a safe house, Lucy. I appreciate the thought, but human cops would just be cannon fodder if the king attacks us. Read the police report on what his power did to Doyle, and think what that would have done to a human being."

"I've seen the reports," she said.

"That's how they persuaded you to come down," I said.

She nodded. "He can turn light into heat and project it from his hand; that's like crazy."

"He is the King of Light and Illusion; he can do many things with light, especially daylight," Doyle said.

"Like what else can he do with light?" Lucy asked.

Doyle shook his head. "I'm hoping he hasn't regained all his old abilities; if he has, then it could go badly no matter where Merry is."

"Well, aren't you just a bundle of cheer," she said.

"Instead of being able to spend time with Merry and our children, I have spent the last day and night negotiating with one high court of faerie or another. The king's courtiers have assured me that he will wait until the DNA tests come back. If they show that none of the babes are his, then he will acknowledge he has no claim on them, or Merry."

"Merry was already pregnant when he . . ." She stopped as if afraid she'd said too much.

"It's okay, Lucy, but the geneticist has informed us that it may not be that simple. The king is my great-uncle, and the sidhe of both courts have been intermarrying for centuries; we could share a lot of genetics. It's probably not enough to prove paternity, but enough to confuse the issue if my uncle wishes not to give up his claim."

"He won't give up," Doyle said.

"Is it true that if he's not able to have children, then he has to relinquish the throne?" she asked.

I fought to keep my face neutral. I hadn't known that the human police knew that, or any human knew that.

"The blank face from both of you is answer enough," she said.

I cursed softly inside my head—sometimes in trying so hard not to give something away, the very effort screams your answer. The big question was: Did the police know that it wasn't a matter of stepping down from the throne, but execution, for having cursed his court with infertility a century after Taranis knew he was infertile? The old idea that your health, prosperity, and fertility came from your king, or queen, was very true in faerie. Taranis was fighting for his very life. Did Lucy know that?

"What happens if he steps down?" she asked.

"He ceases to be king," Doyle said.

"That part I figured, but is he exiled from faerie?"

"No, why do you ask?" I said.

She shrugged. "Because exile would explain why he's so desperate to prove one of the babies is his."

"I think it's simpler than that, Lucy. I think he just can't stand the thought of not being absolute ruler of the Seelie Court after all these centuries. I think he'd do anything to keep his throne."

"Define *anything*," she said, and I didn't like the very shrewd look in her brown eyes. She was smart and very good at her job.

One of the babies made a sound from the cribs. Lucy had ignored them except for a brief glimpse at the cloth-wrapped bundles. She was here on business, not to see babies, but the noise made us turn to find out which baby was waking up.

It was Bryluen, moving fitfully in her basket like a crib within a crib. Doyle picked her up with his big, dark hands. The baby looked even tinier. Some of the fathers had been awkward holding them, but Doyle held our daughter with the same physical ease and grace with which he did everything. Bryluen's eyes were open enough to gleam in the light like dark jewels.

"May I hold her?" Lucy asked, and the request surprised me.

Doyle looked to me, and I said, "Of course. We're waiting for the nurse to bring the wheelchair; they won't let me walk out, and most of the other men are helping load the gifts."

Lucy didn't seem to hear me as Doyle laid Bryluen in her arms. Lucy didn't know how to hold the baby, which said she'd never really been around them. Doyle helped move her arms into place, and once she had the baby tucked into the crook of her arm she just stared down. Lucy's face got this happy, almost beatific glow to it, as if the world had narrowed down to the baby in her arms.

I hadn't expected Lucy to be that entranced with babies, but maybe she was having that "I'm in my midthirties and the clock is ticking" moment.

"Detective Tate," Doyle said.

She never reacted, just started humming softly and rocking Bryluen gently.

"Detective Tate," he said again, with a little more force to his voice.

When she didn't react this time, I moved closer to her and said, "Lucy, can you hear me?"

She never reacted, as we hadn't spoken.

"Lucy!" I said it sharply this time.

She blinked up at me as if she were waking from a dream. She stared at me, trying to say something, but she had to blink twice more to finally say, "What did you say?"

"I need to get Bryluen ready to go downstairs." I took the baby from her arms, and she was reluctant to let her go, but once she wasn't holding the baby Lucy seemed to recover herself. She shook visibly, like shaking off a nightmare, and said, "Wow, I just had that sensation like someone walked over my grave."

I nodded. "It happens."

She shivered again, and when she looked at me her eyes looked normal. Detective Tate was in there again.

"I'm sorry, Lucy, and I hope it doesn't get you in trouble with the higher-ups in your department, but we need to take more precautions against my uncle, and Maeve Reed's estate is more magically guarded than any safe house would be."

"We'll have police wizards on the detail, Merry."

"The last time you and I worked together, one of the bad guys was one of those wizards," I said.

"That's not fair, Merry."

"Perhaps not, but it's still true."

"You're saying that you don't trust the police?"

"No, I'm saying that no matter how safe you think you are, you're probably wrong."

"That sounds pretty hopeless," she said.

"I thought it sounded realistic."

She smiled, but it wasn't entirely a happy one. "We'll put extra patrols in your neighborhood. Call and we'll be there."

"I know that," I said.

"Promise if anything goes wrong you'll call the police and not try to handle it yourselves."

"I can't promise that."

"Because you're not allowed to lie," she said.

I nodded.

"You'll handle this internally, if you can, won't you?"

I nodded again, cuddling Bryluen to me.

She turned to Doyle. "Don't you or any of the people she loves play hero and get killed when we could have prevented it, okay?"

"We will endeavor not to," he said.

"I mean it. Merry loves you, and I don't want to hold her hand while she mourns you, or Frost, or Galen, or any of you guys. We're the police; it's our job to risk our lives to protect and serve."

"It is our job, as well, where Merry and the babes are concerned."

"Yeah, but Merry won't be devastated if we get hurt, and police dying in the line of duty won't lose the babies their dads."

He gave a small bow from his neck. "I will remember what you said, and thank you for putting our lives above yours for Merry's sake."

"I don't want to die, none of us do, but it's our job to stop this bastard from hurting her again."

"And ours," he said.

She frowned and made a little push-away gesture. "You're going to do what you're going to do; I'll tell them I tried."

"We really do appreciate you coming down, Lucy."

She smiled at me. "I know you do. I just really want to get this guy."

I realized that Lucy had taken my rape more personally, because we were friends. It made me care for her even more, and say with real feeling, "Thank you, Lucy."

She smiled a little wider. "I'll leave you to get the little tykes ready to leave, and go join the cops helping to keep back the crowd."

"I assume the press," I said.

"And just people wanting to see the little prince and princess; it's not every day that America gets newborn royals."

"True," I said, and smiled at her.

She smiled back and then left us with, "I'm not usually into babies, but she's a cute one."

We thanked her, and once the door closed behind her, Doyle and I looked at each other. He came to stand beside me, and we both looked down at Bryluen.

"Mustn't bespell the humans," I said to her.

She blinked those exotic-looking eyes at me. The little knit cap was tucked over most of her red curls and completely hid the horn buds. She was tiny and perfect, and already magical.

"Do you think she understands?" I asked.

"No, but that answers one question."

I looked up at him. "What question?"

"Maeve Reed has a human nanny for her baby, but we cannot risk human caregivers."

"You mean we can't risk the human caregivers being ensorcelled by the babies."

"Yes, that is what I mean."

I looked down at our little bundle of joy. "She's part demi-fey, or part sluagh, one has the best glamour in all faerie, and the other is some of the last of the wild magic left in faerie."

"There is wild magic about, my Merry." He motioned at the tree and the wild rose vines.

I smiled. "True, but I've never seen a baby bespell someone that quickly and that well. Lucy has a strong will, and was likely wearing some protections against faerie glamour just as a precaution. Most police that deal with us do."

"Yet Bryluen clouded her mind and senses as if it were nothing," Doyle said.

"It was very quick and well done. I've known sidhe with centuries of practice who couldn't have done it."

He placed his hand gently on top of her head, so very dark against the multicolored cap. Bryluen blinked up at us. "They are going to be very powerful, Merry."

"How do we teach them to control their powers if they have them this early, Doyle? Bryluen can't understand right from wrong yet."

"We will have to protect the humans from them until they are old enough to learn control."

"How long will that be?"

"I do not know, but we know now that they have come into the world with instinctive magic and there is no waiting until puberty for their powers to manifest."

"It would have been easier if their magic had waited," I said.

"It would, but I do not think our path was ever meant to be easy, my

Merry; wondrous, beautiful, exciting, thrilling, even frightening, but not easy."

I raised Bryluen to lay a kiss upon her cheek. I loved her already; she was mine, ours, but I was a little frightened now. If she could make humans like her, want to hold and rock her, what else could she make them do? Child psychologists say that children are born sociopaths and have to learn to have a conscience. It happens around the age of two, usually, but until then there's no conscience to appeal to, no way to understand that something is wrong or right.

I held our beautiful little sociopath and prayed to the Goddess that she wouldn't hurt anyone before we'd had time to teach her that it was wrong.

The scent of roses filled the room, and it wasn't just the clean sweetness of the wild rose vine, but that richer musk that is more from cultivation than nature. It was a heady scent, and reassurance from the Goddess. Normally, it would have been enough to lay my fears to rest, but this time there was a kernel of unease that stayed inside my heart. How could I doubt her, after all she'd shown me, all she'd awakened around me? But it wasn't the Goddess I doubted, it was more just worry. I was a new mother, and mothers worry.

CHAPTER

NINE

Maeve Reed, the Golden Goddess of Hollywood since about 1950, came to the hospital to escort us home to her house. We'd lived in her guesthouse when we first moved in with her, but as more fey had flocked to us, Maeve had moved us into the main house with her and left the guesthouse to new exiles from faerie who weren't as close to her. She was an exile herself, so she understood the confusion of being cast out from faerie and being thrust into the modern world.

Though very few exiles had succeeded as well as Maeve Reed at adapting to this brave, new world. The guard outside opened the door, and I heard Maeve's voice. "So happy you loved my last movie. Congratulations on your baby, he is adorable." Her voice was warm and utterly sincere, and in part it was the truth, but she had been a great actress for decades and could turn utter sincerity on and off like a well-oiled switch. I doubted I would ever be that skilled at being "on" for the public, and being merely mortal I wouldn't live long enough for the centuries of practice that had helped her get so very good at it.

She came breezing into the room with a casual wave of her hand that was too big a gesture for the room but would have looked great in a photo, as would the brilliant smile on her face. She was dressed in an oyster-white pantsuit that flowed and moved with her; a silk shell in a deep but subdued blue helped her not look quite the six feet that she was, forcing the eye down once it had started up those long legs. She smiled at me and I had a moment of catching the edge of the smile she'd used on the fan outside. It was a good smile, and sincere in its way, because she was genuinely happy that the woman liked her film, and meant the congratulations, but . . . the moment the door closed behind her the smile vanished, and she had a moment where it was as if she laid down some invisible burden across her shoulders. Nothing could make her less than gorgeous with that perfect pale gold tan, the perfect blue eyes in subdued but equally perfect makeup, those cheekbones, those full, kissable lips, but she had a moment of looking tired. Then she straightened up and those high, tight breasts pressed against the blue shell, perky forever without any need for cosmetic surgery.

Her gaze went to the fruit tree that was shedding its blossoms like a pink snow, and the roses on the other side of the room. "Ah, the new wonders. The nurses asked me when the plants would be going away."

"We aren't sure," Doyle said.

"Doyle, Frost, I stopped by the nursery first and the babies are beautiful."

"They are," Doyle said, as if to say, *Of course.*

"Welcome home, Maeve," Frost said.

She wasted a few extra watts of smile on him, but she didn't mean it. He wasn't pure sidhe enough for her; most of my men weren't. She'd made no secret about the fact that she'd have had sex with Rhys or Mistral, if they and I had been okay with it. Among humans it would have been an insult; among the fey if you found someone attractive and didn't let them know, it was an insult. She was afraid of Doyle, not because he'd done anything to her, but because she'd spent too many centuries seeing him as my aunt's assassin. She'd lost people she cared about to him long ago, so she never flirted with him. He was fine with that.

Then she turned to me, and the look on her face was suddenly cautious. She'd actually texted me before she came, asking if I was angry at her for neglecting me. I'd reassured her via text but realized I'd need to do more reassuring in person.

I held my hand out to her, and she came to me smiling, but it was a different smile, less perfect than on film, letting me see the uncertainty in her eyes. I valued that I got to see her when the cameras weren't rolling and she let down her guard.

"I'm so sorry that I couldn't come sooner. I saw the babies in the nursery and they are so beautiful."

"You had to fly back from Europe just to see us."

She took my hand in hers, studying my face. "How are you feeling, honestly?"

Her hand was warm, the bones long and delicate as I rubbed my fingers down them. "What's wrong, Maeve?"

"The media circus is in full swing outside, Merry." A frown showed between those perfect brows and those famous blue eyes. If only her legion of fans were ever allowed to see her eyes when they weren't hidden by faerie glamour to appear more human; as beautiful as she was now, stripped of all illusions she was even more so.

"You say that like the media is entirely your fault. I'm the first American-born faerie princess; I've lived with cameras and reporters all my life."

"That's true, but combine your fame with mine and it's worse than I've seen it, and Merry, I've seen it at its worst." She squeezed my hand in hers. I wasn't sure if it was to reassure me, or herself, or maybe neither; maybe it was just the comfort of another hand to hold.

People say they want to be famous, but there is a level of fame that becomes almost crippling. I'd had the literal weight of the press break a window from trying to get a better view of me with Doyle and Frost once. Some of them had been cut, nothing serious, but they had rained glass down on us and the other customers in the shop.

"You are actually frightened," Doyle said.

She looked up at him and nodded.

Frost came forward to lay his hand on my shoulder. "Is Merry in danger?"

"Police have moved them all back enough that we can exit, and other patients can get into the hospital, but I have never seen so many reporters."

"You have been the reigning Goddess of Hollywood for decades, and you have never seen so many of them." Doyle made it a half-question.

"No, I have not," she said.

"Then it will help boost the money that your newly released film makes, which is what your producers, and all of us, wanted," I said. I raised my hand and laid it over Frost's where he touched me.

"I don't think our publicist could have envisioned this," she said.

"We could send you home and sign the papers for the reality TV show. That would bring in more money," I said.

"No, we don't want cameras in our house, not like that."

"Then you're the major breadwinner for our court in exile, Maeve. It behooves us to do as much as possible to help promote your career. The rest of us couldn't earn what's needed, especially not to live in the style to which you're spoiling us. We could say yes to the reality show and bring in more money than we can from being private detectives," I said.

"I earned thirty million dollars for my last film, Merry; I think I can afford you all, though admittedly the Red Caps eat more than I thought possible," she said with a smile.

Frost didn't hear the joke in her words. "They range from seven to thirteen feet tall and are big enough to fill out such frames. It takes fuel to make a warrior as big as an ogre run."

She raised her smile and aimed it at him, but it wasn't a flirting smile now, more the "isn't he cute not understanding" smile. "I was making a slight joke, Frost."

He frowned. "I did not think it was funny."

"Nor I," Doyle said.

She looked from one to the other of them, and then turned to me, laughing. "They can be so terribly serious sometimes."

"If you want jokes, best turn to Rhys or Galen," I said. I leaned my body back against Frost as I said it, letting him know I valued him, but it was true that humor was not the strong suit for my two main loves.

Frost wrapped his arm across the front of me, pulling me closer. I let Maeve's hand go so that I could grip his arm with both of my hands, holding on and leaning hard against the solidness of him. It was as if the strength of him seeped into me just from him holding me this close. I loved him more and more every day, and took more comfort from his presence in my life. I'd lost him once, or thought I had, and it frightened me that I loved him even more now, because when I thought he was gone forever it had been a near-killing sorrow. I knew if I lost him now it would hurt even more, and that was frightening, but I couldn't hold back from him either, because love can die from being withheld, like a flower that is so beautiful you hide it away from the sun trying to make it last longer; but every flower needs sun, and being in love requires risking yourself. It can require risking everything you are, not just in battle, but emotionally. Sometimes you have to risk it all to gain it all. I basked in the warmth of Frost's love and let him feel mine.

He hugged me tighter and leaned down to place a gentle kiss on the top of my head, resting his cheek against me. "I love you, my Merry," he whispered.

"And I love you, my Killing Frost." I turned my head, rising so we could kiss. I'd purposefully waited to put on lipstick, because we all tended to kiss a lot, and we didn't want to face the cameras with lipstick smeared across our faces like clown makeup.

"Seeing the two of you together makes me hope that I'll find another love of my own life someday," Maeve said.

Frost and I broke the kiss to look at Maeve. She had lost her human husband, the director who had discovered her back in the fifties, to cancer.

"I am sorry we could not save him, Maeve," I said.

"Even the magic of faerie can't heal a human that near death," she said.

I started to go to her to hug her, but Doyle surprised us by moving toward her. He held out his hand. "I know what it is to lose someone you love, and all the magic in the world does not ease the loss."

Maeve hesitated, then put her hand in his dark one. "All those years of seeing you stand beside the Queen of Air and Darkness, you were her Darkness, a bringer of blood and death; you gave no clue that you were actually a romantic."

"And achingly lonely," he said, "but neither was helpful as the right hand of the queen."

"But you helped Merry give me a chance to have a child with my husband, and now I have Liam."

"The magic that helped you grow fertile was Galen and Merry's doing, none of mine."

"You kept her alive long enough to do the spell, and that Galen could not have done," Maeve said.

Doyle acknowledged it with a nod, and then Maeve moved slowly into him and put her arms around him. He was stiff and a little unsure, but he patted her as she hugged him almost as awkwardly.

There was a flash from the window behind us. Doyle moved so fast it was hard to follow, as if the gun had just appeared in his hand and was pointed at the window, as he moved toward it. Frost had shoved me behind him. He had a gun in one hand and a blade in the other.

Maeve yelled, "It's a camera, Doyle; don't shoot them."

"Unless they can fly, it cannot be reporters," he said. There was another flash of light. I couldn't see past Frost's body and knew better than to even peer around him. He was guarding me; I had to let him do his job, but I wanted to see, badly.

Doyle cursed. "Anu's Breasts, they're on window-washing equipment, two of them."

"Well, someone has to work the controls while the other one takes pictures, or film," Maeve said as if it were just an everyday occurrence. Maybe it was for the Golden Goddess of Hollywood, but we'd never had reporters climbing down the windows of a hospital before.

Doyle shut the curtains, cutting out the sunlight with them so the room was suddenly dim.

"Thus it begins," Maeve said.

"I hate paparazzi," Frost said.

We all agreed with him and then called hospital security to let them know they'd been breached.

TEN

Doyle had negotiated three days for me to recover my strength from giving birth, and then Aunt Andais, the Queen of Air and Darkness, got to speak to me directly. She wasn't going to use the telephone, because she wanted to see me while we spoke. We weren't going to use the computer for a Skype face-to-face either. Aunt Andais didn't even own a cell phone, and computers were for her staff, but for her it was the old-fashioned way: a mirror. The sidhe could speak through reflective surfaces of more than one kind, but mirrors were the easiest and clearest view. We chose the antique mirror in the dining room. One, because it was large and had been as big as one wall of the room once, before wild magic had expanded the room to the size of a small football field. The French doors showed a forest that had never existed in California. The clearing and forest were new lands of faerie, or old lands returned. We'd been so happy when it had happened, and then Taranis had walked into that bit of fairyland, knocked me unconscious, and stolen me away. Now there were locks on the French doors, and two guards posted at all times. If Taranis kidnapped me again, it wouldn't be through this opening.

The mirror was still large enough to act like a huge flat-screen TV, so that the queen would get a good view first of me, and then, if that went well, the babies, but since some of us could use mirrors to travel from one point to another we weren't risking the babies until Aunt Andais had shown herself sane, or at least sane-ish. I'd take the "ish" because asking for more than that would mean I'd never speak with her.

I debated on what color maternity dress to wear. It wasn't a casual concern. Andais was very into fashion, but more than that, she had taken insult from my choice of clothing in the past. Her feeling insulted had led to my being hurt, or even bleeding, so we put serious thought into what I would wear to sit before the queen. Shades of rich, dark green were some of my best colors. They brought out the green in my eyes, but Aunt Andais didn't always like to be reminded that my eyes were the color of the Seelie Court, and not the Unseelie. So, no green, which took out several of my maternity dresses. The red one was almost the color of fresh blood, not something we wanted my torture-loving aunt to think of when looking at me. The purple dress was at the dry cleaner. That left us with a soft floral print, royal blue, or a rich, salmon pink. Pants were a no-go; I was still too sore to want to wear them. We finally decided on the pink, saving the blue in case we had to do television earlier than we'd planned.

I sat facing the mirror, in the same large thronelike chair that I'd used to do business with the goblins months ago, before I started showing. It was the closest thing we had to a throne. The only downside to it was that my feet couldn't touch the floor, so I felt like a child. There was no footstool in the house that wasn't hard plastic and cheap looking. No one made velvet and wood stools for the queen to put her feet on anymore. Funny how things like that had gone out of style.

It was Kitto who came up with a solution. "I'll be your footstool."

He stood there gazing up at me, the only man I'd ever been with who was significantly shorter than my five feet even. He had moonlight skin like mine, like Frost's, white and pale and perfect as a winter's morn. His hair was a black almost as dark as Doyle's, but as Kitto's hair had grown out it had gotten wavy, so that it fell to his shoulders in an artful tangle of waves and curls as if it couldn't quite decide. I'd taught him how to take care of his longer hair, so that it looked artfully tousled, not messy. If he'd been taller he could have passed for pure Unseelie sidhe, except for three things. His eyes were huge, dominating his face, almond-shaped and a wondrous bright blue that swallowed his entire eye, except for the black point of his pupil; the color was sidhe, the shape and form were not. But more than the eyes, the line of shining scaled skin that grew down his back along his entire spine showed him not pure sidhe. The scales were flat, smooth, in colors of pink, gold, ivory, and small flecks of black, but so bright in color that the line of it looked more like a purposeful decoration than the scales of a snake. It was his back scales that made me wonder if Bryluen's wings might be partially from Kitto; goblins didn't have wings, but her wings were almost the same color as his snake skin. We wouldn't know until the tests came back. If Taranis hadn't been pushing we wouldn't have cared so much about who was the biological father or fathers of the babies, but to prove it wasn't Taranis, we had to prove who it was. Kitto's Cupid's-bow mouth hid a forked tongue, and he had to work hard not to slur his s's, and the last bit of difference was two long, retractable fangs that tucked up against the roof of his mouth unless he chose to bring them down. He was one lover that I could never allow to bite me, because snake goblins were venomous, and his father had been one. If Bryluen could possibly be his daughter, I'd want to watch for those when her teeth started coming in, because even baby vipers have venom.

"The queen may try to frighten you, Kitto," I said.

"I am a stool for your feet, Merry. Footstools can't hear, or talk, or interact with anyone. I can ignore her, because I can just be the object I'm acting as."

I wasn't sure how I felt about him being just a piece of furniture for my feet. It must have shown on my face, because Kitto took my hand in his; his hand was the same size as mine, the only man in my life for whom that was true.

"I will be honored to act for you in this, Merry. I remember when the high kings, even among the humans, had virgins who held their feet so they did not touch the ground when the king sat upon the throne. It was an honored position, but you were not allowed to address the women at all. You had to treat them as the footstool for the king, and thus they were a part of the throne. If the queen speaks directly to me at all, it will be breaking protocol. I think she may talk to you about me, but I do not believe she will address me; besides, I am just a small goblin and she has never thought highly of me."

I couldn't argue that. There was some debate about what Kitto would wear, but not about his acting as my footstool. The other men agreed that he would wear the metal and cloth thong that I'd first seen him in; it was a lovely piece of workmanship, and it showed off his scales beautifully. Among the goblins if you had an extra bit of beauty, it was natural to dress to show it off. Though the fewer clothes you wore, the less dominant you were among the goblins; it was a way of showing visually that you were opting out of the near-constant battles for supremacy in the goblin court. By dressing as he had when I first met him, Kitto had been advertising that he was not a leader and didn't want to be. There was no need to fight him, because his scanty clothing was a white flag of sorts. It had also marked him as a potential victim, if someone wanted to claim him as a sort of mistress, or concubine; there really was no good human word for a man in his situation, and among the goblins there was no word that differentiated between male and female for the role. Goblins didn't care what sex you were, only how big, how strong, how tough. If a female was able to beat the shit out of enough other goblins, then she could rise as high in their ranks as a male. It was just rare, because their women, like most human women, had less muscle mass, size, and strength to back up their threat. It put women at a serious disadvantage in their culture, but then that was true among a lot of cultures.

The rest of the men had gone for the elegant warrior look. Doyle was in his signature black, but he'd put in the diamond stud earrings, to go with his usual silver rings that climbed up to the tops of his delicately pointed ears. He stood at my side, behind the throne, like a piece of the night made handsome and dangerous flesh.

Frost was at my other side in white and silver to match his skin, hair, and eyes, so that he was coldly elegant like a man carved of ice and snow. If Goddess could have taken winter and formed it into flesh and beauty, it would be the Killing Frost. His face was set in arrogant lines, the expression he wore when he was hiding his emotions. We would all hide our emotions tonight.

Rhys turned from where he was standing by the mirror and said, "Frost and Doyle look like bookends, light and darkness, balanced at your side, Merry."

I glanced up and back at the two men and could only agree. It was in moments like this that I still marveled that these two men, the ones who had seemed the most remote, untouchable by any emotion I understood, were now my greatest loves and fathers to my children.

Rhys was in white as well, but whereas most of the men had chosen medieval dress or some older fashion, he was in modern dress pants with a pale blue T-shirt loose over them, and his cream-colored trench coat; he'd even added his white fedora pulled down at a rakish angle over his long white curls. He was wearing a new eye patch in a pale blue that complemented his remaining eye and made all three of the different shades of blue brighter and deeper.

"You look good, Rhys," Galen said as he went to take his place beside the chair, "but I can't tell if you're doing Sam Spade in *The Maltese Falcon* or a sexy ice cream man."

Rhys grinned. "Well, I always go for sexy, and who doesn't like ice cream, but film noir is where I get most of my clothing inspirations."

Galen grinned back. "I just wear what I'm told to put on." That wasn't entirely true, because he had colors he preferred, but he was probably one of the least picky beyond that. He'd had less than a hundred years of my aunt choosing clothes for her guards, and he had never been a favorite, or far enough out of favor, for her to pay special attention to his appearance. That had given him freedom that the other guards had not had to find their own personal sense of style. Rhys's style was personal, but he'd only been able to indulge his film noir kick here in California with me; before that the queen had dressed him to show off his muscles, somewhere between a pornographic warrior and disco. I'd always thought she did it to humiliate Rhys, or that she didn't know what to do with him.

Galen was in pale green pants, untucked dress shirt, and a darker green tailored jacket. His pale curls with the one long braid always looked green, but his skin often looked just white; in the colors he'd chosen today his skin, eyes, and hair were all green. Only his soft tan dress shoes spoiled the solidarity of his color. He looked good in the outfit, but he didn't look spectacular. Had he not cared? Had he thought the queen would pay more attention to everyone else, as she always had? Or perhaps he had chosen green defiantly, because it made it impossible not to think "pixie," which was what his father had been—a pixie who had seduced one of the queen's ladies-in-waiting, back before she'd exchanged them for gentlemen-in-waiting.

The queen had executed Galen's father for his audacious seduction. How dare a lesser creature of faerie touch the sidhe of her court—and then the lady had come up pregnant and it turned out the queen had killed half of a fertile couple. Galen had been the only child born into the Unseelie sidhe once they arrived on American soil. She would not have killed Galen's father if she had known in time. Her temper coupled with her absolute power had cheated her court out of more babies, as her temper and power had cheated her out of being welcomed into our home to see our babies like a normal aunt.

Now Galen was the father of royal triplets, and he'd dressed to remind the queen of his father. Galen wanted her to remember what her anger and arrogance had cost her, and him, once. It was both brave and smart of him. Brave because he was rubbing the queen's nose in her mistake, and smart because it might remind her that a mistake here and now might cost her more.

It was very unlike Galen, so much so that I had to ask, "Who chose your clothing tonight?"

He walked toward me, smiling. "I did." But again there was a new look in his eyes, harsher, more sure of itself. I had mourned it earlier, but now I welcomed it. I needed all the help I could get negotiating with the queen.

I raised my hand and Galen took it, raising it to kiss first my hand, and then lowering his tall frame to kiss me gently on the lips. We didn't want to muss my bright red lipstick. He drew back with lipstick on his mouth, like a scarlet shadow of my smaller mouth between his lips.

"You'll want to rub that off," I said.

He shook his head. "I'll wear your lipstick proudly, my Merry. Let her see that I am in your favor, and that I am one of the Greenmen who prophecy said would bring life to the court."

"And remind her that your father might have brought more life to the courts if she hadn't killed him," I said, still holding his hand.

"That, too," he said. He squeezed my hand and stepped back because everyone else was spilling into the room at once. The prearranged time for the call was close, and we needed everyone in place so we could look impressive for our queen.

Mistral came first, looking impatient and tugging at his tunic. It was dark burnished gold with brighter gold and silver thread worked into the puff sleeves and cuffs, and in a more elaborate pattern across the chest. The pants were a color between tan and gold and bloused over the rich dark brown leather of his knee-high boots. The boots and pants he'd worn before, but the tunic had spent many long years put away, because it was a reminder of the power and magic he had lost. As he walked into the room it was as if lightning reflected down his long, unbound hair. Strands of it had turned gold, yellow, silver, a white so bright it nearly glowed. Some of that was a permanent color change, just a single strand here and there among the gray, but the flashing, reflected light that moved through all his hair came and went like lightning does.

His hair had changed in the last twenty-four hours, as if something had returned more of his power to him. He'd been holding Gwenwyfar, rocking her to sleep, when we'd noticed the first flash of light in his hair.

Now he strode into the room tugging at the tunic, and the colors in it brought out the strands of color in his hair, but I didn't really think it showed off the flash of light. I thought solid black clothing might show-case the lightning display more, but we'd think about that for another night when we wanted to be impressive, or frightening.

Kitto came in, wearing his metal thong. He was smiling and said, "Nicca and Biddy are watching the babies." That meant we could concentrate on meeting the queen without worrying that the babies would cry and need us, which was especially good since the pink dress was not a dark color. If the babies cried, any of the babies, sometimes my milk came down and the nursing bra wasn't enough to stop it from staining. It was a mark of the blessing of the Goddess that I could nurse my children, but it was not convenient for looking serious and in charge.

Kitto went down on the floor so that my feet in their purple and pink flats could rest on his bare back. I'd felt that acting as my footstool had been degrading to him, but now that I felt him solid under my feet it just felt right, as if he grounded me, centered me. I felt less of an impostor dressed up to play queen, and more . . . queenly.

Sholto was the last of the fathers to stride in through the door, and he was in black, an outfit almost identical to the one he'd worn in the hospital when he wanted to be certain to be seen as a king. His white-blond hair was unbound around all the blackness and gleaming jewelry, so he looked both beautiful and frightening, which was the effect he wanted.

Behind Sholto came the guards, who were now just guards for me. We had all discussed it and decided that though our customs didn't force me to limit my sexual attentions to the fathers of my children, there were already too many of them and not enough of me. So not every handsome face, beautiful body, dangerously armed guard, male or female, who came through the door was my lover. Honestly, most never had been, but sometimes it's good to finalize the rules of a relationship, even one with a group as large as ours.

They fanned out around the room in their warrior garb, some in actual armor, but most in modern clothing with body armor under or over the clothing. Though in truth if the Queen of Air and Darkness wanted you dead, armor wouldn't save you. Her name was not an idle title but named her two main powers. She could travel through the dark to anywhere else that was dark, and hear her name spoken in the dark. She could see in the dark without any light to aid her. The air she could make heavy, thick, until you could no longer breathe it and it felt as if your chest were being crushed by the weight of her magic. Andais was truly the Queen of Air and Darkness.

What good was armor against such magic? But they wore it all the same, because sometimes it's not about whether it will actually stop the bullet or the blade, but more about drawing a line in the sand at your enemy's feet. We hoped it would show Andais that we meant to fight rather than submit. All of us were exiles from her court, and almost all of us had suffered at her hands, some more than others. There were a handful of guards that Doyle had decided would not stand with us tonight, because he feared that their memories of what Andais had done to them would make them unable even to stand their ground, let alone fight if the need arose.

We had found therapists for the most damaged of our refugees from faerie. They had been diagnosed with post-traumatic stress disorder, or PTSD. I wouldn't have been surprised if most of us had a touch of it. You don't have to be the one being cut up to be traumatized; watching it is enough sometimes. Those who were most fragile were barred from the room and given duties elsewhere. They could help keep the amazing crush of media from climbing the wall around Maeve's estate, or help patrol the grounds looking for each new bit of faerie that appeared. It was as if the old lands were emerging in puzzle pieces in this bit of America where they had never existed, though faerie wasn't a place you could reliably find on a map. It was more an idea, or ideal, of wild magic that had a mind and will of its own. Faerie moved at its own whim, and that of the Goddess and Her Consort. So the grounds were patrolled, search-ing for each bit of wild magic as it manifested. Already the lands inside the walls were much larger than ordinary senses said the walls could contain, which was wonderful, but Taranis had stepped through on the new lands, and so might the queen. The danger of that meant guards had to be posted, to warn the rest of us if either of them was seen. I think we all felt that we would lose a pitched battle against either the king or the queen, but if the alarm was given first, then even if the guard who dis-covered the breach died, there would be more warriors coming to defend us. And when I said "us," I didn't mean just my babies and me. Maeve and one other of our female guards had given birth here in this new Western kingdom of faerie. We'd run away from faerie to save our lives, and now faerie was coming to us, building itself around us. Doyle and

I had given up our crowns to the Unseelie Court to save our Killing Frost, but the Goddess and the land of faerie itself wasn't done. If we could not rule the Unseelie, it seemed likely we'd get a chance to rule something else, something new, something here.

I hadn't refused Detective Lucy Tate's offer of a safe house just because I thought it would get the nice policemen killed. I had refused because wild magic was everywhere around me and the fathers of my babies. In a human safe house surrounded by human police, we wouldn't be able to hide just how much of the old powers were returning. What would the police have done if they'd woken up with their safe house growing an extra room overnight, or a new door that led to a forest that had never existed on the West Coast of America?

So we stayed inside Maeve's walled estate and let it grow and become magical. I thought about the tree and roses in my hospital room. It had been miraculous even to the sidhe when such things first began appearing around me. Inside faerie some had faded, but others had remained and grown. Outside faerie they had faded over time in the beginning, but lately not so much. I hoped they faded, because we weren't certain what the humans would do if they found out just how much magic was following me around.

Doyle and Frost's positions at my back to left and right had been easily agreed on, but where the other men would stand had been more of a debate. Sholto had won the right to choose his place, because he was a true king in his own right and the Goddess herself had handfasted us and crowned me as his queen. The only issue had been when he tried to insist on standing higher than Doyle or Frost. I had to put my foot down on that, and he'd let me win with almost no argument, which meant he'd made only a token try. He chose to stand beside Doyle on the right of my chair. Rhys had wanted to mirror him beside Frost, until the others pointed out that because of his being six inches shorter than everyone else, he'd be mostly hidden behind whoever was in front. Mistral stood beside Frost, mirroring Sholto. That left Rhys beside Sholto and Galen beside Mistral. Kitto under my feet would not seem to be one of the fathers, and I'd told Royal he couldn't stand at my side tonight. For one thing, Sholto was convinced that Bryluen's wings were from his father's side of the genetics. Even more importantly, if my third baby had truly been fathered after the twins were conceived, that gave credence to Taranis's paternity claim. I didn't want to help Taranis and his team of lawyers stake a claim to my children. I loved Bryluen already, but there was part of me that stared at her red curls, so like my own, and thought, *So like Taranis's hair.* I prayed to Goddess that it was not so, but when so much wild magic and Deity intervention is everywhere, many things are possible, both good and terrible.

"It's time, Merry," Doyle said, his deep voice soft. He laid a hand on my shoulder as if he felt my nervousness.

I put my hand up to cover his, and said, "Then let us begin. Cathbodua, please let my aunt know we are ready to speak with her."

Cathbodua stepped forward from the guards that stretched in a semicircle behind us. She had been part of my father's guards once, the Prince's Cranes, but when he was assassinated the entire female guard had been given to Prince Cel, the queen's son. It had been against the rules and customs to simply transfer them to Cel. Once his master was dead, a guard was supposed to have a choice of either transferring his loyalty to another royal or going back to "private service" and being just another noble of the Unseelie Court. We had learned only in the last year that none of the women had been allowed a choice, and Prince Cel had made them into his personal harem. Some had become his torture victims, as some of the male guards had been for the queen, but some were not so easily victimized.

Cathbodua moved toward the mirror in a rustle of feathers, her raven cloak spreading out around her like the feathers it had once become. She still couldn't transform into full bird guise, but she could communicate with ravens and crows and a few other birds to help spy out the land and look for danger. Her hair was as black as the feathers, so that it was hard to tell where one began and the other ended. Her skin was moonlight skin like mine, like Frost's, like Rhys's, but somehow when you looked at her you thought bone white, not moonlight. She was beautiful as all the sidhe were beautiful, but there was a coldness to her beauty that did not appeal to me. But then I wasn't dating her; as a guard she was excellent, and that was all I required of her.

She touched the side of the mirror, and I heard the distant cawing of crows, like hearing your own phone ringing in your ear, knowing it's louder on the other end.

We had all bet that Andais would keep us waiting, but we were wrong. The mirror fogged as if some invisible giant breathed along the glass, and when it cleared there she sat.

She sat on the edge of her huge black-silk-and-fur-draped bed. It was rich and sensual, and a little threatening, as if there would be pressure to live up to such a bed, and the price for failing expectations might be harsh, or maybe that was just me knowing my aunt far too well.

She was wearing a black silk robe so that her ankle-length black hair mingled with the robe and the sheets, until it was as if her hair was formed out of all that silk and dark fur. Her skin was whiter than white, framed by all that raven darkness, except for one spill of honey-and-white fur to her left that spoiled the effect and showed her hair black and almost normal across it. It wasn't like her to not notice that one bit of pale that spoiled the intimidating effect of her visual.

Her face was almost free of makeup, and without the black eyeliner she usually wore her triple-gray irises weren't as striking, again leaving her eyes almost ordinary. Her beauty didn't need makeup, though without it she was a cold, distant beauty as if carved of ice and raven's wings. That was a strange thought, with Cathbodua standing beside the mirror in her raven wing cloak, but though both women might have begun as similar battle goddesses, where they had gone from their beginnings had made all the difference. It had made one a queen for a millennium and left the other to diminish until she was barely more than human. It is not where you begin, or what gifts you begin with, but what you do with them that matters in the end.

"Greetings, Aunt Andais, Queen of Air and Darkness, sister of my father, ruler of the Unseelie host."

"Greetings, niece Meredith, Princess of Flesh and Blood, daughter of my beloved younger brother, mother of his grandchildren, and conqueror of hearts."

I had chosen my words carefully to remind her that I was her niece and she might value my bloodline if not the rest of me, but she had given an answer as careful as my own, and as nonthreatening. It wasn't like her.

"Aunt Andais, I'm not quite sure what to say next." She was too far off script for me, and when in doubt truth is not a bad fallback plan.

She smiled, and she seemed tired. "I grow tired of torturing people, my niece."

I fought to keep my face blank, and felt Doyle's hand tense on my shoulder where I touched him. I forced my breathing even, and spoke in a normal voice. "May I be so bold as to say, Aunt Andais, that both surprises and pleases me."

"You may, since you already have, Meredith, and you are not surprised that torture no longer pleases me, you are shocked, are you not?"

"Yes, aunt, quite so."

She laughed then, head back, face shining with it, but it was the kind of laugh that slithered down your spine and tickled goose bumps from every inch of your skin. I'd heard that laugh as she cut people's skin with a blade while they screamed.

I swallowed past my suddenly thudding pulse, and knew in that moment that I never wanted her around my babies. I never wanted them to hear that laughter, not ever.

"I see that look upon your face, Meredith. I know that look."

"I don't know what you mean, Aunt Andais."

"Determination, decision, and not in my favor, am I right?"

"In your moments of clarity, aunt, you see much."

"Yes," she said, face growing somber, "in my moments of clarity, when I do not let my bloodlust have full rein, and carve my unhappiness and lust from the bodies of my courtiers."

"Yes, Aunt Andais, when you're not doing that," I said.

She held her hand out to someone out of sight of the mirror. Eamon, her favorite lover for the last hundred years or so, came to take her hand.

He was as pale of skin, as black of hair, as she; a little taller, broader through the shoulders, six-plus feet of sidhe warrior, but the face he turned to the mirror held that calm, even a kindness, that had often been all that stood between Andais and her worst instincts. He'd grown out a thin, neat Vandyke mustache and goatee, but it was still more facial hair than I'd ever seen my aunt allow at our court. Beards and such were for Taranis and his golden throng. Andais preferred her men clean shaven; many of the men couldn't even grow facial hair.

Eamon sat on the bed beside her, putting his arm across her shoulders, and she leaned into him, as if she needed the reassurance of the touching. It was a show of weakness that I never thought she would allow me to see.

"Greetings, Princess Meredith, wielder of the hands of flesh and blood, niece of my beloved," Eamon said.

In all the years that he had stood by her side in mirror calls to others, I had never heard him greet, or be greeted, by anyone. He had been an extension of Andais, nothing more.

"Greetings, Eamon, wielder of the hand of corrupting flame, consort of my Aunt Andais, holder of her heart."

He smiled at me, and it was a good smile, a real one. "I have never heard myself called that last before, Princess Meredith; I thank you for it."

"It was a title I suspected you deserved long ago, but I had never known for certain until today."

He hugged Andais, and she seemed somehow diminished, smaller, or I just had never appreciated how big a man Eamon was, or perhaps a bit of both.

Eamon raised his eyes a little and spoke. "Greetings, Doyle, wielder of the painful flame, Baron Sweet-Tongue, the Queen's Darkness, consort of Princess Meredith."

"And to you, Eamon, all graces and titles deserved and earned to you, as well."

He smiled. "Now, I do not know whom to greet next, Princess Meredith. Do I give formal acknowledgment to Lord Sholto, who is a king in his own right, or to the Killing Frost, who is dearest to you and the Darkness, or to Rhys, who has regained his own sithen again, and no offense to Galen the Green Knight, but our protocols have nothing to cover so many consorts or princes."

"If it is a formal greeting for all of us, then Sholto should be next," Frost said.

I reached out to touch his hand where it sat on the pommel of the sword at his waist. He always touched his weapons when he was nervous. He rewarded me with a smile, and that was enough.

"I will waive such niceties," Sholto said. "For my fellow consorts to acknowledge my title is enough." He gave a small bow from his neck toward Frost, who acknowledged with a bow as low as Sholto's but no lower. There had been a time when you had to know just how low to bow to each level of noble, and to get it wrong was an insult. I was glad such things were in the past. How had anyone gotten anything done?

"Such calm, civilized behavior," Andais said, in a voice that held distaste, as if it wasn't a compliment at all.

Eamon hugged her, laying his cheek gently against her hair. "Would you rather they fight and demand every title we could paint upon them, my queen?"

She ignored his question and spoke, in a voice that seemed as diminished as the rest of her. "Why have you not come to kill me, Meredith?"

I fought to keep my face neutral, and watched Eamon look startled, and the first unease cross his face. What was worse, then his face went back to that handsome, unreadable mask that had allowed him to live and thrive in Andais's bed for so long. Perhaps that last comment had been over the line even for him, chastising his queen in front of others.

I found my voice and said, "I was pregnant with my father's, your brother's, grandchildren and would not risk them for vengeance."

She nodded and put her arm around Eamon's waist, to be held closer. "I went mad after you killed my son and turned down the crown of my court to save your lover, Meredith. Did you realize that?"

"I was aware that you seemed . . . unwell," I said.

She gave that horrible laugh again, and her eyes were fever bright. "Unwell; yes, I have been unwell."

Eamon held her closer, but his face remained unreadable. Whatever happened here, if she went back to being her usual sadistic self, he would survive. Eamon was not our enemy, but he could not afford to be our friend either.

"Meredith, Meredith, the look on your body, your tight control. Do you not understand that after centuries even the fight for control shows to my eyes?"

"I do know that, Aunt Andais, but control is all I can offer."

"Control is all any of us can offer in the end, and I lost mine," she said.

"You seem better now," I said.

She nodded. "It took me months to realize I was trying to force you to send my Darkness to me. I knew if anyone could slay me, it would be him, but day after long day he did not come. Why did you not send him to me, Meredith?"

We had actually discussed sending Doyle to assassinate her, but I had vetoed it. "Because I didn't want to lose my Darkness," I said.

"Your Darkness, yes, I suppose now he is 'your Darkness.'" Anger showed on her face.

I didn't like the "suppose" in that sentence. "Doyle is one of the fathers of my children, which makes us a committed coupling now."

She sat up a little straighter in the curve of Eamon's arm. "Yes, yes, he is yours as a consort, Meredith. I mean nothing by it, beyond the fact that I thought he would be sent to end my pain, but he did not come, and gradually the madness and grief left me. Eamon risked much to bring me back to myself. I tortured Tyler to death one night. I valued him, and I have missed him since, and that helped me realize how far I had fallen."

Tyler had been a barely legal teenage lover. He'd been a human brought into the Unseelie sithen to be her slave, in the bondage-and-submission sense, not in a bought-and-sold sense. Tyler had been good looking in a vapid sort of way; he had been entirely too much pet and not enough person for my tastes, but he had pleased Andais, met a need that was real for her. Apparently he had been more important to her than even she knew.

"I am sorry for your loss, Aunt Andais."

"You sound as if you mean that."

"I would not have wished death by torture on anyone. I had no quarrel with your slave, Tyler. I simply did not understand him or his interactions with you enough to comment."

"Such careful wording, my niece; you never liked Tyler."

"He disturbed me, because you wanted him to disturb me. I know it was part of your games to control me, or amuse yourself, but I was never afraid of Tyler, and he never harmed me. If I hadn't found some value in him I wouldn't have helped your guards and Eamon protect Tyler the night that you almost whipped him to death."

There had been a night in the private chambers of the queen when she had chained Tyler to the wall of her bedroom, and it had gone from a pain-filled game to a near-death experience for him. Eamon had shielded the human with his own body, trying to bring Andais back to sanity in time to save Tyler and keep her from stripping the flesh even from Eamon's bones.

The other guards had been forced to kneel and watch the torture, but what had begun as forcing her celibate guards to watch her have sex with her pet had turned into true life and death. I had watched Rhys, Doyle, Frost, Galen, Mistral, and so many others bloodied and dreadfully injured trying to come to Eamon's aid. In the end I had stepped forward and hoped only to give them time to gather themselves, to think of a way to stop her, but the Goddess had blessed me, and the queen had been stopped by the blessing of the Goddess through me. It was not my power that had done it; I never had illusion otherwise. The best I could claim was that my faith and courage had been rewarded. That night Aunt Andais had been poisoned deliberately to drive her into her full bloodlust in hopes that she would be painted so mad that her nobles would see that Prince Cel, her son, should come to the throne sooner, but I had interfered, and the plan had backfired.

"But you were not there this time, Meredith. You were not in the court that the Goddess and Consort gave to you and Doyle. If you had been, Tyler might still live."

Was she truly going to make this my fault? It was like her self of old; she took little blame for herself and had seen even less attached to Cel, her late son.

Eamon didn't try to soothe her this time, but sat with his arm almost stiffly around her, as if he wasn't sure whether she still welcomed it.

"Would you not have given up your crown to have the man you loved by your side again?" I asked. I wasn't sure it was the right thing to ask, but it was all I could think of to say.

I smelled roses, and knew the Goddess was with me. She either approved of what I'd said or would aid me if the queen did not. Something brushed my cheek and I looked up to find pink and white rose petals falling from empty air. The petals began to collect in my lap like floral snow.

Andais made a sound between a scream and an inarticulate curse. "Pink and white petals, not red, not the colors of our court, but of that golden throng that thinks themselves so superior to us, why, Meredith, why the Goddess of the Seelie and not the Dark Mother?"

"The Goddess is all women, all things, or that is what She has shown to me." I kept my voice calm, but surrounded by the scent of roses in the summer heat of a meadow, in the midst of the soft-petaled rain of roses, I couldn't be upset. Her blessing was too close to me, and it felt warm, safe, like home is meant to be, but so seldom is.

Andais sat up, moving out from the curve of Eamon's arm. "The gardens that have returned to our sithen are full of bright and happy colors. Your Seelie heritage has contaminated our kingdom. You would reshape us in the form of that other world of lies and illusions. You've seen what Taranis considers truth, Meredith. How can you wish our court to become a fairy-tale land that is not real?"

"I did not wish these changes on your court, Aunt Andais. The Goddess returned and with Her the wild magic, and it goes where it will, changing things as it goes. No one of flesh and blood can control the wild magic of faerie itself."

"Would you have returned us to our former dark glory if you could have chosen, Meredith?"

The fall of petals began to slow, but my lap was full of them already. "I do not know, and that is the truth. I had no affection for the court of my uncle; if I had a home in faerie it was the Unseelie Court, and as you remind me, my uncle has made me dread his court even more. So no, aunt, I would not make the Unseelie Court over into that glittering place of lies."

My pulse had sped, not from Andais being so close, but from the thought of Taranis. I mercifully didn't remember most of the attack, but I remembered enough.

Frost and Doyle both laid a hand on my shoulders at the same time. Sholto and Mistral each laid a hand on mine, and I took their hands. Galen went to one knee beside me, his leg almost brushing Kitto, who had remained motionless and still as the footstool he pretended to be, so still that I had almost forgotten him. He had the gift of being that still even when standing beside me. Galen laid his hands on my knee through the layer of petals. He gazed up at me, giving most of his back to the mirror. It was both an insult and a sign that he didn't see her as a threat, or it would have been if one of the other men had done it, but it was Galen and I doubt he thought beyond comforting me. Rhys had taken a half-step forward, so that his hands were free if she was as rash as Taranis had been when he got angry over a mirror call. Galen seemed oblivious to the danger. He had not changed completely. I was both relieved and afraid of what I would find when I raised my eyes from his sweet face to look at my aunt.

I expected anger, disdain, but what I saw was pain, and the closest I'd ever seen to sympathy except when my father died. "It was not my intent to remind you of what he did to you, niece. Our lawyers have told me of what the Seelie king is trying to do, and for that I am sorry, Meredith. I believe Taranis is madder in his own way than I am, or was. At least I come to my senses. He lives in his delusions."

"I appreciate your sentiments, Aunt Andais, more than I can say."

"I made a bargain with you, Meredith, that if you produced a child I would step down for you. Now you have produced three. It is beyond my wildest hopes. I also know that there are two babes from other couplings in your exiled court; again it is more than I hoped for. Come home, Meredith, and the throne is yours, for I gave my word and I cannot go back upon it."

Galen's hand tensed against my knee; the rest of the men went very still where they touched me. Rhys stayed in his forward position. I felt the guards at our backs shift as if a wind had touched them. Turning down Andais never went well.

I fought to keep my voice even. "I do not believe that I would live long upon your throne, Aunt Andais. There are still too many among our court who see my mortal blood as the doom of them all."

"They would not dare harm you for fear of me, just as they have not harmed me during my madness for fear of worse from me, Meredith."

There was a certain logic to what she was saying, but in the end I believed I was correct. "To rule either court, the nobles must take oath to the new ruler, and bind themselves to her or him. At our court it is a blood oath, and I proved on the dueling grounds that to share my blood made my opponents mortal."

"That was unexpected when you killed Arzhul."

"He certainly did not expect the blood oath to make him killable by bullet, or he would never have allowed me a gun against his sword."

She smiled, and looked satisfied. "You were always ruthless, Meredith; why did I not see your worth sooner?"

"You hated my mixed blood as much as any in court, Aunt Andais."

"You're not going to bring back up the time I tried to drown you when you were six, are you? It's very tiresome to be reminded of it, and I would take it back if I could."

"I appreciate that you would take it back, but your belief that I am not worthy to be an Unseelie noble, let alone rule there, is shared by many at the court. They fear taking oath to me, Aunt Andais, for fear that my mortality will cancel out their immortality permanently. Since I cannot promise them it will not happen just as they fear, I think they will choose my death over theirs, or worse, my death over slowly aging like a human."

"For fertile wombs, Meredith, you might be surprised how many would accept you."

"I think that not all the sidhe at your court are as wedded to having children as you are, aunt."

"Perhaps, but have I proved myself calm enough to be allowed a glimpse of my great-nieces and nephew?"

I fought the urge to look at Doyle for reassurance. Rhys glanced back at me and gave me the look I needed. He thought she had been good enough to see the babies, or at least hadn't done anything bad enough to not have earned a glimpse of them. I gave a small nod and then said, "Yes, we will have the babies brought into the room so you may see them tonight, Aunt Andais."

I worded that last carefully, because if I had said, *You may see the babies*, she could interpret it as being allowed to come visit in person, and that she hadn't earned yet.

I gave the order for the babies to be brought into the room. One of the guards went to fetch our nurses and our children to be paraded before their great-aunt, who had nearly killed me when I was little because she thought me not pure-blooded enough, like a mongrel puppy that your prize-winning bitch had dropped. You didn't keep the mistakes, and Andais had seen me as that, or worse. My father had found us, rescued me, fought with his sister, and taken me and all his courtiers with him into the human world. He had chosen exile to keep me safe. I didn't understand what it had cost him until I spent my own three years alone and exiled, hiding here in Los Angeles. My father had loved me dearly; my aunt . . . didn't love me at all. How could I ever trust her around our babies? The answer was obvious: I couldn't.

ELEVEN

Bryluen fit in my arms as if she had been made to tuck into the curve of my elbow. I lowered my face over that tiny face; the dark ginger of her eyelashes lay on her alabaster skin like decoration, almost too perfect to be real. I'm told all mothers think their babies are beautiful; how do you know if you're seeing the truth, or it's some illusion made of love and baby hormones? There are types of glamour that have nothing to do with faerie and everything to do with love.

Galen had taken Gwenwyfar in his arms, and then sat back down by my legs, careful not to bump my "footstool" so that Kitto wouldn't move and ruin his safe pass before the queen. Sholto held Alastair, but stayed standing beside my chair. He rocked the baby automatically when Alastair started to fuss. Once he believed that Bryluen was his, he had joined in caring for all the babies, as if, one being his, they were all his.

"You forget how very tiny they are," Andais said, and her voice was softer, gentler than any time I'd ever heard her.

I looked up and realized that I'd forgotten she was there; for just a moment there had been nothing but the baby in my arms and my feeling of utter contentment. I'd discovered that sometimes being around the triplets was like being drugged with something slow and pleasant, but I hadn't expected the effect to continue with my aunt still on the "phone."

"I remember that look from when Cel was little. He always had that effect on me to a certain extent. Looking at you now, I wonder if it was more than just motherly affection."

"What do you mean?" I asked.

"Your eyes are unfocused; you look almost drugged."

"Bryluen did have a very strong effect on a human friend of ours, so much so that we've decided no human nannies or babysitters for her," I said.

"Perhaps my great-niece's glamour affects more than just humans, Meredith. You would not knowingly let yourself become this distracted in front of me."

"No, Aunt Andais, I would not."

She had a thoughtful look on her face, and laid a hand on Eamon's thigh where it was hidden under his own silk robe. "Do I dare attribute some of my worst mistakes to magic? Was my own son able to throw glamour over my eyes as . . . Bryluen just did to you?"

"I do not know, Aunt Andais, I cannot speak to it."

"Nor I with any certainty," she said, but she kept touching Eamon, stroking his thigh not in a sexual way, but more for comfort. I knew that touch helped keep our minds free of glamour from the King of Light and Illusion, Taranis, and I wondered if she was touching Eamon for comfort, or because there was glamour coming through the mirror from Bryluen and me.

Doyle put his hand back on my shoulder, and I could think even more clearly. It was a sharpening of focus that let me know I hadn't been at my best just seconds before, and the fact that I hadn't realized that was not good. We would have serious negotiations today and later with other relatives, allies, and enemies. I couldn't be besotted with baby glamour while dealing with all of it. How powerful was Bryluen's effect on the people around her?

"For the idea that my mother's blindness to my son's machinations was magic, I thank you, Meredith, and Bryluen. It's Cornish for 'rose,' a sweet name for a little girl."

"It was a compromise between the men," I said.

She looked past me to one of the men at my back and said, "So, Killing Frost, you wished to name your new daughter after the love you lost centuries ago, Rose?"

I felt him tense without need of touching him, so his startle reflex must have shown over the mirror to her. Rose had been the name of the woman and her daughter he had loved centuries ago when he was merely Jackul Frosti, Little Jackie Frost. It was love for them, desire to protect them that had made Frost grow from a minor player in the procession of winter into the tall, commanding warrior, because little Jack Frost couldn't protect his Roses. The Killing Frost could, but in the end, time had taken them away from him. They'd been human and mortal and died as all mortal flesh is doomed to do.

Andais laughed, a high, delighted, wicked peal of laughter. Perhaps it was actually a pleasant laugh, but we'd all heard it so many times when she was enjoying cruelty that it could be nothing but unpleasant to our ears.

Doyle reached across with his free hand to touch Frost and steady him. His reaction must have been even worse than I'd thought for Doyle to show such weakness before the queen. It wasn't always wise to show how much you truly cared about anyone in front of her.

"So the rumors are true, my Darkness and my Killing Frost are lovers," she said.

I actually glanced behind me then, to see what was prompting her to say that, and found the men holding hands behind my chair.

Rhys said, "Once a man could hold the hand of his best friend and not be thought his lover."

She looked at Rhys, eyes narrowing; it was a look that typically began something bad, a bad mood, a bad event, an order we would not want to follow.

"Are you saying that they are not lovers?" Andais said.

"I am saying, why does it matter, and you shouldn't believe every rumor the human tabloids put out."

Galen was still sitting at my feet, beside Kitto, who had stayed almost immobile. Galen was holding Gwenwyfar, so as he leaned back against my legs he had to brush against Kitto's curls. The baby's hand brushed the long hair, and though she was too young to do it, Gwenwyfar grabbed a tiny fistful of Kitto's curls.

It couldn't have hurt, because the baby didn't have the strength for it yet, but it was probably the one thing that Kitto would have reacted to. He raised his face enough to gaze up at Gwenwyfar. I couldn't see Kitto's expression, but it was almost certainly a smile.

"So, little goblin, you make yourself useful, so the princess does not send you home."

I felt Kitto's reaction up through the soles of my feet on his back. It was a startle as bad as Frost's had been, but Kitto had always been terrified of the queen. Frost had loved and hated Andais; Kitto simply feared her.

"It is against protocol to speak with the royal's footstool," Rhys said. Once he had hated all goblins because one took his eye, so the fact that he stepped up to distract her from Kitto made me love him more. He had come far to value Kitto enough to risk himself for the goblin.

She gave him a narrow look. "You have grown bold, Rhys. Where does this new bravery in the face of your queen come from?"

Rhys stepped closer to the mirror, drawing her eye and partially blocking her view, so Galen could pry Gwenwyfar's tiny hand from Kitto's hair and the goblin could go back to being an immobile piece of furniture, and hopefully beneath the queen's notice.

"I don't think I'm braver, my queen, just understanding the value of those around me more than I did before."

"What does that mean, Rhys?"

"You know my hatred for the goblins."

"I do, but this one seems to have won your favor; how?"

Eamon was utterly still beside her, as if he would have left if he thought it wouldn't attract her attention. She had played sane, but her nearest and most dear love was acting like a rabbit in the grass hoping the fox won't find it, if only it can be still enough.

"It was Kitto who shopped for an extra crib, blankets, toys, everything, when the news came that we were having triplets and not just twins. He made certain we came home to a house that was ready for all the children, and that Merry had everything she needed."

"Any good servant will do as much," Andais said.

"True, but Kitto helps tend the babies not out of duty, but out of love."

"Love." She made it sound distasteful. "Goblins don't understand love for that which is small and helpless. Newborn sidhe are a delicacy among the goblins, you know that better than anyone standing here except for my Darkness. The others were not with me during the last Great War against the Goblins, but you and he know what they are capable of."

He glanced back at Doyle and then back to the mirror. I couldn't see his face, but his voice was fierce and bitter, "Now, my queen, remember I was at your side. I remember that the atrocities weren't all goblin work."

"We didn't eat their young," she said. Her eyes had darkened and were beginning to have that first hint of shine, her power beginning to rise. It could also be a sign of anger, or even anxiety, but it usually meant magic was on the rise.

"No, most goblin flesh is too bitter to eat," he said, and there was a finality in his voice. He'd left all pretense of placating her behind. It was simply the truth, and my joking Rhys had decided to leave humor for honesty, the kind of honesty that royals do not always welcome.

I was shocked enough myself, because I hadn't known that my people, the sidhe, had tasted goblin flesh enough to know the bitter or sweet of it. I held Bryluen closer to my face, smelling the sweet clean scent of her to hide my face, because in that moment I wasn't certain I could have kept it neutral.

Bryluen opened those huge almond-shaped eyes, all swimming blue, and I had a sensation like falling. I had to literally drag myself back from the brink. I lowered my baby away from my face and avoided direct eye contact with her. It wasn't just glamour, she had power, did our little Cornish Rose. How much, and how did we teach her not to use it willy-nilly? How do you explain to a newborn the concept of abuse of power?

"We vowed never to speak of some things, Rhys," Andais said, in a voice that crawled along the spine and raised the hairs on the back of my neck.

Alastair began to cry, high and piteous. He waved small fists as he did it. He couldn't be hungry—we'd made sure that everyone had nursed or had a bottle before this call, so we wouldn't have to deal with it. Sholto began to rock him side to side. Alastair didn't like to be bounced the way Gwenwyfar did, and Bryluen liked to be held up on the shoulder and have her back rubbed while you rocked her. Three days and the babies were already so different, so individual. I'd been told that multiples were like each other, but I was beginning to wonder if that was just because most of them looked alike, so people expected it.

Sholto began to rock Alastair in wider arcs, so his upper body turned from side to side. The movement began to quiet the baby.

"We vowed, but we did not swear," Rhys said. If he had given his sworn word he couldn't have spoken of it, because to be an oathbreaker was one of the few "sins" among the fey. An oathbreaker could be cast out of faerie forever.

Andais was looking at the crying baby. "I have seen the girls, but not the boy. Would you bring him closer so I might?"

It was Doyle who said, "If you will stop trying to unsettle us, my queen, perhaps, but if your behavior of the last few minutes continues, then what is the point? We do not want our children raised in an atmosphere of fear and uncertainty."

"How dare you question my behavior, Darkness?"

He shrugged with his hand on my shoulder, and the other still holding Frost's hand. "And this is exactly why we do not want the babies raised around you, or your court. I thought Essus a fool when he took Merry and his retinue and left the Unseelie Court, but now I see it for wisdom. Even if Merry could have survived in our court as a child, she would have been a different person now. I do not think that person would have been better, or kinder."

"You cannot be kind and rule the sidhe, or the goblins, or the sluagh, or anyone inside or out of faerie. Kindness is for children and human fairy tales."

"Kindness where possible is not a weakness," Doyle said.

"In a queen it most certainly is," she said.

"You have seen Merry on the battlefield; do you think her kindness made her less ruthless, or less dangerous, my queen?" he asked, and his voice was lower, crawling down into those vibratingly low tones that had frightened me once. Now it made me shiver for a different reason, a much more fun reason, because three things make a man's voice lower, and all are testosterone based—heavy exercise, violence, and sex.

"Do you think it is wise to remind me that I watched her slaughter my son in front of me?"

"Do you think it wise that you reminded Frost of the loss of his first love?"

"Frost cannot punish such impudence as I can," she said.

"And there you go again," Rhys said.

She looked back at him. "What are you talking about?"

Eamon moved beside her and spoke low and clear, in the kind of voice you use to calm wild animals or talk jumpers off ledges. "My queen, my beloved, he means that if you keep threatening punishment they have no reason to share your nieces and nephew with you. Your brother's grandchildren are before you; do you want to be a part of their lives, or do you prefer to be the Queen of Air and Darkness, frightening and unyielding to all insults?"

"I have already offered to give up being the Queen of Air and Darkness if Meredith will but take the throne."

"So you would rather be Aunt Andais to Essus's grandchildren than queen of all?"

She seemed to think about it for a moment or two, and then she nodded. "Yes, to see my bloodline continue, to have three descendants of our line who are already displaying such power, for that I would step down."

It wasn't just descendants, but powerful, magical descendants. She'd already seen the lightning mark on Gwenwyfar's arm and watched it spark at Mistral's touch. Alastair had displayed no overt talent as the girls had done, but she seemed willing to take it for granted that he, too, would be powerful. If any of our children proved without magic, by her standards, she would still see them as useless, as not worthy, as she'd decided with me when I turned six and she tried to drown me.

Eamon laid his hand over hers, cautiously. "But, my beloved, it's more than stepping down from the throne; Meredith and her consorts want to feel safe around you, and at this moment, they do not."

"They should not. I am the Queen of Air and Darkness, ruler of the Unseelie Court. The fact that people fear me is part of the point, Eamon; you know that."

"For ruling our court, perhaps, and for keeping the Golden Court in check, absolutely, but my love, perhaps being frightening is not the best way to be Great-Aunt Andais."

She frowned at him as if she didn't understand the words, The words made sense, she could hear them, but I wasn't certain she could grasp their meaning.

She finally said out loud, "I don't understand what you mean, Eamon."

He tried to pull her into his arms as he said, "I know you do not, my love."

She pushed away from him. "Then explain it to me, so I will understand."

"Aunt Andais," I said.

She looked at me, still frowning, still not understanding.

"Do you regret the loss of Tyler?"

"I said so, didn't I?"

"You did."

"Then what are you talking about, Meredith?"

"Will you regret not being Aunt Andais to our children?"

"I am their aunt, Meredith; you cannot change that."

"Perhaps not, but I can decide whether you are aunt in name only, or whether you actually have a place in their lives so they know who you are in a pleasant way; or will you be on the list of people that we warn them about? Do you want to be a bogeyman to your nieces and nephew? If you see your Aunt Andais, run. If she comes for you, call for help, fight back. Is that the legacy you want in their lives?"

"They could not fight me and win, Meredith; even you could not."

"And that is not the point of what I said; the fact that you think it is means you are not welcome here."

"Do not make me your enemy, Meredith."

"Then apologize, Aunt Andais."

"For what?"

"For reminding Frost of past pain, for trying to frighten Kitto, for every threat, every hint of pain and violence you've spoken since this conversation began."

"A queen does not apologize, Meredith."

"But an aunt does."

She blinked at me. "Ah," she said, "you want me to be some cheerful relative that comes with gifts and smiles."

"Yes," I said.

She smiled, but it was an unpleasant one, as if she'd tasted something bitter. "You want me to be other than I am around your children?"

"If by that you mean pleasant, kind, and just a normal aunt, then yes, Andais, that is what I want."

"It is not their heritage to be any of those things."

"My father, your brother, thought otherwise, and he raised me to be all those things."

"And it was love and kindness that got him killed, Meredith. He hesitated, because he loved his killer."

"And perhaps if you had raised your son, as my father raised me, to be kinder, considerate, happy, then neither of them would be dead right now."

She startled as if I had slapped her. "How dare you . . ."

"Speak the truth," I said.

"So I must be this false self, this fiction of a cheerful, smiling auntie, or you will try to keep me out of the lives of my nieces and nephew?"

"Yes, Aunt Andais, that is exactly what I mean."

"And if I said there is always darkness through which I can step and visit as I will, what would you say?"

Doyle said, "I would say that if it is death you seek, come unasked, unbidden, unannounced, and we will grant that wish."

"You dare threaten me, my own Darkness."

"I am no longer your anything, my queen. You cared for me not at all except as a visible threat by your side—'Where is my Darkness, bring me my Darkness'—and then you would send me to kill on your behalf. I have a life now, and a reason to keep living, beyond just the fact that I do not age, and I will let nothing stand between me and that life."

"Not even your queen," she said, voice soft.

"Not even you, my queen."

"So either I concede to your ridiculous demands or I lose all contact with the babes."

"Yes," I, Doyle, Frost, and Rhys said at the same time. The others nodded.

"Once I would have threatened to send my sluagh to the Western Lands and find you, or the babies, and bring all to me, but now the King of the Sluagh stands by your side and no longer answers to me."

"You sent me to the princess, my queen."

"I sent you to bring her home, not to bed her. You I did not choose for her."

"You gave her the choice of all your Raven guards, and I am that, as well as King of the Sluagh."

She looked at me, and there was threat and anger, and everything I wanted to keep away from our babies in her face. "You have stripped me of most of my threat, Meredith. Even the goblins answer to you now, rather than to me, and that I did not intend. That was your doing, niece of mine."

"Essus, your brother, made certain I understood all the courts of faerie, not just the Unseelie. He wanted me to rule all, if I ruled any."

She nodded and looked thoughtful, the anger gone as if she could not stay enraged and think at the same time, and that was probably truer than was pretty to think about.

"You are right, Meredith; it was you who bargained with the goblins so wisely, and you who seduced the sluagh to your side, and you who won the loyalty of my Darkness, and my Killing Frost. I did not see you as a threat to my power, but only as a pawn to be used and discarded if it did not serve me, and now here we are with you more powerful than I ever envisioned, and that is without a crown upon your head."

"I did not have your magic to protect me, aunt; I had to find power where it was offered for it was not within me."

"You wield the hands of flesh and blood, niece; those are formidable powers on the battlefield."

"But if all I depended on was my magic, then I would not have Doyle, or Frost, or Sholto, or the goblins, or any of what I have won. I have killed only to save my life and the lives of those I love. My ability to kill, no matter in what horrific way, is not where my power lies, aunt."

"And where does your power lie, niece?"

"Love, loyalty, and when forced being utterly ruthless, but it is kindness and love that have won me more power than any death I have dealt."

She made a face, as if she smelled something bad. "Your hands of power may be Unseelie Court magic, but you are so"—and here she rolled her eyes—"the descendant of all those bloody fertility deities in the Seelie Court. Love and kindness will win the day, oh yes, oh my, my ass."

"The truth is in the results, aunt."

"I have ruled for over a thousand years; kindness and love will not see you rule for that long."

"No, because I shall not live that long, Aunt Andais, but my children will and their children."

"I've never liked you, Meredith."

"Nor I you."

"But I am beginning to truly hate you."

"You're late to this party, Aunt Andais; I've feared and hated you most of my life."

"Then it's hatred between us."

"I believe so."

"But you want me to come and pretend otherwise in front of your children."

"If you wish to be their aunt in truth, rather than just by blood-line, yes."

"I do not know if I have that much pretense in me."

"That is for you to decide, aunt."

She patted Eamon's hand. "I understand what you were trying to tell me now. I will never be other than your aunt by bloodline, Meredith."

"Agreed, Aunt Andais."

"But you would give me the chance to be more to your children."

"If you behave yourself, yes."

"Why?"

"Truth, you are powerful enough that I would rather not go from hating each other to trying to kill each other."

She laughed so abruptly it was more of a snort. "Well, that is truth."

"But there is one other reason I'm willing to do this, Aunt Andais."

"And what would that be, niece Meredith?"

"My father told me stories of you and him playing together when you were children."

"He did?"

"Yes, he did. He would tell me of you as a little girl with him a little boy, and his face would soften and the memories gave him joy, and in hopes that my father's sister is still inside you somewhere, I will give you a chance to show Essus's grandchildren the part of you that made my father smile."

Her eyes were shining again, but it wasn't magic; tears glittered in her tricolored eyes. She swallowed hard enough I could hear it, and then she said, "Oh, Meredith, nothing you could have said would have hurt me more than that."

"I did not mean to cause you pain."

"And I know that you mean that, and that is the cruelest blow of all, my niece, my brother's daughter, because you remind me of him. He should have killed me and taken the throne when Barinthus urged him to; so much pain could have been saved."

"You were his sister and he loved you," I said.

The tears began to fall down her face. "I know that, Meredith, and I will miss him forever." She blanked the mirror with a wave of her hand as she began to cry harder.

CHAPTER

TWELVE

W ell, that was unexpected," Rhys said.

"Merry made her cry," Cathbodua said, and came to drop to her knees in front of me, her raven-feathered cloak spilling around her like shiny black water. The cloak always moved as if it were made of different things than it appeared to be, as if it were more liquid than solid sometimes, but then once it had given her the gift of shapeshifting, so maybe that was it.

I felt Galen shift where he sat by my legs. He didn't always like Cathbodua. I felt Kitto flex underneath my slippers; he would have flinched if he'd not still been pretending to be an object. He was afraid of Cathbodua, though she'd not done anything to him to make him afraid; it just seemed to be an on-principle sort of thing for him. It seemed to be the same reason Galen didn't like her.

Cathbodua wasn't that close to either of them. She'd knelt far enough away from me to keep everyone in the room in view. Battle goddesses, even fallen ones, always seem to remember that you never look away from anyone who could hurt you, and that meant everyone in the room.

"I have only seen one other person who could move the queen as you just did, and that was your father, Prince Essus. Him I would have followed forever, and today I see that you are your father's daughter."

"Thank you, Cathbodua; that makes me happy to hear, for I loved and respected my father."

"As well you should have, Princess, but I will offer my oath to you."

"I have not asked an oath of service from anyone," I said.

"No, you have not; it was the queen who forced Prince Essus to take our oath to him. He would have trusted to our loyalty and love of him."

Bryluen fussed in her sleep and I raised her to put her against my shoulder. She liked to be upright sometimes. I said, "Andais doesn't trust love, only fear."

"Essus understood that those who follow out of love are more powerful than those who follow out of fear."

"There is no loyalty in fear, only resentment," I said.

"You have been fair and gentle with those of us who would allow it, and fierce and ruthless with those who would not. I ask that you would take my oath so that I may serve you, Princess Meredith, daughter of Essus."

"Once you give oath you are bound to me forever, or until my death, and I may not be as much my father's daughter as you think."

"You are more ruthless than he was, and if you fight, you kill your enemy. I have never seen you offer mercy to anyone who tried to kill you or those dear to you."

"Shouldn't that give you pause, before you tie yourself to me, Cathbodua?"

"No, because if your father had held your edge of harshness he would have slain his assassin and not let love stay his hand. He would have been forced to kill his sister and become king, and so much pain, death, and useless bloodletting would have been avoided."

"Are you saying my father was weak?"

"Never, but he was softer than you are, Princess."

I laughed. "I think most of the nobles would not agree with you."

"Then they have not been paying attention since your hands of power manifested, Princess Meredith."

"I kill because I am not the warrior my father was, and I never will be. I am too small to fight as he could."

"Does it matter why someone has the will to win?" Cathbodua asked.

"I think it does," I said.

"I agree with Cathbodua," Galen said.

I looked down at him holding Gwenwyfar, sitting close enough to touch Kitto, his long leg close to the edge of the raven cloak as it pooled on the floor. He had that serious look in his eyes again; it was partly tiredness maybe, but his eyes looked older than they had before, as if his near-eighty years of life were catching up with him.

"Results are what matter, Merry, not motives. I think our friend Detective Lucy would say, leave the motives to the lawyers and the psychiatrists."

"We are not police officers, just private detectives who help them out on crime involving our people."

"That's not what I mean, Merry," he said, turning more toward me with the baby nestled and sleeping in his arms.

Doyle said, "I think Galen means that you will not try to win the battle with flair, or by some chivalrous code. If forced, you simply destroy your enemy; there is no mercy in you when lives are at stake, though outside that you are very merciful."

"My father was six feet tall and muscled, and had centuries of training as a warrior, and one of his hands of power was usable over a distance. He could afford mercy in battle; I can't."

Bryluen moved against my shoulder, making a small sound. I started rubbing her upper shoulders in small circles, being careful of her wings lower down, though they seemed remarkably flexible. They were definitely more skin and reptile scales over bone than butterfly scales over exoskeleton. That strengthened Sholto's view that sluagh genetics had given her the wings. I was still reserving judgment until the genetic tests came back.

"But that's it exactly," Cathbodua said.

It made me turn back to her. "What do you mean?"

"Essus thought as of old, when we could afford battles and assassinations, but we are in modern-day America now, and we need a modern ruler to see us through this strange new land of technology and social issues. You are the future, Princess, and for the first time in centuries I think our race has a future."

"You mean the babies," I said.

"Not just yours, Princess, but Maeve's son, and Nicca and Biddy's little girl. We are fertile once more thanks to you."

"And all this because the queen cried," I said.

"No, because you made the queen cry."

"If I were as ruthless as you say, I would have sent Doyle to assassinate the queen months ago."

"You want him alive more than you want her dead; that's love, Princess."

"Doesn't that make me soft?"

"No," Galen said, "because I know I would do anything to keep our babies and you safe, anything. Holding Gwenwyfar in my arms, seeing you there with Bryluen, doesn't make me feel soft. It makes me feel fierce, as if for the first time I have things I'm willing to fight for, to kill for, if I have to, and it's love that's given me this new . . . resolve. I will not fail you again through hesitation, or lack of will; I will be the man you and our children need me to be."

I could see that resolve in his face, so sure, so firm, so . . . resolute. I was happy to see it, because I'd feared for my gentle Galen in this sea of brutal politics, but at the same time it made me a little afraid, because I wasn't sure that deciding to be harsher would automatically give you the skills to be that. I just didn't know.

"Take my oath, Princess; let me give you my vow," Cathbodua said.

"You wish to serve me until either your death or mine?"

"Yes, and if Goddess wills it, the babes in your arms will be as worthy of my oath as you and your father."

"I pray that it is so," Doyle said.

"So do I," Frost and Mistral said together.

Everyone agreed, and I said a silent prayer. "Please, Goddess, let our children be worthy of the loyalty and love of their people."

Rose petals began to fall from the air above my head like a sweet-scented *yes*. Guards moved from behind us to join Cathbodua where she knelt. The rose petals began to spread through the room as if the entire ceiling were raining roses.

I took their oaths, and I prayed to be worthy of them, because in the beginning most leaders mean well; it is later when the best of intentions twist into something darker. I knew that Andais, Taranis, and my grandfather, Uar the Cruel, were as much a part of my genetics as my father, Essus. There was more insanity than sanity in my family tree; I hoped that everyone kneeling in front of me remembered that.

CHAPTER

THIRTEEN

Most of the guards went about their business, because otherwise the hallway outside the dining room wouldn't have been big enough for us to walk from there to the nursery. There were enough people in the house now that sometimes it felt claustrophobic, so I'd made it clear that outside of special circumstances, like impressing the queen or guarding me from her, less was more when it came to my retinue. So it was just me, the triplets, and their fathers, except for Mistral, who had gone off with the other guards to tend to something. He didn't really enjoy the nursery duties and often tried to be somewhere else when diapers, bottles, and the like came up. I'd been debating whether I should make him do more of it or let it go. The other men were more than enough, so he wasn't absolutely needed, but still, he was their father; shouldn't he help?

The door at the far end of the white marble hallway opened, and Liam Reed, all of thirteen months old, saw us and grinned. Suddenly the hallway didn't look stately, or cold, or like people in ball gowns should be gliding down it; it just looked like home.

If you've ever wondered why toddlers are called toddlers, all you had to do was watch one who was new at walking. Liam toddled toward us with one of the human nannies chasing behind. He was still unsteady after a month of walking, but he was getting quicker at it. He came staggering toward us as fast as he could, saying, "Babies, babies, babies!" He had a huge grin on his face and was just so excited. He'd been that way since we brought the triplets home. Kadyi, Nicca and Biddy's daughter, who had just started sitting up last week, was apparently not "baby" enough for Liam anymore, because he was fascinated with the newborns.

Liam was as blond and blue-eyed as his mother, Maeve Reed, pretended to be for the human media, and so far he was just a really pretty baby with straight golden blond hair and big, pretty, very human-looking blue eyes. His skin was the pale constant gold of Maeve's, like a pale but perfect suntan, easily passing for human.

Rhys scooped him up and said, "You want to see the babies?"

"Babies!" Liam said, at the top of his voice.

Gwenwyfar and Bryluen both protested with tiny cries. Galen and I started patting and rocking them automatically. It had been only a few days, but for a chance to sleep I'd learned to do what I could to soothe them. Only Alastair stayed quiet and deeply asleep in Sholto's arms as we walked toward the nursery.

Rhys held Liam up so he could see Gwenwyfar first. "Baby!" Liam said, again at the top of his voice.

Gwenwyfar started to cry.

"Shhh," Rhys said, "remember use your quiet voice."

Liam turned a solemn face to Rhys, then leaned over Bryluen and said much more softly, "Baby."

I smiled and moved her so that Bryluen could look back at Liam. He reached out very gently and touched her curls, tracing the tiny horn buds, which he seemed fascinated with, and almost-whispered, "Pitty." Which meant pretty.

"Yes, Bryluen is very pretty."

"Bree-lu," he said, trying to wrap his toddler words around her name. He'd been trying for three days and that was the closest he'd managed.

I smiled at him. "That's right, Liam. This is Bryluen."

"Bree-lu-non."

"Bryluen," I said.

He screwed his face up into a picture of concentration and then blurted out, "Bree!"

We all laughed, and I said, "Bree will do."

Liam smiled up at all of us, and then gazed back down at Bryluen, and said, happily and still a little too loud, "Bree!"

She stared up at him with those big, solemn eyes. He reached down and tried to pat her cheek but missed and poked her in the eye. Bryluen started to cry.

Liam yelled, "Sorry, baby!"

Alastair finally woke up and joined the girls crying. Liam's nursemaid offered to take him from Rhys, but Liam wrapped his arms around Rhys's neck and started to cry. "No, don't want to go!"

Maeve glided gracefully into the hallway, calling above the crying, "What happened?"

Galen said, "Liam poked Bryluen in the eye, by accident." He had to raise his voice, too.

Maeve went up to Rhys and he started to hand the boy to her, but Liam clung to Rhys, screaming, "No! No!"

Maeve stopped trying to get him from Rhys, and once he settled back into Rhys's arms he stopped yelling, tears still wet on his face as he gave a petulant face to his mother. She had been in Europe filming for most of the last five months and had been home for only three days. Liam called her Mommy, but he didn't always act like she was Mommy.

Maeve couldn't keep the hurt out of her face for a moment, and then she smiled brightly.

Rhys said, "Liam, go to your mommy."

"No, baby room," Liam said, very serious, very certain of what he wanted and what he didn't.

"I think he wants to go to the nursery and watch the babies," I said.

"It's okay," Maeve said. "I flew in for his first birthday and then had to leave again."

"You shouldn't have to support us all, if it means you're apart from your son," Doyle said.

"For centuries we were just like the human nobility; no one saw their own children. They were all raised by nannies and caretakers," Maeve said.

"But you are not content with that," Frost said.

Maeve shook her head, and tears sparkled in her eyes. She shook her head a little more vigorously, and then managed a voice that held nothing but good cheer. "I'll join you in the nursery in a few minutes." Then she walked back out the way she'd come and left us with Liam and the babies. At least they'd quieted, and we weren't listening to high-pitched newborn cries echoing off the marble walls.

"It's not right that she's sacrificing her time with Liam for us," Galen said.

"Agreed," Frost said.

"Yes," Doyle said.

Rhys was drying the tears off Liam's face. "He doesn't mean to hurt her feelings."

"I know," I said. Liam had spent much of the last few months falling asleep across my ever-growing stomach, so that at the end he'd looked like the arch of a rainbow, but his nannies couldn't get him to settle down like I could. He'd put his little hand on my stomach and say, "Babies," as if he'd been waiting for them to finally come outside and be able to play.

I wasn't sure what to do with the fact that Liam had bonded with our little family group while Maeve was away. I wasn't even sure there was anything to be done, but it seemed like a topic for a family discussion. We actually had family meetings to discuss the complicated intricacies of our happy home. Most of the time it really was happy, but with this many people involved it didn't just stay happily-ever-after without a lot of discussion and work. I was learning that happily-ever-after was the beginning of the next chapter, not the end of the story.

CHAPTER

FOURTEEN

That night I dreamed. It seemed to be just a dream, not Goddess-sent or prophetic, but a dream like millions of people everywhere have every night. It began well, with my father getting to meet my babies, his grandchildren, but in the way of dreams, what is comforting begins to disturb. It's nothing you can put a finger upon, but the wonderful begins to unsettle you, and you know something is wrong with what you're seeing, you just don't know what yet . . . but you will.

In all the long years since my father's death I had never once dreamed of him, and yet there he stood, tall and handsome with his fall of black hair loose around his legs like a curtain of black water, flowing and moving as he held Bryluen in his arms. The wind played in his hair but didn't tangle it, the way it did for Doyle and Frost. They'd said the wind liked them, and the wind in my dream liked my father.

It was strange, but I never forgot he was dead, even in a dream with him smiling down at me. He was dead and this wasn't real, could never be real again.

"Meredith," he said, smiling, "she is beautiful, my little girl."

"I wish you were here to hold your grandchildren for real, Father."

He laid a gentle kiss on Bryluen's forehead and then raised his face, frowning slightly. "What is in her hair?"

I came closer, and he lowered the baby enough for me to spread her red curls and show the tiny horn buds. He startled, and if I hadn't been standing close he might have dropped her, but I took Bryluen in my arms and moved back. I thought, *I need to put her in her cradle*, and one appeared.

"I thought she was the one, she looks so like us, but if she has horns she can't be ours."

I laid Bryluen in the cradle and looked up at my raven-haired father with his tricolored eyes, completely different from Bryluen's large blue ones. He looked nothing like me, or the baby. It had saddened me as a child that I hadn't looked more like my father.

"What do you mean she looks like us? She looks nothing like you, Father."

He held Alastair in his arms now. The black hair did look more like my father, and all newborns look slightly unfinished so that people can see what they want to see in their features. I think it's a way of making everyone feel included, like the baby belongs to everyone.

He leaned over Alastair and frowned. "Is he spotted like a puppy?"

"Yes," I said, and went to take my son from his arms. He didn't fight when I took Alastair. I put him in the cradle behind me. Bryluen wasn't there, she was safely away, and even as I thought it, Alastair vanished from the cradle, too.

I knew he would be holding Gwenwyfar when I turned back, and he was; he was unwrapping her from the blanket she was swaddled in, but she hadn't been swaddled when we put her down for the night. She hated to be confined like that, and as if my thinking it had caused it, she started to cry, flailing small sturdy arms, tiny hands in fists as if she would fight the world.

He ran his big fingers through her hair.

"She doesn't have horns, if that's what you're looking for," I said.

He lifted Gwenwyfar free of the blanket and looked at the skin that the onesie left bare. "She looks sidhe," he said.

My pulse was beating too fast as I moved to take my daughter from him. He let me do it, I think because she was crying. She quieted in my arms, and I moved back to lay her in the crib. She vanished, and I knew that they were safe. I didn't think they'd been in the dream for real, but just in case I'd wanted them safely away, because I knew that whoever this man looked like, he wasn't my father.

I thought, *This isn't real, it's just a dream.* That should have been enough to shatter the dream. I waited for it to unravel and to wake up in my bed sandwiched between Frost and Doyle, but the dream held.

I had never tried to break a dream with magic, but now I reached outward, tentatively, and found that I could feel the edges of the dream almost like a plastic film that I could press against. Press against, but not break.

"So it is true, you are able to travel through dream."

"I don't know what you mean," I said, but my pulse was in my throat. Something was terribly wrong.

"You travel in your dreams to help your soldiers," he said.

"I don't know what you mean."

"You cannot lie to me in dream, Meredith. Your soldiers wear your sign."

In the final battle with my cousin, Prince Cel, I had been protected by the National Guard, and all of them who had been wounded, or had been touched by my blood, seemed to be able to call upon me when I slept. If they were in danger of their lives they could call me to them, and the Goddess gave me the means to show them to safety or bring them the help they needed. Some of them wore the nails that had been part of the shrapnel in the bomb my cousin had set to kill me. They had tied leather cords around the nails and wore them like a talisman, and through those nails they could call me. The black coach of faerie that had been a limousine when I was first called home was now in the desert, a black armored vehicle of whatever kind was needed. It traveled without a driver and went where it was needed, because I had told it to help them, and somehow it did. The coach had always been wild magic, never fully understood or fully controlled by anyone, but it had listened to me.

"Who are you?" I asked.

He walked toward me looking as my father would if he had never known pain, never been wounded, never died, but the smile was wrong. It was his face, but it wasn't my father's smile.

I backed away, so that his outstretched hand wouldn't touch me. "Who are you?"

He held out his hand. "Come to me, Meredith, but take my hand, and we can step out of this dream."

"And where will we appear once the dream is finished?" I asked.

"Someplace wonderful."

I shook my head. "Liar."

"We cannot lie outright, Meredith; you know that."

"Drop this guise and show me your true face."

"Take my hand."

"Drop this disguise and perhaps I will."

He stepped closer to me, hand still held out toward me. "Who do you want me to be?" he asked.

"Show yourself as you truly are, and stop tormenting me with my dead father's face."

"I thought the sight of Essus would comfort you," he said, and frowned as if he didn't understand, and maybe he didn't.

"You were wrong; show me your face." My voice was strident, not with anger, but fear.

"If you let me hold you now, it will be as if Essus were here to embrace you one last time. I can give you that, Meredith; my powers have returned. The Goddess has blessed us both again."

"The Goddess gives Her power where She will. I do not question it, but one man's blessing is another's curse; drop this illusion and show me . . ." I stopped, because the moment I said *illusion*, I knew; Goddess and Consort help me, but I knew.

One moment I was staring up into the face of my dead father, and next it was Taranis, the King of Light and Illusion. He was all red and gold of hair, his eyes like green petals of some exotic flower, tall and commanding, and truly one of the most handsome men to ever grace the high courts of faerie.

"Come, Meredith, embrace me as one of the fathers of your children."

I screamed.

FIFTEEN

He grabbed my wrist and started to pull me to him, but I thought, *I need something to hold on to*, and my other hand found smooth wood to grip, a carved banister leading up to nowhere, but it was a handhold, and I made my choice that I'd let him break my arm before I let go.

"Meredith, I'd never hurt you."

"You raped me!"

"Lies, Meredith, all lies. I saved you from the Unseelie monsters. You have a babe that grows horns, and another spotted like a dog, but our daughter is perfect. They are twisted of body, and it is a miracle you have survived."

His eyes began to glow as if every green petaled layer of his iris were turning to green flame, and I was falling into that flame. I wanted to touch his hair, colored like all the brilliance of a fiery sunset. My hand loosened on the banister behind me, and then a single rose petal fell and landed on the mound of my breast. I was not a victim.

He held my wrist; so be it. I opened my hand and laid my palm against his skin and called one of my hands of power. His skin began to writhe as if it were turning liquid where I touched him.

He yelled and let me go. "What is this?"

"The hand of flesh is my hand of power, as my father carried it before me."

Taranis's arm began to roll up on itself, as the bones and muscle began to spill out to the surface, turning inside out, and spreading up his arm.

"Stop this!" he yelled, but even as I watched, the flowing skin had stopped just short of his shoulder. If he'd laid the arm against other bare skin it would have spread, but he had jerked away quickly enough that it hadn't turned his entire body inside out. The hand of flesh could do that, and had. It had been one of the worst things I'd ever seen, but I was half sorry it hadn't done just that to Taranis.

"This is dream; you don't have this power outside of dream." He was staring at his arm, and the horror on his face as he looked up at me made part of me . . . happy.

"You knocked me unconscious and nearly killed me before you mounted me last time. I was too hurt to fight back."

"This is not real!" He yelled it at me.

"I don't know, uncle dear; perhaps when you wake up your arm will be healed, or perhaps it will be a reminder to you to stay away from me, my babies, and everyone I hold dear, because if you ever touch me by force again, in dream or reality, I will destroy you, Taranis."

"It isn't real," he said, but his voice was uncertain.

"For your sake, I hope not," I said. "Honestly, for my own sake, I hope it is."

"I saved you, Meredith; why do you hate me?"

I wished for a sword, and one was in my hand. The hilt was cool and perfect. You had to look close to see the carved tiny bodies melting into each other as the only warning for what might happen if you touched the sword. It was Aben-dul, once my father's centuries before I was born, and it fit my hand as it had the first time it appeared to me in reality. It had never just appeared in my hand before, but this was a dream—anything was possible.

"Where did that come from?" And now he was afraid, and that made me fiercely happy.

"You can stop me from leaving this dream, but you can't stop me from creating what I need inside it."

"You shouldn't be able to do that," he said.

"You said it yourself, uncle: I have traveled through dream to soldiers who held relics of my blood and pain. The Goddess comes to me in my dreams. I hold my father's hand of power and a sword of Unseelie grace, but I am Seelie as well as Unseelie. I hold the wonders and nightmares of both courts inside me, uncle dearest."

"Stop calling me that; I am the father of your baby."

I wrapped both hands around the sword and only the fact that I carried the hand of flesh kept me safe from the magic of the blade, and got into the stance that I'd learned so long ago. I hadn't kept up my sword practice, because I'd realized as a teenager I was never going to choose a blade as my weapon in a duel, and I was never going to challenge anyone to a duel, and so long as they challenged me I chose the weapons, but I knew how to hold a sword. I knew enough to bleed him unless he killed me first, but I'd blasted the arm that held his hand of light; if I was lucky, I'd crippled his magic. If I'd been certain the sword would work here as it did in the real world, I could have used my hand of flesh without touching him, but I wasn't sure enough to risk using it as anything but a sword.

"I was pregnant when you raped me, you psychotic bastard! Now break us both free of this dream, or I swear by the Summerlands, and the Darkness that Swallows the World, I will do all in my power to kill you, uncle dearest."

"Do not call me that, Meredith; you are my queen and will be my wife."

I started forward, doing a feint with the sword. He jerked back, his wounded arm useless at his side. "Come, uncle, let us embrace and I will finish what I began with your arm."

He vanished from the dream, and a second later I woke in bed with Doyle and Frost looking down at me. Doyle was pinning my arms down across my body, because the sword Aben-dul was still in my hands.

CHAPTER

SIXTEEN

"Merry, Merry, do you know who we are?"

"Doyle, Frost," I said, my pulse so hard in my throat that it choked my voice down to a whisper.

Frost smoothed my hair back from my face and asked. "Do you know where you are?"

"We are in Los Angeles, in Maeve's house, in our bedroom."

Frost smiled down at me. "Do you remember that we love you?"

I smiled up at him. "Yes, that I always remember." Just gazing up into his face and answering that question helped slow my frantic heartbeat and chase away the last clinging terror of the nightmare.

Doyle's deeper voice turned me to look at him. "If you remember that, then relax your arms, so that I know you will not strike out with the sword you hold in your hands."

I realized that my arms were tense underneath his, as if I meant to use Aben-dul once I was free of the strength that held me down. I fought to relax my arms, but it was as if the thought of not being ready to strike when the need arose frightened me, as if I expected Taranis to appear in the room once I was unarmed. There was a chance that even accidentally touching someone who did not carry the hand of flesh would turn them inside out. I didn't want to hurt my lovers, but . . . The fear wasn't rational.

Normally, I would have said that with Doyle and Frost beside me I was utterly safe, but Taranis had nearly killed Doyle with his hand of power. If he still had a hand of power. If the damage I had caused in dream had truly happened to him in reality, then he might have lost his greatest weapon, because often when our hands were damaged, the hands of power went with the injury. Or sometimes the magic became so wild that it wasn't safe to use, like a fire that you meant to use to cook your dinner, but that got out of hand and burned down the house instead.

"Some thought has gone through your eyes, our Merry," Doyle said.

"I had a dream," I said.

"It was not a Goddess-sent dream," Frost said, "because when you cried out in your sleep we were both able to wake and watch over you."

"And there are no flower petals raining down from nowhere," Doyle said.

"But though we awoke," Frost said, "we could not rouse you, as if it had been a dream from the Goddess."

"If it was not the Goddess, then what held you so tight to this dream?" Doyle asked.

"My uncle entered my dream and trapped me there."

"You mean Taranis?" Doyle said, and I saw the fear on his face now. Good to know I wasn't the only one.

"Yes."

They both leaned over me, too close, and even though I loved them both it was as if I couldn't get enough air. I started to try to sit up, but Doyle still had my arms pinned with the sword, and suddenly I was panicked. It took everything I had not to struggle and lash out at the two men I loved most in the world, because they were too close and were holding me down, and my rapist had been in my dreams.

"I need room." I managed to choke the words out.

"We are in our room," Doyle said.

"Move away from me, please," I said.

They exchanged a look over me, but Frost moved back as I'd asked. Doyle did not. "You seem not yourself, Merry. We have seen spells placed inside others we loved that turned them against us. I would not risk your using this sword upon anyone you love."

"I need to be armed with his touch still fresh upon me, Doyle," I said, fighting not to strain against the ease with which he held my arms and the sword down, harmless.

Frost slid off the bed and came back with one of his own blades. Normally I would have been more distracted by the nude beauty of him in the silver cloud of his hair, but somehow men and the things that went with them were all confused with images of a very different man, the one in my dreams, but not the man of my dreams. One of the men of my dreams sat on the bed and offered me his blade, hilt first. It would have been a knife to him, but to me it was as big as a short sword. Sometimes I felt very much the hobbit to their elves. That ordinary-world thought helped me push back the panic.

"An exchange, our Merry," Frost said gently.

"It is a fine blade, but not a fair exchange for this one," I said.

"No one but you in this room can touch that blade and keep sanity and life, so let it go and take up Frost's knife, and then tell us what happened in the dream."

I breathed deeply, forcing myself to take even breaths, and then I let it out slow, counting as I did so. *Control your breathing and you control nearly everything else, but first gain control of yourself; always begin there.* Those had been my father's words to me. That helped calm me, too.

I let go of Aben-dul, and it lay heavy across my legs, but my hands were empty enough to wrap around the hilt that Frost was offering. Doyle moved back then, sliding off the bed; after a moment Frost echoed him. I had room to sit up, and some weight that had been trying to make me panic and lash out at them eased. It wasn't a spell put on me by Taranis, but it was his damage. He'd raped me, and there were moments when even the most beloved of my partners had to give me space, and time to work through the issues of that attack. I was happy I didn't remember most of it, didn't remember the sex, only waking afterward with the concussion that almost killed me and my unborn children.

"I wish we did not have to ask, Merry, but what happened in the dream?" Doyle said.

I took in another deep breath and counted it out slowly, then nodded. I told them about the dream, everything that had happened in it.

"Do you believe that the injury to his arm will follow him out of dream?" Doyle asked.

"I do not know."

"That is not possible," Frost whispered.

"Once the king could use dream to seduce and bed a woman, and the children that came from those dreams were real enough," Doyle said.

"Are you saying he was able to get women pregnant from just visiting them in their dreams?" I asked.

They both nodded.

I must have paled, because they moved toward the bed, then hesitated and looked at each other, then back at me. "We would comfort you if you would allow it, Merry, but we do not wish to rush this moment," Doyle said.

I nodded, but I didn't really want to be touched right that second. I gripped the hilt in my hands tighter, so that the leather-wrapped metal dug into my hands a little, helped remind me that I was awake and not trapped.

"I will take comfort in a little while, but right now just explain to me how he could do that in just a dream."

"Once he was the Lord of Dreams, but that was centuries before we came to the Western Lands. I do not believe that he can make dreams as real as he once could," Doyle said.

"Do not tell her that, for we do not know. He should not have been able to use his hand of light through the mirror when he nearly killed you, and that was months ago. The Goddess returns and wild magic follows in Her wake," Frost said.

Doyle nodded. "And the magic is like most of our powers, like nature itself; the storm does not mean to tear down your house, but it still might."

"Which means that we have no way of knowing who will have gained powers from the return of the Goddess," I said.

"Sadly, no," Doyle said. He gave me a very solemn look.

"What?" I asked.

"If you damaged his arm in this reality, then he may seek revenge outside of dream."

Frost said, "Or he will be so terrified of Merry that he will not come near her."

"It could go either way, true," Doyle said.

"I didn't know he had ever been able to enter dreams," I said.

"Once upon a time," Doyle said.

"The queen could enter nightmares, or speak to us through them, as well," Frost said.

"So he was the Lord of Dreams, and she was what, the Lady of Dreams?"

They both shook their heads, and I was feeling better, because I was a bit distracted by them both standing there nude. Sadly, I still had weeks to go before we could have sex. It had been too long.

"Merry, did you hear what we said?" Doyle asked.

I blinked and had to think; had I heard anything that those lovely mouths had been saying in the last few minutes? I finally said, "No, I'm sorry, but your being nude distracted me."

They smiled at each other, and then at me. I would have said, *Don't be conceited*, but it was just truth that the two of them standing there nude, bodies not even ready for such things, had made me think of sex, and longing. I still ached too badly to do anything about it, even if the doctors hadn't warned against it, but that my body was interested again was nice. After being hugely pregnant for so long, and so ill with the triplets, it was nice to feel something close to normal and think that maybe my body could get back to doing something besides having babies.

"You're going to have to repeat everything you just said. I will endeavor not to be distracted, but perhaps if you sat down and put the sheet across your laps, that might help my powers of concentration."

Their smiles turned to mischievous grins, but they did as I suggested and sat down on the sides of the bed that had become theirs, Frost to my left and Doyle to my right. Once they had piled the sheet in place, Doyle said, "She was the Queen of Nightmares, for she was never merely a lady of the nobility, Merry, but always destined to be more."

"But the king was once just a lord?" I asked.

They both nodded, Frost's hair spilling forward around his bare shoulders. His ponytail had come undone in the night, as it often did. Even braiding didn't always hold it, as if the hair itself didn't like to be bound.

"Who was the royal family of the Seelie Court, then?" I asked. It had never occurred to me that Taranis didn't descend from a "royal" line like Andais did, but then he'd been king for over a thousand years. I wasn't thirty-five yet; it was a little before my time.

"They were killed in the last great war between the two main courts," Doyle said.

I stared up at him. "Then why isn't our queen the high queen of everything in faerie?"

"Because the remaining Seelie nobles preferred death to the Golden Court being swallowed into the Court of Nightmares, which was one of the Unseelie names back then."

"Why didn't my aunt just slaughter them until the survivors surrendered? It is one thing to say you would rather die, but if you see enough people die before you, most relent, or so I'm told," I said.

"Not always," Doyle continued, "but though we had won the war, our side was sore hurt, and if we had continued the fighting it might have meant the destruction of all the sidhe."

"So a Pyrrhic victory," I said.

"If the fighting had continued, yes."

"I did not know things were so dire," Frost said.

"What do you mean, you didn't know?" I asked.

"Belief and need did not turn me into the Killing Frost until Taranis was already king. The first battles I fought in were against the goblins when the courts of the sidhe joined forces against common foes."

I knew that once my tall, commanding Frost had been little Jack

Frost, a child-size embodiment of the hoarfrost that he painted on windows and the edges of things as he followed in the train of the Winter King. But people thought his work beautiful and paid attention to it, and once mortals pay attention and begin to believe or tell stories about something, it grows stronger, more alive. Just as love and belief made the toy rabbit in the Velveteen Rabbit story into a real bunny, so, too, had the man beside me gone from something that danced over the snow, barely more than a thought of cold and icy beauty, to the Killing Frost beside me. For my Frost, it had been the love of a mortal girl named Rose. She was long in her grave, but it was for love of her that Frost had been willing to grow tall and strong enough to build a life with her. I owed her a thank-you, and since I could not give it, when we had a second daughter to name and Frost suggested "Rose," no one had argued. We'd just found the prettiest version of it, Bryluen, Cornish for "rose."

I kept one hand on the knife he had given me, but reached out my other hand to touch his thigh where it lay peeking from the covers.

"I forget sometimes that Darkness and the Killing Frost were not always paired beside the queen."

He put his hand over mine and gave me a smile that held everything I wanted to see in that moment: tenderness, love, and a gentleness that harked back to his first form that had skipped across the snow and decorated the world in icy beauty.

"There were small battles between the sidhe courts after that, and in those a very new Frost fought against me."

I turned to look at Doyle. "Are you saying the two of you fought each other directly?"

He smiled. "No, I saw him across the battlefield a time or two. He was a shining thing and hard to miss, but he was new to battle and they had not schooled him to arms as I would have before allowing a newly risen warrior to take the field."

"I believe that the Seelie saw me as an accident. I was the first lesser fey to become sidhe in a long time. You do not train lesser fey the way you train sidhe."

"True enough even among the Unseelie, but I believe they expected you to die in those small battles; no need to waste training on cannon fodder."

Frost started rubbing his thumb over my knuckles where I still touched his thigh. "You are probably right, but I survived and they began to teach me."

"If you were once Seelie, then how did you get exiled from them?"

"A human serving girl spilled hot soup on the king's hand. It would have healed in minutes, but he hit her, and when she didn't fall down and cower, but kept her feet and glared at him, he started to beat her." He rubbed my hand over and over, his eyes staring at nothing, empty with remembering.

"You saved her," I said.

"I stepped between them, because I could not watch him kill her, and I didn't understand the other nobles just watching."

"You hadn't been noble long enough," Doyle said. "You didn't understand the privileges of rulership."

"I still don't, but our queen taught me not to stand between her and her victims." He shivered, his broad shoulders huddling in upon himself as if the Frost could be cold, but some chills go beyond temperature and reach the heart and soul.

Doyle reached across me to touch Frost's shoulder. "We all learned not to risk the queen's mercy." It was a saying among the Unseelie; to be *at the queen's mercy* had come to mean any hopeless situation, and to avoid being at the real queen's mercy you would do much, or not do, as the case may be.

Frost looked up and met the other man's eyes. They looked at each other and there was such pain in Frost's face, and such long sorrow in Doyle's. It was as if I had caught a glimpse of the long centuries that had made them the men they were now, and the friends they were to each other. They had been forged in fires of battle and torment.

In that moment I was so glad they were mine, so glad I could keep them safe. Once Queen Andais had said that any man who wasn't father to my children would be forced back into her Raven guard, there to be celibate again except for servicing her. It showed how distracted her son's death had left her, that she believed she could make that threat and still have me come home to accept the crown, to force all the guards I had come to consider mine back to be tortured by a madwoman for all eternity. Everyone wants to be immortal—even I did—but there were times when living forever and healing most injuries could have serious downsides, and being tortured forever was one of those.

That thought made me say out loud, "Once the genetic tests come back and prove conclusively who the fathers are and aren't, do you think the queen will demand her Raven guards back?"

"She has stated that many times," Doyle said.

"But most of them have taken oath to Merry now," Frost said.

"Does one oath supersede the other?" Doyle asked.

"That's why Cathbodua did it," I said.

"You mean offered her oath?"

"Yes."

We all thought about it for a few moments, and then Doyle said, "The queen has been too busy trying to die to think about living, but if she believes either that she will live and need her guards, or that by demanding that all her Ravens come home we will help her die, then she might call all those who are not father to your children back to the Unseelie Court."

"What would we do?" Frost asked.

"I cannot send them back to death and torment," I said.

"Cathbodua was free to give her oath anew, because all the princes were dead, but the male guards shouldn't have been able to make such a vow to Merry while the queen still lived," Doyle said.

"You mean literally, the words wouldn't have come out their mouths, or that some curse for oathbreaking should have happened?" I asked.

"The latter."

"How do we know it has not?" Frost asked.

"Because Sholto and Merry are the ones who brought the Wild Hunt back to life, and that is what hunts oathbreakers among us, but you felt no sense of wrongness as they made oath to you, did you?"

I thought about it, and then shook my head. "No, nothing felt wrong, and Sholto was with us when it happened."

"How can the oath to the queen be mute?" Doyle asked.

"Did you take your oath willingly?" Frost asked.

Doyle nodded.

"I did not, but it was the only avenue left open to me, the only safety from the king's mad pride."

"You're saying if the oath was coerced, then it's not a true oath," Doyle said.

"Perhaps," Frost said.

"If they're oathed to me for real, then they can't be forced back to the queen."

"The oath can't force them back, but her rage and madness could."

We had a moment of just sitting there thinking about it all. I finally said, "Being held sounds very good right now."

"Then let us put away our weapons and huddle together," Doyle said.

"The Darkness does not huddle," Frost said.

"Nor does the Killing Frost," Doyle said.

"I promise not to tell; just hold me, and tell me how to keep the king out of my dreams."

I placed the relic, Aben-dul, on top of the headboard. We'd put it back in the weapons locker later. It was far too dangerous to leave lying about. Frost took back his knife, and we lay down with the two of them wrapped around me, and their long arms touching each other. The Darkness and the Killing Frost might not huddle, but I did, and unless there was a way to keep Taranis out of my dreams, I'd be doing more cuddling and less sleeping from now on. I'd never suffered from insomnia, but I was willing to learn.

CHAPTER

SEVENTEEN

The babies were all asleep in their cribs. Once I calmed down from the dream, I had to see them. I knew in all reason that they were safe, but fear isn't always about reason; maybe fear is never about reason, but some fears are reasonable. I feared my uncle, and my aunt, that was reasonable, but I also feared that my babies had somehow been left inside my nightmare—not reasonable.

Kitto stood beside the crib with me. We held hands as we gazed down at Bryluen. She was curled into a tiny ball, as if she were still asleep inside me, trying to find room between her bigger siblings. We walked to Gwenwyfar, to see her white curls almost gleaming in the glow of the night light. Alastair was flopped on his back, arms and legs akimbo, as if he'd played hard and just collapsed where he was the way Liam did sometimes. Were boys so different from the very beginning than girls? I honestly didn't know; there'd been no babies around me growing up, so my learning was all books and classes, and on-the-job training.

Kitto wrapped his arm around my waist, and I slid my arm across his shoulders. They were broader than when he'd first come to me, from Doyle's insistence that the smaller man hit the weight room and even weapons practice. Kitto wasn't expected to take his place among my guards, but Doyle wanted all of us to be able to defend ourselves. I had even joined the practice until I got too big with babies to move well, and the doctors started worrying that some of the training might cause premature labor. As soon as I healed I'd be back to it, because defending myself sounded awesome after my dream about Taranis. But then I had defended myself, hadn't I?

"I swear to you, Merry, the babes have slept peacefully for hours."

I hugged him. "You need to sleep, too, you know?"

He smiled up at me and then gazed at the babies, our babies. "I never thought I'd belong anywhere. I was tolerated among the goblins as long as I served a stronger warrior or his lady as their submissive toy, but if they tired of me, or one got jealous of me with the other, then they could cast me out, and masterless I was anyone's meat."

I put both my arms around him and held him close, resting my head on the top of his black curls; they were soft in texture, not like pure goblin hair, which ran to coarseness. "You're ours now, Kitto."

He hugged me back. "I have a family like I read about in books."

"The goblins aren't much for reading," I said.

"Most are not, but my first mistress taught me how to read, and after that being able to read was an asset to my other masters and mistresses— as much as the sex sometimes."

"So you read them to sleep?" I asked.

"Or read contracts to them, or modern newspapers."

"I didn't know the goblins cared about what was happening in the outside world."

"Some do."

I held him close, rubbing my cheek in the softness of his hair. I thought about all the long centuries that he had managed to survive in a culture that valued brute strength and power on the battlefield, and sex. It sounded like a desperate and lonely existence.

I tried to lighten the mood, because I needed it, too. "Good that you are learned, and fabulous at sex."

"Sometimes I was too good at the sex," he said.

I moved back enough to look into his face. "What do you mean? It's not possible to be too good at sex." I smiled when I said it, but he didn't smile back.

"Several masters and mistresses became jealous that their lovers preferred me to them, and cast me out because of it."

I gave him wide eyes and tried to think my way through that. I finally said the truth. "I'm amazed the jealous lovers didn't just kill you for it."

"Some tried, but the lovers that valued me stopped them, or even fought them in my defense."

"You are very good in bed," I said.

He smiled up at me. "But not that good, you're thinking, not by goblin standards."

"They like it very rough," I said.

"In public, but in private many of them prefer gentler sex."

I'd experienced that difference myself with Holly and Ash, the other goblins in our lives. If anyone knew they enjoyed gentle sex, their reputation would be damaged, so I said nothing, not even to Kitto.

"And if their secret got out that they'd enjoyed that with you, they would be ruined."

"It would be seen as weakness, and that is always challenged among my people."

"Your mother was sidhe, Kitto; we are your people as much as the goblins."

He smiled, and it was a happier one this time. "I was not raised sidhe, Merry, so I will always think of myself as goblin. The sidhe were these impossibly beautiful, magical beings, and the fact that I carried their skin and hair appealed to the goblins that had a fetish for the touch of sidhe flesh."

"It is a serious fetish among the goblins," I said.

"It's what led to so many rapes in the wars between the two races. The sidhe will not voluntarily share themselves with a goblin."

I leaned over and kissed him softly, gently, but thoroughly. "This is one part-sidhe princess who volunteers eagerly."

His face lit up, filled with happiness. "And I will serve you in any way I can for as long as you will have me."

"Kitto, I'm not planning on casting you out, you know that, don't you?"

His happy looks slipped a little around the edges. "If my goblin king calls me home, Merry, there is nothing you can do but let me go."

"You are sidhe now; I have brought you into your power, which means the goblins can't call you from my side, Kitto."

He cuddled tighter against me, rubbing his cheek against the crook of my neck like a cat cuddling closer. He shivered, and not in a happy way.

I hugged him tight. "What's wrong, Kitto? What are you afraid of?"

"I am a goblin with a sidhe hand of power, but Holly and Ash have hands of power, too, and they have stayed in the goblin kingdom."

"They would be insane to try to join the Unseelie kingdom with the queen so unstable," I said.

"True, but the fact that they didn't try to join the sidhe after coming into their magic means that magic alone may not be enough to keep me at your side."

I buried my face in the softness of his curls. I breathed in the scent of him, felt the gentle strength of him, and thought about him not being here by my side. It was a painful thought.

"Has someone said something to you?"

"Have you asked what Holly and Ash are doing with the new hands of power that you helped give them?"

"No, should I?"

"Yes," he said, with his lips soft against my neck.

"Tell me," I said.

"If they find out that I told on them, they will not like it, and their hands of power are much stronger for combat than mine."

He turned in my arms, so he could cuddle even closer to me. He shivered, and it wasn't from happiness at being held. He was afraid of the twin warriors, and he should have been. It suddenly felt like Kitto wasn't close enough to me; sometimes even a robe and pajamas kept the skin hunger and comfort from being fed.

I let go of him enough to open my robe and reach for his shirt. He helped me take it over his head with a smile I could see from the pale glow of the night light. We wrapped our naked upper bodies around each other, his arms wrapping around my waist inside the thin shelter of my robe. The front of him, still in shorts, pressed against my thigh. I could feel that just that much undressing had made his body start to react, but I knew I didn't have to tell Kitto that there would be no sex tonight; he wouldn't push, but be content that I wanted to touch him so closely.

"Now, tell me," I whispered against his curls.

I felt his smile against my neck, and that made me smile in the dimness of the nursery where the babies lay content and safe, despite my dream.

"They are using their newfound magic to fight duels."

"I thought Holly and Ash were so feared even among the goblins that no one would challenge them."

"They are, but there are some insults that no goblin could allow to stand if he or she wanted to keep their reputation, and to lose your reputation is to sign your death sentence among us."

"You mean they're starting the fights," I whispered.

"I mean, they are goading others into challenging them to duels, for they are not only fierce and ruthless warriors, but much craftier than most give them credit for."

I held him in my arms, feeling the warmth and solidness of him, and was afraid for him. He felt so small, delicate as my own more mortal form, and I knew that I would have died quickly among the goblins if I'd had to defend myself from insults.

"They may be nearly as smart as they are strong," I said.

Kitto's breath was hot against my skin as he whispered, "Ash is; I'm not certain about Holly, but he follows where his brother leads and that is enough to save him from mistakes he would make otherwise."

"Do you think they will challenge Kurag, Goblin King, and win the throne from him?"

"They could," Kitto said.

"I have a treaty with Kurag, but not with the twins," I said.

"Yes," he whispered.

I moved back enough to look into his face. "You think they won't honor the treaty agreement," I said.

"I fear they might not."

"Sex with me awakened their hands of power, gave them the blessing of the Goddess," I said.

"Yes, and they are grateful, but I do not believe that Ash is ever so grateful that he would allow it to interfere with his own ambitions."

I nodded. "I know they mean to seat one of them on the goblin throne."

"Kurag knows it, too," Kitto said.

"Why does he not challenge them and be done with it, then?" I asked.

Kitto studied my face. "You know the answer to that as well as I do."

"He fears he will lose," I said.

Kitto nodded.

I let that thought roll around in my head for a minute, and then said, "He's right to be afraid."

"I believe he will lose if he fights them fairly and openly," Kitto said, voice still low so that we didn't wake the sleeping babes.

"Goblin society allows only fair and open fighting. A king who lets someone else do his killing is soon a dead king," I said.

"We must all fight our own battles, that is true; so a king could not hire an assassin, for to be found out would be a death sentence, and likely a long and painful death."

"So what are you saying, Kitto?"

"I am saying that not all assassinations are paid killings."

I frowned at him. "You're being too obtuse for me, Kitto."

He sighed and said, "Kurag is much smarter than he lets most see, and has used it to his advantage politically for years. I believe he might manipulate others into trying to kill the twins for him, and his hands would look clean of their blood."

"But you say the twins are manipulating people into dueling them already; doesn't that feed into what Kurag wishes?"

"No, for the twins are only finding fights with goblins they believe they can beat. They avoid the handful of warriors that they are unsure of on the battlefield."

"You think Kurag might try to arrange a fight between the twins and someone who might be able to kill them," I said.

Kitto nodded.

"Kurag is my ally only for another few weeks, and then the treaty with him ends," I said.

"Unless you bring over more of the half-sidhe among the goblins, yes," Kitto said.

"I am not allowed sex for six more weeks, according to my doctors," I said.

"And by that time the treaty will be over and Kurag will not have to help you against your uncle, or your aunt, if they decide to attack you and yours."

"Are you saying that I should support Kurag in his effort to get the twins killed, or the twins in killing him?"

"I am saying that Kurag fears your enemies and will escape the treaty as soon as he can, and that the twins may not honor a treaty with you. Two of those that insulted them so they had to stand challenge were also sidhe-sided goblins and had made it known that they wished to bed you and gain their own magic."

"You're saying that now that Ash and Holly have their hands of power, they may not want me to give such power to any other goblins," I said.

He nodded. "They do not fear me, for my hand of power only allows me to bring someone through a mirror call against their will, and close the window at will. It is powerful, so I'm told, but it is mostly useless in a duel. Other sidhe-sided may gain other things that are more battle useful."

I wrapped him closer in the circle of my arms, folding my silk robe over both of us. I think the robe would have tied around both of us, we were both so small.

"It is always a gamble which magic will come to a person," I said.

"I've learned that some powers run in bloodlines, as you have the hand of flesh like your father before you."

"True," I said.

"If you had been able to keep fucking them, I think they would still be tied to you more, but when the doctor told you not to risk it with the babies . . ." I could feel him shrug in the circle of my arms.

"You think they want to be free of me?"

"Holly does," Kitto said. "Ash will do whatever will give them the most power."

"It will be six weeks before I can have sex with anyone, according to the doctors."

"And longer before you would risk such roughness in bed as they or Mistral prefer," Kitto said.

I petted Kitto and tried not to betray with even the stillness of my body the secret I'd been keeping. Holly and Ash were perverted by goblin standards. They actually liked gentle sex, and Ash enjoyed giving oral sex, which was a sign among the goblins that he considered himself subservient to me, or anyone he would go down on. It had taken me weeks to convince Kitto to allow me to go down on him, for he feared that it would hurt my reputation among the goblins, and we still needed their threat to keep our enemies in check, or at least to give them pause about attacking me. If the goblins learned the kind of sex that the brothers enjoyed, their reputations would be ruined. It could cost them their lives, because if you were perceived as weak, the challenges to combat could come so fast and often that eventually you would fail, and there was only one cure for failure in a duel among the goblins—death. I was lucky that the sidhe gave other options, or I would have died long before I escaped to Los Angeles.

Kurag, Goblin King, and Niceven, Queen of the Unseelie Demi-fey, had both agreed to forgo their price of treaty until after the babies were born. The goblins would have to wait until I was cleared for sex and had had it successfully with some of the fathers of my children, but Niceven could ask for her blood price to continue sooner. It was but a bit of blood offered to their tiny mouths, but the wild magic that had returned with my own late-blooming hands of power had given wings to the wingless among them, and given extra powers to some among them who had shared my blood and then my bed. Legend had said that some among the demi-fey could change to human size, but we had thought that lost with so much other magic among the fey, until we'd met demi-fey who could do it. I still thought they would be the perfect assassins, though Niceven said that they had never acted as such. I wasn't sure I believed her.

"You've thought of something that makes you sad, or worried," Kitto said softly.

"The demi-fey can demand their bit of blood again sooner than the goblins can demand their bit of flesh," I said.

He snuggled his face against my shoulder and stroked a hand down my back. "You fear the demi-fey, don't you?"

"Remember the case we helped the police solve? That proved to me that the demi-fey can be just as insane and dangerous as any of us." I shivered at the thought of what had almost happened, when our tiny murderer had tried to cut the babies from my body and destroy what she could not have, a regular life with the human she was in love with. They say lovers want the world to love with them, but love thwarted can turn as ugly and dangerous as any hatred I'd ever seen.

He kissed my shoulder. "I am sorry, our Merry, it was careless of me not to remember."

I shook my head, my longer hair sliding over the silk, which meant I was moving more than I thought, as if I could shake the memory of that evil from my mind, but it was too recent a memory to fade. I had been in my first trimester with the babes then, and it had been the case that made the men veto any other cases for the Grey and Hart Detective Agency until after the babies were born. So many things had been waiting for the babies, and now we stood surrounded by all of them. Triplets, the first ones born to the sidhe in more centuries than anyone could remember.

Now, everything and everyone that had been waiting for the births would be wondering when to approach me, and how, and if they wanted to continue with treaties, alliances, or . . . There were those among Taranis's court who had been waiting to see if my children were born deformed monsters, which was what the Golden Court had believed happened to all sidhe who joined the Unseelie Court. It wasn't true, but like all truly ugly rumors it was strongly believed by many.

Now that the babies and their first pictures were disproving the rumor, we would see how serious the Seelie nobles had been about doing anything to have children of their own. If I could truly give them babies they would do much, including perhaps killing Taranis for me. I much preferred his death by his own nobles to risking the men I loved in battle against him, and me battling him . . . it was too ludicrous to think about. He'd kill me. He would just kill me. Of course, what he wanted to do to me was to force me to be his queen, because he thought his rape had gotten me with his child. That he thought that was reasonable was just one more example of his insanity.

I stood there wrapped in the warmth of my robe and Kitto's arms, surrounded by our three children, and I wanted to feel content and happy, but there was still too much work to do, too many deaths to accomplish, because I finally owned that only the deaths of at least one of my relatives would bring safety to me and mine.

One of the babies shifted in their crib, making a small sound like the mewing of a kitten or the soft rustle of a bird. Kitto and I tensed, waiting to see if the noise grew and the baby woke, but the movement quieted and the room was full of that contented sleepiness that babies can give off, so you struggle to stay awake around them like being covered in dogs on the couch.

As if my thoughts had called them, I heard a snuffling at the door. The quiet voice of one of the guards came. "No, pups, you'll wake the babies moving around in there."

I looked toward the door. I could see the vague shapes of larger dogs, and the smaller ones; their eyes shone in the light in a way that those of normal dogs did not, but they were the dogs of faerie, and they did a lot of things that normal dogs didn't do.

I spoke softly. "It's all right, let them in."

"As you will, my lady." And the door was opened so the mass of dogs could spill inside. There were so many of them that their wagging tails made a sound, like wind, or the softest of clapping. I'd never had so many dogs in so quiet a room to understand that wagging tails actually make noise. It made me smile.

My two faerie greyhounds, Mungo and Minnie, pressed close like silk over muscle; the pack of terriers and small lapdogs that seemed to always roam the house and grounds milled around our ankles and calves. The smaller dogs started yipping, and one terrier gave a full bark.

"Hush," I said.

"You'll wake the babies," Kitto said.

The door pushed further open, and two more dogs entered. Two large black shapes, like all black Rottweilers, but they weren't Rotties, they were hellhounds, the black, raw stuff of faerie's wild magic made flesh and blood. Most of the dogs had begun as them, like black placeholders that would shift to a different variety of dog once they were needed, though Doyle said that if they remained in this form for long enough they would simply be hellhounds. They actually had nothing to do with hell and everything to do with being wild magic, powerful guardians, and hunting down those who had betrayed or threatened faerie. If you had a pack of them behind you, you might think Christian demons were chasing you. Doyle's father had been a phouka, a shapeshifting faerie, but his mother had been a hellhound, so he could actually turn into a shape very similar to the pair that strode into the room. The other dogs went silent and gave way as the two came to bump against Kitto and me, only Mungo and Minnie stayed on either side of me, hunched, but touching me from behind. They acknowledged the bigger dogs' dominance, but not their place at my side, which was a fine line to walk in dog politics, but so far they'd managed it without fights. I had no illusions who would win a fight between my two slender sight hounds and the more massive guard dogs. Kitto and I both touched the great black heads.

"Big fellas," Kitto said, affectionately.

But then an even bigger shape pushed his way through the door, and the hellhounds gave way to him, as everyone else had given way before them.

"No," I whispered, "that's the big fella."

Spike was one of the biggest dogs I'd ever seen; he could nearly look me in the eye just standing, as tall as a modern Irish wolfhound with the same wiry coat, but broader, beefier. He was the true figure of the dogs that the Romans said could bring down the horses that pulled their chariots and then, if their masters didn't call them off, could slay the charioteer, too. They'd been so fierce that ransoms had been paid in an exchange of dogs. The great dogs had been pitted against lions in the arena, and the dogs had won enough matches to make it a good sport.

Spike strode into the room with an attitude that wasn't sight hound at all; they tend to be more uncertain, nervous, whereas he carried himself more like a German shepherd, and the way he sized up a room was more Doberman. He just had *working guard dog* in every purposeful pad of those great feet. In good light his coat was a wonderful mix of pale brindle stripes. He had a "sibling" that was short-haired to his wire coat, so that his brother looked like a pale tiger, which was what we'd named him, so it was Tiger and Spike.

"Aye," Kitto said, "he is."

The great dog came to me and I put both my hands on the big head and ruffled him. He gave a big tongue-lolling grin, as goofy and happy to be petted as any of the smallest terriers. I put my forehead against his rough, warm fur and whispered, "Did you hear us up, Spike?"

He snuffled me, as if to say yes, or maybe he was just taking a bigger hit of my scent.

Kitto had moved out of the circle of my arms so I could greet Spike. He wasn't afraid of the smaller dogs, but the wolfhounds seemed to give him and all the goblins pause. I'd learned that the wardogs hadn't just killed Romans, but had actually been used in the great wars between the sidhe and goblins, and they had been one of the few things that could bring true death to the immortals. They looked like dogs, but in effect they were living, breathing manifestations of the wild magic of faerie itself, so in effect they were magic made flesh, and that meant they could kill goblins, sidhe, all of us. I put my face over those gigantic jaws and trusted he wouldn't crush my throat with one bite.

Kitto moved away, and some of the smaller dogs followed him, so that he knelt in a swirl of them, petting them, and the sounds of their happy panting, snuffles, snorts, and quiet dog noises filled the room.

The two big, black dogs walked to the cribs and began to sniff them. Kitto got up and went to them. "Hush, you'll wake the babies."

The big black dog put its nose resolutely against the crib bars and looked back at me. It wasn't a dog look in those dark eyes, and as I gazed into them there was a spark of red and green like Yule fires banked and ready to come to life and fill a room with everything the holiday was meant to be, and so seldom was. I smelled roses, and then I smelled pine, like Christmas trees, and I wasn't surprised when I looked back to find Frost coming through the door. When the wild magic had first come here in L.A. he had sacrificed himself, become a great white stag; for a time we thought we'd lost him forever to that form, not dead, but not human enough to know that I was pregnant with his child, not human enough to hold me or love me.

He came to hold my hand now, and I smiled up at him, so happy that he stood beside me now. He bent and kissed me, whispering, "The God called me to your side."

I nodded.

Kitto came to stand on my other side but didn't try to take my hand. I reached out to him, and the smile that flashed joyful across his face was so worth that small gesture. "What's happening?" he whispered.

"Magic," I said.

The black dog snuffled Bryluen's onesie-covered body. She stared at him, eyes intent, not afraid, and then the big nose touched her bare face. The rush of magic washed over us in a skin-tingling, hair-raising wash of warmth that filled the world with the scent of pine and roses, and the scent of spring like a wash of fresh rain that brings the first flowers.

The black fur ran as if it were water moved by wind, and where that wind touched it the fur turned the green of grass and leaves, fur growing slightly longer, thicker, more wiry-looking. The shaggy green head was bigger than the baby it lay beside, but it raised that head and looked at us. Its tongue lolled out happily, and the overly wide eyes held both happy dog and something else, something more.

"Cu Sith," Frost whispered, and it was, the great watchdogs that used to guard our faerie mounds, our sithens. One had appeared in Illinois and attached itself to the Seelie Court, and a second had appeared here in L.A. when the wild magic created new lands of faerie inside the walled estate. The first one had run away to take up its post among the Seelie and spent a lot of time protecting the servants from King Taranis's rage. Taranis was afraid of their Cu Sith, partly because of what it was, and partly, I thought, because it didn't like him, and a Cu Sith was the heart of any sithen it guarded. It was a way of saying that his faerie mound didn't like him much.

Spike raised his head skyward and gave one long, deep baying howl. The other dogs joined him, one, two at a time, so that it was like a choir, each voice rising and blending with the next, so that we stood in the center of that beautiful, mournful, joyful noise. It reminded me more of the sound of wolves than dogs.

Gwenwyfar began to cry, and the other black dog went to her crib and looked back at us whining, as the howls reverberated and faded in the small room. We lowered the crib and the big black dog sniffed her. She cried harder, striking out with tiny legs and waving small fists. The dog snuffled her harder, rolling her a little with its muzzle; one of her tiny fists must have touched the fur, because white began to spread from its nose backward like a white snow covered the bare earth, except that this snow was shaggy fur, and the dog turned huge saucerlike eyes upward. Its great jaws were full of razor-sharp teeth, and though it looked like a big, white dog, there was just enough different about its eyes and mouth to make you think, *Not quite a dog*. It was one, and it wasn't.

"Galleytrot," Kitto said. He was right, it was known as a ghost dog, something that chased travelers on lonely roads and haunted lonely places. As the Cu Sith was the bright, high court of faerie, so the galley-trot was the scary story told around the winter fire, and a warning to stay in groups, because alone, things that weren't human could find you and steal you away. When the wild magic had come, the only other galleytrot had come to the hands of the goblin twins, Holly and Ash. There was no way for them to be Gwenwyfar's fathers; they had come to my bed too late. Galleytrots weren't exclusive to the goblins, but they were certainly more Unseelie than Seelie Court. Gwenwyfar might look perfectly Seelie, but her true heritage showed in the white dog at her side, as Bryluen's showed in her green dog. If theGalleytrot had come to Bryluen, I'd have wondered more if her possible goblin heritage might come from the twins.

Kitto said, "There's no dog for Alastair."

The door opened, and it was Doyle with another black dog at his side. The dog went to Alastair's crib, and Frost lowered it for him. I took his hand in mine again, and Doyle took his other one, so that Frost stood in the middle of us as the black dog sniffed the baby. Alastair stared into the big face like Bryluen had, and then the dog touched his face, gently. Alastair made a soft sound and then the fur ran with colors, but something was different with this one, because it wasn't just the fur that changed, but the dog began to shrink, as if the big black body were being erased, or condensing down.

"What is it?" Kitto asked.

Doyle bent down and picked it up, ruffling its long ears. "A puppy," he said.

"But a puppy what?" Kitto asked.

I touched the long, trailing ears; they were silky. "Hound of some kind," I said.

The puppy began to whine and wriggle. Doyle put it on the floor, but it began to whimper and cry. Alastair started to cry, too.

Doyle frowned for a moment, then picked the puppy up and set it in the crib. It licked Alastair's face, and the crying stopped. It walked around him and settled on the other side, its white and red puppy body stretched the length of his, Alastair's hand touching its back.

"He's too little to have reached out for the puppy," I said.

"Perhaps," Doyle said.

"We can't leave the puppy in with him, it's not housebroken," I said.

"It's his puppy, Merry."

"Do you know what kind of dog it is?"

"As you said, a hound."

"The other two dogs are guard dogs; what can a puppy do?" Frost asked.

The puppy gave a contented sigh, and Alastair made a similar happy sound. "Maybe every boy needs a dog," Doyle said.

"Did you have one when you were little?" I asked.

He smiled. "I did."

I frowned at him. "What kind of dog?"

He shook his head. "Let's say it was a present from one of my aunts."

Since two of his aunts had been hellhounds, with no human form, I had to ask, "Are you saying that one of your cousins was your puppy?"

He smiled. "Dog was my other form; think of it as more a best friend than a boy's dog."

I looked down at our son and the "puppy." "Are you saying that Alastair will be able to shapeshift?"

"I do not know, but let him keep the puppy, and we'll see. It was once one of my symbols." I knew he was referring to the fact that once he had been the god Nodens, a healing deity known for having dogs at his sanctuary that could lick a wound and heal it, among other things.

"Magical dogs; I assumed the dog was you, but you're saying . . ."

"I was not the only dog in my temples," he said.

We looked back down at our son and the puppy. The Cu Sith had lain down in front of Bryluen's crib, and the galleytrot had done the same to Gwenwyfar's.

My hounds bumped me and I stroked their silky heads. Spike put his head into the crib and sniffed both the baby and the puppy. It opened sleepy eyes and licked his nose. Spike rose back up and "smiled" at us, tongue out, so that he lost all his dignity and looked like the big, goofy hound he could be at times.

"Spike approves," I said.

"He does," Doyle said, smiling.

"He's your son," Frost said, sounding pleased.

Doyle took his hand in his and said, "Our son."

Frost's whole face lit up with the happiness of that shared phrase. "Our son," he said.

I moved so that I could wrap my arms around both their waists, and we hugged my two men and me. There were other men in my life, and I loved them, but these were the two who made my heart sing the most. If I'd been human enough, I might have felt guilty about that, but I wasn't, and I didn't; it was just the truth of my heart.

Kitto petted the puppy and kissed the baby, then put the side of the crib back up. "Good night, little prince."

We left the babies to sleep content with their new protectors, and new best friends, because Doyle was right; every child needs a dog.

EIGHTEEN

Two mornings later I woke to magic breathing and prickling along my skin. I had a moment of staring into the darkened bedroom and then Frost had me around the waist and was lifting me out of the bed, holding me one-armed behind him, while he pointed a sword at the other side of the bed. I gripped his arm where he held me, but I couldn't see the threat around his body, and where was Doyle? Why wasn't he with us?

Frost said, "Doyle, Doyle, it's me, it's your Killing Frost, and our Merry."

A low, deep growl came from the other side of the room. It was a sound to raise the hair on your neck and tighten your body, ready for fight or flight.

"Doyle, do you know me? I am your lieutenant, your right hand, your Frost, do you not know me?" Frost's voice got lower as he spoke, a gentling voice.

The deep, bass growl came again, and I knew in that moment that Doyle was in the room with us. He was just in his dog form, a black dog the size of a small pony.

"Doyle," I said, softly, hesitantly.

He growled again.

Frost leaned ever so slightly so my feet could touch the floor and he could turn himself full toward the threat that was our dearest love. He spoke very carefully as if he were afraid to even move his mouth too much. "Very slowly, we back to the door. When we reach the door, turn the knob carefully, and open the door slowly."

"No sudden movement," I whispered.

"Yes," he said.

The door started opening behind us, and I hissed, "Stop."

It was Usna's voice that said, "What is that?"

"Doyle," I whispered, because I knew that he would hear me. Usna's mother had been cursed into cat form, and it had left him with a lot of very feline traits, including calico-colored hair and skin and extremely good hearing, especially for higher-pitched noises, like women's voices.

"Why is he threatening you?"

"Hush. Usna, when I say so, open the door and grab Merry through," Frost said carefully as he backed us closer to the now partially opened door. He changed our angle slightly to take advantage of the crack in the door.

"What about you?" I asked.

"I will come with you, but your safety is all."

I wasn't sure I agreed with that, but if Frost was actually going to have to fight Doyle in his hellhound/phouka form I wasn't sure I could bear to watch. Why was Doyle still stalking us, growling? It was like a nightmare, and then I had an idea.

"He's dreaming," I said.

"What?" Frost asked, moving us agonizingly slowly closer to the door.

"Doyle is dreaming. He's not awake."

From the other side of the door, Usna said, "You mean he's sleepwalking?"

"Yes."

"He has never done that before," Frost said, and that meant in centuries of friendship Doyle had never done such a thing, so why now?

"The king trapped me in dream," I said. We were almost to the side of the opening. I touched Frost's bare back gently, changing our angle slightly to leave room for Usna to open the door wide enough for us both to escape.

"You escaped," Frost whispered.

"I had to fight, and my father's sword came to me."

"And we had to prevent you from attacking us with it," he said, slowly.

"Shit," Usna said.

"Yes," Frost said.

That evil, frightening growl echoed along my spine, much closer this time. We had to wake Doyle, but how? What had brought me back to myself?

"You and Doyle touching me brought me back."

"If you're close enough to touch," Usna said, "you'll be too close."

I agreed, but . . . I peeked around Frost's body to see the great black dog. It took a moment for my eyes to distinguish it from the darkness of the room, and then it moved, and I could see the shape of the great beast like a piece of the night formed into something of muscle and skin and fur, and a slow, thundering growl. It stepped one paw closer, and the light from the door fell on it. The paw was bigger than my hand. Its lips curled back and teeth gleamed in the light from the hallway behind us.

I moved slightly out from behind Frost, and said, "Doyle, it's me, your Merry."

"Do not . . ." Frost began, and then the dog rushed toward us from less than four feet away, and there was no time for words.

CHAPTER

NINETEEN

Frost had a naked sword in his hand; he could have run the dog through, but he didn't, and the great black shape smashed into him, driving them both against the door and slamming it shut with us trapped inside.

Usna was yelling and pounding at the door. Other voices were joining his, but they couldn't help us, not in time. Frost's hands were holding the dog's throat, keeping those huge, snapping jaws from his face, but even as I watched, the jaws got closer to him.

If it had been some monster sent by Taranis to kill us, I would have picked up one of the many guns in the room and shot it, but it was Doyle, and lead bullets can kill the fey, all of the fey, even the sidhe. I stood there like some helpless princess from one of those foolish stories, and watched the men I loved most locked in a death struggle.

I cursed under my breath and moved toward the bed and my weapons that were still in their nighttime sheaths on the headboard. Frost had moved me too fast for me to grab either my gun or my sword, and I needed one of them. I could wound Doyle to save Frost; I wasn't sure I could kill him to do the same, but maybe lead would break this evil spell.

I moved slowly, not sure if it would attract the great dog, but he was too intent on killing Frost to notice me. I stopped going slow and bounced onto the bed, crawling toward my weapons.

Every hair on my body stood to attention; I smelled ozone, like before a close lightning strike, and had a second to throw myself flat to the bed before the lightning crashed through the upper part of the door and over my head, missing me by inches and leaving me gasping and stunned.

There was a hand on my back, another stroking my hair. Doyle's voice came like a human version of that deep growl, so low it could make me shiver in happy anticipation, but this time it was relief. He was human again, ours again.

"Merry, are you hurt? Did we hurt you?"

I started to say no, but realized I wasn't sure. I didn't think so, but it wasn't until I propped myself up on my elbows, with his hands still petting me, that I was confident enough to say, "No, I'm fine, just frightened."

"I am so sorry." Mistral crawled onto the bed, coming to my side. He was dressed in modern body armor over a black T-shirt. Leather biker pants with extra padding clung to his lower body, spilling into boots that matched them. Since his powers of lightning had returned he couldn't wear his centuries-old metal armor, not and use his major hand of power. His gray hair spilled over his face like clouds to match the smell of lightning that still clung to him and the room.

Doyle turned on him. "You are all strong enough to break a modern door easily; why didn't you try that before you nearly killed Merry?"

His eyes were the sickly green of tornado skies as he looked at the other man. "Doors were stouter things once; I have been on the wrong side of doors that I could not break open without magic."

"Did you even try?"

The green in Mistral's eyes began to swirl with anxiety like clouds do before a storm. "No," he admitted.

"It's all right, Mistral," I said.

"It is not all right," Doyle growled, and his voice still held the bass growls of the great black dog. It made me look at him, as if I needed my eyes to confirm that he hadn't changed back, but he was still there: tall, dark, handsome, and very human. But I reached out to take his hand in mine; I needed the touch of his skin against mine to be certain what was real.

"I'm not hurt, Doyle," I said, shaking his hand in mine.

Frost came to his knees beside the bed. "Alas, I am."

I kept Doyle's hand, but I sat up to see my other love. The front of his body was covered in blood. I let go of Doyle and slid to the floor beside him. "What happened?"

"I happened," Doyle said.

I glanced up at him, and then down at Frost's bloody body. "But how?"

"People think only cats have claws; dogs will cut you up while you keep them from biting your throat out," Usna said, rubbing one hand down the white, red, and black skin of his arm, as if remembering some old wound. His gray eyes were the most human thing about him and most of his face was as white a skin as Frost's and my own, but the edge of his face and neck were patterned with the same red and black spots, as if he'd been the cat his mother had been at his birth. I'd never asked if Usna had been born a kitten or a baby; it had never occurred to me to wonder until that moment.

I turned back to Frost and realized Usna was right. He'd been ripped in great bloody furrows from midchest to thighs; even his arms were marked up, though the worst was his chest, shoulders, and one leg. It took me a moment to realize he'd thrown a knee and thigh up over his groin to keep the great claws from tearing up such tender bits.

"I've sent for a healer," Usna said.

Doyle knelt on the other side of him. "I am so sorry, Frost."

"What happened to trap you in your dreams?" Frost asked, in a voice that held a hint of pain, which meant it hurt even more than I thought, otherwise he'd have hidden it better.

"Nightmares, and it was the Lord of Dreams . . . I guess, King of Dreams now."

"Taranis," I whispered.

"Yes," Doyle said.

"Two nights ago he attacked Merry, tonight you; we must find a way to keep him out of our dreams," Frost said.

"Agreed," Doyle said.

"But how?" I asked.

No one answered me, but my cell phone went off. I jumped and scrambled to get it from the bedside table, because it was Rhys's ring, and he was in charge of security while we slept tonight.

"Tell Mistral to control his anxiety," Rhys said with no hello.

"What?" I asked.

"There's a funnel cloud forming in the air about half a block away. It came out of a clear California night, so tell the storm god to calm down or our neighbors are really going to hate us."

"Shit," I said.

"Yes, now tell him to control himself, now!"

I told Mistral what Rhys had said, but even as I spoke the sickly storm green of his anxious eyes began to fill with movement, and I heard the first crack of thunder above us.

"Control yourself, Mistral," Doyle ordered.

"I am trying, but it's been centuries since I had the weather react to me. I'm out of practice."

Rhys yelled on the phone, "Tell him to practice fast—the tail of the funnel is reaching for the first house."

"Mistral!" I said.

"I'm trying!" His eyes were full of wind and storm.

TWENTY

The men were yelling at him, Doyle was ordering him. Mistral stood there, big hands clenched into fists; the effort of controlling his magic showed in the muscles in his arms as if stopping the storm had weight that he needed to lift with his body and not just his mind.

I went to him and touched his arm. It made him startle and look down at me with wide eyes. I could see the storm in his irises like tiny movie screens so that I saw the funnel cloud begin to reach for the earth below.

Someone said, "Let him concentrate, Merry."

"We need fair weather," I said, and went up on tiptoe, touching the side of Mistral's neck, and he bent toward me, hands still in tight fists; as he bent lower I was able to slide my hands around his neck, touch his face, and stare into the wonder of Mistral's eyes.

The terrible tension in his shoulders loosened, and then he raised his arms to hold me. We kissed and his lips were as gentle as any man in my bed for an instant, and then his arms enfolded me, lifted me off my feet, the kiss growing into an eagerness that was almost like feeding, as if his mouth had been hungry for mine. His arms tightened into a near-crushing weight, and he kissed me as if he meant to climb inside me through my mouth, forcing me to open wide for him. One arm held me in that so-tight grip and the other found the back of my hair and tightened until it was nearly painful. He let me know with his hands, his arms, his mouth, how much he wanted me, how much he'd missed me these long weeks, and how great his need was for the way we made love.

I gave myself over to the thrill and strength of that kiss, those arms, this man. He drew back enough to look into my face, his eyes almost wild with need. His eyes were a rich dark blue like the sky at dusk after a storm has blown everything clean.

He pressed his mouth against mine again in that passionate, almost painful kissing, turning with me in his arms to kneel on the bed, and begin to crawl us farther onto it. I managed to turn my lower body to the side, so that when he pinned me to the bed it was only part of me pressed under the solid weight of his upper body.

I fought free of his kisses and managed to say, "I cannot have intercourse yet, Mistral. The Gods know I want to, but the doctor says no, not yet." My voice was breathless, my heart loud in my ears, my body thick with the rush and beat of my own pulse.

He laid his head on the bed and made an inarticulate sound, half groan and half yell. He spoke with his face still pressed to the covers, hair pooling over him so I could see nothing but the gray fall of hair. "I shall go mad soon."

I touched his hair, smoothing it back until I could see the side of his face. "It's only five to six more weeks, and then I can make love again."

He rolled an eye up and the color was his more typical gray now. "Perhaps you should start with someone gentler than I, our Merry."

I smiled and smoothed more of his hair back so I could see that handsome profile. "Perhaps, but believe this, my Storm King, I want you as badly as you want me."

He studied my face and then smiled. "That is good to know."

"Rhys said the sky is clear, and it's a beautiful California night," Usna said.

I leaned and laid a much more gentle kiss on Mistral's lips. "We just needed his mood to lighten; fair mood, fair weather," I said.

"That was good and quick thinking, Merry," Doyle said. "I would not have thought of it in time."

"I don't think you kissing Mistral would have had the same effect," Usna said.

Doyle frowned at him, but Frost collapsing to the carpet made us all move toward him. He said, "I am all right, I just need to lie down," which meant he didn't feel well at all.

Hafwyn came through the door, and I realized that until she appeared I hadn't known if Usna had called a doctor or called someone who could heal with magic. *Healer* could mean either in this house.

Doyle knelt with Frost's head in his lap, smoothing the other man's hair and saying, "I am so sorry, Frost."

I held Frost's hand and felt it tighten as Hafwyn began to explore the wounds.

"You were not in your right mind, Darkness; I know you would never hurt me."

"Not deliberately," Doyle said, touching Frost's face gently.

"This is two attacks in our dreams in almost as many nights; what can we do to protect ourselves?" I asked.

Frost's hand tightened enough that I could feel that crushing strength, and I said, "Easy, my Killing Frost, easy." I touched his face as I said it.

He loosened his grip. "I am sorry, Merry."

"It's all right, it must hurt a great deal for you to react so."

"Nay, it does not." I realized that despite the strength in his hands in my and Doyle's grip his face was stoic, and only the cording in his arms showed the muscles he was using to hold on and not react to the pain. I cursed myself for revealing his pain when he was covering it so well, my brave man.

I leaned down and kissed him. He gave me startled eyes as I leaned back. I couldn't explain why I'd kissed him without compounding the mistake, so I just smiled at him and let him see how much I loved him.

That made him smile even as Hafwyn's slender fingers finished exploring the claw marks.

His body reacted to the kiss, and nude he could not hide it. He was not one of my men who enjoyed pain. Everyone's need had grown over the months of enforced celibacy. I'd even been forbidden oral, or really any sexual contact, once the doctors told me that any orgasm might bring on premature labor. It hadn't been worth the risk, but now that the babies were on the outside, we wouldn't endanger them.

"I can't have intercourse for weeks yet, but I could do oral and hand on some of you," I said. If I'd been human it would have been too bold in the situation, but no one in that room was human.

"That is very generous of you, Princess," Hafwyn said, "but it is not our way to offer sex without hope of pleasure in return." She wasn't chiding me, just stating cultural norms, as people do.

"I can orgasm from touching a man, especially oral."

Hafwyn looked at me, head to one side like a curious bird. Both her graceful eyebrows arched at me in surprise. "Truly?"

I smiled. "Truly."

"I'd forgotten what it meant to be a goddess of fertility."

"What do you mean?" I asked.

"Sex is a much broader pleasure for certain goddesses."

"I am no goddess," I said.

She made a small gesture with her head, almost a shrug. "As my princess wills, so shall it be, but there are some humans who live because a bit of metal that once pierced your flesh touched them, and now they use those objects to heal others."

"It is magic, yes, but it is not deity," I said.

She averted her eyes, laying out fresh bandages. "If you say so, then of course it is true."

"Hafwyn, seriously, there can be no talk of gods and goddesses for any of us."

"I know that if we are worshipped in this country it is grounds for our exile as a people," she said, still not looking at me, "but to not speak of a thing does not make it less true."

I didn't know what to say that, because I'd been thinking it as the soldiers that I'd healed had come back here on their leave, or when their tour of duty was up. They had come to me like a kind of pilgrimage, and those who had natural psychic abilities were growing in power, just as priests and priestesses did of old when the sidhe had been worshipped. We were ignoring it if we could, but eventually someone in the government would come to speak to us. I didn't think they'd kick us out of the country, but they would have to do something—but what? How do you forbid people from worshipping in a country where freedom of religion is one of the rights that people believe helped found the country?

I decided to change the subject back to something more pleasant and less confusing. I kissed Frost's hand. "I can pleasure you again, our Frost."

"I am too injured to do you even that much good, our Merry," Frost said, his voice holding some of the pain.

I squeezed his hand. "And I am sorry for that."

"I am more sorry, and will wait until our Frost can join us," Doyle said.

"No, Doyle, you do not have to wait for me."

"I will wait for you, Frost." Doyle made it sound very final.

"Very noble, Darkness, but will you be happy in your nobility as others take their turns first?" Mistral asked.

"Happy, no, but content to wait until Frost is healed so the three of us can be together, yes."

"You are certain?" Mistral asked, and I was almost sure what he would ask next.

"I am," Doyle said.

"I think Merry should begin with someone gentler than myself," he said.

I turned around so I could see him more clearly, and let him see the surprise on my face.

He smiled. "I want you, but I want rough even with just oral and I would prefer you be with others who are less demanding first. I would not want to be accused of souring you on the whole thing by my violence."

"You know how much I enjoy having sex with you, Mistral."

"I do," and his smile widened, filling his eyes with the unclouded blue of a spring sky. "But I also know that birth is a trauma to a woman's body, and would prefer you healed a bit more before we test if our idea of rough sex is pleasant to you."

I nodded. "It is logical."

"And noble of you, Mistral," Doyle said.

"Perhaps, but it will bother me to see other men have pleasure when I could have put myself first."

"Then it is truly noble," Doyle said.

Mistral gave a nod that was almost a bow.

"There was a time when I would have tried to jump the queue, but Cathbodua is in my bed and that is enough for me," Usna said.

"Then who?" Doyle asked.

"Are you not limiting your affections to the fathers of your babies now?" Hafwyn asked.

I looked at Doyle and said the truth. "Yes, for this, the fathers."

"You won't know for certain who the fathers are until the tests come back," she said.

"The Goddess has shown me for Alastair and Gwenwyfar, and I think I know for Bryluen."

"But the Goddess did not show you for certain," Hafwyn said.

"No," I said.

She nodded and said, "I will be able to heal much of this, but not all today."

"How long?" I asked.

"Three to four days," she said.

"In four days, Merry," Doyle said.

"Four days," Frost said.

The looks on both their faces tightened things low in my body that hadn't been getting used for a while. It felt good, but my body let me know that Frost wasn't the only one who was hurt. The doctors said I was healing remarkably fast, but giving birth was a trauma to the body as much as any wound, so I'd want to be careful.

"In four days, my Darkness, and my Killing Frost."

"In four days," Doyle said, and the heat in his eyes made me shiver happily.

CHAPTER

TWENTY-ONE

There were so many things that needed my attention, but I left Doyle to talk to the queen about how to keep Taranis out of our dreams, then left the other fathers with the babies, and I had the first hours of being just me, just Merry, in months. Being pregnant had been what I was for so long: unescapable, wonderful, terrifying, physically over-whelming. The fact that I was pregnant was the first thing people saw about me, thought about me, and during the second half of the preg-nancy it was all I thought about myself. Trapped under the weight of triplets, I had been unable to even get out of bed if I was on my back, though lying on my back hadn't really been an option at the very end; it was like being crushed. So I'd slept on pillows, sitting up, which meant I had slept badly, and been exhausted, and . . . I loved the babies, but I was so glad to have them in our arms instead of being forever pregnant.

Maeve Reed was back in her master suite, which I'd used for most of the last year. We'd moved to one of the larger guest rooms in anticipation of her return. It was still a large room, bigger than my apartment in Los Angeles had been. When I said *we*, I meant Doyle and Frost. None of us had spoken of it out loud, but gradually they had moved in and had no other room to call their own. Some of the other men slept with us occasionally, but most of them were as broad through the shoulders as Frost, and what had fit in the bigger bed upstairs was a tight fit here. Since I was planning sex and not sleep, the bed would have been fine, except that Frost was resting in it, because sleep would help him heal faster, so I went to the extra room.

It was one of the other guest rooms in the palatial mansion that Maeve Reed had owned since the 1950s. It was actually one of the smaller bedrooms, but one wall had a bank of windows that faced east, and two skylights, so the room was almost always light and airy and seemed bigger than it actually was. It also had a bathroom complete with shower, which was important for cleaning up afterward. If the room had been bigger I would have moved the three of us in here when we had to leave the master suite, but the shower was narrow enough that some of the men had trouble not bumping their shoulders against the walls. The bathroom in the bedroom that had become ours was much bigger, as was the entire room, but I liked the smaller bedroom better.

I sat on the edge of the bed in a forest-green silk robe, which had been one of the few pieces of clothing that had fit me until right at the end of the pregnancy, and then even the robe hadn't tied over the babies and me. Now it was laced tight. One of the things hardest to explain is that pregnancy makes your body a stranger in a way. You've known it your whole life and yet at some point in pregnancy it's like some stranger has moved in and your body isn't yours anymore. It doesn't react the same way, feel the same way, and there are movements inside you that you know are not your muscles, your fingers and toes wiggling, but other people with their own brains and wills and personalities growing like little strangers inside you. You hope that you'll be friends and like each other, as well as love each other, but you can't really know, not for certain. I'd seen too many people in my family hate each other, kill each other. When that is part of your family's repeated history it destroys a lot of illusions that most women have about their babies and everyone being perfectly happy and loving. That was for Hallmark holiday commercials, not for any reality I'd ever experienced with my actual blood relatives.

I sat with my robe tied tight around a waist and a body that looked,

almost, like me again, and wanted to be just me, just Merry, with someone, for an hour or two.

There was a knock on the door, not a soft one either. I said, "Come in."

Rhys opened the door, smiling. Galen was behind him, sort of looming with his six inches of extra height. I didn't normally think of Galen
as that tall, because he seemed smaller compared to the other guards, but
now I realized he was as tall as most; only Rhys was under six feet.

I smiled but fought not to frown. "I thought you were supposed to
decide which of you it was going to be."

They glanced at each other as Galen closed the door behind them.
"We were," Rhys said, "but we spent months sharing your bed, so we . . .
tied."

"Tied?" I asked.

"Rhys tried to pull rank, and I wouldn't let him without a fight."

I looked at Galen and didn't try to keep the surprise off my face.
"Really?"

"Really," he said, and his usually good-natured face was set in serious
lines.

"Really," Rhys said.

I looked from one to the other of them. "How serious a fight were you
willing to have?"

"I wasn't backing down," Galen said, and he said it as if it were simple
fact and not a total shock.

"I think he might have requested a duel," Rhys said.

Galen looked uncomfortable then, and more his normal self. "I don't
know if I would have taken it that far."

"Now you tell me," Rhys said, smiling.

Galen rolled his eyes, and then the kidding faded, and he turned that
serious, handsome face to me. "But short of a duel, I wasn't giving up the
first chance to touch you in months."

Rhys turned so that only I could see his face. He raised eyebrows at
me, but there was something new in his face as he said, "It was the most
angry I've ever seen him, outside of a fight to save your life, or ours."

I looked up at him, and suddenly his face was uncertain. "The only one who could tell me no today is you, Merry. Do you want just Rhys? If you do, then I'll leave."

I shook my head. "No, it's all right, I mean . . . stay, both of you stay, though with no intercourse allowed and not even being able to do oral sex on me, I'm not sure what both of you will be doing." I laughed and held my hands out to them both. "It's an embarrassment of riches to have you both."

Galen grinned, and the two men exchanged a look. They'd had months of literally sharing my bed and my body. They worked almost as well together as Frost and Doyle, though since they didn't love each other, the energy wasn't the same. It was good, but not as good, but then more love makes everything better.

CHAPTER

TWENTY-TWO

The clothes came off in an eager rush of hands and kisses, and left them nude and me wearing only the forest-green panties that matched the robe. I wanted to be as naked as they were, wanted to rub as much of my skin on theirs as possible, but my body wasn't healed enough from giving birth, not yet.

They laid me down between them and covered my body with kisses and caresses. Just that brought small eager sounds from me, making me writhe, body arching up against their hands like a cat, except I was lying on my back and arching things up toward them that cats didn't offer their owners. Rhys's hand slid down the front of my panties at last. I cried out just from that, arching my pelvis upward toward his hand.

Rhys put his other hand on my hip. "Easy, we need to be gentle, remember."

I blinked up at him and had a moment of wanting to argue, but my body was already letting me know that I might have been a little overeager, writhing around. It didn't hurt, but I ached.

"I'm sorry, I do remember, it's just been so long."

"It's been a long time for us, too, Merry," Rhys said, leaning in to kiss me. His hand wasn't down my pants anymore; he'd moved to keep from hurting me while I moved too much.

"We need to be slow, not fast," Galen said with a grin.

"Goddess help me, but I don't feel slow, or gentle; I feel crazed with the need to have you touch me everywhere."

"And we would like nothing better, but if we hurt you we'll never forgive ourselves," Rhys said.

"Not to mention that Doyle, Frost, and the rest will kick our asses," Galen said, smiling.

"They'd try," Rhys said.

"I'd put up a good fight," Galen said, "but eventually they'd win."

Rhys's face closed down; it was beyond serious.

"What?" I asked him.

He shook his head. "Nothing."

"Liar," I said.

He grinned. "Now we're not allowed to actually lie."

"But we're allowed to exaggerate until you'd believe the moon was made out of green cheese," I said.

"But we're allowed to lie by omission," Galen said.

Rhys frowned at him. "Don't help me."

I studied his face. "You think you could win against Doyle and Frost."

"I know I could."

I gave him a look.

He smiled, but it left that one tri-blue eye unhappy. "I could bring death with my touch to non-fey when I was just Rhys. You've seen me do it."

"But you killed the goblin that tormented you and Kitto; that's fey."

"I couldn't have done that before you and the Goddess brought me back into my power," he said.

"I don't think Doyle and Frost would let you get close enough to touch them," Galen said.

"I wouldn't have to touch them now."

"What do you mean?" I asked.

"I was Cromm Cruach; I lived for blood and slaughter, and I was good at it. I have a sithen of my own again, Merry. It's disguised as an abandoned Los Angeles apartment building, but it's a piece of faerie that came into being, because you brought me back to what I was; I don't have to get close enough to touch someone to cause their death."

"How do you know that, for certain, I mean?"

He looked away then, and I had to reach up, touch his face, and turn him back to me. "Rhys?"

"Let's just say that my sithen is in a bad section of L.A. and I'm blond and blue-eyed and don't exactly look like I belong."

"Someone attacked you," I said.

"Someones," he said.

"Who?"

"Let's just say that the gang problem in that section of downtown isn't an issue anymore."

"You didn't do it to defend yourself," Galen said.

I looked from one to the other of them. "What do you mean?"

"They hurt one of the people living near your sithen, didn't they?" Galen asked.

Rhys shrugged. "Don't make it sound all noble."

"I wasn't."

Rhys looked at him. "Don't disapprove either."

"I wasn't."

"If you have a point to make, make it soon," Rhys said, and he didn't sound altogether happy.

"I saw the flowers and gifts they leave by your building," Galen said.

"I would have known if any of you were close to my sithen."

"Apparently not," Galen said.

"You scouted me," Rhys said, and again he wasn't happy.

It was Galen's turn to shrug and give a little smile. He was pleased with himself.

"I'd believe that Darkness visited me, but not you."

"The only one of us better at personal glamour than me is Merry."

"True, you never need a disguise to do undercover work back when we are all working at the Grey Detective Agency. Sholto's pretty good at it, too."

"Good enough that both of you, and Sholto, went inside the Seelie sithen to rescue me with only your glamour to hide you from the king and his nobles." I grabbed Galen's hand and then took Rhys's. "And you in your fake beard and hat. You could have gotten all of you killed."

"But we didn't," Rhys said.

"But now you're telling me that you killed an entire gang. You risked yourself to do it, Rhys; don't tell me you didn't."

"I wasn't in much danger; that whole immortal thing, remember."

"Bullets can hurt you, Rhys, all of you, it's lead; cold iron can kill us, and steel hurts—no, don't give me that immortal crap. You could have died." I sat up. "Did you at least take some of the other guards with you as backup?"

The moment he looked away I knew he hadn't. I grabbed his arm. "Don't ever risk yourself like that again, not alone. We're a court, a court of faerie, Rhys; that means we fight our battles together."

"I was willing to risk my own life, Merry, but no one else's. Let's be honest: If you lost me you'd survive, but if I got Doyle or Frost killed, you'd never forgive me."

"Yes, I love Frost and Doyle the most, I'm more in love with them, but that doesn't mean I don't love you. Don't you ever think that I could lose you and it wouldn't hurt. How dare you think so little of me, Rhys. How dare you believe that my heart isn't big enough to love more than just two men." I was yelling at him.

He held his hands up in front of him. "I'm sorry, truly, but I did what I thought was best."

"If I'm the royal here, the would-be queen, then you don't get to make decisions like that without consulting me, is that clear?" I was yelling again.

"It's clear, I'm clear, checking with the queen before I clean up any more neighborhoods."

"You could have died!" And I burst into tears like some hysterical pregnant woman. Stupid hormones.

CHAPTER

TWENTY-THREE

forgave him when he made me yell for a much more fun reason, and the first orgasm in months filled my body, flowed over my skin, and brought me screaming. I screamed his name while his fingers brought me, and my nails carved my pleasure in red scratches down his arm, and across Galen's back, because that was what was under my fingers when Rhys's hand pushed me over that delicious edge.

My skin had not glowed until that last push of pleasure; only then had my pale skin filled with moonlight glow like the clouds had finally been blown away and the light of a full moon could bathe the world in its luminescence. My skin ran with power and I could see swirls of greens and golds from the corners of my vision and knew it was the colors of my own eyes alight with magic.

My magic brought theirs, and Rhys's skin was an answering shine to mine, so that it was two moons entwined, filling the world with a light so bright it would make mortals shield their eyes for fear of losing sight, or mind, from the beauty of it. His one eye glittered like three jewels, carved sapphires in a range of blues from palest blue, as if the sky could burn with its own color, a blue so rich, as if cornflowers could explode with their own beauty, and then the color of the ocean where it runs shallow and warm, as if the sun truly did rise from the water in a burst of glory.

He leaned over and kissed me with lips that were the soft pink of sunrise to the ruby glow of my own. I saw his hand held above us; there was red shining on his fingers as if the color of my lips had been spread like slick fire across his hand. It was my blood from bringing life into the world, and it glowed like every other part of us, thick with magic and the grace of Goddess.

He lifted away from the kiss and there were afterimages of the colors of our lips like a Doppler effect that you could see with your naked eyes. My hands fell back to the bed, all of me limp; my eyes fluttered back into my head with the pleasure of it, and I could see the light of my own irises inside my nearly closed eyes, so that when I tried to open them the world was edged with emerald and molten gold fire. The term *afterglow* had a whole new meaning for the sidhe.

The bed moved, but I couldn't see past my fluttering eyelids and the radiance of my own eyes and skin, as if my own magic blinded me.

Someone kissed me, and I knew from that first touch that it was Galen, because the sky didn't glow the pale green of spring leaves, but that was the color that joined mine, so that the greens of my eyes and the green of his seemed to blend and flow together as we kissed. Where his hands touched me the light flared. I couldn't see it, I could feel it, so that a thrumming warmth followed at his touch, and when he slid his body cuddling close to mine, that warmth pulsed between us, until I couldn't breathe for a minute, and when I did it was a gasp, as if I were already putting my mouth around things much deeper than his kiss could ever be.

He whispered against my lips, "I want to feel your mouth around me."

I breathed out, "Yes . . . please."

He got up on his knees beside me. The fire was beginning to fade so that he looked less magical and more just Galen, but that had been magical enough to me since I was fourteen. My own glow was fading so that I could see him without the shine of my own eyes clouding my vision. He smiled down at me, and I gazed up the long length of him. The one thin braid spilled down the side of his body, the tip of it curling around his groin, so that I reached for the braid first.

"I miss when all your hair was this long," I said.

"I'd grow it long again for you."

I smiled up at him. "I would like to make love to you just once with all that wavy green hair surrounding us."

He grinned. "Did you have a crush on me, or my hair, when you were young?"

"You, but the hair was beautiful. Why did you keep just the one tiny braid?"

"Because the queen's commandment was worded in such a way that I could cut all the rest, so long as I kept some of it this long."

"It was still a horrible risk, Galen. She could have found a reason to punish you for cutting that long hair that she's so fond of."

"And that proves we are high court sidhe; that's really why we grow our hair out, Merry, and why anyone not of the court is forbidden long hair. It's just another way to say we're better than everyone else."

"The custom didn't even start until after the Unseelie began to lose their powers," Rhys said, as he walked toward the bed, a towel folded in his hand.

"I thought it was older than that," I said, still running Galen's braid through my fingers.

"No, the queen decreed it to make sure that at least visually we would be different from the rest of the Unseelie Court."

"You're all sidhe, tall, elegant, gorgeous, and that's true no matter what hair you have," I said.

"True, but the nobles were afraid, Merry. Our power, our magic was what made the rest of the fey, the ones who called themselves Unseelie, let us rule them. Without that our rule was in jeopardy."

"Forbidding the non-sidhe from growing their hair past their shoulders didn't change that," I said.

"People, even the fey, are very concerned with appearance, Merry. We looked different. We were allowed a privilege that the common folk were not. I believe it did help set us apart."

"Just having long hair doesn't make us sidhe," Galen said.

"No, but it was a visual reminder of power. People are more likely to follow you if you look impressive."

"True leaders can rule if they are in rags, my father always said."

"Essus was always wise, and correct, but since not all nobles of the court were true leaders it helped for all of us to look impressive and powerful."

"Even if we were not," Galen said.

Rhys nodded. "Even if some of us were not."

I noticed he said "some of us." I was betting he didn't consider himself one of the powerless ones. Rhys had been one of the lesser lights in the court during my lifetime, but I was learning that once upon a time he had been very major indeed.

"What's the towel for?" Galen asked.

"In case we want to bring Merry again, while she screams her pleasure around our bodies."

Galen had a look that was almost pain. "In case, why wouldn't we?"

"We don't want to make her sore."

Galen nodded. "Oh, right, sorry, I'm a little distracted."

"A little," I said, and slid my hand over his balls to cup them loosely in my hand.

He went very still and then looked down at me, eyes slightly wide.

"I want you more than a little distracted," I said, and moved in toward his body, letting the braid drop to his side. I leaned in toward the soft, waiting part of him, my eyes rolled upward so I could watch his face. His body was already partially erect before I got a lick along the shaft of him. His body gave that involuntary quiver that I loved, because it was something that they couldn't control, a sign of pure eagerness.

Licking him meant that he was mostly erect by the time I slid my mouth over the ripe head of him and down that long, thick shaft. He wasn't as hard as he could get, but from one spill of my mouth over him, to come up for air, and then down again, he was harder yet—hard and eager.

I slid my mouth over him again, and he flexed inside my mouth, that eager involuntary twitch against the roof of my mouth. It made me tighten my hand around the base of him and make soft, eager sounds around him as I began to drive my mouth harder and faster over him.

"Goddess," Galen said, his eyes closed, and he reached outward, as if searching for something to steady himself with, but there was no headboard to this bed.

Rhys climbed onto the bed and grabbed Galen's hand. Galen turned and looked at him, eyes wide, and managed to gasp out, "Thanks."

"You can return the favor," Rhys said, grinning.

Seeing the two of them on the bed hand in hand both excited me and made me want to make Rhys work for it. I started sucking harder as I slid over Galen, and then taking as much of that delicious hardness into my mouth as I could and still be able to suck on him.

Galen's hand convulsed, and I watched Rhys's arm flex, muscles cording as he held the other man steady on the soft surface of the mattress.

"Now you're just being mean," Rhys said, with another grin.

I couldn't actually smile with Galen in my mouth, but my eyes smiled for me, and Rhys shook his head at me, smiling, too.

Galen began to burn for me as if the spring leaves could swallow the sun and make it shine out through the fresh, pale green of those first fragile leaves. Each green curl was edged with sunlight; the thin braid sparkled as if thin gold wire had been woven in with the green. I'd seen Galen shine before, but never edged in gold, as if sunlight and molten metal were edging the moonlight paleness of him.

Every inch of him was shining and thrumming with energy, including the part that I was going down on, so that it was like a reverse hummer, his body humming with energy inside my mouth and down my throat as I pushed it those last few inches so that it was impossible to suck anymore, or swallow, or breathe. I didn't stay down that far long, but the sensation of that power vibrating across my tongue, between my teeth, and down my throat was incredible. When I had enough air to make sounds they spilled from my mouth in eager, excited whimpering noises. Gods, it felt so . . . good!

My skin began to fill with moonlight again, an answering moon to the sunrise of Galen's power. He made a harsh sound and managed to gasp, "Close, I'm close."

We'd been doing this together often enough that he knew to warn me so I could decide whether I was swallowing or he was finishing by spilling on me. I tasted the first sweet hint that he was very close.

Rhys's skin began to run with shining white light, his arm cording with muscle as Galen's grip on his hand tightened and strained his own muscles to hold on. Then from one minute to the next Galen's body spasmed, and he cried out, and I plunged that vibrating thrumming down my throat as far as I could, burying my mouth against his body so that every delicious inch of him was in my mouth, down my throat, so thick, filling me up, and that was it: I orgasmed with him in my mouth, my body bucking with him as deep inside my mouth as he would have been between my legs. I felt the flexing as he came down my throat in a hot spill of power and grace. I came up off him enough to scream my orgasm around his body. It made him cry out again, back arching, head thrown back, eyes closed, the muscles on his arm etched in bold relief under his skin as he held on to Rhys's hand to hold himself on his knees, upright, as a second orgasm took him.

Rhys's skin shone brighter and I saw the glimmer as his threefold blue eye began to glow. Galen gasped out, "Enough, enough, Consort save us, too sensitive, stop, stop, stop."

I came up off him smiling, trailing an edge of saliva and a bit of him from his body to my lips. He collapsed slowly to his side, letting go of Rhys's hand and half-laughing.

Rhys slid his hand through my hair, and I found myself staring at his body, muscled and lean from all the extra time he spent in the gym. No other guard paid as much attention to weights and diet so that the six-pack of his abdomen was carved into his flesh. He was already thick and ready, held tight in front of those amazing abs.

He used his hand in my hair to direct me toward all that yummy goodness, and just that extra bit of dominance from him sped my pulse, started my eyes glowing; my hair was spun garnets and rubies wrapped around the shining white metal of his hand. He pushed himself between my lips and I had to open up wide enough so he didn't catch himself on my teeth. He began to push himself in and out of my mouth in shallow strokes, nothing that would make me choke, just enough to make me eager for more. I opened my mouth wider, relaxing my throat, and he felt it, because he began to push himself deeper inside me. Now when he thrust deep there was that moment when I couldn't breathe and my body knew it. Whereas with Galen I had been in total control of how deep, how long, all of it, Rhys had changed the rules with his hand in my hair, at the back of my head, and his own thrusting hips. I made eager noises for him, but not for long and not as loud as for Galen, because he thrust too deep for me to breathe, and without breath there is no sound, just my eyes too wide rolled up to stare into his face, as he looked down at me with a look that made me shudder and finally try to scream my pleasure around him. He moved back far enough so I could scream around him, and then thrust himself deep and hard down my throat, and this time he held my head so I couldn't come back up right away.

He let me up, and I gasped, catching my breath in harsh, overeager breaths, and then he thrust himself into my mouth and down my throat again. He found a rhythm that was just hard enough, just fast enough, just deep enough that it was nearly the perfect blend of force and pleasure.

Rhys liked gentler, but he knew I didn't, and he'd learned to adapt himself to what I wanted and needed. I rewarded him by screaming my pleasure around him, and then he thrust one last time, deeper, forcing my mouth tight against his body so that every last inch of him was shoved as deep inside my mouth as he could get, and whereas with Galen it had been my control, my choice, so I hadn't fought, this wasn't, and I started struggling just a little. Rhys stared down at me, holding me in place until my eyes watered, and when he drew me back I coughed and choked. He drew himself completely out of my mouth.

"Is it too much?"

I shook my head, coughed, and said, "No, it's amazing."

"Do you want me to finish that way, or on those beautiful breasts of yours?"

"On," I said.

He tightened his hold in my hair; if it had been Mistral I'd have asked for tighter, but Rhys was already rougher than he preferred and I appreciated that. He forced himself into my mouth and down my throat again, and this time he was harder, faster, deeper, so that I had to fight for breath, fight not to choke too much; if his hold on my hair had been tighter it would have hit that switch and I could have taken more, but he wasn't quite rough enough to make me enjoy all of it.

He noticed and drew back. "Am I hurting you?"

"If you tighten your hold on my hair, take control even more, I'll be able to enjoy it more."

He looked a little skeptical, but he did what I asked, fingers digging into my hair until it was painful, but for me that translated into finally relaxing into it, giving myself over to the hand in my hair, Rhys's strength, the thrust of him plunging down my throat as he held me where he wanted me, and began to use my hair as a lever so that he thrust into my mouth and drove my mouth down on him at the same time. It rolled my eyes back into my head and spilled emerald and gold light inside my closed eyelids, so bright that it was like daylight with my eyes closed.

He pulled me off him, hand painful in my hair. I opened my eyes enough to see him stroking himself with his other hand. He spilled in a hot wave of shining white, as if moonlight could be made solid enough to pour down my breasts and drip across them in glistening lines.

He helped me lie down beside Galen, and then he collapsed on the other side of me. "Give me a minute and I'll get you a washrag." His voice was breathless with effort and orgasm.

"I'll get it," Galen said. "You rest." I tried to focus on him enough to see the smile I could heard in his voice, but I couldn't focus that much yet.

Rhys's hand found mine and we lay there holding hands, relearning how to breathe and letting the fire and light of our bodies began to fade back to something resembling human-normal.

"I so needed that," I managed to say.

"Me, too," he said.

I squeezed his hand. "Thank you for being rougher than you wanted to be."

"I knew that would make it better for you, and if you can't have intercourse, you need to have the best I can give you."

"That was good, bestest," I said.

"I love you, Merry."

I turned enough to smile at him. "I love you, too, Rhys."

"I love you both," Galen said, coming back from the bath with a rag.

"Don't say that where the reporters can hear you. They're already foaming at the mouth about Doyle and Frost."

Galen grinned. "Dude, I love you like a brother. A brother that I get naked with and fuck the same woman silly with, but like a brother, totally."

Rhys and I laughed, and then he said, "Totally."

"Very bromance of you both, but it's starting to run down onto the sheets."

Galen brought the washrag. Rhys cleaned me up; he had made the mess, as he said. I used the towel he'd brought to dry off, and then we curled up on the bed, with Galen's tall frame curled around the back of me and Rhys tight against me in front, so that we spooned perfectly. Galen's long arm came over me and hugged along my arm that was holding around Rhys's waist, because regardless of sexual orientation most fey had no problem with simple touch. We snuggled under the sheet with the sunlight filling the room and started to doze.

"How can I be so tired?"

"You had triplets less than a week ago," Rhys said.

"I'm tired because the babies don't really sleep yet," Galen said, his voice muffled as if he'd plunged his face into the pillow. If he'd been shorter he would have buried his face against my hair, but if he did that we couldn't spoon because it moved his body out of position; we'd tried.

"How much of the baby care is falling on you?" I asked.

"Kitto is always there; he helps a lot."

"What about the rest?"

"Rhys does his share," he said, and hugged us both with the one long arm.

"I find it restful. It always cleared my head to go hold a baby."

"Really?" I asked.

"I did some of my best planning rocking babies to sleep."

"I know you had other children before this, but there are no stories of you as a deity having any."

His body was tense now, and the doze was no longer relaxing. "It was too long ago, and I didn't tell my stories to the bards. Holding my son in my arms while he died didn't feel like something I wanted to be remembered for."

I hugged him tight, and Galen hugged us both. "I'm sorry, Rhys," he said.

"I led him in battle, my son. He was tall like his mother, dark-haired like her, too. He was handsome and strong and brave and everything a father wants in his son. He followed me into a battle and he died there. Killed by one of the human inventions, explosives with iron filling. I hunted down every member of the tribe that had fought against us. I killed them all, down to the last baby. I destroyed them as a race, do you understand that, I killed their entire people, even the children, while their mothers begged for mercy. My grief was . . . terrible, and I tried to quench it in blood and death, and do you know what I discovered?"

"No, I don't," I said, voice soft. We held him while he told the awful things in an almost unemotional voice, the way to tell terrible things when they still hurt too much to feel.

"That killing them didn't bring my son back, and it didn't make the grief any less. I killed an entire race of people, centuries of culture and invention all gone, because they followed a different god than me, and they dared to fight against me. I forbade anyone to mention the name of their tribe. I wiped them from history itself, and when my vengeance was as complete as I could make it, then my rage left me. All that was left was my sorrow, and that was why I destroyed them, not because of what they had done, not really, but so I could focus my grief into vengeance and not feel the pain of his loss."

We held him, because it was all we could do. I made comforting noises, but it was Galen who said, "I would die to protect the babies now; I can't imagine how much I'll love them in a few years. I understand why you did it."

I wanted to look behind and see Galen's face, but I couldn't manage it; of all the men in my life he was the one I thought would be horrified at what Rhys had done, not agree with it.

"I pray to Goddess and God that you never know such grief, but remember this, Galen, it's going to hurt no matter what you do, and vengeance just postpones it. I realized in the end that I was angry with myself, blamed myself, because I had wanted that fight. I led him to his death. I was his father and I failed him, and that was why I killed all of them. Once I understood that, I didn't want the bards to sing of it. I didn't deserve any stories. I had made certain that that tribe of people passed out of all memory, all history, so I did the same for me. It seemed fair."

"But we have the stories of Cromm Cruach," I said.

"Oh, Merry, that wasn't my first name."

"What was your first name?" Galen asked.

Rhys shook his head, his hair tickling against my face. "No, that name, that person, is gone. He died with the last breath of a people that he destroyed for a mistake that was his own. I buried that name with the children I slaughtered, because when they were all dead I understood that they were no more important than my son, but they were no less important either. They could have grown up and been good men, good women, but I stole that chance from them. They were mortal and had only a short time to live anyway, and I stole what few years they had, because my immortal son had managed to die at the hands of human technology. I am deeply ashamed of what I'd done, so I destroyed my name, my stories, my history in a sort of penance, though even that was such hubris, thinking that the dead could be appeased by punishing myself."

We held him close, we murmured what comfort we could think of, but in the end what comfort is there? Then I thought of something, and had to know. "It took me almost fifteen years to find the murderer of my father. Cel was trying to kill me and all of us at the time, so it was self-defense, but I'm still glad I killed him."

"Has it lessened your grief for your father?" Rhys asked.

I thought about it. "Yes, yes it has. I feel like I avenged him."

"If my son had died at the hands of a true enemy, another sidhe worth fighting with all the magic and grace I had back then, maybe it would have been more satisfying, but I attacked people who could not hope to defend against me; I was a truly terrible power to be reckoned with on the battlefield, and I didn't attack most of them in battle. I hunted them down in the streets, the mountains, anywhere they ran to hide; I found them, and I killed them."

"Cel was already your enemy, Merry," Galen said. "We all wanted him dead, because we were afraid the queen might actually give him the throne."

Rhys said, "You didn't kill Cel just to avenge your father, Merry; you killed him to keep all of the Unseelie safe from him, and that is worth killing for."

"You know, most people's pillow talk isn't about battle and killing," I said.

"Boring people," Galen said.

"Very boring," Rhys said.

"I don't know, sometimes I think it might be nice to be a little boring if it would keep us from having to kill people, or keep them from trying to kill us."

To that there was nothing to say, because we all agreed, that would be nice. "'May you live in interesting times.' It sounds so positive, but it's not," I said.

"That's an Arabic curse, you know: 'May you live in interesting times,'" Rhys said.

"I thought it was Chinese," Galen said.

"Either way, Merry's right; a little boring routine might be nice for a lifetime."

"If you want boring and routine, you're in the wrong bed," I said.

He turned in my arms so he could look at me. "Am I? Well, then let's do something that's not boring, or routine, shall we?"

I laughed. "We just did that."

He grinned. "Let's do it again." He looked across me at the other man. "Unless you aren't up to it again this soon."

Galen grinned back. "You're the older man in this bed; I'm a young one, I'll keep up."

"Old, really?"

"Yeah, really."

"If I could have intercourse, you could actually prove who can keep up, but you can't just keep doing me by hand and have me suck you; I'll strain a muscle in my tongue."

That made them look down at me, surprised, and then they laughed, we all laughed, but when the laughter stopped we did one more round of "not boring, and not routine," and lying between the two of them with the radiance of our bodies making colored shadows on the ceiling, so that our magic was brighter than the sunlight itself, I owned that maybe I didn't want boring and routine anything, but safety for me and the babies and the men I loved, that I did want. Can you be safe and live an interesting life? Maybe not.

CHAPTER

TWENTY-FOUR

Queen Andais was on the large mirror in the dining room again, but it was a very different call. She was wearing a sleek black pant-suit that covered almost all of her; only the lack of a shirt underneath the vest left more cleavage than Auntie Andais should probably have been flashing around her nephew and nieces, but the outfit was such a concession that I wouldn't have dared complain. This was as much as she dressed for a press conference; it was a big step in the right direction.

Her consort, Eamon, was at her side in a tailored black suit, but he'd added a round-collared white shirt with pencil-thin black stripes under his vest so he was showing far less chest.

Doyle was at my side, along with Mistral, Rhys, and Galen. Kitto was back in his place under my feet as my footstool. I'd let him know that this was an informal conference and he could pass on his role, but he had said, "I still do not believe that I am so lucky as to be one of the fathers of the babes, and I would have a place at your side, Merry, even if it is under your feet." What could I say to that?

Kitto was wearing yoga pants today, shirtless, no shoes, because the men were working out after the call. Doyle had insisted everyone learn how to protect themselves at least a little, no exceptions. Doyle and Galen

were in jeans, and it was slacks for Rhys and Mistral, because their weap-
onry needed a belt and fitted waistband to fit properly. They'd change
after the phone call. Doyle's weapons blended in with his all-black clothing, but Galen's blue jeans and green T-shirt showed every weapon he
had. Mistral and Rhys were in suits with jackets designed to go over
weapons, so it was less obvious. One of the exiled lesser fey here in L.A.
had built them all leather holsters that were magically less visible under
clothes, but the men had decided they wanted the queen to see that they
were armed. Well, except for the pregnant lady. I knew how to use a gun
and a sword, but when my doctor approved it I was joining the training.
It probably wouldn't have helped me against Taranis, but I wanted more
options if there was ever a next time. I was wearing one of the purple
dresses that was actually fitted around the waist. It was good to be back
in real clothes again, though the strappy black sandals with their stiletto
heels were just for show. I so wasn't ready to walk in anything like that
yet. We'd learned that Kitto liked feeling heels in his back during sex, so
he was very okay with the shoes.

"You must make Taranis afraid of you, Meredith; only fear will hold
him in check." She'd requested to see the babies, but we were talking
business first.

"He's already attacked Doyle, and we believe that was motivated out
of fear. The king would not willingly meet him in a duel," I said.

"Yes, he feared the Queen's Darkness, but he does not fear Doyle in
the same way. He feared me, Meredith, and my Darkness as an extension
of me, but without my protection and threat he sees Doyle as only your
strong right hand; chop that hand off and it makes you even weaker than
you are. You must make Taranis fear you, Meredith, you and no other, if
you are to rule the Unseelie Court. If he does not fear you, then it is only
a matter of time before the Seelie try to take your throne and combine it
with theirs."

"He's made it clear that he would welcome me as his queen," I said,
and looked carefully at nothing when I said it, because I couldn't keep
the emotion out of my eyes and Andais had used my emotion against me
for years.

"I thought about using his rape of you as a reason to challenge him to a duel."

That made me look at her again. "I didn't think you cared that much about my fate, Aunt Andais."

"It's not your fate, Meredith, it's the insult of him thinking he could kidnap and attack my heir with no retribution."

"Of course, it's an insult to you," I said, and just shook my head. She didn't understand that she'd just admitted that what happened to me was important only because it showed a lack of respect for her.

Eamon laid a hand on her shoulder and looked at me. His face showed that he at least understood, and understood that she didn't. I tried to tell him with my eyes that I appreciated it. Andais went on talking, oblivious.

She said, "It is, but I believe Taranis is actually insane. He has convinced himself that you went willingly with him and were kidnapped from him by the evil Unseelie. The King of Light and Illusion seems to be truly deluded."

"I agree," I said.

"He babbles of taking you as queen if he can only strip you of the abusive Unseelie that are poisoning your mind against him. If I wanted to strip you of your protection I, too, would begin with the Princess's Darkness. It really doesn't have the same ring as the Queen's Darkness, does it?"

"No, Aunt Andais, it does not."

She looked just past my shoulder to where Doyle stood, as he had once stood by her, though he had his hand on my shoulder, a gesture I don't think I'd ever seen him make to her. I raised my hand to lay it over his.

"No need to remind me that I neglected my Darkness."

"I didn't touch his hand to remind you of anything, Aunt Andais; I did it because I wanted to touch him."

She made a small movement with her mouth that meant she was unhappy, and then smoothed it into a smile. She really was trying, on this first call since I'd laid down my ultimatum that she behave like a sane person or she couldn't see the babies.

"I believe that, though I do not understand it."

What I wanted to say was, *How sad for you*, but my aunt had never taken well to pity. She didn't understand it and always saw it as an insult, and she certainly never gave pity to anyone. She was pitiless in the true meaning of the word.

I looked past her to Eamon with his own hand on her shoulder. I was sorry for him, too, and if he had been mine I would have reached up and touched his hand, as I did Doyle's, but he wasn't mine to worry over, and he loved Andais utterly. I'd never understood why, but I knew it to be truth.

"You are the Queen of Air and Darkness, my aunt; all fear you. How do I make Taranis fear me?"

"You disfigured him in the dream, Meredith; that did frighten him."

I tensed, holding tighter to Doyle's hand, my heels involuntarily digging a little harder into Kitto's back. "I told you that I used my hand of power on him in the dream, but not what hand of power I used. How did you know that?"

"Darkness is not the only one with spies at the Golden Court, Meredith. Taranis's sleep is troubled, for he keeps seeing his arm melted and crippled from your magic. If you would do that in reality to someone that he could see, a constant visible reminder, it would be a good start to his fearing you."

"Are you actually suggesting that I pick some random Seelie sidhe and partially cripple or disfigure him, just as an object lesson to Taranis?"

She nodded.

I saw Eamon's hand tighten on her shoulder, as if to caution her. She patted his hand absentmindedly but did not hold on to it.

"There is no one I hate that much at the Seelie Court," I said.

She frowned at me. "It's not about hate, Meredith, it's about practicality. You asked how to frighten Taranis; well, I'm telling you how to do that. If you don't want my help, then do not ask for it; it is most irritating to suggest things and watch you make that face."

"I wasn't aware I was making a face, Aunt Andais; I will try to school my expression better from now on."

"And there you go again, that tone in your voice, never a word out of place, but your tone says, clearly, 'You are a fucking psycho bitch and I hate you.'"

"I would never say such a thing, Aunt Andais."

"No, you would never say it, but you think it hard enough."

"I don't believe I've ever said, or even thought, those exact words about you, my aunt."

"Then what words would you say aloud, if you dared?"

"Are you simply incapable of having a conversation where you don't threaten me or imply something unpleasant?" I asked.

She startled visibly, and this time she did reach for Eamon's hand. "I . . . I hadn't thought about it, niece of mine. I have spent many centuries where my threat was all that kept me and my court safe. You see what Taranis will do if he does not fear another royal."

I nodded. "I do understand that. So you're saying that it's just habit for you to threaten people?"

She seemed to actually think about it for a moment and then said, "Yes, I believe it is."

I sighed and squeezed Doyle's hand. Mistral moved closer to me and laid his hand on my other shoulder. I reached up and took his hand, too. It helped steady me to touch them, though I knew that Mistral did not understand why such casual touch pleased me so; he was the least affectionate of the fathers outside the bedroom, but once he'd accepted that I liked and needed it, he'd tried to do more. I appreciated his efforts and did my best to tell him so.

"That must be very lonely," Galen said.

We all turned to him slowly, like you do in a horror film, because that was pity and you did not let the queen know you pitied her, ever.

She looked at him, head to one side like a crow about to peck the eye out of a corpse. "What did you say?" Her voice made it plain that she didn't believe he'd repeat himself, and that he certainly shouldn't repeat it.

"If people are afraid of you, how do they love you?" he asked.

"Love," she said, and made it sound like a very different kind of four-letter word.

"Yes," he said, softly.

I wanted to say, *Stop this, don't make her look at herself that closely*, but hadn't I done just that the last time we spoke to her? Had my boldness made him bolder, too?

"I do not need to be loved, Galen. I need to be obeyed. I need my people to follow me unquestionably."

"Everyone needs to be loved, my queen," he said.

"Now you remember I'm your queen; how convenient and how too late."

"Too late for what, Aunt Andais?" I asked. My heart was thudding in my throat, and I had to swallow past it to speak clearly. Galen had been one of her lesser guards; he had no special place in her esteem, which meant he had no cards to play here. What was he trying to accomplish?

"If Merry disfigured members of the Seelie Court, they could go to the human media. They would think her a monster, and they'd be right."

She frowned and gave him a very unfriendly look. "Perhaps being thought a monster is the price a queen must pay to keep her people and those she loves safe."

"Perhaps," he said, "but Meredith must win the media's love, or the Golden Court will win their sympathy and all the good work you've done over the years in America will be undone. Haven't you wished for Taranis and his people to be as reviled and feared as we once were?"

She still didn't look happy, but there was a considering look on her face. He had her thinking, which in this case was good. "Go on," she said, voice still unhappy, but under that was another tone. I couldn't quite interpret it, but it wasn't anger.

"What if we make Taranis the monster in the press? What if we use the modern media to win the hearts and minds of viewers to our side?"

"Viewers? I don't understand."

"We've been offered a television show."

"We had decided not to take it," Doyle said.

Galen turned to Doyle. "But don't you see? Taranis will never be able to control himself forever. If we give him enough on-camera rope, I think he'll hang himself."

"You want him to attack us on camera," I said, staring at him.

"I think I do, yes, I do."

"He could hurt or even kill one of us, not to mention endangering the human camera crew," Rhys said.

"True, it's a risk, but maybe we don't have to make him fear Merry, but fear looking bad on TV. He's the King of Light and Illusion; he prides himself on being desirable, right?"

"He does," Doyle said.

"What would he do if he saw himself on film being monstrous and terrifying?"

"The cameras could capture your deaths on film very nicely," Andais said in a voice thick with disdain.

"Or capture us fighting for our lives and defending ourselves."

"You're planning to kill him on camera," Andais said, and she sounded astonished and almost happy.

Galen nodded. "If he attacks us, yes, why not?"

She laughed, head back, her hand in Eamon's swinging, almost like a child skipping beside you.

"We'd be up on murder charges, for one thing," Rhys said.

"Maybe, but the camera crew would be our witnesses, don't you see?"

"It is possible, but Taranis would have to lose complete control on camera," Doyle said.

"And we would have to have the camera crew in the house with us for weeks, months before the chance might come," Mistral said. His hand was tense in mine.

I turned and looked up at him. His long gray hair had more glittering strands of gold, copper, and silver, as if the "light" were getting stronger with his anxiety.

"The thought of them filming us truly bothers you," I said.

"Yes, do you honestly want them filming everything here?"

"There are things that we do, or that happen around us, that we might not want on camera," Doyle said.

I turned and looked at him. He was right, but . . . "No, Mistral, I don't, and Doyle is right."

"If we just want to kill the king, then let's do it. Why do the television show? Why give the courts proof we did it? We could go back home and simply execute him for what he did to Merry."

"I like this plan," Doyle said, and his deep voice was a little deeper with emotion. I knew he'd wanted to slay Taranis for raping me. It had been tempting to let him do it.

"No," I said, "no, the risk is too great." I squeezed his hand in mine and looked up at him. "I will not lose you to vengeance."

"He's tried to kill me twice, Meredith; if he attacks us on camera my life may still be forfeit."

"Then no," I said, "no. We will not lure him here to help us kill him on camera, and we will not go home and slay him there. We will leave the mad king alone."

"He won't leave us alone, Merry," Galen said.

"The boy is right," Mistral said.

"He's going to hunt us in our dreams, Merry; we can't protect ourselves there, so bring him out here where our power is greater."

"What power do we have that is greater?" I asked.

"You are Princess Meredith NicEssus, the first faerie princess born on American soil, and now you have triplets. You are a media darling, or have you forgotten that the police had to help us drive out through the press and people?"

"I haven't forgotten."

"Merry, you are *the* face of faerie right now. If you take this moment and run with it, really embrace it, you will have the power of the media."

"They're already trying to climb the walls and using telephoto lenses on us, Galen. I'm not sure I want more."

"You asked what power we have that is greater than Taranis; well, that's it. You can be the biggest star, the biggest illusion in all faerie, because we pick and choose what they see. We can take this moment and show the Unseelie as good and loving, and eventually the king will lose it and have to come to us. He won't be able to resist, because above all else he has to be the star, the center of attention."

"He always has been a media slut," Rhys said.

"No," I said, "just no; I just want to enjoy my children and the men I love. I don't want more attention."

"You can do what the queen suggested, and maim someone with your hand of flesh, but then you will be the bad guy. Let's just for once make the Seelie Court the bad guys."

"This is conspiracy before the fact," I said.

"No, it's not. We won't do anything to lure him here or set him up; he will come on his own, because he won't want anyone, not even you, to outshine him, Meredith. His ego is too big to stay away."

"It could take months for him to finally break down and come here," I said.

"It could, but we'll be getting paid pretty handsomely the whole time, and maybe Maeve can stay home with Liam, so that he starts thinking of her as mommy, not just his mother."

"Oh, don't go and spoil it now," Andais said.

"Spoil what?" Galen asked.

"You had a lovely plan to kill the king, and now instead of fear or revenge, your motive is all love and sunshine; please, just let me have a few more moments of thinking that there is an Unseelie heart trapped in that overgrown pixie body."

The smile left his face, and he looked . . . cold. "Trust me, my queen, I am Unseelie." And just as Andais had accused me of my words being mild but my tone being insulting, so now Galen's words were fine, but the tone was . . . ominous, even threatening.

She looked at him, and there was something in her face I'd never seen before when she looked at Galen. She "saw" him, considered him in a way I don't believe she ever had before. Andais had a very binary way of look-ing at most men. They were either barely considered, victims of the moment, or potential lovers. He'd been her victim before, as had we all, and he'd been barely considered for most of his life, but now I watched that third choice cross through her eyes.

"If the genetic tests do not come back with your genetics listed, then perhaps I'll give you a night to prove just how Unseelie you are, Galen Greenknight."

He tensed, visibly, his newfound boldness stumbling. My heart was back in my throat, and I was clutching Doyle's hand a little. Mistral had actually moved a little apart from us, so that he was at Rhys's back, as if he thought she might try some violence, and in a way he was right, because she didn't have sex without violence. She was like the anti-vanilla, Auntie Vanilla, and once I thought of it, it was funny and I laughed.

I laughed and I couldn't stop laughing. I laughed so hard it began to ache in places that even sex hadn't bothered. I laughed until tears ran down my face, and I heard other laughter. Galen came to stand by my chair, taking my hand and joining me in helpless laughter, but we were the only ones. Everyone else stayed silent, and when I could wipe the tears away enough to look at the mirror I saw why: The queen was not amused.

She was on her feet with Eamon far enough behind her that she, or maybe he, was out of reach. Her tricolored eyes sparked like lightning behind gray clouds. *The storm isn't overhead, but it's coming.*

"I will not be laughed at, Meredith, not by anyone." Her voice had crawled down into that low purr that should have meant sex but usually meant torment for someone.

I managed to say, "You are the least vanilla person I know, Auntie Andais; you are anti-vanilla, Auntie Vanilla, get it?"

Rhys gave a small snort as he tried not to laugh. Even Mistral made a small noise; only Doyle stayed impervious to my dangerous silliness.

"No," she said coldly, "I do not 'get it.'"

Guards spilled into the room, some sidhe and some Red Caps. They had begun to train together, working on battle strategies that played to their mixed strengths. The goblins had fought like shock troops for the Unseelie sidhe for centuries, but never shoulder to shoulder with them.

Goblins had been used as cannon fodder, never truly as another warrior to fight beside. Now they spread out in front of us, sidhe and goblin, side by side. They stacked themselves around us in a move that was obviously practiced, making themselves a shield of flesh between their "queen" and her "kings." I hated that they might have to sacrifice themselves for us, but that was what it meant to be bodyguards, especially royal guards. Once it had been Doyle and the rest who were the sacrifice for Andais, and the female guards in front of me scattered among the men had been expected to do the same for Prince Cel.

"I allowed you to flee to the Western Lands and my niece's more tender care, but do not let it go to your heads, my guards. None of you are would-be kings. If I call you back to the court, you are oath-bound to answer and return to me." I couldn't see her through the bodies of our guards, but hearing the tone was enough to steal away the last bit of my laughter, even with happy tears still wet on my face.

Galen took my hand in his; he looked grim. Doyle, Mistral, and Rhys had all moved up around my chair, but they were still behind the wall of guards. In a real battle we might lead from the front, but in moments like this princes and kings did not stand in front of their bodyguards. I had spent months learning this lesson as I watched the men I loved risk themselves again and again to keep me and the unborn children safe. Now, they were having to learn the lesson. I looked at my three warriors standing so certain, so ready, and hidden from the threat. I knew that it would chafe on them more than it had on me, because a year ago they would have stood between the danger and Queen Andais; now they stood beside me.

A voice even lower than Doyle's came from that tall wall of guards. "We are goblin; you cannot call us back to your side, Queen Andais, for that has never been our place." It was Jonty, the leader of the Red Caps. He was smallish for his people, only a little over eight feet tall; some of the men in the line were closer to thirteen feet, like small giants, or average-sized ogres. Their skin color ranged through every shade of gray, yellow, and two golds that were almost brown. The sidhe warriors, so tall and commanding, looked small interspersed between them.

"You are Kurag the Goblin King's problem, not mine, but the men and women you stand beside—they are mine." Her voice went down another note to a purring, sexual depth, but it didn't excite any of us who were sidhe, because we knew that it promised violence, not sex, at least for us. I'd begun to realize that violence was a kind of sex for my aunt. She was truly like one of those sexual predators who are wired so that images of violence hit the same centers of the brain that "normal" sex does for the rest of us.

I projected my voice to be heard. It would have been more impressive if I hadn't been hiding behind my guards, but it would have to do, because Andais wasn't the most stable person, and I wouldn't risk myself betting that, one, she couldn't do magic through the mirror, and two, she would remember that she valued my fertile womb, if nothing else.

"They are not yours, Aunt Andais, not anymore."

"Do not let your fertility go to your head, Meredith. It may keep you and your lovers safe, but the rest are on loan, nothing more. Until you sit on my throne, the Unseelie sidhe are mine."

"They are oathed to me now, Aunt Andais."

"They cannot be oathed twice, niece. That would make them foresworn."

"The Cranes, my father's female guards, were never asked to make oath to Prince Cel; you just ordered them to guard him, so they were free to make oath where they will."

"They were oathed to my son," she said.

"No, they were not," I said. I would have liked to see her face, but I trusted the guards to do their job and stared at their broad backs, Galen's hand still in mine.

"Cel gave them a choice and they swore oath to him."

"Who told you that?" This was from Cathbodua, who stood at the end of the line that shielded us.

"Cel and the captain of the Cranes, Siobhan."

"They lied, then," Cathbodua said.

"Why would they have lied about that?"

"His reasons were his own, always, Queen Andais, but I swear to you that no one standing here today ever took oath to Prince Cel."

"I neglected much where my son was concerned, and I regret that."

Cathbodua went to one knee. "I am honored to hear you say that, Queen Andais."

One guard taking a knee was often a sign for all, but no one else knelt, and after a time Cathbodua got to her feet and joined her fellow guards again.

"I will grant that the female guards are free to be with you, Princess Meredith, but the men are mine."

"They took oath to me, as well, Aunt Andais," I said.

"Yes, remind me of our blood ties, Meredith, because you do grow tiresome so quickly."

"As do these moments between us, for me, auntie."

"Do not call me auntie."

"As you wish," I said. My voice was as neutral as I could make it.

"I will call all my Ravens home to roost, Meredith, and they will come."

"No, we won't." This from Usna, who stood beside Cathbodua. His normal joking voice, as if nothing were really serious, was missing. It was a very grim cat that stepped from the line.

"How dare you tell me 'no' and 'won't.' I will carve those words into your flesh."

"We all made oath to Merry; we are no longer your Ravens. You cannot call us home, and we are no longer yours to torture at your will," he said, and his voice sounded sad now. I realized that he did not believe that anything would keep him safe from Andais. Usna spoke bravely, but he didn't believe in that safety.

"Then you are all foresworn." She almost yelled it.

I spoke then, standing up as if that would help. Galen squeezed my hand tight as if afraid of what I would do. "They are oathed to me, which does make them foresworn."

"Then they will be punished for breaking their oath," she said.

"By exile from faerie? Isn't that the usual punishment for being foresworn?" I said.

"No!" She yelled it.

"Yes," I said, clearly, calmly.

"You can't all have chosen exile from faerie," she said, and her voice held shock.

"We are exiled from the Unseelie Court," Usna said, "but we are not exiled from faerie, for wherever Princess Meredith goes, faerie follows."

"That is not possible," Andais said.

"You have seen it yourself, Queen Andais," Cathbodua said. "She brought the gardens of the Unseelie Court back to life. Faerie is alive and spreading for the first time in over a thousand years."

Doyle spoke then. "The night itself must have told you that faerie is alive again."

"My power has whispered rumors to me," she said, and her voice was growing calmer. That could be a good thing or a bad thing; one can never tell with psychopaths.

"Then you know that faerie has come to the Western Lands and we are no longer exiles, but pioneers on the frontier of new fairylands," Doyle said.

"I cannot let anyone defy me like this, Darkness; you know that I am only as powerful as my threat."

"I am sorry for that, my queen."

"I must call one home and make his punishment terrible enough to prevent any others from joining your quiet rebellion."

"I do not know what to say to that, my queen; it is almost reasonable, and for you very reasonable."

"Send Usna to me, and I will leave the rest in place," she said.

I watched Usna reach out and take Cathbodua's hand. I was about to say something in their defense, but she spoke first. "I am pregnant with Usna's child."

"You are lying to save him," Andais said, voice certain.

"The little stick says I am with child, and the only man I have lain with is Usna."

"Little stick, what little stick can tell you you are pregnant?"

I said, "Cathbodua, do you mean a home pregnancy test?"

She looked behind to find me, and nodded.

"When did you find out?" I asked.

"Just before this meeting."

I'd had enough. I stepped forward with Galen's hand in mine. The Red Caps and sidhe in front of us glanced at each other, and then the sidhe looked to Doyle, and the Red Caps looked to me. Whatever they saw on both our faces, it made them move aside so we could come forward and face Andais.

"We have another fertile couple among the sidhe; it is something to celebrate, Aunt Andais, not punish."

She stared at me, and there was a look on her face that I couldn't understand, but it looked almost pained. On anyone else, I might have said it looked afraid, but Andais feared no one, least of all me.

"It is love that has made them fertile," Galen said. I glanced up at him, but he looked only at the queen. He looked handsome, commanding standing there, as if something had stripped away the last bits of childhood and brought him into the man he was always meant to be.

"The crow and the cat do not love each other; it is lust that has made a child." Her voice was thick with disdain.

"I didn't mean their love for one another, but Meredith's love for them."

"Are you saying they, too, are her lovers? Is no one safe from your lusts, Meredith?"

Rhys stepped forward. "Meredith loves them as a ruler is supposed to love her subjects."

"You cannot rule by love," she said, and her beautiful face was creased with angry lines, as if the monster inside her were starting to peer out.

Galen said, "But they oathed themselves to Meredith because she has shown them love and caring, the way Prince Essus did to his guards."

"Do not wave my brother's memory at me and think it will make me relent. Meredith has brought it up too often of late."

Doyle came to stand on the other side of Galen. "Prince Essus stood between you and those you would harm more than once. I don't think any of us understood what a good and strong influence he was on you until we lost him."

"I would allow Essus liberties that no one else dared."

"You loved your brother," Doyle said.

"Yes, yes, I loved my brother, but he is dead and gone."

"But his daughter stands before you; his grandchildren are in the other room waiting to see their great-aunt Andais. Meredith is truly NicEssus, the daughter of Essus, for she has shown the same nobility, kindness, intelligence, and love that he did. He would have made a fine and generous king."

Her eyes were wide, and I realized that the shine in them now wasn't magic, but unshed tears. "But for a few years of time he would have been eldest and king."

"Yes, King Essus," Doyle said.

One lone tear trailed from her eye. "You have made me cry twice, Meredith, daughter of my brother, mother of my nieces and nephew, bringer of life to the sidhe, creator of new fairylands, and they tell me you do all this by love. Is that true, niece of mine? Are you all sunshine and love? Are you all Seelie sidhe and there is none of the Unseelie's blackness inside you?"

"I do my best to rule through fairness and love, but I am also the wielder of flesh and blood; those are not Seelie powers, my queen."

"I saw what your hand of blood can do when you killed my son."

"I did not flinch when Cel tried to kill me; that was my father's mistake. If he had not loved Cel, he would not have hesitated in his own defense and my father would be here to see his grandchildren."

"Do you not think I have thought of that, Meredith, since I learned of my son's treachery?"

"You ask if I am all sunshine and love, and I tell you this, aunt, I do not rule by love and fairness alone."

"What then, kindness?" She made it an insult.

"Ruthlessness. I am more ruthless than my father. You can take credit for that, Aunt Andais, for you allowed sidhe after sidhe to challenge me to duels when I had no magic to defend myself. I had to become ruthless to survive, because you would not protect me. You would not acknowledge that the duels were attempts to assassinate me, attempts done either on Cel's orders or to curry favor from him. If you had only reached out to me, protected me, if not for myself, then for your brother's memory, but you did not. Essus taught me kindness, honor, love, fairness, justice, but you, dear aunt, you taught me ruthlessness—and hate."

She smiled then, and nothing she could have done in that moment would have frightened me more. It caught my breath in my throat and made my skin run cold. Galen moved closer to me, folding me in his arms.

"Then perhaps Essus and I have forged a fit ruler for the sidhe, at last. Perhaps it is Taranis who should fear you, Meredith."

"I do not understand, Aunt Andais."

"I will let it be known that my Ravens, and Cel's Cranes, have oathed to you out of love and loyalty the way rulers gathered followers thousands of years ago. I will let it be known that sidhe among your guards that have not been in your bed are with child. I will make certain that the Seelie know we have a new goddess of love and ruthlessness, for it was not only I who taught you that last lesson, Meredith. Your mother's neglect and Taranis's madness helped forge you into the ruler you are today."

I hugged Galen closer and nodded. "I will agree with that, Aunt Andais."

"I will make certain Taranis knows that." She gave a short, abrupt laugh. "You may be right after all, Galen Greenknight; perhaps love is frightening enough all on its own without any torture needed."

She laughed again, and then just walked out of sight of the mirror. It was Eamon who came forward, reaching to blank the glass. He spoke to me before he did it. "Princess Meredith, Prince Galen." And we were staring at our own startled reflections before I could give him his title in return.

TWENTY-FIVE

Maeve Reed stalked around the main bedroom in a pair of cream slacks, cut wide so they swung enough to give glimpses of the pale taupe stiletto boots underneath. The boots matched her tailored suit jacket, the dress shirt buttoned up to her neck was almost pure white, and her thin man-style tie was metallic gold and cream to pick up the gold of her chain-link belt. The chain was tied into a loose knot to trail across her hip, swinging to cross her groin as she moved, more like jewelry for the waist than an actual belt.

"You look wonderful in this outfit," I said.

She stopped stalking the white carpet and turned to look at me. "You think so?" She trailed long, slender hands down the chain links, which drew the eye down to her groin again. It wasn't accidental, but it wasn't exactly flirting with me either. Maeve had made her living in Hollywood for decades; sex appeal had been one of the commodities that had helped her stay at the top, especially back in the fifties, when she'd have been considered too tall, too thin, and not curvy enough to be a sex symbol. Now she was very chic and very in, but then Maeve Reed, the Golden Goddess of Hollywood, had been one of the reasons the fashion had changed from curvy to a thinness that was almost impossible for a human woman to duplicate without starving herself. The sidhe were built differently, like fashion models with a bit more body fat so they still had breasts and ass, but they could eat a Thanksgiving feast every day and not gain weight. Humans couldn't, and yet they tried.

"I had to go into the studio today. I'm a movie star; people expect an effort."

"You don't have to explain it to me. You could have just dressed to be around the house. It's your clothes, your house, wear what you want."

She looked at me, blue eyes narrowing. She was using glamour to appear more human, hiding her very inhuman eyes with their tricolor blue and copper and gold lines that went out like miniature lightning bolts, changing her golden skin to a human tan, and even making her straight waist-length hair more yellow than her natural white-blond. I never understood why she darkened her hair; it was within human bounds either way. The skin and eyes she'd had to make more human, but the hair could have stayed.

"Why do you make your hair more yellow-blond than it is naturally? Humans have hair both colors."

"The yellow-blond looks better on camera," she said.

"Oh, that makes sense." I sat on the edge of the bed, swinging my feet, because I was far too short to sit and reach the ground. I was still wearing the purple dress, though I'd changed to a pair of black low-heeled pumps. I might get back into the stilettos in a few weeks, but right now having to fight my body on heels that high and thin just took too much effort. I'd lost most of my weight in an almost magically short time, but I still wasn't quite myself. The extra cup size in my breasts alone made me feel unbalanced. I'd been generously endowed before, but now it was a true embarrassment of riches.

"I'm sorry that you disagree about hiring lesser fey to work in the house, Meredith, but I just don't see the point in it. There are plenty of humans in L.A. needing jobs. If we hire only fey, then the media will accuse us of racism."

"Really?" I asked.

Maeve nodded. "Trust me on that."

"I do trust you, but we can't have human nannies around the triplets,

or more specifically around Bryluen. Her ability to fascinate seems automatic; until she's old enough for us to teach her to control it, humans are
nearly helpless around her."

"She's a baby, it can't be that bad."

"Come to the nursery and see for yourself. Perhaps your more pure
sidhe blood will keep you proof against Bryluen's glamour."

"I'm not just sidhe, Meredith; I was a goddess and I'm still worshipped in a way as a celebrity, so if your babe cannot bespell me it's not
really a good test."

"But if she can, then it's a very good test," I said.

Maeve looked thoughtful and then said, "Good point. Who is taking
care of her besides you?"

"Kitto . . ."

"A goblin has no resistance to sidhe magic; of course he would be
ensnared by her."

"Kitto is also half sidhe and has come into his hand of power."

She waved it away. "He was raised goblin; he will never be as sidhe as
he is goblin."

"Why should that make a difference to his magic resistance?" I asked.

"You were taught certain skills from childhood, skills that your little
man was not."

I slid to my feet, settling the skirt in place. "Don't call him a little man."

"Why not? He is the smallest of your men."

"If you were sidhe, yes, but you've lived with the humans long enough
to understand it's an insult."

"What do you mean, if I were sidhe?"

"If Kitto's goblin upbringing undermines his ability to be sidhe, then
a similar argument can be made that your centuries of exile out among
the humans have made you more human than you would have been had
you stayed in faerie as a member of the Seelie Court."

"I was the goddess Conchenn; how dare you compare me to some
sidhe-sided goblin?"

"The goblins are every bit as fey as any sidhe, and this attitude of looking down on them because they have no magic, when it is the sidhe that stole their magic in the first place, really *is* racist, and arrogant. It's like an abusive spouse who blames his wife for not being able to walk gracefully, when he's the one who broke her leg."

"That is not a fair comparison, Meredith. The goblins and the sidhe were at war; they would have won had we not done the spell that took their magic."

"So I'm told by both sides, but that was a very long time ago, Maeve, a very long time ago."

"You weren't there, Meredith; you didn't see your friends die at their hands."

"No, but I have seen that the sidhe-sided goblins do fine magic once they're brought into their power."

"Your goblin twin lovers, Holly and Ash, are quite frightening. That you've armed them with your hand of flesh and blood respectively makes them very dangerous."

"I did not share my hands of power with them, it just happened to be their latent magic."

"Are you sure of that?" she asked, and gave me a very direct look out of those famous blue eyes.

"Kitto's hand of power isn't one of mine."

"He can bring people through a mirror even against their will; that is almost useless as a hand of power."

"It helped him and Rhys kill the goblin who tormented both of them," I said.

"His hand of power is so useless there is no name for it."

"It's incredibly rare, but it has a name: the hand of reaching," I said.

"The hand of reaching allowed small armies to be brought through a reflective surface. Your goblin cannot do that."

"Perhaps not, but the name is for the ability, not the degree of power."

"It needs a new name, something grand," she said.

I shrugged.

She frowned at me. She frowned a lot, actually; if she'd been human she'd have had frown lines by now, but she was sidhe and would never truly wrinkle. She could get some lines here and there, but she'd never have the lines of her unhappiness carved into her face like most people would.

"It's not just me who thinks the twins have only inherited your own magic, Meredith, nor am I the only one who thinks Kitto's hand of power is weak."

"I know that," I said, "but the others don't say it to my face as much."

"You are their ruler; they dare not speak their minds to you."

"And you are Maeve Reed, the Golden Goddess of Hollywood, and you don't plan on going back to faerie, even if Taranis lifted your exile."

She looked startled for a second, and then smiled. "How did you know that? I wasn't even certain myself until recently."

"I may not be your ruler, but I try to be your friend, and friends notice things."

She looked embarrassed then. "I am sorry, Meredith; I've been rude by human standards, and you're right. I've been exiled long enough that human culture is more natural to me than any in faerie, so my apologies."

"Please don't treat Kitto as less than the others anymore. He is my lover and maybe one of the fathers of my children. I would ask that you respect him for that, if for no other reason."

She gave a nod that was almost a bow, but not quite. "If you wish the goblins to be thought better of, then you do need to bring one into a power that isn't one of yours, and is more impressive than mirror-whatever."

"I've been discussing that with Doyle, Rhys, and the others. When I am able to have sex again, I will try to do just that."

Maeve shuddered. "I honestly don't know how you can have sex with Holly and Ash. Kitto, I sort of understand, he's like this beautiful min-iature man, and he's kind to the point I'm amazed he survived among such a savage race, but the twins . . . they are savages, Meredith."

"What they are, or are not, is my business. I'm not asking you to compromise your racial purity."

She sighed and rolled her eyes. "I didn't mean it like that, Meredith. You seem determined to take insult."

"And you seem determined to give it."

We stood there looking at each other, almost glaring at each other. I was tired of Maeve's attitude issues. She hadn't been like this before she went to Europe to make the last movie. I didn't know if something had happened on the trip, or if it was something that had happened here, but something had changed, and not for the better.

"I do not mean to give offense," she said.

"I'd believe that if you didn't keep doing it. What happened in Europe, Maeve? Or what did you find here when you came home to make you angry with me, and my men?"

"My son treats you and your men as his parents, more than me. That hurts, Meredith."

"I am sorry for that, and we are willing to take the reality show offer to help you afford to stay home more."

"I told you at the hospital what I made on my last film, Meredith; there is no way that a reality TV contract will come close to that. We will be giving up our privacy for nothing. If anything, the cameras will record that Liam doesn't think of me as his mommy except as an empty word. Do you think I want to be humiliated like that on national television?"

"You're making it sound like Liam is dumping you for someone else. He's a baby, he doesn't understand."

"I am Maeve Reed, the Golden Goddess of Hollywood; I can't be seen as losing to anyone, not even the first American-born faerie princess."

"You aren't talking about Liam now, are you?"

"I've been a sex symbol since the early sixties, Meredith, and yet you have all the attention of the most desirable men in the household. I understand why, but my image is everything for my job. My agent and my publicist think that a reality show here could harm the image that I've built up over decades. I'm one of the most desirable, and desired, women in Hollywood, but I can't compare to you in my own home."

"Is that your agent and publicist talking, or just you?"

"All three of us."

"Are you serious?"

"Yes, Meredith, perception is everything in this town. If people believe that someone like you is this much more desirable than me, it will hurt my earning power, and maybe my box office draw."

"What do you mean, 'someone like me'?"

She blinked those big, beautiful eyes at me and did an expression I'd seen her do in a dozen films. I'd learned that was one of the ways she hid her true feelings in the real world. I didn't know if other actors did it, but she did; she acted to hide. It was her version of a cop face: actor face.

"Answer me, Maeve; what did you mean, 'someone like me'?"

"Someone who isn't a movie sex symbol," she said.

I shook my head. "That's not what you meant."

"Now you're telling me what I mean, as if I don't know my own mind?"

"Do you think the reason that Bryluen can bespell my mind so easily is because I'm not pure enough sidhe, just like Kitto?"

"I did not say that."

"And that is you avoiding answering the question; very sidhe of you, because we don't lie outright. We just prevaricate until the listener reads into our words whatever they want to hear, and we let them believe it."

"You're overthinking this, Meredith."

"Am I?"

"Yes, and that was a clear answer," she said.

"The one you just gave, yes, it was, but it's not the answer to my question, is it?"

"Drop this, Meredith, please. I'm sorry if I implied anything."

"What if I don't drop it?"

"What is wrong with you today, Meredith?"

"I could ask you the same thing."

"I had a meeting at the studio and they're already trying to pressure me to go right back to filming. I told them I wanted some time with my son, but I'm one of their solid moneymakers and any year without a Maeve Reed film hits their profits."

"You haven't been home a week yet," I said.

"If I leave again, Liam is going to just forget who I am."

I went to her then and touched her arm. "Can you say no?"

"I can always say no."

"Will it hurt your career, or put you in breach of a contract?"

She smiled and put her hand over mine where I was touching her arm. "You understand more than most people do about what really goes on at this level of 'stardom.'" She raised her hand to do one set of quote marks.

"I've watched what you've been through in the last year. I'm amazed at how badly you get treated sometimes."

"I have true power in this town; imagine what happens to actors who don't."

"It must be brutal," I said.

"Hollywood will eat you, if you let it."

"I wonder if reality TV stars have as big a challenge?"

"I don't know, honestly; I only meet them after they've become stars and then it's about their publicists trying to keep them in the news. I don't know how different it is in the beginning, but you wouldn't be like most reality stars. You're already famous."

"And that fame, like all my noble titles, doesn't pay the bills."

"You could go back to being a private detective."

"That won't help you say no to the studio. For that, we need more money than a detective makes."

"Thirty million dollars, Meredith; that is what I made for my last film. Nothing you can do will bring that kind of money in. I'm sorry, but it just won't."

"We have offers for a million here, a few hundred thousand there."

"What's the million dollars for?"

"They've been after me for a while to be a centerfold."

"No, no, because I know some of your publicity offers are from family-oriented things. You can be the sexy young thing, or the beautiful mother with babies, but you can't do both in the media, not in this country anyway."

"I'd appreciate your advice on the offers coming in, then, because I'm tempted to go for the most money. I hadn't thought about building an image."

"I'd be happy to help, but you will have to choose what kind of image you want to project."

I laughed. "Isn't it a little late for me to be the perfect mother since I've just given birth to triplets out of wedlock?"

"It's not that making the mother image hard to sell, it's the multiple fathers, and the fact that rumor has it that Frost and Doyle are lovers, too, that has really hurt their image in the mainstream media."

"Very homophobic," I said.

"Yes, it is, but it's still the truth."

"Can I be the sexy young thing having just given birth to triplets?" I asked.

It was her turn to laugh. "I don't know; I've never seen anyone recover their figure as fast as you who wasn't full-blooded sidhe. You're built human, but you're certainly getting your figure back more like a sidhe."

"Especially with triplets," I said.

She laughed again. "Yes, especially with triplets. The human media will want to know your secret for postbaby weight loss."

"There's no secret; apparently it's just good genetics."

"They won't want to hear that, Meredith. They want some exercise plan, or better yet some magic food, or pill, that will make them all pre-baby thin without any effort on their part."

"I'm getting my figure back without much effort, but every other good thing in my life has come with a lot of effort."

Her face sobered, and she hugged me. "I know that, and I'm sorry that I've been taking my mood out on you."

I hugged her back. "Now I'm supposed to say, 'That's all right,' but it's not. I will never again be anyone's whipping girl for their issues." I hugged her tighter and looked up into the face that had launched a thousand blockbuster movies. "Not even the most beautiful movie star in Hollywood."

"Do you really think so?" she asked, looking down from all that six-plus feet height in her high heels.

I smiled. "Of course I do."

She leaned down, and I went up on tiptoe to meet her kiss. It was a chaste kiss by fey standards, though if some paparazzi had gotten a picture they'd have sold it for a bundle, and the rumor would have been that Maeve and I were lovers. We had made wonderful magical love once, but it wasn't what we were to each other. I wasn't sure if we were extended family, or if she was a member of my inner circle of courtiers. Once such things had been more formalized, and they still were at the Seelie Court, but less so at the Unseelie, and if this was a court then it was the most informal of all.

She smiled down at me, her pinkish lipstick slightly smeared. I wasn't wearing lipstick, just not bothering with glamour so my lips looked red. Humans would assume I was wearing something, but the proof was in the kissing, and the only lipstick smeared was hers.

I pulled out of the embrace with a smile.

"I appreciate you letting me choose lovers from among the new sidhe guards," she said.

"They are free to choose and so are you."

"It's been a long time since I was surrounded by people who truly felt that way. Among humans and the Seelie there is always a price to pay, or strings attached."

"The Unseelie who are not under the queen's direct control are more like the rest of the fey. Sex is another need, like food."

"Yes, but your steak doesn't have feelings and emotional baggage; people, even the sidhe, do."

I nodded. "I can't argue that. The lesser fey treat it more sensibly."

"I think you'll find, Princess, that the lesser fey treat sex with the sidhe sensibly, because they expect it to be a onetime thing, or a fling. Very few non-sidhe ever become a marrying match for the sidhe."

"My grandmother did," I said.

"Your grandfather wanted to end his curse, and only willing marriage to another fey would do that."

"At least the curse didn't demand a love match. My grandfather wasn't called Uar the Cruel for nothing; he'd have never found someone to love him."

"How are his sons, your uncles?"

"They've seen modern doctors and nothing seems to be able to stop the venom from dripping out of the pores of their fingers, but modern plastic gloves have helped. They don't accidentally poison people now."

"Good, they did nothing to earn their curse. I always thought it was unfair that Uar's curse manifested in all his children being born with that birth defect," she said.

"Agreed, but then are curses ever fair? I mean, most of the fairy tales have a grain of truth, and so many of them talk about a curse on the prince, or princess, spreading to everyone in the castle, or kingdom."

"I've never actually known that to happen. I think the human fairy tales were supposed to be a warning to rulers to be fair and just, or their kingdom suffered, but most kings didn't see themselves in such stories."

"Really, so there's no truth to 'Sleeping Beauty,' or 'Beauty and the Beast'?"

"'Sleeping Beauty' is the old sleeping warrior idea, and that's real enough, but 'Beauty and the Beast' isn't based on anything that I'm aware of."

"There are Raven warriors asleep under the Tower of London," I said.

She looked at me, eyes narrowing. "How do you know that? The queen did not tell you, and I know Taranis didn't. She felt it unjust that only her people were used, and he was too cowardly to offer up his own guard as sacrifice at the end of the last great human and fey war."

"The Goddess showed me in a vision that some of the Queen's Ravens sleep an enchanted rest underneath the human tower. They're the ravens the legend refers to, not the birds."

"When the last Raven leaves the tower, then England will fall," Maeve said.

I nodded.

"If England is ever in danger of truly being conquered, then the Ravens are to wake and defend the country, that's really what it means."

"Why didn't they wake during World War Two?"

"If the Germans had touched English soil they might have."

"Who is trapped under there?"

"You mean names?"

"Yes."

She shook her head and all her smiles were gone as she looked at nothing, her eyes full of remembering. "We do not speak their names, and will not until they rise again to fulfill a bargain that should have been shared between the two high courts of faerie. That our king refused to sacrifice any of his golden throng should have told us all what kind of man he was. Instead the story was put about that the warriors sealed up were all monsters that even the dark court was happy to be rid of, when in truth they were some of the best warriors among the sidhe, and no worse men than the rest."

"But you will not speak their names?"

"I will not, for Taranis made all of us at the Seelie Court vow never to speak their names until they rise to complete the treaty between human and fey."

"Was it very hard to pretend to be a starlet back in the fifties when you had all those centuries behind you, inside you?"

She gave me a look, a considering look, and let me glimpse the fine burning intelligence that she usually hid. She didn't pretend to be stupid, but she didn't show everything either.

"That is a very good question. One that in all the decades of interviews I've never been asked."

"I found it hard to pretend I wasn't Princess Meredith when I came to L.A. Even I found all my secrets hard to keep, hard not to share with someone."

"I told some of my secrets to Gordon. I wish he'd lived to see Liam. I think he's going to grow up to look like that handsome man I first met."

By the time I'd met Maeve's late husband he'd been riddled with the cancer that would claim his life, and the man who had been young in the sixties wasn't young three, almost four decades later. He had been a dying shell of the handsome director who had won Maeve's heart, but her dearest wish had been to have his child. Galen and I had done a fertility rite and the Goddess had blessed us with the energy to give Maeve and Gordon Reed their last wish as a couple. He'd died months before Liam was born, but he'd gotten to hear the heartbeat, see sonograms, and know for certain he had a son.

"I'm sorry that you lost Gordon."

"You gave us our son, Meredith; you have nothing to be sorry for."

"Shall we visit the nursery and the children?"

She smiled. "Yes, let's. If I'm going to remind Liam that I'm Mommy, I need to see him more."

"Am I supposed to apologize again for Liam's behavior?"

"If you had been raised in faerie courts and never left them, you would never have said that."

"Not apologized, or not felt like I should apologize for something that isn't my fault?" I asked.

"Both," she said, and smiled softly, but it was sad around the edges and left her eyes almost haunted.

I took her hand in mine, squeezed it. "I am sorry that you have had to spend so much time away from your son."

"If you hadn't said that, and meant it, I probably wouldn't say this: The movie I just finished filming is an amazing chance for me to stretch myself as an actress. If you and the others hadn't been here for Liam I wouldn't have taken it, or I might have tried to take him and a nanny with me, but he was better here at his home with his family. I just need to figure out how to be a bigger part of that family."

"I am very glad you think of us as family, Maeve."

"You have brought me back to faerie, or brought faerie back to me, after centuries of thinking I had lost it forever."

"I can't imagine losing it for so long. Three years of exile was hard enough for me," I said.

"But you truly are an American faerie princess, Meredith, so very American in your ideals. Like letting your guards have a choice when it comes to their lovers."

"I think that was what my father hoped when he sent me to public school and encouraged me to have friends outside the fey community."

"I never really knew Prince Essus, but he seems very wise. Not a single guard will say a bad thing about him."

"Have you tried to get them to?" I asked.

She made a waffling gesture halfway between a nod and a shrug. "A bit. I wanted to see if they were just speaking nicely for his daughter, but it seems as if he truly was as good as his press."

"Why would you care if my father was as good as he seemed?"

"Honestly?" she asked.

"Yes."

"Your uncle on your grandfather's side beat me and exiled me for refusing to marry him. Your grandfather was Uar the Cruel, and he earned that name. Your mother is narcissistic to the point of being delusional, and your uncle is the same. Your aunt on your father's side is a sexual sadist and a sociopath, or maybe even a psychopath; her son, your first cousin, was worse than his mother. He'd have been a sexual serial killer if the women of his bodyguards hadn't been immortal and able to heal nearly any injury. I've taken more lovers from among them than you have, and they hate the late Prince Cel with a fine and burning passion."

"We all knew that Andais was tormenting her guards and others of the court. She was very public about most of it, but I didn't know what Cel was doing with his guards. He was much more private about it."

"I think he hid it from his mother."

"She enjoys torturing people," I said.

"I've had more pillow talk about some of the horrors he did to the women, and I believe he was discreet because Andais might have stepped in and interfered with his fun."

"What's sauce for the goose is sauce for the gander," I said.

She shook her head. "No, Meredith, what Cel did to some of his private harem . . . I'm so glad you've found them a therapist."

"I'm glad they were willing to go."

"They didn't think they had a choice when they started."

"What?"

She smiled. "They thought you ordered them to go to therapy, and by the time they realized you hadn't meant it that way, most of them were benefiting from it, so they kept going."

"I would never order someone to go to therapy. I mean, you can order them to go the appointment, but you can't make them actually work their issues."

"You ordered them to talk to the therapist, and after what Cel did to them if they disobeyed him, or Andais did to anyone who disobeyed her, they worked their therapy as if their lives depended on it."

I shook my head and sighed. "They are all so much more damaged than I knew. Wait, is that why some of the female guards stopped going to therapy a few weeks ago?"

"Yes, they finally realized that you hadn't meant it as an order. A few of them tested to see if you meant it as a suggestion and when you didn't get angry about it, a few more stopped going."

"Most of them haven't stopped going," I said.

"As I said, Meredith, they worked hard at their therapy for fear of what you'd do to them if they didn't, and it worked strangely well for many of them."

"I didn't think you could force someone to do therapy like that."

"Neither did I, but it seems to be working for them."

I frowned, puzzling, and finally shook my head. "If it's working, it's working."

"You are surprisingly practical about very impractical things."

"Do I say thank you, or is that a problem?"

She smiled. "Neither, but the same guards who speak of Cel in hate-filled tones say wonderful things about your father. I think most of them are still in love with him, both as a good leader and as a man."

"I was actually thinking earlier that my family has more crazy than sane in it. Though you forgot that my grandmother was wonderful and caring, as were her parents, my great-grandmother and -grandfather."

"You're right, I did forget. Because your grandmother was half human and half brownie I counted her as less, but I shouldn't have, because it seems like the insanity comes from the sidhe side of things."

"We're not the most stable people," I said.

"I think it's living for so long, Meredith. Our bodies don't age, but maybe our minds do."

"Are you saying that Taranis and Andais have a version of dementia?"

"Maybe, though Cel wasn't that old by sidhe standards."

"I think Cel was always weak and twisted, but his mother indulged him, let him think he could do no wrong, and that cemented his crazy."

She studied me again as if looking for a flaw, or a hint, or something I couldn't guess at. "You are your father's daughter, and that is a good thing."

"I am my grandmother's, too, and that's a good thing as well."

"Yes, yes it is." She brushed off her hands as if brushing the topic away. "Let's go see the newest babies—though with Nicca and Biddy's daughter, Kadyi, and Liam, there are a lot of babies."

"Did you hear that Cathbodua and Usna are expecting?"

She looked startled, and then she laughed again. "No, I hadn't heard; that's wonderful and just fun, that the cat and the bird are having a baby."

"Andais said something similar, the cat and the crow."

Maeve's face sobered. "I would not be compared to the Queen of Air and Darkness in any way."

"I didn't mean to upset you."

She shivered, rubbing her hands up and down her arms. "It's all right, you didn't . . . it's just so many of us seem to go mad as the centuries pass, it makes me worry."

"Worry about what?" I asked.

"About my own sanity, I suppose."

"You have never shown any sign of the madness that haunts some of the noble lines of faerie."

"Oh, it's not just the noble lines, Meredith; some of the lesser fey are just as unpredictable, they just don't have the power of life and death to indulge their insanity."

It was my turn to study her. "What makes you say that?"

"The Fear Dearg, for one; you know we have one of them living here in Los Angeles."

"I've met him," I said.

She shuddered. "I remember the wars against them. It was like their entire race was as bad as Andais, Taranis, and Cel combined. It's why we took their magic away."

"The Fir Dhaeg said the sidhe also took their females, so though they live forever they're dead as a race."

She nodded, rubbing her arms again. "We could not work a spell to kill them, or destroy their evil entirely, but we destroyed what we could of them."

"The Fir Dhaeg said that I could give him back his name. That the curse the sidhe placed upon them could be cured by a royal chosen by Goddess and faerie."

"I do not know the details of the curse, but all curses must have a cure; it's part of the balance. Nothing is truly forever, nothing is that is made cannot be unmade, and that which is unmade has the possibility of being reborn."

"What happened to the Fir Dhaeg females? Doyle would not tell me details after we met the one here in L.A."

"We could not destroy them, Meredith, for they were as much a part of faerie as the sidhe, but we were able to kill them at a price."

"What price?" I asked.

"That we would take in their essence, absorb them. We would tie the Fir Dhaeg to the sidhe forever, so that if they reincarnated they would come back as one of us. The hope was that our bright blessings from the Goddess and Her Consort would cleanse their evil, but I wonder sometimes if the opposite happened."

"What do you mean?" I asked.

"I wonder sometimes if the Fir Dhaeg contaminated the sidhe with their darkness."

"Taranis and Andais were already king and queen by then; you can't blame their evil on the Fir Dhaeg."

"I suppose not, but I remember the day that it was done. The females didn't die; they faded and the energy went somewhere, Meredith. What if it went not into the land, or sky, or plants, or water, but into the ones that did the cursing? Andais was part of that spell; your father was not."

"You're saying that in cursing the Fir Dhaeg, Andais may have . . . what, become one herself?"

Maeve shrugged. "Maybe, or maybe she was mad even then and we just hadn't realized it."

"Faerie chose her to be queen of the Unseelie Court, so she was fit to rule once," I said.

"She was a great war leader, so yes, she was fit once."

"Have you discussed your theory with anyone else?"

"No, by the time I thought of it I was in exile. I had a lot of time to think upon old things while I was alone."

"I'll share your theory with Doyle and see what he thinks."

"Remember that he was a part of the spell, too."

"Doyle is not evil," I said.

"I didn't say he was, but being around evil changes a person, even if you're killing it on the battlefield."

I tried to read her face and couldn't. "Why tell me this?"

"I don't know; perhaps I've wanted to tell someone my idea for a very long time."

"You lived in the high court of faerie for centuries, Maeve, and then in Hollywood for decades; you don't say things without understanding how it will affect people, or how you hope it will affect people, so what's your point? Why tell me? Why now?"

"I don't know, and that is the honest answer; it just seemed time."

I shook my head. "I wish I believed that."

"I would never mean to make you doubt Doyle."

I laughed then. "I don't doubt Doyle; nothing you could say would make me do that."

She controlled her face, but for just a moment I saw she was unhappy. Why would she want to divide me from Doyle? Out loud I said, "Do you have an old grudge against Doyle?"

"Why would you say that?"

"He's been the left hand of the queen for centuries, and their court was often at war with yours, so just answer the question. Do you have a grudge against him?"

"If I had to choose a king to follow I would prefer the energy of sunlight and life, not darkness and death."

"Doyle was who faerie crowned as my king."

"Your Unseelie king," she said.

I nodded. "And faerie crowned me Sholto's Queen of the Sluagh."

She couldn't hide her distaste. "They are the stuff of nightmares."

"True, but the Goddess saw fit to make me their queen all the same."

"I would wonder who faerie would choose for you if it were the Seelie throne you were sitting upon, or a new throne of faerie. Who would be that king for you, Meredith?"

"Since we gave up the crowns that faerie offered us, and I can't go back to visit Sholto's kingdom for fear of Taranis, I don't think it matters. I think I've turned down too many thrones for the Goddess to offer me another."

The first pink rose petal fell from empty air and floated down between us. We watched it fall slowly to the floor.

"You are surrounded by miracles, Meredith."

"The Goddess blesses me with Her presence."

"I think She's happy to have someone worth blessing again."

Rose petals began to fall like a flurry of candy-colored snow. I stood in the center of it holding my hands up, raising my face toward the fall of petals. I thanked the Goddess for Her attention and Her blessing, and the rose petals fell faster until it was a blizzard of cotton candy petals.

Maeve Reed, the Golden Goddess of Hollywood, once the goddess Conchenn, fell to her knees and began to weep.

TWENTY-SIX

By the time Maeve recovered herself, the rose petals had almost stopped falling. Only a few of them trailed me to the nursery, like pink snow flurries. Two of the new Diplomatic Security Services, or DSS, guards had trailed us from outside Maeve's bedroom to here; now they stood at the door in bodyguard pose, one hand holding a wrist, or just arms free, but strangely at attention. They were on duty while all the rest of the guards were at blade and hand-to-hand training. The human guards had tried to participate, but the difference in strength and speed had made it . . . awkward. Though some of the humans had persisted.

It also meant that the only people left to tend the babies were human. Liam came running to us as we entered the triplets' nursery. "Mommy! Come see, babies!" he yelled, and grabbed Maeve's finger so he could drag her farther into the room.

Her whole face lit up, not with magic, but with happiness that he'd run to her, not me. She'd been spending as much time with him as she could in the last few days, and just like that, he was running to her more. A tightness I hadn't realized was there eased as I watched him pull her forward.

One nanny was diapering Gwenwyfar on the changing table. Alastair was in his crib with most of the dogs crowded around it, and him. Liam's nanny, Rita, was in one of the two rocking chairs, holding Bryluen, and that was where the little boy led Maeve. Rita's dark head was bent low, giving only a glimpse of her smile, as she gazed down at the baby. Rita was short for Margarita, and she was a pretty, dark, older woman, very shy. She rarely spoke and when she did, she didn't like to hold eye contact. I wasn't sure if she was just naturally that shy, or if it was being in the presence of Hollywood stars and princes and princesses of faerie. Danika, the second nanny, was as tall as Maeve with thick blond hair that fell to the tops of her shoulders. She did a serious yoga workout every day, and used the weights when the guards weren't in the room. She hadn't bulked up, just made her curves more firm. She moved with a physicality that reminded me of the guards. Apparently she'd gone through college on an athletic scholarship, and the habit of it hadn't left her. Rita was only a few inches taller than me, in her early forties, and had given up the fight for the gym a few years ago, so she was just comfortably round. She'd been a nanny when she was Danika's age, but a divorce had forced her out to work again. It had also made her interested in live-in positions like this one.

How did I know all this? Galen had told me; he'd apparently won her confidence with all his time in the nursery. She'd never seen a man who loved his children so much, and she'd informed me I was a lucky woman.

Danika glanced up and said, with a smile, "Ms. Reed, Princess Meredith."

"Hello, Danika. Hello, Rita," I said.

Maeve said, "Rita, are you all right?"

I walked farther into the room so I could see Rita more clearly around Maeve's tall form. Rita kept smiling and rocking Bryluen but never looked up at Maeve. In fact, she didn't react at all, as if she hadn't noticed us come into the room.

"Rita, Rita!" Maeve raised her voice a little.

"Bree likes 'ita to rock her," Liam said.

Maeve waved her hand between Rita's face and Bryluen's gaze. The nanny didn't react. Maeve kept her hand above the baby's face, completely blocking them both from looking at each other.

"Rita, can you hear us?" I asked.

Danika walked toward us holding Gwenwyfar. "What's wrong with her?"

"Rita!" Maeve said sharply, her hand still held between them.

Rita startled, almost as if she'd been asleep, her arms starting to unfold as if to drop Bryluen, but she recovered instantly and held the baby closer. The baby started to fuss.

"What's wrong? Did I doze off? I'm so sorry, Ms. Reed, I've never done that before."

Maeve straightened up. "It's okay, Rita, I know . . . it's not your fault."

"But I fell asleep with the baby in my arms." She looked at me. "I am so sorry, Princess, so sorry, I would never . . ."

"It's okay, Rita, honestly," I said.

She was completely beside herself, thinking she'd nearly dropped Bryluen because she fell asleep. I waited for Maeve to explain, but she didn't, and I didn't either. I wasn't sure how to explain it, and I definitely didn't want the media to know that one of the triplets was already so magically powerful that she could bespell people with her gaze. No, that bit of information was not something I wanted in the tabloids.

Maeve told Danika to take Rita to her room and make her take a short nap. Maeve took Bryluen from her. I took Gwenwyfar from her, so she could escort the still-apologizing Rita away.

Liam said, "Bree likes 'ita."

We looked down at the little boy. "Does Bryluen like Rita better than Danika?" I asked.

He nodded.

"Why does she like her better?"

He looked very serious, as if he were thinking hard, then said, "'ita plays."

"Rita plays more than Danika," I said.

He nodded, smiling.

"Do you and Bryluen tell Rita what to play?"

"Bree does," he said, smiling.

"And does Rita always play the way Bree wants?"

He nodded solemnly.

Maeve looked down at the baby in her arms. "Her gaze has a weight to it, Meredith."

"What do you mean?"

"I can resist it, but she just seems such a beautiful child. It's peaceful to look at her."

"It's a compulsion, isn't it?"

Maeve nodded, face very serious, as she looked at me. "We'll interview some nonhuman nannies. I'll call the agency and see if they have any available. If they don't have any, then we should ask in the larger fey community."

"Agreed, and until we find someone, Rita shouldn't help take care of the triplets anymore," I said.

Bryluen started to fuss, and Maeve rocked her back and forth. The baby quieted almost immediately, big eyes growing sleepy. "None of the humans should be around her much, Meredith."

"How did you know that Bryluen likes to be rocked that way, side to side, not up and down?"

Maeve stared down at the tiny baby. "I . . . I don't know. I just knew that's what she wanted."

"Can you stop rocking her?" I asked.

Maeve stopped, and Bree started to fuss; more rocking and the fussing stopped again. "She cries every time I stop."

"Try stopping anyway," I said.

Maeve tried, but eventually she started again. "No, I can't stop, not for long."

We stared at each other and for the first time I was afraid of Bryluen, because magic usually gets more powerful with age. She was only a week old; what would she be like in a few years?

"Maybe none of us should take care of Bree by ourselves," I said, softly.

Maeve went to the crib with the most pink on it. It had been purchased while I was in the hospital, and Kitto had let the clerk talk him into pink ribbons and little lambs. She was able to lay Bree down, but the moment she started fussing Maeve moved to pick her up.

"Don't pick her up," I said, and I held Gwenwyfar closer to me.

Maeve turned away, but the baby began to cry and she turned back.

Liam was at the crib now. "Pick her up, Mommy, she wants up."

Maeve picked Liam up and held him so he could see into the crib better. She was able to walk away with the toddler in her arms, but he wasn't happy.

"Mommy, pick Bree up, not me!" He started to push to be put down. She let him down and he ran to the crying baby. She turned to go in that direction, too.

"Pick Alastair up," I said.

She went to my quietly sleeping son and lifted him slowly. He slept through it, though the dogs began to whine around her feet, especially his puppy.

Maeve turned to me. "I can resist her demands now."

Liam had his tiny hand through the crib bars and had her hand in his. "Up, Bree. Up, Mommy!"

Maeve and I looked at each other. "She's only a week old, Meredith."

"I know."

"If it gets worse, stronger . . ."

"I know," I said.

"Why does holding the other babies act as charm against it?" she asked.

"I don't know."

"There have been stories of some being so beautiful from babyhood on that all that saw them were entranced, but I thought that was an exaggeration; now I'm not so sure."

"Do we have anyone here who was that compelling, this young?"

She held Alastair close, and thought. "Aisling. Stories tell how people loved him even as a baby."

"I saw one of our women claw her own eyes out, so he couldn't control her with his beauty."

"A human woman?"

"No."

"Lesser fey?"

"No, sidhe."

Maeve shivered, so violently that Alastair protested with a small cry. His puppy came and whimpered at her feet. "Did it work?" she asked.

"Did what work?"

"Did scratching out her own eyes stop him from having power over her?"

"She was able to stop answering questions truthfully, but she was still besotted with him, still magically infatuated. He told her the last sight she would ever see, ever remember, was his face, and she wept. She wept into her hands all blood and gore." I raised Gwenwyfar so I could smell the top of her head, that clean, pure smell that seemed to make everything all right.

"He was forbidden to use his charms in battle; it was deemed too horrible to make your enemy love you," Maeve said.

"I didn't really understand what his power was. I mean, I knew the stories, why he was veiled, but I didn't really understand until it was too late. I agree, some things are too terrible to use."

"You wield the hands of flesh and blood, Meredith. They are two of the most horrifying powers the sidhe have ever commanded. How can it be more terrible than that?"

"It's not lust, but love, obsession that he causes. She screamed when she saw him, when they kissed, as if it were the most horrible sight in the world. I never want to order anything done that causes that sound from another person."

"She was part of a group that was trying to kill you and the men you love, Meredith; you had no choice."

"It's pretty to think so, but in the end there are always choices, Maeve. People decide what lines they will not cross, I just found another one, that's all."

"You look haunted, Meredith."

I nodded. "I don't feel bad about much that I've done, or had others do, but that one bothers me."

Maeve came and used one arm to hug me to her, so that she encircled the babies and me in her arms. "I am sorry for that then, Meredith, truly sorry."

I realized I was crying, and wasn't sure why; maybe it was postbaby hormones, or maybe the thought that my wonderful babies, my children, might have frightening magic hadn't occurred to me. Most magic didn't manifest in the sidhe until puberty, but both girls had already shown power. Gwenwyfar with her lightning birthmark that actually caused a sort of static shock sometimes, and Bree with this, whatever this was. I held Gwenwyfar and pressed my head against the sweetness of Alastair's dark hair, and wept while Maeve Reed, the Golden Goddess of Hollywood, held me. In the end, faerie princess or box office queen didn't matter as much as being two women, two mothers, two friends. Maeve joined me in the tears, and I doubted she could have said why she was crying either.

TWENTY-SEVEN

I left Maeve in the nursery to make sure Bryluen didn't bespell the nannies, and went in search of the fathers who were doing the most baby duty. I wanted to know if they'd had any problems, or noticed that Rita was being manipulated by our baby daughter. The guards were doing weights, weapons practice, and hand-to-hand, in separate groups, so I went to the weight room first. It was easier to ask questions there.

I had two guards with me, because I went nowhere without them since Taranis had kidnapped me. I couldn't complain about the extra security, but it meant that some of the guard had to miss the workouts at times. Saraid and Dogmaela paced just behind me and to each side. Saraid's hair was as glitteringly gold as Frost's hair was silver; her eyes were blue with a white starburst around the pupil, as if someone had drawn a shining white star in the middle of the blue of her iris. Dogmaela's more ordinary yellow hair seemed pale compared to the glittering braids that Saraid could boast, and her eyes, three rings of green and gray, seemed almost human-normal, but they were both tall and slender with fine muscles showing in their bare arms. Saraid was six feet even, and Dogmaela two inches shorter at five-ten. Her yellow hair flowed free, held back from her face by a metal helmet that was so not modern, but if no one made her wear modern equipment Dogmaela had a habit of reverting back to more familiar things. She did keep her sidearm, a modern Beretta .45, and according to Doyle she was one of the most accurate with a pistol. She liked her helmet and her familiar sword at her side, but she'd embraced the modern weapons wholeheartedly. Except for the color of her hair and eyes, Saraid looked like a very modern Hollywood model/ actress in skinny jeans tucked into knee-high boots, and a tailored mannish suit jacket that didn't quite hide the sword she had strapped to her back, but distracted the eye from the two guns and extra ammunition that fit along her long, slender torso.

The women stayed outside the door, as the other guards had stayed outside the nursery. Rhys and other guards were inside the weight room, and that meant that the workout areas were one of the safest places in the house and grounds.

There was a big sign over the door to the weight room. It read, *IF YOU DON'T KNOW HOW TO USE A MACHINE, ASK FOR HELP. DO NOT BREAK THE MACHINES! THIS MEANS EVERYONE: SIDHE, RED CAPS, GOBLINS, DEMI-FEY, EVERYONE!*

I knew Rhys had made the sign after one of the Red Caps had stripped all the cables out of one machine, and one of the newer sidhe guards had damaged another, all in the same week. I could hear his voice without even going through the doorway, not the words he was speaking, but the rhythm of his voice. The room had been a ballroom back in the day when houses had them, because it was the only room with ceilings tall enough for the Red Caps, since they averaged between seven and thirteen feet tall. Maeve had let us buy what Rhys felt was needed for training the guards, so the once-elegant ballroom was filled with state-of-the-art padding, enough free weights to make Mr. Universe happy, and a forest of machines. The latter were mostly mysterious to me, because they'd been purchased after I got pregnant. I'd never spent a lot of time with weights, but I'd been forbidden to use anything but the lightest hand weights for so long that it was like a foreign land to me now. The machines were all taller than me, with interchangeable handles, pulleys, and attachables, and I had no idea what most of them did. I wasn't the only one overwhelmed by Rhys's fully equipped room.

"How can you use all this cold iron?" a woman's voice protested. I could glimpse Rhys through the maze of machines, but the woman was sitting down and I couldn't tell from her voice who it was, over the machines' mechanical clatter and the clink of the weights.

I nodded to the guards as I walked past. I'd learned that etiquette in the weight room meant you didn't say hello when someone was lifting, unless they spoke first. If they were into the zone of their workout, just having to talk too much could throw them out of it. Rhys had explained all this to me. I'd never lifted weights seriously enough to experience a "zone," but I trusted Rhys to know what he was talking about.

Most of the guards in the room were the newer ones who had only come from faerie in the last few months, but they were all tall and slender, with a play of muscles under their mostly pale arms, long legs moving the leg press machine easily. I didn't usually still feel like the short ugly duckling, but seeing them in the tank tops and shorts, or even just sports bras for some of the women, I suddenly felt far too round, and much too short, and just awkward as I walked across the special padded floor in my three-inch heels. I'd felt pretty good about myself until that moment, and then it was as if all the childhood years of being told I wasn't sidhe enough came spilling back. No one had said anything, or even lifted an eyebrow at me; sometimes it's just the inside of your own head that is the problem.

I squared my shoulders, made sure my posture was perfect, and kept walking toward Rhys with a smile on my face. My insecurities in that moment were my own.

Of course, I wasn't the only one who didn't look like everyone else. There were three Red Caps in the room, too. They were all between seven feet, short for a Red Cap, and thirteen feet, which was almost as tall as they got. The tallest and the shortest were shades of gray, but the middle one was the yellow of aged ivory. I wasn't close enough to see their true red eyes, but they were Red Caps; the eyes would be scarlet. The yellow-skinned one was Clesek, but I couldn't recall the names of the other two. They all wore the short, round caps that gave them their name, but right now the caps weren't red, more brown, the color of dried blood. They were all stuffed into sweat suits that strained to fit over their bodies. It was like trying to find workout clothes for the Incredible Hulk. They'd originally worked out in their undergarments, but Maeve had too many humans working in the house and they were uncomfortable with nearly nude giants striding through the hallways. They were in the far corner using the special free-weight bars that we'd had to get, so they could carry more weight than regular barbells without breaking; I hadn't even known that there were special bars to hold weights once you got up to four to five hundred pounds and more. The fact that human beings with no fey ancestry needed special bars like that amazed me a little, and made me feel even weaker. I was so not the strongest person in this room, not in any way.

I heard Rhys say, "The metal makes us have to work harder, because not all our magic works."

The woman's voice: "It's harder than I thought it would be."

"Good," he said.

The Red Caps saw me and dropped their weights with a clang that vibrated the room as they went down on one knee. They didn't have to do that during exercise, I'd told them all that, but the Red Caps were very devoted.

I stopped and called out to them. "It's all right, you don't have to bow in the weight room, remember?"

"You are our queen, we must show proper respect," Clesek said. He gave a narrow-eyed stare at the sidhe. "They should show it, too."

"It's dangerous in the weight room, Clesek; we discussed this," I said.

"Which of you dropped it?" Rhys yelled it, as he came striding through the machines wearing midthigh-length compression shorts and a tank top that was more straps than shirt so that the muscled beauty of his upper body was more revealed than hidden by it. The shorts showed off assets, too, but in the gym you were supposed to be paying attention to other things. His hair was back in a ponytail held by multiple hair ties spaced a few inches apart along its length so that it was almost a braid, but not quite.

Since he was six inches taller than me, I didn't think of him as short, but as he went for the Red Caps, he looked small. It made me wonder how tiny I looked standing next to the biggest of the goblins.

His voice boomed out, filling the room. One of the visiting human soldiers had called it a drill sergeant voice. "You do not drop the weights! If you have to drop the weights, then it's too heavy for you, and you do what?" He was pressed nearly into the Red Cap's chest, but his voice thundered through the suddenly quiet room. Everyone had stopped exercising to see someone else get dressed down.

The Red Cap mumbled something.

Rhys did that big voice again. "I can't hear you!"

"Lower the weights. But it wasn't too heavy for me. We needed to show respect to Queen Meredith," the Red Cap said. He looked sullen. His scarlet eyes narrowed in an unfriendly manner, though part of it was the color. Bloodred eyes with no whites in them could make the Red Caps look angry, or at least unfriendly, easily and often.

"But the humans on TV just let the heaviest barbells drop," one of the other Red Caps said. This one was a gray so pale that he was almost white. He also had one of the most human of faces, not exactly handsome, but not the frightening fanged expression that most of them had once had.

Rhys turned and got up in the face of the second Red Cap. It was almost funny to see the huge Red Cap's shoulders slump, head ducking, shame-faced at the much smaller man's angry rant.

I heard one of the sidhe closest to me say, "She's not our queen yet."

I turned and found one of the very newest refugees from faerie. Our policy had been to take in any fey who wanted to leave faerie and come to the Western Lands, but a few of the recent sidhe were making me doubt the wisdom of that.

Fenella was just a fraction under six feet tall, with hair that fell like a gold and yellow cloak to her ankles when it was unbound; now it was in two long braids that had been looped back in upon themselves so they glittered as she moved, one moment more gold, the next like sunshine spun into rope, with the beauty of her face shining through the light and jewel-bright glory of her hair. She wasn't called Fenella of the Shining

Hair for nothing. She blinked her tricolored eyes at me. At first you thought her eyes were white with two circles of yellow shades, until you realized that the white around her pupil was actually an incredibly light yellow like winter sunlight, then butter, and the brighter yellow autumn leaves. I'd always thought that her eyes would have looked better with less spectacular hair, or that she needed eyes that were as amazing as the hair.

"Do you have something to say to me, Fenella?" I asked.

"No, Princess, I do not."

"If you will not say it to my face, then please refrain from saying it behind my back."

She startled, as if too caught off guard to hide it under centuries of courtly manners, or maybe I wasn't worth the effort.

"Will you not allow us any privacy, even to our own thoughts?"

"Your thoughts are your own, but when they spill out your lips and I can hear, they are no longer private."

"Very well, Princess Meredith. I find it disquieting that the goblins bow to you and call you queen when you are not a queen . . . yet."

"I am not the official goblin queen, that is true, but I am Queen of the Sluagh."

A look of distaste flitted across her face. "There was a rumor that you were Shadowspawn's queen, but those of us in the Seelie Court had not believed it."

"First, never call King Sholto by that name again; you know it is an insult. Second, why not believe it?"

"You are of the same bloodline as our king. It is a pure sidhe line, and even your mother's lineage speaks to the light, but I suppose you cannot help the corruption of your father's blood."

"Are you trying to be insulting?" I asked.

She looked surprised, and I was almost certain it was genuine. She just didn't understand the insult. "I have given offense; I am sorry, Princess, but your mother speaks endlessly of the corruption and vileness of your father, so I assumed that you felt the same."

"And if I did, then why would I have stayed at my father's vile and corrupt court, when I could have been with my mother at the Seelie Court?"

Fenella seemed to think about that, and watching her eyes while she did it, I realized something I hadn't before. She wasn't that bright, not stupid by any means, but not a deep thinker. Sometimes I thought that Taranis wasn't that deep a thinker either; maybe his court reflected that?

Then a smooth voice came from the other side of the tall machine. "Most of us never blamed you for preferring to rule in hell, rather than serve in heaven, Princess."

Trancer was inches above six feet, maybe six-five, and thin, even by sidhe standards, as if he'd been stretched just a little too much. His arms looked firm, but not muscled. If he'd been human you could have taken it to mean he wasn't very strong, but among the fey, even the sidhe, what you saw was not what you got.

"My father loved me, my mother didn't; a child goes where she's loved," I said.

"Love. What do the Unseelie know about love?" Fenella said.

Trancer touched her arm, and I watched her think about why he'd just cautioned her with that touch. I looked up into his tri-blue eyes. His hair was a more ordinary golden brown, waving just below his shoulders. The Seelie men let the women have the longer hair.

How many times had Trancer had to save his wife from speaking out of turn, or too boldly? How many centuries had he minded her, protected her from herself? I spoke to him, as I said, "Love is very important to most of us, don't you agree, Lord Trancer?"

He gave me a long look. "Yes, Princess Meredith, we do."

"I just don't see why we have to exercise," Fenella said, and there was a childish whine to her voice that went along with the lack of understanding I'd seen in her eyes.

Rhys said, "Because all of the guards exercise, that's the rule."

"But we were never guards," she protested.

"Now, dearest," Trancer said, "you know that we have to find a way to be useful."

"I can set a fine table, and host a banquet, but I don't think I will be very good at guarding anyone with strength of arms. Magic has always been enough in the past."

Secretly I agreed with her, but I was letting Rhys and Doyle handle what to do with the fey who were seeking refuge with us. We had so many now that we did need them to pull their weight, but I doubted sincerely if I would ever trust Fenella to guard me or mine from anything. I would reserve judgment on Trancer, but . . . I wondered how well Fenella had done at weapons practice. What do you do with immortal beings whose major talents were being beautiful courtiers and toadies? What use were they in modern Los Angeles? I suppose that there were Hollywood equivalents of the job description, but Lady Fenella and Lord Trancer wouldn't know the modern world enough to adapt, and I wasn't a big one for sycophants, maybe because I'd never been powerful enough to have any, and now I didn't trust them.

"Then think of it as getting into practice for losing the baby weight."

"I won't need that," Fenella said.

"I thought you came into exile in the Western Lands so that you could get pregnant," Rhys said. He put an arm across my shoulders, drawing me in against his body. I slid my arm around his waist automatically, and just holding and being held helped me feel less short, less round, less bad about the changes in my body since the babies. The circle of Rhys's arms eased most of the anxiety that had started. Was it baby hormones still? It wasn't like me to allow anyone to make me feel that unhappy with myself.

"We did," Trancer said, beginning to rub his hand in small circles on his wife's back.

"Then getting a habit of exercise will help her get her girlish figure back afterward," Rhys said, smiling.

"But I will not need to exercise to lose my weight. It will just go."

"I may have lost my weight faster than most human women, but I'll still have to exercise when the doctor clears me for it."

"But you're much shorter than me, and I'm told that makes it much harder to lose weight."

"I don't think it's just about height," a voice said. It was Biddy just coming into the gym. She was six feet of broad shoulders and muscles, even after having her baby only two months ahead of my triplets. She was built more like a very tall human, and she put on muscle better than most of the sidhe, even the men, but then she was half human. Her hair was cut very short in a mass of brown curls. She'd chosen to cut it when she refused the late Prince Cel, and had been warrior enough and willing to do enough damage to make her *no* stick. She'd told me she'd keep her hair short to remind herself that she was stronger than she knew, and that no one would ever hurt her again.

"I'm having to work to get back to my fighting weight. I guess after three hundred years the metabolism slows down," she said with a grin.

"You're half human; I'm not," Fenella said.

"You know, Fenella, I'm beginning to wonder why you left faerie," I said.

Those yellow eyes narrowed. "I came here to get with child, not to sweat and guard . . . you."

Trancer's hand stopped moving in those small useless circles on her back. His smile looked frozen. "Now, dearest . . ."

"Merry had triplets. The last set of triplets among the sidhe was at least eight hundred years ago," Biddy said. Her solid brown eyes, so very human, were darkening with the beginnings of anger. She would get angry for me.

"Yes, triplets, like a litter of dogs," Fenella said.

Biddy said, "Bitch."

"Exactly," Fenella said.

Rhys made a small movement forward, but I held him tighter around the waist.

I didn't need to be protected; I had the power to do it myself now. "You know, Fenella, if you don't want to be one of my guard, that's fine; I don't think you're suited to the position."

"I can stop lifting these things?" She motioned at the weights.

"Yes, and in fact pack your bags and go back to the beach house."

"There is no fairyland at the beach house. It's just ordinary land."

"Princess Meredith, my wife didn't mean . . ." Trancer began.

I held up a hand and stopped him midsentence. "The beach house is lovely all year round, and maybe going back there will remind your wife that all the fairyland around this house is here because of me."

"The Goddess returned Her blessing to us," Fenella said.

"No," Biddy said, "the Goddess returned Her blessing to Merry, and Merry shares it with the rest of us." She stood very tall, looking down at the other woman from where she still sat on the front of the weight machine.

Fenella opened her mouth again, but Trancer actually put a fingertip against her lower lip. "My love, we will go to the beach house, as the princess bids. She is, after all, the ruler here in the Western Lands."

Fenella pouted with her lips still against his finger, but she didn't try to talk again, which was a relief at this point. She was the perfect example of exactly why I hadn't tried to stay at the Seelie Court. Yes, she was less astute than some of the nobles, but her attitude was about average. I wasn't pure enough, sidhe enough, and more than the Unseelie, the Seelie put great stock in physical purity.

"Pack and go, now," Rhys said, voice low. His skin began to hum with power, and about the time I noticed that, I could see the white glow of his power sliding almost cloudlike under his skin. I glanced upward and saw that the three circles of blue had begun to swirl, as his magic began to unsheathe itself.

"We will, my lord," Trancer said. He got his wife to her feet and began to ease out from among the machines and us. I realized that "us" didn't just include Biddy. The three Red Caps were looming behind us like the mountains were on our side, my side. I reached my free hand out and touched the closest Red Cap, who happened to be Clesek. I wanted them to know how much I valued them, and had since the night they risked themselves in battle to help me save the men I loved.

Clesek's cap was suddenly a bright scarlet instead of the dried brown it had been. The first thin trickle of blood began to drip down the side of his face from his round skullcap. The Red Caps had once dipped their caps in fresh blood often enough to keep them scarlet, but random slaughter for dipping purposes had been forbidden since the fey immigrated to America. I'd known that to be a war leader among them you had to have enough magic to cause your cap to bleed on its own, but what I hadn't known was that a sidhe with the hand of blood could give them back that ability and make all their caps bleed. That was why they called me their queen, and why they bowed, and why they had risked everything to help me, and had joined me in exile here.

Fenella hissed, "Unclean, Unseelie magic that."

I stopped touching Clesek, because I didn't want him to bleed enough to get the new padded floor bloody, but I'd had enough of the Seelie for today. "Yes, yes it is Unseelie magic, Fenella, and you might want to remember that the next time you insult me."

"Are you threatening me?"

Trancer tried to pull her toward the door, saying, "Hush, my dearest."

"Yes, yes, I think I am. I can come to you as a goddess of fertility and joy, or I can come as the dark goddess who brings the winter and kills the crops. That was the face of the goddess that the Seelie brought down upon themselves, centuries ago. You have learned nothing." And that last sentence echoed in the room in a way that human voices did not. Pink and white rose petals began to fall from thin air around me, Rhys, Biddy, and the Red Caps, but the fall of flowers stopped short of the two Seelie nobles.

Their eyes went wide and I saw fear on their faces. "She meant nothing by it, Princess, please."

"She meant everything by it, Trancer." My voice was almost mine, just the faintest echo of the Goddess around the edges of my words.

"We will pack and we will go to the edge of the sea, and await your pleasure to bid us return to this new bit of faerie," he said, pulling his wife backward toward the doorway.

"You do that," I said. The petals were thick as a snowstorm, but spring warm, so that I watched their frightened faces leave through a pink snowfall.

"It is not our place to say so, but they do not deserve your blessing," Clesek said.

Rhys hugged me. "I love you, our Merry, just as you are." And just like that, I started to cry again; stupid baby hormones. The rose petals fell so fast it was like being inside some magical snow globe that had been shaken by a giant. What did the Christians say—if God be with me, then who can be against me? That was true, but it still hurt to know that no matter how many wonders I performed, I would always and forever be too short, too human, too Unseelie for the most of the Golden Court to ever accept me. But then hadn't six out of sixteen of the Unseelie noble houses been against me the last time I stood in open court there, too? If the Goddess herself could not make them see their own bigotry, then there was no cure for it.

There was a soft kiss on my cheek. I looked up and found that Rhys's face was pressed to the top of my hair, and no one else was close. The Goddess had kissed my tears like my own mother never had. I whispered my thanks, and the petals began to slow. I was almost ankle deep in petals now; that was enough.

CHAPTER

TWENTY-EIGHT

Rhys and Biddy both offered to escort me to the outdoor area where Doyle was conducting the hand-to-hand training, but I told Rhys to stay and supervise the weight training. Biddy wasn't on full duty yet, and she helped run the household along with her husband, Nicca. I didn't want to put her back on guard duty; it wasn't where she was best used. Both of them were content when they realized Saraid and Dogmaela were just outside the door.

Rhys kissed me good-bye and gave me over to the two female guards. I'd already asked him my question, and he'd had no problem with Bryluen, and the two human nannies weren't needed when he, Galen, and Kitto were on duty, so he hadn't seen them with the littlest of our babes. It was interesting that Maeve and I both felt Bryluen's magic, but Rhys didn't. He was a death deity, and Maeve and I were both fertility, sex, and love. If that made us more susceptible to my daughter's glamour, then Galen would also have an issue, but Doyle and Frost might not. Come to think of it, Galen was the only one of the fathers who was spring and fertility, though he wasn't as close to Maeve's and my magic as a couple of the other guards. Adair and Amatheon weren't fathers, or my lovers anymore, but their magic was closest; I might see how they fared babysitting if Galen had more issues than the other fathers. If he didn't, then

I might ask one of the female sidhe and see if Bryluen had more power over women, though I couldn't think why she should.

"If you don't mind me saying so, Princess Meredith, you seem unusually solemn," Saraid said.

I glanced at her and smiled. "I don't mind, Saraid."

"You have everything any woman could want, and more; what do you have to be so sad about?" Dogmaela said.

"Dogmaela," Saraid said, making a caution of the other woman's name.

"No, it's all right, Saraid, truly. I may not answer the question, but you can all ask me anything."

"That is a most democratic attitude, Princess," Saraid said.

"I may be a faerie princess, but I'm also American. We tend to like democracy."

"I've been following your politicians in the media," Dogmaela said, "and I do not find all of them very democratic. In fact, many of them seem as if they would be happy to have a dictatorship if they could be in charge."

I laughed. "Very accurate of some of them, I grant you that."

"Well, you laughed, so that's a good thing," Dogmaela said, and she smiled. She was one of the guards who had gone to therapy with the same work ethic she'd applied to learning to shoot modern firearms.

Saraid had been one of the women who stopped going to therapy when she found out it wasn't mandatory.

"Is Uther coming over this week for movie night?" I asked.

Saraid ducked her head and grinned, that special stupid-faced, almost drunkenly happy grin. I loved seeing it on that angelically beautiful face, because Uther had been my friend back in the days when I'd been hiding as just plain Merry Gentry, a human with some fey ancestry. He'd been one of my coworkers at the Grey Detective Agency for three lonely years while I hid in L.A. on the shores of the Western Sea to keep my cousin, Cel, and his friends from killing me. Uther Squarefoot was the legal name on his license, and he was thirteen feet tall, with magnificent curling tusks, and a face that was almost more wild boar than human. He was a Jack-in-Irons, one of the solitary faeries, but still of the Unseelie Court, because the Seelie Court wouldn't touch any fey who was ugly. But Saraid had found in Uther the first gentleness she'd known in a man for centuries. He had found in her the wonderment of being loved by a truly beautiful woman. There were only two Jacks-in-Irons in the entire United States, and no one had ever seen a female one, so Uther had been lonely in a way that mere friendship couldn't fix. When he'd found out I was sidhe, he'd very politely asked me to help him break his fast for female companionship, but I was mortal and not sure I could survive his attentions. I wasn't sure what Saraid and he did together on their dates, but whatever it was satisfied them both, and they'd been a couple for almost six months.

"He is, my lady."

"Good," I said.

She gave me a shy smile, those star eyes full of a contentment that I had feared I might never see in the faces of the women who had been abused by my cousin. It made me smile back.

"You are truly pleased when the people around you are happy, aren't you, Princess?" Dogmaela said.

I glanced back at her. "Yes, I am."

She shook her head. "You are your father's daughter, Meredith, and it is a blessing for us all."

I touched her arm. "If I had known that none of you had been given a choice to go from serving my father to serving Cel, I would have tried to free you sooner."

Dogmaela looked frightened. "Oh, Meredith, no, the evil bastard was already trying to kill you through his toadies; if you had tried to take us away from him years ago, he would have seen you dead, or worse." She patted my shoulder. "No, things happened as they were meant to, and now we are here and you are the ruler your father hoped you would be."

I stopped walking, so they did, too. I looked at both of them. They'd been part of my father's personal guard, the Prince's Cranes, for centuries, and certainly through my childhood, but it had never occurred to me that they would know something I'd wanted to ask my father.

"People keep asking me why my father trained me to be a ruler when it seemed I would never wear a crown. I had no answer, but you were there. You were his guard, his confidants—did he intend me to take the throne, do you know?"

Dogmaela shook her head. "I was not a close favorite of Prince Essus, so I do not know what was in his heart."

Saraid was very quiet, face careful and empty.

"You know something; please tell me."

"He raised you the only way he knew, and that was to be a ruler, Princess Meredith, but he did not plan on assassinating his sister, your aunt, or her son, his nephew, to put you on the throne."

"What did he intend for me then?"

"I was closer to him, but he did not confide in me about you, except to worry for your safety. He spoke of you getting your doctorate in biology of some kind and being the first American-fey doctor; that thought pleased him."

I smiled, and nodded. "He wanted me to be a doctor at one point, a medical doctor."

"I believe that course of study takes many years by human standards; that seems to imply he did not plan on you vying for the throne."

I nodded. "I think you're right, but he told his sister that I would be a better queen than Cel would ever be a king."

"I heard him tell her that," Dogmaela said, "and she was furious with him. Had it been anyone but Prince Essus, he would have been tortured for such talk."

"She always did have a soft spot for her brother," Saraid said.

"She was afraid of him," Dogmaela said.

"No," Saraid said.

"She feared his power, Saraid. She knew he was one of the few in the courts strong enough to take the throne from her."

"To kill her, you mean," Saraid said.

"Yes, that is what I mean."

"My father loved his sister, and she loved her brother," I said.

They looked at me.

"They were devoted to each other, in their own ways," Saraid said.
We all just agreed.

"If only he hadn't loved his nephew," Dogmaela said.

"He might still be alive to see his grandchildren," I said, and the thought made my chest tight, my eyes hot.

"But if our prince, your father, had lived, these would not be the grandchildren he would see," Dogmaela said.

I looked at her.

"You speak nonsense, Dogmaela."

"No, Saraid, if Prince Essus had lived, then Meredith would never have had to hide in the Western Lands, and the queen would never have sent Doyle to find her. He would never have brought her back to be guarded and bedded by the Queen's Ravens, so she would never have had sex with them, or fallen in love with Frost and Galen, and well, all of them. For that matter, if she'd gone on to be a doctor, would she have been able to bring the Goddess's blessing back to us, or would we all still be slowly fading as a people?"

Saraid and I stared at her. I wanted to say, *Dogmaela, you're a deep, philosophical thinker; I didn't know that.* But that seemed vaguely insulting, as if I'd thought her stupid before, and I hadn't, but . . . "Are you saying that my father had to die for me to help bring life back to faerie?"

"It's something I've talked to the therapist about, and yes, I think so. I would never have traded our prince, your father, for anything, but it is a way I've made sense of his death and everything that came after. If it was all so that you would save us, Meredith, bring our people and faerie itself back to life, then that makes all the pain worth something, don't you see?"

"That's just talk," Saraid said. "If it makes you feel better, then believe it, but Prince Essus did not martyr himself so that Meredith could bring the Goddess back to us and save the sidhe from themselves."

"I never said that our prince agreed to die to save us, Saraid, but it is a way at looking at all the pain and horror, and having some sense from it."

Saraid shook her head. "And this is why I stopped going to the therapist."

I wasn't sure how I felt about Dogmaela's comforting therapy reasoning. I wasn't even sure I thought it was comforting to me, but if it gave Dogmaela peace of mind, then I didn't want to argue with it.

"I'm sorry, Princess Meredith, I didn't mean to upset you. I have been thoughtless."

"I encouraged you to go to the therapist, Dogmaela; what you take from it has to work for you, not me."

She looked at me, seemed to study me. "If I may be so bold, Princess, perhaps taking your own advice might not be a bad idea."

"What do you mean?"

Saraid said, "No, no, you are not going to tell the princess she needs therapy. We are going to escort her to Captain Doyle and anywhere else she needs to go, and that is that."

Dogmaela dropped to one knee as the Red Cap had done in the weight room. "I beg your pardon, our princess."

"Oh, get up, you did nothing wrong, Dogmaela, and neither did you, Saraid. You're allowed to be different people and deal with your traumas differently. Right now I just need to talk to Doyle and Aisling."

"Aisling, why do you seek him?" Saraid asked.

"That is my business."

Saraid dropped to her knee beside Dogmaela. "We have offended you."

"Oh, get up." And with that I started down the hallway as fast as my high heels could take me. I made them jog a little to catch up with me, and then they dropped back to their bodyguard position half a pace behind and to each side. That was how we walked through the sliding glass doors and out into the Southern California sunshine, where Doyle was teaching hand-to-hand combat, and all I wanted to do was run to him and wrap the strength of his arms around me. I didn't, because it might have undermined his authority, but it took more control than a would-be queen likes to admit.

Doyle stood under the shade of a huge eucalyptus tree that rose at least thirty feet high and spread out like a canopy. Most eucalyptus didn't have such a magnificent top, but this one was simply one of the prettiest ones I'd ever seen. Doyle had paced off a circle months ago that started under its shade and then spread out into the bright California sun. That circle of shade and light had become the unarmed combat practice area, because the Red Caps who practiced with the guard were too big to be thrown around inside any room the house could boast, so they got thrown around outside where they couldn't break things. Though, honestly, most of the guards who practiced with the Red Caps couldn't throw them around; it was more getting thrown around. The sidhe were quicker and more agile than the biggest of the goblins, but they weren't stronger.

The white, oversized tank top made a startling contrast with Doyle's skin, but the fitted exercise shorts were black so that it was almost hard to see them against his long legs. He was dressed like a hundred personal trainers in L.A., but the clothes were the only thing that was ordinary. No other trainer was going to have skin the color of night with purple and blue highlights when the sunlight hit it just right, and the pointed ears and ankle-length braid made him look like some elven prince from a fairy tale trying to blend into a modern gym. If Doyle wasn't different enough, the circle around him was full of the towering figures of Red Caps.

There were actually more Red Caps than sidhe standing and sitting around the circle. It was a first; the sidhe always outnumbered anyone else. Then one of the sidhe got up from where he'd been sitting on the ground, and the sunlight sparkled across his bare upper body as if he'd been sprinkled with gold dust. I knew that he had yellow and gold blond hair braided tight to his head, because he'd shoved it all up under a thin face mask that covered him from the chin up, leaving only holes for his eyes and mouth. It was far too hot even for the thinnest mask they'd been able to find, but it was the best solution we'd found so far to make sure Aisling's face wasn't exposed. He was why there were so few of the sidhe here. The Red Caps feared nothing, so they said, which meant they couldn't admit to worrying that Aisling's beauty would bespell them.

Dogmaela and Saraid moved in front of me, turning their backs on the practice and blocking my view entirely. "Princess, you should not be here; none of us should," Dogmaela said.

"Aisling is one of the people I need to speak with; please move aside."

"None of the female guard will risk seeing him bare of face, Princess Meredith, and we would be poor bodyguards if we let him bespell you," Saraid said.

"True love protects from his magic," I said. "I think you and I will both be safe, Saraid."

It took her a moment to understand what I'd implied, and then she blushed, which was not something you saw much among the fey. It made me laugh, not at her, but just happy for her and for Uther. He was like the ugly stepsister who had won the beautiful prince, and it couldn't have happened to a nicer guy.

"We are not certain that anything protects from Aisling's beauty, and he seems to have grown in power since he helped bring the dead gardens back to life," Dogmaela said.

I remembered that night. Galen and several of the sidhe who had once been vegetative deities had been absorbed into the very trees, rocks, and earth. When they came back out, they'd gained in power, or regained old powers once lost. But Aisling's sacrifice had been the most spectacular. A tree limb had pierced him through the chest, and he'd hung there. I'd thought he was dead, and then his body had exploded not into flesh, bone, and blood, but into a flock of songbirds that flew out into the garden to be lost in the dead trees. Their songs had been the first life heard in that lost place in centuries. Later Galen and all the rest appeared, melting out of the very walls and floor of the Hallway of Mortality, the queen's personal torture chamber. The hallway's cells had opened, and some had dissolved, and there were flowers and trees growing there now.

Aisling had survived all that and come back into more of his powers, or so some of the women believed. Since none of us could risk gazing on his face, I'm not sure any of us knew for certain whether Aisling had gained from his own sacrifice, or if everyone assumed it, because it was so true of the other men that had been taken by faerie and returned to us that night.

"I've seen Aisling with his shirt off before, and it hasn't affected me."

The two women glanced at each other, and then Dogmaela said, "I would not risk staring at any part of his body without a covering."

"Hafwen told us what happened when he revealed his face to Melangell."

I looked down at the dry grass. "I was there, I remember."

"Melangell clawed her own eyes out, so she would no longer be able to see him," Dogmaela said.

"I was there," I snapped at her.

She dropped to one knee, head bowed. "My apologies, Princess Meredith, I did not mean to offend."

"Get up, Dogmaela; I don't want any of you to abase yourself like that."

Saraid said, "Prince Cel expected that and more from us, so forgive us if we still fall back into decades of habit."

"I forgive you, but Dogmaela, please stand up."

"I angered you," she said, head still bowed.

"I regret what happened to Melangell. I didn't understand what I was asking when I told Aisling to use his magic on her, and a leader should know what a weapon does before using it."

They both looked at me, Dogmaela still on the ground. They exchanged another glance. It was Saraid who said, "Melangell meant to kill Galen that night. You were within your rights to do what was needed to find out the plan to assassinate you and your consorts."

"You did nothing wrong," Dogmaela said. "I just don't wish to suffer Melangell's fate by accident."

"I would not willingly use Aisling's beauty against anyone ever again."

"Why not?" Dogmaela asked.

"Because it wasn't lust that he filled Melangell with, it was love, as if she were forced to be in true love with him all at once, even though they hated each other." I hugged my arms tight trying to hold myself.

"You feel guilty," Saraid said, voice full of a soft awe.

"It was a terrible thing to do; why shouldn't I feel bad?"

They exchanged another look.

"Stop that," I said.

"Stop what?" they both asked.

"That look, just talk to me. I am not my aunt, or my dead cousin, I am not even my narcissistic mother, or egomaniac great-uncle, or my grandfather, Uar the Cruel; just talk to me, please, and for the love of Goddess, Dogmaela, stand up."

She got to her feet, started to glance at Saraid again, and then looked at me instead. "Regret is not an emotion we are accustomed to seeing in the royal family."

"No, they usually enjoy their cruelty," I said.

"We would never say that to you," Saraid said.

"I'm saying it, about my own family, but I am not them. I know a few months here doesn't erase decades of abuse, but I swear to you that I do not take pleasure from causing other people pain, or humiliating them."

"We believe you mean what you say," Saraid said.

I smiled, but it wasn't a happy smile. "You believe I mean it now, but you're wondering when I'll go crazy like my relatives and change my mind, is that it?"

"Time has taught us caution, Princess, that is all," Saraid said.

Dogmaela put her hands on her hips and then said, "I fell back into old, unhealthy habits, and I'm sorry for that, Princess Meredith. You deserve better than that, because you have shown yourself to be fair and sane, and . . . I am sorry."

I smiled at her. "It's all right, we're all learning as we go."

"That is true," she said.

"I still don't want to see Aisling's bare skin," Saraid said.

"Nor I," Dogmaela said.

"Then stand where you can't see him, but I'm going to speak with Doyle and eventually with Aisling. If you don't want to guard me while I do that, then you need to find guards to replace you."

They exchanged another look, and then Dogmaela looked embarrassed and said, "I'm sorry, Princess, it is a very old habit. The other Cranes were the only beings we could look to for help once the queen gave us to her son."

I thought the phrase was interesting: *gave*, like you'd give away a possession, or a puppy. You didn't give people away. It just wasn't supposed to work that way.

I had to go up on tiptoe to hug her. She stiffened, and didn't hug me back at first, and then patted my back awkwardly. "I'm so sorry, so very sorry."

She hugged me back then, and whispered, "Thank you for saving us."

I drew back with tears threatening in my eyes again. I didn't like this new emotional me, and really hoped that the hormones would even out and I'd regain more control, but the look on Dogmaela's face was worth a happy tear or two.

Galen came up to us smiling. He was shirtless, showing his flat stomach and the compact muscle that was underneath every bit of him. He didn't lift as seriously as Rhys did, and he didn't do the more extreme nutrition, so his body looked less defined, but wearing only a loose pair of shorts there was no way for him to hide the muscles that were inside all that smooth, pale green skin. Maybe it was being surrounded by so much grass, trees, and plants, but his curls looked very green, that one tiny braid still the only memory of when his hair was almost to his knees.

"Is everything all right?" he asked, reaching his hand out toward me. It was as natural as breathing to take his hand and stand at his side.

"We're fine," I said, and leaned into him, going up on tiptoe to meet his kiss.

Dogmaela mumbled, "Fine," and turned away to hide her own emotions, I think.

"We don't think it's safe that the princess be here with Aisling," Saraid said.

Galen grinned then. "She's safe enough."

"I think it's careless," Saraid said.

"If you're in love, really in love, then Aisling's magic has no power over you," Galen said.

"The princess told us the old wives' tale about true love keeping you safe from him," Saraid said.

"Meredith said that Saraid, you, and she would be safe," Dogmaela said. She'd wiped quickly at her face, and turned a stony, unreadable face to us, though she was as careful as Saraid not to look toward the practice area.

Galen drew me into his arms, grinning wider. "Then the three of us are safe as houses, but Dogmaela might want to go somewhere else."

She nodded. "I will, with Meredith's permission. I have not even an old wives' tale to keep me safe from the Terrible Beauty of him."

Aisling had once been called Terrible Beauty, though the Gaelic equivalent of it, and since I didn't know what country Aisling had started out in, I didn't know what his original Gaelic name had been. Saying *Gaelic* was almost like saying *Romance language*; some were so different from each other.

"You may go, Dogmaela; I think I'm safe enough." I knew I was smiling, and it was my own version of that stupid-faced, I'm-so-in-love smile.

She darted a glance at Galen, me, and then finally at Saraid. "Are you sure you want to stay?"

Saraid shook her head. "No, I'm not, I . . ." She glanced at me and then back to her sister guard. There was something close to pain on her face.

"Go, Saraid," I said. "Go if being near Aisling makes you this uncomfortable."

"It's okay," Galen said, his face sober, worried even. "Merry is in good hands." He hugged me closer to him, and I wrapped my arms around the slim smoothness of his waist.

"I just don't want you to think I hold my personal safety above that of the princess. I would lay down my life for her."

"I believe that, Saraid," Galen said. "We both do, but this is not life and death."

"You're dismissed, Saraid, Dogmaela; now go with my blessing," I said.

"And mine, if it matters," Galen said.

"It matters," Dogmaela said, smiling, a little sadly.

She and Saraid exchanged another glance; then they bowed, arms crossing their chests so their hands rested over their hearts, turned, and left.

"Why do they do that, touching their hearts, do you know?" I asked.

"It was Cel's idea, to show that he owned not just their bodies but their hearts."

I looked up at him and must have looked as horrified as I felt.

He hugged me tight against the front of his body, and I pressed my cheek against the warmth of his chest and wrapped my arms tight around his waist, holding on.

"I'm so glad you killed Cel," Galen whispered against my hair.

"So am I," I said, breathing in the scent of his skin and the slight dew of sweat, but it wasn't a masculine smell, it was almost like sweet cut grass.

"Now if you could just kill a few more of your relatives, we could live in peace."

"The queen is behaving herself," I said.

"All right, just one of your relatives then," he said.

I drew back enough to look up into his face. "Since when did you get so bloodthirsty?"

He smiled, but his green eyes were empty of it. "When he hurt you, and then when he tried to sue for visitation rights with our babies. He needs to be dead."

I hugged him as tight as I could, gazing up at him, studying his face. I didn't know why, but I was suddenly frightened for him. "Promise me you won't do anything foolish, Galen."

"I'm your bodyguard; it's my job to keep you safe. I'm the father of your children, and a husband in all but name; that gives me all the right I need to do anything to protect or avenge you, my Merry."

"If the king tries to kidnap me again, then do whatever you can, or want, but just promise me you won't go off and try to beard the tyrant in his lair, so to speak?"

He kissed me, and I kissed him back, but I studied his face as he drew back from it. "Galen, promise me."

He smiled at me, fingers tracing the edge of my cheek. "I can't."

"Don't get hurt, or worse, please, Galen. I've lost enough people in my life, all right?"

He hugged me tight again, and gave me a little shake. "I love you, Merry, and I love our children. I want to be here for you and them."

"Then don't do anything stupid, okay?"

"Me, stupid?" He gave me that look that was charming and self-deprecating, and in that moment I didn't trust it at all. I was suddenly so afraid for him that my chest was tight with it, as if I couldn't breathe past it.

"Remember, I don't want you to die for me, Galen; I want you to live for me."

He grinned. "I already live for you."

I would have pushed it, but Doyle yelled a warning, and Galen took me to the ground with him on top of me. I got a glimpse as I was falling backward of one of the Red Caps flying over us, tumbling through the air, before Galen's chest blocked my view of everything.

CHAPTER

THIRTY

could feel Galen's heart pounding underneath my hand where it was trapped against his bare chest, as his arms wrapped me close, pressing me between his body and the rough grass, his body a shield to protect me. I knew it was his job, but in that moment all I could think was, if he actually gave his life for mine, I wasn't sure I'd ever recover from the loss.

His chest filled my vision; I could see nothing but the edges of grass and sun haloing us. I felt him move and knew he was looking around. What was happening?

I heard voices yelling, "Is she all right? Merry! Is she hurt?" I felt and heard people running toward us. Funny how much you could feel vibrating through the ground when you were lying on it.

A deep rumbling voice said, "Don't worry about me, I'm fine."

Galen got to his feet and helped me stand. There were enough Red Caps standing around that they put us in the shade as if a grove of small trees had magically sprung up around us. Doyle was there, taking my other arm, while Galen still held me.

"Are you hurt?"

"No, startled, that's all." I looked at him, knew something was different, and then realized the white tank top had been badly ripped down the front, so that it flapped around him as he moved.

"No one gives a tinker's damn if a goblin gets hurt, it's all about the sidhe." It was the Red Cap that I'd seen go overhead. He was only about nine feet tall, with skin a deep charcoal gray setting off the scarlet of his eyes like rubies. His face was smooth and strangely pleasant, and though his mouth was almost lipless, it wasn't a bad mouth. Considering all the Red Caps had once had a mouth full of jagged teeth, or even fangs, it was a very good mouth indeed. His round skullcap was almost black.

"Hello, Talan," I said.

His brilliant red eyes narrowed. "I would not have been thrown so, before your magic changed me."

Doyle let go of my arm, taking a half step in front of me. "Do not blame Merry for your lack of prowess on the battlefield," he said in a voice that held an edge of growl to it. It wasn't his dog form coming out, just that first rush of testosterone, before the real fight began.

Talan started forward, but another figure was already there, moving between Doyle and the Red Cap. Jonty's skin had been the color of dust when I met him; now it was a nearly silver gray, shining almost metallic in the sunlight. He was shorter than Talan, but broader through shoulders and back. His biceps were as round as medium tree trunks; the weight lifting that Doyle had insisted on for all of them had made Jonty lean and filled him out at the same time, so that he was even bigger than he'd started, but now you could see the muscles with no extra flesh to hide them, and he was simply massive. The cap on his head was fresh scarlet and bleeding. His cap bled whether I was around or not, which was one of the reasons he was the leader of the Red Caps.

"Apologize to Merry," Jonty growled.

"I will not apologize for the truth."

"Merry didn't make you a whining bitch, Talan; you were always that." I saw Jonty plant his back foot.

Doyle motioned and Galen was moving me back. I didn't argue; if the two Red Caps were going to actually fight I didn't want to be standing less than ten feet behind them. Twenty feet would be about minimum safe distance. Galen seemed to agree with me, because he kept moving

me back until we were near where the fight had started at the practice
circle.

Only Aisling was left kneeling in the center of the circle. His hands
were held up to his face as he rocked forward, those glittering shoulders
hunched as if he huddled around some great pain. He was hurt, badly
hurt, because the warriors of faerie do not show pain unless it is too great
to bear.

Galen and I went hand in hand to him. There was blood in a spatter
of glittering crimson on the grass in front of him. He must have heard
us, because he folded in upon himself, burying his face against his knees.

"Aisling, how badly hurt are you?" Galen asked.

"Don't look at me!" He yelled it, voice high with fear and pain.

Galen dropped my hand and moved toward the other man. "Talan
couldn't have done anything to mar your beauty, Aisling, not without a
weapon. Even a Red Cap can't hit one of the sidhe that hard," Galen said,
and he put a note of joking in his voice.

Aisling's voice came muffled. "You're half right, Galen. He didn't mar
my beauty, but he hit me hard enough to do harm."

"Aisling, how hurt are you?" Galen touched one of those bare
shoulders.

Aisling screamed, and scuttled away on knees and one hand. "Don't
touch me! Goddess help me, don't touch my bare skin."

"True love is proof against your magic, Aisling. Let me see how hurt
you are; you will not bespell me."

Aisling thrust one hand back as if to ward off a blow, and the other
hand stayed at his face. I realized that he was covering his face, and that
I could see the complicated braids that held all that yellow and gold hair
tight to the back of his head. The mask that had been covering his hair
and his face was gone. A thrill of something close to fear went through
me from the bottoms of my feet to the top of my head. Galen might have
been sure that true love would protect him, but he was immortal, and I
wasn't. I knew that the immortal sidhe were not proof against Aisling's
power, but he wasn't allowed to show his face to any human, no matter

how in love they might be. Mortal blood just didn't protect against magic as well as immortal.

Galen reached out and grabbed Aisling's outflung hand. "Let me help you, Aisling." Galen's voice held pain; he could never stand to see someone so distressed without wanting to make it better.

Aisling's hand made a fist, and he went very still. "You are a good man, Galen; do not let me hurt you by accident."

"Let me see what is bleeding on you." Galen knelt beside the other man, his hand still holding his arm.

Aisling cried out and jerked free of him, crawling away from Galen, using both hands to scramble faster, and looked directly at me. He hadn't realized I was standing just behind them.

THIRTY-ONE

We had a long, frozen moment of staring at each other. I waited to be bespelled, but though his skin was what the sidhe called sun-kissed as mine was moonlit, and though his face, like the rest of him, seemed to be sprinkled with gold dust, still there were others in faerie whose skin was more beautiful to me. The blue of his eyes was the color of a late-spring sky, but then part of Rhys's eyes were a similar color. Aisling did have spirals in his eyes, as if someone had tattooed them on his irises, so that the spirals took attention away from the sky blue, but again there were others in faerie with more unusual eyes. I don't think I would have been so critical if I hadn't grown up being told he was so beautiful that to gaze upon his bare face was to fall in instant, irresistable lust, if not actual love. I tried to see the lines of his face and found him beautiful, but I thought Frost was fairer of face. Maybe I was prejudiced, but though Aisling was amazing, his was not the most amazing face I had ever seen. I had my father to compare him to, as well, and I still thought my father was one of the most handsome men I'd ever known. Maybe I was prejudiced, but then isn't that what love, all kinds of love, is supposed to do?

I smiled, and Aisling let out a wail of despair and hid his face behind both of his hands.

Galen said, "Merry."

I smiled at him, that face that I had loved since I was fourteen. "I'm fine."

Doyle called out, "Merry!"

I turned and watched that tall, dark body stride toward us. He was moving so fast that his long braid bounced and I could see the flash of it as he stepped. The torn white shirt looked like some prop in a strip club, artfully ripped to give glimpses of his chest and stomach. The sunlight glittered off the silver earrings in the high, graceful points of his ears and caught the glint of the nipple ring on the left side. I just watched him and enjoyed the view, and the fact that he was mine, and I was his.

I turned back to Aisling, who still had one hand held up in front of his lower face like some movie harem girl, so that only those blue eyes with their spiral shapes showed. I smiled at him, and he closed his eyes as if in pain. He raised his other hand and hid even his eyes from view.

I realized he was saying, "No, no, no," over and over again.

Doyle grabbed me and whirled me round to face him. He searched my face with nearly frantic eyes, and whatever he saw there calmed him, because he smiled. We wrapped our arms around each other and kissed. We kissed long and thoroughly, until I could wrap the sun-warmed feel of his body around me like a perfume made of flesh and warmth and love.

We broke the kiss and came away from each other's lips smiling. "I love you, my Merry."

"And I love you, my Darkness."

His smile widened, and he ran his hand along the edge of my hair. "Let us comfort our fallen man."

I nodded.

We went to him still holding hands. "Aisling," Doyle said, "Merry is not bespelled by you."

He just shook his head, hands still covering almost every bit of his face.

Doyle knelt beside him. "I saw your face when Talan struck you and ripped your mask off, and I was not bespelled either."

"You saw what happened to Melangell," he murmured through the shield of his hands.

Doyle touched his arm, and Aisling jerked away from the touch. Doyle touched him again.

"Don't touch me!"

Doyle grabbed both his upper arms and held him tight when the other man tried to flinch away. "Your skin is just skin to me, Aisling, no more or less beautiful than all the sidhe."

Aisling just kept shaking his head, hiding behind his hands, and whispering, "No, no, no."

I knelt beside Doyle and touched Aisling's shoulder. He tried to move away, but Doyle's grip was too firm. If he wanted to escape from Darkness he would have to fight.

I petted his shoulder the way you'd comfort a friend. "It's all right, Aisling; I've looked into your face and I'm not befuddled, I swear."

"Look at me," Doyle said.

"No."

"Aisling, look at me."

He lowered the one hand just enough to gaze over it at Doyle. "You have not harmed me, Aisling."

He closed his eyes and whispered, "You don't understand."

Doyle put a hand on either side of Aisling's face and gave him all the concentration out of those black eyes. "Drop your hands, Aisling, drop them."

Those spiral eyes were too wide, almost wild like a horse that is about to bolt, but he slowly let the other hand fall away. Doyle held his face between those two, big, dark hands and gazed directly into his face. "You do not have to hide from us, my friend."

I touched his arm and said, "You don't have to hide anymore, Aisling, not from us."

Aisling started to tremble, and then to shake as if he were freezing cold instead of kneeling in the warm sunshine. One single silver tear trailed down from the corner of his eye, and then another, until the tears seemed to be racing down his face. Doyle rose high on his knees and kissed him on the forehead.

Galen came to kneel on the other side of Doyle, and when he moved his hands from Aisling's face, Galen kissed his forehead, too. "You're safe," he said.

I hugged Aisling. "You are safe with us."

His shoulders started to shake, and then he started to cry almost hysterically. His arm came around me and around Galen on the other side, so that he held all three of us with Doyle in the middle, and we held each other and we held him, and let him cry.

The Red Caps and sidhe who had been about to have a fight all trooped back into the house quietly, faces averted for the most part. Only Jonty risked a look; he nodded at me, and I nodded back. We were left alone in the warm sunlight, with the smell of eucalyptus filling the dream of eternal summer with a crisp, healing scent. We laid everyone's discarded shirts underneath the shade of the big tree, so we wouldn't be lying on the scratchy, dry grass, and put Aisling in the center of us, so that we could all touch his bare upper body. We petted and stroked him, not as lovers do, but just to fill the terrible skin hunger that he'd had to deny for so long. Babies who don't get enough touch will fail to thrive and die, even if they are well fed and otherwise well cared for; touch is so much more important than most people want to admit.

We touched his back and shoulders at first, and then he rolled over and we ran our hands over his chest and stomach. The three of us gazed into the spiral of his eyes, traced his face with our fingertips. I got within inches of him until I could see that the black spiral lines were formed of tiny birds all flying out of his eyes. I remembered that moment in the dead gardens when his body seemed to have exploded into tiny song-birds. I traced the line of his cheek and said, "Have the spirals always been tiny birds?"

"Not in a very long time," he said, softly.

Galen peeked over the top of his head, so that he was staring at him upside down from inches away. "I don't remember them ever being tiny birds."

Aisling laughed, and it filled his face with a joy that I had never seen there; even behind his veil he had been a solemn man.

"It has been longer than your lifetime, Galen, since Aisling had birds in his eyes," Doyle said.

The happy glow faded around the edges, and then without looking at any of us, he said, "Would you unbind my hair and . . . touch it, please?"

I glanced at Doyle and Galen. They both nodded, and Galen smiled. We had Aisling sit up so that we could take out the pins that held all those small braids tight to his head. Even with three of us doing it, it took a while to undo all the braids. We ran our fingers through the gold and blond of his hair. It didn't shine with its own light the way Fenella's hair did, but it gleamed, catching every bit of light that filtered through the leaves above us.

His hair fell in ankle-length waves, thick and warm, not as soft as Galen's, or Frost's, or even Rhys's, closer to Doyle's texture. Aisling lay down on his stomach and let us pet and play with all that shining hair until we made a cloak of it fanning out around him.

He gave a deep, contented sigh and rose up on his elbows. "Some of the nobles of the Seelie Court contacted me. They offered me the throne."

"When?" Doyle asked.

"A few days ago."

"Why did you wait to tell us?" Galen asked.

"Because I thought you would cast me out, and I have nowhere left to go."

I smoothed his hair back, piling it into my lap like a pet, until I could see the side of his face. "I would not cast you out for the machinations of other nobles. You have no more control over the different factions within the courts than I do."

He glanced at me. "You aren't angry?"

"No," I said.

"You have two factions within the Seelie Court that want you on the throne."

"Sir Hugh's contingent and the king himself, but I know that there are Seelie nobles as there are Unseelie nobles who see me as unfit for either throne."

"They fear that your mortal blood will steal away their immortality as it did on the dueling grounds."

"I know that, and honestly for all I know they may be right."

Aisling looked at me, obviously surprised. "You're worried about it, too, then."

"Yes."

"Will you take the throne then?"

"The Goddess and faerie itself crowned Doyle and me as rulers of the Unseelie Court, but the Seelie sithen did not recognize me when I entered it."

"You were part of the wild hunt, Merry; you can't be queen of any court and lead the hunt," Doyle said.

"You mean ever?" I asked.

He smiled and shook his head. "No. When you ride with the hunt, especially if you are the huntsman, it is your only title. You lay the crown aside to lead it, and pick it back up only if you give up being the huntsman."

"You were the huntsman once, I remember you said so."

"I was, but not of the same wild hunt that you and Sholto led."

"I never saw more than one wild hunt and that was the sluagh," Galen said.

"As there were once many more faerie mounds, so with the wild hunts," Doyle said.

"I remember when Darkness led his own wild hunt and was the huntsman for our queen," Aisling said.

Doyle stroked a hand through the other man's hair. "You are older than I am, my friend; you would remember."

"What did you tell the nobles who offered to make you king?" I asked.

"I told them I would not betray you, or Doyle."

"What did they say to that?" I asked.

"They told me to think upon it before answering."

"If you want the throne, Aisling, take it," I said.

He looked startled. Doyle said, "Merry!"

I stroked the hair so gold and warm in my lap. "No, Doyle, you've seen how some of the Seelie nobles treat me. They've come here in hopes that I can help them get with child, and many of them still treat me like some mongrel. People follow you for only three reasons; love, fear, or loyalty. No one at the Seelie Court loves me, or fears me, and I'm not certain there's much loyalty to anything there except whatever, or whoever, will further their own pursuit of power."

"Lord Hugh wants a baby with his lady," Doyle said.

"But he also wants to be close to the throne, and if he put me on it, he would be," I said.

"There has never been a welcome for Merry and me at the Seelie Court," Galen said.

"Are you both serious that Merry should just give up the golden throne?" Doyle asked. He was looking from one to the other of us.

We both nodded. "Besides, Doyle, the Seelie sithen recognized Aisling when the Seelie first came to this country. Taranis exiled him; because of that his own sithen wanted to crown a new king. The sithen has already chosen Aisling as king; let it stand."

"What if the sithen has changed its mind after over two hundred years?" Aisling asked.

"Then you will be welcome back here in the Western Lands," I said.

"Aren't we forgetting something?" Galen said.

"What?" I asked.

"The king would have to be dead for Aisling to take this throne."

"That works for me," I said.

"Me, too," he said.

"Me, three," Doyle said.

"If I agree, it seems like a plot," Aisling said.

"I've wanted him dead since he took Merry," Galen said.

"Oh, yes," Doyle said.

"For hurting Merry I would happily slay him, too," Aisling said.

"If the sithen still wants you as its king, then be the king of the Seelie, Aisling. The sithens will let a hereditary monarchy rule, but the start of every lineage is chosen by each kingdom. I believe that when we stopped letting the land choose its own ruler, that was the beginning of our decline as a people."

"When the Irish stopped letting the great stone choose their kings, that was the beginning of their undoing, as well," Doyle said.

I stroked his arm, because I knew that his people had been among the Irish and he still felt for how much they'd suffered at the hands of the English, though I'd only learned his feelings on it in the last year. Doyle had been such a mystery, not just to me but to most of the court. He had been the captain of the guard, and the Queen's Darkness, her left hand, her assassin, but it was as if all that had kept him from having feelings, or being entirely real. In his own way, Doyle had been as lonely as Aisling.

"You would truly let me take the golden throne, when you could unite the two thrones of the sidhe for the first time in centuries?"

"It's a pretty thought that I could unite us, but I think there is too much fear and hatred between the Darkling throng and the golden one. Oh, Aisling, six of the noble houses declared themselves against me. I'm not certain I can safely rule even the Unseelie throne, but I know that the Seelie throne is too dangerous for me and the babies, and the men I love. I would not risk all that I hold dear for any throne, so be king if you can; the sithen has chosen you and that should stand."

He studied my face and finally said, "You really are the most extraordinary person, Merry."

"I am a practical person in this, or a selfish one. I do not wish to lose any more of the people I love, not just for power."

"That's right, you and Doyle both gave up the Unseelie crowns given to you by faerie itself to save Frost's life."

We smiled at each other, and we reached out at the same time to take each other's hands, which made us smile more. "What is more important than love?" Galen said.

We looked at him, and I held my other hand out to him. He took it with a smile. "Nothing," I said.

"I'll disagree," Aisling said.

We all looked down at him where he still lay propped up on his elbows. "What's more important than love?" I asked.

"Safety," he said.

We were all silent for a moment, and then we all nodded. "The power to keep that which you love safe," Doyle said.

"It always comes back to power," Aisling said. "It has to, because without power you can't protect what's yours."

"I can't argue with you," Galen said, "but damn, that was a mood killer."

We laughed, even Aisling. "You are charming, Green Knight."

"It's part of my magic."

Aisling looked up at him. "Truly?"

Galen nodded. "Apparently."

"To be charming in a friendly way, not a romantic way?" Aisling asked.

"Yes." He smiled, and shrugged. "I think it's what helped me not get killed in a duel years ago. People just liked me, even when I was a political disaster and didn't have enough powerful friends to protect me."

I drew Galen down to me so we could kiss, and said, "I'm so glad you're magically likable; I would have missed you."

He grinned. "I love you, our Merry."

"And I love you, too, my Galen."

"I'm jealous," Aisling said.

We all looked at him. He added hastily, "I don't mean of Merry in particular, but of your being in love, and being able to lie with a woman. I haven't dared break my long fast for fear of bespelling some poor woman."

"I guess it is ironic that to be safe to have sex with anyone, you'd need the woman to already be in love with someone else."

"Something like that," he said, and gave a half laugh, but it was more bitter than happy.

Doyle patted his back. "I'm sorry, my friend."

I remembered why I'd wanted to talk to Aisling. I told him about Bryluen's effect on Rita the nanny. He sat up, spilling his hair all around him, face serious as he listened. "It is highly unusual for one so young to exhibit such powers."

"So you didn't have to worry about hiding your face when you were a baby?"

"No, not until I reached my teens, and then the year that I grew six inches, my shoulders filled out, and I suddenly looked more my age, and that was the beginning of this. I thought I was just very good with women, and then I started attracting women I didn't want to attract, and we began to figure out what was wrong."

"Your power is the closest to what Bryluen is doing; can you see if you sense anything?" I asked.

"I will happily look at the baby, but I'm not sure what I can tell you; as I said, my powers didn't manifest until I was in my teens. It's very unusual that both your daughters would be displaying powers almost from birth."

"They are going to be very powerful," Doyle said.

"I believe you are right," Aisling said. He began to gather his hair back from us, and to braid it almost absentmindedly. "I will need a covering for my face before I go to the nursery."

We finally used the remains of Doyle's shirt to make a mask that went around his lower face and tied securely enough to make Aisling happy with it. He left his hair in two long, thick braids. It reminded me of the way Saraid had worn her hair, though his was longer and seemed thicker. I hadn't petted her hair, so I wasn't sure on the thickness. We walked toward the house with Doyle and Galen holding my hands. Galen held out his hand to Aisling. I couldn't be certain, but I thought he was smiling under the white mask when he took the offered hand. We walked four abreast out of the practice circle, and as soon as we left the magical spell that kept the reporters from seeing inside it, we heard a yell of, "Hey, Princess!"

I looked, and I knew better, but they'd have pictures of me with the three men wearing nothing but exercise shorts—well, pants for Aisling, but either way three mostly nude men and we were all holding hands. There'd be rumors about Galen and Aisling being more than friends soon, because no one in America could understand that men could hold hands and just be friends. I loved my country, but it was a weird culture when it came to touching.

CHAPTER

THIRTY-TWO

Aisling sat in the nursery rocking chair holding Bryluen. He'd gone
back to his room to change, so that he wore his usual gauzy veil
wrapped around his head; only his eyes showed bare to the world. The
veil was layers of nearly transparent gold cloth so that you could see that
all that hair was in multiple braids snugged tight to the back of his head.
He wore a silk T-shirt that was only a few shades lighter gold than the
veil, and then the dress slacks were a darker gold. Just seeing the outfit
let me know that Maeve had picked it out. She liked layers of gold and
cream. I'd have put him in blue to see if it would bring out the color in
his eyes. In the gold his eyes looked grayer than I knew they were.

I knew that Maeve was helping a lot of the sidhe shop for modern
clothes; one, because she enjoyed shopping, and two, because she would
often use the shopping trip as a way of getting to know them and seeing
if she wanted to sleep with them. That hadn't been an option with Aisling
for her, because Maeve was still grieving for her dead husband; that
would not keep her safe from his magic.

She stood across the nursery watching him as he rocked Bryluen. The
look on Maeve's face was speculative, and the look was enough; she
would have pursued him as a lover if she could have done it safely.

She caught me watching her, and smiled brilliantly at me. It was her public smile, beautiful, vibrantly sincere, and it was her version of a "blank cop face." She could hide any emotion behind that shining smile. I knew it, and she knew I knew it, so either she didn't care, or her emotions were so strong about Aisling that she couldn't hide it any better from me. Or maybe I just knew Maeve that well now?

Little Liam was playing near her feet, rolling a ball along the floor for the dogs to chase. The terriers chased it in a happy, barking, snarling pack. No dogs were allowed in the exercise room, so when Rhys was there his terriers had started coming to the nursery, or following Liam around, or Galen, or me. Minnie and Mungo, my own pair of greyhounds, were pressed to my side, so I could play with their ears and stroke their heads. They usually didn't press like this unless they sensed I was nervous. Why was I nervous? Because watching Aisling made me wonder if we were going to have to veil our daughter like Aisling. The thought of having to hide her sweet face from the world, so we could save the world from her, was somehow horribly sad.

Maeve came to me and touched my shoulder. "Your face, so sad; what did you just think to take the light from your eyes?"

I looked up at her and shook my head. How could I say in front of Aisling that the thought of Bryluen sharing his fate of having to hide his face for all his life seemed awful?

Maeve looked where I was looking and her eyes showed that maybe she knew me as well as I knew her now. She drew me into a hug and whispered, "We will not have to hide her cute little face."

I didn't so much return her hug as hold on to her. What was wrong with me today?

Aisling stood up with Bryluen in his arms and came to stand next to us. "Merry, why the tears? She is lovely and powerful, but no reason for such sorrow."

I heard myself saying my fears out loud, while the crying grew. Aisling helped Maeve hold me while I cried. Bryluen stared up at me with those big, solemn eyes and I realized that there were distinct lines in her irises; they were still blue, but it was as if someone had drawn faint lines that were dividing the color up. Was this how a tricolored iris started to change? I realized that I'd never seen a baby with triple irises. I was the last baby born to the sidhe in America, so I didn't know if Bryluen's eyes were just going to be blue with pale circles like Aisling's spirals of birds, or whether this was the beginning of her irises separating out into different colors. For some reason that made me cry harder, as if the fact that I didn't know what it meant for her eye color was just another symptom of me not knowing about her magical powers, or Gwenwyfar's for that matter. How was I supposed to raise them if I didn't know the answers?

Maeve took Bryluen and let Aisling hold me while I wept. It was close to the way he'd cried earlier in the garden, but there I'd had Doyle and Galen to help me comfort him; here a man who had never been my lover, or even a close friend, held me tight while I cried so hard my legs gave out and he was left holding all my weight as if I were fainting. Part of me knew it wasn't logical, and stood aside in a sort of horror that I would show such weakness to someone who didn't even love me, but the rest of me was consumed with a near-hysterical grief.

I just had no idea what I was grieving about.

THIRTY-THREE

Then there were other arms holding me from behind, helping Aisling hold me, and it was Galen, dressed and showered from practice. "Merry, what's wrong? What's happened?"

I shook my head, too lost in my hysterics to answer, and honestly I had no good answer.

Aisling was trying to explain when another set of arms reached in and took me from between both of them, lifting me so I could curl against his chest, as he held me. Doyle's hair was damp from the shower, loose of its braid so it could dry faster. I wrapped my arms around his neck and buried my face against his shoulder and neck. I breathed in the scent of his skin, the soap and shampoo and the fresh smell of the clean shirt, so that it all mingled together to make him smell so good and fresh and real, and . . . just the scent of him began to calm me, as if I could breathe easier when he held me close.

"Let us go visit our Killing Frost," he said in that deep, rumbling voice of his, that seemed to vibrate through my body as if the deep, thick sound of it could fill me up and leave no room for anything else.

He walked out of the room and down the hallway, moving effortlessly toward the room where Frost was still resting, healing from the last time Taranis had tried to kill my Darkness, or force him to kill us.

Taranis was mad, insane in a very real way; how do you keep yourself safe from someone who can enter your dreams and turn them into nightmares?

Doyle was so strong, and I felt so safe as he carried me down the hallway, but it was an illusion, because no matter how good you were with a sword or gun, or how much magic you had, death could still come, could still carry you away. I could not protect anyone, not really, and by that same thought, they couldn't protect me. Eventually, we all lost.

I kept my face buried against Doyle. I breathed in the scent of him, and didn't look up as he adjusted his hold on me and opened the door to our bedroom. He kicked the door closed behind us, and I heard Frost say, "What has happened now?"

What *had* happened now? It wasn't just me. We were all getting . . . battle fatigue, hadn't they called it once? Doyle started to explain what little he knew, and I just let their voices wash over me. It didn't matter, nothing mattered, because no matter how hard I tried, or what I did, I couldn't defeat all our enemies, I couldn't find us a safe haven in the midst of it all. Even here in the Western Lands, as far from my family as I could travel, they would not leave us in peace.

Doyle laid me on the bed between the two of them, my favoritest place in the world to be, and for once I felt nothing but a dim numbness, like trying to sense the world while wrapped carefully in cotton and put away somewhere so I wouldn't break.

Frost was above me, propped up on one arm. He touched my face, traced the still-wet track of my tears, and said, "Merry, our Merry, what has happened to make you weep so?"

I stared up into that heartbreakingly handsome face, those gray eyes, and I saw again that image that sometimes showed in them, like the inside of some magical miniature snow globe. It was a winter-barren tree on a hillside with snow all around it, but for the first time there was a mist of pink buds, the promise of blossoms to come. For no reason that I could name, the sight of that promising pink blush of life made me start to cry again.

I wept as if my heart would break and spill out of my eyes in shattered pieces on the sheets, and their hands tried to comfort me and save the pieces I was crying away. The light and the dark hands touching me, caressing, their voices saying all the things you say when the people you love are in pain. I started to yell at them, tell them that they were wrong, that it wouldn't be all right, that it would never be all right. I told them they were lying to themselves if they believed it would be all right. I screamed and cried and fought, and it wasn't them I was fighting, it was everything else, but as so often happens it's your nearest and dearest who take the brunt of your rage.

Arms found me that wouldn't let go, that held me so tight that I couldn't push them away or struggle free. I was pressed against a chest, held in arms so strong that it felt as if nothing could move them or tear them from me. Strength like that could have made me panic, but when Taranis had done what he did, he hadn't held me tight; the injury had done that for him. He was a man who didn't know how to hold on to anything, or anyone, but himself. The man who held me now knew how to hold and keep and protect, and I gave myself over to that strength. I collapsed into the dark solidity of his arms, my head pressed against his chest, arms limp at my sides as I let myself cry in a way I hadn't allowed myself yet. I cried until there were no more tears, and I felt empty like a seashell that held only echoes of what it had once been.

I ended up lying on top of him, my head on his chest so I could hear the sure beat of his heart, while one arm held me close and the other stroked my hair. Doyle's deep voice rumbled up through his chest as he whispered, "Merry, Merry, Merry."

The bed moved and I knew it was Frost; then his hand stroked my back, and he said, "I would do anything to take this pain from you."

I turned my head so that my other cheek lay on Doyle's chest while I looked at Frost. He lay on his side beside us, his hand still laid gently on me. Tears shone on his face, his eyes looking darker gray than usual like clouds before it rains, heavy and dark, or maybe that was just how I felt.

"I know that," I said, and my voice was still thick with tears.

He lay down beside Doyle, who moved his arm from holding me to let Frost slip into the circle of his arm, and put his arm across me and hold me against Doyle's body. Frost's head lay on Doyle's shoulder, one long leg going over Doyle's legs, so we lay entwined, the three of us. I loved seeing two such big, physical men hold each other, and hold me like this. It made me feel safer and more complete than anything ever had.

Yet even here with them, the fear wasn't gone. It was pushed back, but it was like a battle; being here with them meant I was safe and happy for now, but the next wave of invaders was coming. Maybe that was always true of life? I'd had a professor in college who said we were all temporarily able-bodied; at the time I hadn't understood, but I did now. Were we all just temporarily happy? Or were we all just temporarily sad? I guess it depended on how you looked at things.

I reached out and traced the tracks of tears on Frost's cheek. "Why are you crying?" I asked.

"Because you are, and I love you," he said.

I laid my hand against his cheek, and my hand was so small that I couldn't cover the whole side of his face even with my fingertips spread.

"I do not love you less because I do not cry," Doyle said.

I moved my head enough so I could see his face. "I know that," I said.

"We both know that," Frost said, and moved his head just enough so he could meet the other man's eyes, so that we were both gazing up at Doyle.

He looked down at both of us, from inches away, and suddenly he smiled bright and glorious in the darkness of his face. "I had given up such dreams as this."

"As what?" I asked.

He hugged both of us with the arm he had around each of us. "This, the two of you in my arms, gazing at me like that. It is more than I ever hoped to have again, one person to love and be loved by, but to have both of you is such riches as no man would ever expect in one lifetime."

I smiled at him, and I knew that Frost was, too, but I glanced to see that smile, those gray eyes gazing up at our tall, dark, and handsome man.

"I, too, had no thought of ever being this happy again," Frost said.

"I've never been this happy," I said.

They both looked at me. "Not even when you were in love with Grif-fin?" Frost asked.

"I wasn't in love with Griffin when my father made him my fiancé, but he was handsome and sidhe, and my father's choice."

"So it was a political coupling, not a love match?" Doyle asked.

I nodded, my chin resting on his chest.

"We all envied him," Frost said.

I turned to look at him. "You and the other guards talked about it?"

"No," he said, and seemed to think about it, and finally said, "I can only say, I envied him."

"I didn't think you even liked me," I said.

He smiled. "I will admit that it wasn't you, our Merry, but more any woman at that point, but when I saw you look at him with your face shining with love, then I envied him you."

I sighed. "I did grow to love him, but looking back at all of it I don't think he ever loved me. If he'd gotten me pregnant we would have married, and I'm not sure when I would have figured out how little he valued me."

Doyle raised his hand from my body to touch my hair, and Frost laid a kiss on my shoulder. "We love you," Frost said.

"I know that, and I love you, but it is true love, not some infatuation made up of sex and magic. It is loving you that's let me look back at his behavior and realize that he must never have truly loved me."

Frost laid his face against mine, and Doyle kissed the top of my head. Doyle lay back down and cuddled us both tighter in his arms. "Whatever comes, we can see it through together. For all the blessings that we have in our lives right now, there is nothing I would not do to defend us, and our children." He smiled again, that bright surprise of a smile.

"The babies are a wonder to me," Frost said, softly.

Doyle rose so that he could lay a quick kiss on his lips, and then I rose so he could share that kiss between us. "I've never been in love with someone I called friend before, Frost; it is everything we were as friends and now all this, and to be fathers together"—he hugged us again—"I am happier than I can remember."

Frost got that almost-shy smile that he only seemed to get when the three of us were alone, and it was usually from something that Doyle said, not me. I wasn't sure why it worked that way, but I knew it did.

He turned to me that pale handsome face, those serious gray eyes. "Whatever comes, Merry, we will face it together, with the other fathers at our side. Never has such might been joined in one purpose among us; we will prevail against all that stand against us. We can do this."

"How can you be so certain?" I asked.

He smiled. "Because such love as ours cannot be without purpose, and if it were wasted by death or tragedy this soon, it would be without purpose, and I do not believe the Goddess and the Consort so cruel as that."

The first pale, pink rose petal fell from empty air to land on Doyle's shoulder. A second joined it as I said, "I am sorry that I lost faith for a moment. I love you both more than I have words to say; you are my hearts, and I will not despair again if the two of you are with me." I touched Frost's face again and gazed into those eyes. "I am blessed by Goddess and the Consort in so many ways; how dare I give in to sorrow."

The petals kept falling, as if we were inside an invisible snow globe that was full of summer warmth instead of winter cold.

"The Goddess and Consort are with us, Merry, with us in a way that they have not been in centuries," Doyle said.

"But magic is returning to our enemies, too," I said, and I felt that hard knot in my stomach again. I realized that I was afraid of Taranis, truly afraid.

The rose petals began to slow, but the scent of a summer meadow with the wild roses sweet and thick-smelling in the heat was stronger.

"There is a purpose to that, as well, I think," Doyle said.

I knew he was right, so why couldn't I let go of my fear?

"In another few days I will be completely healed, and then the three of us can celebrate our happiness again," Frost said.

"Does it sound odd to say that I've missed you both terribly when we've spent most of the last year sleeping next to each other?" I asked.

"No," they said together, and then they laughed, a wonderful deep, shared masculine sound that I loved.

"You are meeting Sholto two days from now at the beach house, correct?" Doyle asked.

"Yes."

"Then it's our turn," Frost said.

I looked from one to the other of them, and felt a deep, happy shiver run through my body that finally spilled out enough to make me writhe.

Doyle laughed again, "Oh, don't do that again; my self-control is only so good."

Frost sat up, pulling away from us. "You and Merry can have sex now, and in a day or so we can all be together."

Doyle caught hold of his wrist and held him beside us. "No, my friend, we will break our fast together."

"You do not have to wait for me," Frost said.

"If I loved only Merry, then there would be no point to waiting, but I love you both, and that is worth waiting for," Doyle said. His face was fierce as he said it.

Frost gave that shy smile and then looked down, his silver hair spilling forward to hide his face. "You shall make me cry again, Darkness."

Doyle smiled, not fierce this time, but gentle. "That you both cry for love of me delights me."

We both looked at him, and I didn't have to see Frost's face to know we were giving our Darkness almost the same look from both our faces. We loved him. He loved us. I loved Frost. Frost loved me. It was all more wonderful than I had ever dreamed. Doyle was right; as long as we were together, nothing would stop us. I believed that, I honestly did, but . . . but I was still afraid. I was beginning to wonder if Dogmaela was right. Maybe I did need a therapist. My father had taken me to one as a child, because I'd had flashback nightmares about Aunt Andais drowning me, or trying to drown me. She'd done it because no sidhe could die by drowning. Her reasoning had been that if she could drown me, then I wasn't truly sidhe, and so I would be no loss. The therapist had helped me process it all; maybe the right one could help me again.

I gazed at the two men in my bed. They were worth fighting for, even if that fight was against the issues in my own head. I knew Maeve had seen someone after her husband died of cancer, and the therapist had helped her deal with the grief. I had everything I could ever want and more, but I felt like I was grieving something; maybe it was time to find out what.

I kissed them both, long and thoroughly, then went to find Maeve and apologize to Aisling for falling apart all over him. He would tell me not to worry about it, that it was his honor or something, but he wasn't my lover, or my love, so I'd apologize, because that level of care should come with love attached to it somewhere.

THIRTY-FOUR

The three of us, and then the five of us, talked for hours about everything that was worrying me. Doyle, Frost, Galen, Rhys, and Mistral had all had different points of view that helped me think and helped us all plan. Maeve had joined us in interviewing lesser fey for nanny duty. We thought we'd found some possible candidates. We'd done what we could to plan about the babies, especially about Bryluen's powers. Aisling had helped reassure us that we did not need to veil her; he said her power did not come from her face. So she was still a concern, but that particular fear was gone. We'd gone back to the days when I had no hand of power and kept bags of antinightmare herbs tucked into our pillows; so far either it was working, or Taranis had not tried to invade anyone else's dreams. It was odd that we really couldn't know if the herbs worked, only if they didn't. I realized that having real sidhe magic had made me arrogant like the rest of the nobles, and I'd thrown out almost all the anti-fey practices I'd used for years to keep me safer around my relatives. It seemed odd that I, of all people, would forget that there are so many more kinds of magic than just sidhe, but I had. I was part human and part lesser fey through my brownie heritage. I needed to remember all the parts of myself, not just one.

We planned, we talked to Sholto via mirror about our plans, and then two days later I was standing on a windswept beach waiting for him. One of his titles was Lord of That Which Passes Between, and that was why we were at the edge of the sea where the water met the sand in swirling, whooshing waves. The edge of the surf is one of the between places, neither dry land nor water, but both, and neither. The edge of a woods that bordered a meadow or a plowed field would probably be where he started, hundreds of miles away in Illinois, because that was a place that was neither wild nor tame, a place between. He was also able to control the recently dead, animating them until their bodies were well and truly dead, and he could call a taxi out of nowhere, or any kind of transport that spent its time going between places.

The wind was cold off the water—not winter cold, it was L.A., but still plenty cold as it whipped my short skirt around my thighs. I was happy for the thigh-high hose with their lace edges, because it was at least something between my legs and the wind. I was standing on the next-to-last step on the long stairs that led from the house on the cliff above to the pale sand. The high-heeled pumps would look awesome as I walked back up the stairs, but they weren't meant for protection from the elements. I'd dressed for cute and sexy, not standing beside the ocean in the early-morning chill. Even in June, Southern California could have mornings that felt more like Midwestern fall.

"Princess Meredith, please take my jacket." Becket, one of the human DSS guards, held out his suit jacket, which left most of his arsenal of weapons very visible against his white dress shirt. His tie was like a black stripe down his chest, held in place against the wind with a tie bar, so generic I wondered if it had come standard government issue. He was broad through the shoulders, and without the jacket on, the shirt sleeves seemed to strain just a touch over the muscles of his arms, which meant his jacket was going to be huge on me.

His partner, Cooper, said, "Let her have mine, Becket; yours will swallow her."

Cooper was a few inches taller, a few years younger, and a lot more slender. If I hadn't had so many sidhe to compare him to I'd have used words like *willowy* and *graceful* to describe Cooper, but he was only human, and that put more bulk on his thin frame, and meant that he'd never have the speed or dancing grace of the nonhuman guards. His hair was truly black, and he had the skin tone to match. Becket was one of those blonds with a ruddy complexion as if he'd burned years ago and never been able to get rid of all of it. He had his pale hair cut so close to his head that it was as if he had started to shave himself bald, but stopped most of the way through. Coop's hair was thick, and longer on top than any of the other diplomatic specialists assigned to us. I wondered if he put hair gel in it and went out to clubs in his spare time.

He helped me slip into the jacket. It was still warm from his body, and smelled faintly of nice aftershave. I was betting he fought to keep his hair long enough to style. I didn't blame him, but it was just interesting. He was also one of the few of the men who weren't married or in a serious relationship.

Becket and most of the others had been eager to have a diplomatic assignment in the States so they could be with their loved ones more. It was hard to maintain a relationship from halfway around the world, and usually in a place too dangerous to bring your family. Los Angeles was dangerous, but not in the same way as Pakistan.

"We really appreciate you asking for us this morning, Princess Meredith," Coop said.

"You're welcome, Agent Cooper, Agent Becket." I wrapped his jacket around me. It covered me to midcalf, as if I'd borrowed my father's coat to wear, but I was warmer, and that seemed more important than looking sexy, for now.

"Not to look a gift horse in the mouth," Becket said, "but why us?"

I smiled at him, because I'd already learned that he could never quite leave well enough alone. He had to ask that one more question, take that one more small chance. Cooper would never have asked.

"I saw you practicing with the other guards."

He looked embarrassed, rubbing his big blunt-fingered hands down his sides. "Yeah, that wasn't such a great idea."

"I told you that before we did it," Cooper said.

Becket shrugged those big shoulders. "Hey, how do we tell the princess here that we can take care of her, if we don't know how we stack up against her main guards?"

"That was the reasoning that made me agree to it," Cooper said, but he didn't look happy about it.

"You both acquitted yourselves well," I said.

"Acquitted ourselves well; if that means got our asses handed to us, then I'll agree," Becket said.

I laughed, and a distant flight of seagulls seemed to laugh back at me, as they arched their wings and let the wind carry them closer to us.

"Yeah, it was pretty embarrassing," Cooper said.

"Becket's turn of phrase was what made me laugh. You both did well in practice—Doyle said as much, and he never gives praise unless it's earned."

"Yeah, your . . . main . . . person," Becket stopped and looked across me at his partner.

Cooper said, "Captain Doyle is reserved about a lot of things when we're around."

"And by 'we,' he means humans," Becket said.

Cooper frowned at him. "I said what I meant, Beck."

Becket shrugged. "We're the odd people out here, Cooper. The princess knows that; why not say so?"

I smiled again and let the banter go on around me. Doyle hadn't liked me coming out to the beach house without him or Frost, but our shared man was still healing, and I'd felt that we needed to use the human guards more, at least the ones who had braved hand-to-hand practice with Doyle and the others. I had brought Saraid and Dogmaela with me, but they were inside the house. One of the other female guards needed a word with them. The shared abuse had made many of the guards more comfortable talking to each other, so I'd let them handle it. I'd also reminded Doyle that there were other sidhe guards at the beach house. We'd started putting anyone we weren't sure was entirely trustworthy here first. The main estate was building more rooms, but there were still more sidhe than rooms. The other sidhe had been very insulted that I'd come down to the beach with only the human guards, until I'd asked them if they thought humans were lesser beings, bearing in mind that I was part human. To that they'd said the only thing they could—"Of course not," which was a lie, but a political lie. When everybody knows it's a lie, it isn't like lying at all, just doing what I wanted them to do, and we could all live with that. The sidhe had been impressed that Becket and Cooper had joined practice at the main house. That the men had even tried to hold their own with the fey had earned them points with me and with Doyle. He'd said, "They aren't bad, and for humans they are really quite good." If Becket only knew what high praise that was from him, he'd have been happier about it.

"It's okay, Agent Cooper, you and the rest of the human guards are the outsiders at the house."

"See, told you so," Becket said.

"But it's not just because you're human, it's because you're new. We don't know you yet, and you don't know us; that makes you all the odd people out. There's a learning curve when new sidhe join the guards, too," I said.

"You usually give very good eye contact, but you're staring at the horizon while we're talking. What are you looking for, Princess Meredith?" Cooper asked.

"King Sholto."

"What?"

"You asked what I was looking for, and I answered the question."

"I thought his title was Lord Sholto," Becket said.

"He's the only sidhe noble with a different title in another court," I said.

"Is Lord, or King, Sholto coming in by boat?" Cooper asked.

"No," I said.

"Then why are you looking out at the ocean for him?"

"He is coming from the ocean, just not by boat," I said.

"Okay, I'll bite; if he's not coming by boat, how is he getting here?" Becket asked.

"He'll walk," I said.

"Princess, you don't do this often, but when you do, it's like pulling teeth to get you to answer a straight question."

I turned and looked at Cooper, and thought about it. "I'm sorry, you're right. I've spent the last few months with just other fey, and we aren't always known for straightforward information sharing."

Becket gave a snorting laugh. "That's an understatement."

"Becket," Cooper said, voice sharp.

"It's all right, Agent Cooper, truth is truth."

"All right, then if King Sholto isn't coming by boat, how is he going to walk here?"

"Magic," I said, and went back to staring at the edge of the water.

"Can you elaborate, please?"

I smiled, and thought about it. "Do you know what his title is as lord among the sidhe?"

"He's the Lord of That Which Passes Between," Cooper said.

"Exactly," I said.

"What does that mean, Princess?" Becket asked, and he sounded impatient now.

I sighed, and shivered for a minute even in the borrowed jacket. "The edge of sea and shore is a place between, which means he can use it to travel to me."

"You said he was going to walk; do you mean he's going to walk onto the beach like magic?" Cooper asked.

"Not *like* magic, it *is* magic."

"You mean literally 'oooh' magic?" Becket said, making a finger-waving gesture when he said "oooh."

"Exactly," I said, smiling. I liked Becket. He made me remember that I missed being around people who weren't sidhe, or fey, or familiar with the high courts. It was a more formal world, and I'd been surrounded by people who had lived in it for centuries, and it had made me lose some sense of myself that wasn't sidhe, or even brownie. I'd forgotten that being human could be fun, and that though I'd hated being exiled to Los Angeles without any way to interact with another sidhe, and losing all of faerie had been like a living death, I'd found a part of my humanity that had gotten lost at the Unseelie Court. I'd grown up with a house full of sidhe and other fey, but I'd gone to school with humans—American humans—and our neighbors had been the same. I hadn't realized until this last year that being raised outside faerie had given me more of a connection to my human grandfather's culture, and having the ambassador and his men in the house had made me realize I'd gotten sucked right back into the culture of the courts. It was a different culture than either the Seelie or Unseelie, but it was still not a human way of looking at things. The soldiers who had visited hadn't helped me understand that, because they'd come more as priests and priestesses seeking answers. That hadn't been normal enough to make me realize that I was in danger of losing something important. My human great-grandfather had been a good man, from every story I'd ever heard. He'd been a Scottish farmer who had been special enough to fall in love with the family brownie, not a type of fey known for their beauty. I didn't want to lose that part of my heritage again. I'd actually begun to wonder if I needed to work at the Grey and Hart Detective Agency just to remember that I was more than a faerie princess. I was a person, I was Merry Gentry, or had been for three years until the queen had sent Doyle to these Western Lands to find me and bring me home. Now I had sidhe lovers, and faerie had come to us. I had almost everything I'd been homesick for, plus three children, and the magic of the Goddess returned, but in all that wonder I didn't want to forget that I was part human, too, and part brownie. I wanted to find a way to honor all those parts of me, and share that with our children.

"You look very serious all of a sudden, Princess; what ya thinkin' about?"

I glanced at Becket and smiled. "That I'm part human, not just sidhe, and I need to be reminded of that."

"I don't understand," he said.

"Are you saying we remind you what it's like to be human?" Cooper asked.

"No, you remind me that I *am* human."

He gave me a look, one dark eyebrow rising. "Forgive me, princess, but you aren't exactly human."

"My great-grandfather was."

"And your grandfather is Uar the Cruel, one of the high nobles of the Seelie Court, who is mentioned in myth and folklore going back hundreds of years."

"My great-grandmother was a brownie."

"And your father was Essus, Prince of Flesh and Fire. He was worshipped as a god before the Romans conquered Britain."

"Agent Cooper, are you saying that the noble side of my heritage is more important than the non-noble side?"

He looked startled. "I wouldn't say that. I mean, I didn't . . . I didn't mean that."

"She so got you, Coop," Becket said.

"I didn't mean to insult you, Princess, but you can't just say you're human with the pedigree you have."

"I didn't say I'm just human, but I'm not just sidhe either, and I want my children to understand that they're more than just sidhe. Through me they're brownie, and through Galen they're pixie, and Doyle gives them phouka. I want them to understand that they are more than just sidhe of either court. I want them to value all parts of their heritage."

"It sounds like you've been thinking about this," Cooper said.

I nodded. "For a few days, yes."

"So you want your kids to grow up being more human?" Becket asked.

"Yes," I said. A shimmering caught my eye at the edge of the sea. One moment it was just the waves and the sand, and the next Sholto just stepped out of nowhere and started walking up the beach toward us.

"Holy shit!" Becket said.

Cooper had started to reach for his gun, and then forced himself to relax, or at least pretend.

The wind caught Sholto's hair, streaming it out around him in a pale blond halo that intermingled with the black of his cloak, so that he strode toward me in a cloud of silken hair and dark cloth. The three yellow rings of his eyes had already begun to shine as if they were carved of gold, citrine, and topaz. It almost distracted from the beauty of his face, the broad shoulders, the sheer physicality of him as he strode toward me.

"You can try to be human, Princess, but that's not human," Becket said.

"Oh, Agent Becket, you have no idea how not human he is." Then Sholto was there, sweeping me into his arms, kissing me as if he hadn't seen me in months, instead of just days. I wrapped myself around him, and he put his hands under my ass and started up the stairs, his mouth still married to mine. He climbed smoothly, easily, as if he could keep kissing me forever, whether he was climbing a set of stairs, or a mountain.

Becket called after us, "I don't know, Princess, I think the glowing eyes give it away."

I broke from the kissing long enough to look over Sholto's shoulder and let the men see that my own eyes had started to burn.

They looked startled, but it didn't stop Becket from saying, "Humans don't glow, just so you know."

I might have said something pithy back, but Sholto ran his hand through my hair and kissed me again, and nothing seemed more important than giving all my attention to the man in my arms.

CHAPTER

THIRTY-FIVE

We passed the sidhe in a hurried rush. Some of them looked astonished, others . . . *hungry* was the only word I had for it. They all watched us pass, though; Unseelie culture didn't demand that they look away. In fact, in all fey culture, if someone was trying to be attractive or sexy and you didn't pay attention, it was an insult; no one insulted us.

Sholto and I made it to the bedroom before the clothes began to come off, but barely. In fey culture we could have been nude in front of the guards and it would have been taken in stride. Nudity taboos were more human, and both the Seelie and Unseelie courts were closer to the rest of the fey; nudity meant just without clothes on, neither good nor bad.

I did toss Cooper's jacket off to one side so it wouldn't be in danger of getting messy. If I'd been thinking more clearly I'd have thrown it back to him before we got to the bedroom, but I wasn't thinking clearly about anything. It was all hands, and mouths, and the weight of Sholto above me as he pressed me to the bed. It wasn't a time for thinking, it was a time for feeling his smooth skin under my fingertips, his muscles under my hands, him pulling my top over my head in one eager motion so he could stare down at my breasts in the lacy bra I'd chosen for him.

"Your breasts were magnificent before, but now they are beyond amazing," he said in a voice that was low and almost hushed, the way people talk in museums around works of art.

"Hopefully they won't stay this big," I said, gazing down at more mounding creamy goodness than I'd ever thought possible on my own body.

He shook his head, all that pale hair sliding around the blackness of his clothes. "No, Meredith, they are beautiful, you are beautiful."

"I'm just not used to them this big. I pass a mirror and it startles me. The belly is gone, but the breasts are still out to here." I laughed.

He drew his gaze up to look into my eyes. The glow in his eyes was just a faint shine now, like a fire banked for the night, hot just near the center of the wood.

"Whether your breasts stay this magnificent size, or become the beautiful, pale mounds that they were, they, and you, will still be as desirable."

I hadn't realized until that moment just how much the body changes were still bothering me. You want to be able to breast-feed, especially when you have a baby like Bryluen who might not be able to take formula. I'd expressed milk for her before I came on this little booty call. The others could have formula in a pinch, but Bree couldn't. It wasn't all natural, and only that was safe for her.

"Such a serious face, Meredith; what are you thinking about that steals the light from your eyes?"

I sighed. "The babies, Bryluen in particular." I looked up at him, touching his arms where they were tented on each side of my body, while the rest of him sat sideways on the bed, most of his long legs still off the side of it.

"I'm sorry, Sholto, you deserve better than a distracted me. Would it be odd to say, this is the longest I've been away from the triplets, and I'm both excited for the time away and weirdly missing them. That doesn't make any sense at all, does it?"

He smiled, and it was gentle. I wondered if I was the only one who got to see that particular smile. "It means you will be a good mother, are

a good mother. You are, what's the phrase, wired right for motherhood."
He suddenly looked very serious, almost sad.

I stroked my hands up and down his bare arms; he'd taken off his
near-medieval-looking tunic but was still wearing a very modern black
undershirt. It was one of those designed more for working out than just
wearing, but the stretchable material fitted his muscular upper body like
a glove, tucked into the top of black breeches that matched the tunic that
was now on the floor.

"Now why is your face all serious?" I asked.

He looked at me, smiling, but it was tinged with something not
happy. "To another female in my bed I might lie, but that is not our rule."

"No," I said, "honesty between us, always."

"As my queen commands," he said, smiling more now.

I smiled back. "As my king requests," I said.

We smiled at each other with that special happy softness that couples
have when they use one of their endearments that they use with no one
else.

"Then I will speak honestly to my queen. I had feared that perhaps
you would not be wired to be a mother."

I studied his face, trying to read more of his thoughts. "Why would
you think that?"

"Your own mother is not the most maternal of women. Your aunt
was devoted to her son, but cruel and horrible to almost everyone else.
Your uncle, the king, is little better. Your grandfather is Uar the Cruel."
He shrugged, and raised a hand so he could take my hand in his.

"You were worried that my family is mostly crazy, so would I be
crazier than I seem, too?"

He began to rub his thumb over my knuckles. "Have I said too much
honesty to you, my queen?"

I smiled up at him and squeezed his hand. "No, I was thinking the
very same thing earlier this week, but not about me, about the babies."

I sat up and shared my fears with him. It might have been more logical to share them with Doyle, or Frost, or one of the fathers who actually
lived with me, but sometimes it's not about logic in relationships, it's

about the people, and in that moment Sholto gave me an opening to talk that no other man in my life had managed. I'd noticed that it worked that way a lot; the man you thought would be perfect for this or that wasn't always the one who worked best for it.

He wrapped his arms around me, pressed me to the slickness of the modern undershirt, my hands trailing a little lower as I hugged him back, so I felt the nearly velvet texture of his leather trousers, still tucked into the knee-high boots. I pressed the side of my face against the firm strength of his chest. I could hear his heartbeat against my cheek. It was a good, steady sound, the kind of sound you could plan your life around if you were looking for a center to your world. Sometimes I felt I had too many centers to my world, and the triplets had just amplified the sense of too many people pulling me in too many directions.

His voice vibrated up through his chest against my face as we held each other. "Your idea of raising them with more non-sidhe and humans is sound, and they will already be visiting my court. That will certainly expose them to a wider world of faerie than the high courts can offer."

I leaned back enough to see his face, sorry that I couldn't keep the beat of his heart in my ear, but my desire to see his face was greater.

"In a few days, or weeks, we'll know which of the babies is yours; don't you mean that child will visit your court?"

He looked down at me, his face arrogant and almost heartrendingly handsome. It was the face he wore when he was hiding his emotions. Why did he feel that he needed to hide from me about this?

"Do you want only my genetic child to visit the sluagh?"

"No, I want them all to understand just how diverse their world is, but I hadn't talked to you about it, and I didn't want to assume."

Some tension went out of his arms, his shoulders, and that release traveled through my arms, where I held him. His face went from arrogant and model perfect to smiling broadly at me. He looked so joyous that it made me smile back.

"Only one babe may be mine genetically, but they are all a part of you, Meredith, and I love you." He touched my lips with a fingertip, as if

I'd made some motion to speak. "I know you are not in love with me, nor I with you, not yet, but I do love you more than any woman before you."

I kissed his hand and used mine to move him so I could speak. "I am honored to have such a place in your heart, Sholto."

"This sounds like the beginning of a 'let's just be friends' speech."

I laughed then, and he looked puzzled.

"Oh, Sholto, no, I do not want to friendzone you. I love what we have together. I love that we do things in the bedroom that no one else can do with me, because no one else has the diversity of your equipment."

He laughed then, joyous and somehow masculine, that sound. I liked the tones of men laughing when they were happy enough not to worry how it sounded, or who heard them. Good that I did, since I was likely to be surrounded by men for the rest of my days.

"That you list my extras as part of what you love about me makes me love you even more."

"Good, because I love that you want to take all the babies to see your kingdom. I love that you spend more time in the nursery helping with them than half the other men, even though you don't live at the house all the time. I love watching your face when we're alone and how many different expressions I get to see that I'd never seen at court, or when other people are with us. I love the look on your face when you hold the babies. I love how your arms feel when you hold me, and the sound of your heart when I press my cheek against your chest."

"And this would be when Rhys or Galen says, 'But you aren't in love with me.'"

"But you aren't in love with me, either," I said.

"True," he said, and he pulled me close again. "And they are, and it is always hard to love more than you are loved."

I snuggled up against his body and said, "That sounds like experience talking."

"It is. I had many a serious crush on noble ladies of both courts, but I was the Queen's Perverse Creature, as Doyle was her Darkness, and Frost her Killing Frost. I feared someday that she would say, 'Where is my Creature, bring me my Creature,' when she wanted to send the sluagh out to frighten or kill her enemies." He held me tight and said, "Before you came to me, Meredith, I feared I would simply become the Queen's Creature."

"Doyle is the Queen's Darkness," I said, softly.

"Yes, but it is frightening and romantic for the Queen to say, 'Where is my Darkness, bring me my Darkness,' and someone would bleed or die at his hand."

"You and your host have made men lose their minds at the sight of all of you in full strength, and bled many, killed many."

"What is that old children's rhyme, 'Sticks and stones may break my bones, but words will never hurt me'? Anyone who says that doesn't understand the power of words. They can cut deeper than any knife, hit harder than any fist, touch parts of you that nothing physical will ever reach, and the wounds that some words leave never heal, because each time the word is thrown at you, labeled on you, you bleed afresh from it. It's more like a whip that cuts every time, until you feel it must flay the very skin from your bones, and yet outwardly there is no wound to show the world, so they think you are not hurt, when inside part of you dies every time."

I hugged him as tight as I could. "I love you, Sholto, King of the Sluagh, Lord of That Which Passes Between, Lord of Shadows, I love all of you, and would not have you any other way than you are."

"Oh, Meredith, Meredith, Meredith, I do love you more and more."

"I cannot offer you to make love yet, but I want to touch and be touched by you. I want to feel all those wonderful extras do the amazing things that only you can do. I want all of you, touching as much of me as possible."

The shine in his tri-gold eyes brightened as if someone had set a match, and the golden-yellow flame was coming alive again. "Whatever my queen desires," he said, and took me in his arms again, but this time the skintight shirt wasn't flat against his body. Bumps and bulges stretched the fabric and began to move, pulsing and writhing under the shirt. It was still tucked into his pants so they couldn't escape, and then the edge of the shirt appeared from his pants, and I realized that his extras were pulling the shirt loose from the inside. The first tentacle peeked out of the cloth, wriggling free like a snake spilled out of a bag. Once analogies like snakes in a bag had frightened me, made me not want to touch Sholto. Now, just the sight of the tentacles beginning to appear at the edge of his shirt and pants tightened things low in my body, anticipating the pleasure to come.

He let the thinner, lower tentacles roll the shirt up slowly, exposing his stomach below the belly button, which was smooth and showed that he'd been working out with the rest of my warriors, but above that round indentation that I'd licked more times than I could count now was the first fringe of thin tentacles that were as pearl white as the rest of his skin, but with darker red tips. I knew that those tips had tiny, delicate suction cups on them. The thought of what Sholto could do with them made me shiver with anticipation.

The shirt rolled up a little more to reveal the first grouping of longer, thinner tentacles that grew in groupings around his ribs and upper stom- ach. I knew that they were a hundred times more sensitive and flexible than any fingers. They helped roll the shirt up, but it was the larger, heavier tentacles at the far edge of his chest that did most of the lifting. The medium tentacles rolled the cloth, while the thicker ones lifted that roll upward, until they themselves were revealed in all their glory, thick and white with a marbling of gold along their lengths. They sat just below his nipples, thick and heavy like leprosy-pale pythons, except they stretched and grew in size more like other body parts that were very sidhe, very human male. Once the tentacles had always been this real, and only his ability to use glamour and illusion had hidden them, but now unless he willed it they were like a very realistic tattoo. The Goddess and God, returning their grace to us, had manifested for each of us according to what we most needed, or what was most useful to them.

"The look on your face as I revealed them, Meredith, it is a look I have waited all my life to see on another sidhe's face."

I reached out, and one of the thickest tentacles wrapped around my hand and wrist. The image may have brought snakes to mind, but these felt almost rubbery, like petting a dolphin, except not wet. I squeezed where the tentacle wrapped around my hand, holding "hands."

"Now that you have the tattoo you might be able to find another sidhe lover," I said, gazing down the length of the undulating tentacles, like a bed of exotic sea creatures waving in the current, except this current was his body, his muscles, his thoughts.

"But they would only love me with the tattoo in place hiding my extras." He ran his hands through both sides of the graceful movements of those other body parts.

My gaze followed his hands down through all that potential until he came to the band of his pants, where he caressed his hands over the only bulge that was still hidden behind cloth. I let out a shuddering sigh, because I knew that the promise of that bulge was everything a woman could want.

"The heat in your eyes never flinches, just sharpens as you see things you like more, but there is nothing on me that you do not enjoy in some way." He started drawing me closer with the tentacle I was holding "hands" with.

I half crawled and half let him pull me across the bed toward him where he stood beside it. My heart was racing, my body already wet, though right now that was a mixed blessing, a messy mixed blessing.

"I am so sorry that I had any issues at first," I said.

He smiled and wrapped another tentacle around my other wrist. He wasn't holding hands this time; he wrapped around my wrist like a rope, or a chain made of muscle and skin. The one I'd been holding twisted in my grip and he suddenly had both my wrists bound. It caught my breath in my throat, sped my pulse even more.

"Just as I need someone who sees all of me as desirable, you need bondage."

"We can't be rough yet," I said, but my voice was already lower, almost choked, just from him holding my arms out to my sides, and feeling the unbelievable strength as he held me. I knew I couldn't get away if he didn't want me to, and that was part of the thrill, but I also knew that if I asked he would let me go instantly, and that was one of the reasons I trusted him to do bondage with me. It was all about trust and desire, and understanding yourself and your lover.

"I'll never be rough compared to Mistral, but you wouldn't want that rough every night." He pulled me over the bed, my body sliding helplessly toward him. There was nothing I could do to stop that muscled strength. Luckily I didn't want to escape; I so wanted to be caught.

He smiled, and it filled his eyes with that darkness that wasn't fey, or human, but just male. It made me shiver, but not with fear.

"No," I whispered.

"How long has it been since you had any bondage?" he asked, pulling me close enough that some of the smaller tentacles could trace across my skin in teasing lines.

"You know how long," I said, my voice a little hoarse.

"Do I? As you said, I don't live with the rest of you; how do I know what you are doing?" He made it light, teasing, but sometimes when we tease there is a truth to it.

"Do you want to live with us?"

"It is not want, Meredith. I cannot leave my kingdom and move to yours." He forced my hands straight out to my sides, until it was almost uncomfortable. His tentacles stretched effortlessly outward to hold me, while the smaller ones traced teasing lines, careful not to go inside my bra or panties.

I found my voice and said, "I have no kingdom of my own."

"Perhaps not, but you have a court of faerie, and more magic gathers to you every day."

I didn't know what to say to that, so I said nothing and just gave myself over to the sensation of him touching me, and being held so terribly, wonderfully tight. I began to pull. I knew I couldn't break his grip by just struggling, but sometimes struggling is the best part, or the best part until the man pins you and makes the struggling impossible.

I closed my eyes and pulled harder.

"You can't get away," he said, voice full of that arrogance that big, athletic men can have.

"I know," I said.

"Then why try?"

I opened my eyes and let him see that my eyes had started to shine, just from this. "Because I like to struggle, and you like to feel me struggle."

"True," he said, and it was almost a whisper. One of the thinner tentacles trailed the edge of my bra, and another the band of my panties.

"Please," I whispered.

"Please what?" he asked, but the look on his face said he knew exactly what I wanted.

But I played the game and said, "Slide inside my bra and panties, touch me, suck me, make me come."

"And what do I get out of it?"

"I'll return the favor," I said.

He grinned, and then it turned into a smile that was full of as much lust and eagerness as anyone could have wished for, and I did wish for it.

"Ladies first," he said.

It took me a second to realize what he meant, and then he slipped those long, thin pieces of himself inside my clothing and began to caress and tease along my breasts, and at the top edge of my panties, not really sliding inside them, but only playing just inside the band, when I knew he could go so much farther down.

He began to suck on my breasts, a small suction "mouth" wrapping around my nipples. Other parts of him slid a little farther inside my panties, tickling and caressing and finally sliding lower to tease, caress, and begin to bring that near-magical pleasure that usually takes someone's mouth, but Goddess had shaped Sholto so that his mouth could be kissing mine, while other parts of him kissed me, so much lower down.

He drew back from my lips, his eyes glowing brighter, the circle of yellow around his pupil beginning to glitter like molten gold, the amber circle gleaming, and that last circle of pale yellow like elm leaves in autumn shimmering in rich, golden sunlight. His hair spread out around him like a cloak of new snow with just a hint of yellow, like snow reflecting the light of the rising sun. His skin began to blaze as if the moon were rising inside him to shine a cold, cool light that played out the tips of the smallest tentacles like shining rubies, and the largest ones that held me so tight were marbled with colored lightning, soft red, softer violet, bands of gold like the colors of his eyes. He was a thing carved of light, and color, and magic. It vibrated down his body, so that his skin hummed against mine, and the weight of pleasure began to build between my legs, and my breasts. It quickened my breath, and those shining ruby tips sucked harder, deeper, and that heaviness between my legs burst into pleasure and power, spilling through my body in a wash of light that decorated the room in the twin shines of our moon-bright skin, and when I threw my head back to scream my orgasm, my hair shone like spun rubies and garnets woven in cool fire across my face.

He didn't stop with my screams of pleasure, but kept sucking, stroking, until one orgasm followed another, and I could see the spark of power from my own eyes like emerald and melting gold, until I was blinded by the colored fire of my own magic.

Sholto brought me until I was a quivering, shaking thing, and only the pull of his body held me upright. He laid me down on my side, on the bed. I lay there shivering with happy aftershocks, my eyelids quivering so hard that I couldn't open my eyes and was literally blind with pleasure.

I sensed the bed moving like a distant thought, but I couldn't think what it might mean. I couldn't do anything but lie there and let the aftershocks of pleasure have their way with me. The light in my eyes and hair had faded enough that I could see the colors of the actual room in bits and pieces, when a hand smoothed my hair back from my face. I blinked and tried to focus, to see; I knew it was Sholto, but in that instant he was a pale blur of movement and colors seen through the fluttering of my eyelids.

He leaned in and kissed me, soft, but there was still magic in him, so that the kiss vibrated and tickled across my lips. It brought a soft moan from me, and then he lifted my head and put a pillow ever so gently underneath. He stroked fingers down my cheek, and I was able to turn toward his touch. Parts of me were beginning to work again, but the languorous edge of orgasm still held most of me delightfully immobile.

He ran a fingertip across my lower lip, and I opened my mouth. I wasn't sure if I meant to kiss him or just to touch more of him, but he took it as invitation, finger sliding between my lips. I closed my mouth around him, and the movement was so much like sucking on other things that it was almost a shock to feel the bone and hardness of finger, when part of me had already started to think about other, bigger things that had no bones, but only round, solid, flesh.

He pulled his finger almost out of my mouth and then slid it back in until his knuckle met my mouth, and then he pulled out again, and began to slide in and out, and then two fingers for me to suck and lick, and then three. He had to be careful with his fingernails not to cut me as he began to plunge his fingers in faster, and then four and he couldn't go in deep now, because he was too wide and the fingernails were harder to be careful with. I rolled my eyes up to him, and found him nude and eager. The tentacles were like a dream painted across his skin, a tattoo of exquisite detail, but his body was lean and solid, and human looking. I'd asked before, so I knew that the tentacles got in the way of his view when I was in certain positions, and he liked to watch me while we made love.

Now he knelt above me, his body as muscled and sculpted as any sidhe in my bed. He folded his thumb in with his fingers and shoved all of it into my mouth. I opened as wide as I could, and still he could only push in to the second knuckle of his hand; there was just no way to go deeper when he was that wide. He started to back out, but I grabbed his wrist and urged him to push in farther. His eyes widened, but he didn't argue, just kept pushing his hand into my mouth, pushed, pushed, until my mouth was impossibly wide and it was uncomfortable, but there was something about that discomfort that I enjoyed. He finally shoved his hand as hard and far into my mouth as he'd ever gotten it, and I finally had to tap his arm and let him know that I was done, I could take no more.

He drew his hand carefully out of my mouth, and before I could completely catch my breath, the hand that had been so deep in my mouth was wrapped around that long, solid, quiveringly eager part of him, and the rounded head was against my lips like an invitation.

I opened my mouth for him, because after that much of his fist inside me, I wanted as much of the rest of him inside me as possible. I mounded the pillow up so that my mouth was like an offering to that long, hard piece of him. It felt so much better than just fingers; it seemed to complete something in me to feel him slide between my lips, across my tongue, and then not too deep, before he pulled out, but I grabbed his ass and started pushing him in and out faster and harder than he and I usually preferred, but Sholto had said it earlier—it had been a long time for me. Months of not daring to risk an orgasm throwing me into labor, months of having to be so careful, so safe. I didn't want to be either today.

He followed my urgings and begin to slide himself deep into my throat, pushing until he buried himself as deep against my mouth as he could, and I had to fight my body, force my throat to relax around all that hard flesh. I urged him on with my hands on his body, with the shining that began in my skin and eyes, that set my hair blazing like spun rubies around the edges of my vision. The tattoo across the moonlit white of his skin glowed with the colors I'd seen on them so that his human shape ran with colors in a pale rainbow play of red, violet, shades of gold that mirrored his eyes that stared down at me as he plunged himself fast and faster into my mouth and down my throat.

I began to have to time my breathing for the top of his stroke, grab a quick breath and then he was down, plunging inside me, gagging me almost, and then pushing past even that, cutting off my air. He found a rhythm that was deep and slow, which gave me more time to breathe at the top of his stroke, but also meant he was deeper, longer down my throat, so that I began to have to fight my body not to panic at the lack of air, and even that filled a need, so that I wrapped my hands around the tightness of his ass and held him tight with him plunged so deep inside me that my mouth was sealed against the front of his body and I fought my body not to gag, not to panic, as it asked to breathe, and all the time our bodies shone bright and brighter, painting the room in shadows and light.

He vibrated across my tongue, down my throat so that the deep, plunging thrum of him seemed to calm the panic and just make me want to hold him inside me as long as I could. Then between one downstroke and the next, the orgasm hit me, one made up of the feel of him inside my mouth; all that thick, vibrating flesh brought me almost as if he had been shoved between my legs. It made me set my nails into his body as my body writhed around him; when he drew out enough for me to breathe, I screamed my orgasm around him.

He cried out above me, and then he shoved himself down my throat one last time. I felt the involuntary movement as his body pulsed and he spilled himself down my throat so far back I couldn't taste him but only felt the sensation of warmth. So far down that I didn't so much swallow as he poured himself down my throat, while I rode my own orgasm, nails digging into his ass, the rest of my body almost convulsing around him, helpless and eager for him.

When he was done, he drew himself out enough for me to breathe in a gasping rush of air. He collapsed over me on all fours, arms on the other side of my head and the pillow I rested on. His head hung down, his hair spilled around us both like a shining, silken tent. He pulled himself out of my mouth as I let my head roll farther down the pillow.

He found his words first and said in a voice that was still breathless with effort, "Oh, my God and Goddess, that was amazing."

"Yes," I said, "yes, it was."

He moved his head enough so we could look at each other, so he was looking at me almost upside down as he said, "I love you, Meredith."

I smiled up at him and said the only answer there ever was for such a moment: "I love you, too, Sholto." Rhys and Galen would argue that I didn't love them as much as I loved Doyle and Frost, and that was true, but in moments like this I did love the man I was with, maybe not always in the way he would wish, or want, but it was true: still real, still love.

Sholto moved so that he could lie beside me. I curled into the mound of his chest, the curve of his arm, the hollow of his shoulder, and was content.

THIRTY-SIX

We slept, and I dreamed, but I wasn't alone in this dream. Sholto walked beside me, his bigger hand clasped in mine. We had to hold hands, because the rose vine tattoos on our forearms were real again, alive again, binding us together with the vine that moved like something much more alive than any normal rose. Its thorns bit into our flesh, and bound us with flesh and blood and life. Sholto was crowned once more with a wreath of living herbs and tiny white, pink, and lavender flowers. I felt the crown on my own hair and knew it was mistletoe and white roses. I was dressed in a flowing white dress, and Sholto in white tunic and breeches, tucked into silver-gray boots. I wondered, *Why am I still barefoot?*, and between one step and the next I felt flat sandals on my feet. Apparently, I'd just needed to ask.

"Meredith," Sholto said softly, "where are we?"

We stood in the middle of a flat plain with short, scrubby grass and harsh, dry weeds. The ground that showed between the plants was pale and dry tannish brown; there wasn't much water on this ground, but it wasn't the barren sand and rock I'd seen before. In fact, when I looked up there was a small house in the distance. It looked old and weather-beaten, but "normal," or maybe *American Midwest* was a better phrase.

"There's a road with power lines behind us," Sholto said.

I glanced back and found he was correct. It was drier and more desolate, but it felt like Midwestern farmland, and indeed there were distant houses scattered around more cultivated fields. The land around this house was barren and the barn near it was literally falling down around the wrecks of farm equipment peeking out from the vines that seemed to be both destroying the wood and holding it together.

"I think we're somewhere in the United States, maybe the Midwest, but it's drier than Missouri or Illinois, different vegetation, too."

"I thought you only appeared in the desert where your soldiers were fighting."

"I did, until now," I said. The sun was bright overhead. If a car came down the road we'd be exposed to view. Up to this point only the soldiers and those fighting with them had been able to see me, as far as I knew, but someone getting pictures with their phone of us standing here like this would be on the Internet in minutes. I pushed the thought away and tried to "feel" who had called me, us, and why? Always before, people's lives had been in danger. What was dangerous here, and who was in danger?

"I thought only you traveled in dream at the Goddess's bidding?" Sholto said.

"That was true, until now." I stared at the house with its ramshackle barn. I thought that was our goal, but I wasn't sure. Appearing here and not in some faraway country had thrown me, and having Sholto with me like this puzzled me more.

"I am the first of your men that the Goddess has drawn with you?" he asked.

"Yes," I said.

He smiled then, and said, "I am honored." The scent of herbs and roses grew stronger as if we walked in a garden surrounded by a bank of wild roses, instead of the barren yard that smelled of sunbaked grass and some bitter weed baking in the heat. It wasn't as hot as some of the deserts I'd been in, but it was still much hotter than Los Angeles.

I smiled at the fact that he was happy to be with me even here, not knowing why, or where. I squeezed his hand a little tighter, which made the vines squeeze a little tighter as if they were happy with us. It should have hurt, but it didn't; as before when we were handfasted by Goddess, it was more pressure than anything, though the blood dripped a little more. The dry ground soaked up the blood eagerly; moisture was moisture to the earth and plants.

"Why are we joined as a couple?"

"I don't know," I said, softly; we weren't whispering, but our voices were hushed the way you did in human churches sometimes, as if you knew God was near.

"Does your crown always manifest in dream and vision?"

"No, almost never."

"Is your soldier in the house?"

"I think so," I said, but I was . . . distracted and puzzled that Sholto had come with me. I'd been asleep and touching a lot of the other men, but they'd never been transported with me. Why Sholto? Why now? Why in our "wedding" finery? I tried to let the questions go so I could hear Goddess's message. If you let your thoughts get too loud, then you can't hear God, or Goddess.

I took in a deep breath, closed my eyes, and stilled my thoughts, but the warmth and solidity of Sholto's hand in mine was a part of that stillness. The wind touched my face, and I raised my head, eyes still closed, and knew that the house was where we needed to go. I couldn't have explained it in words, but "knew" in the same way that the flower knows which way the sun is rising; it is just that simple, and that complicated. I started walking toward the house, leading Sholto by the hand. He didn't question, just came with me, and that was a kind of faith. I wasn't sure if it was faith in the Goddess, or faith in me, or both, but I walked forward believing, and he came beside me the same way. Our blood decorated the ground as we walked, and began to decorate our white clothes as the dry, hot wind whipped my dress around us. It spattered our blood across the white like a Jackson Pollock painting.

Most of the paint had peeled off the house, leaving it shades of weathered gray, the wood pitted and marked as if it had been beaten by small, sharp objects, but I knew that it was just the elements of wind, rain, heat, and time. Houses need love and care just like animals and people; without it, our dwellings begin to fade and die just like we do. No one had loved this house in a long time.

We stepped up on the warped, uneven boards of the porch and I reached out to the screen door. It had been torn long enough that the edges had begun to discolor, the screen going almost brittle with heat and neglect.

The inner wood door was peeling and had warped so badly that I couldn't push it open easily. Sholto put his hand on it and together we opened it. It should have made a horrible racket of breaking wood and scraping metal, but it didn't. The door opened as soundlessly as if it had been recently oiled and opened only moments before, though I knew it had to have been weeks since the door was used. With the silence of the door came a more profound quiet, as if the world were holding its breath. I saw the living room under a layer of gray dust, the floor littered with mail as if months' worth had just been thrown on the floor. There was a couch sagging under a pile of knitted afghans, and a pillow. A small gray cat was curled up on the pillow, blinking huge yellow eyes at us. I wondered if it could see us.

As if in answer to my thought it hopped down from the couch in one graceful arc, padding toward the only hallway that led to the left. It turned and looked back at us, and gave a plaintive meow, tail twitching.

"It wants something," I said.

"I'm more interested in what Goddess wants," Sholto said.

The cat gave him an unfriendly look, then looked at me, dismissing him, or that was how it seemed to me. The scent of roses and herbs grew stronger.

"It's like standing in a sun-warmed garden full of herbs and roses; the scent of everything is stronger. Why?"

"The cat knows where we need to go," I said, and led us toward the waiting cat.

I think he opened his mouth to protest, but in the end he simply followed where I led. He followed me better than almost any of the men, considering he was a king in his own right; it was impressive.

The gray cat walked ahead of us, tail held high, tip twitching slightly. She stopped in front of the first closed door in the short hallway. There was another screen door at the end of the hallway. I wondered if that was the door people came in through, or if no one ever came into the house, or ever left it. No, the cat was too much a pet, too well cared for; it hadn't been alone for months.

The cat put a delicate paw up against the door and looked at me with those intense yellow eyes. It gave another plaintive meow.

A man's voice called out. "Stop it, Cleo, stop wailing outside the door. I left a message for Josh, he'll take care of you."

The cat meowed again and scratched at the door.

"Stop it!" he called out.

I thought I knew the voice. "Brennan," I said, softly.

"Who's there!" His voice sounded strident, almost panicked.

"Brennan, it's Meredith."

"Meredith, you can't be here. I am crazy."

The cat pawed at the door again. I used my free hand to touch the doorknob and open it. The cat slid inside as soon as there was an opening big enough for her slender body. We had to open the door wider for Sholto and me to step through.

The cat was already rubbing back and forth on his boots when he finally saw us. The dark of his desert tan had lightened, but his large brown eyes and short dark hair were the same. The hair was a little longer, but I knew that face now. One hand was around his necklace, and the other was holding a gun. It looked like a Glock, but I wasn't an expert on guns. I recognized ones I'd shot, or the people around me used frequently.

He blinked up at us, confused, as if he weren't sure what he was seeing. "Meredith, you don't look . . . is there someone with you? Are you holding someone's hand?"

"Why can't he see me?" Sholto asked, softly.

I didn't know, but out loud I said, "Yes, I have Sholto with me."

"Why can't I see him clearly?"

"What do you see?" I asked.

"It's like heat in the desert, the air wavering until you start thinking you see things that aren't there in the pattern of it."

I tugged on our bound hands and drew Sholto a step farther into the room. From the look on Brennan's face, Sholto must have simply appeared—one moment a wavering in the air, the next fully formed, solid, and real.

"What the hell!" Brennan exclaimed. He startled enough that the cat backed away from him, hissing, as if his foot had hit her accidentally.

"I'm sorry, Cleo, you okay?" He offered her the hand that had been tight around the charm around his neck, though perhaps *charm* wasn't the right word. It was a long, dark nail, with a leather cord bound around the top of it so that it hung point down just at that small depression at the base of the neck. It still looked discolored as if my blood might still have been on it. It had been part of the shrapnel used in a bomb. Every nail that had bled me had fallen out as I healed people that night, and each soldier who had been healed and gained a nail had kept it as a sort of talisman. I think it had started as superstition for having survived, but it had become more. It had become their cross, their holy item that gave them a direct link to Deity. But somehow, I was that deity. Their prayers that involved that bit of metal went to me, if the need was dire enough, but this was no desert battlefield.

I looked at the gun still in his hand as he tried to persuade the cat to come closer to him. I remembered that he'd said someone else would look after the cat, and I suddenly knew that there were battles being fought in this room.

"You called me, Brennan," I said.

He stopped trying to coax the cat and shook his head. "I didn't call you with blood, metal, and magic this time, Meredith. I got no wounds." He held his hand up as if to show it healed and whole.

"Not every wound leaves blood behind," Sholto said.

Brennan glanced at him. "I remember you from when I visited Meredith in Los Angeles, but I don't remember you with a crown, either of you." He started to motion with his gun, stopped himself in midmotion, and used his free hand. "What's with all this?"

"What were you thinking just a few minutes ago?" I asked.

He shook his head. "It doesn't matter."

"Brennan, you wrapped your hand around the symbol at your neck and you prayed. You prayed for something important enough to call me to your side and bring King Sholto with me. What was it?"

He shook his head again. "No."

"Brennan, you prayed to the Goddess and I'm here; tell me."

He glanced at us both again. "Why are your hands bound together?"

"It's how faerie and the Goddess handfasted us," I said.

"What does that mean, handfasted?"

"It means we are married, but with no official legalities."

"The Goddess herself has wed us," Sholto said. "It is the way all marriages were once between our kings and queens."

I smiled at him and went up on tiptoe to offer him a kiss.

"Oh God," Brennan said, and the sound was almost a sob.

I turned back to him. "What, what is it? What do you need so badly that you were about to shoot yourself?"

He looked at the gun in his hand as if he'd almost forgotten it. "It sounds too pathetic."

"You brought us all the way from L.A.—the least you could do is tell us why," I said.

He nodded as if that made sense to him. "Okay, okay, that's fair." He wrapped both hands around the gun, not like he was going to use it, but more like he was holding on to it as a sort of comfort object. He talked without looking at us.

"Jen is dating someone and it's serious. He's got money, a nice house, great career, hell, even his ex-wife says good things about him. They had a little girl and they seem to share the custody without getting all ugly the way most people do. Jen deserves someone that good. Someone who can give her all the things I can't. Someone who isn't crazy. Someone who doesn't wake up in a cold sweat reaching for his gun."

He looked at us then, and there was anguish in his face. "I could hurt her, by accident. I have flashbacks, nightmares. What if I lash out during one of them? I couldn't stand it if I hurt her. I'd rather die than risk that."

It was Sholto who moved forward and drew me with him. "So you've decided to kill yourself instead of telling this woman that you love her?"

Brennan looked startled, eyes too wide, and then he said, "No, she knows I love her. I told her, but I told her I was no good for her. I'm not good for anyone right now, not like this."

"Did you find a counselor like we talked about when you visited us?" I asked.

"There's a waiting list at the VA and I can't afford it any other way. The farm is dying. My dad must be rolling in his grave seeing how Josh neglected this place."

"Who's Josh?" I asked.

"My brother, kid brother, he was supposed to hire people to work the land after Dad died, but he didn't do anything. He finished his degree and got a good job, beautiful wife, baby. It's like he's turned against everything Dad taught us, or doesn't want to be reminded where we came from. This land has been in our family for nearly four generations, and now we're going to lose it to the bank, because my baby brother couldn't be bothered to take care of it. He lied to me in his letters, on the phone, looking at his face over Skype, and he fucking lied to me, said it was handled. He was handling it."

He laughed, but it was one of those laughs that was so bitter it needed a different word. "How can I drag Jen down with me? I'm about to lose everything. I can't do that to her."

"Does she have a job?" I asked.

"Her family owns a hardware store and a restaurant. She manages the store and helps out weekends in the restaurant."

"How's business?" I asked.

"Good, they're doing good."

"So, how would you drag her down with you? You're not endangering her job or her family's businesses, are you?" I asked.

"No, I mean her family are good people. Her dad offered me a job, but I know she made him do it."

"Is it a job you can do?" Sholto asked.

Brennan looked at him, and then nodded. "Yeah, I mean I worked in their hardware store all through high school. I know the business."

"Then maybe they need the help," I said.

He seemed to think about that. He looked at the gun in his hand, and then at us, and finally at me. "I was about to shoot myself, you're right, because I can't save the family farm. I left a message on my brother's phone telling him to take care of Cleo, the cat, and that I didn't want to see the farm go to the bank."

"You wanted to make sure he felt guilty and knew it was his fault," I said.

"I guess I did. Goddess, that is pathetic." He laid the gun on the side table. He looked up at us. "I guess I'm not going to kill myself today."

I didn't like the "today," but one battle at a time. We'd worry about winning the war later.

"You going to help me save the family farm?" he asked.

I said, "I don't think so. You weren't thinking about money when you were praying just now."

"The hell I wasn't, I was thinking how to get enough money to save the farm."

"Not when you prayed to me," I said.

He frowned and touched the nail again, wrapped his hand around it in a familiar gesture. "I was thinking about Jen, and how much I loved her."

"You called me with love, metal, and magic," I said, smiling.

"Love, not blood, but love."

The scent of roses and herbs was sweet and intense again. "Yes, Brennan, you called me, us, with love."

"I smell roses and . . . a garden."

"Take the job that Jen's father offered you," I said.

"I can't do that to them. Jen is getting serious with a really great guy."

"Better than you?" I asked.

"Not better than me, but better for her."

"Is he stronger than you?" Sholto asked.

"No."

"A better warrior?"

Brennan laughed again, but this time he was amused. "No."

"Is he more attractive than you are?" I asked.

Brennan had to think about that one, but finally said, "We're different, but he's not bad looking. He's handsome in a soft sort of way, if that makes sense?"

"It does," I said.

"So you're stronger, a better warrior, and both of you are equally handsome; how is he the better man?" Sholto asked.

"He's got more money, a better career, and he's not crazy."

"Does she need his money?" I asked.

"No, Jen isn't like that, and I told you her family is doing good. She's practically running the hardware store on her own. That's why her dad wanted me to come work with her; they can't find good help."

"Is she impressed with his career?" I asked.

He smiled. "No, not really. She says he's too ambitious for her. He'll want to move away and not stay, and she can't leave her parents. She loves the store and the town, always has."

"So, the only reason not to take the job, declare your love, and marry the woman is because you are crazy and the other man is not?" Sholto asked.

Brennan seemed to think about it again. "I guess so, but seriously I'm not safe."

"Have you hurt anyone?" I asked.

"No, not yet."

It was Sholto who said, "One of your soldier friends hurt someone."

"How did you know?"

"So you have PTSD," I said. "So do I, so do a lot of us, but we don't all hurt people. We get therapy, we talk to our friends, our family, other soldiers, other survivors, and we heal. We find love." I smiled up at Sholto.

There was a knock on the door, no, a pounding on the door, as if it had shut behind us as tightly as when we tried to open it. We heard someone running around the house, and then the screen door we'd seen at the end of the hallway banged open, and whoever it was came running down the hallway. I thought at first it would be the brother, but then a woman's voice yelled, "Brennan, damn it, you better not be dead, or I am so going to kill you!"

Brennan stood up. "It's Jen."

Sholto and I stood there as a woman with short brunette hair came rushing into the room. She saw him, the gun on the table, and ran at him slapping his chest, finally slapping his face hard enough to rock him.

"Your good-for-nothing brother told me the message you left. I left him in charge of the store and told him if anyone stole anything I'd see him in jail. Josh always was useless."

Brennan just stared at her, too surprised to speak, I think. He glanced back at us, but she either hadn't seen us or couldn't see us.

"Jen . . ." he started.

"Don't you Jen me, Brian Fitzgerald Brennan. You are not going to kill yourself; you are not going to leave me just because you're losing the family farm. It's just land, just a house." She grabbed his arms and shook him. "I'm here, I'm real, and I love you. Don't leave me to marry Tommy."

He was holding her arms, to keep her from shaking him more. "I thought you loved Tommy."

"No, he's nice enough, but he's so boring. I hate to be bored, you know that."

He laughed. "I remember."

"You never bore me, Brian, never. You're the only man who never bored me, even when we were kids."

"I love you, Jen. I'm sorry."

"Sorry you love me, or sorry you almost did something stupid and ruined it all?" She motioned at the gun.

"That last part, because Jennifer Alice Wells"—he dropped to one knee—"if you'll have me, I will do my best to never be boring for the rest of our long and interesting lives."

She started to cry, and so did I.

"I will, I do, you stupid man, yes, I will."

Brennan picked her up around the waist and lifted her off her feet. The gray cat, Cleo, sat on the floor and purred. He put Jen down and said, "Thank you."

"You're welcome," she said, laughing and crying.

"She can't see us," Sholto said, softly.

I shook my head. I thought we'd have to walk out of the house to break the dream, but the room started to fade. The last thing we saw was the two of them kissing. Sholto and I woke naked on the edge of the Western Sea in a bed covered in white rose petals, and sprigs of thyme and rosemary, all covered in the delicate blossoms that still decorated his crown.

Sholto turned to me, smiling. Our hands were no longer bound, but the matching tattoos of the rose vines on our arms shone blue. He raised his arm up so he could watch it glimmer, and then laid his arm next to the glow of mine. "They pray to you for protection and fertility, but what am I?"

"Love, apparently," I said.

"Love?" he said.

I nodded. "You were there, Sholto. She was his true love, and he hers, maybe marriage."

"King of the Sluagh, King of Nightmares, the Queen's Perverse Creature, Lord of Shadows, and behind my back, Shadowspawn, and now you're telling me I'm a deity of love and marriage?"

"Yes," I said.

He smiled, then grinned, and said, "Me, a god of love and marriage," and he threw his head back and laughed until the sound of it danced around the room. Then distant from outside the house came the singing of a mockingbird. It was loud, clear, and sweet, falling from one song to another, and I remembered that it had been a mockingbird that welcomed us back to L.A. the night that Sholto had brought us all back to the edge of the sea. He laughed, the bird sang, and tiny multicolored flowers and white rose petals started falling from thin air.

CHAPTER

THIRTY-SEVEN

Sholto and I got dressed, him back in his mix of modern and museumworthy fashion, the black making his skin whiter, and strangely bringing out more of the yellow in his mostly white-blond hair.

"I always like you in royal purple; it makes your hair even more scarlet, and only green makes your eyes more brilliant." He touched my hair as he said it, gazing down at me as if to drink in the sight of me in one of his favorite colors.

I smiled up at him, putting my hand over his so I could rest my cheek in his open palm. He felt safe and warm, his hands large enough that he could cradle the entire side of my face.

"Why do you think I wore it today?"

His smile lit up his face, not with magic, but with happiness. "I have never had anyone pay as much attention to my preferences as you do, Meredith."

He was over three hundred years old; the thought that I was the first person to ever pay the attention that all lovers deserve made me sad, but I didn't say it out loud, because I didn't want to take the happiness off that handsome face.

I let my smile quirk at the edges and put into my eyes the heat I felt for him.

"We just finished," he said, laughing.

"I am never finished with the pleasure you can give me, Sholto."

His face sobered, his gold-on-gold eyes gazing down at me with a tenderness that was almost frightening, because I only aimed such looks at other men. I loved Sholto, but I was not in love with him, though that might come. I'd learned that my heart was big enough for more than just one great love of my life; maybe it could hold more than two someday?

I let him see the hope on my face, not the worry, and he leaned down to lay another kiss on my lips. I melted into his arms, getting as close as our now-clothed bodies could manage. It felt almost odd to not feel his extras. I must have stiffened, because he pulled back.

"What's wrong?" he asked.

"It feels different without your extra bits," I said.

He looked down at me, and I could see him thinking. "Different good, or bad?"

I frowned. "Just different, but"—I hugged him tighter—"I do sort of miss them when they're not touchable."

He laughed and hugged me close, folding his upper body over me, so my head was pressed into his chest not in a romantic way, but almost in a childlike way. I could forget how much taller almost all of my lovers were, but every once in a while they would do something and I would be forcibly reminded that I was tiny. I didn't feel that tiny, but it was as if Sholto could have folded himself around me twice. His hair fell around our bodies like a pale curtain.

I pushed at him enough to make him rise up so I could see his face. "What is so funny?"

"You're not horrified by the tentacles; you miss them when they're gone. Do you know what a wonder that is to me?"

I touched his face, still bent so close, and smiled. "I have some idea, yes."

The laughter died around the edges and left his eyes haunted. "I would have given anything not to have them when I was younger. It wasn't until the Seelie cut them off and I thought I would never have them again that I realized they were a part of me, as much as my arms and legs."

I held his face between my hands, gazed into those golden eyes, and said, "I'm so sorry they hurt you, and so happy that the Goddess and Consort made you whole again."

"That's just it, Meredith; I didn't realize until they were lost that I wasn't whole without them."

"Sometimes you have to lose a thing to value it," I said, softly.

He nodded, but his face was serious now, the laughter gone as if it were a dream. He stood back up all straight and tall and every inch the sidhe warrior and king. He pulled his dignity around him like a familiar piece of clothing, or a well-used shield. I wrapped my arms around his waist, happy that I got to see inside that shield.

He smiled down at me and hugged me back but stayed standing this time, so it was just his arms across my back. "Well, I value you without having to lose you, my queen."

I smiled, and said, "And I value you, my king, so much."

"I had given up having a sidhe for my queen."

"Would you have taken someone from among your sluagh?"

"I would have had no choice, would I?"

I thought about it. "Humans can be driven mad seeing some of your people, and goblins are, well, goblins. I cannot imagine you happy with one of their women, though Kitto is very dear to me, and if you could have found a female similar in nature to him she might have been quite lovely, and there might be lesser fey who would have been willing."

"I mention it in passing, and you think seriously about it."

"I'm sure you thought seriously about it," I said.

"Not as hard as you might think, my queen. Remember, my throne is the only one in faerie that is not normally an inherited one."

"The goblin throne isn't inherited either," I said.

"True, but they kill the old king and the victor takes the crown. I may retire from my job, and help my people vote another in my place."

"Has any King of the Sluagh ever stepped down voluntarily?"

He laughed again. "Well, no, but we can step down; the goblins do not give their rulers that choice."

"No, they do not."

"Now you look worried; what is wrong?"

"Holly and Ash," I said.

"The goblin twins who are your visiting lovers. You fear they will kill their king, Kurag."

I nodded. "They mean to, eventually, I think."

"It is the goblin way."

"Yes, but I have no treaty with Holly and Ash. I have one with Kurag."

"You brought them into their hands of power, and turned them from sidhe-sided goblins to true sidhe. They must be grateful for that."

"They are both thrilled with the power, but grateful enough to stay bound in treaty to me, knowing that I have enemies at both sidhe courts." I shook my head. "I don't know if they're that grateful."

"Have you not won them over with the pleasures of your body, as you won the rest of us?"

"I might have, but I haven't been able to have sex with anyone for months. The goblin twins weren't tamed enough before I had to stop entertaining them."

"Then as soon as you are able, Meredith, you must invite them to visit you."

I studied his face. "You aren't bothered by me sleeping with them?"

"I always find that euphemism for sex confusing, because the last thing you do with the two of them is sleep."

I smiled. "Fair enough, but my question remains."

"It is politically expedient to keep the goblins as your allies, and that means Holly and Ash must want to be on your side, because you are correct, they will be the next rulers of the goblins."

"I've been wondering how they'll divide up the throne. They can't both be king," I said.

"I think Ash will take the crown, but they will rule the goblins as they have done everything in their lives."

"They will rule together," I said.

"Yes."

"Ash is the more dominant personality, but up to the point where they disagree they are a unit."

"And then Holly lets Ash win the disagreement?" Sholto asked.

I nodded.

"I wonder what would happen if Holly wouldn't give way to his brother?"

"I don't know. I don't think either of them would have survived without the other. Sidhe-sided goblins are physically weaker than most goblins."

"Like your Kitto."

"Kitto is weaker than most," I said.

"You have given him a refuge and a home, Meredith; it is good to see."

"I didn't think you cared for Kitto one way or another."

"I did not know him, but I knew the fate of the sidhe-sided among the goblins and I would not wish that upon anyone."

"You are much kinder than your reputation among the fey."

"The King of the Sluagh needs a fierce reputation to keep his kingdom and people safe."

"That may be true of all rulers in faerie," I said.

He touched my face. "Now you look too serious."

"I am not respected, or feared, enough to keep us safe."

"The Goddess walks with you, Meredith. You have brought back the magic that we lost, and the sidhe are having children once more; those are all things worthy of much respect."

"Many of the sidhe still see me as a mortal abomination, the first sidhe ever born who was mortal and could be killed by normal means."

"You and I are both abominations to them. You with your human mortality, and I showing that the humanoid bias of the sidhe no longer wins genetically. We are both living proof that the sidhe are fading as pure people."

"They do hate us both for that," I said.

"Let them hate us, we know our worth," he whispered, and leaned down to kiss me again. I kissed him back eagerly, because he was right. We knew our worth now. Those who hated us for physical traits we could not change could go hang themselves. Racists are always evil, whether it's the color of your skin they hate, or how many limbs you have, or how fragile you are; it's all hatred and it's all just fear. They hated us because they saw us and thought, *There but for the grace of Goddess go I, or my children.* Sholto and I were the bogeyman in the mirror, and yet he was a king and I was a princess, and those who hated us most were neither. I wondered, did they hate us more because we were different, or because we were different and ruled in faerie and they with their pure, perfect, sidhe bodies did not?

left my hose off so that I could walk barefoot through the sand to kiss
Sholto good-bye at the edge of the surf. He'd protested, "The sand is
chilly, and the surf cold."

"I would kiss you as often as I can, before you go. If that means getting my feet a little cold in the edge of the sea, so be it."

The pleased look on his face was totally worth padding barefoot
through the sand and letting the chill wind have its way with my bare
legs. Sholto had given me his jacket this time, so at least my upper body
was warm enough. I'd protested, "I'll have to give it back to you at the
water's edge, and then I'll be even colder walking back to the house."

"No, keep it until I return. I have other jackets and I love the idea of
you wearing mine. Give it back to me smelling of your skin, and I will be
content."

What could I say to that but yes, and, "You are a terrible romantic,
my king."

He had grinned at me, that grin that made him look younger and
carefree, as if no sorrow had ever touched him. I loved that I could get
that smile from him.

"I thought I was a very good romantic, my queen," he said.

I'd agreed and there had been more kissing. Now, we stopped just short of the waves where they spilled along the sand, and kissed again. An energetic wave found my feet and I startled from the cold. He laughed and picked me up, holding me around the waist effortlessly, my arms around his neck and my bare feet suddenly kicking in empty air while I laughed with him.

I didn't hear the shot; I felt it spin him around and suddenly we were in the waves, the sea like ice water pouring over us. He was on top of me, pinning me, as the waves drew back and left me gasping.

Saraid and Dogmaela were there, bending over us. Saraid yelled, "Princess! Princess, are you hurt?"

"Lord Sholto!"

The next wave came, leaving me spitting water, and coughing. Sholto never moved. I said his name, but I knew. If he could have, he would have been helping Saraid and Dogmaela. He would have been up protecting me, but he just lay there as the next waves came and Saraid dragged me out of the water.

Beck and Cooper were there, guns drawn, looking outward for someone to shoot. Dogmaela had grabbed Sholto and was pulling him farther up on the sand. Saraid had pinned me underneath her on the sand, using her body as a shield, and yelling for reinforcements from the house.

They came, the sidhe, armed, helping shield me from danger, but all I could see was Sholto. Dogmaela rolled him onto his back and I could see the wound that came out a few inches below his right arm. The hole looked big enough to put my fist through. Exit wound, I thought, and then, could he heal it? Could King Sholto, Lord of the Sluagh, heal a high-powered rifle round that might have gone straight through his heart?

Dogmaela was trying to hold pressure on the bullet hole on the entry wound. Someone else knelt and started trying to hold pressure from the other side. I saw them look at each other, and then Dogmaela looked not at me, but at Saraid.

I screamed, "No! Sholto! No!"

Far off I heard seagulls calling in their rough, complaining voices, but there was no mockingbird to sing sweet music. The wind from the sea was cold, and the sea was colder.

CHAPTER

THIRTY-NINE

I sat at the hospital with Galen on one side of me and Frost on the other. He was still hurt, but as he said when he came through the door, "I am well enough for this."

I hadn't let the nurses and doctors take the jacket or the clothes I was wearing, because the jacket was Sholto's and it, and my dress, were covered in his blood. When they all gave up on the beach, I'd gone to him and held him, and he'd bled on me. He'd still been warm, neither death nor the sea had stolen him that far away, so that he still felt like he should open his eyes and smile up at me. But he'd lain in my lap with that stillness that nothing mimics, not sleep, not illness, nothing but the warm dead feel—so alive and at the same time they move in your arms as you hold them, nerveless, flopping like some great doll, so that you know, you know even while life still warms their skin, you know, oh Gods, you know, that it is the last warmth that their skin will ever hold, and the only thing left is the cold, the terrible cold.

Galen held my hand, and Frost had his arm around my shoulders and it helped, but . . . I had prayed to Goddess and the Consort, but the petals that had fallen from the sky had been all white, no pink, just white, and I'd known that there would be no help even from Her.

I was starting to shiver and couldn't seem to stop. A nurse came and kneeled in front of me so she could look into my face, because I seemed to be staring at the floor. "Princess Meredith, please let us take your clothes and get you in something warmer. You're in shock and the cold, wet clothes aren't helping."

I just shook my head.

She pushed a strand of hair back behind her ear to try to get it to stay in the ponytail she'd started her shift with, but she needed to take it out and redo the ponytail, just shoving it back behind her ear wasn't going to fix her hair. I almost told her that, and then realized concentrating on her hair I'd stopped listening to what she was saying.

"I'm sorry, but I didn't hear any of that," I said.

"We have to get you warm, honey, or we'll be admitting you next."

"Can we just take her home?" Galen asked.

"We'd like to get her warm and dry, and have a doctor look at her."

Frost asked, "I thought you did all that before we arrived."

The nurse smiled, sort of an unhappy or maybe frustrated smile. "The Princess wouldn't go into a private area, she just kept insisting she was all right."

Frost hugged me with the one arm across my shoulders and spoke low with his face against my hair. "Merry, you need to let the doctors look at you."

"I'm all right," I said, and even to me it felt automatic.

Galen raised my hand that he was holding up so that he could lay a kiss on the back of it, but I pulled back at the last second. "I have blood on my hands."

"There's no blood on the back of your hand." He held it up so I could look at it. "See, all clean."

I just shook my head, over and over again, and shivered harder. My teeth started to chatter.

"We have to get her dry and warm," the nurse said, her voice sounding like there was no more arguing about it.

"I'm fine," I managed to say between chattering, and even as I said it, I knew it wasn't true. I had no idea why I didn't want to let them help me, except that I hadn't been shot. Sholto had been shot. Sholto was dead, not me. I realized that part of me seemed to think that if I just didn't let them help me, they'd be able to help him more. It made no sense, but that was finally the thought I dragged up into the front of my head, from where it had been hiding in the back of my thoughts, so I was acting on it, but didn't know why.

"Merry," Frost said, "you are not fine. Where does she need to go for a doctor to look at her?"

"Follow me," the nurse said, obviously happier now that someone was being reasonable.

I didn't want to be reasonable. I wanted to be totally unreasonable. I wanted to scream at her, lash out at Frost, scream at the world, and the only thing that kept me from it was that voice in my head saying, "That makes no sense."

I was a princess, a queen actually, Sholto's queen, which meant I had to do better. The last thing I could do for him was to remember I was his wife—funny, but I'd never thought the word *wife* much about Sholto and me, but we had been married by the very magic of fairie and Goddess, and that was about as blessed a union as you could get.

I thought of something I hadn't before. I looked at Frost. "Has anyone told the sluagh that their king is dead?"

"They know," he said.

"Are you sure?" I asked.

He nodded. "Yes." He helped me stand, but the high heels that hadn't seemed that high turned underneath me, and he had to catch me or I would have fallen. A small pain sound escaped him, and I remembered he was hurt, too.

"Frost, you're hurt. I'm so sorry, so sorry . . ." I pushed away from him, but he wouldn't let me go. I pushed against his chest, trying to force him to let me go, but he flinched and I realized I was pushing against his wounds. I started to cry again. "Everyone keeps getting hurt."

Galen picked me up, and Frost let him. "I'm not hurt," he said with a smile.

"Not yet," I said, as I curled my arms around his neck and buried my face against the side of his neck. The tears stopped and I was suddenly exhausted. I started shivering again, trembling in his arms as if I would shake myself apart.

I felt him walking and lifted my head enough to see we were following the nurse and that Frost was behind us. The guards that had been waiting outside the little alcove seating area closed in on either side of us. Usna and Cathbodua were there, her raven feather cloak had morphed into a fitted black leather trenchcoat, but I knew it was partly illusion. I wasn't sure how I felt about her still being on guard duty now that I knew she was pregnant, but it was too hard for me to think about, so I let it go for now. Uniformed police came in at the front and back of the knot of security. They'd given me the breathing room I asked for, but my guards both sidhe and human DSS had been doubled, and the police were determined that I didn't get killed on their watch.

"Where's Doyle?" I asked.

"He's tearing Saraid and Dogmaela a new one," Galen said.

"It wasn't their fault," I said.

"He's really mad at himself, but he's going to take it out on them."

"Why is he mad at himself?"

Frost spoke from just behind us. "Because we both believe if we'd been with you this wouldn't have happened."

I shook my head, fought to talk around my chattering teeth, and said, "That's not true. I don't think that's true."

I tried to think, was there a moment when someone could have done something? Would Doyle and Frost have made the difference? Would that have been much better than Saraid and Dogmaela? Frost had been hurt; he couldn't have been there today, but Doyle . . . would Doyle being there have made the difference, or would he have died, too? That thought was too awful. I pushed it back and started to shake until I could barely keep hold of Galen. He held me closer, tighter, as if trying to share his warmth.

The nurse, whose name was Nancy, yes, Nurse Nancy, led us to a private room. One thing being a faerie princess had always gotten me was a better room at the hospital. Being a princess didn't keep me out of the hospital; in fact, it seemed to put me in more often than if I hadn't been one, but I did usually get a private room. It was the only way to control the media and the gawkers. I'd been newsworthy all my life, and right at that minute I would have traded all of it for Sholto to walk through the door alive.

The police wanted to secure the room, so did the men and one woman of the diplomatic service, but the sidhe pointed out that none of them could look for magical dangers. It was like trying to get a rugby huddle into one room, no one wanted to be left outside, and each branch of guard wanted to search the room.

Nurse Nancy settled it all. "We've got to get the princess out of her wet clothes, so unless you've already seen her naked in person, you have to get out."

All the humans, both goverment issue and police issue, went in an embarrassed mass for the door. There were enough of them that they had a traffic jam at the door. One of the cops stepped back and asked, "Are you sure that just the two fathers are enough protection for her once we leave the room? She had four guards at the beach."

It was Cathbodua who said, "Only Usna and I are leaving of our seven guards. I think five Raven guard should be enough."

"She had four at the beach, remember?" he said.

"Nothing personal, but two of the four were human. This is five of the Raven guard."

Galen sat me on the bed where the nurse told him to, and then she produced a large plastic bag. "We can put your clothes in here, Princess, if the police don't need them for evidence. Then they can go home with you."

I touched the jacket, cold with seawater and wet with blood, and didn't want to take it off. In some part of my mind I knew it made no sense, but it felt as if once I took it off that Sholto would be more lost to me. Stupid, but it was his jacket, he'd put it on me himself, and it was his blood on it—it was his in a way nothing else would ever be again.

Galen bent over and held my chin in his hand, made me look into his eyes. "Merry, you have to get warm, and for that the clothes have to come off. No one's going to take the jacket away."

I nodded, because I was shivering too hard to talk.

Nurse Nancy touched my face. "She's cold and clammy to the touch. We have to get her out of these clothes now."

"We will," Galen said. He sat beside me on the bed and began to slide the jacket off one arm. I let him take it, because it was Galen, and I trusted him to help me keep it.

Frost stood beside me and helped take the other sleeve off, but when he bent a certain way, he hesitated in midmotion as if something hurt.

I grabbed his hand in mine and just looked at him as I sat there shivering in the short skirt and tiny top. Funny how sexy outfits are never good emergency clothing.

Nicca came forward, his knee-length deep brown hair was back in a braid. He'd started wearing it back once Kadyi got old enough to grab hair. Nicca's skin was still the rich brown of autumn leaves, and I knew underneath his very modern-looking clothes were huge moth wings, but like Sholto's tentacles, his wings could be just an incredibly vivid tattoo if he wished. Just that thought made my mind skip a beat, like I'd almost thought too much about it, and now I had to stop thinking altogether.

"Let me help her undress, Frost, please?"

"It doesn't do any good for you to be here if you reopen a wound," Galen said.

Frost frowned like he'd pout, which he'd done a lot once upon a time, but then he found the room's only chair and sat gingerly on the edge of it. Was his back hurt, too? I didn't remember any of the scratches being there, but I was having trouble remembering everything that happened in the last hour, and that was days ago. How could I remember something that far back?

Cathbodua had shooed everyone else out and closed the door behind her. It was then that Nurse Nancy seemed to figure out that five of the men were staying and helping her undress me. "OK, gentlemen, the rest of you can go on out with the rest of them," she said.

Ivi said, "You said we could stay."

"No, I said only the people that had seen her nude could stay."

"Well, then we can all stay," Ivi said. He wasted a smile on her and flipped his nearly ankle-length hair so that the pattern of ivy leaves that climbed all that paler green hair showed clearer. Humans were always thinking that Ivi had somehow decorated his hair with the pattern of ivy vines and leaves, but it was natural, an outward sign of his inner nature.

But Nurse Nancy was made of sterner stuff than some and didn't respond to the flirting. "I know the fey are more comfortable with nudity than most humans, but I didn't just mean that. I meant . . ." The nurse seemed lost for words. She was ignoring the flirting, but her discomfort was real.

Brioc moved where I could see him and where he could help Ivi flirt and intimidate the nurse. Brioc was as tall, slender, and muscled as Ivi, but Brioc's hair was a bright yellow blond, his skin a pale grayish white like some of the Red Caps had, but Brioc was pure sidhe. His skin was the color of cherry tree bark, just like the incredible red of his full lips wasn't due to lipstick of any kind. He was the cherry tree made flesh and blood, as Ivi was for his namesake. Vegetative deities were always interesting. Brioc said, "You meant her lovers could stay."

"Yes, that is what I meant," the nurse said.

"We assumed that is what you meant," Ivi said.

I couldn't see the nurse's face, but I heard her silence, even through my shivering and chattering teeth. "Are you saying that you're all . . . lovers?"

"Yes," Ivi said.

"Ex-lovers," Brioc said, "but yes, so we can guard the princess no matter her state of undress."

Galen and Nicca had peeled off the wet top and the bra. For some reason my bare breasts seemed to galvanize Nurse Nancy. "The hospital gown is on the bed, it closes in the back, just open the door when she's dressed . . . undressed . . . redressed." She fled. Apparently, five lovers was a few too many over the nurse's comfort zone. Under other circumstances it might have been amusing; now it just seemed like another reminder that I would never completely understand human culture.

I was in shock, as in the kind of shock that needed a bedsize heating pad under me, warm blankets, and an IV to give me fluids. I felt fragile and very human ending up in a hospital bed just from shock. There was nothing wrong with me; I hadn't been the one who got shot. I didn't have a scratch on me, though they'd probably been aiming at me. Had the bullet been for me, and Sholto just got in the way? No one wanted to kill Sholto, but plenty of people wanted to kill me.

The bed was warm, I was warm, and I was suddenly so tired. Frost sat beside the bed, his hand in mine, and my eyes were fluttering shut. I managed to ask, "Did they give me something?"

"What do you mean, give you something?" Frost asked.

"To sleep. Did they give me something to make me sleep?"

Galen came to stand on the other side of me, stroking his hand across my forehead. "Yes."

"I'm not hurt. I don't need to sleep."

"We agreed with the doctor," Galen said, voice soft.

"Damn it," I managed to say as my eyes fluttered closed again.

He leaned down to lay a soft kiss on my lips. "I love you, Merry."

"I love you, too," and that was the last thing I remembered, before sleep came and I could not fight it.

CHAPTER

FORTY

The dream began innocently enough, but like all innocence it could not last. I stood in the high, round room of a tower that I had never seen before. There were beautiful tapestries on the walls, rugs bright as stained glass on the floor, and through the room's two windows the sunshine was golden and thick like honey for the eyes. It was beautiful, peaceful, so why was I afraid?

A man's voice came from behind me, "I can keep you safe, Meredith, you and our children."

My throat closed tight, and I couldn't breathe for a second, because I knew that voice. I turned as one does in a horror movie, slowly, unwilling, because you know the monster is right there—behind you.

Taranis stood in a bright swath of sunlight, most of him lost in the light, so that he seemed to be forming from the light itself as he stepped farther into the room. He held his hand out to me, a smile curling his lips, and it was as if that smile were some happy jewel set between the red-gold of his mustache and beard. His hair flowed in matching curls and waves as if his hair couldn't decide how curly it wanted to be. I didn't think I'd ever seen him when his hair wasn't perfectly styled. This careless play was somehow more pleasing, and more real. His eyes looked just a brilliant green rather than the green of many flower petals in every shade of green known under the sky, and those more human eyes smiled kindly at me.

I actually took a step toward him, but I stumbled on the edge of my floor-length skirt. I looked down and found myself in a dress that matched the tower room. I was dressed like some fairy-tale princess waiting to be rescued. My heart climbed into my throat, so that I was choking on it.

"Meredith." And the moment he said my name, the fear receded. I gazed up at him and found this new, more human Taranis comforting. Part of me knew that was wrong, that he wasn't comforting, but it was as if I couldn't think the thought all the way through.

He crossed the room and touched my cheek, ever so gently, with the back of his hand. "Come to me, Meredith, come and be my queen and I will keep you safe from all that would harm you."

His tone was sweet, but his words jarred me, because they did not ring true with my own memories. I moved my face back from that touch and said, "You're part of what I need to be protected from."

He looked puzzled, as if my words made no sense. "Meredith, I would never hurt you."

I looked up into that handsome face and thought, *He would never hurt me, of course he would never hurt me.* I said, "No," not because I believed it in that moment, but as a place to start. No, he was wrong somehow. No, I shouldn't be here. No, just no.

"Oh, Meredith, I want to take care of you, you and our children."

I shook my head. "No . . . not . . ." Not what, I thought? What was he not? What was not true? That was it, something he'd just said wasn't true, but what was it? Why couldn't I think?

He touched my face again, and I started to rub my face against his hand, but stopped in midmotion, because there was nothing familiar about his hand on my face. I had so many men who touched my face, who held me, who kept me safe, but this hand wasn't one of them. This man wasn't one of them. Who was he then, what was he to me? Why couldn't I think?

I shook my head hard enough that he had to move his hand. I tried to back away from him but tripped over the hem of the dress, falling to the floor hard enough that it jarred me, and I tasted blood, from biting my tongue. A single pink rose petal drifted down into my lap, and a tiny drop of blood began to fall from my lip, and it was as if time stretched forever as that drop fell in slow motion down, down, to finally land on that pink petal.

It was as if time, sound, reality all resumed with a rush that should have had a sound to it like the Doppler shift of a car speeding past me in the dark, so near that its wind ruffles my hair, tugs at my clothing, and leaves me gasping at the nearness of it.

I looked up at him, and said, "I know who you are."

He knelt beside me, smiling. "Of course you know me, I am your beloved."

"You are Taranis, King of Light and Illusion; you beat me and you raped me, and everything else is a lie."

His smile faded around the edges; that pleasant face flickered, like a TV set that wasn't quite on one station, so you got the ghost of other images, and then he was back to pleasant, smiling, handsome, but harmless. I could change my physical appearance using glamour, but I couldn't add an emotion to it and make someone feel things they didn't actually feel. Was that all that his illusions were, just personal glamour with the addition of being able to project thoughts and feelings?

"Meredith, Meredith, see how much I love you."

I looked into his face and saw . . . love. He loved me, of course he loved me. He had always loved me . . . and the moment I thought that, I knew it was wrong. I remembered him beating me as a child. I remembered how terrified I had been of him. I remembered reaching out to my mother and she had turned away. It had been my grandmother, her mother, who had saved me from the king's anger.

I shook my head. "It's a spell, it's just a spell, it's not real."

"I want you, Meredith, I need you, that is true. I swear it by any oath you ask of me." He reached out to touch my face again.

I flinched away from his hand, but that put me almost prone on the floor, and I knew that was a bad idea, so I tried to stand, but I got tangled in the long skirts and fell back to my knees.

His hands closed on my upper arms, and he pulled me against his chest. He was so much bigger than I was, as tall as any of my lovers, and broader through the chest and shoulders than anyone but Mistral. He would be stronger than me even if he'd been human, but he wasn't human, he was sidhe, and once had been a god. He held me against his body as we knelt on the floor of the tower and I was happy for how full my skirts were, because I could only feel his chest and stomach against my back; the skirts protected me from feeling anything lower on his body.

I was so scared I couldn't breathe, as if the fear were squeezing my chest too tight for me to draw a complete breath of air.

He whispered my name, "Meredith, Meredith, Meredith," and with each repetition of my name my fear began to fade, until by the time he'd said it a dozen times I melted in against his body, letting his arms wrap around me, so that his big hand held my lower arms and then wrapped my arms and his across my body, so that I was held so close, so safe.

"I need you, Meredith," he whispered; his breath was warm against my hair and face as he bent over me and planted a kiss on my neck. His lips were so warm.

"But give me a willing kiss, Meredith, and then you will be mine."

It seemed so reasonable. I began to turn my head back toward him, and then what he'd actually said came to me. "Willing," I said.

He laid another warm kiss along my neck. "Yes, Meredith, willing. I want you always to be willing, so there are no more misunderstandings between us."

"Misunderstandings," I said.

"Yes, Meredith," he said, and kissed higher on my neck, just under the line of my jaw. His lips were so warm, almost hot against my skin, as if he were fevered. I didn't remember his skin being hot like this last time, and just thinking about that last time made me remember coming to with him on top of me. I remembered the fear, and the pain of the concussion from where he'd hit me. He hit me. He raped me. He did not love me, had never, ever loved me. I wasn't sure King Taranis could love anyone but himself.

I tensed in his arms, because the fear was back, screaming through every nerve in my being. I wanted him to stop touching me. I spoke around the pulse in my throat and it made my voice have to squeeze out around the fear, "Stop, please, stop touching me."

"Meredith, you don't want me to stop."

My name from his lips began to calm the fear again, but him telling me that I didn't want him to stop pissed me off. I knew my own mind, and I did not want him to touch me, ever again.

I remembered coming to with him on top of me. I remembered him naked, and on top of me, and I hated him. I hated him with a fine, burning hatred. "You have hurt me too much and too often, Taranis. Your spell will not work, because I keep remembering how much I hate you and what you have done to me."

His weight was just suddenly more, pinning me harder to the rugs, hard enough that I could feel the hardness of the stones underneath. My fear washed over me so that my skin ran cold with it.

"Will you forgive nothing, Meredith, and remember only the bad?"

"What good memories do I have of you, Uncle Taranis?"

"Meredith, Meredith, hear me, feel me, and know that I love you."

Even with his weight pressing me into the floor, and my fear almost choking me again, that unnatural calmness started to take me over again. It was magic, it wasn't real!

"Is this how you seduced them all, Taranis, through trickery and lies? Are you not the great lover, but just a great liar?"

He squeezed his hands around my wrists until I thought he meant to crush them, and then he slid his knee between my thighs, and the fear robbed me of everything. I couldn't think past the fear as he began to try to worm his way between my legs.

"Stop!"

He leaned his face close, his voice ugly with his rage. "Shadowspawn is already dead. His sluagh will not hunt or protect you now, Meredith.

Your Darkness and your false storm lord will be dead soon, and I do not fear the rest of your would-be suitors."

I knew he meant Doyle, but it took me a second to realize that the third death was Mistral. I was suddenly less afraid, because my anger helped chase it back. "You had Sholto killed. You ordered it."

"He led his wild hunt into the heart of my sithen. I could not allow that to happen again, Meredith."

"Stop saying my name!" I yelled it, holding my anger to me, because even now when he said my name, I could feel the compulsion in it, to just give in, to believe him. But he had me pinned to the floor, his weight on me, and that helped me not to believe he loved me.

"If you but kiss me once, Meredith, you will enjoy the rest, I promise you that."

I kept my face turned away from him. "A kiss, or a willing kiss, uncle?"

"Do not call me that," he said.

"You are my uncle. You are my grandfather's brother. Nothing you do will change that."

"I have never acted as an uncle to you, Meredith."

"No, you tried to beat me to death when I was a child, and you almost beat me to death less than a year ago, and you raped me after you had beaten me unconscious. A good uncle would do none of these things, I suppose."

He used his body weight to keep my body pinned to the floor, and wrapped his big hand around both my wrists where they were still pinned under me. He was freeing up one of his hands; nothing good would come of it. I struggled to free the wrist that he was trying to hold with one hand, and felt his fingers begin to slide. His free hand grabbed a handful of my hair and pulled my head back.

I spoke through gritted teeth as I fought to keep my face down. "A stolen kiss will not win you my affections, not even by your magic. You said it yourself, it must be willing."

"I could have made this pleasant for you, Meredith. I meant it to be, but you are always so difficult!"

"Yes, I am difficult, uncle; you will not win me."

He pulled my hair tight enough that it hurt and growled his anger in my ear. "I will have you, Meredith. You can enjoy it, or you can fight me and I will take my pleasure and not worry about yours."

"Are you saying that I can either enjoy my rape, or not enjoy it?"

His grip in my hair loosened slightly, and some tension went from him, as if by hearing it spoken so bluntly, even he heard that it made no sense.

His voice was calmer when he said, "I can leave this dream now, Meredith. I can free us both of this dream, and call back the assassins that are going to kill Doyle and Mistral, if you will but kiss me here and now."

"I trust Doyle to kill anyone you send against him, and you must fear Mistral very much to target him, so you know what he is capable of; they are not easy to kill."

"Sholto shouldn't have been easy to kill either, Meredith, but he was; think upon that as the minutes tick away. Think upon that and decide whether you would rather your Darkness and your Storm be alive but parted from you, or dead and parted from you forever?"

Fear poured over me again, and the fresh memories of holding Sholto's body on the beach. I didn't think I could bear seeing Doyle dead. I admitted to myself that I would not grieve Mistral as much, but I remembered the moment on the battlefield when I'd thought my cousin Cel had killed Doyle. If I left them, then Doyle would still have Frost; they would not be alone, but I would be. I would be worse than alone.

"One kiss, Meredith, one willing kiss, for the lives of two of your lovers, is that so much to ask?"

"No, not if it were just one kiss, but if I give you a kiss, uncle dearest, then what happens next?"

"I kiss you back, of course."

"I am not stupid, uncle; if I kiss you willingly, what does the spell do?"

"You will no longer be afraid; you will be safe and happy in my arms."

"But for it to work you must win a kiss from me." I laughed, I couldn't help it. "You need to 'Kiss the Girl,'" I said.

"Yes, I suppose I do need to kiss the girl."

"No, uncle, I'm quoting a movie that you've never seen."

"I do not know what you are talking about, Meredith. The assassins are even now in place, and I promise you they will strike, as they did this morning for your shadow lord."

"You don't even know there was a movie of 'The Little Mermaid,' do you?"

"I have read the story by Hans Christian Andersen, if that's what you mean."

"Yes, that is what I mean. I forgot the Seelie Court enjoys reading fairy tales, and laughing at how wrong the humans get things."

"It would be a shame if you kissed me too late to save them, Meredith. I can only offer their safety for a little while, and then the assassins will do their jobs and it will be too late."

"They made a movie of the story. They made a movie of 'The Little Mermaid,' and there was a song in it called 'Kiss the Girl.'"

"What does it matter, Meredith? Why this delay, do you want them dead?"

"You don't understand. By killing Sholto you put them all on alert, and I trust my men, and the human guards, and the human police, to fight."

"It will not be a fight, Meredith, any more than Sholto had a chance to fight."

"What of my babies? What happens to them if I let you bespell me?"

He settled his weight more firmly against me, one knee between my legs. "They are our babies, Meredith. They will come with you to the Seelie Court. They will be princesses and prince here with us."

"You'll never take them to a Disney movie, or read them a fairy tale without showing your disdain for the human who wrote it. You won't love them."

"I will love them, as I love you, Meredith."

"You don't love me!" I yelled it at the floor, the echo of my own voice strident in my ears.

"I love you, Meredith."

"Swear it, swear that you love me truly, swear it by the Darkness That Eats All Things; swear that oath, uncle, and I may give you your willing kiss."

"That is an Unseelie oath, and I will not utter it."

"It is an oath that will hunt you down and destroy you if you break it. The only reason not to take such an oath is that you know you do not love me."

"You will love me, Meredith. You will adore me. Our children will see us as a devoted couple."

"You are not their father! The genetic tests will come back in a few weeks and that will prove that I was pregnant before you forced yourself on me. The tests will prove that you are a rapist, a liar, and infertile, and I will do everything I can to get you convicted of my rape. I will plaster it across the human media, that the great King of the Seelie is so insecure that he has to beat and rape rather than seduce."

"You won't; you will drop the charges against me, Meredith. You will tell everyone that you came to me willingly, Meredith."

Of course I would; he was right, of course.

"You will tell the newspapers and the television that the Unseelie kept you prisoner and it was only when Shadowspawn, Darkness, and Storm were dead that you felt safe enough to escape to the Seelie Court with your babies."

"You always go too far, uncle," I said. "You almost have me under your spell, and then you say something that is so outrageous that even your magic can't make me believe it. You are evil, uncle, did you know that?"

He got both of his legs inside mine, and only the dress with all its layers of petticoats kept him from pressing closer, but even through all the clothing I could feel him against me. I had to swallow past the lump in my throat. I prayed to Goddess that he would not touch me again.

"Do you feel that, Meredith?"

"I don't know what you mean, uncle." It was a lie, but I was not going to play along.

He ground himself in against my ass. "Do you feel me now, Meredith?"

"Yes," I whispered.

"I dressed you for this dream, Meredith; I can just as easily undress you with a thought."

"Don't."

"Kiss me, Meredith, and then you will want me to, and it will not be rape."

"Lust magic is the same as date-rape drugs in human courts, Uncle Taranis. Even if you bespell me, humans have forensic wizards who specialize in understanding spells like this; I have too many friends among the human police. They won't believe that I was willing. Even if you win this moment, the police will free me of your spell eventually, and when they do, you will be jailed, or exiled from this country."

"At worst they would limit me to the Seelie Court, Meredith, and that is where I stay anyway."

"No, uncle dearest, you had a king of another kingdom assassinated; that is an act of war, and that is the one thing that will get you kicked out of this country."

"Only you know what I did, Meredith, and once we kiss, you won't tell."

"You don't believe the human wizards will free me once you have me under your spell?"

"No, Meredith, I don't. Human magic has never been a match for mine. Now, about that dress."

"No," I said.

My clothes vanished and I was suddenly naked against the rugs and the stone. He was still pressed against my ass, but now he felt bigger and harder, eager for his conquest.

"NO!" I pulled my hand free, and I prayed as never before, *Let this work, let my hand of power be real here!* Taranis made his clothes vanish. I had a moment of feeling him naked on top of me, pinning me to the floor, and then his hips began to shift, to hunt for an angle that would let him enter me, and I shoved my hand against his bare arm. The same arm that I had twisted in the last nightmare he'd given me.

His arm began to fold in upon itself. He let me go, and it was his turn to scream, "NO!"

I turned and saw him on his knees, naked, and maybe he was handsome, but all I could see was the monster he was, and his left arm was a curling, deformed thing. I waited for it to reach the main part of his body and turn him inside out so that he wouldn't be able to hide the monster inside, behind the handsome façade. I would make him into the truth of himself, and pull the horror out so all the world could see it.

"Meredith! Help me, Meredith, help me!"

I said, "No."

He vanished, and a second later I woke in the hospital with Doyle bending over me. He wasn't dead. I wasn't trapped with Taranis, and he hadn't bespelled me, and maybe, just maybe, the damage I'd done to him in dream would be real when he woke. Now, all we had to do was stop the assassins from killing Doyle and Mistral the way they'd killed Sholto.

CHAPTER

FORTY-ONE

A sound in the darkened room had frightened me at first, and then I'd seen the nightflyers plastered to the wall around the window, and my heart had lifted, because only Sholto could have brought them to L.A. He wasn't dead? Had it been another dream? No, it had been real. I held Doyle's hand in mine and looked around the room for Sholto.

Galen was on the other side of the bed. "I told you what she'd think when she saw the nightflyers. I'm sorry, Merry, but Sholto is still dead."

"How did they get to L.A. without him?"

"Kitto brought them," Doyle said.

I looked from one to the other of them. "Am I still dreaming?"

Galen smiled. "I could pinch you to prove we're real."

It made me smile a little. I tried to reach for his hand, but I was still hooked to an IV, so he took my hand instead. "No pinching necessary," I said, "but how did Kitto bring the sluagh across the country?"

Doyle answered, "He used his hand of power."

"The hand of reaching only lets him bring someone through a mirror during a call." I looked at the mass of nightflyers covering the far wall and clinging to part of the ceiling. There had to be at least two dozen of them, though the way their flat bodies overlapped it was hard to get an accurate count, but still . . . "It would take hours to bring through this many of the sluagh. How long was I trapped in dream?"

My heart was pounding in my throat again, because though Doyle was here safe beside me, Mistral was not.

"You have only been asleep a short time, Merry; it has not been hours," Doyle said.

"Where is Mistral?" I asked.

"At the main house, in charge of seeing that no harm comes to the babies. A hate group had claimed responsibility for trying to assassinate you, so I made Mistral stay at the house and see to the defenses there. He made me swear I would explain that only duty to our children would keep him from your side."

"Doyle, you and Mistral are in terrible danger. Taranis means to have you both killed, as he killed Sholto. He fears the three of you the most of my men, and he intends to strip me of you, and then try to claim me for himself."

Doyle touched my face, looking very hard into my eyes, as if trying to tell if I was telling the truth, or mad, or still dream befuddled.

"It was not just a nightmare, Doyle. Taranis was in my dreams again."

Galen cursed softly. "Damn it, we let them put you to bed without the herbs in your pillow. I am so sorry, Merry; I should have thought of it."

"We know that it is not a human hate group, but traitors among the sidhe themselves," Doyle said.

"How do you know? Did Taranis invade someone else's dreams?"

"No, but Rhys and Barinthus went to the beach house to make certain the sidhe there cooperated with the police, and forced them all to let the police take their fingerprints."

"Are you saying one of the sidhe at the beach killed . . . shot Sholto?"

"Rhys and the police both quickly realized that the angle of the shot meant it could not have come from the hillside, but had to come from one of the upper windows of the house itself."

"A lot of them didn't want to cooperate with the police," Galen said.

"I understand the murderer not wanting to cooperate with the police, but why did the rest refuse?"

Doyle and Galen exchanged a look, and it was Doyle who said, "They felt that the human authorities had no sway over them. I sent Rhys and Barinthus to convince them that they were mistaken." There was something ominous in the way he said the last; at another time I might have asked how harsh the methods of persuasion had been, but frankly, I didn't care. How dare they not want to help solve Sholto's . . . murder.

"They refused to help when they thought that I'd been the attempted target?"

"They said that Sholto was not their king, and that he died so easily proved he was either not sidhe or contaminated by your mortality."

I just stared at him for a few seconds. "What?"

They exchanged another look between them.

"What was that look just now? You've mentioned almost everybody but Frost; where is he?"

"He's with a doctor," Doyle said.

I started to sit up, and he held me down with one hand on my shoulder. "He is all right, or as all right as when he entered the hospital," Doyle said.

"What does that mean?" I asked, and it was as if the fear from the dream had just been waiting below the surface, because it came bubbling up now. I fought the panic, and knew it was at least partly the nightmare and Taranis, but . . . sometimes there was so much that I felt as if I'd been on the edge of panic for months.

As if talking about him had conjured him, the door opened and Frost was there, looking tall and unbelievably handsome. His hair glinted in the dim light of the room the way the Christmas tree had looked on Christmas Eve when I was little, all gleaming and beautiful as my father turned out the lights because Santa wouldn't come if the lights were on. We celebrated Yule and the winter solstice as a religious holiday, but he wanted me to have a more American holiday when I was very small, and had even been willing for me to go to Christian church with some of my school friends, and to temple with my friends who were Jewish. My father had wanted me to understand my country, not just our people. Frost's hair looked like that long-ago Christmas tree tinsel, and the Christmas mornings I'd seen on television, but that never quite happened to me. I'd so wanted brothers and sisters, and family holidays that hadn't been full of political debate, or photo opportunities for the press. Frost coming through that door made me feel like Christmas morning was supposed to feel, and never had.

Whatever he saw on my face made him smile, that bright, too-wide one that made his face both less model perfect and more amazing all at the same time. Galen moved back so Frost could take my hand and lean in to kiss me. He hesitated somewhere in the middle of standing back up, as if something in the middle of his body had caught, or hurt.

"What did the doctor say?" Doyle asked.

"He gave me some antibiotics and told me not to do anything physically taxing for at least three more days."

"Wait, are you saying that the dog scratches are infected?" I asked.

"It would seem so," he said; he held my hand in his, and smiled down at me.

"You can't get infection from a wound, except through poison, or an evil spell. None of the fey can just get an infection."

"Nonetheless, it is why I am not healing as I should."

"Frost, you . . . I've seen you heal bullet wounds in less time than these scratches. They were deep, but not that deep."

"The doctor assures me that these are natural antibiotics, not man-made, so I should not have an allergic reaction to them, and because I have never had antibiotics before, the infection shouldn't be immune to it, as it might be if I had had more modern medical care."

"Frost, are you saying you're healing human-slow, as slowly as I might heal?"

Frost wouldn't look at me. I looked at Doyle and Galen at the foot of the bed. "Someone talk to me, now," I said.

"Some of the newer sidhe were not happy that Frost isn't healing as he did before he left faerie," Doyle said.

"Before he was with me, you mean," I said. I held both their hands in mine, squeezed them tight.

"It doesn't matter what caused it," Frost said, and his face was still serene, peaceful, even happy.

"You were immortal and unaging. You would have been this beautiful and amazing forever, and loving me has stolen that from you. How? How did just being my lover damage your immortality?"

He raised my hand and rubbed his lips along my knuckles. It felt wonderful, but all I could think was that he would age now. That in loving him I'd killed him.

"We do not know why or how it happened," Doyle said.

"So Sholto dying is my fault; that he couldn't heal it like a nightflyer might, or a sidhe might, is because he loved me? How can that be?"

I wasn't panicked now, I was horrified.

There was a hissing from the nightflyers and one of them slid to the floor and rose upward as if a manta ray could stand. It spoke with the flat, lipless mouth on its underside, gesturing with its tentacles that were so like Sholto's.

"Our queen, it was a fearsome wound; even we might have died of it."

There was a hissing, sibilant chorus from the others.

"Do not blame yourself, and if your mortality did spread to our king, he was still the happiest we had ever seen him."

One of the others peeled itself back enough from the wall to say, "So young and so sad, until you came."

The one that was standing, swaying like a fleshy carpet, was able to walk forward. "We will see you safe, and the killer punished. Your little goblin shamed us into coming to protect you and the babes; it is the last duty we can do the best king in all of faerie."

All the nightflyers were very old, so saying *thank you* was potentially an insult, but I wanted to say something. "What is your name?" I asked.

"Barra, my queen."

"Sholto was the best of rulers in all of faerie, and a good man. I am honored that you, Barra, and so many of the nightflyers have traveled so far to help keep me and Sholto's children safe."

He bowed, and it was clumsy, because among the sluagh they weren't expected to do something that worked so awkwardly for their anatomy.

"The bow is much appreciated, but I know that among your own people that is not a gesture expected of you, and I will not expect it either."

He looked at me with huge dark eyes. "You are wise in our ways."

"I am your queen until you elect another king; I will do my best by you all, until that time."

It was as if the mantle of his body flowed, or waved from top to bottom. "It was voted on; we will elect no new king until we have avenged King Sholto."

"That might be months," I said. "Won't you need a ruler before that?"

"You are our ruler until we have a new king."

I said the only thing I could say. "I am honored, and I will do my best to rule as Sholto would have wished."

Doyle put his hand over his heart and bowed to all the nightflyers. "We are all honored by your presence here, but I do not think it will be months before Sholto is avenged."

We all looked at him. "Rhys's last phone call said that they had linked a fingerprint to one of the sidhe at the beach. Rhys and Barinthus and some of the Red Caps have taken the suspect to the police station."

"Is he the one who shot Sholto, or did he just load the rifle?" I asked.

Doyle looked down at me, and it was an approving look. "Sometimes in these months of you being pregnant I have forgotten that you were a detective here in the Western Lands before I found you."

"Sometimes I feel like I've been pregnant forever, and never anything else, but being a mother doesn't make me not Merry Gentry, private detective."

"We do not know if he pulled the trigger, or if he was part of a conspiracy. Until we are certain we have no other traitors among the sidhe, we will surround you with guards we are certain of, like all in this room."

"We appreciate the trust you show us," Barra said.

"The sluagh have more honor than most of the guard of any court," Doyle said.

Barra gave another of those strangely graceless, graceful bows.

"We need to know everything the suspect knows," I said.

"He is not wanting to talk."

"I'm assuming he's claiming diplomatic immunity as a noble of the court," I said.

"Of course," Doyle said.

"Good," I said.

He looked at me. "Good, Merry? That means the police cannot question him at all."

"It also means that the sidhe has put himself firmly in the hands of faerie, and I am a queen of faerie. We will treat our traitor as a noble of the faerie courts, and he will tell us everything we want to know."

"If you torture him, the police will likely stop you."

I smiled and could feel that it wasn't a pleasant smile. "I don't think we'll have to resort to traditional torture."

"What are you planning?" Galen asked, and he sounded suspicious.

"How much of the sluagh is here in the Western Lands? Is it just nightflyers?"

"No, our queen, we are many. Your goblin sidhe brought many of us through the mirror."

"Even better," I said.

"Merry," Galen said, "what are you planning to do?"

"I am the Queen of the Sluagh, and he's slain my king; I am within my rights to use the sluagh to question him."

"Some of the sluagh seen without magic to protect the mind can cause madness," Doyle said.

"I think he'll talk before that happens," I said.

"Ruthless, and practical," Barra said. "We approve."

There was another hissing sound like a Greek chorus from some Lovecraftian nightmare. It made me smile, because it would likely scare the hell out of our traitor.

"I brought you fresh clothes," Galen said.

I smiled at him. "Then let's get me dressed and go help Rhys question our prisoner."

"Let the doctor say you are well enough to go, first," Doyle said.

"I am well enough."

"Galen, fetch the doctor."

Galen turned without a word and went for the door. One of the nightflyers slithered across the ceiling, poured like thick water down the wall, and crawled sideways out the door. Galen held the door without being asked, as if he expected it.

"There are more guards outside the door, both human and fey. It has been decided that none of your lovers go anywhere without extra guard."

"I agree," I said.

"We will lose no more princes of faerie to this plot," Barra said.

I let go of Doyle's hand so I could hold Frost's with both of mine. "But we will lose this prince of faerie, eventually. I am so sorry, Frost."

Frost smiled down at me. "We will grow old together, my Merry. What could be better than that?"

Doyle leaned in and put his dark hand over our clasped ones. I realized he was crying, the tears gleaming in the lights. "Do not leave me all alone, not both of you, I do not think I could bear it. I would rather age and fade with the two of you than live the rest of eternity without either of you."

We opened our arms and the Darkness laid himself across the bed so we could hold him while he cried, because we would age and he would not.

CHAPTER

FORTY-TWO

Trancer's handcuffs were fastened through the metal ring on the metal table in the interrogation room. His feet were chained to a ring in the floor. His long brown hair was disheveled, but since he couldn't raise his hands to smooth it into place, there was nothing he could do about it. I knew how vain the men of the courts were about their appearance, so it bothered him more than it would have most men, but there were probably things about his physical appearance that bothered him more right now. One tricolored eye was swelling shut, the cheek underneath it was swollen, and his mouth had blood drying at the corner of the opposite side from the other damage, as if someone had hit him on one side, then backhanded him and hit him again. For all I knew that was exactly what happened, but honestly, I didn't care. I hoped it hurt, hoped he was hurting. If he had pulled the trigger and killed Sholto, I planned on him hurting, a lot.

I was strangely calm as I sat across the table from him. I felt icy calm, as if something in me had gone cold and would never be warm again. It was still a type of shock, emotional shock, and I knew that, but thanks to being in shock, I didn't care about that either. It would help me think; it would help me question the man sitting chained across from me without losing my temper. The police hadn't wanted me in here, and as Merry

Gentry, private detective, I wouldn't have been, but I was sitting here as Queen Meredith of the Sluagh, and Trancer was still invoking his rights as a citizen of faerie, so being a queen trumped my PI license all to hell.

No matter what you see on television, interrogation rooms are small, so with Rhys and Doyle standing behind me, and Detective Lucy Tate standing in the far corner along with one local detective it was . . . cozy. Lucy was here as a courtesy since she was L.A. homicide, not Malibu, which was where the beach house was located, but the Los Angeles County Sheriff's department was like most police departments, they both fiercely protected their turf and wanted desperately to avoid blame in high-profile cases. There was always that mix of wanting to be the hero and not wanting to be the scapegoat for a mediaworthy case like this one. It was a thin line to walk, and they were willing to let me help them walk it, for now.

"You told me you and your wife wanted me to help give you a baby; was that a lie?"

I had a moment to see him surprised by the question, before he schooled his face to polite blankness. It didn't work as well with the bruises and blood, but he did his best. He was a noble of the Seelie Court; he knew how to hide his feelings.

"Answer her," Doyle said in a growling deep voice.

"I don't have to answer her," Trancer said.

Detective Ivan stepped away from the wall, running a hand through his short, dark hair. He looked exotic, almost Asian, but not quite. "You don't have to talk to us, local cops, or even Detective Tate here, because your diplomatic immunity means we have no authority over you."

"See, I don't have to answer any of your questions." He sounded far too satisfied when he said it.

"You don't have to answer our questions," Lucy said, "but you do have to answer to your own people."

"The princess is not one of my people."

"Technically, I am a princess of both courts, but I'm not here as a princess."

He actually sneered at me. "What then, as a private detective?"

I smiled, not pleasantly. I clenched my hands together in front of me, because if I lost control of my temper I didn't want to hurt him by accident. No, if I hurt him, I wanted it to be on purpose.

"No, as Queen Meredith."

"Queen of what?" And again he made it disdainful.

"Queen of the Sluagh, married and crowned by faerie itself to King Sholto."

A flicker of uncertainty crossed through the one eye I could read well, but his arrogance climbed back into place almost instantly. "The sluagh are already electing a new king, and then you will be nothing to them. They are not a hereditary monarchy, so even if your babies are Sholto's they gain no hold on the crown of the dark host."

"The sluagh have voted to elect no new ruler until King Sholto's murderer is punished. Until then, I am Queen Meredith the First, of the Sluagh."

I saw the first hint of fear, but he conquered it quickly and was back to arrogance. "I don't believe you."

"It is unprecedented in all their long history, so I can understand you not believing it, but you don't have to take my word for it." I looked back over my shoulder and said, "Doyle, could you ask Barra to come inside, please?"

He went to the door without a word, spoke low, and held the door open. Barra didn't walk in; he crawled sideways around the wall of the door frame and flowed up to hang on the ceiling above me, which put him above the table, and our prisoner—who stared up at the nightflyer with undisguised fear on his face. Good.

But Trancer was made of stern stuff, and though he couldn't quite control his face, his voice was unconcerned. "Almost every type of fey has been exiled at one time or another. One nightflyer in the Western Lands proves nothing."

"Oh, is that all," I said. "Doyle, if you please."

He opened the door again and the nightflyers flowed inside like writhing, fleshy water, until they covered the ceiling and most of the walls.

I spared a glance for Lucy and Detective Ivan; they had both been introduced to the nightflyers and knew the plan. One of the reasons Detective Ivan was the local policeman in the room was that he was the one who had had the least amount of discomfort interacting with them. Lucy had visited with us at the main house, so she knew that fey came in many shapes and sizes.

Trancer wasn't pale, he was gray from fear. He had to lick his lips twice before he said in a strained voice, "They could not have traveled here this quickly."

"You thought that once Sholto was dead no one else could open the way for his sluagh, didn't you, Trancer?"

He just stared at them; the skin near his one good eye had started to twitch. "This is not possible."

"Who is the Queen of the Sluagh?" I asked.

They answered in a hissing chorus, "You are, Queen Meredith." The last syllable of my name hissed nicely in echoes around the room.

"Are you expecting Taranis to rescue you, Lord Trancer?" I asked.

There was the barest flicker of confirmation in his face, quickly hidden between a mixture of ongoing fear and the last bit of arrogance he could muster. "He is the only king I acknowledge."

"But there, you see, Trancer, we have a problem."

"I have no problem, for I am a noble of the Seelie Court and neither the humans nor you have authority over me."

"Actually, we contacted the Seelie Court and they don't give a damn what we do with you. In fact, the various factions seem to be very busy disavowing all knowledge of your actions."

He frowned. "What are you babbling about? The factions all bow to our one true king."

"If you mean Taranis, he is no longer King of the Seelie, or of anyone anywhere for that matter," I said.

"Your lies will not trick me," he said.

"It is true that Taranis was the absolute ruler of his court, and once given the throne it's for life, which means in his case forever."

"Your own words prove that you are lying," Trancer said.

"There are only two things that could dethrone a King of the Seelie," I said.

He blinked at me, and I could see him thinking. "The king is father of at least one of your brats, proving that he is not infertile."

"Ironic, isn't it," I said.

He was recovering himself, burying his fear under centuries of court manners. "King Taranis knows who is loyal to him."

I smiled a little wider. "Perhaps, but since he is no longer king, his loyalty is of absolutely no help to you."

"What are you babbling about, girl?"

The nightflyers moved restlessly and it was as if the ceiling and walls breathed and flexed. It was unsettling even to me, and they were on my side.

"Neither my subjects nor I like you very much, Trancer. I'd try to play nicer with us, if I were you."

He swallowed hard enough that I could hear it, and then said in a much milder tone, "What do you mean that Taranis is no longer king?"

"I told you, there are two reasons that a Seelie ruler will lose their right to rule. One is infertility, but there is one other. It hasn't been invoked in a very long time, but it's still irrevocably tied to rulership of the Seelie Court. Do you remember what it is? Because I do. I remembered it when Taranis invaded my dreams at the hospital."

"He is still physically perfect; his arm was not deformed in reality, only in the dream. He said that he saw it twisted from the corner of his eye, but none of the rest of the court could see it, because it was not real."

"Not the first time, no," I said.

"You are lying now; no one can cause true harm in dream. That power was lost to us long ago."

"Taranis was able to make this dream much more real. I couldn't break free of it. Maybe it was the drugs the hospital gave me to help with the shock I went into after my king died in my arms, or maybe Taranis recovered more of his own power over dreams. I suppose we'll never know, but as he made the dream much more real, and much more frightening, I was able to make my magic much more real, too."

"You didn't . . . you couldn't have."

"I could, and I did. Whatever power, or favor, Taranis offered you to assassinate Sholto, he can't pay it now, because as an ex-king he has no access to the treasury, and no ability to make political appointments or give out noble titles. All he can offer now is his friendship. Is that enough, Lord Trancer? Is the friendship of a fallen king payment enough for you to have assassinated a king?"

"You are just trying to manipulate me into a confession of some sort."

"I do want to know who else is involved in the plot to assassinate King Sholto, Prince Doyle, and Prince Mistral, that is true."

His arrogance slipped away and what color he'd regained went with it, so that he wasn't just gray, but pasty gray, as if he were suddenly ill.

"You're wondering who told me exactly which of my men was being targeted? I could pretend that someone else involved has talked, but the truth is so much better. Taranis himself told me. He confessed everything like a villain in a superhero movie, because he thought he would use a love spell and I would forget everything he told me, or be so besotted with him that I wouldn't care."

My anger rose, and with it my magic, so that my skin began to shine, just a little. It was hard to see in the fluorescent light, but Trancer saw it, because the fear made his one good eye flash white, like a horse about to bolt. I took long, even breaths to control my anger and the power. I glanced at the two police in the corner. Lucy gave the smallest shake of her head, telling me to calm down. Detective Ivan was wide-eyed, his hand going to a gun that wasn't at his hip, because you weren't allowed to bring guns into an interrogation room. Their reaction let me know that my eyes had started to glow, and maybe even my hair was starting to do that ruby luminescence. I worked until I could swallow most of that magic down, and then did my best to speak calmly.

"Taranis would have had me like some drug addict with him as my addiction. He meant to control me and gain control of my children, and for that evil plan he has paid with two of the things he values most in the world: his beauty, and his kingship."

I stood up and leaned a little across the table. "Be careful, Lord Trancer, that you do not pay with the things you hold most dear."

"What do you . . . mean?"

"If you will not name a conspirator, then I have to assume that your wife, Lady Fenella, was an active participant in the murder of my husband."

"She knows nothing, I swear it."

"Make me believe that, Lord Trancer."

He made me believe it, because he really did love his wife. He bargained for her safety, and never tried to bargain for his own, because he knew there was no point. I'd looked into his eyes and seen that he loved his wife, and he'd looked into mine and seen his own death. We were both right.

CHAPTER

FORTY-THREE

We had enough from Trancer's confession to get the human
authorities to limit Taranis to the Seelie Court's sithen, not just
faerie, but inside the Seelie Court's mound only. They actually made it
part of the National Guard unit that was still assigned to keep watch in
Cahokia in case another battle broke out, to report if Taranis stepped
outside the sithen. He had been the King of Light and Illusion, but his
hand of power was twisted in upon itself so he could no longer use light
as a weapon. He could still make illusions with his other hand, so that
you'd believe almost anything he conjured on himself, or that's what our
friends among the Seelie report, but they also report that he can't change
the arm I damaged. No matter how perfect the rest of his illusion is, the
arm remains deformed, foreshortened, with the hand half swallowed up
somewhere close to his elbow. He had been able to stop my hand of flesh
from turning him completely inside out, but from the elbow down he
was a walking example of what my magic could do to even the most
powerful among the sidhe. Everyone's been much more respectful.
Andais said it: People will follow you for love, respect, or fear. I preferred
love, but fear would do.

Andais has continued to be the perfect aunt, until we finally allowed
her and Eamon to visit in person. We made it a media event for the

Queen of the Unseelie Court to visit her nieces and nephew. It was some of the best press that our court has had in, well, ever. Perhaps she behaved herself better because the cameras were watching everything she did, but the tears she shed when she held Alastair were real enough. He looks more like my father every day, so she says. His full name is Alastair Essus Dolson Winter after my father and his two genetic fathers, Doyle and Frost. Wynne, Gwenwyfar Joy Tempest Garland, actually seems to look like Rhys and Galen had a love child, but her magic is all Mistral's. Her first name was the oldest Welsh spelling of Guinevere, Rhys's choice. Then Joy to reflect my nickname, so that we're Merry and Joy, and yes that was Galen's idea, but he and Rhys also chose Garland, both because it's a wreath of flowers and you wear it to celebrate victories and special occasions, but also for Judy Garland, because of Rhys's love of old movies. For Mistral it was either Windy, Storm, or Tempest, and he chose his favorite of the three. We've all been doing our best to teach our budding storm princess how to control her temper and her powers. They seem to be more intense if she's outside where she can see the sky; so far she's only been able to call some clouds and a few raindrops if she throws a tantrum outside, but since Mistral's rage can call tornadoes we're working with a child psychologist to help teach the girls how to control their magic. Alastair seems to be the most normal baby of the three, so far. Our last baby is Tegan Bryluen Mary Katherine. Tegan was Sholto's grandmother's name on his father's side, and Royal is happy with Bryluen because it means "rose" in Cornish and plant names are traditional among the demi-fey. Then Mary for me, and Kitto chose Katherine for his daughter because it could be shortened to Kitty, which looked like his own name. We've actually started calling her Tegan Rose, as if it's one name. She's learning to control her powers, too. Maeve's son, Liam, is still insisting that Rose is his, the way you'd claim a puppy, but I have to wonder if her ability to fascinate might have had a lasting impression on the little boy. We shall see.

I've made it clear that I have no desire to sit on Taranis's vacated throne. The many factions inside the Seelie Court scrambled to try to put their candidates on the throne, but through our friends among their nobles we suggested they let the sithen choose, as of old. Their faerie mound sang with joy when Aisling was finally allowed back through its doors, because now that Taranis was no longer king, all those that he exiled have a chance to return home.

Maeve Reed has no plans to visit, just yet. She's still afraid of Taranis, and rumor has it that he's convinced that he may find a cure for his arm, as the long-ago Lugh of the Silverhand did when he lost his hand in battle and had to give up the throne because of his lack of perfection, until a magical hand of silver was formed and he was made whole again. I think Taranis is lying to himself, but as long as he stays inside faerie and away from us we will let it lie. Do I want him dead for what he did to Sholto? Yes, but I want peace in faerie more. We'll see how Taranis reacts as Aisling's coronation gets closer; it's going to be the first-ever faerie coronation to be televised live.

Andais would still step down and let Doyle and me have her throne, but we still don't trust our safety inside either court, light or dark. I am content ruling the growing Western Lands of faerie, because it is spreading, and more enchanted land keeps appearing, here and there around L.A. They say that Hollywood is magic; they've never been more right.

ABOUT THE AUTHOR

Laurell K. Hamilton is the top-ten *New York Times* bestselling author of twenty-two 'Anita Blake: Vampire Hunter' novels – the latest of which is *Affliction* – and the 'Meredith Gentry' books. *A Shiver of Light* is the ninth novel in this series. Laurell lives with her family near St Louis, Missouri in the USA. To find out more, visit www.laurellkhamilton.org

Deploying License-Free Wireless Wide-Area Networks

Jack Unger

Cisco Press

Cisco Press
201 West 103rd Street
Indianapolis, IN 46290 USA

Deploying License-Free Wireless Wide-Area Networks

Published by:
Cisco Press
201 West 103rd Street
Indianapolis, IN 46290 USA

Printed in the United States of America 1 2 3 4 5 6 7 8 9 0

First Printing April 2008

Library of Congress Cataloging-in-Publication Number: 2001098196

ISBN: 1-58705-790-5

Warning and Disclaimer

This book is designed to provide information about license-free wireless wide-area networks. Every effort has been made to make this book as complete and as accurate as possible, but no warranty or fitness is implied.

The information is provided on an "as is" basis. The author, Cisco Press, and Cisco Systems, Inc. shall have neither liability nor responsibility to any person or entity with respect to any loss or damages arising from the information contained in this book or from the use of the discs or programs that may accompany it.

The opinions expressed in this book belong to the author and are not necessarily those of Cisco Systems, Inc.

Trademark Acknowledgments

All terms mentioned in this book that are known to be trademarks or service marks have been appropriately capitalized. Cisco Press or Cisco Systems, Inc. cannot attest to the accuracy of this information. Use of a term in this book should not be regarded as affecting the validity of any trademark or service mark.

Feedback Information

At Cisco Press, our goal is to create in-depth technical books of the highest quality and value. Each book is crafted with care and precision, undergoing rigorous development that involves the unique expertise of members from the professional technical community.

Readers' feedback is a natural continuation of this process. If you have any comments regarding how we could improve the quality of this book, or otherwise alter it to better suit your needs, you can contact us through e-mail at feedback@ciscopress.com. Please make sure to include the book title and ISBN in your message.

We greatly appreciate your assistance.

Publisher	John Wait
Editor-in-Chief	John Kane
Executive Editor	Brett Bartow
Cisco Representative	Anthony Wolfenden
Cisco Press Program Manager	Sonia Torres Chavez
Cisco Marketing Communications Manager	Tom Geitner
Cisco Marketing Program Manager	Edie Quiroz
Production Manager	Patrick Kanouse
Acquisitions Editor	Michelle Grandin
Senior Development Editor	Christopher Cleveland
Project Editor	San Dee Phillips
Copy Editor	Karen A. Gill
Technical Editor(s)	Greg DesBrisay, Jim Geier, Dr. H. Paul Shuch, Ph.D.
Team Coordinator	Tammi Ross
Book Designer	Gina Rexrode
Cover Designer	Louisa Adair
Compositor	Mark Shirar
Indexer	Tim Wright

CISCO SYSTEMS

Corporate Headquarters
Cisco Systems, Inc.
170 West Tasman Drive
San Jose, CA 95134-1706
USA
www.cisco.com
Tel: 408 526-4000
    800 553-NETS (6387)
Fax: 408 526-4100

European Headquarters
Cisco Systems International BV
Haarlerbergpark
Haarlerbergweg 13-19
1101 CH Amsterdam
The Netherlands
www-europe.cisco.com
Tel: 31 0 20 357 1000
Fax: 31 0 20 357 1100

Americas Headquarters
Cisco Systems, Inc.
170 West Tasman Drive
San Jose, CA 95134-1706
USA
www.cisco.com
Tel: 408 526-7660
Fax: 408 527-0883

Asia Pacific Headquarters
Cisco Systems, Inc.
Capital Tower
168 Robinson Road
#22-01 to #29-01
Singapore 068912
www.cisco.com
Tel: +65 6317 7777
Fax: +65 6317 7799

Cisco Systems has more than 200 offices in the following countries and regions. Addresses, phone numbers, and fax numbers are listed on the
Cisco.com Web site at www.cisco.com/go/offices.

Argentina • Australia • Austria • Belgium • Brazil • Bulgaria • Canada • Chile • China PRC • Colombia • Costa Rica • Croatia • Czech Republic
Denmark • Dubai, UAE • Finland • France • Germany • Greece • Hong Kong SAR • Hungary • India • Indonesia • Ireland • Israel • Italy
Japan • Korea • Luxembourg • Malaysia • Mexico • The Netherlands • New Zealand • Norway • Peru • Philippines • Poland • Portugal
Puerto Rico • Romania • Russia • Saudi Arabia • Scotland • Singapore • Slovakia • Slovenia • South Africa • Spain • Sweden
Switzerland • Taiwan • Thailand • Turkey • Ukraine • United Kingdom • United States • Venezuela • Vietnam • Zimbabwe

About the Author

Jack Unger, the founder and president of Wireless InfoNet, Inc., is a pioneer in the broadband fixed-wireless industry. Since founding Wireless InfoNet in 1993, he has personally designed and installed hundreds of license-free outdoor broadband wireless network sites and consulted on countless others. In 1995, he designed and deployed one of the world's first public outdoor wireless Internet access points-of-presence. This wireless POP is still in service today in Palo Alto, California. In 2001, based on his wireless ISP experiences, Jack created the world's first vendor-neutral wireless ISP training seminar. To date, in this seminar, he has personally trained more than 800 ISP personnel across the United States.

Prior to founding Wireless InfoNet, Jack worked for 14 years in the Silicon Valley telecommunications industry for ROLM, IBM, Siemens, and NEC. Prior to that, Jack worked for 7 years selling wireless communications equipment, including television and radio station broadcast equipment. He has a total of 45 years of wireless experience since his "initiation" into the wireless world as an amateur radio operator at the age of 11. Jack has received A.A., A.S., and B.A. degrees and has completed extensive work in the U.C. Berkeley Extension Telecommunications Engineering Program. He holds FCC Amateur Extra and General Radiotelephone licenses as well as an FAA Private Pilot license. He also served as a volunteer firefighter for 11 years in the mountains of Santa Cruz County, California.

Jack is an experienced technical writer who has written numerous telecommunications hardware and software manuals and close to 100 Cisco IOS Release Notes for the Cisco 2600, 3600, 3810, 4000, and IAD2420 router product lines. *Deploying License-Free Wireless Wide-Area Networks* is the industry's first book written specifically to help wireless ISPs and corporate IT department personnel successfully deploy outdoor, license-free, wireless WANs and broadband wireless Internet access. Jack welcomes your comments, suggestions, corrections, and questions via e-mail. You are invited to contact him at suggestions@ask-wi.com.

About the Technical Reviewers

Jim Geier is the founder and principal consultant of Wireless-Nets, Ltd., a consulting firm that assists companies with the development and deployment of wireless LAN products and systems. His 20 years of experience includes the analysis, design, software development, installation, and support of numerous client/server and wireless network-based systems for retail, manufacturing, warehousing, healthcare, and airline industries throughout the world. Jim is the author of several books: *802.11 Unleashed*, *Wireless LANs*, *Wireless Networking Handbook*, and *Network Reengineering*, as well as numerous articles. He is a voting member within the Wireless Ethernet Compatibility Alliance (WECA), responsible for certifying interoperability of 802.11 (Wi-Fi) wireless LANs. He served as chairman of the Institute of Electrical and Electronic Engineers (IEEE) Computer Society, Dayton Section, and chairman of the IEEE International Conference on Wireless LAN Implementation. He has been an active member of the IEEE 802.11 Working Group, responsible for developing international standards for wireless LANs. Jim's education includes B.A. and M.A. degrees in electrical engineering and an M.A. degree in business administration. You can contact Jim at jimgeier@wireless-nets.com or visit his website at www.wireless-nets.com.

H. Paul Shuch, Ph.D. is the aerospace engineer who is credited with designing the world's first commercial home satellite TV receiver. Paul has served as executive director of the grassroots, nonprofit SETI League, Inc. since its inception eight years ago.

The author of more than 300 publications, Paul holds a Ph.D. degree in engineering from the University of California, Berkeley and has taught on various campuses for 30 years. His teaching and research have won several international awards. Paul is a Fellow of the Radio Club of America and a Fellow of the British Interplanetary Society; he has served on the boards of directors of several nonprofit organizations.

A licensed commercial pilot and instrument flight instructor, Paul serves as an accident prevention counselor for the FAA, as a military program evaluator for the American Council on Education, and as a lecturer for the Air Safety Foundation. He is listed in *Who's Who in Aviation and Aerospace*, *Who's Who in California*, *Who's Who of American Inventors*, *Who's Who in Science and Engineering*, *American Men and Women of Science*, *Who's Who in American Education*, and the *International Directory of Distinguished Leadership*.

Paul lives on a radio-quiet hilltop in central Pennsylvania with his biologist wife, five of their seven recombinant DNA experiments, three motorcycles, two radio telescopes, and an antique MG-TD. He can be found on the web at http://drseti.com.

Jack Unger, the author of this book, is Paul's former student, former employee, fellow radio amateur, and lifelong friend.

Dedications

I dedicate this book to my mother, Virginia Blossom Kaufman-Unger-London and to my father, Milton Unger. Thank you both for loving me unconditionally.

Acknowledgments

Literally thousands of people have made indirect contributions to this book.

First, thanks to all of my public school teachers (from kindergarten through college) who patiently helped me, encouraged me, and taught me how to learn. Next, thanks to the many members of the amateur radio community who showed me how to actually make wireless equipment work. Further, I extend my thanks to the many members of the wireless ISP community who shared their experiences and their ideas with me. Next, thanks to my colleagues, J.V. Rudnick, Bob Fike, and Phil Marcelis, who many times showed me a better way to erect an antenna, route a cable, or configure a wireless router. Last but certainly not least, I'd like to thank my Cisco Press editors, Michelle Grandin and Christopher Cleveland, and my technical reviewers, Dr. Paul Shuch, Jim Geier, and Greg DesBrisay, for graciously contributing their energy, their experience, and their knowledge to this book.

Finally, allow me to make a gentle request of you, the reader. If you find this book helps you to learn more about and to experience the magic of wireless, please feel free to generously pass your new learning along to others who share your interest in wireless.

Contents at a Glance

Contents

Chapter 5   Selecting Antenna Systems 133

Introduction

Thank you for choosing to read this book. I wrote it for the following reasons:

- Wireless is both fun and satisfying. I want to share that fun and that satisfaction with you.

- Wireless allows you to be creative. Using the techniques in this book, you can be both creative and successful with your wireless wide-area network.

- Wireless networks save money. You can be a hero by delivering broadband bandwidth at a lower cost than traditional wired bandwidth. The more people who save money, the better it is for everyone.

- I wanted to fill the need for a practical, license-free outdoor wireless WAN book. The book needed to be based on real-world WAN deployments. The book also needed to be unbiased and vendor-independent—that is, to be free of all marketing and sales material.

Who This Book Is For

This book is for you, if you

- Find yourself intrigued by the magic of wireless

- Want to advance your knowledge and want to learn practical wireless networking skills

- Want to advance in your career and in the wireless field

- Are interested in providing broadband wireless service to others in their community

- Want to save money, have fun, and be creative

How to Use This Book

The chapters in the book are arranged in a logical order. If you have never been exposed to wireless ("exposed to wireless"… "radio-active"——you get it?), you can start reading at Chapter 1 and read right through to Chapter 9. On the other hand, if you just want to look up one particular topic, use the index or the table of contents, locate the topic, and go directly to that page or chapter. Here are the topics covered by each chapter:

- Chapter 1, "An Introduction to Broadband License-Free Wireless Wide-Area Networking," presents basic broadband wireless terminology and history. It outlines the advantages and the challenges of working with outdoor networks. Finally, it discusses the safety issues that you need to address.

- Chapter 2, "Understanding Wireless Fundamentals," helps you understand wireless fundamentals. Even if you have never worked with wireless before, you can be successful if you take the time to learn these fundamentals.

- Chapter 3, "Choosing Your Network Architecture," describes the four basic wireless network architectures, including the advantages and disadvantages of each architecture.

- Chapter 4, "Performing Site Surveys," discusses physical site surveys and wireless site surveys. Site surveys are an important step in building a reliable wireless network.

- Chapter 5, "Selecting Antenna Systems," describes how antennas work and how to use them. Proper antenna selection and use is vital to successful wireless WAN operation.

- Chapter 6, "Evaluating and Selecting Wireless Equipment," helps you to understand the range of features available in wireless equipment. When you understand the features and how they determine your network capabilities, you can select the best equipment for your network.

- Chapter 7, "Installing Outdoor Wireless Systems," explains the techniques to safely install, ground, and test your outdoor wireless systems.

- Chapter 8, "Solving Noise and Interference Problems," discusses the causes of noise and interference and explains the techniques that you can use to minimize noise and interference problems. This chapter also provides some suggestions about how you can cooperate and coordinate with other wireless network operators to reduce interference between your networks.

- Chapter 9, "Providing Broadband Wireless Internet Access," provides extra tips and techniques for those of you who want to be wireless Internet Service Providers (WISPs) and provide wireless Internet access service to your communities.

- Appendix A, "Wireless Standards Summary," provides a summary table of the 802.11 standards. It also includes related standards, such as 802.1x and 802.16.

- Appendix B, "Wireless Hardware, Software, and Service Provider Organizations," contains a listing of organizations that provide wireless hardware, software, peripherals, and services.

- Appendix C, "Answers to Chapter Review Questions," provides answers to the review questions that appear at the end of Chapters 1 through 9.

CHAPTER 1

An Introduction to Broadband License-Free Wireless Wide-Area Networking

This chapter introduces broadband wireless networking terms, summarizes license-free wireless history, and describes both the advantages and the challenges of deploying license-free wireless wide-area networks (WANs).

Differences Between Wired Networks and Wireless Networks

Most of the time, users of a broadband wireless network do not experience a difference between using a wireless network and using a wired network. Your experiences as you design and build a wireless network, however, will be quite different compared to your experiences when you design and install a wired network. Table 1-1 summarizes the differences that you need to be aware of.

Table 1-1   *Differences Between Wired and Wireless Networks*

Network Characteristic	Wired Network	Wireless Network
Visual determination of network connectivity	If you can see the network cable going to a location, that location can be connected to the network.	Wireless networks sometimes connect locations that you *cannot* visibly see. Additionally, wireless networks *might not* connect locations that you *can* see visibly.
Visibility node-to-node on the same network	All of the nodes on a wired network can hear all other nodes.	Many nodes on a wireless network cannot hear all of the other wireless nodes on the same network.
Visibility network-to-network	Wired networks are invisible to other wired networks. The presence of one wired network has no effect on the performance of another wired network.	Wireless networks are often visible to other wireless networks. One wireless network *can affect* the performance of other wireless networks.

continues

Table 1-1   *Differences Between Wired and Wireless Networks (Continued)*

Network Characteristic	Wired Network	Wireless Network
Atmospheric properties	Wired network performance is not affected by the properties of the atmosphere.	Wireless network performance *can be* affected by the properties of the atmosphere.
Terrain properties	Wired network performance is not affected by the properties of the earth's terrain.	Wireless network performance is *strongly affected* by the properties of the earth's terrain.
User connectivity and mobility	Connectivity is possible only to or from those physical locations where the network cabling extends.	Connectivity is possible *beyond* the bounds of physical network cabling.

Wireless Terminology and Evolution

Today, you can design and build wireless networks that possess three characteristics that were not available in the past. These characteristics are broadband capability, wide-area coverage, and license-free operation. The definition of these terms is somewhat vague; therefore, it is important to define the terms clearly. The following sections provide these definitions as well as some wireless history.

Broadband

Broadband is a subjective term that has been used in various ways throughout the communications industry. Broadband is used when new communications technologies are developed that provide enough additional bandwidth for the user experience to feel substantially faster than it felt before.

Most Internet users today have experienced dialing into the Internet at bandwidths ranging from 28,800 bits per second (28.8 kbps) up to 56,000 bits per second (56 kbps). They perceive a faster Internet connection, such as a 1.5 million bit per second (1.5 Mbps) connection, as a broadband connection.

Some users have access to the Internet using a web browser on a cell phone. Their connection bandwidth ranges from 9.6 kbps to 14.4 kbps. Comparing the cell phone connection speed to a dialup 28.8-kbps connection, the cell phone connection feels slow. It certainly doesn't feel like broadband; in fact, it feels like "narrowband."

For the remainder of this book, any wireless connection that has a bandwidth of 128,000 bits per second (128 kbps) will be defined as broadband. Given the Internet experiences of users who have either browsed the Internet using a cell phone or dialed into the Internet, a 128-kbps connection is perceived as broadband.

Wide-Area Network

There is no absolute line between the definition of a local-area network (LAN) and the definition of a wide-area network (WAN). Both terms have been used somewhat loosely. Here's how this book defines them:

- **LAN**—A network that connects stations contained within a single building
- **WAN**—A network that connects stations located in different buildings or in different parts of a city

---

NOTE   Some books use the term *MAN* to indicate a metropolitan-area network or, in other words, a citywide network. This book refers to a citywide network as a WAN.

History of License-Free Wireless Networking

The purpose of this book is to help you deploy broadband wireless WANs without needing to apply to the Federal Communications Commission (FCC) for a license. The following sections provide a historical overview of some of the events that led to the present privilege of using some broadband wireless equipment without needing to obtain a license.

History of Wireless Licensing

Wireless technology has passed through several regulatory phases during its history. In the late 1800s and early 1900s, there were many wireless scientists, experimenters, and hobbyists. In these early days, transmitting distances were limited and population density was low; it was unnecessary to require a license for transmitting. As more wireless stations came on the air, interference between stations became a serious problem. In 1921, the United States government began requiring licenses for all transmitters, including commercial broadcast transmitters, experimental transmitters, and amateur radio transmitters.

Radio system usage continued to grow rapidly during the remainder of the 20th century. The U.S. government continued to regulate radio transmissions and to license radio transmitters. These licensing regulations played a useful role because they allowed many different radio systems to share the available radio frequencies without interfering with each other.

The downside to governmental regulation was that it took both time and money to obtain a license to transmit on a specific frequency. This limited the use of broadband wireless equipment to those companies or individuals who could afford the cost of obtaining the FCC license and purchasing the rather expensive wireless equipment.

In 1985, the U.S. Federal Communications Commission (FCC) issued regulations that, for the first time, allowed the use of broadband wireless transmitting equipment without the need to apply for, pay for, and wait for a license. To operate license free, the wireless equipment had to do the following:

- Operate at low power levels
- Use spread spectrum modulation
- Transmit within three specified frequency bands

Broadband license-free wireless equipment began to be manufactured and sold at a much lower cost than the licensed broadband wireless equipment.

Table 1-2 provides an outline of the wireless events that led full-circle from the days when licensing was not required, to the days when licensing was required, to today, when broadband wireless equipment can be deployed license free.

Table 1-2   *Brief History of Wireless Development*

Year	Event
1600	Dr. William Gilbert detects electromagnetic activity in the human body and describes it as "electricity."
1837	Samuel F.B. Morse invents the Morse telegraph and sends messages over wires by using Morse code.
1865	Scientists, inventors, and hobbyists begin performing experiments with wireless.
1867	Scottish mathematician and physicist James Clerk Maxwell develops the theory that predicts the existence of electro-magnetic waves.
1886	German physicist Heinrich Hertz is the first person to demonstrate the existence of electromagnetic waves as predicted by James Clerk Maxwell.
1896	Italian Guglielmo Marconi demonstrates electric-wave telegraphy.
1901	Marconi transmits the letter "s" in Morse code across the Atlantic Ocean from England to Canada.
1906	Professor Reginald Fessenden broadcasts voice and music in Massachusetts.
1910	The U.S. government requires all ships to be equipped with a wireless telegraph.
1912	The "unsinkable" Titanic ocean liner sinks after striking an iceberg in the North Atlantic. The wireless telegraph is used to summon help from other ships in the area.
1912	The regulation of radio broadcasting is started by the U.S. Department of Commerce, Bureau of Navigation. Transmitting stations simply had to supply the government with a description of their transmitting equipment.
1912	Radio station KQW makes frequent broadcasts from San Jose, California.
1920	Radio station KDKA begins regular commercial broadcasting from Pittsburgh, Pennsylvania.

Table 1-2   *Brief History of Wireless Development (Continued)*

Year	Event
1921	The U.S. government requires all broadcasting stations to apply for a broadcasting license.
1927	The responsibility for regulating radio transmission is transferred to the Federal Radio Commission.
1934	The Communications Act of 1934 establishes the FCC. The responsibility for regulating radio transmission is transferred to the FCC.
1985	The FCC authorizes license-free spread spectrum transmission in three industrial, scientific, and medical (ISM) bands at 900 megahertz (MHz), 2.4 gigahertz (GHz), and 5.8 GHz. Maximum legal transmitter output power is 1 watt (1W).
1994	The FCC begins using spectrum auctions. Corporations bid hundreds of thousands to millions of dollars to buy the right to use specific wireless frequency bands.
1997	The FCC authorizes license-free transmission in three 5.1 to 5.8 GHz Unlicensed-National Information Infrastructure (U-NII) subbands. Maximum legal transmitter output power ranges from 50 milliwatts (50 mW) to 1 W.

History of Spread Spectrum

Modulation is the process of adding information or intelligence to a wireless signal.

NOTE   In the wireless world, the term *intelligence* sometimes has no discernable relationship to the process of using one's brain to make a wise decision.

A modulated wireless signal carries intelligence to the receiver where the intelligence is removed and used. The intelligence might be voice, music, data, or video. For example, the process of *amplitude modulation* adds voice and music to AM broadcast station signals. The process of *frequency modulation* adds voice and music to FM broadcast station signals. The process of *spread spectrum modulation* adds data to broadband license-free wireless signals.

The development of spread spectrum modulation began during World War II. Hedy Lamar (the actress) is credited for inventing spread spectrum modulation. The story goes that she was opposed to the actions of the German military during the war and decided to find a way to transmit and receive messages that would remain undetected by the German military. She devised the spread-spectrum principle of frequency hopping. Frequency hopping changes the transmitter frequency rapidly to prevent the transmitted messages from being detected by anyone except the person intended to receive the messages. The spread spectrum receiver knows the proper sequence of frequency changes and follows them to decode (demodulate) the transmitted message.

Two different types of spread spectrum modulation are in general use today, both of which spread the signal out over a broad band of frequencies:

- **Frequency hopping spread spectrum (FHSS)**—Changes frequency from 8 to 32 times each second

- **Direct sequence spread spectrum (DSSS)**—Stays on one center frequency but spreads out the signal at low power over a wide frequency band

The resulting transmitted signal simply looks like weak noise. Only a receiver that knows how to despread the signal can demodulate it and recover the original intelligence.

Development of License-Free Spread Spectrum

Prior to 1985, the FCC permitted low power, short-range devices such as baby monitors and garage door openers to operate license free. These devices operated indoors or with short-range transmitters and did not cause interference problems with other wireless systems. In 1985, the FCC considered the following points and then decided to allow the operation of license-free spread spectrum systems:

- Spread spectrum signals spread their wireless energy over the frequency spectrum rather than concentrating it all on one frequency. By spreading out the energy, the signals are *less likely to cause interference* to other spread spectrum and non-spread spectrum systems.

- Spread spectrum signals are *less susceptible to being interfered with* than non-spread spectrum signals.

- Low power spread spectrum transmitters operating in the ISM bands will be limited to line-of-sight operation. The *signals will not carry very far*; therefore, many spread spectrum systems can operate in the same general area without causing significant interference to each other.

- Many spread spectrum systems will be used indoors. *The building walls will absorb much of the wireless energy* before it can go very far and cause interference problems.

The first license-free spread spectrum wireless systems were short-range, indoor LANs. These systems were used for applications such as retail price marking and inventory management. Next, wireless equipment manufacturers began to offer spread spectrum equipment with improved antenna systems that could be used for longer-distance outdoor point-to-point links between buildings. These outdoor links offered a low-cost alternative to the expensive leased-line connections offered by the local telephone companies. Soon, cities, school districts, and corporations began to use this outdoor equipment in point-to-multipoint network configurations. By 1995, the first few Internet service providers (ISPs) began to use the technology to provide license-free broadband wireless Internet access to the public. The era of the license-free broadband wireless WAN had begun.

NOTE   Although spread spectrum systems are unlicensed, it does not mean that they are unregulated. The FCC specifies the rules and regulations that govern the manufacture of spread spectrum systems. Equipment manufacturers are responsible for manufacturing equipment that complies with the FCC regulations. Equipment installers are responsible for installing the wireless equipment properly so that it does not violate FCC regulations.

License-Free Wireless Frequencies

In 1985, the FCC authorized the use of license-free spread spectrum wireless equipment in the following three ISM bands in the United States:

- 900 to 928 MHz (900 MHz range)
- 2.4 to 2.483 GHz (2.4 GHz range)
- 5.725 to 5.850 GHz (5 GHz range)

Further, in 1997, the FCC authorized the use of license-free low-power *non-spread-spectrum* wireless equipment in the following three U-NII bands:

- 5.15 to 5.25 GHz
- 5.25 to 5.35 GHz
- 5.725 to 5.825 GHz

Advantages of License-Free Wireless Networks

Following are the advantages of deploying a license-free broadband wireless WAN:

- Cost savings
- Fast deployment speed
- Network architecture flexibility
- Network independence

Cost Savings

Saving money is perhaps the largest benefit of deploying a license-free wireless WAN. After the costs to design and install a wireless WAN are paid, there are no ongoing monthly rental, leasing, or service charges. Contrast this with the charges to lease a broadband line from the telephone company, which can range from $250 to $1000 or more each month. Wireless WANs also have no right-of-way costs. This is the monthly cost to place cable or fiber on telephone poles.

Compared to the cost of leased lines, the monthly costs for broadband digital subscriber line (DSL) and broadband cable Internet access service are more moderate. These costs range from $39 to $300 per month, depending on bandwidth. In many areas, however, neither DSL nor cable Internet access is available. In a few areas, two-way Internet access service is starting to be available via satellite. Costs for this service range upward from $80 per month.

In areas where DSL, cable, or satellite Internet access is available, there is frequently only one provider; many times it's the telephone company offering DSL service. Because of this lack of competition, the telephone companies are now raising their DSL prices. This trend is likely to continue indefinitely into the future.

Fast Deployment Speed

After a broadband wireless network has been designed and the access points deployed, the installation of new wireless end users can take place quickly. Typically, the time needed to install a new end user is a few days. Contrast this with the typical installment time for a new DSL or leased-line end user. The installation time is often weeks or months.

Network Architecture Flexibility

The architectural flexibility of a wireless network is unmatched by any other broadband medium. As long as a line-of-sight wireless path exists to one or more new locations, a wireless link can be deployed or redeployed in as little as one day. Redeployment consists of removing the antenna system and wireless equipment from the old location and reinstalling it in the new location. After antenna aiming is complete, the link should be ready to use.

Network Independence

A wireless WAN is the only network that can be built without relying on infrastructure that another carrier owns. Traditional broadband leased-line circuits rely on using a local loop (copper wire) circuit owned by the local telephone company; the same is true for DSL service. Providing Internet access over cable requires obtaining approval to access cable lines that the cable company owns. Cable companies routinely deny this access to competing ISPs.

In all of these cases, providing broadband service depends on using infrastructure that another company owns. Wireless WANs do not rely on obtaining permission from (and making payment to) any other company or carrier. The choice to use a wireless WAN is a choice to build, own, and operate your own broadband network.

ISPs that want to offer broadband Internet access while maintaining control of their cost structure might decide that deploying a license-free broadband wireless WAN is the only way to proceed profitably.

Challenges of License-Free Wireless Networks

To obtain the most benefit from wireless WANs, you need to understand the challenges to their successful deployment. These challenges are as follows:

- Understanding wireless fundamentals
- Overcoming real-world obstacles
- Maximizing available bandwidth
- Working safely

Challenge of Understanding Wireless Fundamentals

Wireless signals are invisible to the human eye. Making this invisible phenomenon become visible requires some learning and practice.

NOTE   What does it mean to say you can make invisible wireless signals visible? It means that you can make wireless signals predictable, controllable, and usable. You can become so familiar with their behavior that it is almost as if you could physically see them.

Successful wireless deployment requires an understanding of wireless principles. These principles determine the behavior of wireless signals, such as how they do the following:

- Spread out and get weaker as they leave an antenna and travel from point to point
- Lose strength when they hit a tree, hill, or other obstruction
- Reflect off of a building, the ground, and bodies of water

Chapter 2, "Understanding Wireless Fundamentals," contains an explanation of these and other basic wireless principles. The deployment of wireless WANs that provide *reliable* service at anything beyond short distances requires that these fundamental physical laws governing the behavior of wireless signals be understood and followed.

Challenge of Overcoming Real-World Obstacles

The previous section emphasized that it is important to understand wireless principles. After you understand these principles, the next step is to apply that understanding in the real world. Every wireless WAN deployment takes place in a unique and different real-world environment.

NOTE   The previous sentence might sound like a contradiction. How can the real world be real if every wireless WAN is deployed in a unique and different real-world environment? How many real worlds are really out there? Please continue reading for an explanation.

To understand the real world faced by a 2.4-GHz wireless signal, try to imagine that you are a wireless signal. You are five inches long, and you are about to start on a 20-mile journey. Your journey will take you from an antenna on the roof of a ski lodge at the top of a 10,000-foot mountain down to an antenna on the roof of an office building. The office building is located 35 miles away, in the middle of a city in the desert at sea level. Your mission is to carry and to deliver a big (and important) data packet to a computer inside the office building.

You are handed the data packet; then some powerful but invisible force roughly pushes you up to the antenna on the roof. As you reach the roof, the antenna suddenly spins your body around toward the city. The giant unseen force slams you out of the antenna and into the air. You feel strong, but you can't see the city and you have no way of steering yourself. Snow is falling, and you're freezing; the trees below you are covered in white. You hug the data packet tightly against your body. You know you are only five-inches long, but you can feel your chest slowly puffing out; you are expanding. You're getting wider and your skin is getting thinner. You feel yourself brush against the icy snow-covered treetops and some of your strength leaves you. You hug your data packet tighter as you fall. Down, down, down—your body keeps expanding, but now, as you expand, you feel the moisture in the icy air start to bend and warp you. You don't remember ever feeling this cold and swollen. You're weaker. Your chest is so big that you feel like you're about to burst. You suck in a breath but this time you don't feel that familiar icy pain in your nose. Have you gone numb? Then you realize that the air may be getting warmer. The foothills are below you. The snow is gone, but your body is now so big and so thin that it bumps against some of the foothills. You don't have much strength left and now it's getting hot. You grip the data packet as the hot, dry air starts to bend your body and wave you around. You see the city buildings ahead getting closer, taller. The end of your journey is there, somewhere, in that huge mass of steel, concrete, and glass. Closer, closer, your data packet is starting to slip away. You're so thin, so weak. The buildings are hitting you, bouncing you around. There's a roaring in your ears; hundreds of other signals are surrounding you, bumping, shoving, pushing. Your antenna is just ahead, but all of your energy is gone. The packet… the packet…. The antenna is reaching for you…. Almost there…. Almost… there…. In the rooftop cafeteria, a worker suddenly zaps a microwave oven on. Aaaaaaaaaaahhhhh!

In the world of broadband wireless, every journey between two antennas is a unique one. The terrain, the trees, the buildings, the weather, the packet size, and the other wireless signals combine to make the real world different for every wireless signal on every journey at every moment. Understanding the effects that these real-world influences have on wireless signals allows the design and the construction of broadband wireless networks that deliver reliable performance in the presence of all the real-world influences.

Challenge of Maximizing Available Bandwidth

The two preceding sections described the importance of understanding wireless fundamentals and overcoming real-world obstacles. The next challenge to deploying broadband wireless networks is maximizing the available throughput.

During broadband wireless network design, installation, and operation, one consequence always occurs when a mistake is made at any point in the process: the throughput of the network goes down. The throughput of a network going down is a sure sign that one or more problem areas exist that need to be identified and corrected. The goal of this book is to help you design and build a reliable, money-saving, high-bandwidth network and to avoid the common and the sometimes not-so-common mistakes that reduce network throughput.

Challenge of Working Safely with Wireless

A fast, reliable, low-cost broadband wireless network is not beneficial if an employee or a bystander is hurt or killed by a falling tool or a falling antenna. Safety must be the top priority of each person involved in designing, building, and maintaining a wireless network. It is crucial to promote and emphasize safety by conducting and documenting safety meetings that cover the following topics:

- Working with heights
- Working with microwave energy
- Watching the weather
- Using lightning protection
- Using personal safety equipment
- Climbing safely
- Other safety procedures

Working with Heights

Wireless antennas are usually mounted high above the ground on masts, rooftops, and towers. During design and installation, the following safety issues must be addressed:

- **Falls**—A fall from as little as 18 inches can be enough to cripple a person for life. A fall from a roof or a tower is often fatal. Only properly trained personnel should be assigned to install towers and rooftop antenna systems.
- **Falling objects**—The installation process must be safe for the installation personnel as well as for other people passing by who are below the antenna. An object as small as a screwdriver falling from a roof can cause serious injury if it hits somebody below. Imagine the injury that a larger object such as an antenna mast could cause!

Working with Microwave Energy

Wireless networks transmit microwave energy. High levels of microwave energy or the cumulative effects of low levels of microwave energy are known to have adverse effects on the human body. To minimize the chance of injury, network installation personnel must observe the following safety procedures:

- Always turn off the wireless equipment when working around or in front of a microwave antenna. Never point a microwave antenna toward another nearby person.

- Mount all antenna systems high enough so that they do not focus and radiate energy toward a nearby area where people could be present.

- If there is a high-power transmitter located on the same tower as the broadband wireless antenna system, ask that the transmitter be turned off temporarily so that work on the wireless antenna system can be performed safely.

Watching the Weather

Always consider the following weather conditions when deciding if it is safe to work on outdoor antenna systems:

- **Wet conditions**—Water makes surfaces slippery. It is dangerous to work on roofs or towers when it has been raining or when it is about to rain. Make it a rule to direct installation supervisors to stop outdoor antenna work when it is raining or when rain is expected within a short period.

- **Icy conditions**—Like water, ice makes surfaces slippery. Prohibit your installation crews from working outside near towers when it is icy. Remember: Ice that falls from a radio tower can be heavy and sharp. It can damage equipment or smash a skull.

- **Lightning strikes**—When lightning strikes a person, it is not always fatal. Occasionally, the person survives the lightning strike with only burns or scars. It is, however, not wise to run the risk of having an installation crew struck by lightning. When lightning threatens, installation crews should stop work and take shelter inside the nearest building.

Using Lightning Protection

The previous section discussed protecting installation crews from lightning. Wireless equipment, customer property, and customer personnel also need protection from lighting. Last, your company or agency needs legal protection from the possibility of performing negligent work. If lightning hits a wireless antenna and then destroys the wireless users' building or business, you could be sued for damages. Even worse, if lightning hits an antenna system and travels inside the building where people are working, someone could be hurt or killed.

Every responsible adult must realize that each outdoor wireless antenna system installation must include lightning protection. The cost of including a lightning arrestor and a proper ground connection is approximately $50 for the parts and one hour or more of extra installation labor. Following are the benefits of installing lightning protection on each outdoor antenna installation:

- Protecting your customers from serious injury or death

- Protecting your customers' building and equipment from being destroyed by lightning

- Protecting your customers' businesses from stopping while they move their entire business to a new location, replace their network equipment, restore their software, recover their databases, and recover from the revenue losses that occurred because of the lightning strike

- Protecting yourself and your business from being sued for negligence because an antenna system you installed did not contain lightning protection

- Allowing yourself to relax and avoid worry when a lightning storm passes through the area

- Feeling the satisfaction that comes from spending a few dollars more but knowing that you chose to do installations the right way, the safe way, the legal way, and the ethical way

Using Personal Safety Equipment

Every person involved in wireless antenna system installation should be provided with the following personal safety equipment:

- A hard hat to protect his head from falling objects

- Gloves to protect hands from punctures and abrasions

- Safety glasses to protect eyes from injury

- Sunscreen to protect skin from sunburn

Climbing Safely

In addition to the personal safety equipment listed in the previous section, each person who must climb a tower to perform antenna installation or service work should be provided with the following:

- Proper, professional training on safe tower climbing and installation practices. If no one in your organization has received tower safety training, it is necessary to hire an experienced tower or antenna erection company to perform this work.

NOTE   See Appendix B, "Wireless Hardware, Software, and Service Provider Organizations, " for information about organizations that provide tower safety training.

- A safety belt.
- A body harness.
- Boots with a steel shank inside the soles.

Other Safety Procedures

It is beyond the scope of this book to address any or all the other safety challenges that you and your company or organization might face. As you receive additional safety ideas, suggestions, and thoughts, it is wise to follow up and include these issues in your safety policy, your safety meetings, and your safety procedures.

Review Questions

1   This book defines a broadband wireless connection as any wireless connection with a bandwidth of ____.

2   What year did the U.S. government first require licenses for all transmitters?

3   What year did the FCC first allow broadband wireless equipment to be used without applying for a license?

4   What does the process of modulation do?

5   Name one way that a license-free broadband wireless WAN saves money.

6   Why is the real world different for every wireless link?

7   During antenna system installation, what safety practice helps protect workers on the ground from being injured by falling objects?

8   A fall from 18 inches can cripple a person for life. True or false?

9   If you need to work in front of a wireless antenna, what should you do first?

10   Every outdoor wireless antenna system should include a lightning arrestor. True or false?

Understanding Wireless Fundamentals

This chapter describes the wireless fundamentals that underlie the successful design, deployment, operation, support, and expansion of wireless wide-area networks (WANs). This book focuses on the application of these fundamentals in license-free wireless networks; however, these same wireless principles apply to licensed wireless networks and to all wireless signals.

Wireless Propagation

Wireless propagation is the total of everything that happens to a wireless signal as the signal travels from Point A to Point B. Although invisible to your eyes, the wireless signal interacts with everything that it comes near or passes through, including trees, hills, buildings, bodies of water, the earth's atmosphere, people, vehicles, and so on. The better you understand these interactions, the more easily and more successfully you will be able to deploy wireless WANs. First, it is important for you to understand how wireless signals are created.

Wireless communication is possible because changes in the electron flow within a wire cause changes in the magnetic fields and in the electric fields that surround the wire. Magnetic fields and electric fields are invisible, but you can see the results of their presence. If you have ever used a magnet to attract a piece of iron or steel, you have seen the result of a magnetic field. If you have ever seen a bolt of lightning, you have seen the effect of an electric (or electrostatic) field.

When electron streams change direction rapidly within a wire or antenna, the electrostatic and magnetic fields around the wire or antenna change at the same rapid rate. These rapidly changing fields are called electromagnetic waves. The electromagnetic waves do not simply stay near the antenna; they travel away at nearly the speed of light—186,000 miles per second (300,000,000 meters per second). The changing electron flow within the antenna has been transformed into electromagnetic (wireless) waves traveling away from the antenna.

TIP   Keep a mental picture of a moving wave in your mind; it is not a spot or a line; it is a wave. If you drop a rock into a pond, the waves spread out from the point where the rock hit the water. If you place an antenna in free space, the wireless waves spread out from the antenna. Wireless waves pass through air, space, people, and objects. If you can visualize electro-magnetic waves traveling away from an antenna and radiating outward, you will be off to an excellent start toward successfully deploying wireless WANs.

Wireless Frequency

As an ocean wave travels, its height changes; as the front of the wave approaches you, the height increases. When the crest passes you, the height of the wave decreases. The height decreases further as the trough passes you. Finally, the height of the sea is back to the level where it was before the wave appeared. You have just experienced one complete up-down-up wave cycle. Without changes in the wave height, there would be no wave cycle or wave.

Changes in the electron flow in an antenna cause the same changes in the electromagnetic fields around the antenna. Another word for electron flow in a wire is *current*. Without changes in the antenna current, there would be no change in the electromagnetic fields around the antenna; therefore, there would be no useable wireless signal moving outward, away from the antenna. The number of times each second that the current in the antenna goes through one complete positive-negative-positive change-cycle is the same as the *frequency* of the wireless waves that radiate outward from the antenna. If you drew a graph of the current flow in the antenna, the resulting graph would be a sine wave. The positive distance (above the centerline) and the negative distance (below the centerline) represent the *amplitude,* or strength, of the current. The greater the amplitude of the current, the stronger the radiated electromagnetic waves.

Figure 2-1 shows two complete cycles of positive-negative-positive current flow in an antenna. If there are 100 complete cycles in one second, the frequency of the current flow (and the frequency of the resulting wireless wave) is 100 cycles per second. Around 1960, the term *cycles per second* was replaced with the term *Hertz* (abbreviated Hz). The frequency of this wireless wave is 100 Hz.

Wireless signals cycle back and forth so quickly—millions of times each second—that the following abbreviations are used to specify their frequency:

- Kilohertz (kHz): Thousands of cycles per second
- Megahertz (MHz): Millions of cycles per second
- Gigahertz (GHz): Billions of cycles per second

Figure 2-1   *Antenna Current Alternating Between Positive and Negative*

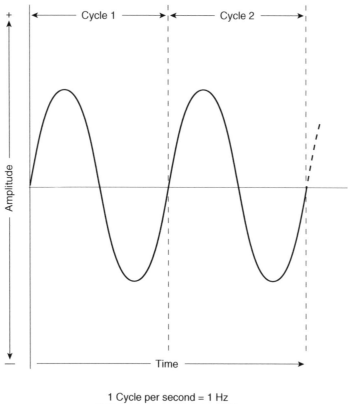

1 Cycle per second = 1 Hz
1000 Cycles per second = 1 kHz
1,000,000 Cycles per second = 1 MHz
1,000,000,000 Cycles per second = 1 GHz

Wireless Wavelength

It is important to be able to visualize the physical size of a wireless signal because the physical size of each signal determines how that signal interacts with its environment and how well it is propagated from antenna to antenna within the wireless network. The signal's physical size also determines how large or how small the antennas that transmit and receive the signal must be; the smaller the signal size, the smaller the antenna.

Figure 2-2 shows two wireless signals on two different frequencies—2.45 GHz and 5.775 GHz. All wireless signals travel through the air at the same speed. That speed is the speed of light, which is 186,000 miles per second (300,000,000 meters per second). The distance that a radio signal travels during a single cycle is called the *wavelength* of that signal. Higher-frequency waves have less time to travel during a single cycle than lower-frequency waves, so the wavelength for higher-frequency waves is shorter than for lower-frequency waves.

Figure 2-2   *Physical Size (Wavelength) of Wireless Waves*

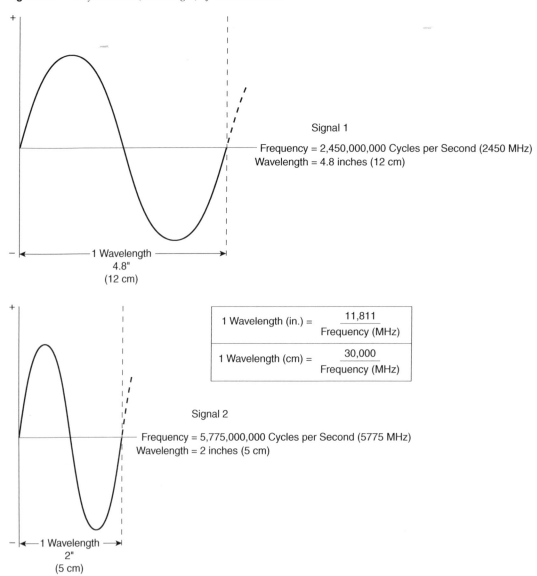

In Figure 2-2, each cycle of Signal 1 (2.45 GHz) has time to travel 4.8 inches (12 cm). Therefore, Signal 1's wavelength is 4.8 inches (12 cm). Signal 2 is changing more rapidly; each cycle of Signal 2 has time to travel only 2 inches (5 cm). Therefore, the wavelength of Signal 2 is only 2 inches (5 cm). There is a corresponding physical wavelength for every wireless frequency. The lower the frequency, the longer the wavelength; the higher the frequency, the shorter the wavelength.

Attenuation

Attenuation is the loss in amplitude that occurs whenever a signal travels through a wire, through free space, or through an obstruction. Figure 2-3 shows a 2.45-GHz (2450 MHz) signal as it encounters a tree. The signal is attenuated; that is, its amplitude is reduced. The amount of signal that emerges on the other side of the tree is much less than the amount of signal that entered the tree. Often, after colliding with an object, the signal strength remaining is too small to make a reliable wireless link.

Figure 2-3   *Attenuation of a 4.8-inch (5-cm) Signal by a Tree*

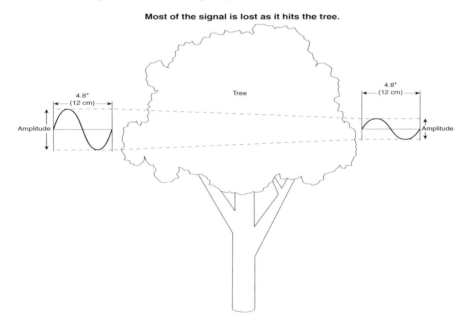

In addition, the shorter the wavelength of a wireless signal, the more it is attenuated when it encounters an object. The longer the wavelength of a wireless signal, the less it is attenuated when it encounters an object. Figure 2-4 shows a signal in the AM radio broadcast band at a frequency of 1000 kHz (1 MHz).

Figure 2-4   *Attenuation of a 984-ft (300-m) Signal by a Tree*

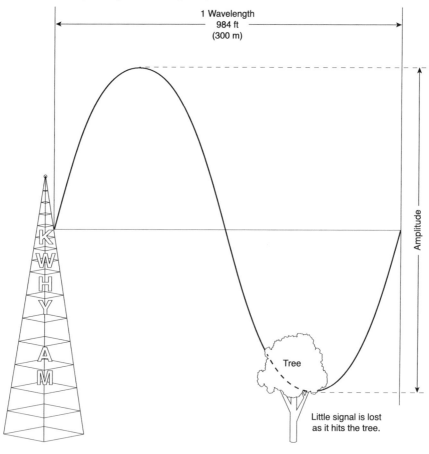

When this signal encounters a tree, the wavelength of the signal (984 ft/300 m) is so much greater than the size of the tree that the amplitude of the signal remains almost unchanged.

NOTE   A sharp-eyed reader will look at Figure 2-4 and says "Sure, the amplitude is still large after the collision. The amplitude of the AM broadcast signal was a lot larger than the amplitude of the 2.4-GHz signal to begin with." Well, sharp-eyed reader, you are correct. Yes, the AM broadcast signal had higher amplitude (more power) to begin with—perhaps 50,000W compared to the 2.4-GHz signal that started out with 4W, but here's the point. Even if the AM broadcast signal started out with 4W, a lot more of it would *still* be left over after encountering the tree, compared to the remaining 2.4-GHz signal. This would be true because the tree is many times larger than the physical wavelength of the 2.4-GHz signal, and the tree is many times smaller than the physical wavelength of the 1000-kHz KWHY-AM signal.

Free-Space Waves

A free-space wave is a signal that propagates from Point A to Point B without encountering or coming near an obstruction, as in Figure 2-5.

Figure 2-5   *Free-Space Wave*

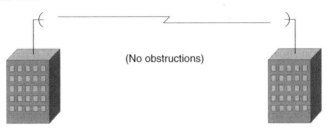

(No obstructions)

The signal arrives at its destination with as much amplitude as possible because the amplitude is not reduced by attenuation from objects. The only amplitude reduction that occurs is the normal reduction due to the signal being propagated through free space. A signal path like this, with no obstructions, is an ideal wireless scenario.

Reflected Waves

When a wireless signal encounters an obstruction while traveling from Point A to Point B, two things normally happen:

- **Attenuation**—In general, the shorter the wavelength of a signal, relative to the size of the obstruction, the more the signal is attenuated.

- **Reflection**—The shorter the wavelength of the signal relative to the size of the obstruction, the more likely it is that some of the signal will be reflected off the obstruction.

The following sections describe two types of reflected waves. One of these two types occurs at microwave frequencies and is important to your understanding of microwave propagation. You might already be familiar with the first type of reflected waves: sky waves.

Sky Waves

The first type of reflected waves is sky waves. Sky waves generally occur at short wave frequencies, where wavelengths range from 328 to 33 feet (100 to 10 m). Sky waves often reflect off the ionosphere—layers of ionized particles that exist from 30 to 300 miles (48 to 482 km) above the Earth, as shown in Figure 2-6.

Figure 2-6   *Sky Wave: Reflected Signal at Non-Microwave Frequencies*

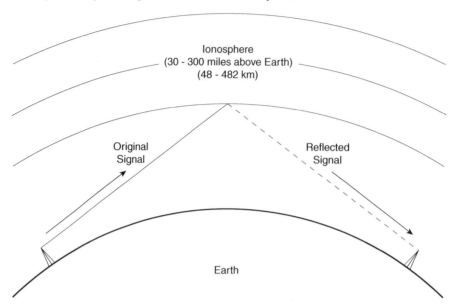

Sky waves arriving via ionospheric reflection make it possible to receive short wave broadcasts from stations located in other countries, thousands of miles away. Sky waves sometimes also make it possible for you to receive AM broadcast stations at night that are hundreds or thousands of miles away. Ionospheric reflection, however, seldom occurs at microwave frequencies.

Microwave Reflections

Microwave signals have frequencies between 1000 MHz (1 GHz) and 30 GHz and a physical wavelength from approximately 12 in. (30 cm) down to less than 1 in. (2.5 cm). Microwave signals reflect off of objects that are larger than their wavelength, such as buildings, cars, flat stretches of ground, and bodies of water. Figure 2-7 illustrates microwave reflection off of a building.

Each time a microwave signal is reflected, its amplitude is reduced. Microwave reflection can be an advantage or a disadvantage. The advantage is that sometimes the reflection (or *bounce*) off of a building or water tank allows a microwave link to work even though obstructions, such as the trees in Figure 2-7, block the direct wave. The disadvantage of microwave reflection is that a phenomenon called multipath can occur.

Multipath occurs when reflections cause more than one copy of the same microwave signal to arrive at the receiver at slightly different times, as shown in Figure 2-8.

Figure 2-7   *Microwave Signal Reflection*

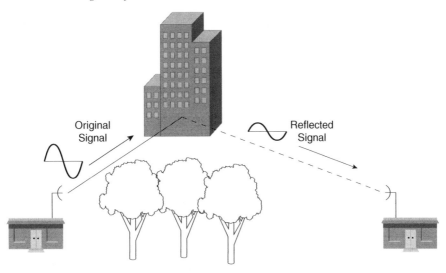

Figure 2-8   *Microwave Signal with Multiple Reflections*

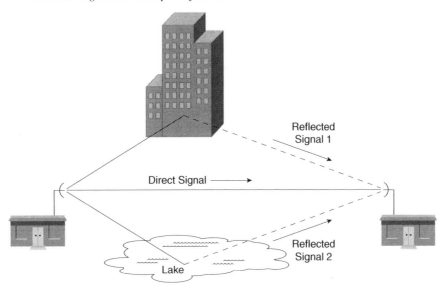

Reflected Signals 1 and 2 follow slightly longer paths than the direct signal; therefore, they arrive slightly later than the direct signal. These reflected echoes sometimes cause problems at the receiver by partially canceling the direct signal, effectively reducing its amplitude.

The link throughput slows down because the receiver needs more time to either separate the real signal from the reflected echoes or to wait for missed packets to be retransmitted. Multipath is a significant problem for designers of microwave networks. Methods that you can use to minimize the effects of multipath are discussed later in the book.

Diffraction

Diffraction of a wireless signal occurs when the signal is partially blocked or obstructed by a large object in the signal's path, as shown in Figure 2-9.

Figure 2-9   *Signal Diffraction Around an Obstruction*

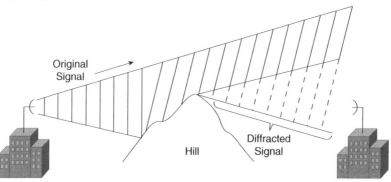

The edge of the hill partially blocks the microwave signal. As the bottom part of the signal intercepts the hilltop, the signal is diffracted, causing part of the signal energy to bend slightly around the hilltop.

The diffracted signal energy is usually attenuated so much that it is too weak to provide a reliable microwave connection. In a few cases, however, the diffracted signal, although weakened, might still be strong enough to allow a connection to be made to a nearby location that would otherwise be blocked.

TIP   Always try to obtain an unobstructed path between the microwave antennas that you set up. Do not plan to use a diffracted signal in place of a direct signal because most of the time, the diffracted signal is too weak to provide a reliable link.

Weather and Other Atmospheric Effects

Microwave signals must pass through the earth's atmosphere (unless you are communi-cating from spacecraft to spacecraft, which is a not-too-distant possibility). The earth's atmosphere is a dynamic environment consisting of regions of constantly changing temperatures, pressures, water vapor, and weather. These changes affect the passage and the propagation of microwave signals. Understanding these propagation changes helps you design reliable wireless WANs.

Precipitation

Rain, snow, hail, fog, and sleet are all forms of precipitation—water or water vapor—that is present in the air. As you evaluate the effect that each form of precipitation has on your wireless WAN, keep in mind that the physical size of a wireless signal plays a big role in determining how that signal interacts with the precipitation that it encounters.

Rain, Snow, and Hail

One cycle of a wireless signal at 2.45 GHz has a wavelength of 4.8 in. (12 cm); one cycle at 5.7 GHz has a wavelength of 2 in. (5 cm). Compared to the size of a raindrop—even a big raindrop in a heavy downpour—these wireless signals are quite a bit larger than the raindrops. As a result, the raindrops do not significantly attenuate these signals. At higher wireless frequencies (at or above 10 GHz), where the signal wavelength decreases to less than 1 inch (3 cm), rain, partially melted snow, and partially melted hail *do* start to cause significant attenuation.

Rain can, however, have other effects on the operation of a wireless system. Wherever a tiny hole exists anywhere in an antenna system, rain usually finds it and gets inside the system. After the rain is inside, the water degrades the performance of the system. Eventually, the system fails completely and the antenna cabling must be replaced. Rain can also make surfaces (such as buildings and leaves) more reflective, increasing multipath fading.

TIP   This is another reason to use nonobstructed paths between your antennas. If you try to "blast through" trees, you are just setting yourself up to have problems.

Ice

Ice buildup on antenna systems impacts the operation of wireless WANs in two different ways:

- Reducing system performance
- Physically damaging the antenna system

A thick buildup of ice on a microwave antenna changes the performance of the antenna and the performance of the wireless link degrades.

Ice buildup also adds substantial extra weight, which increases the chance of antenna system failure, especially under windy conditions. A heavier than normal antenna might bend under the extra weight or might even fall from the antenna tower. Ice can also fall from a higher antenna onto a lower one, damaging the lower antenna or antenna cable.

NOTE   To minimize problems in snow and ice-prone areas, many commercial microwave antennas are protected with radomes that are designed to cover the antenna. Some radomes also have heaters to melt ice buildups. If you are located in an area that has heavy winter icing conditions, you might want to consult with a local two-way radio shop to see what methods it uses to reduce icing problems on its antenna systems.

Wind

Wind can have a significant impact on the reliable operation of wireless WAN systems. The force from a moderate or heavy wind pushes against both the antenna and the tower or mast that holds the antenna in position. Under this force, several things could happen:

- The antenna could turn on the mast or tower, causing signal levels to decrease as the aim of the antenna changes.
- The tower or mast could sway or twist, changing the aim of the antenna and causing signal levels to decrease or to vary.
- An antenna or tower that has not been properly designed, installed, guyed, or maintained could fail in a strong wind—potentially causing physical injury or property damage.

NOTE   *Safety is priority one* in the design, installation, and operation of a wireless WAN systems. Please pay special attention to the safety sections and notes throughout this book. Give them special attention as you design and install your wireless systems.

Refraction

The changes in temperature, pressure, and water vapor content in the atmosphere play a significant role in the propagation of microwave signals—refracting (or bending) the signals. The refractivity of the atmosphere changes depending on the height above ground. The refractivity is usually largest at low elevations, closest to the surface of the earth. The refractivity is usually smallest the higher you go above the earth. This refractivity change (called the refractivity gradient or *k-factor*) usually causes microwave signals to curve downward slightly toward the earth, as shown in Figure 2-10.

Figure 2-10   *Signal Refraction in the Atmosphere*

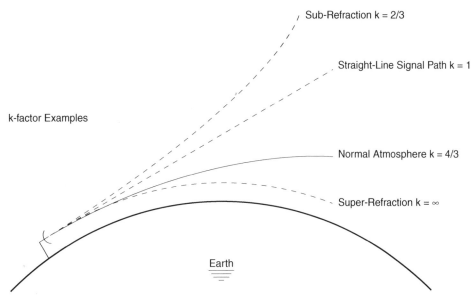

The k-factor can change frequently, such as from hour to hour, from day to night, from weather pattern to weather pattern, or from season to season. Different regions of the earth have slightly different average k-factors. A k-factor of 1 indicates no bending; a signal radiated under this condition travels in a straight line.

A k-factor higher than 1 means that microwave signals bend slightly downward, toward the earth. In most regions, *the median k-factor is 4/3.* A k-factor of 4/3 has the effect of making the radio horizon farther away than the visual horizon. In other words, the length of the microwave path is increased by approximately 15 percent. At times, weather conditions can temporarily cause the k-factor to become infinite. When this occurs, the amount of signal bending equals the curvature of the earth. This effect is called *super-refraction,* or *ducting.* Ducting causes a microwave signal to be propagated for hundreds of miles or until the atmospheric conditions change enough for the ducting to stop.

Changes in the k-factor are a common cause of fading on microwave paths. Sometimes, due to atmospheric conditions, the k-factor is less than 1; for example, the k-factor could be 2/3. This condition, called *subrefraction*, has the effect of bending the microwave signal path upward, away from the earth. Subrefraction reduces signal levels, causing fading at the distant receiver. Over longer microwave paths, the k-factor might be different at different points along the path.

Working with Wireless Power

- Working with wireless WANs requires knowing how to work with wireless power. Following are facts about wireless power:

- Power can be either increased (a power gain) or decreased (a power loss).

- Power can be relative, for example, twice as much power or 1/2 as much power
  or
  Power can be absolute, for example, 1 watt or 4 watts.

- Both absolute and relative power are always referenced to initial power level, either to a relative power level or to an absolute power level.

- Wireless WAN power levels become very small, very quickly after leaving a transmitting antenna.

- Wireless WAN power does not decrease linearly with distance; it decreases inversely as the square of the distance increases. Here are some examples:

  — If we double the distance of a wireless link, we don't have 1/2 of the original power reaching the end of the new link; we receive only 1/4 of the original power.

  — If we triple the distance of a link, we receive only 1/9th of the original power.

  — If a new link is 5 times longer than an existing link, we receive only 1/25th of the power that arrived at the receiver of the original link.

- Wireless power calculations are done in dB, for the following reasons:

  — dB values are logs—that is, they increase and decrease not linearly but logarithmically, just like the way that wireless power increases or decreases.

  — dB values can be used to conveniently represent very small power levels, like the levels of wireless power that arrive at a receiver.

  — Although they are logarithmic, dB values can be added and subtracted together (with each other) using just regular (linear) math. For example: 3 dB plus 3 dB equals 6 dB.

The following sections help you become comfortable using dB to calculate relative power levels and dBm to calculate absolute power levels. Later, you will also use dBi to calculate and compare antenna gains relative to the reference level of an isotropic antenna.

Ratios

Every db value is a *ratio*. This section explains ratios. A ratio is a comparison between two quantities. Ratios use a colon (:) to divide the two quantities. Figure 2-11 uses pennies to show two examples of ratios.

The first example is a ratio of two-to-one (2:1), and the second example is a ratio of 100:1. The first example shows a pile with two pennies next to a pile with one penny—a ratio between the piles of two pennies to one penny, or 2:1. The second example shows a pile with 100 pennies next to a pile with one penny—a ratio of 100:1.

Figure 2-11 *Penny Ratios*

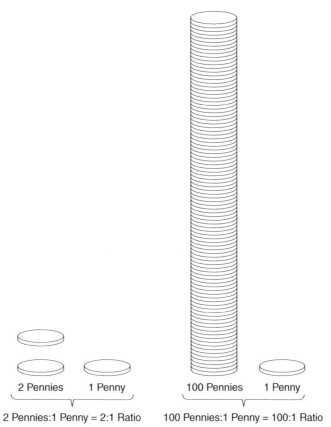

2 Pennies   1 Penny   100 Pennies   1 Penny

2 Pennies:1 Penny = 2:1 Ratio   100 Pennies:1 Penny = 100:1 Ratio

Power Ratios

Figure 2-12 uses two flashlights to show an example of a power ratio.

The flashlight on the left has a power of 40 candlepower (as bright as 40 candles). The flashlight on the right is 10 candlepower. The power ratio, 40 candlepower to 10 candlepower, is 4:1.

NOTE   If you look closely, you'll also notice that the 40 candlepower flashlight beam travels only twice as far as the 10 candlepower beam. Hmmm… four times the power travels only twice the distance? Yes, that is correct. The reason for this will be discussed more at the end of this chapter. You will also see how to quickly and easily determine if you can double the distance of a wireless link. (HINT: Do you have four times the power?)

All power ratios use some quantity as their initial reference point. The flashlight example in Figure 2-12 uses the 10-candlepower level (the smaller flashlight) as the reference point. This 10-candlepower level is abbreviated "FL". + 6 dBFL now means 6 dB (or 4 times) larger than the 10 candlepower reference level, or 40 candlepower (the larger flashlight). As long as the abbreviation (FL) and the power level (10 candlepower) are defined and communicated, then FL can be used indefinitely as a reference level.

Figure 2-12   *Flashlight Power Ratios*

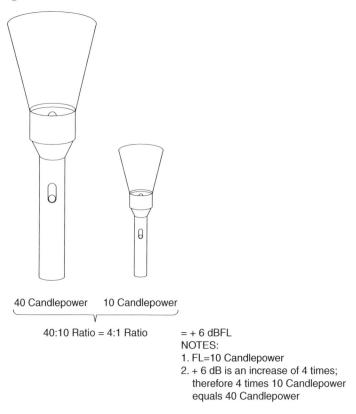

40 Candlepower   10 Candlepower

40:10 Ratio = 4:1 Ratio   = + 6 dBFL
NOTES:
1. FL=10 Candlepower
2. + 6 dB is an increase of 4 times;
   therefore 4 times 10 Candlepower
   equals 40 Candlepower

Wireless Power Ratios

Figure 2-13 shows examples of three wireless power ratios; each uses 1 Watt (1 W) of power as their reference point. The 1-Watt reference point is abbreviated by the "W," the third letter in "dBW." If, for example, you were told that a transmitter had an output of +3 dBW, you would know that the output power was twice (3 dB means two times) greater than (the + sign indicates a power gain) 1 Watt (indicated by the "W") or a total of 2 Watts output.

Figure 2-13 *Power Ratios in dBW (Relative to 1W)*

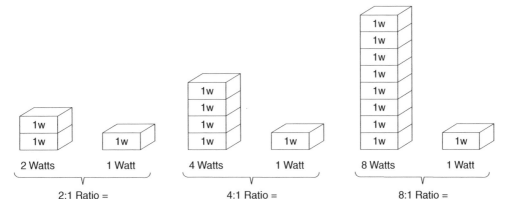

dBm

The most common dB power reference level when working with wireless WANs is dBm. The "m" in dBm stands for 1 milliwatt. A milliwatt is 1/1000 of a watt. There are 1000 mW in 1Watt. 1 milliwatt is 0 dBm. Positive dBm values (such as +30 dBm) indicate power levels greater than 1 mW. Negative dBm values (such as –20 dBm) indicate power levels less than 1 mW.

This is a good place to reaffirm that all absolute-power decibel values contain three things:

- A sign (+ or –) to indicate whether the value is above or below the absolute reference level
- The logarithmic value that represents the ratio of the two powers, in decibels
- The reference-power level, such as the "m" meaning 1 mW

Table 2-1 shows some of the most common wireless power levels (above and below 1 mW).

Table 2-1 *Power Ratios in dBm (Relative to 1 mW)*

Power Level Relative to 1 mW (0 dBm)	Level (+ or – dBm)	Power (Watts)	Power Abbreviation
4000 times more than 0 dBm	+36 dBm	4Watts	4W (4000 mW)
1000 times more than 0 dBm	+30 dBm	1Watt	1W (1000 mW)
Two times more than 0 dBm	+3 dBm	2 milliwatts	2 mW
0 dBm Reference Level	**0 dBm**	**1 milliwatt**	**1 mW**
1/2 of 0 dBm	–3 dBm	1/2 milliwatt	0.5 mW
1/1000 of 0 dBm	–30 dBm	1/1000 milliwatt	0.001 mW
1/4000 of 0 dBm	–36 dBm	1/4000 milliwatt	0.00025 mW

dBm Calculations and Reference Chart

It is possible to calculate a power gain or a power loss in decibels by using the following formula:

dB = 10log(P2/P1)

This says that the power ratio (in decibels) between any two power levels is equal to 10 times the log of the ratio of the two power levels. For example, if you have a transmitter with a power output of 100 mW and you add an amplifier with a power output of 400 mW, the increase in power level (in decibels) is calculated as follows:

The initial power level (P1) is 100 mW.
The new power level (P2) is 400 mW.
The ratio P2/P1 is 400/100, or 4.
The log of 4 (use a calculator here) is .602.
Ten times .602 is 6.02 or, rounding this off, 6 dB.

The power has increased (P2 was greater than P1), so the final decibel value has a + sign (+6 dB) to indicate that there is a four-times relative power gain.

Going the other way, here is an example of a power loss:

The power output of the same 100-mW transmitter suddenly drops down to 25 mW.
P1 is 100 mW and P2 is 25 mW.
The ratio P2/P1 is 25/100 (1/4, or .25).
The log of .25 is –0.602.
Ten times (–0.602) is –6.02, or, rounding off, –6 dB.

The power has decreased (P2 was less than P1), so the final dB value has a – sign (–6 dB) to indicate a power reduction down to 1/4 of the original value.

When you need to convert a power in watts to an absolute power in dBm, use the following formula:

dBm = 10log (Power in watts) + 30

This says that the power ratio in dBm equals 10 times the log of the power in watts plus 30. For example, if you have a transmitter with 1W of output power, the output power in dBm is as follows:

The log of 1 is 0. (Check it on your calculator.)
Ten times 0 is also 0.
Add 30 and the answer is +30 dBm.
1W of power is equal to +30 dBm.

It is usually easier and quicker to use the following reference table (Table 2-2) to find dBm levels; however, from time to time, you should practice using the formulas to keep sharp on how dBm ratios work.

Table 2-2   *Decibel (dB) Reference Chart*

Power Level (dBm) (Relative to 0 dBm or 1 mW)	Power Loss (Relative to 0 dBm or 1 mW)	Power Gain (Relative to 0 dBm or 1 mW)	Comments
–104	40 percent of 1 ten-billionth of 1 mW		
–100	1 ten-billionth of 1 mW		
–85	3 billionths of 1 mW		Threshold where most receivers start working
–40	1/10,000 of 1 mW		
–30	1/1000 of 1 mW		
–20	1/100 of 1 mW		
–13	1/20 of 1 mW		
–10	1/10 of 1 mW		
–9	1/8 of 1 mW		
–6	1/4 of 1 mW		
–3	1/2 of 1 mW		
0 dBm	**No Power Loss**	**No Power Gain**	**0 dBm Reference Level (1 mW)**
+ 3		2 times 1 mW	
+ 6		4 times 1 mW	
+ 9		8 times 1 mW	8 mW
+ 10		10 times 1 mW	10 mW
+ 13		20 times 1 mW	20 mW
+ 16		40 times 1 mW	40 mW
+ 20		100 times 1 mW	100 mW
+ 30		1000 times 1 mW	1 W
+ 40		10,000 times 1 mW	10 W
+ 85		316,000,000 times 1 mW	316 kW (316 kilowatts)
+ 100		10 billion times 1 mW	10 MW (10 megawatts)

Antenna Characteristics

Antennas are the most important part of every wireless WAN. Every WAN covers a wide area. Without an antenna, wireless power travels only a short distance, perhaps a few dozen feet. To successfully deploy license-free wireless WANs, you need to understand the key concepts of antenna directivity and antenna gain.

Antenna Directivity

Antennas radiate wireless power—that is, antennas accept wireless signal energy from the transmission line connected to a transmitter and launch that wireless energy into free space. Antennas focus the wireless energy like a flashlight reflector focuses the light from the flashlight bulb. Figure 2-14 compares the energy radiated from a bare, unfocused flashlight bulb to the focused energy radiated from a flashlight bulb with a reflector behind it.

Notice that in Figure 2-14, the flashlight bulb on the left radiates light energy in all directions. There is no focusing element, and no direction receives more light than any other direction. The light energy radiated from the unfocused flashlight bulb is similar to the wireless energy radiated from a theoretical isotropic antenna. An isotropic antenna radiates wireless energy equally in all directions and does not focus the energy in any single direction.

Figure 2-14 *Focused Versus Unfocused Energy*

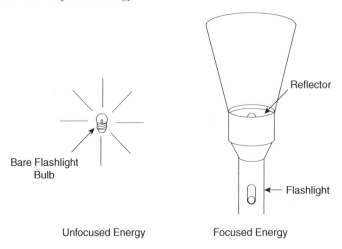

In contrast to the bare flashlight bulb, the flashlight on the right has a reflector behind the bulb. The reflector focuses the light into a beam that comes out the front of the flashlight. The flashlight does not amplify the power or the total amount of light from the flashlight bulb. The flashlight simply focuses the light so that all of it travels in the same direction. By focusing the light, the flashlight provides more *directivity* (beam-focusing power) for the light energy. Similarly, an antenna provides directivity for the wireless energy that it focuses. Depending on their design, construction, and orientation, antennas focus and radiate their energy more strongly in one favored direction. When they are receiving, antennas focus and gather energy from their favored direction and ignore most of the energy arriving from all other directions.

Antenna Radiation Patterns

Antennas exhibit directivity by radiating most of their power in one direction—the direction of their major (or main) lobe. They radiate only a small amount of power in other directions—the directions of their minor (or side) lobes. Figure 2-15 shows a top view of a directional antenna.

Figure 2-15   *Horizontal Radiation Pattern of a Directional Antenna*

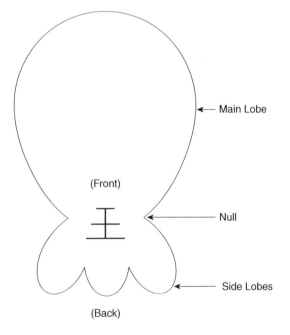

main and the side lobes. A main lobe exists toward the front of the antenna and several side lobes exist toward the back of the antenna. *Nulls*—areas where no power is radiated—exist to the sides of the antenna.

All antennas provide the same directivity on both transmit and receive. An antenna radiates transmitter power in the favored direction(s) when transmitting. The antenna gathers signals coming in from the favored direction(s) when receiving.

NOTE   When receiving, antenna directivity not only gathers incoming signals from the favored direction, but it also reduces noise, interference, and unwanted signals coming in from other directions. Keep this important point in mind as you select antennas for your networks; use antenna directivity to reduce noise coming from unwanted directions.

Figure 2-16 shows another view of antenna directivity: the vertical radiation pattern, when you look at an antenna from the side.

Figure 2-16   *Vertical Radiation Pattern of an Omnidirectional Antenna*

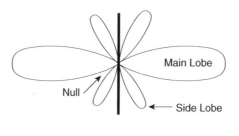

SIDE VIEW

This view shows an omnidirectional antenna with main and side lobes in the vertical direction. An omnidirectional antenna radiates equally well in all horizontal directions around the antenna but has a main lobe in the vertical direction. This main lobe surrounds the antenna like a doughnut.

Antenna Gain

Measuring the power in the main lobe of an antenna and comparing that power to the power in the main lobe of a reference antenna determines the *gain* of an antenna. Antenna gain is measured in decibels, either in dBi or in dBd.

If the reference antenna is a dipole, the measured antenna gain is in dBd. The "d" in dBd means that the gain is measured relative to the gain of a dipole reference antenna.

If the reference antenna is an isotropic antenna, the antenna gain is measured in dBi. The "i" in dBi means that the gain is measured relative to an isotropic reference antenna.

NOTE   Chapter 5, "Selecting Antenna Systems," defines and discusses isotropic antennas and dipole antennas in more detail. For now, the important point to remember is that your wireless WAN uses antennas that have more directivity (and therefore more gain) than either a simple dipole or an isotropic antenna.

Antenna Spillover

Now that you are familiar with the horizontal and vertical directivity of antennas, there is one more point to keep in mind. Wireless power never stops exactly on a sharp line like the main and the side lobe drawings show. Wireless power tapers off—it declines gradually rather than suddenly. In other words, some transmitter power and some receive capability exist outside of the main and side lobes of each antenna.

Antenna Beamwidth

Beamwidth—the width of the main beam (main lobe) of an antenna—measures the directivity of the antenna. The smaller the beamwidth in degrees, the more the antenna focuses power into its main lobe. The more power in the main lobe, the further the antenna can communicate. Beamwidth is specified in two dimensions:

- Horizontal beamwidth around the antenna
- Vertical beamwidth above and below the antenna

Figure 2-17 shows an example of the horizontal pattern of a directional antenna. This antenna has one main lobe that extends outward from the front of the antenna.

Figure 2-17 *Horizontal Beamwidth Showing Half-Power Points*

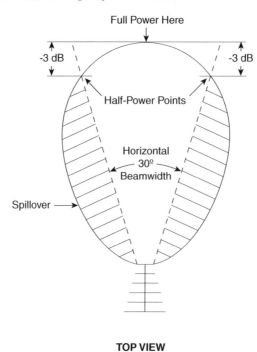

TOP VIEW

(Looking down on a directional antenna)

Figure 2-18 shows an example of the vertical pattern of an omnidirectional antenna. This antenna has one main lobe extending outward in all directions (like a doughnut) from the antenna. The antenna sticks up like a pencil through the center of the doughnut.

Remember from the discussion of wireless spillover that wireless power does not stop and start exactly along a straight line but declines gradually with distance; therefore, a consistent method is needed to define the width of the main lobe. This method is visible in Figures 2-17 and 2-18. The smooth outlines of the main lobes show the approximate intensity of the wireless power at various distances away from the antenna, but the dotted lines inside the smooth lines enclose most of the power of the main lobe. These dotted lines pass through the *half-power points*—the points on each side of the center of the main lobe where the wireless power is one-half as strong as it is at the center of the lobe. The angle between the two dotted lines defines the horizontal or vertical beamwidth of the antenna.

Figure 2-18 *Vertical Beamwidth Showing Half-Power Points*

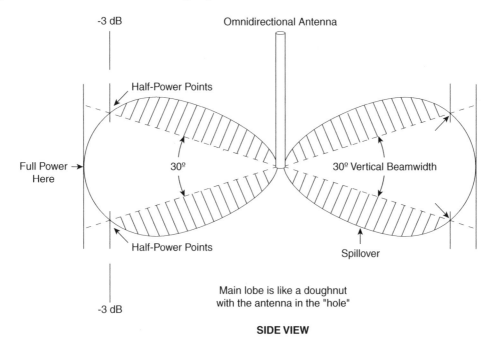

SIDE VIEW

Obtaining Wireless Line-of-Sight Paths

When a wireless signal encounters an obstruction, the signal is always attenuated and often reflected or diffracted. With outdoor wireless WANs, the attenuation from these encounters is usually so great that not enough signal remains to be detected at the other end of the link. When you design a wireless WAN link, it is important to work to achieve a wireless *line-of-sight (LOS)* path. This is a path that has no obstructions to significantly block, diffract, absorb, or attenuate the wireless signal. A wireless LOS path typically requires a visual LOS path plus additional path clearance to account for the spreading of the wireless signal. The following paragraphs describe visual and wireless LOS paths and help you understand how a wireless LOS path is different from a visual LOS path.

Visual LOS Path

If you can see from one antenna to the other, you have a visual LOS path, as shown in Figure 2-19. You might or might not have an unobstructed wireless LOS path.

Figure 2-19   *Visual LOS Path*

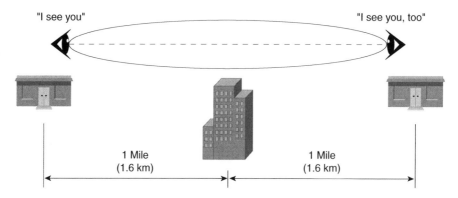

Difference Between Visual and Wireless LOS Paths

How can there be a difference between the visual and the wireless LOS paths? There is a difference because of the vast difference between the wavelength of a wireless wave and the wavelength of a visible light wave. Figure 2-20 shows this physical wavelength difference.

Figure 2-20   *Difference Between Wireless Wavelength and Visible Wavelength*

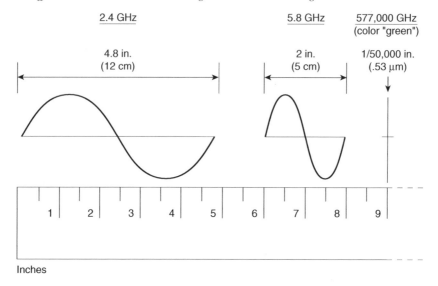

The 2.4-GHz signal has a wavelength of 4.8 in. (12.5 cm). The 5.8-GHz wireless signal has a wavelength of 2 in. (5.3 cm). The light wave, which is green, has a wavelength of 1/50,000 of an inch (.53 micrometers), which is much shorter than either of the wireless signals. The wavelength of the green light wave is only approximately 1/100,000 as long as the wavelength of the 5.8-GHz wireless signal.

NOTE   A lightwave is similar to a wireless wave. Both lightwaves and wireless waves are forms of electromagnetic radiation. Although there is a substantial size difference between the wavelength of light and the wavelength of wireless, they both obey the same laws of physics as they propagate. You might want to think of wireless signals as lightwaves that the eye cannot see.

The shorter the wavelength of an electromagnetic wave, the less clearance it needs from the objects that it passes as it travels from Point A to Point B. The less clearance a wave needs, the closer the wave can pass to an obstruction without experiencing an additional loss in signal strength. The next section shows you how to calculate how close a wave can come to an obstruction without experiencing additional attenuation. This clearance distance is called the *Fresnel zone*. For now, look at the waves in Figure 2-21. Both a green lightwave and a 2.4-GHz wireless wave are traveling the same path and passing by the same building.

Figure 2-21   *Visual and Wireless LOS Paths*

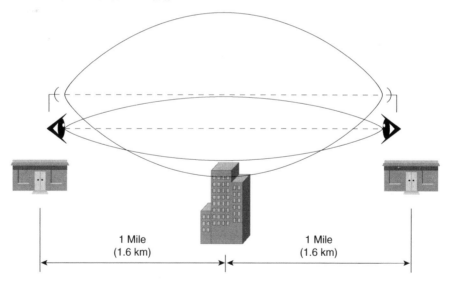

The short wavelength of the green light wave needs to clear the building only by a fraction of an inch to avoid being attenuated. All of the green light wave easily clears the building. The longer-wavelength 2.4-GHz wireless wave has a larger Fresnel zone and needs to clear the building by quite a few feet to avoid being attenuated. The next section provides more information about calculating the necessary Fresnel zone clearance.

Fresnel Zone

The concept of the Fresnel zone (pronounced "frA-nel"; the "s" is silent) provides a method of calculating the amount of clearance that a wireless wave (or a light wave) needs from an obstacle to ensure that the obstacle does not attenuate the signal. Figure 2-22 shows two ways to calculate the Fresnel zone clearance.

Figure 2-22   *Fresnel Zone Calculation*

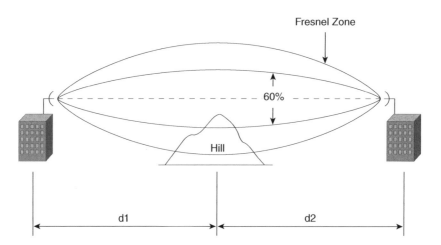

To calculate Fresnel Zone diameter in either English or Metric units:

$$\text{diam} = \sqrt{\frac{\lambda(d1)(d2)}{(d1+d2)}} \qquad \lambda = \text{wavelength}$$

To calculate Fresnel Zone diameter in English units:

$$\text{diam (ft.)} = 72.1 \sqrt{\frac{(d1)(d2)}{f(d1+d2)}} \qquad \begin{aligned} &d1, d2 = \text{miles} \\ &f = \text{GHz} \end{aligned}$$

The amount of Fresnel zone clearance is determined by the wavelength of the signal, the total path length, and the distance to the obstacle. The Fresnel zone is always widest in the middle of the path, between the two antennas. At least 60 percent of the calculated Fresnel zone must be clear to avoid significant signal attenuation. In Figure 2-22, the top of the hill extends so far into the Fresnel zone that 60 percent of the Fresnel zone is not clear; therefore, part of the signal will be attenuated. Figure 2-23 shows the calculation of Fresnel zone clearance for a green light wave over a two-mile path with a hill located at the middle of the path.

Figure 2-23 *Fresnel Zone Clearance for a Green Light*

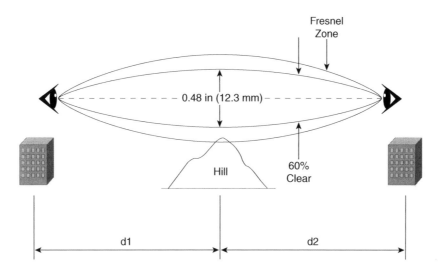

Fresnel Zone Diameter in Feet
d1, d2 = 1 mile
f = 577,000 GHz (Green Light)

$$\text{diam} = 72.1 \sqrt{\frac{(d1)(d2)}{f(d1+d2)}}$$

$$= 72.1 \sqrt{\frac{(1)(1)}{577,000\,(1+1)}} \quad = 72.1 \sqrt{\frac{1}{1,154,000}}$$

$$= 72.1 \sqrt{.0000008666} \quad = 72.1 \;\;(.000931)$$

$$= 0.0671 \text{ ft.} = 0.8 \text{ in.}$$

60% of FZ = 0.6 (0.8) in. = 0.48 in. (12.3 mm)

Figure 2-24 shows the calculation of Fresnel zone clearance for a 2.4-GHz signal over the same two-mile path.

Figure 2-24   *Fresnel Zone Clearance for 2.4 GHz*

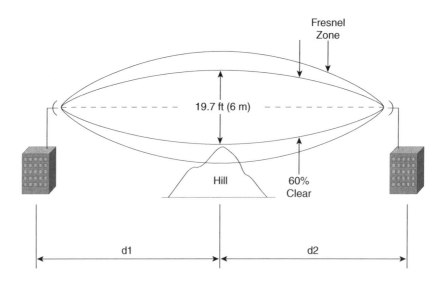

Fresnel Zone Diameter in Feet
d1, d2 = 1 mile
f = 2.4 GHz

$$\text{diam.} = 72.1 \sqrt{\frac{(d1)(d2)}{f(d1+d2)}}$$

$$= 72.1 \sqrt{\frac{(1)(1)}{2.4(1+1)}} \quad = 72.1 \sqrt{\frac{1}{4.8}}$$

$$= 72.1 \sqrt{.208} \quad = 72.1 \ (.456)$$

$$= 32.9 \text{ ft.}$$

60% of FZ = 0.6 (32.9) ft. = 19.7 ft. (6m)

The green light wave in Figure 2-23 must have a clear Fresnel zone diameter that is at least 0.48 in. (1.22 cm), or 60 percent of the calculated Fresnel zone diameter, to avoid being partially attenuated. The required clearance above the hill (the radius of the calculated 60 percent Fresnel zone diameter) is one-half of the diameter, so the green light wave must clear the hill by one-half of 0.48 in., or by 0.24 in. (0.61 cm).

The 2.4-GHz wireless wave in Figure 2-24 must have a clear Fresnel zone diameter that is at least by 19.7 ft (6 m), or 60 percent of the calculated Fresnel zone diameter, to avoid being partially attenuated. The required clearance above the hill (the radius of the calculated 60 percent Fresnel zone diameter) is one-half of the diameter, so the wireless wave must clear the hill by one-half of 19.7 ft, or by 9.85 ft (3 m).

You can see from Figures 2-23 and 2-24 how a visual LOS path can exist that allows you to see from Point A to Point B with no attenuation, whereas a wireless wave traveling the same path *will* experience significant additional attenuation. Many times in your life, you have heard the expression, "Seeing is believing." Figures 2-23 and 2-24 provide a graphic example that, when you are working with wireless, "Seeing is *not* believing." In other words, just because you can see to the other end of a wireless path, do not believe that you have a clear LOS wireless path. The clear, visual LOS path does *not* mean that you have an attenuation-free wireless path. You must calculate the size of the Fresnel zone and confirm that the clearance above any obstacle(s) is at least equal to one-half of 60 percent of the Fresnel zone diameter.

Wireless Link Budget

A wireless link budget calculation totals the signal gains, subtracts the signal losses over the length of a wireless link, and predicts whether the signal level that arrives at the receiver will be high enough for the link to work reliably. If the link budget predicts that the link will *not* work reliably, you can examine the gain of each link budget element to see which elements to change and by how much to get the link to work.

NOTE   The following link budget discussion explains the link budget elements as if the signal path went only one way: from Transmitter A to Receiver B. Wireless WAN links in the real world operate in both directions—with a transmitter and a receiver at each end of every link. Therefore, your two-way wireless links have two link budgets—one in each direction. Due to differences in transmitter power or receiver sensitivity, the link budgets in each direction can be different.

The individual link budget elements are as follows:

- Transmitter power output
- Transmitter antenna system coaxial cable (transmission line) loss
- Transmitting antenna gain
- Free-space path loss
- Receiving antenna gain
- Receiver antenna system transmission line loss
- Receiver sensitivity threshold

Transmitter Output Power

The transmitter generates power and delivers it to the transmitter output connector. This power level is specified in dBm—decibels referenced to 1 mW. Typical transmitter output powers range from 10 mW (+10 dBm) to 1W (+30 dBm). Transmitter output power adds to the link budget.

Transmitter Antenna System Transmission Line Loss

The transmitter antenna system coaxial cable or transmission line carries power from the transmitter output connector to the transmitting antenna. Some power is lost in the cable (and in the cable connectors and lightning arrestor) during this process. The smaller the diameter of the cable and the shorter the wireless wavelength (the higher the frequency), the more power that is lost. Typical power losses at 2.4 GHz are 7 dB for each 100-ft length of 3/8-in. diameter cable. The total transmission line loss is subtracted from the link budget.

TIP   Always design your wireless links to minimize the length of the antenna cables. Place the transmitter and the receiver as close as possible to the antenna. By doing this, you maximize the distance and the reliability of your wireless links.

Transmitting Antenna Gain

The transmitting antenna receives power from the transmission line. The antenna focuses and concentrates this power and radiates it toward the distant receiver. This focusing ability results in an effective power gain in the direction of the antenna's main lobe. For 2.4-GHz antennas, gains typically range from +6 dBi to +24 dBi. The transmitting antenna gain adds to the link budget.

Free-Space Path Loss

You must pay a price to use the magic of wireless. That price is that most of the wireless energy that leaves your transmitting antenna is lost—gone forever. Only a tiny fraction of the transmitted energy ever arrives at the receiving antenna. How much of the energy actually arrives? If you have a 2.4-GHz signal that travels 1 mile, your receiving antenna catches less than 1 ten billionth of the energy that you radiated from your transmitting antenna. All the energy that is lost (remember that there is no wire present) is called the *free-space path loss*. The longer the wireless path and the shorter the wavelength of the wireless signal, the higher the free-space path loss. The free-space path loss can be calculated using the following formula:

$$PL = 96.6 + 10 \log(d^2) + 10 \log(f^2) \ \ dB$$

where f is the frequency in GHz and d is the distance in miles.

If you prefer to use metric units to compute the free-space path loss, here is the formula:

PL = 92.4 + 20 log(f) + 20 log(d) dB

where f is the frequency in GHz and d is the distance in km.

Table 2-3 shows several examples of free-space path loss for the 2.4-GHz and 5.7-GHz frequency bands.

Table 2-3   *Examples of Free-Space Path Loss*

	Free-Space Path Loss at 1 Mile (1.6 km)	Free-Space Path Loss at 2 Miles (3.2 km)
2.4 GHz	104 dB	110 dB
5.7 GHz	112 dB	118 dB

Wireless Is Magic!

If you stop and think about wireless signals for a minute, you will probably agree with the statement, "*Wireless is magic.*" You know—invisible energy waves that carry voices, pictures, and information almost instantly through the air, through you, and even through interplanetary space at distances of thousands, and sometimes millions of miles. Only a tiny fraction of the transmitted energy ever arrives at the receiving end, and yet wireless works! Wireless has seemed like magic to me since I was 10 years old.

Receiving Antenna Gain

The receiving antenna works like the transmitting antenna to concentrate energy, but in reverse. The receiving antenna gathers and concentrates the small amount of power that reaches it at the far end of a wireless link. Think for a moment about the catcher in a game of baseball. The receiving antenna works a lot like the catcher's glove. The larger the glove, the easier it is for the catcher to grab the ball that the pitcher throws. The larger your receiving antenna, the easier it is for the antenna to grab the incoming signal—and the more signal that the antenna grabs. The more signal the antenna receives, the more gain that is added to the link budget.

Receiver Antenna System Transmission Line Loss

The receiving antenna system transmission line carries power from the receiving antenna to the receiver input. Just like with the transmitter antenna system transmission line, some power is lost in the cable during this process. This cable loss subtracts from the link budget.

Receiver Sensitivity Threshold

Each receiver has a *threshold level*—a minimum level of signal where the receiver just starts to operate. The receiver cannot detect signals below this threshold. The receiver antenna system (receiving antenna plus transmission line) must deliver a signal that is at or above this threshold for the wireless link to begin to operate. A typical threshold for an 11-Mbps 2.4-GHz wireless link receiver is around –85 dBm. The smaller (the more negative) this number is, the more sensitive the receiver is. For example, a receiver that has a threshold of –90 dBm is more sensitive than a receiver that has a threshold of –85 dBm.

NOTE   There is a tradeoff between receiver sensitivity and receiver data rate. Generally, the higher the data rate of the receiver, the less sensitive the receiver is. For example, a receiver that has a threshold of –85 dBm at a data rate of 2 megabits per second (2 Mbps) might have a threshold of only –80 dBm at a data rate of 11 Mbps. If you compare the sensitivities of two different receivers, be sure you compare them at the same data rate (or bandwidth) setting.

Fade Margin

The reason for calculating a wireless link budget is to design and build a reliable wireless link. Microwave signals normally interact with many objects in their environment, as discussed throughout this chapter. Therefore, fading is a normal condition for all microwave links. To overcome the effects of this fading and to provide reliable service, every microwave link needs a certain amount of extra signal, over and above the minimum receiver threshold level. This extra signal is called the *fade margin*. Another term sometimes used for this extra signal is *system-operating margin (SOM)*. Most wireless equipment manufacturers recommend a minimum fade margin of at least +10 dB to ensure reliable link performance. In general, the longer the link, the more fluctuation in signal levels and the greater the fade margin needs to be. Figure 2-25 shows a sample link budget calculation, including the calculated fade margin.

Figure 2-25 *Link Budget and Fade Margin Calculations*

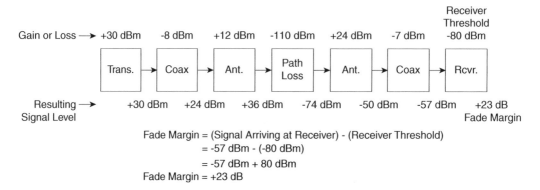

By calculating the fade margin, you can predict the reliability of a wireless link. The 2-mile long link shown in Figure 2-25 has a fade margin of +23 dB. +23 dB is 13 dB more than the 10 dB fade margin needed to make this link perform reliably; therefore, you can conclude that this link is going to deliver excellent reliability.

TIP	It is important that you measure the fade margin of every link that you install. Even though the calculated fade margin might be 10 dB or more, it is possible that installation mistakes or local noise conditions could reduce the performance of your real-world links. After you measure the fade margin, you can be sure that the link will operate reliably. Chapter 7, "Installing Outdoor Wireless Systems," covers the fade margin measurement process in detail.

Doubling the Link Distance

Doubling the distance of a wireless link requires four times more signal power, not twice the power like intuition would suggest. Wireless signal power declines as the square of the distance covered. Doubling the distance of the wireless link requires 2^2, or four times, the power. Four times the power is +6 dB (as shown in Figure 2-13).

After you have measured the fade margin on a link, you can predict how far the link can be extended. For example, the fade margin on the 2-mile 2.4-GHz link in Figure 2-25 is +23 dB. Doubling the distance requires four times (+6 dB) more power. Starting from the 2-mile fade margin of +23 dB and subtracting 6 dB leaves a remaining fade margin of +17 dB. This is 7 dB more than the minimum required fade margin of 10 dB; therefore, you can double the distance of this link to 4 miles and still have a reliable link. Of course, these figures are true only if both the 2-mile and the 4-mile link have unobstructed wireless LOS paths.

If you calculate or measure a fade margin of less than 10 dB (or whatever value of fade margin the manufacturer of your equipment recommends), you need to increase the power or reduce the loss of one or more of the system elements shown in Figure 2-25. You can increase the transmitter power, reduce the transmission line loss, use a larger antenna, or use a more sensitive receiver. Any of these improvements will increase the fade margin and improve the reliability of your link.

Tips for Planning Long Wireless Links

The longer a wireless link, the more important it is to properly design and plan the link so that it will provide you with reliable performance. The following sections provide some reminders to help you plan longer, reliable wireless links. Consider your links that are longer than about 7 miles (11 km) to be long links.

Antenna Height

As you know, the earth is curved. The distance to the radio horizon is 7.75 miles (12.5 km) for an antenna that is mounted 30 ft (9 m) above the ground, assuming a k-factor of 4/3.

Longer link distances require that you mount your antennas higher above the ground to extend your radio horizon. You can calculate the distance in miles to the radio horizon by multiplying 1.415 times the square root of the height of your antenna (in feet) above the ground. You can calculate the distance in kilometers to the radio horizon by multiplying 4.124 times the square root of the height of your antenna (in meters) above the ground.

Fresnel Zone

You know that a wireless wave needs a clearance (Fresnel) zone from objects that it passes close to. You also know that the size of this Fresnel zone is largest in the middle of a wireless path and that the Fresnel zone size increases both with longer distances and with higher frequencies.

The longer your link, the higher above the earth your antennas need to be mounted so that the part of your wireless wave closest to the earth can maintain an adequate Fresnel zone clearance above the earth.

Atmospheric Refraction (k-Factor)

You have learned that the k-factor varies depending on the temperature, the water vapor, and the barometric pressure of the atmosphere. The k-factor is usually greater than 1, bending microwave signals around the earth and extending the radio horizon beyond the visual horizon by approximately 15 percent. Sometimes, however, the k-factor can be less than 1, causing microwave signals to bend away from the Earth and causing the radio horizon to be closer than the visual horizon.

The longer a wireless link, the more regions of the atmosphere the wireless wave passes through and the more frequently the k-factor changes. These k-factor changes result in more frequent changes in your wireless path and more frequent fading. You need to allow a higher fade margin.

Link Budget

You remember that a reliable wireless link requires each receiver to receive a signal that fits both of the following conditions:

- Is above the receiver threshold
- Is high enough above the threshold to fade (usually at least 10 dB) and still remain above the threshold

The transmitter power, transmission line loss, antenna gain, and receiver sensitivity might need to be adjusted to maintain an adequate fade margin. The longer your wireless link, the more variation in signal strength and the more fade margin you need.

A rule-of-thumb that I like to use is to add 1 decibel of additional fade margin (above the original 10 dB) for every additional mile beyond 10 miles of link distance.

Long-Link Strategies

To successfully design, plan, install, and test long links, consider doing some (or all) of the following:

- Get help from wireless equipment vendors to select equipment and antenna systems with appropriate fade margins.

- Consult advanced wireless engineering textbooks (see the books in Appendix B, "Wireless Hardware, Software, and Service Provider Organizations").

- Consult with people (both paid and unpaid) who have more hands-on wireless experience than you do.

- Install the links carefully; pay particular attention to mounting the antennas firmly and aligning them correctly.

- Allow more time to test longer wireless links before placing them into service.

- Monitor your long links to be sure that they are providing reliable service.

- Enjoy the journey. Although long wireless links require you to spend more time and energy to do it right, the rewards for you in personal satisfaction are substantial and long lasting. Have fun with wireless—after all, whether you realize it or not, wireless is having fun with you.

Review Questions

1 How does the wavelength of a wireless signal change as the frequency of the signal increases?

2 When a 2.4-GHz signal encounters an obstruction, what happens?

3 Does ionospheric reflection occur at microwave frequencies?

4 How is wireless power measured?

5 In the abbreviation dBm, what does the "m" stand for?

6 If 1 Watt equals +30 dBm, then 2W equals how many dBm?

7 The main lobe of a non-isotropic antenna radiates power in which direction?

   A In one horizontal direction

   B In two horizontal directions

   C Equally in all horizontal directions

   D Both A and C

8 If you can stand at one antenna and see the antenna at the other end of a wireless link, do you have a line-of-sight wireless path?

9 Tripling the distance on an unobstructed wireless link requires increasing the power how many times?

CHAPTER 3

Choosing Your Network Architecture

This chapter helps you evaluate the four major wireless network architectures and choose the most appropriate architecture for your network. Specifically, this chapter does the following:

- Describes four wireless network architectures: point-to-point, point-to-multipoint, cellular, and mesh
- Explains the advantages and disadvantages of each of these architectures
- Provides examples of each architecture
- Assists you in evaluating, drafting, and designing your own wireless network using one or more of the four architectures

Point-to-Point Architecture

The point-to-point architecture is the simplest of all four wireless network architectures. It connects one single point to another single point, as illustrated by Figure 3-1.

Figure 3-1   *Point-to-Point Architecture*

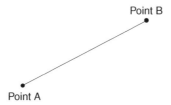

Advantages of Point-to-Point Architecture

The advantages of point-to-point architecture include the following processes that are faster, simpler, and less costly when compared to other wireless network architectures:

- Antenna selection
- Line-of-sight (LOS) determination

- Site surveys
- Hardware costs
- Facility costs
- Installation
- Testing
- Support

Antenna Selection

Point-to-point wireless networks should use directional antennas whenever possible. Directional antennas focus and radiate the signal in just one direction. This directivity has two important advantages: maximizing signal strength and minimizing noise pickup. In a point-to-point network, each endpoint needs to radiate a signal in only one direction; therefore, every point-to-point network should use a directional antenna at each endpoint. Selecting a directional antenna is a simple, straightforward process compared to selecting an antenna for a point-to-multipoint network, for example.

TIP Chapter 5, "Selecting Antenna Systems," contains more information about antenna selection. Please resist the urge to use omnidirectional (omni) antennas in point-to-point networks. Omnis minimize cost and shorten the installation process slightly, but they are more susceptible to interference and they cause unnecessary interference to other wireless networks. Always use directional antennas for both ends of point-to-point links.

LOS Determination

Between each network location, you need a wireless LOS path.

NOTE Remember from Chapter 2, "Understanding Wireless Fundamentals," that a wireless LOS path means that there is *both* an unobstructed visual path *and* an unobstructed Fresnel Zone clearance between the two antennas.

A point-to-point wireless network requires *only one* LOS path. Because only one path is needed, confirmation of this single LOS path is a fairly quick process. More complex network architectures require the confirmation of *many* simultaneous LOS paths; this confirmation is a longer, more complex process.

Site Surveys

There are two types of site surveys:

- **A physical site survey**—Should be performed for every location on a wireless network

- **A radio frequency (RF) site survey**—Should be performed for each hub site on a wireless network

---

NOTE   Chapter 4, "Performing Site Surveys," describes in detail how to perform both types of site surveys.

A point-to-point wireless network requires that you perform physical site surveys for only the two network endpoints. Neither endpoint is a wireless hub site that would require a more complex and time-consuming RF site survey. It is faster and less complex to perform the site surveys required for a point-to-point network than for most other wireless architecture.

Hardware Costs

The endpoint of a point-to-point network communicates with only one other endpoint. Compare this to the more complex hub site of a point-to-multipoint network that communicates with 2 to 30 (or more) endpoints. If only a few network endpoints need to be connected, hardware and software costs are lower for point-to-point network equipment when compared to more complex network architectures.

Facility Costs

Facility costs include the following:

- Renting or leasing space for wireless equipment
- Renting or leasing tower or roof space for wireless antennas
- Electrical power and backup power systems

These costs are lower in a point-to-point network, which requires less equipment space, rooftop space, and backup power.

Installation

Installation costs are lower in a point-to-point network because you need to install only two network endpoints, consequently minimizing the costs for the following:

- Installing the wireless equipment
- Installing the antennas, antenna cabling, and antenna mounting hardware
- Installing the amplifiers (if used)
- Managing the installation process

Testing

Testing is an essential step for every new wireless network. Testing is necessary to ensure that the network is ready to provide reliable wireless service. The test process for a point-to-point network is shorter and less complex compared to the test process needed for a more complex architecture.

Support

Network monitoring and network support are necessary functions in every wireless network. A license-free network can experience sudden throughput deterioration caused by noise, interference, antenna problems, and equipment problems. It is less expensive to support a small point-to-point network than it is to support a larger, more complex network architecture.

Disadvantages of Point-to-Point Architecture

Many successful network deployments eventually result in an expansion of the network to serve more end users. The disadvantages of a point-to-point network architecture occur because this expansion process includes several requirements that might be difficult or costly to satisfy. These requirements include the following:

- LOS path availability
- Backbone bandwidth availability
- Antenna system expansion
- A low-noise hub site
- Ability to upgrade equipment

LOS Path Availability

All current license-free wireless networks operate in the microwave frequency range and transmit at relatively low power levels. When a microwave signal encounters an obstruction, the signal experiences a combination of the following:

- Attenuation
- Reflection
- Diffraction

In every case, the signal is attenuated (reduced in power). Usually, the attenuated signal is too weak to provide a reliable wireless link. To preserve enough signal strength to provide a reliable link, it is important to have an unobstructed LOS path between network endpoints.

Typically, expanding a point-to-point network results in it becoming a point-to-multipoint network. Point-to-multipoint architecture is described in more detail in the next section, but briefly, it consists of one hub location that connects to more than one end user location.

Expansion of a point-to-point network into a point-to-multipoint network is not possible if LOS paths do not exist between one of the old endpoints and all (or most) of the new end user locations. Determining if the needed LOS paths exist requires site surveys and sometimes requires path testing.

TIP   When performing site surveys for a new point-to-point wireless network, always evaluate each network endpoint to see if it could serve as a future hub site for an expanded point-to-multipoint network. For example, a site that is mostly surrounded by trees and nearby hills would have few LOS paths in other directions. The site would not be a good candidate for a future hub location.

Backbone Bandwidth Availability

The expansion of a point-to-point network to become a point-to-multipoint network requires additional backbone bandwidth at the hub site to meet the needs of the additional users. This backbone bandwidth might be either LAN bandwidth (in the case of a corporate network) or Internet access bandwidth (in the case of an Internet service provider [ISP]). A point-to-point network that does not have additional backbone bandwidth available cannot be easily expanded.

Antenna System Expansion

The hub site of a point-to-multipoint network serves many users in several different directions, often using different radios and different frequencies. A hub site antenna system consists of several antennas. When a point-to-point network needs to be expanded, additional antenna space might be difficult to obtain for the following reasons:

- The space might not be physically available on the rooftop.

- Building management might not allow additional antennas because of concerns about the building's appearance.

- The cost of leasing additional rooftop space might be too high to be affordable.

- Zoning regulations might limit the number, height, or appearance of rooftop antennas.

TIP When you negotiate an agreement to install a point-to-point antenna system, try to include permission to install additional antennas, if needed, in the future.

Low-Noise Hub Site

Proper operation of a wireless network occurs only when the wireless equipment receives a signal that is substantially stronger than the noise and interference. A strong signal alone does not make a wireless link work well; a strong signal together with a low noise level make a wireless link work well. In other words, a high ratio of signal to noise (signal-to-noise ratio, or SNR) makes the network work well.

NOTE *Noise* is everything that is not the desired signal. Noise includes undesired signals, industrial noise, natural noise, and so forth.

A point-to-point network uses a directional antenna that is aimed toward only one other antenna. This directivity maximizes the received signal and minimizes interference and noise coming from all other directions.

Upgrading a point-to-point network to a point-to-multipoint network results in changing the antenna system from a very directional one to a less directional one. The new antenna covers a wider area; therefore, it picks up more noise and interference. If the new level of interference and noise is too high, the SNR might be too low for reliable point-to-multipoint operation.

TIP Make it a habit always to look and plan ahead. When you perform a physical site survey for a point-to-point network, consider performing radio frequency (RF) site surveys also. By examining the level of wireless noise, you can determine if the noise level is low enough to allow a point-to-multipoint hub to be placed there in the future.

Ability to Upgrade Equipment

The features and configuration capability of wireless equipment varies widely. It is always good to re-use wireless equipment instead of throwing or giving it away when the network is upgraded.

Some point-to-point equipment can be reconfigured to work in a point-to-multipoint network, but other equipment cannot be reconfigured. If you expect that your point-to-point network might need to be upgraded to a point-to-multipoint network, be sure to select equipment that has reconfiguration capability.

Examples of When to Use Point-to-Point Architecture

The following examples describe situations in which a point-to-point architecture is the most appropriate choice.

Two Network Locations Only

Point-to-point architecture is best when you have only two locations that need to be connected and the network most likely will not be expanded in the future. Point-to-point architecture minimizes the costs, deployment time, and experience level needed to get your network up and running.

Longer-Than-Normal Links

If you need a network link that is longer than normal, point-to-point architecture is the best choice.

NOTE   Ahhh, but just how long is a normal link, you ask? In general, a normal link can be as short as one block or as long as 10 miles (16 km).

If you are planning a link that is longer than normal, such as a 15- or a 30-mile (24- to 48-km) backbone link, plan on point-to-point. A long link needs the following:

- High-gain antennas to focus all the signal strength toward the other end
- Directional antennas to reduce the interference and noise coming from all other directions
- Antennas mounted high above the ground to prevent the earth from intruding into the Fresnel zone

The antenna systems used for a point-to-multipoint network are too broad to use on a long point-to-point link. Their gain is too low and their beamwidth is too wide to provide the high signal strength and low noise that a long point-to-point link needs.

High Noise Level

When a particular location has a high noise level, it is likely that only a point-to-point link will work at that location. A high-noise location needs the higher signal levels and lower noise levels that only a directional high-gain antenna can provide. A point-to-multipoint antenna system would be overcome by the noise.

Path Obstructions

Often, a site has many nearby obstructions, such as tall mountains or tall surrounding buildings. A site like this might work as an endpoint on a point-to-point network or even as an endpoint on a point-to-multipoint network. The site might not be a good location for a point-to-multipoint hub site.

Point-to-Multipoint Architecture

A point-to-multipoint wireless network can be an economical way of providing connectivity from a single hub site to many end user locations. The wireless equipment at the hub site is referred to as the *access point*. The equipment at each end user location is generally referred to as the *customer premises equipment (CPE)* or *client equipment*. Point-to-multipoint architecture is often used, for example, to provide connectivity between buildings that are located in a campus environment. Another use of point-to-multipoint architecture is to provide wireless Internet access service from one ISP location to many end user locations. Depending on the number of locations that need to be connected, the hub site might be divided into several sectors to increase network capacity.

NOTE Think of a sector as one slice of a whole pie. Each sector faces in one specific direction and serves only the users who are located in that direction.

Each sector usually has its own dedicated radio, antenna system, and frequency. Figure 3-2 shows a diagram of a typical point-to-multipoint network with no sectorization.

Figure 3-2   *Point-to-Multipoint Architecture (No Sectorization)*

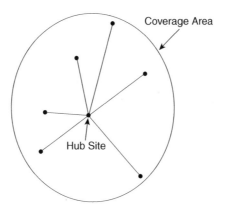

Figure 3-3 shows a diagram of a typical point-to-multipoint network with a three-sector hub site.

Figure 3-3   *Point-to-Multipoint Architecture (Three Sectors)*

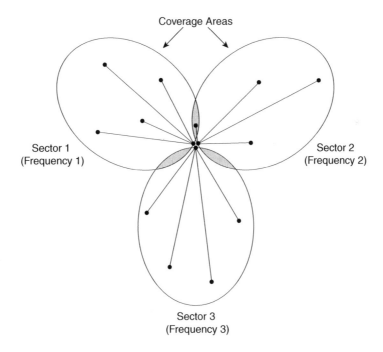

A point-to-multipoint network can have one to six (or more) sectors. Most networks have two or three sectors. Although no specific rules exist for deciding how many sectors to build, it is important to plan to meet both the current and the future bandwidth needs of your users. If you have 100 heavy business users on an 11-megabit per second (Mbps) wireless network, you should plan to build more than one 11-Mbps sector to avoid network congestion and slow performance. If, on the other hand, you have only five residential users on an 11-Mbps network, one sector might be enough to meet the bandwidth needs of these users.

Advantages of Point-to-Multipoint Architecture

The advantages of point-to-multipoint architecture are as follows:

- Cost effective for many users
- Scalable
- Open for the testing of new technology

Cost Effective for Many Users

Point-to-multipoint architecture is a cost-effective way to serve many end users from one central site; all the end users share the same central site equipment. When a new user needs to be added to the network, the only new equipment that needs to be purchased is for that one new user. No new hub site equipment is needed. Compare this to a point-to-point network in which *two* radios would be needed if *one* new user needed connectivity to an existing point-to-point wireless network.

Scalable

A point-to-multipoint network is easily scaled up for more users. Every time a new hub site radio (or hub site sector) is added, several end user locations can be added.

Open for Testing of New Technology

A point-to-multipoint network that has a sectorized hub site makes the testing and introduction of upgraded hardware or software possible. For example, with a three-sector hub, new software can be installed and tested on just one of the three sectors. End users on the other two sectors can continue to use the older software until the new software has been tested and verified. When the new software proves to be stable, it can be installed on the other two sectors.

Disadvantages of Point-to-Multipoint Architecture

The disadvantages of point-to-multipoint architecture, when compared to point-to-point architecture, include the following:

- Bandwidth management
- Antenna selection
- LOS determination
- Site surveys
- Initial hardware costs
- Facility costs
- Installation costs
- Testing
- Support

Bandwidth Management

The bandwidth management process is more complex within a point-to-multipoint network because many users are sharing the access point (or sector) bandwidth.

Antenna Selection

Access point antenna selection is more demanding in a point-to-multipoint network. If the area to be covered is a relatively small area (one mile [1.6 km] in diameter, for example) and if the number of end users is small (for example, 20 or less), a simple one-sector access point using an omnidirectional antenna might be all that is needed. More often, however, the following conditions are present:

- The area to be covered is several miles/km in diameter with trees, buildings, or other obstructions present.
- The number of end users is 20 or more, and the number of end users is expected to increase.
- The level of interference is high, as it likely will be if other unlicensed networks exist in the same general area.

When any of these conditions occurs, proper design and selection of the antenna system components are especially important. Improper antenna design or selection limits network throughput and prevents the network from delivering satisfactory wireless service.

LOS Determination

The requirement for LOS paths to all the potential end users complicates the selection of a hub site location for a point-to-multipoint network. The time needed to verify the existence of these line-of-sight paths can be substantial. The more potential end users that are on the network, the more time that will be needed to verify LOS.

NOTE   As this chapter is being written, many wireless manufacturers have begun to advertise wireless equipment with near-line-of-sight or non-line-of-sight (both abbreviated as NLOS) capabilities. The NLOS definition is vague and is used loosely at this time.

Few point-to-multipoint NLOS systems have actually been installed and operated under real-world conditions at the present time; therefore, it is not yet possible to verify the accuracy of these advertising claims. For more information, please see the NLOS discussion in Chapter 6, "Evaluating and Selecting Wireless Equipment."

Site Surveys

Compared to a point-to-point network, a point-to-multipoint network serves many more end users; therefore, the network site survey times are longer. More importantly, the time needed to perform adequate hub site surveys and to select the best hub site locations is longer. Chapter 4 describes the physical and radio frequency (RF) site survey processes.

Initial Hardware Costs

The initial hub site (access point) hardware costs for a point-to-multipoint network are higher than for a point-to-point network. These higher costs occur because of the need for more antennas, antenna cables, connectors, equipment cabinets, power supplies, and backup power systems. Often, the cost of the access point wireless equipment is also higher. Total hardware costs (including CPE) for a point-to-multipoint network with 20 users can range from $8000 to more than $100,000.

Facility Costs

An access point (hub) site probably costs more to use per month than a point-to-point site. Rental or leasing rates might be higher due to the possible need for more equipment and rooftop antenna space, as well as the greater amount of electrical power consumed.

Installation Costs

The installation costs for a point-to-multipoint access point site are higher than for a point-to-point site. The reason is simple; the labor cost is higher to install more equipment, cabling, antenna systems, and power systems.

Testing

An access point in a point-to-multipoint network serves many customers located over a wide geographic area. The test time needed to confirm reliable coverage over this area can be substantial. Reliable wireless coverage requires more than end users being able to hear the access point. It also requires the access point being able to hear the end users. It might take days, weeks, or months to test and adjust an access point so that it provides reliable two-way service throughout the coverage area.

Support

The support costs to maintain a point-to-multipoint network are substantially higher than for a point-to-point network. These support costs include monitoring network performance, maintaining network hardware, responding to possible interference problems, and maintaining network security.

Examples of When to Use Point-to-Multipoint Architecture

Point-to-multipoint architecture is the best choice when many end users are located in the same general area, such as in the same small city or in the same part of a larger city.

Cellular Architecture

When point-to-multipoint networks are connected to the same backbone network and designed to allow the same frequencies to be re-used in different areas, the result is a cellular network. The backbone network might be either wired or wireless. Figure 3-4 shows a diagram of a cellular network that includes three point-to-multipoint networks.

Figure 3-4 *Cellular Architecture*

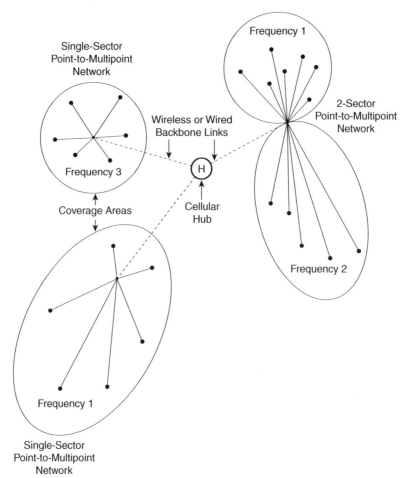

Advantages of Cellular Architecture

The advantages of using a cellular architecture are as follows:

- Expands the geographical coverage area
- Increases the network capacity
- Leverages the use of network resources
- Provides redundant end user coverage
- Allows roaming

Expands the Geographical Coverage Area

Each point-to-multipoint network (or sector) within a cellular network is considered to be one cell. A cellular network with multiple cells can cover a larger geographical area than a single point-to-multipoint network. A wireless Internet service provider (WISP) that wants to extend coverage to a new area can add a new wireless (or wired) backbone lnk and then install one or more new wireless access points in the new area.

Increases the Network Capacity

Each additional cell in a cellular network increases the number of end users that the network can serve. For example, a cellular network with two cells can serve twice as many end users as a single point-to-multipoint network.

Leverages the Use of Network Resources

A cellular network allows the sharing of network resources between large numbers of end users. These resources include backbone bandwidth network administration, maintenance, and monitoring. These resources are typically supplied from the same network hub location.

Provides Redundant End User Coverage

Cells in a cellular network might be designed to overlap each other. If cells do overlap, end users might be able to obtain service from an adjacent cell if one cell is temporarily out of service. Sometimes, this requires re-aiming the end user's antenna. These resources are typically supplied from the same network hub location.

Allows Roaming

Roaming refers to the capability of an end user to move out of the coverage area of one cell and into the coverage area of another cell while retaining network connectivity. For example, cellular telephone networks are designed to provide roaming capability for mobile telephone users. In contrast, only a few outdoor networks that are used to provide Internet access service offer roaming.

NOTE   The 802.11b access points typically provide a roaming feature. This roaming feature works well within small, well-designed, indoor wireless LANs. This same roaming feature does *not* usually provide satisfactory roaming between large, outdoor wireless cells.

Disadvantages of Cellular Architecture

There is one primary disadvantage of a cellular architecture: it is important that nearby cells re-use the same spectrum space without interfering with each other. During installation, it is important to verify that mutual interference between cells is low.

Re-Using Limited Spectrum

License-free wireless bands have a limited amount of frequencies (spectrum space). A cellular architecture must be designed to re-use this spectrum space in a noninterfering fashion. Cells that use the same frequency (in a direct sequence spread spectrum system) or the same hopping sequence (in a frequency-hopping spread spectrum system) must be isolated from each other far enough so that interference between the cells does not reduce the throughput of the cells.

Verifying That Interference Is Low

One crucial task during the installation of a cellular network is to identify and eliminate interference between cells that are close together (and even between cells that are farther apart). Throughput testing confirms that interference between cells is low enough for satisfactory network operation.

Cells that use the same frequency should be throughput-tested simultaneously. The test process is as follows:

Step 1   Perform a throughput test (upload a file) from the farthest end user location to the access point location for one cell. Make a note of the throughput.

Step 2   Go to the nearest adjacent cell that uses the same frequency or hop sequence. Perform the same throughput test from the farthest end user location to the access point of the second cell. Make a note of the throughput.

Step 3   Perform the two throughput tests simultaneously and note the throughput from each end user location. If the throughput stays the same for both end user locations during the simultaneous test, enough isolation between the cells exists for satisfactory operation.

Step 4   If the throughput between either end user location and its corresponding access point is reduced when both tests are running simultaneously, you must increase the isolation between the access point antenna systems. Increasing the isolation might be as simple as redesigning one of the cell site antenna systems or as complicated as moving the cell site locations farther apart.

TIP	Be sure to allow additional test time when you are building and testing a cellular network. Take the time needed to test and minimize interference between cells. Failure to confirm during installation that the cells do not interfere with each other might make it necessary to interrupt service to the end users later and to redesign the network.

Examples of When to Use Cellular Architecture

Cellular architecture is the best choice when more end users exist than a single point-to-multipoint network can cover or when end users are located in different geographical areas—areas that just one point-to-multipoint network cannot cover. Cellular architecture is the most frequently selected method of expanding a point-to-multipoint network.

Mesh Architecture

Mesh architecture is a multipoint-to-multipoint architecture with one or more Internet interconnection points. In a mesh network, each network node can connect to any other network node that is turned on and within wireless range. Mesh networks are usually deployed in areas where many end users are located relatively close to each other, such as from one block up to one mile apart.

Each mesh network node performs two functions:

- As a wireless router/repeater
- As an end node

Packets can travel through several intermediate wireless nodes to reach the desired end user node. If one or more of the intermediate nodes is down, the packet is dynamically rerouted through other intermediate nodes. Figure 3-5 shows a diagram of a mesh architecture network.

Figure 3-5   *Mesh Architecture*

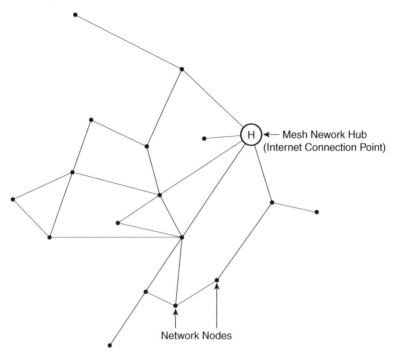

Advantages of Mesh Architecture

The advantages of mesh architecture are as follows:

- Near-line-of-sight coverage
- Routing redundancy
- Simpler network design process
- Simpler antenna installation

Near-Line-of-Sight Coverage

A clear LOS microwave path is always desirable between nodes in a wireless network. In many areas, clear LOS paths are difficult to achieve due to obstructions such as trees and buildings. In areas where LOS paths are partially obstructed, mesh architecture might allow reliable connectivity. This occurs because the network nodes are placed close enough together to allow reliable node-to-node-to-node communication in spite of the obstructions attenuating the signal strengths. The denser the obstructions, the higher the signal attenuation and the closer together the mesh nodes need to be placed.

Routing Redundancy

In a mesh network, every wireless node is a wireless router or repeater. Operating as a router, each node is capable of dynamically calculating the best available path to each distant node. If one node is down (due to failure, being turned off, or being blocked by an obstruction), network traffic is rerouted through other nearby nodes. This on-the-fly rerouting capability provides a measure of network routing redundancy.

Simpler Network Design Process

Point-to-multipoint and cellular network architectures require a moderately complex network design process to ensure that LOS paths exist between each end user location and the wireless access point. The network design process for a mesh architecture network is somewhat simpler. The node-to-node-to-node capability of a mesh network, where each node serves as a relay point, simplifies the network design process. As long as the network designer ensures that each node can communicate with at least one or two nearby nodes, network design can proceed without needing to verify the existence of longer LOS paths.

Simpler Antenna Installation

In a point-to-point or cellular network architecture, each end user location normally uses an antenna that is highly directional and that points back toward the wireless access point. This is desirable because of the need to maximize the signal strength and minimize the interference between the end user and the access point. Successful installation of this directional antenna requires that the appropriate high gain antenna be selected, mounted at or above a specific height, and then pointed in the specific direction of the access point. Each antenna installation must be completed with a fairly high level of precision and accuracy. In contrast, the antenna installation at a mesh network end user does not require the same high level of precision. In a mesh network, the typical end user antenna is not a directional antenna; it is an omnidirectional (omni) antenna. An omni allows the end user node to communicate in more than one direction so it can connect to more than one other node. The same omni antenna can be used at each end user location; it can normally be mounted at a standard (rooftop) height and does not need aiming in a particular direction.

Disadvantages of Mesh Architecture

The disadvantages of mesh architecture are as follows:

- More wireless nodes needed
- Progressive network deployment process
- Difficult bandwidth management

More Wireless Nodes Needed

In a mesh architecture, wireless paths are shorter than in other network architectures. This means that if the number of network nodes is equal, the coverage area of a mesh network is less than the coverage area of a point-to-multipoint network.

Progressive Network Deployment Process

A mesh network relies on the availability of point-to-point-to-point wireless repeating. This means that if a wireless node is installed beyond the range of the nodes that have already been installed, the new node will not be able to connect to the mesh network to obtain service. To prevent this problem, you must deploy a mesh network progressively within a particular service area. Deployment must begin near the Internet access point and continue outward toward the far edge of the mesh.

Difficult Bandwidth Management

Each end user node in a mesh network has dual roles:

* Wireless router or repeater
* End user node

The wireless bandwidth available to each end user node is shared between providing Internet access for that specific end user and providing backbone access for the other end users who are connecting to the Internet through that node. The more hops that exist between an end user and the Internet access point, the less bandwidth that is available to that end user. Managing this shared bandwidth dynamically with continuously changing customer bandwidth needs and backbone bandwidth needs is a challenge for the mesh network software.

Examples of When to Use Mesh Architecture

Mesh architecture is most appropriate when a number of end users are clustered closely together and numerous LOS obstructions exist. Throughput requirements of the users should also be fairly modest, such as up to a few hundred kilobits per second (kbps). One such environment would be a residential housing development where many trees obstruct the LOS paths between the houses. The short path lengths, alternate routing paths, and relatively modest throughput needs of the residents would make a mesh network the appropriate architectural choice.

Selecting the Preliminary Network Architecture

The presence of LOS paths between the proposed network locations is the major determining factor in selecting a network architecture and designing your network. Your final network might be a combination of the four architectures described in this chapter—that is perfectly all right. The terrain and the obstructions in every area are unique. This means that your final network architecture will also be unique. It will be constructed with LOS paths that fit around and over the obstructions in your area.

To select the most appropriate network architecture for your wireless WAN and design your actual wireless network, follow these steps:

Step 1   Map the locations of the end users.

Step 2   Evaluate point-to-point architecture.

Step 3   Group users by proximity.

Step 4   Evaluate point-to-multipoint architecture.

Step 5   Evaluate cellular architecture.

Step 6   Evaluate mesh architecture.

Step 7   Draft preliminary network architecture.

Step 8   Confirm hub site availability.

Step 9   Confirm end user site availability.

Step 10 Confirm site usability.

Steps 1 through 6 will help you select the most appropriate network architecture for your wireless WAN. Steps 7 through 10 will help you design your actual wireless network.

Step 1: Map the Locations of End Users

Obtain a topographical (topo) map that covers all the areas where potential network end users are located. A topographic map shows the terrain elevation at each location. Figure 3-6 shows a representation of a topographic map for the (fictional) area of Pleasantown, in the state of Harmony.

Figure 3-6   *Topographic Map of Pleasantown*

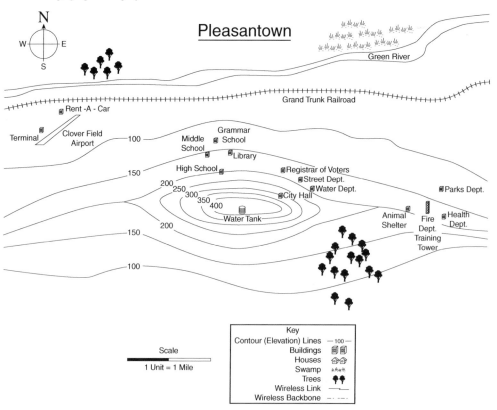

TIP   Topographic maps are available from map stores, bookstores, or (in the United States) the
             offices of the U.S. Geological Survey (USGS). For some areas, mapping software is
             available that makes it easy to prepare a custom topographic map for your area. See the
             "Wireless Link Planning Software" section of Appendix B, "Wireless Hardware, Software,
             and Service Provider Organizations," for a list of sources for maps and mapping software.

It is helpful to know the elevation of each end user location as well as the elevation of the
terrain between the locations. This information helps to determine if an LOS path exists
between the locations. On your map, mark the position and the approximate elevation of
each end.

Step 2: Evaluate Point-to-Point Architecture

If only a few end-user locations exist, point-to-point architecture is often the best architectural choice. For example, Figure 3-7 shows the area around the Pleasantown airport.

Figure 3-7   *Point-to-Point Network*

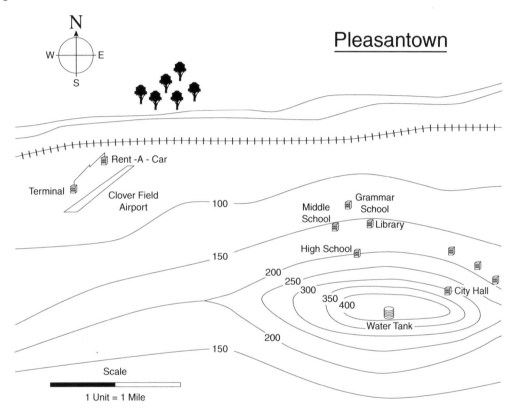

The airport terminal and the airport rent-a-car location need a broadband wireless network connection. These are the only two points that need to be connected. They are both at the same elevation and no obstructions stand between them. The LOS path, simple site survey, and low hardware cost make this an ideal situation for a point-to-point network. If your situation is roughly similar to this example, point-to-point architecture should be your choice. If, however, you have more than a few network end point locations, point-to-point might not be your best choice. Go to Step 3 to continue the evaluation and selection process.

Step 3: Group Users by Proximity

The existence of LOS paths is the most significant factor that affects your network architecture. There is a higher likelihood that end users who are located close to each other will have an unobstructed LOS path to a common access point location. Keeping this in mind, look at Figure 3-6 again. A number of end user locations exist that are close together and have shared LOS paths to access point locations.

In downtown Pleasantown, the grammar school, middle school, high school, and library are within one mile of each other. Also downtown, the Registrar of Voters, City Hall, Street Department, and Water Department are close together. On the east side of town, the animal shelter, the Fire Department training tower, the Health Department, and the Parks Department are within one mile.

Now, look at your own map and see if there are end user locations that are close together and that can be grouped together. If you have one or more such groups, plan on using either point-to-multipoint, cellular, or mesh architecture. Go to Step 4 to continue the architecture evaluation.

Step 4: Evaluate Point-to-Multipoint Architecture

Point-to-multipoint architecture provides economical service to a number of end users who all have an unobstructed LOS path to one high-level access point site. Figure 3-8 provides an example.

At the east edge of Pleasantown, the Animal Shelter, Health Department, Parks Department, and Fire Department training center are all located close together. The top of the Fire Department training tower is high enough to provide an LOS path to each of the other three locations. Together, these four locations can be grouped together into one single point-to-multipoint network. The access point antenna for the network can be mounted on top of the training tower.

On your map, identify any group (or groups) of users who appear to have LOS connectivity to a shared access point location. Consider this group as a potential point-to-multipoint network. The following list directs you to the next step:

- If you have just one group of users and they all appear to have an LOS path to a shared access point location, plan on using a point-to-multipoint architecture. Go to Step 7.

- If you have more than one group of users, each with its own access point location, go to Step 5.

- If many of your end users don't have an LOS path to an access point location, go to Step 6.

Figure 3-8   *Point-to-Multipoint Network*

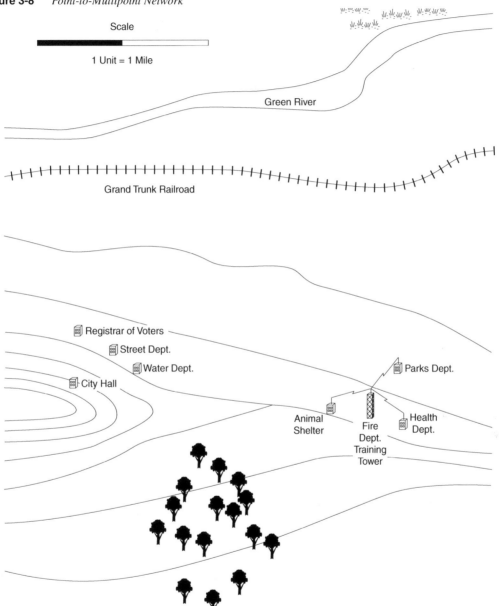

Step 5: Evaluate Cellular Architecture

Sometimes, an area might have more than one point-to-multipoint network, with each network served by its own access point. If several of these access point locations are then connected, the result is a cellular network.

Multiple Point-to-Multipoint Networks

Figure 3-8 identified one point-to-multipoint network at the east edge of town (Fire Department, Parks Department, Health Department, and Animal Shelter). If you look at the end user locations near the center of town in Figure 3-9, you see several other potential point-to-multipoint network possibilities.

Figure 3-9   *Multiple Point-to-Multipoint Networks*

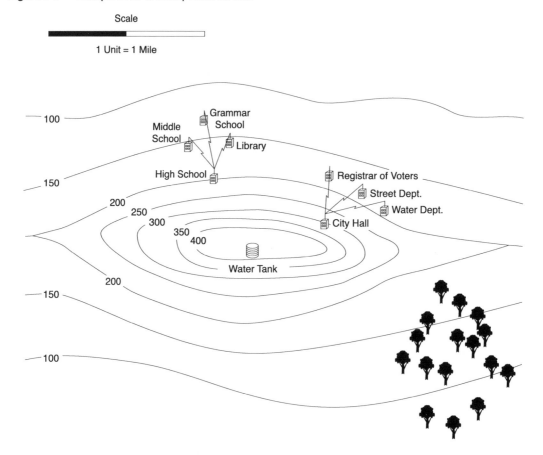

City Hall is located on the side of the hill approximately at a 300-foot (91 m) elevation. The Registrar of Voters, Street Department, and Water Department are each about one mile from City Hall and the elevation of each is about 175 feet (53 m). From the roof of City Hall, there is an LOS path to each of the other three locations. Together, these four locations can be combined into one point-to-multipoint network. The access point can be placed inside City Hall and the antenna can be placed on the roof.

Another point-to-multipoint network exists near the high school. From the roof of the high school (elevation 200 ft [61 m]), LOS paths exist to the library, grammar school, and middle school. An antenna system on the high school roof can supply connectivity to the other three locations.

Access Point Connectivity

Pleasantown now has three new access points, one for each of the three new point-to-multipoint networks. The access point antennas are on the Fire Department training tower, the City Hall roof, and the high school roof. If these three access points are connected together through a common location, a cellular network is created. Refer to Figure 3-10 to see if this is possible.

Figure 3-10 *Cellular Network Options*

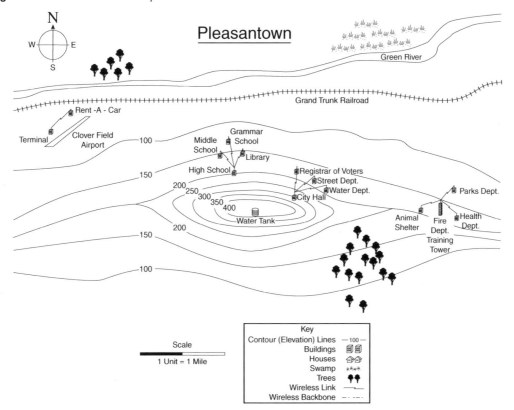

Do any locations exist in Pleasantown that have LOS paths to all three existing access points?

- The Fire Department training tower might be one possibility, but the LOS path from there to the high school is long (about 3.5 miles [5.6 km]), and the path is obstructed by City Hall.

- City Hall has LOS paths to both the Fire Department training tower and the high school. City Hall is one candidate to serve as the hub of a cellular network that would connect and serve all three of the point-to-multipoint networks in town.

- Another cellular network hub location is possible. The water tank on the top of the hill is located at an elevation of 400 ft (122 m). From the top of the tank, it is easy to see the high school, City Hall, and the Fire Department training tower. The tank can serve as the hub of a cellular network. Because the hilltop is the highest point around Pleasantown, it would also allow future expansion of the cellular network to new locations as the area grows.

On your map, identify any locations that appear to provide wireless connectivity to all your wireless access point locations. If you can identify one or more cellular hub site locations, plan on using a cellular architecture for your broadband wireless WAN, and then go to Step 7. If cellular architecture doesn't fit your area, go to Step 6.

Step 6: Evaluate Mesh Architecture

Occasionally, a group of potential wireless network end users are located close together, but they don't have LOS paths to a shared access point. Under these conditions, none of the previous network architectures provide reliable wireless service. One alternative is to evaluate mesh architecture as a possible solution.

Recently, Forest Shadows Estates was carved out of the woods southeast of Pleasantown. Many Forest Shadows Estates residents want broadband Internet access, but they are beyond digital subscriber line (DSL) range, and the cable television company does not offer Internet access.

Because of the number of trees in the area, none of the houses have an LOS path to any of the wireless access point locations in Pleasantown. Some houses have an LOS path to another house and some houses do not. The distances between the houses are short; therefore, in spite of the high attenuation caused by the trees, enough wireless signal remains to allow each house to connect to at least one other house. Mesh architecture can provide connectivity to the Internet if at least one point on the mesh network can be connected to the Internet. Two possible ways to bring Internet connectivity to a hub point on a Forest Shadows Estates mesh network are as follows:

- Purchase a leased line from the local telephone company. The line will cost $500 each month, or a total of $6000 each year.

- Erect a tower and install a point-to-point wireless link connecting the mesh network to the water tank on the hill. If the water tank was already acting as the hub of the cellular network that served Pleasantown, it will be a simple matter to add connectivity from the water tank to a new tower in Forest Shadows Estates. The cost of the tower and the wireless link to the water tank will be $6000.

- Either broadband option will work to connect the Forest Shadows Estates residents to the Pleasantown WAN. The subdivision builder evaluated these two options and decided to pay for the building of the tower and the installation of the wireless link; the results are illustrated by Figure 3-11.

Figure 3-11 *Mesh Network Connected to Cellular Network*

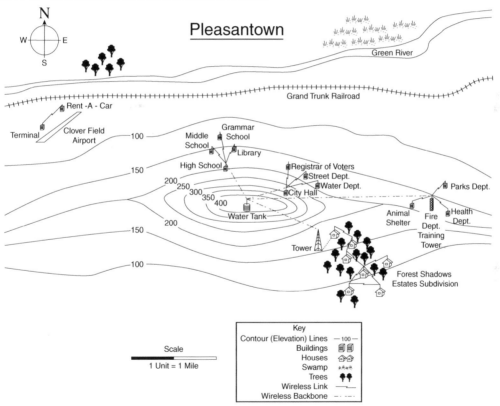

- The builder reasoned that it would be better to pay $6000 one time, own the equipment, and charge the residents each month for Internet access. "Besides," he thought, "the new interstate highway will soon be built and it will pass along the edge of Forest Shadows Estates. I'll be able to lease antenna space on my new tower to three or four cellular telephone companies, and that will bring me an additional three or four thousand dollars of income each month."

- If your potential end users are located close to each other but they have no LOS path to an access point, mesh architectures can successfully connect all or most of your end users. Keep in mind that backbone connectivity is also required to and from at least one node on the mesh network. Go to Step 7.

Step 7: Draft Preliminary Network Architecture

By now, you are aware of the terrain in your area and you know the major obstructions that you need to go around or over. You should have a clear idea which network architecture is best for your proposed WAN. Keep your network design as simple as possible, although it is okay to combine several architectures if that is what you have to do to provide service to all of your end users. Draw straight lines on your map to connect your proposed hub and end user locations.

Measure Compass Headings

Measure the approximate compass headings from the hub site(s) to the end user sites.

TIP   Use a protractor placed over your map. If you are using mapping or topographic software, use the compass tool to determine the headings.

The heading from end user site to hub site will be 180 degrees opposite to the heading from the hub site to the end user site. Start with the estimated heading from hub to end user and either add or subtract 180 degrees. (Choose either one—whichever is easier for you to visualize and calculate. The result is the same.) For example:

A heading of 50 degrees from hub to end user will have a heading of 230 degrees (50 degrees plus 180 degrees equals 230 degrees) from end user to hub. A heading of 300 degrees from hub to end user will have a heading of 120 degrees (300 degrees minus 180 degrees equals 120 degrees) from end user to hub.

Measure Distances

Use the scale of miles on your map with a ruler or the mapping software compass tool to determine the distance from hub sites to end user sites and mark these distances on your map. If you are using point-to-point or mesh architecture, estimate and mark the distances between end user locations.

Make a note of any path distances that appear to be beyond the common range of wireless equipment. Although you have not yet selected the wireless equipment that you will use, some general rules follow:

- Path lengths greater than approximately 7 miles (11.3 km) frequently need some kind of special attention, such as higher antennas, larger antennas, or extra amplification (when legal).

- Point-to-point networks can span distances as long as 30 miles and sometimes longer. To achieve these distances, there must be *no obstructions* to the LOS path, and the end points must be substantially higher than the height of the terrain. Five hundred feet or more of antenna height might be needed. Long links like this are easiest to build if one or both ends of the link are located on hilltops or on the tops of tall buildings.

- Long links that have obstructions, such as mountains, along the way need intermediate repeater locations.

Inspect LOS Paths

Physically drive (or walk) between your hub site locations and your end user locations. If you have a point-to-point or mesh network, drive between end user locations. The purpose is to look for obstructions such as tall buildings, tall trees, water tanks, bridges, or radio towers that were not visible on your map. These tall obstructions could cause attenuation and make the path unusable.

If you find obstructions, mark their location and their approximate height on your map. Calculate the Fresnel Zone clearance needed at that point along the wireless path.

TIP	Use the formula and the example in Figure 2-24 in Chapter 2 to calculate the Fresnel Zone clearance needed.

If your inspection reveals the presence of significant obstructions, you must revise your network architecture. You can either add intermediate repeater sites or redesign the network to use shorter LOS paths.

Make a Frequency Plan

In a point-to-multipoint network with more than one sector or in a cellular network, the same frequency (direct sequence spread spectrum) or hopping sequence (frequency hopping spread spectrum) might be re-used on more than one link or sector. It is important to isolate network segments that share a frequency or hopping sequence from each other. Lack of proper isolation results in interference and throughput reduction. See Chapter 5 for information about isolating antennas on different sectors.

Step 8: Confirm Hub Site Availability

If you are using point-to-point architecture, go to Step 9. Otherwise, you will be using a network architecture that requires one or more hub sites. Inquire as to who owns or manages the buildings where the hub sites are located. Contact the building manager, explain your interest in placing wireless equipment there, and request a meeting to discuss performing a site survey to determine if the site qualifies as a good hub site location.

Step 9: Confirm End User Site Availability

Inquire as to who owns or manages the buildings where the end user sites are located. Contact the building manager, explain your interest in placing wireless equipment there, and request a meeting to discuss performing a site survey to determine if the site qualifies as a good end user site location.

Step 10: Confirm Site Usability

Before concluding that a hub site or an end user site is acceptable, you must perform a site survey. A physical site survey includes determining where and how to mount the antennas, run the cabling, and accomplish the other physical details surrounding the installation. Perform a physical site survey for *all installations*. An RF site survey uses wireless test equipment, including a spectrum analyzer, to examine the RF environment and to confirm that wireless noise or interference is not too high to prevent the successful operation of the new network. Perform an RF site survey for all hub sites and backbone node locations.

Chapter 4 contains a detailed description of both the physical and the RF site survey process. It is important to perform both physical and wireless site surveys before finalizing the design of your network. The site surveys reveal any factors that would prevent successful use of a site, such as the lack of LOS paths, the lack of appropriate antenna-mounting locations, or high noise levels. Chapter 4 also helps you with suggestions about how to revise your network architecture if your site surveys reveal that network revisions are needed.

Review Questions

1 If you have one pair of backbone locations that need to be connected, which network architecture is the most appropriate?

2 What type of antenna—omnidirectional or directional—does a point-to-point network normally use?

3 When a microwave signal strikes an obstruction, what always happens to it?

4 When a point-to-point network is expanded, what architecture is usually chosen? Why?

5 Why is SNR important in a wireless network?

6 What network architectures use sectors?

7 What are the consequences of selecting the wrong access point antenna system for a point-to-multipoint network?

8 What architecture is used to allow frequency re-use while connecting several point-to-multipoint networks?

9 What is the primary disadvantage of cellular architecture?

10 What type of network architecture can be used if end users are located close together and have partially obstructed (non-LOS) paths between each other?

11 What type of routing does a mesh network perform?

CHAPTER 4

Performing Site Surveys

During your preliminary network design process, you selected a draft network architecture based on your preliminary conclusions about the existence of line-of-sight (LOS) paths between specific network locations. Now, you need to evaluate your potential wireless equipment locations to determine if they meet the qualifications that allow you to proceed and to successfully install wireless equipment there. These potential locations might be buildings, towers, or possibly even hilltops with no buildings or wireless equipment. This chapter helps you perform two types of site surveys:

- Physical site surveys
- Radio frequency (RF) site surveys

Performing effective site surveys allows you to determine the following things:

- If the site is 100 percent perfect for your network
- If the site would be acceptable for your network with a few changes to the site, to your network design, or both
- If it is possible to make changes to the site to better meet the needs of your proposed network
- What modifications to make to your network design to fit your network to the site
- If the site is not acceptable for your network because changes to the site or to your network design would be too expensive
- If RF path testing or coverage testing should be performed to gather more information and to determine if the site is suitable
- The specific installation details that must be documented now but used later by installation personnel

Physical Site Surveys

Physical site surveys examine the physical environment of the building, tower, or other location where you want to place either a point-to-multipoint access point or a point-to-point end node. The physical site survey helps you accomplish the following tasks:

- Verify that the locations where you want to place your wireless nodes will actually allow you to place wireless equipment there.

- Determine the best location inside the building or inside the tower equipment vault to place the wireless equipment.

- Verify that your postulated LOS paths actually exist.

- Determine where and how to mount your antenna systems to make successful use of the LOS paths.

- Determine how to design and route the cabling to the antenna system.

- Determine how to protect against damage from lightning by properly grounding the antenna system.

- Document your physical findings and make further recommendations for additions or changes to the preliminary network design.

Reviewing the Preliminary Network Design

Before you travel to a physical site survey location, take time to review the preliminary network design that you created in Chapter 3, "Choosing Your Network Architecture." Make a note of the following:

- The directions that your antennas need to point *from* the site that you are preparing to survey

- *How high* above ground your antennas must be mounted so that the tallest obstacle along your LOS paths does not intrude into more than 40 percent of the Fresnel zone

---

NOTE   It is tempting to skip over this calculation and hope that the antennas will be high enough and that your links will work. Don't fall for this temptation, though. Calculate the Fresnel zone clearances needed, as described in Chapter 2, "Understanding Wireless Fundamentals." If you do not do this now, your wireless network might not provide reliable performance or it might not work at all.

- Determine the approximate antenna gains needed. When you know the gain, you know the approximate physical size of the antenna. Knowing the size helps you evaluate potential antenna-mounting locations and antenna-mounting hardware.

TIP   If you need to calculate the approximate antenna gain, use the link budget formula in Chapter 2.

Contacting Site Management

The first step in performing a physical site survey is to obtain permission from the building or tower manager to check the site to see if it would be a suitable location to place an antenna.

NOTE   You might be performing a physical site survey of an existing wireless tower site instead of a building. The principles are the same, although instead of looking for a flat roof or building wall to mount the antenna on, look for the best location on the tower to mount your antenna.

Locate the building manager, identify yourself, and explain your interest in placing a wireless system in the building or on the tower. You will most likely be asked to speak with the facility manager. Be prepared to provide the following information:

- Your name and your company name
- Who will use the wireless system
- The size and location of the wireless equipment that connects to the antenna system
- The size, appearance, location, and weight of the antenna system

---

TIP   It is helpful to actually bring an antenna with you if possible, or at least to bring a drawing or a picture of the proposed antenna. Most wireless antennas are fairly small, and by showing the antenna size, you help to eliminate concern that the antenna will detract from the appearance of the building.

- How the antenna could be mounted to or on the building
- How the cabling connects the antenna to the wireless equipment
- Whether your wireless equipment will or will not interfere with wireless equipment that already exists on or in the building

---

TIP   This is a good time to ask about the existence of any other wireless equipment in the building or on the tower. When you know about other wireless equipment, you know more about the wireless environment. This knowledge can alert you to the possibility of interference to or from your proposed wireless installation. See Chapter 8, "Solving Noise and Interference Problems," for detailed information about interference.

- The information you need to obtain by doing a physical survey and, if needed, a radio-frequency (wireless) site survey of the building

If management agrees, schedule a day and a time to perform a physical site survey. Allow at least two hours minimum to complete the survey.

If the site already has a number of wireless systems installed or if you plan to install a hub site with one or more wireless access points, schedule several additional hours to perform a wireless site survey.

Physical Site Survey Preparation

Plan to take the following information and equipment with you when you perform the physical site survey:

- A knowledge of the zoning requirements for the city, town, or jurisdiction in which the site is located.
- Distance and direction information to the sites that you hope to provide the wireless link to. You should have this information from your earlier network design work.
- Fresnel zone clearance distances from obstructions along the wireless path.
- A notebook, a pencil, and a pen to record your physical site survey findings.
- Gloves to protect your hands when climbing.
- Sunglasses to protect your eyes from ultraviolet light damage.
- A hat to protect your face from excessive exposure to sunlight, which can lead to skin cancer. Also, if you expect to be on the roof for a considerable period of time during the middle of the day, consider applying sunscreen to your face and hands before going onto the roof.
- A jacket. On a cold day, the rooftop of a building can be much colder and windier than at street level.
- Water. The temperature on the roof of an office building can be 10 to 20 degrees Fahrenheit (5.5 to 11 degrees Celsius) above the ambient temperature, so you can suffer from heat exhaustion on a hot day if you don't drink lots of water.
- A magnetic compass to determine the exact direction toward the other wireless sites.
- A Global Positioning System (GPS) receiver to calculate and display exact distances and antenna direction headings.
- A digital camera to photograph the building, the roof area, and the view in each direction from the roof.
- A flashlight to help you see in dark basements, attics, and crawlspaces.
- A five-foot stepladder to see into (and possibly crawl into) ceiling areas.

Locating a Controlled Equipment Environment

The first step in performing your physical site survey is to find the best location to place the wireless equipment. Some wireless equipment mounts outdoors—at or near the antenna— and connects to the indoor network with fiber-optic cable or with Category 5 (Cat 5) Ethernet cable. Most wireless equipment, however, mounts indoors and connects to the antenna system with coax cable. Therefore, in every case, you need to select an indoor location to house some physical equipment. The indoor location that you choose must provide the following:

- **Accessibility**—The location must allow reasonable access to the equipment for installation and servicing.

- **Security and access control**—The location must prevent unauthorized personnel from gaining access to the equipment and perhaps turning it off or removing it.

- **Power availability**—Sufficient AC or DC power must be available to power the equipment.

- **Temperature control**—The location must not get hot enough or cold enough to exceed the operating temperature limits of the equipment.

- **Humidity control**—The location must not be too wet or too humid.

- **Dust control**—The location should be reasonably clean and dust free to prevent dust or dirt from collecting inside the wireless equipment and causing premature failure.

- **Minimal distance to antenna**—The area should be located as close as possible to the area where the antenna system is located to minimize signal loss in the cabling.

- **Access to cable routing paths**—The equipment location must have access to cable routes that go to the area where the antenna system will be installed. The cable routes might consist of conduit, cable raceways, crawlspaces, drop-ceiling areas, air plenums, or other cabling paths.

TIP   If other wireless equipment is installed in the building, ask where it is installed. If cabling access to that location is good, consider placing your equipment in the same location.

Minimizing the Distance Between the Equipment and the Antenna

In most cases, the performance of your wireless network improves the closer the wireless equipment is mounted to the antenna. This occurs because the shorter the length of the antenna cable, the more signal that reaches the equipment.

As much as possible, choose an indoor location that is as close as possible to the antenna location. For example, if you have a choice between a location that is 60 feet (18 meters) from the antenna and a location that is 350 feet (106 meters) from the antenna, choose the 60-feet-away location because the performance and range of your wireless network is maximized.

If you are evaluating a communications tower as an antenna location, avoid going too high on the tower. Plan to go only high enough to cover the area where your customers are located. Going too high increases your costs for cabling, installation labor, and maintenance labor. In addition, the cost of mounting on a tower frequently is more expensive the higher you go. Going too high also increases the exposure of your system to additional noise and interference.

Gaining Access to the Roof

Most building roofs contain air conditioners and ventilation systems. To install and service these systems, most buildings have a way to reach the roof from inside the building. Roof access methods include stairways to the attic, doors, and roof hatches from the attic to the roof, and ladders attached to a wall. Occasionally, you will find a building with *no* existing roof access. In situations like this, it might be necessary to place your own ladder against an outside wall of the building and climb to the roof.

TIP   Be sure to make a note of situations in which your installation crew will need to ladder the roof themselves. They will need to bring a long ladder with them, and they will need more time to complete the installation because they must use ropes to raise and lower antennas, tools, and equipment up onto the roof.

Routing the Cables

Try to locate the shortest path from the indoor equipment location to the outdoor antenna location. Use existing cable paths whenever possible. One of the most challenging parts of the physical site survey is finding a way to route the cable from the outside of the building to the inside.

TIP   Building managers and owners are concerned about preventing damage caused by water leaking into their buildings. Tell the building manager that you would prefer not to drill holes (and especially not vertical holes that rainwater could pass through) to bring your cabling inside. The manager will appreciate that you are aware of and that you respect the needs of their company.

If possible, try to find and use an existing cable entry hole into the building. These existing holes might be holes for other cables, ventilation grates, electrical conduits, or roof jacks. The building manager can often advise you of existing cable routing paths and answer your questions about which routes are acceptable.

Surveying the Roof

When you are on the roof, take a good look around. Locate any existing antenna installations. Note how the other antennas are mounted to or on the building and notice where their cabling runs. Make a drawing of the rooftop and indicate the height of the roof above ground. Add the locations of the other antennas and any large pieces of rooftop equipment.

TIP Note the location of existing AC power outlets. These will come in handy later, such as during installation when drills need to be recharged or test equipment needs to be plugged in.

Determining Where to Point the Antenna

From the review of your preliminary network design, you know the compass headings where your antennas need to point.

Turn your magnetic compass until the north (N) mark is under the marked end of the compass needle. The needle is pointing toward magnetic North. Mark an arrow on your rooftop drawing showing where North is relative to the sides of the building. The mark at the top center of the compass dial shows the direction that you are facing.

Turn the compass dial until the compass heading for your antenna is at the top center of the dial. Slowly turn your body until the marked end of the compass needle once again is under the N mark. You are now facing in the direction that your antenna needs to point. Mark this heading on your rooftop drawing and walk toward that side of the building to look for places to mount your antenna.

If your antenna is to be mounted on a square or a triangular tower, examine the tower legs and the flat tower faces and select the leg or the face that is pointing the closest to your desired antenna direction.

Determining Where to Place the Antenna

You can place and mount your antenna using several good methods. A flat, clear, horizontal roof area on the side of the building that your antenna needs to face is probably the best mounting location. A flat vertical wall that faces the direction that your antenna needs to point can also be used. The peak or the ridgeline of a roof is the worst location to mount an antenna. Figure 4-1 shows examples of some of the best mounting locations.

Figure 4-1 *Antenna-Mounting Location Examples*

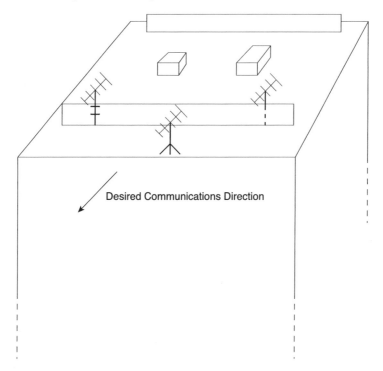

If the roof has industrial equipment such as air conditioners or ventilation equipment, select your antenna-mounting locations to be some distance away or in a location where the equipment is behind the antennas. This way, the equipment won't block the LOS path.

NOTE Chapter 5, "Selecting Antenna Systems," has additional information about antenna-mounting hardware. Chapter 7, "Installing Outdoor Wireless Systems," has more information about installing the antenna support hardware. If you want to become more familiar with these details, look through those chapters now.

Be aware of the visual impact that your antennas will have. Whenever possible, choose a location that will make your antennas less visible from the street level.

Avoiding Nearby Obstacles

From your roof, note any nearby obstacles in the direction that your antenna will point, such as nearby trees or buildings. If the obstacles are higher than (or almost as high as) your antenna, the LOS path that your system needs is obstructed. Add these obstacles to your rooftop drawing, noting the direction, approximate height, and approximate distance. If these obstacles are present, you must either move your antenna to a different, less obstructed part of the roof or raise your antenna until it is above the obstacles.

Avoiding Power Lines

If power lines run along the side of the building near the roof, you must choose an antenna-mounting location far enough away from the power lines so that the antenna and the antenna support mast cannot hit the power lines if the antenna falls.

WARNING   Each year, people are burned and killed when antennas fall and hit power lines. DO NOT EVEN THINK of placing an antenna or a support mast close enough to power lines so that it could hit the lines if it fell over or was blown over.

Avoiding Distant Obstacles

If distant obstacles, such as tall buildings or hills, exist along your LOS path, you likely are already aware of them from your preliminary network design work. If these obstructions intrude into your Fresnel zone, they add additional loss, which can prevent your link from working.

From the rooftop of a four-story building, you can often identify tall buildings up to 10 or more miles (16 km) away. In the morning on a clear day, you might be able to identify tall hills and mountains 25 or more miles (40 km) away.

From your roof, note any distant obstacles and add them to your drawing with the approximate distance, height, and direction. Moving your antenna to a different area of the roof will probably not help you avoid these obstacles. You will need to raise your antenna higher to clear them.

Determining Antenna Height

To determine how high your antenna needs to be above the ground, start with the height above ground of the roof, and then do the following:

- If nearby obstacles exist that you cannot stay clear of by moving your antenna to a clearer area of the roof, add the height needed to clear the obstacle.

- Remembering that 60 percent of the Fresnel zone needs to be clear; if any distant obstacles exist that intrude into more than 40 percent of your Fresnel zone, add the additional height needed for Fresnel zone clearance above the obstacle.

- If your path is longer than approximately 7 miles (11 km), you might need to add additional antenna height to clear the earth bulge, as described in Chapter 2.

- Knowing the total height that your antenna needs to be above the ground, subtract the roof height from the total antenna height. The result is the height that your antenna needs to be mounted above the roof.

Selecting the Antenna-Mounting Structure

You now know the following about your proposed antenna system:

- The direction that the antenna needs to point

- The location on the roof where the antenna will be clear of other antennas, nearby obstacles, rooftop equipment, and power lines

- The height that the antenna needs to be above the roof

- The availability of flat roof areas and vertical walls, which can serve as possible antenna-mounting locations

Make a note of the area that you recommend the antenna system be mounted in. Indicate this area on your rooftop drawing.

Grounding the Antenna System

To be safe as well as legal, all outdoor antenna systems must be properly grounded and protected from lightning.

NOTE   At press time, the National Electrical Code (in the United States) requires that every antenna mast be grounded. Coaxial cable shields must also be grounded. Each conductor of a Cat 5 cable running indoors from an outdoor antenna must be protected with an antenna discharge unit (a lightning arrestor) where the cable enters the building.

The following section is an overview but not a complete treatment of the subject of grounding and lightning protection. The purpose is to give you a basic introduction to lightning protection so that you can determine where to route the ground wire for your antenna system. For more information about the grounding requirements in your area, do the following:

- Consult your local building or planning department to learn what local rules and regulations are in place.

- Talk with an electrician to gain the benefit of his local experience.

- Refer to the National Electrical Code for the latest guidelines.

- Use the additional grounding standards information sources listed in Appendix B, "Wireless Hardware, Software, and Services Provider Organizations."

Providing Protection from Lightning

A lightning protector (lightning arrestor) works by providing a low-impedance path to ground for the high-voltage, high-current electrical energy contained in a lightning strike. All outdoor wireless antenna systems must contain a lightning protector or surge suppressor.

Without a lightning protector, the energy from a direct or a nearby lighting strike travels to the ground by passing through (and damaging or destroying) the wireless equipment and the wired network equipment. The building housing the equipment can also be damaged, and the people within the building can be injured. Even an installed lighting protector cannot provide proper protection unless it connects to a good ground connection.

Locating the Grounding Point

Locating the best grounding point is one of the most challenging parts of performing a site survey because it can be difficult to find a good ground point that allows a short, straight, large-diameter ground wire to be run from the antenna system to the ground. Figure 4-2 shows the ideal grounding scenario.

Figure 4-2   *Ideal Grounding and Lightning-Protection Scenario*

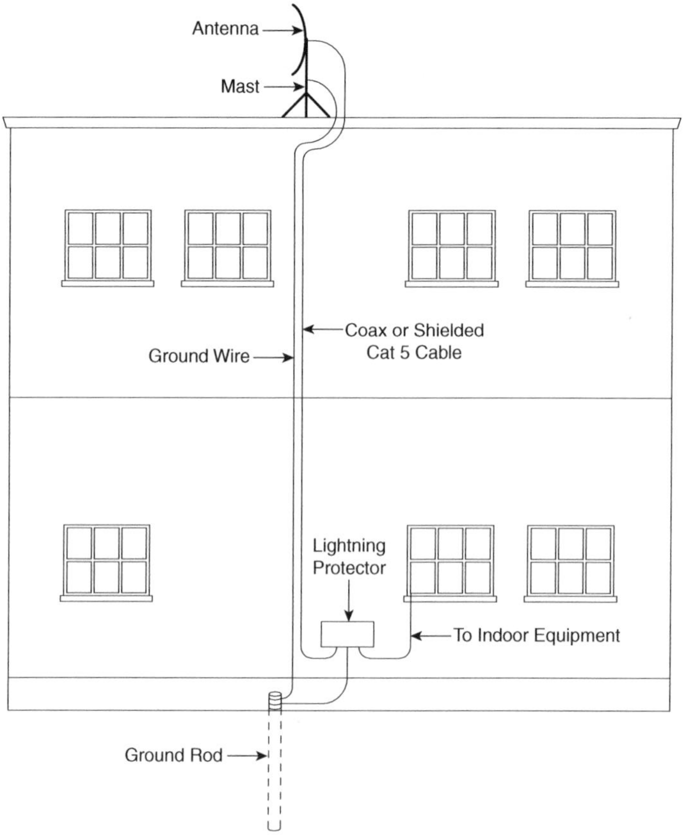

The best ground wire route is to run the shortest possible large-diameter ground wire straight down from the antenna system to an 8-foot (2.4 m) ground rod.

In some situations, the rooftop antenna is located too far away from the earth to allow you to run a short ground wire. One alternative is to ground the antenna system to the building. If there is a rooftop penthouse with air conditioning or ventilation equipment inside, you might be able to attach the ground wire directly to the building's structural steel. Ask the facility manager to help select the best, most direct ground attachment point.

TIP   Resist the urge to use a rooftop electrical ground point such as the frame of an air conditioner or a connection to metal electrical conduit. These electrical ground connections are usually long and indirect and are not designed to provide proper protection from lightning. You must either locate a suitable lightning-protection ground point or plan to have one installed when the antenna system is installed.

TIP   The lightning protector must also be grounded. The most effective location for the lightning protector is at the point where the antenna cable (or the Ethernet cable, if power-over-Ethernet [PoE] equipment is used) enters the building. Again, for effective protection, use an 8-foot (2.4m) ground rod.

Revising the Preliminary Network Design

Based on your physical site survey findings, it might be necessary for you to revise your preliminary network design. Use the suggestions in Table 4-1 as a guide to overcome common site problems.

Table 4-1   *Solutions to Physical Site Problems*

Problem		Solution
LOS Path Problems	There is no LOS path on a single backbone link or end user link.	Revise that link to use an intermediate relay or repeater location.
	There is a lack of several LOS paths to or from a hub site.	Choose a higher hub site location, one with better LOS paths to the end user locations.
Hub Site Antenna Problems	There is no appropriate location to mount antennas at a hub site.	Erect a short tower on the roof to provide additional antenna-mounting space; if that is not possible, move the hub site to a different location.
	More than 100 feet separate the hub site wireless equipment and the antenna system.	Find a new equipment-mounting location closer to the antenna system; or Use an indoor or outdoor wireless equipment architecture that can tolerate long cable runs; or Budget to use more expensive, larger-diameter, lower-loss coax.
	The hub site antenna system design is difficult.	Get help from a more experienced wireless system designer.
Rooftop Cost Problem	The cost for roof space is too high.	Investigate the use of other lower-cost high-elevation locations, such as private homes or businesses, where you can trade Internet access for roof space.

Physical Criteria Evaluation and Conclusion

Your physical site survey findings need to be preserved and communicated. The information that you develop will determine if the site is physically suitable for your wireless network. If the site is acceptable, your survey information can be a guide during the installation process. This is why it is important to clearly document all your findings, comments, and recommendations.

Table 4-2 provides one example of a form that you can use to collect your site survey information. You can modify this form to meet your specific needs. Use the tearout card at the end of this book to make copies of this form.

Table 4-2   *Sample of Physical Site Survey Data Form*

Surveyor Name		Phone/E-Mail	
Site Address		Site Owner	
Site Manager		Phone/E-Mail	
Facility Manager		Phone/E-Mail	
Existing Wireless Equipment		Existing Antenna Locations	
New Equipment Location		Power Source	
Path Length		Fresnel Zone Clearance	
Roof Height		Roof Access Location	
Antenna Location		Antenna Height Above Ground	
Antenna Mounting Hardware Needed		Antenna Heading/Tilt	
Nearby Obstructions		Distant Obstructions	
Cable Type and Length		Cable Entry Point	
Cable Route			
Grounding Locations (Mast and Building Entrance)		Ground Wire Route (Mast and Building Entrance)	
Lightning Protection Description		Lightning Protection Location	
Site Evaluation	Good	Acceptable	Not Acceptable
Comments and Recommendations			
Follow-Up Issues			
Drawings Attached			

Radio Frequency (RF) Site Surveys

The physical site survey process inspects the physical environment where your wireless equipment will potentially be installed. If your physical site survey finds the site acceptable, then your next step is an RF site survey. The RF site survey examines the outdoor wireless environment that your network must work within.

It is a good policy to do an RF site survey for each potential new installation because the license-free frequencies are shared bands. There is always the possibility of interference from other wireless systems.

The consequence of installing a wireless network incorrectly in an area with a high level of interference is simply that the *throughput of your network will be reduced*. Under worst-case conditions, your throughput might be less than if you were using a 14.4-kbps dialup modem. If you plan to install a hub site for a point-to-multipoint network, an RF survey is a necessity. The risk of having your new network not work properly is just too high. Don't take a chance; do the RF site survey and maximize your likelihood of installing a reliable, high-throughput network.

At this point, you're probably wondering if there are ever any situations where you can skip the RF survey without running too much risk that your new system won't work. Yes—you can skip the RF site survey if you install a point-to-point link (or the customer end of a point-to-multipoint link) and you know that the following conditions are true:

- No other wireless systems are in the area on the same frequency to cause interference.
- A clear LOS path exists to the other end of the link.

Overview of the RF Site Survey Process

The purpose of an RF site survey is to accomplish the following:

- Determine if signals are already present in the area that are strong enough to cause interference to your new system
- Document the signal type, strength, direction, and polarization of the other signals present
- Evaluate the site to see if the wireless environment has a low enough level of interference and noise to allow your new wireless system to operate reliably there

You might wonder why it matters what other signals are present. It matters because interference to your system can occur from other systems that are already present in the same area where you want deploy your new system. If you experience interference, the opposite will probably also be true—your system will cause interference to the other system. If you know about other nearby systems, you can plan to deploy your system in a way that minimizes interference and allows successful, high throughput operation of both systems.

NOTE   You can find much more information about minimizing interference in Chapter 8.

RF Site Survey Test Equipment

RF site survey test equipment ranges from PC-based utility programs to full-featured RF spectrum analyzers. You need the following equipment to perform an RF site survey:

- The physical site survey equipment listed earlier in this chapter.

- A spectrum analyzer with an instruction manual. The spectrum analyzer must cover the frequency bands that you plan to use. In some cases, a PC-based site survey utility can be used in place of a spectrum analyzer.

- If your equipment is not battery powered, you need 100 to 200 ft (30 to 60 m) of AC extension cord.

- A 30 dB attenuator that can be placed in the coaxial cable between the antenna and the spectrum analyzer.

- A 6 dBi omnidirectional antenna to check for signals coming from all directions.

- A 10–14 dBi panel antenna to check for signals coming from specific directions.

NOTE   If you already know what type of antenna your link will use, plan to test with that antenna during your site survey.

- A wireless sniffer, protocol analyzer, or site survey utility.

TIP   A wireless protocol analyzer can be added to supplement, but not replace, a spectrum analyzer. For example, an 802.11b protocol analyzer or packet sniffer can be helpful if you plan to deploy multiple 802.11b access points in the middle of a medium-to-large city. The protocol analyzer can help you determine the number of other 802.11b access points in the vicinity, their frequency, and their approximate direction. You should still perform an RF site survey with a spectrum analyzer to locate sources of non-802.11b signals and strong signals outside of the 2.4-GHz band.

How a Spectrum Analyzer Works

A spectrum analyzer is a very-wide-band receiver that can be adjusted to receive across either a wide or a narrow range of frequencies. Spectrum analyzers visually display the signal energy that they find at each frequency. A wide receive range can look at a wide band of frequencies simultaneously, such as from 2400 MHz to 2500 MHz. A narrow receive range examines a single frequency or a single signal all by itself, such as 2442 MHz.

Spectrum Analyzer Input

The spectrum analyzer is a sensitive receiver that is designed to detect low signal levels received from whatever antenna you connect to the input. For example, a signal level of + 20 dBm (100 mW) or higher can overload a spectrum analyzer and permanently damage it. This damage is expensive to repair. To protect the input circuitry, many spectrum analyzers have built-in input attenuators that can be switched ON to reduce the amplitude of strong signals.

TIP   It is a good habit to begin each of your RF site surveys by switching the built-in attenuator ON. After you check the signal levels and you see that none of the levels is high enough to cause damage, you can switch the attenuator OFF.

If your spectrum analyzer does not have a built-in input attenuator, you can buy a low-cost 30-dB attenuator and manually insert it between the antenna and the input connector. When you see that no exceptionally strong signals are present, you can remove the attenuator and continue with your testing.

Refer to the instruction manual that came with your spectrum analyzer to find the maximum safe input level.

Spectrum Analyzer Output

The output from the spectrum analyzer is a graph of signal strength versus frequency. The horizontal (x-axis) of the spectrum display shows the frequency range that is being received. The x-axis is usually divided into 10 divisions. For a wide sweep range, these divisions are adjusted to be large. For example, a setting of 10 MHz per division results in a total receiving range of 100 MHz. For a narrow sweep range, the divisions are adjusted to be small. A setting of 10 kilohertz (kHz) per division results in a receiving range of 100 kHz.

The center frequency on the x-axis is also adjustable. This is either the single frequency being examined or the center of the frequency band being examined.

The vertical (y-axis) of the spectrum display shows the signal strength (amplitude). The y-axis is frequently divided into 8 or 10 divisions. Moving down the y-axis, each line marks a signal level that is 10 times lower (10 dB lower) than the division above it. These signal levels generally range from about 0 dBm (1 mW) down to –100 dBm.

By looking at both the display axis simultaneously and observing the signal's shape (also called spectral output), it is possible to determine the signal strength, the center frequency, the width of the signal, and (with practice) the type of modulation being used.

By using a directional antenna and rotating the antenna in different directions while watching the signal level, you can tell the direction that a signal is coming from.

By shifting your directional antenna from horizontal to vertical polarization while watching the signal level, you can tell whether a signal was transmitted from an antenna that was horizontally polarized or vertically polarized.

NOTE   For additional information about antenna polarization, see the discussion in Chapter 5.

Inspecting a Band of Frequencies

Most RF site survey work consists of examining a wide band of frequencies to determine if other signals are present in or near the frequency band that you plan to use.

NOTE   This is a bit like using a wide-angle lens (such as a 24 mm or a 28 mm lens) on a 35 mm camera. You see a wide area without seeing all the little details of everything in the picture.

The following examples provide practice setting the spectrum analyzer and seeing what the output looks like.

The standard North American FM radio broadcast band ranges from 88 MHz to 108 MHz. FM radio broadcast signals are not spread spectrum signals, but they are easy to see on the spectrum analyzer. That's why they are used in these first two examples.

Figure 4-3 shows the spectrum analyzer output that would be visible when viewing the FM broadcast band in a major city where you will see from 20 to 40 different stations.

Figure 4-3   *Wide Spectrum Analyzer Frequency Coverage Display*

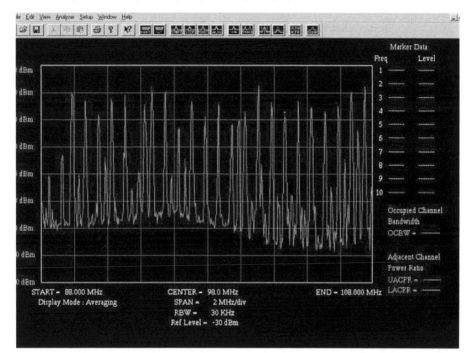

The center frequency is 98 MHz and the span (the frequency range between each x-axis line) is 2 MHz per division. There are 10 horizontal divisions, so the total frequency coverage is 10 times 2 MHz for a total range of 20 MHz. The lowest frequency being received is 88 MHz and the highest frequency is 108 MHz.

Inspecting a Single Frequency

Switching from the inspection of a wide band of frequencies to the inspection of a narrow band of frequencies is easy. Adjust the span control to 200 kHz per division. The center frequency is the same (98 MHz), but the overall frequency coverage is now 2 MHz (10 divisions times 200 kHz per division for a total range of 2 MHz). Figure 4-4 shows the resulting display.

Figure 4-4   *Three-Signal Spectrum Analyzer Coverage Display*

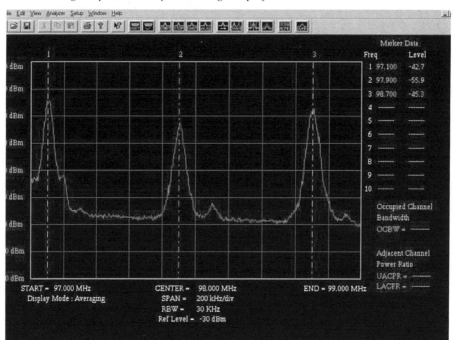

Instead of 40 stations, only the three stations near the 98 MHz center frequency are visible. From left to right, these stations are at 97.1 MHz, 97.9 MHz, and 98.7 MHz.

If you reduced the span per division still further, you would see even more details of the signal at the center frequency. In Figure 4-5, the span is reduced to 50 kHz per division and the center frequency is set to 98.7 MHz (the frequency of the right-hand station in Figure 4-4).

NOTE   This is like using a telephoto lens (such as a 200 mm lens) on a 35 mm camera. You see a magnified view of one object without seeing much of the landscape or the context that surrounds that object.

Figure 4-5   *Single-Signal Spectrum Analyzer Coverage Display*

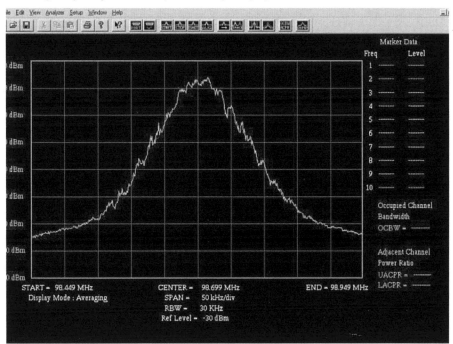

Figure 4-5 shows only the signal of the station at 98.7 MHz. With these spectrum analyzer settings, you can study the characteristics of this one signal more closely. You already know that the modulation type is FM, but you can also determine the following:

- **Signal strength**—The display shows that the signal has a peak signal strength of approximately −34 dBm.

- **Direction**—If you rotate the spectrum analyzer antenna until you see the signal strength peak and then use your compass to determine the direction that the antenna is pointing, you will know the direction that the signal is coming from.

- **Polarization**—If you rotate your antenna from horizontal polarization to vertical polarization and back to horizontal, you can determine if the signal was transmitted from an antenna with a horizontal or a vertical polarization. The position (horizontal or vertical) of your spectrum analyzer antenna that results in the highest signal strength is the same polarization as the signal's transmitting antenna.

Spectrum Analyzer Peak-Hold Feature

The spectral output of a spread spectrum signal is not constant. Spread spectrum modulation was originally designed for use by the military to spread out wireless signal energy and make it harder to detect and decode the intelligence. The varying modulation of a spread spectrum signal causes the signal to continuously change in frequency and in signal strength. After you learn the general shape of spread spectrum signals, you can determine the modulation type of signals that you see.

Unless you have a very expensive spectrum analyzer designed specifically to analyze spread spectrum signals, you must practice using the peak-hold feature on your spectrum analyzer. This feature displays a second output trace that captures the peak signal strength and holds these peak values so that you can examine the signal shape more carefully. Without the use of this feature, it is difficult to see enough of a spread spectrum signal to determine much about it. Using the peak-hold feature allows you to arrive at more accurate and more useful conclusions.

Please go back and look at Figure 4-4 for a moment. It shows three FM broadcast signals. The frequency and the phase (phase is related to frequency change) of each of these signals changed slightly as the signal was modulated. By activating the peak-hold feature of the spectrum analyzer, you get a fuller picture of the signal shapes. In Figure 4-6, peak-hold was turned ON for the same three signals shown in Figure 4-4.

Figure 4-6   *Spectrum Analyzer Peak-Hold Function*

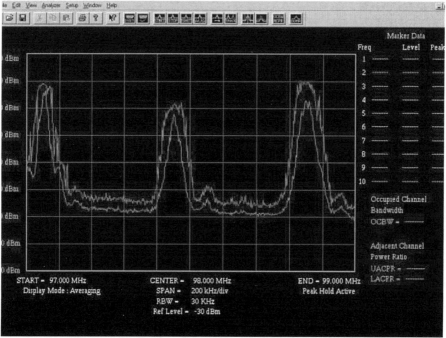

The lower trace in Figure 4-6 shows what the three signals looked like at one moment in time. The upper trace shows (and holds) the peak value that each signal reached during the entire time that the signals were sampled (about 20 seconds). Using peak-hold for your RF site surveys results in a clearer picture of the type of signals that are present.

Inspecting Real-World Signals on a Spectrum Analyzer

From a downtown rooftop in many cities, you can see a variety of signals on (and near) the license-free bands. Many signals are inside the bands and some signals are below or above the band. You need to be aware of all signals because sometimes signals just outside the band can affect your ability to receive signals inside the license-free bands.

One disadvantage of using a PC-based site survey utility instead of a spectrum analyzer is that the utility doesn't have the ability to receive outside of the band. You run the risk of missing strong signals outside the band that could reduce your wireless throughput.

TIP   If you plan to deploy a system on an existing tower that has many transmitters already installed and operating —be advised that this is the most challenging RF environment that you can encounter. If you plan to use a site like this, you must do a thorough RF site survey with a spectrum analyzer. The chances of high levels of RF energy overloading your receiver and reducing your throughput are high.

In addition to your RF site survey, be ready to take other evasive measures; in other words, be ready to add additional filtering to your system to help it perform reliably. See Chapter 8 for information about using bandpass filters.

The majority of the signals that you will encounter outdoors in the license-free bands will be either direct sequence spread spectrum (DSSS) or frequency-hopping spread spectrum (FHSS). Occasionally, you will encounter a combination of several of these signals on the same band at the same time. The following sections show you what these signals look like.

Direct Sequence Spread Spectrum

A DSSS signal is easy to identify when you use the peak-hold feature to allow the signal spectra to fill out. The signal is approximately 22-MHz wide from side to side. The more data the signal is carrying, the faster and wider the display fills. When no data is being carried, no (or little) signal is present. The weaker the signal, the more time it takes to see it and identify it.

Figure 4-7 shows two strong (approaching –60 dBm) DSSS signals in the 2.4 GHz band. One signal is on Channel 1 (2412 MHz) and the other is on Channel 6 (2437 MHz). The peak-hold trace (the upper trace) reveals the two hill-shaped signal spectra.

Figure 4-7 *DSSS Spectrum Analyzer Signal Display*

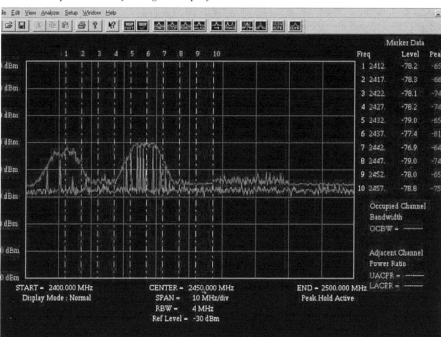

Frequency Hopping Spread Spectrum

An FHSS signal is easy to identify by using the peak-hold feature. The signal hops from 1-MHz channel to 1-MHz channel, throughout the band. The spectrum analyzer peak-hold trace looks like the teeth on a comb, with a signal peak every few MHz, as shown in Figure 4-8.

Detecting Other Signals on the Spectrum Analyzer

Occasionally, you will see other signals and modulation types that you cannot identify or classify. It is important to record and document these other signals. The license-free bands are shared bands that are legally used by a wide variety of end users.

Figure 4-8   *FHSS Spectrum Analyzer Signal Display*

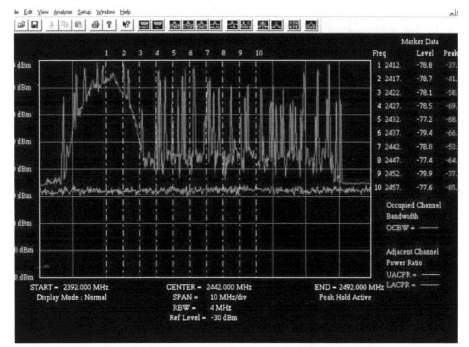

The FCC originally designated these bands for license-free industrial, scientific, and medical (ISM) use on a shared basis with military and licensed amateur radio users.

Additional signal types that you might see include the following:

- Newer forms of DSSS and FHSS modulation, such as multicarrier direct sequence and wide-band frequency hopping
- Wide-band non-spread spectrum signals in the 5-GHz Unlicensed National Information Infrastructure (U-NII) bands
- Military communications and radar systems
- Licensed amateur radio public service and experimental systems

Performing an RF site survey with a spectrum analyzer helps you to accomplish the following:

- Know in advance the RF level in a specific band.
- Work around the RF signals that you see.

- Avoid delays during deployment of your network.

- Avoid creating interference problems for others.

- Promote successful license-free operation by communicating and cooperating with others.

Chapter 8 contains many tips and techniques that can help you deploy your wireless networks cooperatively and successfully.

RF Site Survey Principles

Following are some principles to help you prepare your RF site survey inspection procedure:

- First, if you have never used a spectrum analyzer before, it is best to experiment with it first in your office or shop. Learn how to operate it and practice identifying different types of signals. Learn how to use the peak-hold feature and how to protect the spectrum analyzer from being overloaded and damaged by strong signals.

- Plan to do your RF survey using a two-person test team. Your assistant might suggest questions and test ideas that did not initially occur to you; besides, it is easier to haul all the test equipment up to a roof (or a hilltop) if two people share the workload.

- Plan and list your RF survey steps in advance. Think in terms of taking wireless snapshots of the area. Think about where your end locations are and how your sectors will cover those end locations. You need to check the strength, the antenna polarization, and the signal types present in each of your sectors. For example, if you plan to deploy a three-sector access point on a rooftop in a medium-size city, plan to do the following:

    1 **Take an overall look**—Use the omnidirectional antenna to look at the number and level of signals present within a band of frequencies starting below and ending above the band that you plan to use. For example, if you plan to use 2.4 GHz equipment, you should examine the frequency band from 2.3 GHz to 2.5 GHz. This step allows you to quickly locate strong signals in the band and adjacent to the band.

    2 **Look at each sector**—Use the panel (or directional) antenna to look for signals within the band and within each of your sectors. First, search for signals using the antenna that is oriented for vertical polarization and then search for horizontally polarized signals. This step allows you to identify the presence and the polarization of signals within each of your sectors.

    3 **Take a detailed look**—Narrow the spectrum analyzer frequency sweep and use the panel antenna to take a detailed look at any strong in-band signals that you discover. These signals can interfere with the system that you plan to install. Save a file or a screen shot of these strong signals along with information about their direction, antenna polarization, and the length of the sample interval.

4 **Vary the sampling interval**—Use both long sampling intervals and short sampling intervals. The more quickly a spectrum analyzer display fills up with signals, the more intense the level of RF activity. Experiment using sampling intervals as short as 15 seconds and as long as 30 minutes.

- Do one or two practice sessions from a high, outdoor location before your first real RF site survey. These practice sessions allow you to become familiar with the outdoor RF environment where more than one signal is present simultaneously. You will become comfortable with your RF survey process before your actual site survey when a facility manager could be looking over your shoulder, asking you questions, and judging your professionalism.

- Schedule your actual RF site surveys to take place during the busiest part of the workday, when RF activity and RF interference is highest. Good test periods are in the morning from 8:30 to 10:30 a.m. (0830 to 1030) and after lunch from 1:00 to 3:00 p.m. (1300 to 1500). The more potential wireless signals that are present during your testing, the more meaningful your test results will be. Allow at least two to four hours for each survey location. It is important to have enough time to set up and thoroughly investigate and document the signals that are present.

- Choose your test location to be as close as possible to the location where you would like to permanently install your antenna system; for example:

  1 If your antenna system will be on a building rooftop, test from the section of the roof that has the clearest possible view (ideally, 360 degrees). Nothing on the roof should obstruct the LOS path toward your endpoint locations.

  2 If you are testing on a hilltop, find a clear spot that is about 100 feet away from towers or buildings. The towers and buildings can obstruct the LOS paths of incoming signals.

  3 If you need to locate your antenna system on an existing tower to obtain a LOS path, use an antenna with a radiation pattern that is similar to your actual antenna. If practical, place the test antenna in the same tower location where your real antenna will go. Your test antenna should be exposed to the same local and distant RF environment that your real antenna will be exposed to.

NOTE   If you are not certified as a tower climber, you need to hire a properly certified tower climber to safely climb the tower and mount the test antenna. Even with a certified tower climber, it is still your responsibility to make sure that the climber always uses the appropriate safety equipment.

RF Site Survey Process

Before you begin your RF site survey, here are some additional explanations about the way wireless equipment works. These explanations help you understand what to look for and why.

Observing Signal-to-Noise Ratio (SNR)

The *signal-to-noise ratio (SNR)* is the single most important condition that must be met before a wireless signal can be successfully received and decoded. Simply stated, the level of the received signal must be high enough and the noise level low enough to allow the receiver to separate the signal from the noise. If the signal level is too low or the noise level is too high, the incoming data will be lost. The more often that incoming data is lost, the slower the network throughput and performance. On the other hand, the higher the SNR, the better and faster the network performs.

At this point, it is important to understand what the definition of noise includes. Noise is everything other than the desired signal; therefore, noise is the total of natural noise, manmade noise, signals from other networks, and even signals from other access points in your own network. Again, noise is everything other than your one desired signal at every moment in time (every receiver timeslot).

Access Point Vulnerability to Noise

A low SNR at any point in a wireless network results in slow (or, in the worst case—no) data throughput on that particular wireless link. The worst place to have a low SNR is at the hub site (the access point) of a point-to-multipoint network. The reason should be obvious. If an access point (AP) receiver is bombarded with high noise levels, that AP will find it difficult to receive and decode the signals from all the network endpoint transmitters in the network. The throughput to and from all the users of the network will be drastically slowed down.

Unfortunately, point-to-multipoint access points are the most vulnerable to noise for the following reasons:

- They are often located near the center of a metropolitan area where they are exposed to a high concentration of noise sources.
- They are usually located atop high buildings where they can pick up noise from a long distance away.
- They use wider beamwidth antennas (when compared to the narrower beamwidth of point-to-point antennas) that receive noise from a wider and larger area.

The more noise that an AP receiver is exposed to, the lower the SNR will be and the stronger the signals must be for them to be received and decoded. For the signals to be stronger (remember that the amount of power radiated from the antenna systems is limited by the

Federal Communications Commission), the endpoint locations must be closer to the AP location. Therefore, the higher the noise level that an AP receiver is exposed to, the shorter the distance it can communicate and the smaller the cell radius or sector size. This is why it is important to do a site survey and verify that the hub site noise levels are reasonably low. If the noise levels are too high, the range of your newly installed access point might be low, perhaps as low as one-half mile.

Locating Nearby Out-of-Band Noise Sources

Out-of-band noise sources are (as the name suggests) not in the same frequency band that you plan to use. Most often, these transmitters are located just below or above the band and transmit with high power. Following are some examples:

- Paging transmitters
- Cell site transmitters
- Multichannel, Multipoint Distribution Service (MMDS), Multipoint Distribution Service (MDS), and Instructional Television Fixed Service (ITFS) transmitters
- AM, FM, and television broadcast transmitters
- Commercial two-way radio transmitters, especially if they operate near the intermediate frequency (IF) used by your equipment

---

NOTE   Chapter 6, "Evaluating and Selecting Wireless Equipment," describes IF-based equipment in more detail.

Out-of-band interference sources can be strong, either physically nearby or on a nearby frequency. They can overload your receiver and decrease the receiver's sensitivity to desired signals. This in turn reduces the network range and slows the network throughput.

By locating these interference sources early in your network design process, you can do the following:

- Recommend additional test time during installation.
- Recommend the use of a bandpass filter to minimize possible throughput reduction from receiver overload.
- Recommend moving your equipment further away from the high-power transmitters.

Locating In-Band Noise Sources

In-band noise sources are on frequencies within the same ISM or U-NII frequency band that you plan to use. Here are some potential in-band noise sources:

- FHSS networks used by Internet service providers (ISPs) and by corporate, governmental, and educational organizations
- DSSS networks used by ISPs and organizations
- Broadband non-spread-spectrum wireless equipment used in the 5-GHz U-NII bands
- Amateur television (ATV) repeaters used by licensed radio amateurs
- Microwave ovens, cordless phones, Bluetooth and HomeRF devices, indoor wireless access points, wireless video cameras, and other license-free wireless consumer devices

By detecting these noise sources early, while it is still possible to modify your network design, you can minimize the impact of noise and interference. Table 4-3 provides techniques to help your network coexist peacefully with various noise sources.

Table 4-3   *In-Band Noise Source Coexistence Techniques*

In-Band Noise Source	Coexistence Technique
FHSS networks	Locate your access points away from the existing FHSS access point locations. Plan to use antenna systems with the opposite polarization. If you are planning a FHSS network, coordinate your hopping sequences with the existing FHSS network. Be aware that if you deploy a DSSS network without adequate RF isolation, you will experience a severe throughput reduction.
DSSS networks	Locate your access points away from the existing DSSS access point locations. Plan to use antenna systems with the opposite polarization. If you are planning a DSSS network, coordinate your frequencies with the existing DSSS network. Be aware that if you deploy an FHSS network without adequate RF isolation, you will experience a throughput reduction.
Broadband non-spread-spectrum U-NII equipment	If possible, select your frequencies so they do not overlap the existing U-NII network frequencies. Locate your access points away from the existing U-NII equipment access point or endpoint locations. Plan to use antenna systems that have the opposite polarization.

Table 4-3   *In-Band Noise Source Coexistence Techniques*

ATV repeaters	If using DSSS, choose operating frequencies that do not overlap the ATV frequencies; specifically, do not choose frequencies that overlap the repeater audio subcarrier or video carrier frequencies. Locate your access points away from the ATV repeater location. Communicate with and coordinate with the repeater operator. Remember: This is a licensed repeater and it has priority over your network operation.
License-free wireless consumer devices	In general, when used indoors, these devices do not have a big impact on the operation of your (properly designed) outdoor network. To minimize impact, avoid locating your access point antenna systems close to areas where these devices exist. For example, avoid placing your antennas near an employee lunchroom where microwave ovens are frequently in use.

If your RF site survey reveals a substantial amount of in-band noise, you can do the following:

- Suggest that the operators of the existing networks be contacted regarding frequency or antenna coverage coordination.

- Recommend additional test time during your network installation process to correct any noise problems that arise.

- Recommend redesigning your network and moving your wireless equipment (or at least your AP locations) further away from the existing wireless networks.

Locating 802.11b Access Points

The use of 802.11b DSSS access points is rapidly increasing. These access points were originally designed for use on indoor wireless LANs. More and more frequently, ISPs, community network proponents, and experimenters take these access points, add external antenna systems, and deploy the access points in outdoor locations. In large cities, quite a few of these access points are likely deployed. Your spectrum analyzer can detect these access points as long as the access points are handling traffic. Their transmissions are indistinguishable from any other DSSS transmissions.

Before you decide to deploy an 802.11b (or other DSSS) network in a particular area, you should know how many 802.11b access points are already deployed. A PC-based site survey utility or 802.11b packet sniffer provides this information. Use your panel antenna to discover how many access points are within RF range in each of the directions that you plan to deploy your network antennas.

Documenting RF Site Survey Findings

Your RF site survey must collect enough information to make an intelligent decision about where (and with what antennas) to deploy or, possibly, not to deploy your network. The documentation needed to make this decision should include your printed spectrum analyzer output files marked with the following information:

- Date when the data was collected
- Time of day when the data was collected
- Spectrum analyzer sample times (Was it a 60-second sample or a 60-minute sample?)
- Antenna used to collect the data
- Antenna heading used to collect the data
- Antenna polarization used when the data was collected

No Spectrum Analyzer? Now What?

If you do not have access to a spectrum analyzer or even to a PC-based site survey utility, you still have four choices:

- Rent a spectrum analyzer for two weeks or for a month. This is a good choice if you think you might need to buy one in the future. The rental has the advantage of allowing you to become familiar with one (or more) different models.

- Plan to perform a wireless path test using the actual equipment that you plan to deploy. If this path testing is successful, you can be reasonably sure that the equipment will perform the same way after it is permanently installed. The disadvantage of this choice is that you might have to buy the equipment before you can do the path test. Path testing is described later in this chapter.

- Make the decision to recommend that the site be used even though no RF site survey could be performed. You might make this recommendation if you are located in a rural location where few (or no) wireless systems are deployed. Keep in mind, however, that there is always some risk that interference might be present that will affect the throughput of the network that you install.

- Hire a company that is experienced in performing RF site surveys to perform a site survey for you and with you.

RF Criteria Evaluation and Conclusion

Before you make a decision to select a wireless site based on the results of an RF site survey, take a moment to review the following benefits and shortcomings of the site survey process.

The benefits of performing an RF site survey are as follows:

- It helps you gather information about the RF environment that your new network faces.

- It stimulates you to think about alternative network deployment scenarios.

- It allows you to make reasoned judgments and recommendations about whether to use a particular site.

The shortcomings of the RF site survey process are as follows:

- Each RF environment and wireless equipment combination is unique; therefore, there are no absolute Go/No-Go answers, only relative answers.

- The wireless environment can change after the site survey. New networks can be deployed or existing networks can be removed from service.

RF Site Acceptance

You have designed and conducted an RF site survey, collected and documented data, read the explanation of SNR, and reviewed the shortcomings of the RF site survey process. Now you must decide if a site is acceptable for your network. The best site survey data that you have to help you make your decision is the SNR that you observed, as shown in Figure 4-9.

Figure 4-9   *SNR Spectrum Analyzer Signal Display*

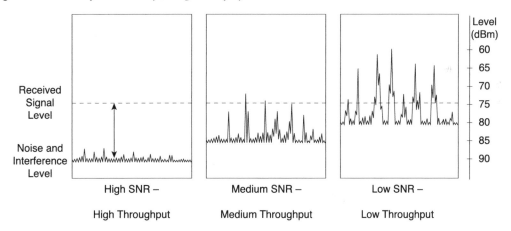

In the real world, the average received signal typically ranges from a low of approximately –85 dBm to a high of approximately –65 dBm. In the Figure 4-9 example, the average received signal level is shown by the dashed line to be –75 dBm.

In the left panel, the noise level is low and the resulting SNR is high. If your spectrum analyzer results look generally like this, you can deploy your network and expect high throughput with little or no problem from noise.

In the center panel, the noise level is moderate. Occasional noise peaks reach and slightly exceed the –75 dBm receive signal level, but they do not occur during every receive data packet and their level is not too high above –75 dBm. If your spectrum analyzer results look generally like this, you can deploy your network and expect good throughput. If you make some effort to reduce the noise level, you should be able to achieve high throughput.

In the right panel, the noise level is high. Noise peaks frequently far exceed the –75 dBm receive signal level. If your spectrum analyzer results look generally like this, your deployed network will deliver low throughput. If you make heroic efforts to reduce the noise level, you should be able to achieve medium throughput, at least until the noise level increases further. In this situation, your best course of action is to attempt to find a site where the noise level is lower.

Table 4-4 provides additional information to help you arrive at a decision about the feasibility of deploying your wireless network at a particular site. If you want still more information before making a final decision, go to the following section and perform path testing or coverage testing.

Table 4-4   *Site Selection Feasibility*

Factor	Excellent	Good	Poor
RF Environment	Friendly—There are no noise sources or only a few obvious noise sources. High SNR values and high throughput can be expected.	OK—There is more than one strong out-of-band interferer and there are only one or two strong in-band interference sources. Medium SNR values and medium throughput can be expected.	Heavy Interference—There are many in-band noise sources. Low SNR values and low throughput can be expected.
Location Desirability	Ideal—This is the best possible site to locate the wireless network equipment.	OK—This location is not perfect, but network coverage and performance are acceptable from this location.	Poor—Physical or RF factors make this location too difficult or expensive to use.
Alternative Locations	Available—Several other locations are available. This location can be selected but does not have to be selected.	Possibly available— Alternative locations might be available. This location might have to be selected.	None—No other alternative locations are available. This location must be selected or no network can be deployed.
More Information and Testing Needed?	No—A definite decision to select this location can be made right now.	Probably—This site could be selected now without further testing and could be made to work.	Yes—More information must be obtained before this site could be selected.

Performing Path Testing or Coverage Testing

There are times when performing path testing or coverage testing using the actual wireless equipment that you plan to deploy might be necessary to provide additional information to support your eventual Go/No-Go deployment decision.

Performing Path Testing

Your RF site survey might not have provided an absolute Go/No-Go answer to the noise and interference question. Questions might remain about the following:

- The duration and intensity of the noise and interference over longer periods of time
- What antenna you should use
- The noise-resistance features of the wireless equipment that you plan to use

In these situations, perform a path test using the selected wireless equipment and antenna. This allows you to test the actual network performance. When the path test is running, be sure to perform throughput testing in both directions and to document the results. For more information, please see Chapter 7 for details about testing point-to-point wireless links.

Performing Coverage Testing

Perhaps, you would like to deploy an access point hub site but you are unsure whether the interference level from other wireless networks in the area would prevent successful performance of your network. Perhaps, you would like to deploy an access point to serve an area that has many trees or many buildings and you are not sure how much of the area your access point will actually cover. In these two situations, it is best to perform a coverage test.

To perform the coverage test, temporarily install an access point with the antenna system that you believe will provide good coverage of the area. Then, use actual customer premises equipment (CPE) and drive around the coverage area. Test the throughput at each location. Document the areas where throughput is excellent, good, borderline, or nonexistent. Plot these results on a map. You now have a coverage footprint for that equipment/antenna combination. You can make changes to the antenna system and retest the coverage. Use your results to determine the areas that you can serve successfully. For more information about testing point-to-multipoint wireless links, see Chapter 7.

Negotiating a Site Lease

After your physical and RF site surveys, if a decision is made to use the site, you need to negotiate a site agreement. The following sections provide some tips that you can use as you prepare to reach agreement with the site owner or manager. These tips are based on a win-win scenario where both you and the site owner benefit from the agreement.

Lease Rates

Monthly lease rates can vary widely depending on the market area where a site is located. In a rural area, you might find rates as low as $200 per month. In a city with high buildings and high population levels, monthly rates might be $1000 per month or higher. This occurs because—at least in the United States—building owners have become accustomed to receiving these high rates from cell phone companies. The owners might not be willing to reduce their price for small ISPs or institutional users.

One possible way to reduce your monthly costs is to ask the building or tower owner if he can use Internet connectivity at the site. If the owner agrees, you might then be able to negotiate a agreement to pay a lower lease rate in return for providing free Internet access to the site.

Finally, when roof space on a building is limited, building managers generally give preferential treatment to tenants who already lease office space within the building as opposed to potential new tenants who only want to lease roof space for antennas and wireless equipment.

Avoiding Interference

When negotiating a contract for space in or on a building, it is appropriate to advise the site manager about the license-free nature of your equipment. You could suffer from interference if other license-free equipment is placed nearby on the roof without first consulting and coordinating with you. Ask that a provision be included in your lease to allow you to approve or disapprove such additional use.

The building management will probably also ask for assurance from you that the wireless equipment that you deploy will not cause interference to equipment that others have already deployed. Be ready to meet with the owners of any equipment already in place and to provide this assurance to building management. Managers of communications antenna tower sites adhere to this principle strictly. The new potential tenant is always responsible for eliminating interference problems caused by their equipment.

Access to Equipment

Try to negotiate 24-hour, 7-day per week equipment and antenna access. Accessing your equipment to provide maintenance and adjustments is required so that you can provide quality service to your wireless customers or end users.

Insurance Requirements

Most locations require you to have liability insurance to cover any possible damage that your equipment might cause. Site owners are rightly concerned about possible damage from water leaks or falling antennas. Most often, liability coverage in the amount of $1 million is required. Costs for this coverage can start below $1000 per year but are often higher.

Consult with several insurance agents in advance to obtain quotes or to confirm that your business insurance policy provides coverage.

Many sites might also ask you to show proof that you carry worker's compensation insurance. This protects the owners from being sued if one of your workers experiences an injury while working on their site.

Work Requirements

Each location will have its own combination of rules and regulations regarding who can perform antenna and equipment installations. In many cases, your personnel will perform all the installation work. In some buildings, the cabling might have to be installed by electrical contractors who are approved by building management. In some cities, you might be required to use union members to install your equipment. Your installation will proceed most efficiently if you accept and respect whatever work regulations are in place.

Tower Site Requirements

A communications tower site is a specialized environment. Many different communications systems are located closely together and need to be managed carefully to ensure that they all operate properly. Site requirements for locating your antenna system on an existing tower can be rather rigid. You can expect to encounter the following:

- **Tower mounting position limitations**—Your choice of where you can mount your antennas on the tower might be limited. Tower management will advise you which mounting positions are open and available. To minimize your installation, maintenance, and monthly costs, plan to mount your antenna(s) at the lowest level that provides complete coverage of your service area.

- **Additional hardware costs**—If you are the first to place antennas at a certain tower height, you might be asked to pay for antenna-mounting hardware, such as antenna support brackets. The brackets (or arms) allow several antenna systems to be mounted horizontally at the same level.

- **Installation personnel requirements**—Many tower sites require that only properly trained tower riggers perform antenna installations. This is more than just a safety issue. Tower management wants to minimize the chance that an improperly installed antenna could fall and damage other antennas on the tower.

- **Strict interference protections**—It is rather unlikely that your low-power license-free equipment will cause interference to any other tower equipment. Once in a while, however, interference can be caused by spurious signals that your equipment generates. If this should ever occur (again, it is rather rare), you will be asked to pay the costs to filter or correct the problem.

Review Questions

1 A physical site survey includes determining how to route cable from the wireless equipment to the antenna. True or false?

2 Before you perform a physical site survey, you should know how high above the ground your antennas need to be mounted. True or false?

3 If there is already wireless equipment operating on a building, you will first discover it during your RF site survey. True or false?

4 Minimizing the distance between your wireless equipment and your antenna system is important. Why?

5 If power lines run near a roof edge, is it okay to mount your antenna near that roof edge? Why or why not?

6 What is the biggest consequence from installing a wireless system in an area with a high noise level?

7 If you have a wireless protocol analyzer, you do not need a wireless spectrum analyzer. True or false?

8 If the operation of license-free equipment causes interference to the operation of licensed amateur radio equipment, the operator of the license-free equipment is responsible for correcting the interference problem. True or false?

9 The length of the spectrum analyzer sampling interval doesn't tell you anything about the level of RF interference in a particular area. True or false?

10 In general, the higher the signal-to-noise ratio on a wireless link, the higher the wireless throughput. True or false?

11 What part of a point-to-multipoint wireless network is the most vulnerable to a high noise level? Why?

CHAPTER 5

Selecting Antenna Systems

Your selection of the proper antenna system is the biggest factor in the success of your wireless network. This chapter helps you select the most effective antenna system for your wireless wide-area network (WAN). This chapter discusses the following topics:

- How antennas focus power
- Basic antenna types
- Antenna polarization and how to use it
- Reasons to combine antennas and how to combine them
- Reasons to isolate antennas and how to isolate them

In a wired Ethernet, the Ethernet cable directs the signal. Ethernet packets can go only where the Ethernet cable goes. In a broadband wireless WAN, the antenna directs the signal. Wireless packets can only go where the antenna system radiates them.

Your antenna system must radiate signals only toward your end users. In addition, to be effective, your antenna system must have the following characteristics:

- Be mounted high enough to achieve a line-of-sight (LOS) path
- Have enough gain to provide reliable link performance
- Be mounted correctly and held in position securely
- Reject noise and interference from other signals and networks

Using Antennas to Focus Power and Reduce Interference

You already know that antennas focus power to and from the end users while reducing interference from other networks and other directions. The next few sections discuss the electromagnetic building blocks that antennas use to focus power. In addition, you will see how to reduce interference using antenna polarization.

Antenna Building Blocks: Lights, Mirrors, and Lenses

Antennas achieve their directivity by using a combination of properly sized and properly spaced antenna elements. These elements are electromagnetic building blocks. Combining the elements in different ways produces different antenna radiation patterns. In some designs, the antenna elements are electrically connected to each other, forming a driven array. In other designs, the elements are placed close together but with no electrical connection, forming a parasitic array.

All antennas use a driven element. The driven element is always electrically connected (via coaxial cable) directly to the wireless equipment. Antennas achieve gain when the driven element is combined with additional element building blocks that reflect, direct, or concentrate the signal.

It is helpful to use the concept of lights, lenses, and mirrors to illustrate how different antenna designs achieve gain as the antenna elements work together to focus transmitted and received energy.

Driven Element: The Light

To create light, a source of electrical energy (such as a battery) is connected to a light bulb. The light bulb converts the electrical energy into light energy.

To create a wireless signal, a source of radio frequency (RF) energy (a transmitter) is connected to the driven element of an antenna. The driven element converts the RF energy into radiated electromagnetic energy—a wireless signal. Every antenna system must have at least one driven element to initiate this energy conversion.

A dipole antenna is one-half wavelength ($\Lambda/2$) long and is frequently used as a driven element. A dipole mounted vertically above the earth radiates energy equally in all horizontal directions. This energy forms a torus (donut-shaped) pattern around the antenna. When the dipole is horizontal to the earth, the donut-shaped pattern becomes bidirectional, radiating energy in just two horizontal directions, off the two sides of the dipole. Figure 5-1 shows a top view of this bidirectional radiation pattern, as well as the bidirectional pattern of light energy radiated from a fluorescent light tube.

Both the horizontal dipole and a horizontal fluorescent light radiate most of their energy off the sides. They radiate little or no energy off the ends. When this bidirectional property is combined with other antenna elements or, in the case of the fluorescent light tube, with other optical elements, a more concentrated, more focused beam of energy results.

Figure 5-1   *Bidirectional Radiation Patterns*

Top View(s)

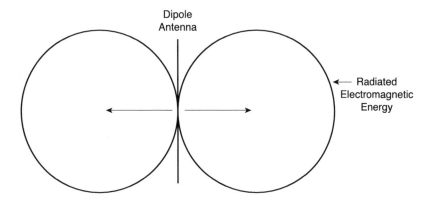

Dipole
Antenna

Radiated
Electromagnetic
Energy

Bidirectional Patterns-Energy Radiated in Two Directions

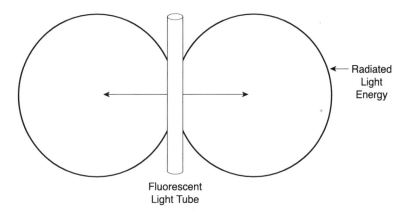

Radiated
Light
Energy

Fluorescent
Light Tube

Figure 5-2 shows two vertical antennas. The lower antenna has a single dipole, half-wavelength-long driven element. The top antenna has four half-wavelength-long driven elements. The four driven elements are mounted one above the other and connected together electrically. Because all four driven elements are in a single line, this antenna is called a collinear array.

Figure 5-2 *Multiple-Driven Element Radiation Patterns*

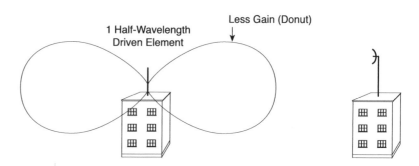

Side View(s)

When two or more driven elements are electrically connected and placed end-to-end (a collinear array), the vertical radiation pattern changes. The donut-shaped pattern flattens out into a pancake shape. The pancake-shaped pattern extends farther away from the antenna than the donut-shaped pattern.

Stated technically, the antenna with the pancake-shaped pattern has more gain compared to the antenna with the donut-shaped pattern. The transmitter power supplied to the antenna hasn't changed, but the end-to-end driven elements concentrate that transmitter power into a narrower but longer coverage area (a narrower vertical beamwidth). A receiver located inside this coverage area can be located farther away from the antenna and still receive a good signal.

NOTE	Another way to look at this is to imagine that the donut around a single half-wave vertical antenna is a jelly donut. When more half-wavelength elements are added, it is like a giant foot came along and stepped on the donut, squashing it down. The jelly squirts out beyond the donut. The radiation pattern of a gain antenna is like the jelly in the donut—it spurts out farther and flatter than the donut. The energy radiated from a four-half-wavelength-long collinear array spurts out about twice as far as the energy from a single half-wavelength-long vertical antenna.

Reflector: The Mirror

Some antenna designs use a reflector along with the driven element. A reflector is an antenna element that is about 5 percent longer than the driven element. The reflector is placed parallel to the driven element and about one-quarter wavelength ($\lambda/4$) away from the driven element, as Figure 5-3 shows.

There is no electrical connection between the driven element and the reflector. When electromagnetic waves leave the driven element, they encounter the reflector. Because the reflector is both physically and electrically longer than the waves, the waves bounce off of the reflector and turn back toward the driven element. The reflected waves join the non-reflected waves to form a stronger signal pattern in the direction away from the reflector. The effect is similar to placing a curved mirror behind a light bulb. Most of the light energy is reflected in one direction, away from the curved mirror.

Together, the driven element and the reflector combine to make the antenna more directional, with more gain in the forward direction and less gain in the backward direction.

Figure 5-3   *Effect of a Reflector*

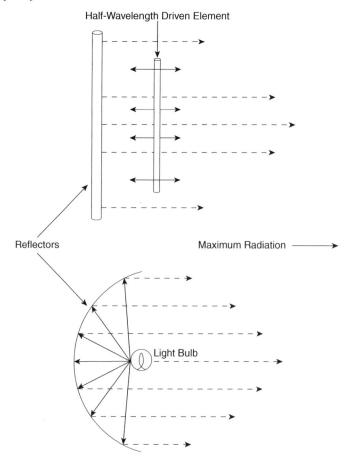

Half-Wavelength Driven Element

Reflectors

Maximum Radiation ⟶

Light Bulb

Top View(s)

Director: The Lens

Some antenna designs use a director along with a driven element. A director is an antenna element that is about 5 percent shorter than the driven element. The director is placed parallel to the driven element and about one-quarter wavelength (λ/4) away from the driven element. There is no electrical connection between the driven element and the director. When electromagnetic waves leave the driven element, they encounter the director. Because the director is physically and electrically smaller than the waves, the waves tend to travel toward the director. The director concentrates the waves into a tighter beam. This is similar to using a lens in front of a light bulb to concentrate the light energy, as shown in Figure 5-4.

Figure 5-4   *Effect of a Director*

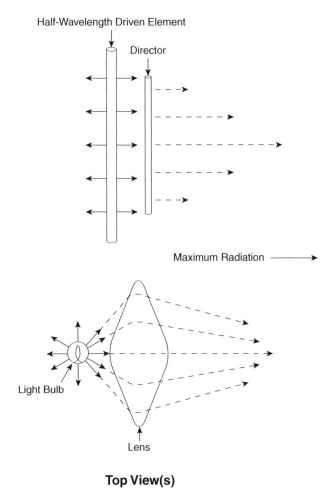

The director has a concentrating effect on the electromagnetic waves similar to the way a lens concentrates light waves. The waves are concentrated in the direction of the director. This gives the antenna directivity and gain in the forward direction.

NOTE   Many antennas make use of both reflectors and directors. When both of these elements are combined with the driven element, the result is a highly directive high-gain antenna. The Yagi antenna (discussed shortly) is one example.

Antenna Polarization

This section describes antenna polarization and provides several examples to help you select the best polarization for your particular wireless system environment.

Definition of Antenna Polarization

Two electromagnetic fields leave a transmitting antenna and arrive at a receiving antenna: an electric field (also referred to as the E-field) and a magnetic field (also referred to as the H-field). The E-field and the H-field are perpendicular (at a 90-degree angle) to each other, and each field is also perpendicular to the direction that the electromagnetic wave is traveling.

The E-field exists in the same plane (with the same orientation) as the plane of the antenna elements. By definition, the plane of the E-field is the polarization of the antenna. If the antenna elements are vertical relative to the surface of the earth, the E-field is vertical and the signal is vertically polarized. If the antenna elements are horizontal relative to the surface of the earth, the E-field is horizontal and the antenna is horizontally polarized.

In your networks, you can use any of the following four types of polarization to maximize reception of desired signals while reducing noise and interference from undesired signals:

- Vertical polarization
- Horizontal polarization
- Circular polarization
- Cross polarization

Vertical Polarization

Vertical polarization is used in many wireless WAN deployments. Figure 5-5 shows the orientation of the E-field of a vertically polarized antenna relative to the antenna and relative to the surface of the earth.

Figure 5-5   *Vertical Polarization*

Top View

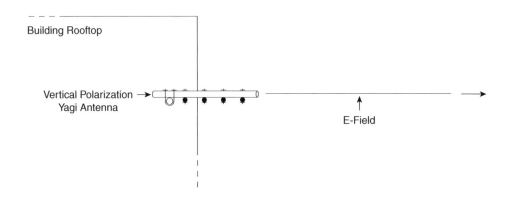

Side View

With a vertically polarized antenna, the E-field is vertical, relative to the surface of the earth.

Horizontal Polarization

Horizontal polarization is used in some wireless WAN deployments. Figure 5-6 shows the orientation of the E-field of a horizontally polarized antenna relative to the antenna and relative to the surface of the earth.

Figure 5-6 *Horizontal Polarization*

Top View

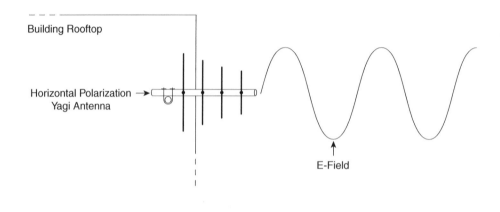

Side View

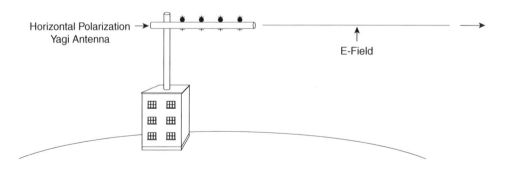

With a horizontally polarized antenna, the E-field is horizontal, relative to the surface of the earth.

Circular Polarization

Occasionally, circular polarization is used in a wireless WAN. Figure 5-7 shows the orientation of the E field of a circularly polarized antenna relative to the antenna.

Figure 5-7   *Circular Polarization*

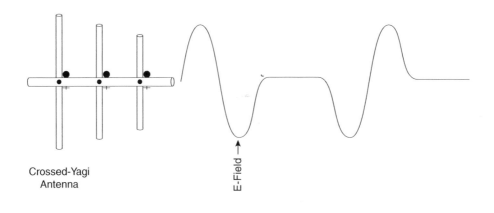

Side View and Top View (Identical)

Crossed-Yagi
Antenna

E-Field

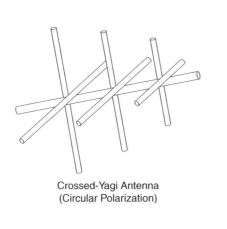

Crossed-Yagi Antenna
(Circular Polarization)

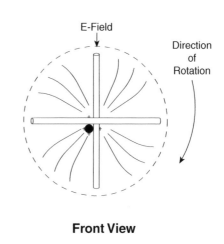

E-Field

Direction
of
Rotation

Front View

With a circularly polarized antenna, the E-field is constantly rotating relative to the antenna. Depending on the antenna construction, the E-field might be either right-hand circularly polarized or left-hand circularly polarized, depending on the direction (or sense) of rotation. The E-field from a right-hand circularly polarized antenna rotates clockwise as it leaves the antenna. The E-field from a left-hand circularly polarized antenna rotates counterclockwise as it leaves the antenna.

Cross Polarization

Cross polarization and circular polarization sound similar but they are not the same thing. As explained in the previous paragraph, circular polarization describes the orientation of the rotating E-field relative to the antenna. In contrast, cross polarization occurs when the E-fields of two antennas are at right angles to each other, such as when one antenna is horizontally polarized and one antenna is vertically polarized. Another example of cross polarization is when one antenna is right-hand circularly polarized and the other antenna is left-hand circularly polarized.

Most antennas have a cross-polarization discrimination (XPD) of about -20 dB. This means that the antenna discriminates against (attenuates) cross-polarized signals by about 20 dB. A signal attenuated by 20 dB is reduced to about 1/100th of its original power level. For this reason, you need to use the same antenna polarization at both ends of your wireless link or suffer a 20-dB reduction in signal strength.

Sometimes, you can use XPD to your advantage. If you need to reduce the level of an interfering signal, you can orient both (or all) of your antennas to be cross polarized relative to the polarization of the interfering signal. You will reduce the level of the interfering signal by 20 dB or 99 percent, as shown in Figure 5-8.

Figure 5-8   *Cross Polarization*

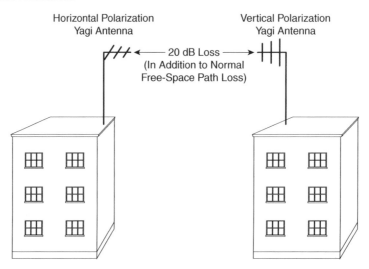

In addition to using cross polarization to reduce the level of interfering signals, you can use cross polarization to do the following:

- **Reuse frequencies**—You can cross polarize your antennas to reduce noise from other parts of your own network, thereby allowing you to reuse the same frequency at other access points (APs).

- **Avoid overload**—You can cross polarize to attenuate strong out-of-band signals and thereby reduce overloading and desensitization of your receiver. Desensitization reduces the size of your system coverage area.

Polarization Selection Examples

The examples in the three sections that follow illustrate typical uses of vertically polarized, horizontally polarized, and circularly polarized antenna systems.

Example 1: Cost-Effective Deployment

Initially, for a fast, simple, and low-cost deployment, a vertically polarized omnidirectional (omni) antenna is often used, as shown in Figure 5-9.

Figure 5-9   *Vertically Polarized Omnidirectional Antenna*

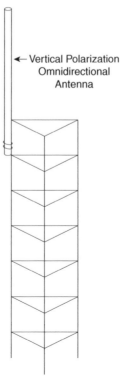

←Vertical Polarization
Omnidirectional
Antenna

A vertical omni is the fastest, lowest-cost way to deploy an outdoor wireless WAN. If the antenna is mounted high enough to be clear of nearby obstacles, it is relatively easy to cover a circular area with a radius of two or three miles.

There are, however, several significant disadvantages to using an omni:

- **Exposure to noise**—Using an omni exposes the AP receiver to a high level of noise. All the vertically polarized noise and interference sources within the antenna coverage area are received all the time. You cannot discriminate against or reduce any of the noise sources.

- **Coverage area limitations**—Using a low-to-moderate gain omni (+6 to +10 dBi) limits the coverage area to a few miles. Using a higher gain omni (such as +15 dBi) enlarges the coverage area in theory but, in practice, the flatness of the pancake radiation pattern concentrates most of the energy toward the far edge of the coverage area. This makes it difficult to simultaneously cover the end users who are located closer to the antenna.

Because of these limitations, using a vertical omni as a quickly deployed, low-cost antenna system is not recommended except in a small town where there are no significant present (or future) noise and interference sources.

Example 2: Noise Reduction

Compared to the previous vertical omnidirectional antenna example, a better, more noise-resistant AP antenna system uses three horizontally polarized sector antennas, as Figure 5-10 shows.

Figure 5-10 shows an AP with three sectors. Each sector covers about 120 degrees and uses a horizontally polarized sector antenna.

Horizontal polarization reduces the noise and interference coming from the vertically polarized antennas by 20 dB. This occurs because of the cross polarization discrimination (XPD) between the horizontally polarized and the vertically polarized antenna systems.

The three-sector antenna system has an additional advantage compared to an omnidirectional antenna system. An omni is exposed to noise from a 360-degree coverage area. Each sector of a three-sector system is exposed to noise only from a 120-degree coverage area. The noise reduction advantage should be 2/3, or 66 percent.

Downtilting provides even more noise reduction and signal-to-noise ratio (SNR) improvement for the three-sector system. Downtilting allows orienting the main lobe of each sector antenna down away from the horizon and toward the majority of end users in that sector. This increases the signal level to and from end users in the sector while reducing the distant noise coming from beyond the sector.

Figure 5-10   *Horizontally Polarized Sector Antennas*

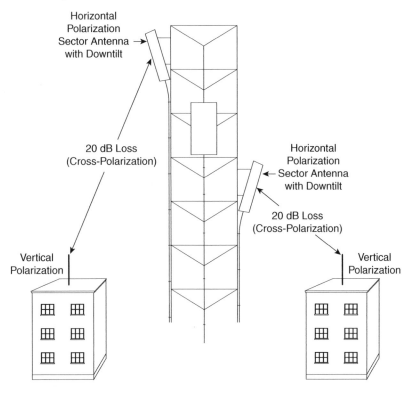

NOTE   A more detailed description of sector antennas is coming up in the next few pages, so stay
tuned in.

One final advantage of a sectorized antenna system is that it can start out with one radio and
one three-way power splitter to connect all three sectors to the one radio. Removing the
splitter and adding two more radios expands the AP to serve three times the number of users
without needing to change the antenna system in any other way.

Example 3: Multipath Resistance

In an urban environment with many buildings, many incoming signal reflections are possible,
and multipath can be a problem. Circularly polarized antenna systems, as Figure 5-11 shows,
can prove beneficial.

Figure 5-11 *Circularly Polarized Antenna in a Multipath Environment*

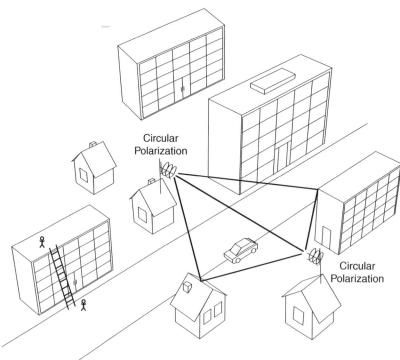

When a circularly polarized signal is reflected, the polarization sense changes. For example, a right-hand circularly polarized signal becomes left-hand circularly polarized. Circular polarization can reduce multipath effects because a once-reflected signal arrives at the receiving antenna with a reversed polarization sense. The XPD of the circularly polarized receiving antenna attenuates the reflected signal by –20 to –30 dB. This severely attenuated multipath signal is too weak to interfere with the direct signal and cause receiver errors.

TIP   Use circular polarization conservatively and only in environments where multipath appears to be a bigger problem than noise and interference. Circular polarization provides only –3 dB of XPD from horizontally and vertically polarized signals. By using circular polarization, you will experience interference from and cause interference to any nearby horizontally and vertically polarized antenna systems.

Surveying Common Antenna Types

You need to be able to identify different types of antenna systems for the following reasons:

- **Antenna selection**—To select the best antenna for your particular application, you need to know what antenna types are available and what the characteristics are of each type.

- **Interference reduction**—You will most likely deploy a wireless network in an area where one or more other wireless networks already exist. You need to be able to identify the antenna type, polarization, and coverage pattern that these existing networks are using. This information allows you to select antennas for your own network that will minimize interference from (and to) the existing networks.

The sections that follow describe the antenna types that are most frequently used for outdoor wireless WANs:

- Omnidirectional antennas
- Yagi-Uda (Yagi) antennas
- Corner reflector antennas
- Parabolic antennas
- Panel antennas
- Helix antennas

Omnidirectional Antennas

An omni antenna radiates equally in all horizontal (azimuth, or compass) directions, but it exhibits directivity in the vertical direction by concentrating energy into a donut or pancake-shaped pattern.

Most often, omnidirectional antennas are vertically polarized, although horizontally polarized omnis are also available. Horizontally polarized omnis generally cost more because their construction is more complex and they are manufactured in smaller quantities.

Figure 5-12 shows both vertically polarized and horizontally polarized omni antennas.

Figure 5-12   *Omnidirectional Antennas*

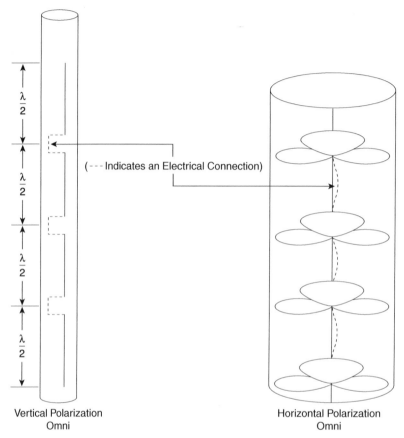

The vertically polarized omni consists of four vertical 1/2 wavelength (λ/2) driven elements, placed end to end, and connected electrically. The main lobe of the omni is shaped like a pancake, with a gain of about +6 dBd (decibels referenced to a λ/2 dipole) or +8 dBi (decibels referenced to an isotropic antenna) for stations that are located within the main lobe.

The horizontally polarized omni consists of four cloverleaf-shaped antennas, placed one above the other and connected electrically. This omni pattern, although horizontally polarized, is also pancake shaped with a gain of +6 dBd (or +8 dBi).

NOTE   Figure 5-12 shows one typical design of a horizontal omni. There are also other horizontal omni designs.

Yagi-Uda (Yagi) Antennas

The Yagi-Uda (usually called simply a Yagi) antenna is named after Hidetsuga Yagi and Shintaro Uda. This antenna consists of a dipole driven element, usually with a single reflector and one or more directors. Figure 5-13 shows a Yagi antenna.

Figure 5-13   *Yagi-Uda (Yagi) Antenna*

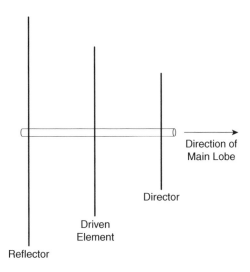

Top View (When Antenna Is Horizontal)

Direction of Main Lobe

Director

Driven Element

Reflector

Side View (When Antenna Is Vertical)

A Yagi antenna is made up of the following antenna building blocks:

- The driven element (DE) is a $\lambda/2$ dipole.

- The reflector is slightly longer than the driven element, has no electrical connection to the DE, and acts like a mirror to reflect the radiated energy back toward the DE.

- The director is slightly shorter than the DE, has no electrical connectivity to the DE, and acts like a lens to focus the radiated energy away from the DE.

The main lobe of the Yagi extends out from the front; the front is the end of the antenna that the director is on. A Yagi can be mounted either vertically or horizontally, depending on the polarization that you need. Figure 5-13 shows a three-element Yagi; however, Yagis are often constructed with many more elements. At 2.4 GHz, Yagis with 10 or even 20 elements and gains as high as +20 dBi are available.

NOTE   A Yagi antenna is sometimes mounted inside a long, tubular radome. (Radomes are
            discussed in more detail later in this chapter). These yagis are still directional toward the
            far end (away from the mounting end) of the tube. Do not make the mistake of thinking that
            these antennas radiate off the sides like omnidirectional antennas do.

Corner Reflector Antennas

A corner reflector consists of a dipole-driven element mounted in front of a parasitic (no
electrical connection) reflector. Instead of a straight reflector, like a Yagi, the corner
reflector is a sheet of metal bent into a corner shape, as shown in Figure 5-14.

Figure 5-14   *Corner Reflector Antenna*

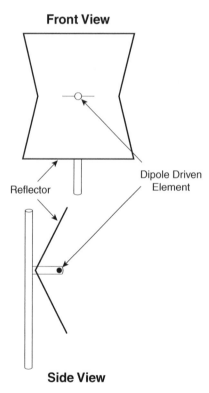

The main lobe of a corner reflector extends out from the front (the driven element) side of
the antenna. The angle of the reflector can be 45, 60, or 90 degrees. The antenna in Figure
5-14 is horizontally polarized because the driven element is horizontally polarized. By
rotating the entire antenna 90 degrees, the main lobe becomes vertically polarized. The gain
of a corner reflector might be as high as +15 dBi.

NOTE   Occasionally, you might see a corner reflector design that uses a series of rods or rib-shaped elements for the reflector instead of a solid metal reflector. The rods are arranged in a corner pattern just like a solid metal reflector. These antennas perform about the same as a solid-back corner reflector, but they are lighter and present less resistance in high winds.

Parabolic Reflector Antennas

A parabolic reflector antenna (or dish antenna) usually consists of a dipole-driven element mounted in front of a parabolic-shaped reflector. Some more expensive parabolic antennas use a waveguide feed instead of a dipole-driven element. Figure 5-15 shows two parabolic antennas, one with a solid reflector and one with a grid reflector.

Figure 5-15   *Parabolic Antenna*

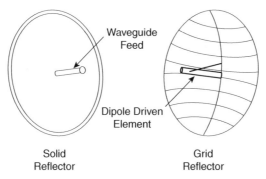

The main lobe of a parabolic antenna extends out from the front (the driven element) side of the antenna. By rotating the mount of a parabolic dish 90 degrees, you can select either vertical or horizontal polarization.

The larger the diameter of the reflector, the higher the gain of the antenna. Typical 2.4-GHz parabolic antenna gains range from +18 to +24 dBi.

A grid parabolic has less wind resistance, a lower front-to-back (F/B) ratio, better XPD, and a lower cost than a solid parabolic antenna.

Panel Antennas

A panel antenna typically consists of an array of driven elements mounted in front of a flat, metallic reflector. The entire antenna is covered with a plastic or fiberglass cover. A panel antenna is usually only a few inches wide. Depending on the gain, the height and width might vary from 6 inches (15 cm) on a side up to and beyond 30 inches (76 cm) on a side. Figure 5-16 shows two panel antenna examples.

Figure 5-16   *Panel Antennas*

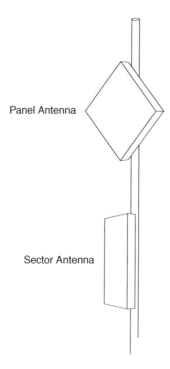

The horizontal and vertical beamwidths of the main lobe of a panel antenna might or might not be symmetric. An example of a symmetric beamwidth is an antenna with a 30-degree horizontal and a 30-degree vertical beamwidth. A non-symmetric example is a sector antenna with a 60-degree horizontal beamwidth and an 8-degree vertical beamwidth. Keeping these respective beamwidths in mind, a panel can be rotated 90 degrees to utilize either horizontal or vertical polarization. This type of panel antenna is often called a sector antenna because it is specifically designed for use in sectorized AP antenna systems.

Panel and sector antennas have moderate to high gains, from +8 to +20 dBi. They have a clean, uncluttered appearance, moderate prices, and are available with a wide variety of radiation patterns. For these reasons, panel antennas are gaining wide acceptance for use in wireless WANs.

Helix Antennas

The helix is a circularly polarized antenna with a circular, helically wound driven element that is shaped like a spring. The driven element usually has from 5 to 20 turns; each turn is one wavelength (λ) in circumference, with individual turns spaced one-quarter wavelength apart along the length of the antenna. The driven element is mounted in front of a metallic reflector that can be either circular or square and either solid or mesh, as Figure 5-17 shows.

Figure 5-17   *Helix Antenna*

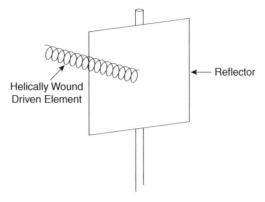

Depending on the direction that the driven element is wound, the helix produces either left-hand or right-hand circular polarization. Helix antennas have typical gains of +12 through +17 dBi; the more turns, the higher the gain.

TIP   Remember this when using circular polarization: The antennas on both ends of the link need to use the same circular polarization sense (both right-hand sense or both left-hand sense).

Combining Antenna Systems

There are a number of reasons to combine antennas or to connect more than one antenna simultaneously to the same piece of wireless equipment. Often, antennas are combined to modify the directivity and the gain of an antenna system. For example, the horizontally polarized omni in Figure 5-12 is made up of four horizontally polarized omni antennas placed (stacked) close together and electrically connected. When these four antennas are stacked together to create one antenna system, the gain goes up by +6 dB and the vertical beamwidth of the main lobe narrows by a factor of four. (Donut-to-pancake—remember?) You might have situations in which you need to combine antennas to create a custom coverage pattern.

Multipath fading is sometimes a problem in wireless WANs. To reduce the problem of multipath, some wireless equipment includes the capability to monitor two antenna inputs and to switch to the signal from the best antenna on a packet-by-packet basis. A two-antenna system is called a diversity antenna system. At some point, you might need to set up a diversity antenna system. The sections that follow describe techniques and provide examples to help you successfully combine antenna systems or set up diversity antenna systems.

Feeding Power to Combined Antenna Systems

You can use a number of methods to feed power to combined antenna systems. The power feed technique that is the most practical for wireless WAN use is to use a *power divider* (sometimes called a *power splitter*). Power dividers are used to feed equal amounts of power to individual antennas within an antenna system. Figure 5-18 provides an example of a two-port power divider.

Figure 5-18   *Using a Power Divider*

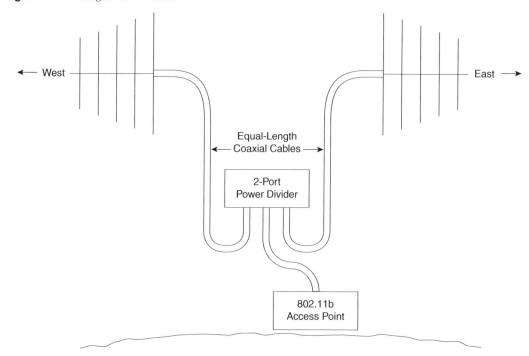

Figure 5-18 shows a two-port power divider dividing the power from one 802.11b AP and sending one-half of the power to each antenna. Two, three, and four port dividers are commonly available.

Bidirectional Antenna Systems

In Figure 5-18, the AP is operating as a low-cost repeater. It is located on a mountain to provide a backbone connection between two communities. It repeats between one community that is located to the east and one community that is located to the west.

An omnidirectional antenna would be a poor choice for this repeater because much of the energy would be radiated (and wasted) in directions other than east and west. To avoid interference from other directions and to maximize link distances to the east and the west, a custom antenna system is needed that focuses the radiated energy toward only the east and the west. The antenna system in Figure 5-18 provides the necessary bidirectional coverage.

The spacing between the two antennas is not critical as long as the two antenna patterns don't interact with each other. If the two antennas are mounted back to back on the same tower or mast and separated vertically by at least 10 feet (3 meters), the antenna system should perform as expected.

NOTE   Keep in mind that splitting power between two or more antennas reduces the range of each antenna. Also, using a single access point as a repeater reduces the throughput by 50 percent.

Diversity Antenna Systems

The primary fading mechanism affecting outdoor microwave links is multipath fading. To minimize system outages due to fading, some wireless equipment incorporates a diversity antenna-switching feature. Diversity means having a signal available from a second (diversity or alternate) antenna system. If the signal from the main antenna system fades or is degraded, the signal from the diversity antenna system can be selected.

Space diversity is the primary diversity technique used in low-cost wireless LAN equipment. This requires that the main and the diversity antennas be separated far enough so that when the signal arriving at the main antenna fades, the signal arriving from the diversity antenna does not. To achieve this uncorrelated fading behavior in an outdoor WAN deployment, a vertical separation between the antennas of 10 to 200 wavelengths is required. At 2.4 GHz, this is a vertical separation of 4 feet to 80 feet (1.2 meters to 24 meters). The more the separation, the better the reduction in multipath fading. Figure 5-19 shows a diversity antenna system.

Figure 5-19   *Diversity Antenna System*

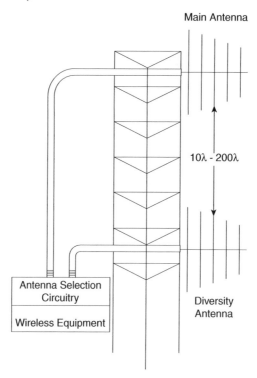

Many 802.11b access points include a diversity feature. These access points were originally designed for indoor use, although many organizations and service providers now deploy them in outdoor WANs. Before activating the diversity feature on your access point, you should do the following:

- Study your documentation carefully so that you understand how your particular equipment implements diversity switching.

- Avoid the temptation to use different types of antenna systems or to point the two antenna systems in different directions. The diversity feature is not designed to function properly this way.

TIP   If you need to cover two different directions with one access point, use two antennas—a two-port power divider and the primary antenna port on your AP. Disable the diversity feature.

- Determine the best spacing to use for deploying the diversity antenna. A rural or suburban point-to-point link benefits from vertical separation between the main and the diversity antenna. A point-to-multipoint antenna system in an urban area benefits from horizontal separation to discriminate against multipoint reflections from buildings.

- Plan to mount the AP as close as possible to the antennas and midway between them. This reduces the cost of antenna cabling.

- If in doubt, disable diversity and use one antenna.

Isolating Antenna Systems

The scarcest and most valuable resource that is needed by individuals and groups who want to deploy license-free broadband wireless WANs is license-free spectrum—frequencies that can legally be used without spending hundreds of thousands of dollars to buy a license.

The quantity of available license-free frequencies is not increasing, but the number of people who want to use these frequencies is increasing. The result is that the same spectrum space will be used repeatedly. The knowledge and the ability to re-use frequencies and to avoid interference determines who is successful in the license-free wireless business and who is not. Any interested individual can put an outdoor wireless system on the air; however, providing reliable service with it is not a plug-and-play operation.

This section suggests techniques that allow you to re-use the license-free frequencies successfully by isolating antenna systems from each other.

Benefiting from Antenna System Isolation

Moving antenna systems away from each other creates isolation between the systems. As the antennas move farther apart, the signal level that each antenna receives from the other antenna is reduced. Armed with this knowledge, you can use physical antenna separation to provide isolation between different parts of your network, and you can also isolate your network from other networks. Antenna system isolation provides the following major benefits:

- Noise reduction from other networks
- Noise reduction from your own AP transmitters network

Noise Reduction from Other Networks

Antenna separation between your antenna(s) and the antennas of other, nearby networks allows you to operate on the same frequencies that the other networks are using. For example, using direct-sequence spread spectrum (DSSS) in the 2.4 GHz band, there are only three non-overlapping channels; these are channels 1, 6, and 11. If you are using these frequencies and a neighboring network is also using one or more of them, the networks interfere with each other. The networks can interfere with each other even if they are 5 to 10 miles (8 to 16 km) apart. Without effective antenna isolation, packets from each network collide and the throughput of both networks suffer.

In addition to packet collisions between your network and other license-free networks, you can also experience slow network performance caused by licensed transmitters. All wireless receivers are susceptible to being overloaded by strong, nearby signals. Licensed transmitters that are located on the same site as your license-free equipment might be legally transmitting with fairly high power levels. Even though they are not transmitting on the same exact frequencies that you are using, they might overload your receiver and cause your incoming packets to be lost. The result is the same as interference from other same-frequency trans-mitters—your network throughput decreases. Antenna isolation is the easiest, lowest-cost method to minimize noise and interference problems as you design, deploy, and operate your wireless WAN.

Noise Reduction from Your Network

When you deploy more than one sector at the same physical location, noise caused by your transmitters in your other sectors can cause receiver desensitization, coverage area reduction, and decreased throughput. This is true whether you are using direct-sequence spread spectrum or frequency-hopping spread spectrum equipment.

If you are deploying direct-sequence spread spectrum (DSSS) equipment, you might reach the point where you need to use more than three frequencies at the same physical location. If you deploy a second wireless access point, you will most likely need to re-use one or more of the three non-overlapping frequencies (channels 1, 6, and 11). In either of these situations, using antenna isolation techniques, you will be able to successfully re-use frequencies.

If you are deploying more than one sector of FHSS equipment, you will be following the manufacturer's recommendations to utilize the same hopping set but different hopping sequences for co-located sectors. This practice minimizes but does not eliminate the throughput reduction caused by collisions between your sectors. The use of effective antenna isolation techniques reduces these collisions further.

The following sections help you determine how much isolation you can obtain by separating antennas both vertically or horizontally.

Vertical Separation Isolation

Separating antennas vertically on a mast or on a tower is fairly straightforward. It requires mounting the antennas (the antennas might or might not be similar to each other) one above the other. This method requires no extra hardware.

Isolation between the two antenna systems is obtained via two mechanisms. The total vertical separation isolation is the sum of these two mechanisms. Figure 5-20 demonstrates the mechanisms, and the list that follows describes them in more detail.

Figure 5-20   *Vertical Separation Isolation*

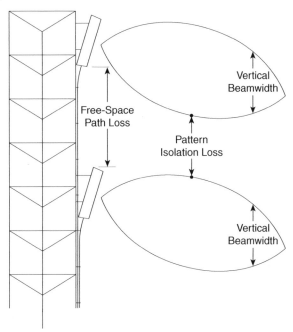

- **Free-space path loss (FSPL)**—You will remember from the discussion of free-space path loss in Chapter 2, "Understanding Wireless Fundamentals," that free-space path loss is the price that must be paid to enjoy the magic of wireless communications. Of all the wireless energy that leaves a transmitting antenna, only a tiny percentage ever arrives at the receiving antenna. Most of the energy is simply lost in space. Now (when you need some antenna isolation) is the time that this loss can be your gain. After leaving an antenna, a 2.4-GHz signal experiences about 49 dB of FSPL in the first 10 feet (3 meters). In other words, only about 1/100,000 of the signal remains after it has traveled 10 feet.

NOTE Experienced wireless engineers differentiate between an antenna's near field and an antenna's far field. In an antenna's near field, the signal strength varies in a more complex fashion, and other nearby objects can affect the signal strength. Both an antenna's published specifications and true FSPL calculations apply only in the antenna's far field. For the purpose of this book, however, the discussion of antenna isolation is still a useful one and close enough to reality that it is a practical design and planning tool.

- **Pattern isolation loss**—If both antennas have clean radiation patterns without significant minor lobes extending upward or downward and a fairly narrow vertical beamwidth, a significant amount of additional isolation is possible between the patterns of the antennas.

Table 5-1 shows the approximate total vertical separation isolation values that can be obtained when the FSPL isolation and pattern isolation loss are combined.

Table 5-1 *Vertical Separation Isolation Values (dB)*

Vertical Separation in Feet (Meters)	Total Antenna-to-Antenna Isolation (in dB @ 2.4 GHz)
1 (0.3)	43
2 (0.6)	55
3 (0.9)	62
4 (1.2)	67
5 (1.8)	74
10 (3.0)	83
15 (4.6)	90
20 (6.1)	95
50 (15.2)	112
100 (30.5)	124

Horizontal Separation Isolation

Obtaining horizontal separation isolation for antennas mounted on the roof of a building is straightforward, as Figure 5-21 shows. One extra support mast is required compared to mounting both antennas on the same mast.

Figure 5-21 *Horizontal Separation Isolation*

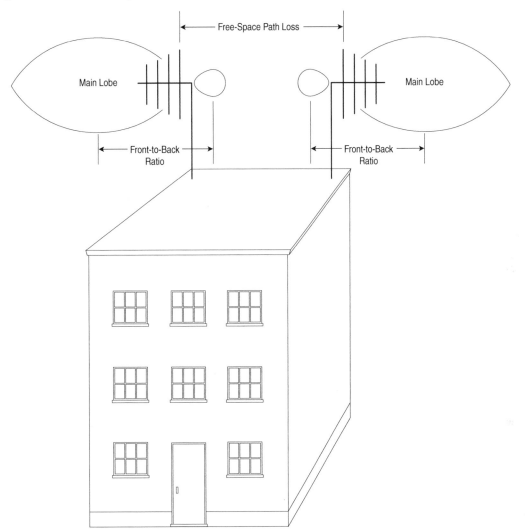

In Figure 5-21, the rooftop antennas are mounted back to back. The maximum isolation possible from horizontal separation is the sum of the front-to-back ratios of both antennas plus the free-space path loss shown in Table 5-2.

NOTE	What is the front-to-back (F/B) ratio, you ask? This is a good place to define it. F/B ratio is another power ratio in dB—just like the power ratios using dB that you looked at earlier in this book. The F/B ratio is the ratio between the energy in the main (front) lobe of an antenna divided by the energy in the back lobe of the antenna. Good antennas focus and radiate most of their energy from the front of the antenna and very little of their energy toward the back. The higher the F/B ratio (for example, +20 dB or +30 dB), the better the antenna and the less interference that will be experienced to and from signals in back of the antenna.

Table 5-2   *Horizontal Separation Isolation Values (dB)*

Horizontal Separation in Feet (Meters)	FSPL Isolation (in dB @ 2.4 GHz)
1 (0.3)	29
2 (0.6)	35
3 (0.9)	39
4 (1.2)	41
5 (1.8)	43
10 (3.0)	49
20 (4.6)	55
30 (6.1)	59
50 (15.2)	63
100 (30.5)	69

Cross-Polarization Isolation

Earlier in this chapter, Figures 5-8 and 5-10 provided examples of using XPD isolation. XPD isolation is mentioned again here in the context of the other antenna-isolation techniques. Keep XPD isolation in mind and use it frequently as you design and deploy your outdoor wireless WANs. It can add up to –20dB of additional isolation.

Obstruction Isolation

To maximize and maintain the performance of your network, it is sometimes necessary to use obstruction isolation. Buildings and other large objects reduce the strength of microwave signals through absorption, diffraction, and reflection.

When you need additional isolation between antenna systems, position the antennas in such a way as to place a building (or part of a building) between the antennas, as shown in Figure 5-22.

Figure 5-22   *Obstruction Isolation*

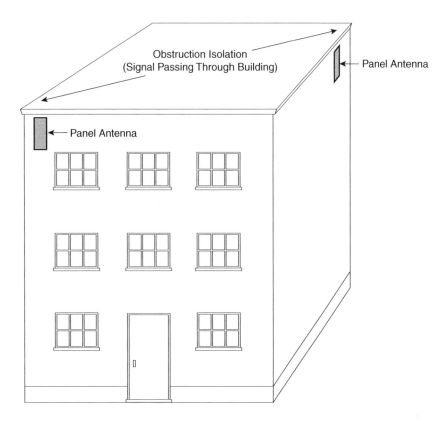

The construction of each building is different, so it is difficult to estimate the amount of isolation that a building provides. If you estimate an average of –8 dB for each exterior wall and –4 dB for every interior wall, the isolation provided by the building in Figure 5-22 might total between –30 and –40 dB.

Sector Antenna Systems

Chapter 3, "Choosing Your Network Architecture," described sectors as similar to pieces of pie, but sectors are never exactly wedge shaped. In practice, sectors can be shaped like a circle, an oval, a fan blade, or whatever shape you need to cover a specific area. Figure 5-23 shows examples of access point locations with sector antenna systems consisting of one, two, three, and six sectors. Your antenna system for each sector needs to be selected and aligned to maximize the coverage within that sector and minimize the noise and interference from all other sectors and areas.

Figure 5-23 *Sector Coverage Examples*

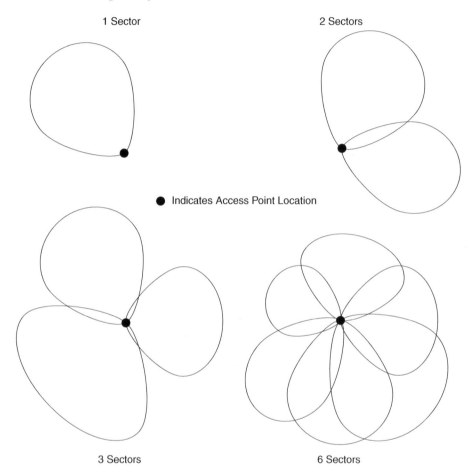

When you choose to build a sectorized access point, you gain the following advantages:

- **Scalability**—You can increase the capacity of your system. You can start small, perhaps with just a single sector serving a few users. As the number of users grows, you can add more sectors. By converting omnidirectional coverage to three-sector coverage, you can triple the capacity of your hub site.

- **Reliability**—You can select the gain and the pattern of each sector antenna to provide the highest signal level for end users in that sector. You can also choose the polarization and adjust the downtilt of each sector antenna to reduce interference from other networks. By designing a good sector antenna system and installing the sector antennas correctly, you reduce the noise level and improve the reliability of your service within each sector.

Selecting Sector Antennas

Sectorization always yields dividends compared to a non-sectorized antenna system. For the best performance from your sectorized system, consider the suggestions in the sections that follow as you design your system and select your antennas.

Low-Noise Access Point Location

Although a sectorized system handles noise and interference far better than a non-sectorized system, it is still important to select a low-noise access point location. Even the best sector antenna design might not provide satisfactory service if it is installed in a high-noise location.

TIP   For help in choosing a low-noise location, review the wireless site survey information in Chapter 4, "Performing Site Surveys."

Sector Orientation

Coordinate the orientation of your sectors to provide effective, scaleable coverage of your service area. For example, if many of your end users are concentrated in a downtown area, plan to use more than one sector to cover that area. For example, if you decide to use a total of three sectors to cover the downtown area, then each sector should cover 1/3 of the total area. If the total downtown area extends 180 degrees when viewed from your access point location, each sector antenna should have a horizontal beamwidth of 45 to 60 degrees.

Sector Radius

The radius of each sector plays a direct role in choosing the proper antenna for that sector. A sector with a small radius requires a low-gain sector antenna. A sector with a large radius needs a high-gain antenna. Use the formula for link budget in Chapter 2 to determine how much gain you need to cover your sector. Remember to allow a fade margin of at least 10 dB.

Polarization

Choose the polarization of each of your sector antennas. Each sector should be cross polarized when compared to the polarization of the strongest source of noise and interference within that sector. It is okay to use different polarizations in different sectors.

Horizontal Beamwidth

Choose the horizontal beamwidth of each sector to be from 75 to 100 percent of the width (in degrees) of the sector. There is no absolutely correct formula; however, one rule of thumb is to choose a sector antenna with a horizontal beamwidth equal to *75 percent of the sector width*; for example, a 45-degree horizontal beamwidth antenna is often chosen for a 60-degree sector.

Remember from Chapter 2 that horizontal beamwidth describes the width of an antenna's main lobe at the half-power points. This means that an antenna with a 60-degree horizontal beamwidth still radiates a substantial amount of power beyond a 60-degree angle.

TIP   If you prefer to have a substantial overlap between sectors to provide a little redundant area coverage when frequency re-use is not an issue, choose a horizontal beamwidth equal to the sector width.

Vertical Beamwidth

Choose the vertical beamwidth of each sector antenna based on the radius of the sector. A sector that has a larger radius needs a wider vertical beamwidth to cover the sector. A sector that has a smaller radius needs a smaller vertical beamwidth.

Downtilt

Choose sector antennas that can be mechanically downtilted to allow you to center the main lobe of the antenna in the middle of the coverage area of each sector. More downtilt is needed in sectors that have more elevation differential between the end users and the sector antenna. For example, in a 5-mile radius sector, an antenna that is mounted 500 feet higher than the elevation of the end users must be downtilted more than a sector antenna that is mounted only 150 feet higher than the end users.

F/B Ratio

Select a sector antenna with the highest possible F/B ratio consistent with the cost of the antenna. Higher F/B ratios result in more interference rejection off the back of the antenna. More interference rejection allows a higher signal-to-noise ratio and better performance in the forward direction.

Size, Weight, and Appearance

Choose a sector antenna that has a size and weight that can be safely and securely mounted in or on the available mounting area or tower.

Choose an antenna that has an appearance that is acceptable to the management of the site where the antenna is to be located.

TIP   If you need to paint an antenna to make it blend in with a building, be sure to select paint without metallic content. Metal in the paint reduces the performance of the antenna.

Quality and Cost

Sector antennas range in cost from $50 to more than $500. Choose a sector antenna that balances quality and cost. A more expensive, higher-quality antenna will have the following features:

- Higher-quality materials for a longer life
- A cleaner radiation pattern with fewer side lobes to cause interference
- More constant performance characteristics across the band, including gain and standing wave ratio (SWR)
- A mounting system that is easier to install and adjust
- Fewer internal parts to minimize the chances of failure

Other Antenna System Components

An antenna system has several other parts, such as these:

- **Feed system**—The feed system carries power to and from the antenna. The feed system is coaxial cable (coax) or, in rare instances, waveguide.
- **Coaxial connectors**—Connectors transfer power between different sections of the feed system.
- **Mounting hardware**—Mounting hardware connects the antenna to the antenna supports. The mounting hardware must hold the antenna firmly in place, including any uptilt or downtilt. Mounting hardware also secures feedlines to masts, towers, and buildings.
- **Covering**—Antenna coverings are called radomes.

The sections that follow cover the antenna system components in greater detail.

Feed Systems

99 percent of the time, an antenna feed system consists of coaxial cable plus connectors, jumpers, and lightning arresters. 1 percent of the time, a feed system consists of waveguide. Waveguide is heavy, expensive, and low loss compared to coax. A full description of waveguide is beyond the scope of this book; however, in brief, waveguide is like running a rectangular, circular, or elliptical metal pipe up a tower to connect the radio and the antenna. Wireless energy is carried inside the waveguide until the energy reaches the antenna.

Consider the following coax characteristics when selecting the proper coax for your antenna feed system:

- Impedance
- Loss
- Size
- Type
- Power-handling capability
- Upper frequency limit

The sections that follow cover each characteristic and provide recommendations for selecting coax transmission line that is suitable for your purposes.

Impedance

Most radios are designed with an antenna impedance of 50 ohms (50 Ω). The coax for these antenna systems needs to have a characteristic impedance of 50 Ω.

NOTE   It is becoming increasingly popular to integrate a radio directly into an antenna and run Ethernet cable from the outdoor radio/antenna combination down to the indoor network equipment. This configuration avoids the coaxial cable losses that would otherwise occur. These integrated systems use shielded outdoor Category 5 (Cat 5) Ethernet cable and no coaxial cable.

Loss

Coaxial cable is rated in decibels (dB) of loss per 100 feet at each frequency. For example, good quality, low-loss 0.4-inch (1 cm) diameter cable (the most frequently used size) has a loss of about −7 dB per 100 feet at 2.4 GHz.

The sum of the coax cable losses at each end of a wireless link plays a role in determining the distance over which the link operates. See the link budget discussion in Chapter 2 for the link budget distance computation and the maximum loss that the coax can contribute. The most important consideration in selecting the proper coax for a particular installation is to avoid excessive loss at the same time you avoid excessive cost.

Size

Coax is available in a wide range of diameters from about 1/16 of an inch (1.58 mm) up to over 1 inch (2.54 cm). The larger the diameter, the lower the loss. Also, the larger the coax diameter, the heavier and more expensive the cost of the coax.

Type

In addition to standard coaxial cable, the following additional cable types are available:

- **Plenum**—Plenum cable is manufactured using material that meets building code standards for being placed into horizontal air plenums. Plenum-rated cable materials do not give off toxic fumes and can be safely placed into air ventilation plenums that carry breathable air.

- **Riser**—Riser cable is manufactured using material that meets building code standards for being placed into vertical riser systems that run between floors of a building. Riser-rated cable materials burn slowly and inhibit the spread of fire vertically from floor to floor in a building.

- **Direct burial**—Direct burial cable is manufactured using material that resists the spread of moisture through the cable. When water intrudes into standard cable, it typically spreads along the cable. When this occurs, cable losses rise significantly, and the only way to correct the problem is to replace the entire cable. In contrast, direct burial cable resists the intrusion and spread of moisture and can be directly buried without experiencing moisture problems.

- **Flexible**—Flexible cable is significantly more flexible than standard cable. Use flexible cable where cable needs to make sharp bends or where cable needs to flex, move, or rotate.

Power-Handling Capability

Coaxial cable has limits on the amount of power that it can handle before failing. Fortunately, all commonly used cable types handle many times more power than the maximum legal 1-watt (W) transmitter output power allowed in license-free systems.

Upper Frequency Limit

Although, in general, larger-diameter coax with lower loss is better than smaller diameter coax, there is a maximum cutoff frequency limit when the coax size becomes so large that the coax begins to behave like waveguide. If you deploy 5-GHz equipment, discuss this size limitation with the manufacturer or distributor of your wireless equipment. In general, at 5 GHz, use coax with a maximum diameter of 0.9 inch (2.3 cm). Larger diameter coax is not recommended.

Feed System Connector Locations and Types

Coaxial connectors perform many functions in wireless systems. Although many different connector types are available, in practice, only a few different types are used. The most commonly used connector is the N connector.

When you know the location of a connector, you can often predict the type of connector that is used. Coaxial connectors are used in the following locations:

- **Wireless equipment inputs and outputs**—This is the area with the largest variety of possible connectors. FCC rules specify that wireless equipment manufacturers must use connectors that are not generally available. The reason for this rule is to make it difficult to use the equipment with antenna systems (and amplifiers) that do not meet FCC certification requirements. The FCC is concerned that equipment operators will add amplifiers that transmit at illegally high power levels.

NOTE   Unfortunately, the FCC concern appears to be justified. A small number of license-free network operators do apparently transmit at power levels that exceed FCC regulations. Sometimes these operators have not taken the time to become familiar with the FCC rules. Other times, the violators know the rules but choose to ignore them in the belief that they will not be caught. These operators appear not to care about the interference that their overpower operation can cause to other wireless networks. At press time, it has been reported in the U.S. that the FCC has begun to enforce the power level rules more widely. Lawbreakers beware!

- **Pigtails**—Typically, short, small-diameter "pigtail" connecting cables are used to bridge from equipment connectors to the rest of the antenna system. These pigtails have an equipment-specific connector on one end and a standard larger-diameter connector on the other end. The larger diameter connector is typically an N connector.

- **Jumpers**—Jumpers are generally short, larger-diameter connecting cables. Jumpers are usually used between different peripheral devices as well as between large-diameter antenna cable runs and the antennas themselves. Jumpers generally use N connectors.

- **Peripherals**—Peripheral devices, such as lightning arresters, are placed between the wireless equipment and the antenna system. These devices generally use N connectors.

- **Antenna cable runs**—Coaxial cable runs from wireless peripherals up to antenna systems generally use N connectors, although some equipment manufacturers occasionally use other large-diameter connectors.

Antenna-Mounting Hardware

Although there are exceptions, most antennas are designed to mount around a vertical pipe, mast, or tower leg using a U-bolt, as shown in Figure 5-24.

Figure 5-24   *Antenna U-Bolt Mounting Hardware*

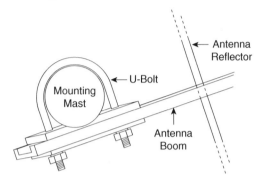

A U-bolt bracket typically mounts through two holes in the antenna boom or other antenna-support element. The U-bolt then clamps around the antenna support mast or tower leg. When the U-bolt is tightened, it grips the mast and holds the antenna firmly in position.

Antenna Coverings

Many antennas operate for years outdoors, uncovered and exposed to the weather. In some harsh environments, antenna coverings are used to either minimize damage to the antenna from the weather or reduce the wind resistance of the antenna system.

When antenna coverings are used, the coverings are called radomes. Radomes are made out of nonconducting material (such as fiberglass) to prevent the radome from altering the radiation pattern of the antenna. Some radome advantages are:

- Preventing moisture and precipitation from corroding the metallic parts of the antenna and degrading antenna performance
- Covering the antenna to reduce snow and ice buildup
- Covering the antenna to reduce wind loading on the antenna, the antenna mast, and the tower

Review Questions

1 When comparing light energy to wireless energy, a light bulb can be compared to what antenna element?

2 The orientation of an antenna's E-field determines what characteristic of the antenna's operation?

3 Relative to each other, the E-field of a vertically polarized antenna and the E-field of a horizontally polarized antenna are what?

4 Omnidirectional antennas are available with either vertical or horizontal polarization. True or false?

5 A diversity receiving system can automatically select the best signal from one of two antennas. True or false?

6 When using a diversity system, the two antennas must always be the same type and point in the same direction. True or false?

7 Anyone who deploys an outdoor license-free wireless system can provide reliable wireless service. True or false?

8 A strong signal arriving at your receiver from another wireless network increases your network throughput. True or false?

9 How much is the typical cross-polarization isolation between a horizontally polarized and a vertically polarized antenna?

10 A sectorized antenna system does not allow you to serve more end users. True or false?

11 In a sectorized antenna system, all the sector antennas should be identical. True or false?

12 Sector antennas in a sectorized antenna system should always be mounted perfectly vertical. True or false?

CHAPTER 6

Evaluating and Selecting Wireless Equipment

The equipment that you select for your broadband wireless wide-area network (WAN) plays a major role in the reliability, scalability, and profitability of your network. This chapter helps you evaluate and select your wireless network equipment.

This chapter does not list feature information vendor by vendor. The quantity of information would be overwhelming and the listing would quickly become outdated. Instead, this chapter aims to help you understand the features and characteristics that are available on wireless equipment. When you understand the features and their significance, you will be in a position to select the equipment that best meets your network needs.

Any New Features This Week?

Wireless equipment is evolving rapidly. Wireless hardware and software features change each week. I have attempted to describe all the significant wireless hardware and software features that were offered (by at least one equipment manufacturer) at the time I wrote this chapter in 2002. Because of rapid equipment evolution, I suggest that you supplement the information presented here with your own feature research.

This chapter contains the following major sections:

- A description of the equipment selection process.

- A brief explanation of the International Organization for Standardization (ISO) Open Systems Interconnection (OSI) seven-layer reference model. An understanding of this model helps you understand how various wireless features fit into your network.

- A list of equipment features, arranged by OSI layer. Following each feature is an explanation of the feature.

- A summary of the features that are the most desirable for wireless backbone equipment, access points (APs), customer premises equipment (CPE), wireless network cards, mesh network nodes, and amplifiers.

- A discussion of compatibility issues that can cause problems when mixing wireless equipment from different vendors.

- Suggestions about evaluating and receiving vendor support.

Overview of the Equipment Selection Process

Your equipment purchase can involve spending only a few hundred dollars, or it can involve spending hundreds of thousands of dollars. The more money that you plan to spend, the more important it is that you include all of the following steps in your selection process.

Reviewing Your Wireless Network Needs

Before you select your wireless equipment, take the time to review your wireless network needs:

- How many wireless end users do you want to serve?
- What network architectural elements do you want your wireless network to include?
- Do you need only point-to-point links or will you deploy point-to-multipoint APs?
- Do you need wireless backbone bandwidth?
- Do you need mesh network nodes or repeaters?
- What features will your wireless network need so that it can connect to your wired network?
- Will you need routing or only bridging?

After you have reviewed both the wireless network features and the wired features that you need, you are ready to begin researching specific wireless equipment features.

Researching Equipment Features

Now that you know your network needs, you can begin listing wireless equipment that matches your needs. The most difficult part of the research process is not learning what features a particular brand of equipment offers. The most difficult part is learning what features are *not* offered or which features do not work the way you expect them to work.

If you have not worked with wireless equipment before, it can be difficult to get an accurate picture by looking only at press releases and advertising flyers. Press releases are typically loaded with attractive buzzwords that promise wireless performance and wireless benefits that are sometimes exaggerated or theoretical. Advertising flyers and spec sheets do not lie about equipment performance, but they sometimes omit information that would reveal performance shortcomings.

Evaluate equipment that offers the specific features that you need, such as distance and bandwidth capabilities, but before you decide to buy, visit a network where that particular vendor's equipment is deployed.

Visiting Deployment Sites

After you have researched equipment features, you will have one or more equipment vendors who can provide equipment that appears (at least on paper) to meet your wireless needs. It is appropriate and proper for you to ask the vendors to recommend one or two existing wireless networks that have deployed their equipment. Visit these sites and talk with the network operators who have deployed the equipment.

Your visit will allow you to learn what features work especially well and what features do not work as expected. You will learn which expectations were exceeded (the good news) and which expectations were not met (the not-so-good news). You will learn if the equipment is easy or difficult to manage. You will also learn if vendor support is poor, good, or outstanding. This is information that you cannot obtain from a spec sheet or an advertising flyer. With the benefit of this information, can make an accurate and informed decision about which equipment to purchase.

Testing Wireless Equipment in the Lab

When you have completed your site visits, there will probably be one or two vendors that you think would be good equipment providers. At this point, consider making a small equipment purchase consisting of either a pair of wireless units or one AP and one CPE unit.

Set up these units indoors and become familiar with them. Configure the units and measure their throughput in both directions. Learn to use the diagnostics.

TIP

Practice safety when you are working near wireless equipment. High amounts of microwave energy can cause damage to the human body, so minimize your exposure to this type of energy. Do not point a directional antenna at yourself or at any other nearby person. Turn the wireless equipment off any time you are not testing it. Remember: When you double the distance between yourself and a wireless antenna, you reduce the amount of radiation reaching you to one-fourth the previous level. Whenever possible, maintain as much distance as possible between yourself and a wireless antenna.

When your indoor testing is complete and you are comfortable with the units, proceed to outdoor testing.

Testing Wireless Equipment Outdoors

Testing wireless equipment outdoors allows you to test the range, throughput, and reliability of the equipment in the presence of real-world noise, interference, and weather.

For your outdoor testing, perform the following steps:

Step 1   Pick two locations that are as far apart as the maximum link distance that you expect the equipment to cover. For example, if you plan to build a wireless cell with a 4-mile (6.4 km) radius, pick an AP location that is high enough to have at least two line-of-sight (LOS) paths that are at least 4 miles long.

Step 2   Test using an AP antenna system similar to the one that you expect to use in your actual network deployment.

Step 3   Temporarily set up the CPE at first one and then the other of your two test locations.

Step 4   Test during the busiest part of the day and repeat the throughput tests that you performed indoors. It is important that you test the throughput from the CPE to the AP. This is an important test of the AP's capability to receive in the presence of noise and interference. For more details about throughput testing, see the description in Chapter 7, "Installing Outdoor Wireless Systems."

Step 5   If possible, repeat your performance testing several times over a period of several days or weeks. The equipment performance should remain constant throughout the entire test period.

Your outdoor testing will not tell you how many customers the AP will handle at full load, but it will give you a good preliminary performance indication. If all your test results are good, proceed to the following purchase decision step.

Making Purchase Decisions

Your testing should bring you to the point where you are most comfortable with the performance of one or two brands of wireless equipment. You can now make your purchase decision and be fairly confident that the equipment you buy will meet your performance expectations.

OSI and TCP/IP Reference Models

Several different but similar layered data architectures have been developed to allow reliable data transfer between different computer systems and between different networks. When you understand a little about the service layers and the protocols that these architectures use, you will be in a good position to understand the similarities and the differences between different brands of wireless equipment.

The seven-layer ISO OSI reference model was first proposed around 1983 to allow connectivity (or interworking) between different computer systems. Prior to the OSI reference

model, computer systems made by one manufacturer could not easily communicate with computer systems made by other manufacturers. The intent of the OSI reference model was to allow computer systems to successfully communicate with each other even though different vendors manufactured them. Figure 6-1 shows the OSI reference model alongside the
TCP/IP architecture.

Figure 6-1   *OSI and TCP/IP*

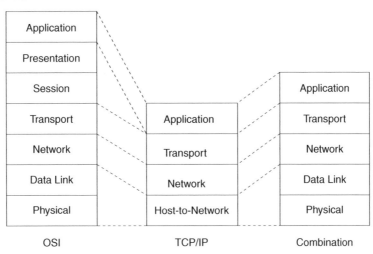

Beginning in the 1970s, the United States Department of Defense began promoting computer networking between university research departments and government installations. One of the primary goals of this internetworking effort was to develop a survivable network—one that would be able to continue communicating even if some of the network nodes or some of the communications links were destroyed. This new networking effort was based on two primary protocols: the Transmission Control Protocol (TCP) and the Internet Protocol (IP). TCP performed transport layer functions equivalent to the transport layer in the OSI model. IP performed network layer functions that were equivalent to the network layer (Layer 3) in the OSI model. When application layer (Layer 7) protocols (Telnet, FTP, SMTP, and so on) and physical (Layer 1) and data link layer (Layer 2) protocols were added, the result was an architecture that effectively contained five layers. Figure 6-1 shows the TCP/IP model alongside the OSI reference model for comparison.

The TCP/IP architecture is functionally equivalent to the OSI reference model. The major similarities and differences are as follows:

- Both models have an application, a transport, and a network/Internet layer.

- The TCP/IP model does not have a session layer (Layer 5 of the OSI reference model) or a presentation layer (Layer 6 of the OSI reference model).

- Both models have a lower layer that connects the upper layers to the actual physical network. In the OSI reference model, the lower layer (Layer 1) is called the physical layer. In the original TCP/IP model, the lower layer was called the host-to-network layer. In present-day use, TCP/IP networks use the combination of a Layer 2 sublayer called the medium access control (MAC) sublayer along with Layer 1 to provide connectivity over the wireless link.

Virtually all the wireless equipment features that you evaluate operate at the physical, data link, and network layers of the OSI and TCP/IP reference models. The wireless features and functionality (modulation type, data rate, and so on) take place at the physical layer. Access to (and sharing of) the wireless medium takes place at the data link layer. Routing takes place at the network layer.

Peer Protocols

Peer protocols run across the Internet but provide communication only between same-layer processes. One example of this same-layer communication process is a Hypertext Transfer Protocol (HTTP) web browser running on the application layer of one network. The HTTP browser retrieves information from its peer web server running on the application layer of another network. Although the HTTP communication is application-layer-to-application layer (peer-to-peer), both networks communicate downward through their lower network layers.

Services

Information is passed from the top (application) layer of one network down through the lower layers. Each layer provides a set of services for the layer just above it and utilizes the services provided by the layer just below it. The set of services between two layers is referred to as the *interface* between the two layers. For example, Layer 6 provides services for Layer 7; Layer 5 provides services for Layer 6; and so on. In this way, Layer 7 (the application layer) can communicate all the way down to Layer 1 (the physical layer).

The following list illustrates how services and protocols operate. When your web browser uses HTTP over a wireless network, the information flow is as follows:

1 The HTTP information request originates at the application layer on the originating network.

2 The HTTP request travels downward from the application layer (using the services provided by all the intermediate layers) to the physical layer on the originating network. The physical layer uses the appropriate wireless *protocol* (for example, the appropriate direct sequence spread spectrum modulation or DSSS) to communicate the request over the air wirelessly to the physical layer on the other network.

3 The physical layer on the other network uses the DSSS protocol to receive the request from the originating network. The physical layer then passes the information up through its interface to the data link layer. Using higher and higher layer services, the request passes upward until it eventually reaches the application layer. There, the HTTP protocol processes the request and replies with a response.

4 Using services of lower and lower layers, the response travels downward to the physical layer. Using the Layer 1 DSSS protocol, the response is transmitted over the air back to the physical layer of the originating network.

5 Using services, the originating network passes the response upward to the application layer where the HTTP protocol receives the response to its original request.

Basic Packet Structure and Frame Types

Packet switching store-and-forward techniques underlie the operation of layered architectures. Packet switching uses an underlying data structure, called a *packet*. A packet is like a hamburger on a bun. Although the exact packet structure varies from layer to layer and protocol to protocol, most packets contain a data payload section. The data payload is the hamburger in the middle of the bun. Other fields encapsulate (surround) the data payload and make up the bun. The bun typically provides the following:

- Source and destination address information
- Packet numbering information
- Packet acknowledgment information
- Error detection and correction information

Figure 6-2 shows this general packet structure.

Figure 6-2   *General Packet Structure*

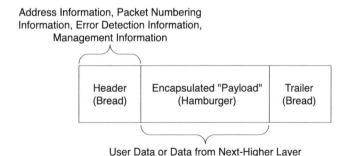

Packets prepared by Layer 2 (the data link layer) are called *frames*. Not all frames contain payload data. Wireless APs and wireless stations exchange three types of frames, each with the following functions:

- Data frames carry user payload data (the hamburger) between different wireless network nodes.

- Control frames carry information such as request-to-send (RTS) and clear-to-send (CTS) messages as well as frame acknowledgments (ACK).

- Management frames carry association and authentication requests and responses in addition to beacon information.

Application Layer Functions and Protocols

The application layer is where the end user programs run. Telnet, Simple Mail Transfer Protocol (SMTP), File Transfer Protocol (FTP), and HTTP are examples of application layer protocols. Wireless equipment that you evaluate will likely have network management software that operates at the application layer level.

Transport Layer Functions and Protocols

The transport layer's job is to provide reliable communications from application to application regardless of the lower-layer protocols and communications links. The transport layer encapsulates data from the application layer (and the session layer, if used) and passes it down to the network layer.

Typical transport layer protocols are TCP and User Datagram Protocol (UDP). Wireless equipment that you evaluate does not usually have features that operate at the transport layer level.

Network Layer Functions and Protocols

The essential network layer protocol is IP. In addition to IP, the network layer often utilizes other routing protocols such as Routing Information Protocol (RIP) and Border Gateway Protocol (BGP).

The network layer encapsulates data (the hamburger) from the transport layer between IP source, IP destination, and IP routing information. Packet routing typically goes from intermediate network to intermediate network before the packets finally arrive at their destination network.

Data Link Layer Functions and Protocols

The data link layer includes the logical link control (LLC) sublayer and the MAC sublayer. The data link layer normally performs a wide variety of functions, including segmenting the bit stream into frames, error handling, flow control, and access control.

Examples of data link layer protocols include Point-to-Point Protocol (PPP) and Spanning Tree Protocol.

LLC Sublayer Functions and Protocols

The LLC sublayer makes up the top half of the data link layer and interfaces to the network layer (above) and the MAC sublayer (below). The LLC Sublayer encapsulates the Layer 3 data by adding sequence and acknowledgment numbers. The LLC Sublayer might provide different service options, depending on the network software.

MAC Sublayer Functions and Protocols

The MAC sublayer makes up the bottom half of the data link layer. The MAC sublayer interfaces to the physical (wireless) layer and provides the following functions:

- **Reliable delivery**—The MAC sublayer provides a reliable delivery mechanism that looks for an acknowledgment for every frame that is sent. If an acknowledgment is not received, the MAC sublayer retransmits the frame.

- **Access control**—The MAC sublayer controls access to the wireless channel. The two basic types of access control are carrier sense multiple access with collision avoidance (CSMA/CA) and polling. CSMA/CA is a distributed coordination function (DCF) because the decision about when to transmit is distributed to all wireless stations. Each wireless station listens before transmitting. If a station hears that the frequency is busy, it backs off (waits) a random amount of time and tries again. When the frequency is clear, the station proceeds to transmit. In addition, a request-to-send/ clear-to-send (RTS/CTS) mechanism can be enabled. Large packets are more likely to collide; therefore, stations that have packets larger than the RTS/CTS threshold must request and receive clearance from the AP MAC before they can transmit their packets. Finally, in networks that have heavy traffic and many end users, a point coordination function (PCF) can be used. One single point (the MAC in the AP) coordinates transmissions from all stations. The PCF polls each wireless station and then tells each end user when it can transmit.

NOTE   You might have heard of wireless networks with a hidden node problem. This problem can occur in a network that uses DCF. In most wireless networks, certain wireless stations cannot hear all the other wireless stations. Under heavy traffic loads, several stations might try to transmit at the same time. This can happen even when the stations are using RTS/CTS. When stations transmit at the same time, collisions occur and network throughput drops drastically. The solution to hidden-node problems is to use wireless equipment that can support PCF.

- **Encryption**—The MAC also provides encryption. The most frequently used encryption method is wired equivalent privacy (WEP).

MAC control frame subtypes include RTS, CTS, and ACK. Examples of management frame subtypes include Beacon, Probe Request, Authentication, and Association Request.

Physical Layer Functions and Protocols

The physical layer transports encapsulated data from the data link layer and transmits it wirelessly to the distant network. There are several physical layer wireless standards. There are also many proprietary physical layer wireless protocols. In addition to your wireless feature evaluation, you will evaluate physical layer wired-interface features such as Ethernet and serial port features.

Physical Layer Wired-Interface Features

This section describes the wired-interface feature options that you will encounter when you begin to research and select your wireless equipment.

NOTE   No wireless equipment vendor offers all the listed features in any model of their wireless equipment—nor should they. Each wireless network is built to serve a specific set of end user needs. These end user needs dictate the best set of wired and wireless features for that particular network. Each feature listed in the following sections is offered on at least one brand and model of wireless equipment. It is important that, as you consider the available features, you keep your wireless network needs in mind. Your equipment research involves finding the best match between your network needs and the wireless equipment feature set offered on a particular model of wireless equipment.

Your physical layer wired-interface feature evaluation includes some or all of the following:

- Low-speed data ports
- Ethernet ports
- High-speed data ports
- Voice interfaces

Low-Speed Data Ports

Most wireless equipment contains at least one low-speed port, such as the following:

- **Low-speed serial data ports**—On some equipment, a low-speed serial data port is used for initial system configuration. The serial port speed generally ranges between 4800 bits per second (bps) and 19.2 kilobits per second (kbps).

- **Low-speed user data ports**—Early wireless modems were frequently designed to transport only low-speed serial data over the wireless link. Port speeds range from 4800 bps to 128 kbps.

- **Dialup telco interfaces**—Dialup telco interfaces provide low-speed dial backup connectivity for times when a higher-speed primary link, such as a T1 or digital subscriber line (DSL) link, is unavailable.

Ethernet Ports

Ethernet interfaces allow network data to access the wireless network. Wireless equipment can include one or more of the following Ethernet interfaces:

- **10Base-T**—This is the most common Ethernet interface.
- **100Base-TX**—This interface is found on higher-speed wireless equipment.
- **Ethernet hubs or switches**—This interface is found on some wireless APs.

High-Speed Data Ports

In addition to Ethernet interfaces, it is often desirable to use wireless bridges or routers to transport other high-speed non-Ethernet data streams. To transport these streams, wireless equipment can include the following interfaces:

- **Digital subscriber line (DSL) interfaces**—DSL interfaces enable a wireless bridge or router to extend or share a DSL connection.

- **Cable interfaces**—Cable interfaces enable wireless equipment to extend or share a cable Internet connection.

- **Asynchronous Transfer Mode (ATM) interfaces**—ATM interfaces enable wireless equipment to connect to and from an ATM network.

- **T1/E1 interfaces**—T1/E1 interfaces enable wireless equipment to extend a 1.544 megabit per second (Mbps) T1 line or a 2.048 Mbps E1 line from point A to point B, for example, between two private automatic branch exchanges (PABXs). Some models of wireless equipment provide T1/E1 connectivity only. Other wireless equipment models provide simultaneous wireless Ethernet and T1/E1 connectivity.

TIP   Telecommunications managers who want to provide both Ethernet and voice-PABX connectivity between buildings find wireless equipment that simultaneously provides both Ethernet and T1 connectivity to be especially useful.

- **T3/E3 interfaces**—45-Mbps T3 interfaces enable full-duplex wireless equipment to provide T3 connectivity between two points.

- **Optical Carrier 3 (OC-3) interfaces**—155-Mbps OC-3 interfaces enable full-duplex wireless equipment to provide OC-3 connectivity between two points. Wireless OC-3 equipment usually has the capability to carry several T1 or E1 circuits in addition to the OC-3 circuit.

- **Optical Carrier 12 (OC-12) interfaces**—622-Mbps OC-12 interfaces allow full-duplex wireless equipment to provide OC-12 connectivity between two points.

TIP   Remember that, in general, there is an inverse relationship between wireless bandwidth and wireless distance; as bandwidth goes up, distance goes down. OC-12 wireless equipment typically operates only over distances up to approximately 1312 ft. (400 m).

Voice Interfaces

Voice interfaces enable wireless equipment to carry voice in addition to data. The following types of voice interfaces are possible:

- **Voice over Internet Protocol (VoIP) interfaces**—VoIP interfaces allow IP telephones to connect directly to the wireless equipment and to make on-network voice calls. Making calls to the public switched telephone network (PSTN) requires the use of an external telephone gateway.

- **Talkback/orderwire interfaces**—A talkback interface (sometimes called an *order wire*) provides a two-way voice circuit. Maintenance personnel normally use this circuit for end-to-end voice communication over the wireless link while servicing the wireless equipment.

Wired-Interface Security Features

Physical layer wired-interface security features limit user access to the system administration console via a serial port or an Ethernet port. Successful entry of a password is required before gaining access to system administration functions. Additionally, some equipment allows a management station IP address to be configured. Attempts to access the system administration console from other IP addresses are refused.

Physical Layer Wireless-Interface Features

Wireless features operate at the physical layer; therefore, your wireless-interface feature evaluation covers a broad range of features. The following sections cover these feature categories:

- **NLOS**—Non line-of-sight and near line-of-sight equipment capabilities
- **Wireless frequency bands**—Propagation characteristics and equipment availability for each of the license-free bands
- **Modulation types**—Various types of modulation used by license-free equipment
- **Bandwidth and throughput**—Tradeoffs between data rate, data throughput, and link distance
- **Noise and interference-reduction features**—Receiver and antenna features that improve signal reception abilities
- **Security**—Physical layer wireless security features
- **Miscellaneous wireless features**—Transmit and receive features that can play a significant role in the performance of your wireless network operation

Non Line-of-Sight Features

In the broadband wireless industry, there is no agreement about the exact meaning of the term *NLOS*. Here are two common ways that NLOS is used:

- **Near line-of-sight**—When equipment vendors state that their equipment has *near*-LOS capabilities, they are claiming that it operates satisfactorily even when there is a partially obstructed line-of-sight path, as long as there are not too many obstacles to the line-of-sight path. For example, perhaps a few trees are intruding into the Fresnel zone.
- **Non line-of sight**—When equipment vendors state that their equipment has *non*-LOS capabilities, they are claiming that it operates satisfactorily even when there is an obstructed line-of-sight path. For example, perhaps buildings, trees, and hills are completely blocking the path.

Because there is no standard definition of NLOS, the process of evaluating NLOS performance claims is a challenging one. Almost all vendors of NLOS equipment (either accidentally or intentionally) exclude information about the range of their NLOS equipment. The
impression is left with the customer (you) that the NLOS equipment has the same communications range as LOS wireless equipment. This is never the case; the range of NLOS
equipment is always substantially less than the range of equipment that is operating over a
true, unobstructed LOS path.

Now, you will learn about features that actually improve performance in NLOS environments. Two significant challenges that an NLOS environment presents for wireless
equipment are as follows:

- **Multipath**—Any equipment feature that improves performance in a multipath
  environment also improves performance in an NLOS environment. These features are
  as follows:
    — Diversity antennas
    — Circularly polarized antennas
    — Smart antennas that constantly adjust their beamwidth to receive and
      transmit energy directly to and from each individual end user antenna
    — Adaptive equalization
    — Multicarrier modulation, such as OFDM

  Whenever possible, always try to design your wireless WANs to use LOS paths. You
  will achieve more reliable coverage at longer distances.

- **Attenuation**—Attenuation losses in a non-LOS environment are the reason that the
  communications range in an NLOS environment is less than in a LOS environment.
  The following equipment and network features reduce attenuation and improve
  NLOS performance:
    — Receiver sensitivity
    — 900 MHz frequency band
    — Mesh networks

Wireless Frequency Bands

The following sections describe the license-free frequency bands, including the propagation characteristics and the power levels of each band.

900 MHz

900 MHz is the lowest-frequency industrial, scientific, and medical (ISM) band. The total
width of the band is 26 MHz. Signals in this band have a wavelength of approximately
12 inches (30 cm). These signals have the capability to pass through some obstructions
without being completely lost. For example, they can pass through light trees and diffract

over one low hill and still be strong enough to be received several miles away. 900 MHz is the best band to use when there are just a few obstacles to the LOS path. Table 6-1 shows 900-MHz power levels.

Table 6-1   *Power Levels for the 900-MHz Band*

Band	Maximum Transmitter Power	Maximum Antenna Gain	EIRP (Equivalent Isotropic Radiated Power)
902 to 928 MHz	+30 dBm (1 Watt)	+6 dBi	+36 dBi (4 Watts, relative to an isotropic antenna)

2.4 GHz

2.4 GHz is the middle ISM band. The total width of the band is 83 MHz. Signals in this band have a wavelength of approximately 4.8 inches (12 cm). These signals have little capability to pass through obstructions without being lost. Passing through one wall can result in 10 to 12 dB of attenuation. Attenuation from trees varies depending on the presence of leaves and whether the leaves are wet or dry but, on average, the attenuation from trees is approximately .5 dB per meter. One 30-ft (10-meter) diameter tree (the tree canopy/leaves are 30 feet across, not the tree trunk) results in about 5 dB of attenuation; 6 dB of attenuation reduces the length of a wireless link to 1/2 of its previous length. You can see that passing a 2.4-GHz signal through a few trees can easily reduce the usable length of the wireless path to a few hundred feet. Table 6-2 shows 2.4-GHz power levels.

Table 6-2   *Power Levels for the 2.4 GHz Band*

Band	Maximum Transmitter Power	Maximum Antenna Gain	Maximum EIRP
2403 to 2483 MHz (Point-to-Multipoint)	+30 dBm (1 Watt)	+6 dBi	+36 dBi (4 Watts).
2403 to 2483 MHz (Point-to-Point only)	+30 dBm (1 Watt)	(3-to-1 Rule) For every 3 dBi (above +6 dBi) of antenna gain, reduce the transmitter power by 1 dB. (For example, for a +9 dBi antenna, reduce transmitter power to +29 dBm.)	Depends on antenna size. With a +24 dBi antenna and +24 dBm of transmitter power, +48 dBi (64 Watts) is possible in a Point-to-Point (only) link.
2403 to 2483 MHz Wideband frequency hopping spread spectrum using from 15 to 74 hopping frequencies	+21 dBm (125 mW)	+6 dBi	+27 dBi (500 mW).

3.5 GHz

The 3.5-GHz band is not available for use in the United States; however, some frequency subbands between 3.3 and 4.0 GHz are available for use (usually on a licensed basis) in a number of other countries. This band is mentioned here because equipment for this band is, in many cases, similar to equipment for the 2.4-GHz band. Signals in this band have a wavelength of approximately 9 cm (3.4 in). The propagation characteristics are somewhat similar to the 2.4-GHz band, although attenuation from trees and other obstructions is higher.

5 GHz

There are four license-free subbands at 5 GHz, although two of these bands overlap each other. There is one ISM band from 5725 to 5850 MHz (5.725 to 5.850 GHz), and there are three Unlicensed National Information Infrastructure (U-NII) bands: 5150 to 5250 MHz, 5250 to 5350 MHz, and 5725 to 5825 MHz. The ISM band is 125 MHz wide, and each U-NII band is 100 MHz wide. Signals in the 5-GHz subbands have a wavelength of approximately 2 inches (5 cm). Each 5 GHz subband is wider than the entire 2.4-GHz band; therefore, it is possible to build 5-GHz wireless equipment that provides more bandwidth and more throughput than equipment for any other license-free band. The attenuation from trees at 5 GHz is about 1.2 dB per meter; therefore, each 30-ft (10-meter) diameter tree (crown) that blocks an LOS path reduces the length of a wireless link by approximately 75 percent. Table 6-3 shows 5-GHz power levels.

Table 6-3   *Power Levels for the 5-GHz Band*

Band	Maximum Transmitter Power	Maximum Antenna Gain	EIRP
ISM 5725 to 5850 MHz	+30 dBm (1 Watt)	+6 dBi	+36 dBi (4 Watts). Note that point-to-point systems can use an antenna with more than +6 dBi gain with no transmitter power reduction.
U-NII 5150 to 5250 MHz	+17 dBm (50 mW)	+6 dBi	+23 dBi (500 mW; indoor use only per FCC regulations.)
U-NII 5250 to 5350 MHz	+24 dBm (250 mW)	+6 dBi	+30 dBi. (1 Watt).
U-NII 5725 to 5825 MHz	+30 dBm (1 Watt)	+6 dBi	+36 dBi (4 Watts) Note that point-to-point systems can use an antenna with up to +23 dBi gain with no transmitter power reduction.

60 GHz

The 59 to 64-GHz ISM band was approved for use in the United States in 1999. The total width of this band is almost 5 GHz. Signals in this band have a wavelength of about 2/10 of an inch (1/2 cm). Signals at this frequency are attenuated by the presence of oxygen in the air; therefore, the maximum wireless link distance is approximately half a mile (800 m), assuming that a LOS path is available. Obstructions completely block the signal. The advantage of this band is that equipment is available that provides point-to-point raw data rates up to 622 Mbps. In addition, the oxygen absorption means that the likelihood of interference from other networks is low.

Modulation Types

This section covers the following information:

- A quick review of the modulation process
- A direct sequence spread spectrum (DSSS) description
- A frequency hopping spread spectrum (FHSS) description
- An orthogonal frequency division multiplexing (OFDM) description
- A brief mention of other spread spectrum and non-spread types of modulation

Understanding the Modulation Process

Chapter 1, "An Introduction to Broadband License-Free Wireless Wide-Area Networking," defined *modulation* as the process of adding intelligence to the signal. The modulation process creates a change in some combination of the amplitude, the frequency, or the phase of a signal. Many types of modulation exist, including amplitude modulation used by commercial AM broadcast stations and frequency modulation (FM) used by police departments and fire departments, for example.

Spread spectrum modulation was originally designed for use by the military to camouflage the existence of and the content of military communications. Descriptions of the two types of spread spectrum modulation follow.

Direct Sequence Spread Spectrum (DSSS) Modulation

DSSS modulation simultaneously widens (spreads) a data signal out and reduces the amplitude (technically, it reduces the power density) of the signal. The resulting modulated signal resembles a low-level noise signal that is widely dispersed around a single frequency. The modulated DSSS signal is wider than the bandwidth of the original data. For example, an 11-Mbps raw data rate signal becomes a 22-MHz-wide DSSS signal. In the 2.4-GHz frequency band, there is enough room for three nonoverlapping 11 Mbps-wide signal channels. Each time a DSSS signal is transmitted, the wireless energy is centered around only one frequency; therefore, DSSS modulation is a *single-carrier* modulation scheme.

Frequency Hopping Spread Spectrum Modulation

Frequency Hopping Spread Spectrum (FHSS) modulation does not spread its signal energy out, but it rapidly shifts the energy from frequency to frequency. A narrowband FHSS signal is transmitted first on one narrow (1-MHz) channel and then quickly shifted to another channel, then another, and another, and so on. The rapid frequency hopping gives this type of modulation its name. The two following types of FHSS are now allowed in the 2.4-GHz band:

- **Narrowband frequency hopping**—Narrowband FHSS signals are 1 MHz wide. They hop using a total of 79 different frequencies. The signal can hop between these frequencies in 78 unique hopping patterns or hopping sequences. 802.11 standards define narrowband frequency hopping.

NOTE   Hopping sequences are sometimes different in different countries. Check with your national telecommunications authority for the regulations in your country.

- **Wideband frequency hopping**—Wideband FHSS signals can be up to 5 MHz wide and can hop using a total of less than 75 different frequencies. Typical wideband FHSS systems use far less than 75 frequencies; one such system uses 43 frequencies with a signal that is 1.7 MHz wide. Wideband frequency hopping systems are relatively new and are just beginning to be deployed in outdoor wireless WANs.

FHSS equipment changes its center frequency each time it hops; however, each time it transmits, the wireless energy is still centered on only one frequency. FHSS is, therefore, a single-carrier modulation scheme.

Orthogonal Frequency Division Multiplexing Modulation

Orthogonal Frequency Division Multiplexing (OFDM) modulation transmits bursts that use more than one carrier frequency simultaneously. Compared to a DSSS signal, an OFDM signal has the following characteristics:

- Occupies the same amount of bandwidth
- Uses 52 carriers instead of one carrier
- Carries more information with each transmitted burst
- Is more resistant to multipath fading

802.11a equipment uses OFDM modulation and operates on the 5-GHz band; 802.11g uses OFDM on the 2.4-GHz band. OFDM is a *multicarrier* modulation scheme because it transmits using more than one carrier simultaneously.

Other Spread Spectrum Modulation Types

Other types of spread spectrum modulation are now legal to use. These versions are proprietary to particular manufacturers and do not interoperate with 802.11b, 802.11a, or 802.11g systems.

One example of a proprietary spread spectrum modulation type is multicarrier DSSS. Rather than using just one DSSS carrier, multicarrier DSSS uses several simultaneous carrier frequencies to transport data. This multicarrier approach is a hybrid combination of single-carrier and multicarrier modulation.

Other Nonspread Spectrum Modulation Types

In the ISM bands, the FCC originally required that spread spectrum modulation be used. Recent rule changes now allow additional modulation types. In the U-NII bands, nonspread spectrum modulation types are permitted, and equipment manufacturers use proprietary digital modulation schemes to offer a variety of high-bandwidth point-to-point and point-to-multipoint systems.

Bandwidth and Throughput

It is important for you to understand wireless throughput so that you can meet (or exceed) the expectations of your wireless end users. This section describes the following:

*   The difference between the wireless data rate and the wireless throughput
*   The tradeoff between throughput and distance
*   Examples of low, medium, and high throughput equipment

Comparison Between Data Rate and Throughput (Including Simplex Versus Duplex Throughput)

There is a common misunderstanding regarding the bandwidth, the data rate, and the throughput of a wireless device:

*   Bandwidth refers to the raw data rate of the device.
*   Throughput refers to the actual amount of end user data that the device can transfer in a given time interval.

The result of this misunderstanding is that wireless network users are frequently disappointed in the wireless throughput (data transfer speeds) that they experience.

Understandably, wireless equipment manufacturers want their equipment to look as attractive as possible to potential buyers. For this reason, they usually use the raw data rate in their sales and advertising material. An 802.11b AP, for example, provides a raw data rate of 11 Mbps.

Wireless users have a different expectation; they are interested in how fast a web page or a file downloads. They are interested in the capability of the wireless device to deliver their data. When the wireless users' 802.11b AP delivers just 5.5 Mbps of data throughput, they feel that there must be a problem with the equipment.

Most frequently, the real data throughput potential of a half-duplex wireless network is approximately 50 percent of the raw data rate. An 802.11b AP operating at the maximum 11-Mbps raw data rate has a maximum throughput potential of about 5.5 Mbps. This difference between raw data rate and actual throughput has several causes, including these:

- The framing and signaling overhead
- The half-duplex turnaround time between transmit and receive
- The lower efficiency inherent in the transmission of small packets

Collisions between wireless users and interference from other networks can reduce the throughput below 50 percent. Chapter 8, "Solving Noise and Interference Problems," discusses this issue in more detail.

Remember that your end users rely on you to set their throughput expectations realistically. When they measure their throughput and discover that it meets or slightly exceeds the throughput that you told them to expect, they will judge your wireless network performance to be good.

Tradeoff Between Data Rate and Distance

As you evaluate wireless equipment, you will invariably compare different equipment brands based on how long of a link they can support. Link distance is important; however, during your comparison, it is important that you compare apples to apples. When you compare two brands of wireless equipment side by side, you must compare their link distances at the same data rate. Other factors being equal, the higher the throughput (or the higher the raw data rate), the shorter the communications range. Table 6-4 lists the typical outdoor link distances from an 802.11b AP (using a standard low-gain omnidirectional antenna).

Table 6-4   *Examples of 802.11b Data Rates Versus Distances*

Data Rate	Distance in Ft. (m)
11 Mbps	500 (152)
5.5 Mbps	885 (270)
2 Mbps	1300 (396)
1 Mbps	1500 (457)

As the data rate increases, the maximum AP link distance decreases. AP data rates automatically fall back to the next lower level when the AP detects the signal quality decreasing as the link distance increases.

Sub-1 Mbps Data Rates

Two types of wireless systems operate at sub-1 Mbps data rates:

- Low-speed (such as 4800 bps to 128 kbps) wireless modems that provide a point-to-point wireless extension for an RS-232 serial data system.

- 128 kbps to 1 Mbps point-to-point or point-to-multipoint wireless Ethernet bridges or AP systems. These systems are useful for Internet access.

1-Mbps to 11-Mbps Data Rates

Most point-to-multipoint wireless WAN systems are in this category. This category also includes both 802.11 (2 Mbps) and 802.11b (11 Mbps) systems.

12-Mbps to 60-Mbps Data Rates

This category includes both high-bandwidth point-to-point backbone equipment and point-to-multipoint equipment. Here are some examples:

- Point-to-point equipment is available with bandwidths of 12 Mbps, 20 Mbps, 24 Mbps, and 45 Mbps.

- Point-to-multipoint equipment is available with shared, aggregate bandwidths of 20 Mbps, 40 Mbps, 54 Mbps, and 60 Mbps.

- 802.11a WLAN equipment is becoming available. However, as this book was being written, this equipment was not yet appropriate for use in outdoor wireless networks. The power level was too low, and there is no connector to attach an outdoor antenna.

Over 60-Mbps Data Rates

The higher in frequency wireless equipment operates, the more bandwidth that is available. Products that provide more than 60 Mbps of bandwidth operate almost exclusively in the 5.3- and 5.8-GHz U-NII bands, although a few short-range products operate in the 60-GHz band. Products that operate in these bands have aggregate bandwidths of 90 Mbps, 100 Mbps, 155 Mbps (OC-3), 200 Mbps, 480 Mbps, 622 Mbps (OC-12), and 872 Mbps. All these are full-duplex products.

Noise and Interference Reduction Features

Noise is defined as anything and everything other than the desired signal. Interference reduces the throughput of a wireless network. Interference has many sources, so it is important that you consider and utilize all possible noise-reduction features.

NOTE   Chapter 8 is devoted completely to the topic of understanding and minimizing the effects of noise and interference. Refer to Chapter 8 for additional information as you read about the following interference-reduction features.

In the outdoor wireless environment, many potential interference sources exist. You can use a few equipment characteristics to provide some help in minimizing the effects of interference.

The following interference-reduction features operate at the physical layer to help reduce the effects that interference can have on both AP and CPE throughput.

Receiver Selectivity

Selectivity is the capability of a receiver to reject signals that are not exactly on the desired receiving frequency. No receiver is perfectly selective; no receiver has the capability to completely reject all off-frequency signals; therefore, all receivers are susceptible to being overloaded by nearby, strong off-frequency signals. These off-frequency signals can be within the license-free band (in-band interference), or they can be outside the band (out-of-band interference).

Overloading causes a receiver to become desensitized (to experience a reduced sensitivity) to the desired signals. The symptom of a desensitized receiver is a reduction in the receiving distance. Some receivers allow you to configure a higher receive threshold level. This feature enables you to intentionally reduce the sensitivity and therefore reduce the intensity of the overloading. This feature is similar to a "squelch" control on an FM two-way radio.

It can be difficult for you to compare receiver selectivity and to predict overload resistance because most manufacturers do not publish overload specifications. Keep the following general guidelines in mind as you evaluate wireless equipment:

- Wireless equipment that is designed for outdoor WAN use should be less susceptible to being overloaded when compared to indoor wireless LAN equipment.

- Wireless equipment that is designed for indoor LAN use is likely to be more susceptible to being overloaded when used outdoors.

- All wireless equipment might need to have an external bandpass filter added when there are one or more strong, nearby transmitters such as FM, AM, or television broadcast transmitters.

Multipath Resistance

Multipath fading is a fact of life at microwave frequencies. *Multipath* is caused when signal reflections cause several signals (echoes) to be received almost simultaneously. Equipment features that minimize the effects of multipath include the following:

- **Antenna diversity**—Antenna diversity helps minimize multipath by using two separate antennas. The antennas are separated from each other, and when the signal fades, one antenna receives a stronger signal than the other antenna. The receiver automatically selects the strongest antenna signal on each incoming packet, so fading is reduced.

- **Circular antenna polarization**—Circularly polarized antennas discriminate against multipath interference. Equipment that offers the option of using a circularly polarized antenna provides more protection against multipath compared to equipment without a circularly polarized antenna.

- **OFDM**—Equipment that uses orthogonal frequency division multiplexing modulation provides more immunity to multipath interference compared to non-OFDM equipment.

Multipath interference is worse in a physical environment where you find many obstacles that reflect wireless signals. The center of a city with many tall, flat, reflective metal building surfaces is a high multipath environment. If you plan to deploy wireless service in a high-multipath environment, use as many multipath-reduction features and techniques as possible.

Miscellaneous Interference Reduction Techniques

There are many sources of noise and interference besides multipath. The following miscellaneous features help reduce the distance-robbing effects of noise and interference:

- **Selectable antenna polarization**—Interference from other wireless systems is usually either vertically polarized or horizontally polarized. Equipment that allows you to select either vertical or horizontal polarization allows you to minimize interference from other systems by selecting polarization opposite to other, interfering networks.

- **Smart antenna technology**—Smart antennas enable the antenna pattern beamwidth to be automatically adjusted under software control. In this way, the antenna pattern can be automatically steered to minimize or avoid interference. Smart antenna technology is a relatively new technology that is just beginning to appear in license-free wireless WAN equipment.

- **Smart radio features**—Smart radio features include the radio's capability to automatically scan the available frequencies and to choose the frequency with the least amount of interference. Automatic power adjustment is another smart radio feature. The wireless equipment measures the strength and the quality of the received signal and adjusts the transmit power level up or down to maintain the desired link quality. Using only the amount of power needed minimizes the interference to other wireless systems.

Physical Layer Wireless Security Features

There are a number of physical layer wireless security features as well as many higher-layer security features. The following sections describe the main physical layer security features.

Antenna Pattern/Signal Strength

Although not immediately obvious, antenna directivity provides a certain measure of security. Unauthorized wireless users must physically position themselves in an area where a usable signal exists. This is another reason to carefully consider where you radiate your signal. Rather than broadcasting it everywhere, use directional antennas to radiate only into the areas where your end users are located.

Modulation Type

Like antenna directivity, modulation type is a not-so-obvious security feature. If a wireless network uses DSSS, a hacker must use the same DSSS modulation type. Likewise, if a network uses FHSS, a hacker must use FHSS. If a network uses another proprietary modulation type, an unauthorized user must use the same proprietary modulation type. Therefore, proprietary modulation types provide a higher level of physical layer security than 802.11b, for example.

Network ID (SSID, ESSID)

Several different logical networks can exist in the same physical space. Wireless packets contain a service set identifier (SSID), extended service set identifier (ESSID), or network ID to specify the logical network that a wireless station belongs to. The ESSID is a basic network security feature. If a wireless station does not possess the correct ESSID (or network ID), it cannot connect to a wireless network.

Miscellaneous Wireless Features

This section describes miscellaneous transmit and receive features. Although these features cannot be neatly classified into a specific section, their presence or absence can play a significant role in the performance of your wireless network operation; evaluate them carefully.

Miscellaneous Transmit Features

The following miscellaneous transmitter features can affect the design and performance of your wireless WAN:

- **Transmitter output power**—Most license-free wireless equipment is limited by Federal Communications Commission (FCC) regulations to one watt (+30 dBm) of transmitter output power. Available transmitter output power levels typically vary from 1 watt (1W) down to 200 mW, 100mW, 50 mW, and 30 mW.

TIP   The role of transmitter power in the successful operation of a wireless network is often misunderstood. Many people believe that more power is always better; however, this is not true in many cases. Your best approach is to transmit with only the amount of power that you need to cover your desired service area. Transmitting with too much power results in a transmitting range that is larger than your receiving range. This causes unnecessary interference to other networks. The owner of the other networks might then feel the need to retaliate with excessive transmitter power, which can lead to a cycle of escalation in which everyone loses.

- **Configurable transmitter power control**—A few models of wireless equipment allow you to configure the transmitter output power; however, for most wireless equipment, the power output is not configurable. Only one or two equipment models exist where the AP automatically configures the transmitter power of the end user nodes. The purpose of automatic power control is to use only the power needed for a reliable link. Avoiding the use of excessive power minimizes interference between the end user nodes.

Miscellaneous Receive Features

The following receive features affect the performance of your wireless WAN in many ways:

- **Receiver threshold**—A receiver starts working (receiving and decoding an incoming signal) when the signal reaches the receiver threshold level. Signals below the threshold are either not received or are received with numerous errors. Signals above the threshold are received with a low error rate. The low error rate allows the wireless link to deliver maximum throughput. If you are comparing two different receiver thresholds, the receiver with the lower threshold receives over a longer distance. For example, a receiver with a –85 dBm threshold is better than a receiver with a –80 dBm threshold.

NOTE   When comparing receiver thresholds, compare the threshold values at the same data rate. Comparisons at different data rates are invalid because as the data rate goes up, a receiver's threshold goes up. Stated another way, as the data rate goes up, the receiver becomes less sensitive.

- **Noise figure**—Receivers create noise in their circuitry. *Noise figure* refers to internal noise or the relative lack of internal noise created by the receiver. The lower the internal noise, the better a weak signal is received. A 3-dB noise figure is better than a 6-dB noise figure, for example.

Miscellaneous Transmit/Receive Features

The following features, when present, apply on both transmit and receive:

- **AP and bridge**—Some wireless APs can be used either as an AP (connecting to many end users) or as a bridge. An AP with bridging capability provides you with more network flexibility than an AP without the capability to work as a bridge.

- **AP and repeater**—Most APs can serve both as an AP and as a repeater at the same time.

- **Number of wireless ports**—Most wireless equipment has one wireless port. Some equipment has more than one wireless port. Multiport equipment can operate simultaneously on more than one frequency or more than one band. One example is an AP that has one 2.4-GHz and one 5-GHz wireless port.

- **External antenna connector**—Wireless WAN equipment must always be connected to an antenna that has LOS paths to the end users. Except in the case of CPE that has the radio integrated with the antenna, this means that the wireless equipment must have a connector for an external antenna. Equipment that is designed to be used indoors often lacks a connector for an external antenna.

- **Split (indoor/outdoor) hardware architecture**—Indoor/outdoor architecture splits the wireless hardware. The microwave part of the equipment is placed outdoors, near the antenna. The low-frequency part of the equipment is placed indoors. The two halves of the radio are connected with either coax or fiber. With a split architecture, coax cable losses between the microwave section and the antenna are almost eliminated, consequently improving the wireless performance.

- **Integrated antenna/radio**—With increasing frequency, wireless equipment (especially 802.11b) equipment is becoming available with the radio physically located inside the antenna. Integrated equipment has the same advantage as split-architecture equipment—eliminating transmission line losses to improve wireless performance. The connection from the antenna/radio to the end user network is made with Ethernet cable. Power-over-Ethernet (PoE) to the antenna and radio is provided using the nondata conductors in the Ethernet cable.

- **Multifrequency management commonality**—A few equipment vendors now offer a wireless equipment family that operates on different frequency bands but can be managed from a common management platform. This equipment provides management economies for those wireless ISPs that need to deploy wireless systems on different bands.

- **Antenna alignment aids**—Some equipment, especially split architecture or integrated antenna and radio equipment, provides visual or aural antenna alignment aids. These aids, typically a series of LEDs or an audible tone, help the installer align the antenna for the highest signal level without leaving the antenna location.

- **Availability of FCC-certified antenna systems**—Most equipment vendors provide at least one antenna system that is FCC-certified for use with the equipment. Some vendors provide a number of certified antenna systems. The more vendor-certified antenna systems are available, the more flexibility you have to use an antenna system that provides the service-area coverage that you need.

Data Link Layer Features

The sections that follow describe features that operate at the data link layer.

Bridging Features

Bridging takes place at the data link layer and is based on the MAC addresses of the end user equipment. The typical wireless bridge contains a table of MAC addresses and bridge ports. Packets are forwarded to the correct bridge port based on the MAC address table information. Your data link layer feature evaluation includes the following features.

MAC Address Table Size

The MAC address table of a wireless bridge is finite in size. The table might be large enough to contain one or two thousand MAC addresses or small enough to contain only one. In most cases, the MAC address table size is larger than the number of simultaneous end user connections.

Number of Simultaneous Connections

Each wireless AP or bridge is designed to connect to only a specific number of end users at the same time. In general, the more simultaneous users it supports, the higher the cost of the wireless bridge or AP.

TIP   Sometimes, an equipment vendor's advertising confuses the MAC address table size with the number of simultaneous end user connections. For example, an advertisement might state that one AP can support up to 1000 users. The ad might fail to mention that only 128 of the users can be connected at the same time. This type of error can be caused by an error on the part of the person preparing the advertisement. This person might be unclear about MAC address table size versus the number of simultaneous connections. If you see claims like this that appear to be excessive or too good to be true, ask the vendor to confirm that the advertised information is correct.

A wireless bridge is designed to support many wireless users, typically from 50 to several hundred. One special type of wireless bridge is called an *Ethernet converter.* Originally, an Ethernet converter was designed to bridge between one Ethernet port (on one computer) and a wireless WAN. Currently, Ethernet converters are available that support bridging between up to eight computers and the wireless WAN. This expanded Ethernet converter is called a *super Ethernet converter (SEC)*.

Spanning Tree Protocol

Most wireless point-to-point bridges implement the 802.3 Spanning Tree Protocol. In bridged networks, it is important to avoid routing loops (more than one simultaneous path). The 802.3 Spanning Tree Protocol senses the presence of routing loops and disables one route to avoid looping.

Switching

Wireless APs occasionally contain a built-in switch. The switch allows Ethernet connectivity from the AP to a number of Ethernet devices without needing to purchase an external switch.

Support for VLAN Tagging

Virtual LAN (VLAN) tagging allows the definition of a VLAN, as opposed to a geographically located LAN. Support for VLAN tagging allows the wireless device to support the operation of a VLAN.

MAC Sublayer Features

The MAC layer is a sublayer of the data link layer (Layer 2) in the OSI reference model. MAC features can be either standards-based or proprietary. In all cases, the primary purpose of the MAC sublayer is to provide reliable data delivery over the inherently noisy and collision-prone wireless medium. The MAC sublayer performs the following general functions:

- **Error control**—The MAC sublayer implements a frame-exchange protocol with an acknowledgment procedure. This procedure maximizes the chance that every packet is delivered error free across the wireless link.

- **Congestion management**—The MAC sublayer works to minimize congestion on the wireless medium. The MAC sublayer utilizes several methods to determine which station is allowed to gain access to the wireless medium. The 802.11b MAC specifications contain both a CSMA/CA contention-based access scheme and a polling-based access scheme. Most 802.11b equipment does not implement the polling feature.

- **Packet aggregation**— The MAC sublayer can maximize throughput by aggregating several small packets together into one larger packet. This reduces the number of times the wireless equipment must switch back and forth between receive and transmit (the switching time is also called the *turnaround time*), thereby making more time available to pass data traffic.

- **Data protection**—Encryption (in general) can take place at several different layers; however, WEP encryption takes place at the MAC level. 64-bit and 128-bit WEP encryption schemes are in common use.

Data Link Layer Security Features

The following sections analyze data link layer security features that might be offered by the equipment that you are evaluating.

MAC Address Access Control Lists

When providing wireless Internet access, it is desirable to deny access to any end user whose account is not current or who is not authorized to use your network. Most APs allow you to configure an access control list (ACL). Unless the ACL contains the specific MAC address of an end user, that end user will not be allowed to connect to the AP.

Protocol Filtering

Protocol filtering permits you to deny bridging based on the Layer 2 packet protocol. Protocols such as IPX, NetBEUI, DECNet, or AppleTalk can be denied.

MAC Address Pair Filtering

In bridged networks, it is occasionally desirable to provide filtering for specific address pairs. The filtering can either allow a connection between two specific MAC addresses, or it can deny a connection between two specific MAC addresses.

Authentication

Authentication is the process that a network uses to determine if an end user is allowed to connect to the network. Authentication schemes require an exchange of management frames between the authenticator (the network) and the end user who is requesting network access. Simple authentication schemes provide minimal security, whereas more complex schemes provide higher levels of security.

Several network layers are typically involved in the authentication process; however, because Layer 2 plays a prominent role, authentication is outlined here.

Open-system authentication is the least secure; it simply requires a station to identify itself to an AP and request that it be granted authentication.

A more secure authentication system is shared-key authentication using WEP. The shared key is distributed to all stations that are authorized to use the network. The stations use the shared key to respond to challenge text sent to them by the AP. If a station responds to the challenge text correctly, the AP grants network access.

A more secure authentication system is based on one of the 802.1x authentication types defined in the Extensible Authentication Protocol (EAP). EAP is defined in RFC 2284 and includes a number of different authentication methods. 802.1x requires using three entities:

- A supplicant (the station requesting authentication)
- The authenticator (typically the AP)
- The authentication server (such as a Remote Authentication Dial-In User Service [RADIUS] server)

EAP implementations typically allocate a new encryption key each time a wireless user begins a new session. A number of wireless vendors provide proprietary authentication features that are based on EAP and 802.1x. In the future, 802.11i wireless standards will likely evolve out of the current 802.1x standards.

Encryption

Sending an unencrypted packet over the air increases the chances that an unauthorized person could intercept and decode the packet. A variety of encryption schemes make it harder for this to occur. In addition to WEP encryption (already described), other available encryption schemes include the following:

- **Data Encryption Standard (DES)**—A 64-bit encryption standard with a user-selected encryption key.

- **Triple DES (3DES)**—Uses three 64-bit keys. The first key encrypts the data, the second key decrypts the data, and the third key re-encrypts the data.

- **Advanced Encryption Standard (AES)**—The most current U.S. Government-approved encryption standard. It uses a Rijndael (pronounced "rain-doll") algorithm with either a 128-bit, 192-bit, or 256-bit encryption key. AES requires a math coprocessor; therefore, it might not be compatible with existing 802.11b hardware. The upcoming 802.11i standard includes AES.

Data Link Layer Proprietary Security Features

Some currently available wireless products contain a combination of proprietary Layer 2 security features and industry-standard security. It is beyond the scope of this chapter to list these product combinations here; however, they include combinations of encryption, per-session key exchange, and frame authentication to provide high levels of security.

Network Layer Features

Routing takes place at the network layer. All wireless equipment currently available performs bridging; however, some models of wireless equipment also perform routing. Just as there is a wide range of routing features available with conventional (wired) routers, there is also a wide range of features available with wireless routers.

NOTE   Later in this chapter, there is an additional discussion of the advantages and disadvantages of selecting wireless equipment that includes routing.

Routing Features

The following sections contain descriptions of some of the routing protocols and features that are often available in wireless routers.

Static IP Routing

Every wireless router includes static IP routing. Static routing enables you to configure permanent IP routes.

Dynamic IP Routing

Some wireless routers include dynamic IP routing. These routers support one or more dynamic routing protocols. The most common of these supported protocols include the following:

- **Routing Information Protocol (RIP) v1 and v2**—RIP is an interior routing protocol. It is a distance-vector metric protocol that routes packets based on the number of routing hops needed to reach the destination. RIP is relatively easy to implement, but it does not take into account the bandwidth of each hop.

- **Open Shortest Path First (OSPF)**—OSPF is also an interior routing protocol. It is a link-state metric protocol. OSPF routes packets based on the shortest distance, the least delay, and the most bandwidth available to reach the destination.

Dynamic Host Configuration Protocol Server

A Dynamic Host Configuration Protocol (DHCP) server allows the allocation and reuse of IP addresses as end users need them. The DHCP server allocates an address when a DHCP client logs on. When the client logs off, the IP address is returned to the address pool, ready to be reused when another client logs on.

Network Address Translation

Like DHCP, Network Address Translation (NAT) expands the pool of usable IP addresses. NAT allows the use of a pool of private nonroutable IP addresses within a network. When IP traffic needs to be routed over the Internet, NAT translates the nonroutable addresses to an Internet-routable address.

Point-to-Point Protocol over Ethernet

Point-to-Point Protocol over Ethernet (PPPoE) allows an ISP to authenticate end users. Some wireless routers support PPPoE by passing PPPoE packets to the PPPoE server.

Bandwidth Management

Wireless equipment occasionally includes bandwidth management features. This allows the bandwidth available to and from each MAC or IP address to be throttled or limited to a specified level. This feature allows you to manage your total available bandwidth, to offer different service levels to different groups of end users, and to serve more end users. Some equipment allows end user bandwidth to be throttled at different speeds in different (downstream and upstream) directions.

NOTE   Some wireless routers allow you to allocate bandwidth based on either the IP address of the end user or the MAC address of the end user.

Quality of Service (QoS)

Quality of service functionality is not one, but a set of features that work together to prioritize different service levels for different users. One use, for example, is to prioritize the handling and thereby reduce the latency for voice over IP (VoIP) packets.

Roaming

Roaming is the ability of an end user to move from AP to AP within the same subnet while maintaining a network connection. 802.11b APs usually include roaming capabilities. The vast majority of wireless WANs provide service to fixed end user locations; therefore, roaming is not used. If you need to design or deploy a wireless WAN that includes roaming, you should evaluate the following:

- **Reassociation speed**—The length of time it takes for an end user to be switched from one AP to another.

- **Tunable parameters**—Any other AP parameters that are designed specifically to enable smooth roaming.

- **Compatibility issues**—AP-to-AP communication standards are not specified in 802.11b. If you anticipate building a network that supports roaming, you should plan to buy all of your APs from the same vendor.

Network Layer Security Features

The following network layer security features are often available on wireless routers.

IP Address Access Control Lists

Some wireless routers allow specific IP addresses to be included in an ACL. Addresses in the list can either be denied or allowed network access.

Firewalls

Wireless routers sometimes contain firewall features. These features allow traffic to flow outward from a local network to the Internet. Traffic flowing inward from the Internet to the local network is filtered or blocked.

Virtual Private Networks

Virtual private network (VPN) features include IP Security (IPSec) encryption capabilities and tunneling capabilities, such as the Point-to-Point Tunneling Protocol (PPTP).

Application Layer Features

Application layer features play a significant role in the network design, configuration, management, monitoring, and security of your wireless network.

Network Design

Many factors of network design, including terrain, distance, buildings, trees, and the presence of other networks, influence the design of your network. Sometimes, relatively expensive tools (such as spectrum analyzers) are needed to assist during the network design process. Sometimes, however, inexpensive tools are available to help you with network design.

Some wireless LAN equipment vendors include site survey utility software along with their wireless equipment. These usually display signal strength, noise level, signal-to-noise ratio (SNR), and signal quality information. Although these utilities are often designed for indoor use, they are useful to show you how well a signal from your AP is being received at different locations within your desired outdoor coverage area. These utilities are also useful for antenna alignment. Sometimes, low-cost (or free) hardware-specific utilities are available that function like a low-cost spectrum analyzer. Although these low-cost utilities do not have the full range of regular spectrum analyzer features, they do cover the entire 2.4-GHz band and show which channels are in use by other networks.

Network Management

Network management system (NMS) capabilities vary widely between different models of wireless equipment. Look for some of the following features:

- **Access method**—Methods used to access the NMS include serial port access, telnet access, generic Windows browser access, and proprietary Windows-based software. Generic browser access is probably the easiest method to use.

- **Wireless link statistics**—An NMS that provides statistics for each individual wireless link in a point-to-multipoint system is important to allow effective network monitoring. At a minimum, the following statistics should be available for each end user link and each AP: signal strength, noise level, and percentage of packets that need to be retransmitted.

- **Graphical usage statistics**—Make network management easier. You can identify light or heavy traffic patterns, perform usage-based billing based on either IP or MAC address, and see when bandwidth usage peaks.

- **Simple Network Management Protocol (SNMP)**—SNMP-based NMSs are fairly standard today. Some wireless equipment uses proprietary management software; however, many third-party management programs can manage SNMP-based systems.

- **Antenna-alignment utilities**—Generate wireless link traffic and allow the system administrator to see real-time statistics while turning the antenna to receive the highest signal.

- **Flood ping capability**—Floods a network with ping packet traffic. This test allows the system administrator to test the wireless link while simulating a traffic load.

Application Layer Security Features

The capability to interface with Remote Authentication Dial-In User Service (RADIUS) servers is possibly the most important Layer 7 security feature for wireless equipment.

Major Network Feature Decisions

Your network feature decisions have a major impact on the equipment that you choose to purchase and on the success and profitability of your wireless WAN. The following sections describe those decisions.

Market Versus Equipment Cost

The market that you choose to serve—commercial, residential, or some mixture of the two—largely determines the price range for the wireless equipment that you purchase, install, and resell. If you serve primarily residential users, you need to purchase lower-cost equipment. If you provide higher-value service by providing more bandwidth and additional value-added services to businesses, you can select higher-cost equipment with a larger feature set.

802.11b Compatibility—Yes or No?

If you choose to use 802.11b equipment for your wireless WAN, you gain some significant advantages and, at the same time, you face several disadvantages. The following sections discuss these advantages and disadvantages.

Advantages of 802.11b Compatibility

The advantages of using 802.11b equipment include the following:

- **Cost**—802.11b equipment is available at the lowest cost of any wireless equipment.

- **Availability**—802.11b equipment is widely available.

NOTE   At the time of this writing, 802.11a equipment that is operating in the 5-GHz U-NII bands (with bandwidths up to 54 Mbps) is beginning to become available. This equipment is currently designed for use in indoor LANs and not in outdoor WANs. Further product development might make outdoor versions available in the future.

Disadvantages of 802.11 Compatibility

The disadvantages of using 802.11b equipment outdoors include the following:

- **Security**—Although newer security mechanisms are being developed to supplement the current wired equivalent privacy (WEP) security, there is a somewhat greater chance of security being compromised because many people are familiar with 802.11b technology and more hacking tools are available.

- **Interference**—As more 802.11b APs are deployed, spectrum congestion and interference between wireless networks become more of an issue.

- **Support**—Most 802.11b equipment sold today is designed for low-cost in-home use. The level of vendor support for this equipment is likely to be low, especially when the equipment is used in an outdoor WAN environment. Vendors focus on supporting the equipment in its intended (indoor LAN) use and not in the outdoor WAN environment.

Bridged Versus Routed WANs

Every wireless WAN is interconnected with a wired network that includes routing. During the design phase of your wireless WAN, you need to determine how your WAN will interoperate with your wired network. Based on your determinations, you will select wireless equipment that either performs bridging only or that performs both bridging and routing. The following questions can help you decide whether to purchase wireless equipment with built-in routing or whether to use external routers (or perhaps, no routers):

- **IP-based network services**—What advanced IP-based network services are already provided in your existing wired network? What IP-based network services will you need to provide immediately over your wireless network when it is first placed into service? What additional IP-based services (such as voice-over-IP) will you want to offer later to your wireless network users?

- **Edge routing**—Relative to your existing core routers, where do you need edge routing? If edge routing is (or will soon be) needed, is it better to select wireless equipment that includes this routing functionality initially, or is it better to select wireless bridges and add external routers later between a customer's wireless bridge and their LAN?

- **Multiple wireless backbone links**—If you anticipate using multiple wireless backbone links to provide extended wireless area coverage, you are more likely to deploy routing within the wireless backbone. You might decide that selecting wireless equipment with built-in routing is more practical or economical than using external routers.

Backbone Feature Decisions

Your backbone supplies the bandwidth that your APs distribute wirelessly to your end users. The following sections describe some key decisions that you will make as you select backbone equipment.

Backbone Capacity

Your first backbone decision is to determine how much throughput you need. This throughput decision is affected by the following factors:

- **Market needs**—How much throughput do your markets require? A backbone link that serves businesses located in several cities needs to provide more throughput than a link that serves only one or two small residential areas.

- **Number of users**—The number of wireless end users and the nature of their needs determine the amount of throughput that your backbone needs to provide.

- **Simplex versus duplex backbone**—Backbone equipment can be either simplex or duplex. A duplex backbone can provide up to 50 percent more throughput than a simplex backbone. Duplex backbone costs are generally higher because a duplex link contains two complete transmitting systems and two complete receiving systems.

- **Overselling ratio**—Internet usage is bursty. Most Internet users use bandwidth intermittently; therefore, ISPs can oversell bandwidth knowing that not all users will be on all the time. The number of times that you resell the same bandwidth (your overselling ratio) affects the amount of backbone bandwidth that you need. Your ISP experience combined with your observation of the usage patterns on your network help you determine your best overselling ratio and your backbone bandwidth needs.

Wired Versus Wireless Backbone

If economical wired backbone connectivity is available at your wireless AP location, it makes sense for you to use that wired connectivity. If wired backbone connectivity is not available or if the cost is too high, a wireless distribution system is the logical choice.

License-Free Versus Licensed Backbone

After you choose to use a wireless backbone, it is important for you to evaluate and compare the cost and the bandwidth of licensed wireless backbone equipment with the cost and the bandwidth of license-free wireless backbone equipment.

The advantages of using a license-free wireless backbone are

- **Cost**—The cost is generally lower.
- **Availability**—Equipment is generally available more rapidly.
- **Licensing**—There is no licensing cost, licensing paperwork, or licensing delay.

The disadvantage of using a license-free wireless backbone is that interference from other license-free networks is a possibility, and it is your responsibility to ensure that license-free equipment does not interfere with licensed equipment.

Given these advantages and disadvantages, it makes sense to use a license-free wireless backbone if you are reasonably certain that interference levels (both from other networks and from your own network) will remain reasonably low.

Dedicated Versus Shared Backbone Bandwidth

Wireless backbone links can be either of the following:

- Dedicated to providing only backbone bandwidth.
- Shared between backbone bandwidth and last-mile bandwidth. Examples of shared bandwidth include mesh networks and 802.11b repeaters that both connect end users and provide backbone connectivity for other APs.

Heavy bandwidth demands at one AP can cause slow performance at other APs. If possible, try to avoid sharing wireless link bandwidth between backbone use and last-mile access use. If you choose to share backbone bandwidth, you might find it necessary to use additional routers throughout the backbone to allocate and manage the bandwidth demands.

AP Feature Decisions

The list that follows describes some of the key decisions that you need to make as you select your AP equipment:

- **Frequency band**—Your choice of frequency band is probably the most important equipment decision that you will make. The difference in wireless propagation characteristics and interference levels between the license-free bands means that a poor decision here might result in an unusable network. Before making this decision, you should review the propagation characteristics of each band (discussed earlier in this chapter). You should also perform a wireless site survey (see Chapter 4, "Performing Site Surveys") to determine potential interference levels on a frequency band before you select equipment for that band. The information in Chapter 8 can help you if you find high levels of interference.

- **NLOS environment**—If you are considering buying equipment that operates in an NLOS environment, you need to either rule out or verify the range claims that the equipment manufacturer has made. You can do this by visiting an ISP that has the equipment deployed in an NLOS environment that is similar (such as the same density of trees and the same type of obstructions) to yours.

- **Modulation type**—Your choice of modulation type (DSSS, FHSS, or proprietary) is an important factor in the ultimate success of your network. Choose a modulation type that is compatible with the level and the type of interference in your coverage area.

- **802.11b or proprietary**—Every organization needs to match its budget to its mission. If your budget is modest, the lowest-cost indoor 802.11b equipment might be your only choice. A somewhat larger budget allows you to choose higher-cost 802.11b equipment with expanded feature and management capabilities. An even larger budget allows you to choose from the full range of wireless equipment.

- **Hot spot use**—802.11b APs deployed for hot spot use should be 802.1x-capable to implement improved security and to interface to external authentication and accounting servers.

- **End user polling**—Some APs implement end user polling as an option to the 802.11b CSMA/CA and RTS/CTS collision-avoidance mechanisms. If you plan to serve more than about 25 busy end users from one AP, polling increases your network reliability and performance.

- **Bandwidth management**—A few APs contain a bandwidth management capability that allows you to set bandwidth for each end user link. If the AP that you choose does not include this feature, consider adding this capability with an external bandwidth manager.

- **Support**—Vendor support is important when your wireless customers are looking to you to provide reliable Internet service. Talk with other wireless network operators to assess the availability of driver and firmware upgrades, as well as the response time and quality of support from their equipment vendors.

CPE Feature Decisions

Price is often the top consideration in the selection of CPE. The competition between broadband DSL and cable Internet access providers has driven the cost of broadband service down. It can be difficult for broadband wireless companies to compete at these low price points. For this reason, wireless providers constantly seek to lower the cost of CPE. Business users usually understand that they need to pay for value received; in contrast, residential users often seek to pay little (or nothing) for their CPE. Try not to cut too many corners in seeking and deploying low-cost CPE. Although cost is important, it is more important to deploy reliable, supportable, and manageable networks. The following discussion can help you make these cost-benefit decisions:

- **Wireless card versus external radio-based CPE**—Traditionally, license-free broadband wireless equipment is mounted indoors with a coaxial cable running to the outdoor antenna. In the drive to minimize CPE costs, wireless IPSs often choose to install wireless network interface cards (NICs) in their customers' computers, rather than purchase full-size (and higher priced) wireless bridges or routers. If you choose to deploy NICs in customer computers as CPE, recognize that some customers might expect you to provide no-cost PC support indefinitely, and this can be a costly situation for you. Also, be aware that the software tools needed to adequately monitor the quality of the customers' connection might not be available. This, too, can increase your customer support costs and raise your costs above the level where you can make a reasonable profit.

- **Separate versus integrated radio and antenna**—An alternative to the traditional wireless model is the integrated radio and antenna model. To reduce CPE costs and installation costs, wireless ISPs are now using (wherever possible) integrated radio and antenna equipment. These integrated units combine the radio and the antenna into one plastic or fiberglass enclosure that is mounted outdoors in a location with an LOS path to the AP. The integrated unit connects to the end user PC or network through either an Ethernet cable or, in a few cases, through a universal serial bus (USB) connection. The wireless performance is better because there is no coaxial cable loss between the antenna and the radio.

- **Split radio architecture**—There is one additional equipment configuration for you to evaluate: the split architecture. Split architecture actually divides the wireless unit into two physical pieces: an indoor section and an outdoor section. The indoor section contains the lower-power, lower-frequency circuits. The outdoor section contains the higher-power, higher-frequency circuits and mounts just below the antenna. Split architecture provides the benefits of the integrated radio and antenna architecture but also allows a greater choice of antennas because the antenna and radio are not built into one unit. Split architecture is often the most expensive configuration; however, it might be the best in terms of both performance and flexibility.

Wireless Network Card Decisions

If you decide to deploy wireless 802.11b cards as the customer CPE or if wireless cards plug into the AP that you are using, you must evaluate the following wireless card characteristics:

- **Transmitter**—Outlined earlier in this chapter; wireless cards share these same characteristics. The key characteristic is transmitter power output. The ideal transmitter would have a power output of 100 to 200 mW with a software-configurable power level.

- **Receiver characteristics**—Also outlined earlier, the better the receiver sensitivity (when combined with good selectivity), the better your wireless system performance will be.

- **External antenna connector**—An antenna is the key element in any wireless system. A wireless card needs to have a connector that allows an external antenna to be attached.

- **Form factor**—The most frequently used wireless card form factor is PCMCIA; however, other form factors are sometimes used. These other form factors include industry-standard architecture (ISA), peripheral component interconnect (PCI), and Compact Flash (CF).

Mesh Network Feature Decisions

You can evaluate mesh network equipment using the same considerations that you do for all other wireless equipment. Keep the following differences in mind, however:

- **Network deployment process**—Deploying a mesh network is different from deploying a point-to-multipoint network. Every mesh network node serves as a repeater and relay point for other network nodes. Nodes that are located farther away from the Internet connection must be relayed through closer network nodes. Before distant nodes can be deployed, nodes must be deployed closer to the Internet node. To provide coverage to an entire geographical area, the area must be *seeded*. Some nodes must be installed initially even if no end user is available to pay for the cost of the node.

- **Bandwidth and throughput limitations**—Mesh networks share backbone bandwidth with last mile bandwidth, which can reduce the amount of bandwidth to each end user. Be sure to factor this throughput limitation into your evaluation process and into your business plans.

- **Maximum hop limitations**—The multihop nature of mesh networks increases network latency and reduces network throughput. You will be limited to a maximum number of hops, so be sure to factor this limitation into your business plan.

Wireless Equipment Environmental Decisions

Remember environmental considerations when evaluating wireless equipment:

- **Operating temperature range**—All wireless equipment is designed to operate correctly between certain specified temperatures. Indoor equipment is designed to operate within a narrower temperature range than outdoor equipment. If you choose to use indoor equipment outdoors, be sure to provide cooling for it in the summer. In severe winter climates, it might also be necessary to add a heat source to keep the equipment warm.

- **Radio frequency (RF) immunity**—Many models of broadband wireless equipment are not designed to be used in a high-level RF environment. For example, locating a wireless LAN AP designed for home use in the equipment vault of a mountaintop transmitter site can lead to operating failures. The high-power transmitter energy can either come down the antenna cable and overload the AP receiver, or the energy can pass through the plastic case of the AP and disrupt the AP operation. If you plan to deploy equipment like this, plan to use an external bandpass filter in the antenna system. Also plan to mount the AP in a shielded and grounded metal equipment case. As an alternative, you can select equipment designed for high-RF environments. This equipment is usually designed for mounting in a standard 19-inch metal equipment rack.

Wireless Amplifier Feature Decisions

Wireless network operators often add external bidirectional amplifiers to their wireless systems. *External* means that the amplifier is external to the wireless equipment. Bidirectional amplifiers actually contain two amplifiers: one to amplify the transmitter signal and one to amplify the incoming received signals.

In the United States, FCC regulations require that external power amplifiers be marketed and sold only as part of a complete legally certified radio-cable-amplifier-antenna combination. The purpose of this regulation is to minimize the use of illegal overpowered equipment. Excess transmitter power raises the noise level, increases interference, and makes it harder for other, legal networks to operate correctly. Unfortunately, some wireless WAN operators ignore this regulation and intentionally use external power amplifiers in violation of FCC regulations. This behavior can result in heavy fines and equipment confiscation and also decreases the usability of the license-free bands for everyone.

NOTE   Illegal amplifier use is not the answer to making your WAN operate over longer distances. Often, a power amplifier actually decreases the receiving range of your WAN. In addition, using illegally high transmitter power causes substantial interference to other network operators who are operating legally. Finally, if illegal amplifier use increases, the FCC might be forced to step in with new, more restrictive regulations that could reduce license-free operating privileges for everyone. Resist the urge to amplify. Proper wireless network design and proper antenna system design provides you with the best network performance.

The following sections explain how external amplifiers work and how to use these amplifiers properly.

Transmit Amplification

On transmit, an external amplifier increases the transmitter power that reaches the antenna. This is useful when the power output of the transmitter is low and the cable length between the wireless equipment and the antenna system is long. Without an amplifier placed at the antenna, the high cable loss results in little signal reaching the antenna.

Here is an example of the correct way to use an amplifier. Start with a transmitter that has an output of 50 mW (+17 dBm). If the antenna cable has a loss of –14 dBm, the power reaching the antenna system is (+17 dBm – 14 dBm) = 3 dBm (2 mW). This is a low level of transmit power. If an amplifier with +14 dB of gain is added at the antenna, the +3 dBm that reaches the amplifier is amplified by +14 dB, resulting in a total of (3 dBm + 14 dB) +17 dBm (50 mW) reaching the antenna. The amplifier has added back the power that was lost in the antenna cable.

Receiver Amplification

On receive, an external amplifier mounted at the antenna performs two functions:

- It helps to overcome the signal loss that occurs in the antenna cable.
- It sets the SNR of the receiving system.

These two functions can lead to a small improvement in receiver performance if the amplifier has a good, low-noise design. In addition, a properly designed antenna should be used with the amplifier. If the antenna system design is poor, the amplifier can actually reduce the receiving range of the system.

Up/Down Converters

Up/down converters translate wireless signals from one frequency band to another. If the 2.4-GHz band is crowded in your area and the 5.8-GHz band is less crowded, you might want to use a 2.4-to-5.8 converter. Here is how this works. Each AP and end user station is equipped with a converter. Then, the following occurs:

- During transmit, each 2.4-GHz transmit signal is upconverted (translated up in frequency) to the 5.8-GHz band.

- During receive, the 5.8-GHz signal from the other station is downconverted to the 2.4-GHz band.

Using lower-cost 2.4-GHz equipment, communication actually takes place on the less crowded 5.8-GHz band. The advantage of this approach is that it usually costs less than buying more expensive equipment for 5.8 GHz. The disadvantage of this approach is that only a few manufacturers supply frequency converters, so your choice is limited. Converters need to be mounted at the antenna.

Compatibility Issues

Several compatibility issues can reduce the reliability of your network and consume troubleshooting time. If you are deploying an 802.11b network, never assume that different brands of wireless cards and wireless APs will work reliably together. Even hardware that is wireless fidelity (WiFi)-certified sometimes has firmware, software, operating system, and feature differences that can result in certain equipment combinations that do not work together. In most cases, equipment manufacturers do not cause these issues intentionally. There have, however, been a few instances in which large equipment vendors have intentionally created incompatibilities to boost the sales of their equipment and hinder the sale of lower-cost competitive equipment.

Watch for the folowing incompatibility issues:

- **Operating system software**—New features might not work with older software versions, or older features might not work in newer software versions. This situation can require that you upgrade all your wireless equipment software simultaneously.

- **NIC firmware**—Upgrades might have features that do not work even though they did work in earlier versions. NIC firmware might work when matched with older versions of AP software but not with upgraded AP software versions.

- **MAC incompatibilities**—Different brands of equipment that should work together do not work together or some of the features do not work.

- **NIC drivers**—Drivers might not be available for your OS or, if available, they might not be upgraded to work with newer versions of your OS.

- **USB**—There might be incompatibilities between wireless USB devices and certain PC operating systems.

- **Network management**—Network management software and diagnostics software can be unavailable or can be limited in their capability to manage mixed-equipment networks.

- **Timing**—Equipment that has timing designed for indoor (several hundred foot) distances might not work outdoors at longer (several mile) distances.

Here are some of the things that you can do to minimize the loss of time and money caused by these incompatibilities:

- **Standardize**—As much as possible, standardize on one brand of equipment for your APs and your CPE. Minimize the mixing and matching of different wireless equipment brands that talk to the same AP. Using a different brand of equipment is fine for wireless backhaul links; however, the fewer types of AP/CPE equipment that you use, the more efficiently you will be able to support that equipment and the more reliable your service will be.

- **Test time**—Be sure to plan for enough test time between the time that you build an AP and the time that you begin service from that AP. The more dissimilar your equipment, the more test time you need.

Wireless Support Issues

The quality of support from wireless vendors varies widely and ranges from excellent to none. In addition, technology changes rapidly; new software, new hardware, new firmware, and new drivers constantly become available. To maximize your chances of receiving effective support, do the following:

- **Research**—During your equipment research process, be sure to visit other organizations that have deployed the equipment you are considering. Ask the organizations to comment about the quality of vendor support they are receiving, including warranty support.

- **Realistic approach**—There still is no free lunch. Be realistic with your support expectations. You deserve to be notified by your vendor when equipment problems are discovered. You should rightfully expect that your vendor would not discontinue support for equipment that you have purchased; however, after your warranty period has expired, it is not unreasonable for a vendor to charge for software upgrades or new and improved hardware. Expect to pay a reasonable amount to receive a high level of continuing vendor support. You need your equipment vendor to make a profit so that it will continue to be there when you need it.

- **Support groups**—A number of online support groups are available for specific brands of wireless equipment. Find a discussion group for your equipment and join it, if possible, even before you purchase your equipment. You, your end users, and the entire industry will benefit from this helpful and friendly sharing of information.

Review Questions

1 Why is it important to visit an actual deployment site before you purchase wireless equipment?

2 The electromagnetic waves that we call wireless exist at what layer of the seven-layer OSI reference model?

3 How is a packet like a hamburger sandwich?

4 Why does a wireless network need a big MAC?

5 Wireless bandwidth and wireless throughput are the same thing. True or false?

6 The communications range under NLOS conditions is about the same as the communications range under LOS conditions. True or false?

7 DSSS equipment hops from frequency to frequency. True or false?

8 Other things being equal, the higher the data rate, the shorter the communications distance. True or false?

9 If you start receiving interference from another network, the best thing to do is to get an amplifier. True or false?

10 Any 802.11b equipment works with any other 802.11b equipment. True or false?

CHAPTER 7

Installing Outdoor Wireless Systems

The correct installation of outdoor wireless systems is vital to reliable network operation. In broad terms, the three stages of successful installation are as follows:

- Planning and preparation
- Installation
- Testing and verification

This chapter provides information and guidance for you as you plan and install your outdoor wireless equipment and antenna systems.

Preparing for Outdoor Wireless Installations

Successfully installing outdoor wireless equipment requires, more than anything, a consistent and efficient installation process. That process includes the following components.

Planning

Plan your installation process to be as consistent as possible from installation site to installation site. Installations should be as similar to each other as possible. Try to use the same:

- **Wireless equipment**—Have one or two basic customer premises equipment (CPE) packages (such as one package for a single-PC end user and one package for a multiple-PC end user). The fewer end user packages, the lower your inventory and support costs.

- **Cable**—Use only a few types of cable. One type could be 0.4-inch (1 cm) diameter coax and the second type could be outdoor Category 5 (Cat5) Ethernet cable. Using fewer cable types reduces your inventory, tool, training, and connector costs.

- **Antennas**—Use only a few CPE antenna packages. Package 1 might be a +8-dBi panel antenna for end users within 1 mile (1.6 km) of your access point, package 2 might be a +14-dBi panel antenna for users within two miles (3.2 km) of your access point, and package 3 might be a +21-dBi parabolic antenna for end users located between 2 miles (3.2 km) and 5 miles (8 km) from your access point.

- **Test techniques**—Use one test technique to verify the performance of your point-to-point links. Repeat the same basic test at various locations throughout the coverage area of each point-to-multipoint sector that you install. Several suggested tests are described at the end of this chapter.

- **Documentation**—Use the same access-point documentation process (and documentation paperwork) for each access-point sector that you install. Use the same CPE documentation process for each customer installation.

Collaboration

In a perfect world, 100 percent of the installation details would be decided during the site survey process, well in advance of the actual installation. The actual world is still a few percentage points short of being perfect (quite a few points short, actually); therefore, installers often find that they need to make some installation decisions during the actual installation process. The installer must become a collaborator with the person who performed the site survey (perhaps you are one and the same person) and constructively contribute to fill in the details that the person performing the site survey did not address.

Safety Training

Safety training is required for all installation personnel. The training should cover all the following:

- **Height awareness**—This includes heights and the possibility of being injured or disabled by working above the ground.

- **Tower safety**—If your company expects you to do tower work, it should train you in tower climbing techniques and tower rescue techniques.

- **Government regulations**—These are Federal and State Occupational Safety and Health Administration (OSHA) rules and regulations.

- **Personal protection equipment**—Hats, boots, eye protection, gloves, sunscreen, radiation monitors, and other personal protection equipment are all essential.

- **Hoisting techniques**—This involves using ladders, ropes, and pulleys safely.

- **Microwave safety techniques**—This involves avoiding the injury caused by excessive exposure to microwave radiation from antenna systems.

- **Weather restrictions**—The weather conditions should cause you to stop working and take shelter. You should stop work and go inside when it is raining, snowing, lightning, and when there are high winds.

Availability and Use of Proper Tools

The proper tools (portable drills, hand tools, ladders, ropes, buckets, safety equipment, and so on) need to be available to all installation personnel. In addition, training needs to be provided in the safe and skillful use of all tools. Managers are responsible for both providing the necessary tools and verifying that training has been completed.

Professional Work Attitude

A professional installer does more than just collaborate with the person who performed the site survey. He interacts with many people and needs to possess and to express the following:

- **Positive attitude**—A constructive, positive, can-do approach to solving the problems that can occur during installation
- **Personal interaction skills**—The ability and willingness to work in a respectful, helpful, and friendly fashion with customers, facility managers, installation crewmembers, other trades people, city employees, and others who are involved in various aspects of the installation process
- **Responsibility**—A willingness to accept responsibility for the successful completion of each installation job
- **Attentiveness**—The ability to remain focused on the details of the job, the dynamics of personal interaction, and the adherence to safe work practices and habits

Verifying the Installation Documentation

A site survey, properly performed in advance of installation, should supply you with all the information shown in Table 4-2 of Chapter 4, "Performing Site Surveys." This information is summarized here:

- **Equipment location**—The location where the main wireless equipment will be located.
- **Antenna mounting location**—The location and the mounting method for the antenna system.
- **Antenna alignment information**—The antenna direction and the uptilt or downtilt angle, if any.
- **Cabling details**—The cable type, route, and building entry point.
- **Grounding location**—The grounding wire type, route, and ground connection point location.

- **Equivalent Isotropic Radiated Power (EIRP) calculation**—The equivalent power that will be radiated from the antenna. You need to recalculate this level and verify that the Federal Communications Commission (FCC) power limits will not be exceeded. See Tables 6-1, 6-2, and 6-3 in Chapter 6, "Evaluating and Selecting Wireless Equipment," for a summary of the legal power levels. Table 7-1 provides several examples of EIRP calculations for point-to-multipoint systems.

Table 7-1   *Equivalent Isotropic Radiated Power Examples*

Transmitter Output Power Level	Power Gain or Loss	Resulting Power Level	Antenna Gain	Resulting EIRP	Legal? (Yes or No)
1 Watt (+30 dBm)	3 ft (1 m) of small diameter coax with a total of –1 dB of loss	+29 dBm	Antenna with a gain of +6 dBi	+35 dBi	Yes
100 mW (+20 dBm)	Amplifier with a gain of +14 dB	+34 dBm	Antenna with a gain of +8 dBi	+42 dBi	No
25 mW (+14 dBm)	Amplifier with a gain of +14 dB	+28 dBm	Antenna with a gain of +8 dBi	+36 dBi	Yes

Installing Tower-Mounted Antenna Systems

Only properly trained personnel should perform tower work. If your company chooses not to train its employees to perform this work, it needs to contract this work to properly trained and properly insured antenna installers. The contracted installers should use proper climbing and hoisting tools to safely install, repair, or modify your tower-mounted antennas. If your company chooses to obtain tower training for you, your training needs to teach you the proper tools, techniques, and practices to use when you install tower-mounted antenna systems.

The goal of antenna system installation is to safely install the proper antenna (the antenna with the correct directivity, gain, wind-loading, and appearance) high enough off the ground to provide a reliable line-of-sight (LOS) signal path. The antenna must remain in the air, weatherproofed, and pointed in the proper direction indefinitely. The wireless equipment, all other connected equipment, and all nearby people and buildings must also be protected from lightning damage, physical damage, and injury.

Working in High-RF Environments

Installers who do antenna installation work on pre-existing towers have one advantage and one disadvantage when compared to installers who do only nontower antenna installation work. The advantage is that tower antenna installers do not usually have to worry about installing the tower. Tower installation includes designing the tower, digging a hole for the base, installing the base and the guy-wire anchors, erecting the tower sections, installing the guy wires, and installing the tower grounding system.

The disadvantage that tower antenna installers have to face is that they often must work in high-intensity radio-frequency (RF) environments. High RF environments include commercial AM, FM, and television broadcast station transmitting sites. In environments like this, it is necessary to protect both the wireless equipment and the installation personnel.

Microwave Radiation Won't Kill You...Immediately

Sometimes, you might need to work in high RF environments such as building rooftops with transmitting antennas for five or ten different wireless services. When you work in these environments, you need to take the same precautions to protect yourself that tower personnel must take.

Protecting Your Personal Safety

The long-term health effects of exposure to high and low levels of microwave radiation are not fully known or understood. Controversy will probably continue for a number of years until we (human guinea pigs) can say conclusively that exposure to microwave radiation is (or is not) harmful to our health. Until more is known, you should practice prudent avoidance. This means that you should act to be aware of sources of RF radiation and intentionally limit any and all unnecessary exposure to RF energy. Following are some ways to do this:

- Use external antennas on wireless devices (such as wireless cards in your laptop or your customer's laptop) whenever possible.

- Keep as much distance as possible between yourself and transmitting antennas. Do not get in front of a directional transmitting antenna when the transmitter is on.

- Turn off all transmitters when you are not using them. (This includes cell phones; they transmit even when you are not making a call.)

- If you work in a wireless lab, use a nonradiating "dummy load" whenever possible during the testing of wireless transmitting equipment.

- Use a headset on your cell phone; then place the cell phone as far as possible away from your body.

- Avoid making fun of people (like me) who tell you that exposure to wireless energy can cause health risks. Sure, health nuts like me could turn out to be wrong, but on the other hand, are you willing to bet the health of your unborn children on it? Now, please... Turn off your pocket or belt-carried cell phone when it doesn't absolutely need to be on. (The world won't end if you pick up your cell phone messages from voicemail every 30 minutes.) Play it safe.

Monitor and limit your exposure to high RF levels. Personal RF monitors are available that can be worn on your belt. These monitors provide an audible warning when RF levels exceed safety thresholds. Some products also continuously log RF exposure levels.

If your job responsibilities require you to work regularly in high-RF environments, your safety tools should include a personal RF monitor, and your company's safety program should include both RF safety training and RF exposure-level monitoring.

If your personal monitor indicates that your RF exposure is too high, you might need to request that one or more transmitters be scheduled to be turned off long enough for you to complete your installation work.

Protecting the Wireless Equipment

Just as humans might be injured by exposure to high levels of wireless energy, wireless equipment can also be damaged, either temporarily or permanently. Wireless equipment that is installed in high-RF locations needs to be protected with bandpass filtering. Bandpass filtering attenuates (reduces) the level of out-of-band RF energy and protects wireless receivers from being overloaded and desensitized, with a corresponding decrease in their ability to receive weak signals.

Tower Equipment-Mounting Scenarios

Most of the time when you need to do a tower-mounted antenna and equipment installation, you are installing access point (AP) equipment rather than CPE equipment. Figure 7-1 illustrates the three typical AP equipment-mounting configurations, which are as follows:

- Mounting the wireless equipment inside and the antenna system outside (Figure 7-1a).
- Mounting the wireless equipment outside, below the antenna, on the tower (Figure 7-1b).
- Mounting the wireless equipment inside of the antenna itself. This configuration is coming into wider use, especially for CPE (Figure 7-1c).

Figure 7-1   *Inside/Outside Equipment-Mounting Configurations*

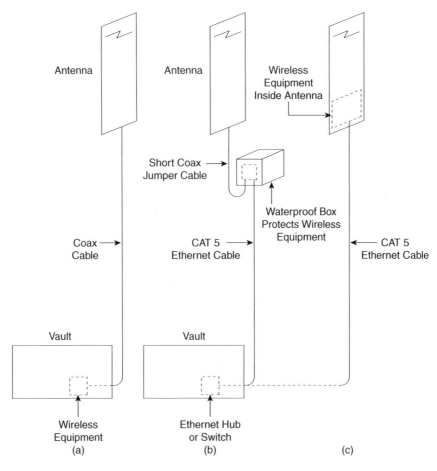

Mounting Wireless Equipment Inside

At submicrowave frequencies (below 1000 MHz), wireless equipment is traditionally mounted inside the building or inside a special equipment shelter (vault or hut). Coax cable then runs outside, up the tower, and to the antenna. The wireless equipment is inside, protected from the weather, and accessible for maintenance and servicing. The only disadvantage of mounting the equipment inside is the transmit signal that is lost in the coax cable running from the equipment to the antenna and the receive signal that is lost in the coax running from the antenna to the equipment. At submicrowave frequencies, this is not a serious problem; however, in the license-free microwave frequency bands, this signal loss becomes high.

Mounting Wireless Equipment on the Tower

In the 2.4 GHz and 5 GHz license-free bands, wireless equipment is often mounted outside to overcome the high coaxial cable signal loss. The wireless equipment is mounted as close to the antenna system as possible—normally on the tower, just below the antenna. The equipment is connected to the antenna with a short (3 ft or 1 m) jumper cable. A variation of this configuration is to mount the wireless equipment inside the wireless antenna. The nonwireless equipment port is connected to the network equipment (inside, on the ground) with outdoor-rated CAT5 Ethernet cable.

Installing Rooftop-Mounted Antenna Systems

Most of your installation work consists of installing rooftop-mounted antenna systems at customer locations, both businesses and residences. The installation includes the following steps:

1 Building a base on the roof for the antenna mast

2 Installing and waterproofing the antenna

3 Attaching the cable and weatherproofing the connection

4 Raising the mast and aiming the antenna

5 Running the cabling to the equipment

6 Installing lightning protection, including grounding the mast and cable

7 Testing the completed installation

8 Documenting both the installation and the testing results

The following sections provide more detail in each of these areas.

Building the Roof-Mounted Antenna Base

All roof-mounted antenna masts need a base that holds them in place. Ideally, the mast base should be a nonpenetrating type; no holes should be drilled in the roof to mount or secure the base. A nonpenetrating base prevents leaks in the roof caused by imperfectly sealed nails or screws.

NOTE   If you use a wall-mounted mast or a small dish-type antenna mount, you can disregard this antenna-base section. Use the appropriate wall-mounting hardware to attach your antenna mount to the wall.

Several commercial mast bases are available; however, most installations can be done using a base that you can build yourself. This lowers the overall cost of the installation. To build your own flat-roof base, use two 5-ft lengths of pressure-treated 4 × 4 lumber and do the following:

1 Raise the two 4 × 4 pieces of lumber individually to the roof and place them in a T shape. Connect them using one T-shaped bracket and two right angle brackets, as shown in Figure 7-2. Align the stem of the T to point toward the edge of the roof and toward the far end of the wireless link.

Figure 7-2   *Building a Flat-Roof Mast Base*

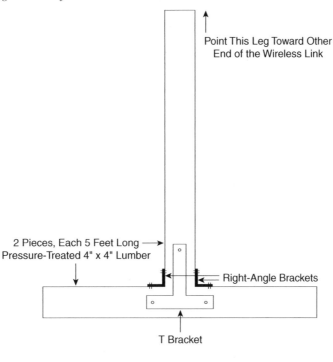

Top View

TIP   If you need to mount an antenna base over the peak of a roof instead of on a flat roof, you can still use the wooden T base. Cut the leg of the T and position the cut over the peak of the roof. Use a right-angle bracket (hammer it slightly flat to match the angle of the peak) to connect the two cut pieces.

---

2 Place a 5-ft tall tripod on top of the center of the base. Move it around until each of the three legs of the tripod is centered on top of one of the three legs of the base. Use one or two 1.5-inch (4 cm) large-diameter hex head screws to attach each of the tripod feet to the wood base.

3 Remove the screw holding the tripod leg that points toward the other end of the wireless link. Hinge the tripod down until it is horizontal on the roof.

4 Insert the mast completely into the tripod, and then place a tool bucket (or other object) underneath the mast to support it in a position raised approximately 15 degrees from horizontal.

Installing the Antenna

When your mast base is prepared and your mast installed, you are ready to attach and connect your antenna. Do this as follows:

1 Lightly tighten the tripod screws so that they keep the mast from rotating inside the tripod.

2 Extend the top section of the mast just enough to make room to attach the antenna onto the top section of the mast. Attach the antenna to the mast and tighten the antenna hardware well so that the antenna will not turn on the mast in a strong wind.

3 Install any mast-mounted equipment such as amplifiers or frequency converters on the mast, just below the antenna. If you need to mount nonwaterproof equipment on the mast (such as indoor CPE or a bandpass filter) you can use an appropriate National Electrical Manufacturer's Association (NEMA) box. NEMA boxes are waterproof and prevent moisture from rain or snow from damaging the equipment. Larger hardware stores should have several sizes available.

4 Attach the cable to the antenna. If you are using mast-mounted equipment, connect the cable to the equipment and connect a short coax jumper between the equipment and the antenna.

Waterproofing the Connections and the Equipment

Because water runs downward, you should, whenever possible, mount the equipment in a position that places the connectors on the bottom. This reduces their exposure to rain and snow. The suggestions in the sections that follow will be helpful as you complete your waterproofing.

Using Drip Loops

Make a drip loop just before the point where each cable connector attaches to an antenna and to any piece of mast-mounted equipment. A drip loop extends below the connector/equipment junction and prevents water from running down the cable and into the equipment. Figure 7-3 shows a drip loop.

Figure 7-3   *Drip Loop*

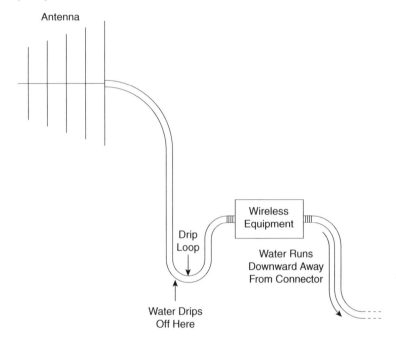

Applying Waterproofing

Several products and product combinations can effectively seal outdoor cable connectors. Regardless of which product you standardize on, to use it effectively, you must "think like water." This means that you must be extremely observant and notice every method by which water could enter your antenna system. Water can find the tiniest pinhole in your cable, connectors, outdoor amplifiers, frequency converters, lightning arrestors, and filters. Water can also enter any antenna that is not correctly designed or sealed. You can use any of the following products to make your connections watertight:

- **Cold-shrink tubing**—Cold-shrink tubing is placed around the connector joint. The cold-shrink tube string is pulled and the tube shrinks around the joint, sealing it.

- **Heat-shrink tubing**—Heat-shrink tubing is placed around the joint and shrinks around the joint when it is heated with a heat gun or a propane torch.

- **Self-galvanizing tape**—Self-galvanizing tape is wrapped around the joint and stretched as it is wrapped. It chemically bonds to itself, forming a waterproof layer. Wrap the tape in the direction that tightens the connector, not in the direction that loosens it.

- **Coax-seal**—Coax-seal is not a tube or a tape; it is semisticky, like a ball of tar. It is formed all around the joint, covering it and keeping out moisture. It remains semisoft so that the connection can be checked or changed in the future.

Cold-shrink, heat-shrink, self-galvanizing tape, and coax-seal all generally seal a joint without the use of additional tape or sealer; however, one or more layers of high-quality black electrical tape is often used as a final outer wrap over the top as an additional moisture-barrier. Black electrical tape is sometimes placed underneath the other products to make it easier to remove the other tape or tube if the joint ever needs to be reworked. See Appendix B, "Wireless Hardware, Software, and Service Provider Organizations," for information about suppliers of these products.

Outdoor wireless equipment and outdoor antennas are designed to be weatherproof. Does this mean that they are always perfectly waterproof? Usually they are, but it is wise to examine them closely and to add a light coat of a liquid sealer over any area where it appears that water could enter. Be especially careful to seal around case-mounted ground lugs and along the edge of any equipment case that lacks obvious gaskets. One liquid sealant that is often used is Scotchcoat, which is available in the electrical department of most large hardware stores.

TIP   Scotchcoat can seep out through the threads around the top of its own can. If you use Scotchcoat, carry the can vertically inside a slightly larger, empty metal can. The larger can will contain any Scotchcoat that seeps out of the original can. Carry both cans vertically because if either can falls over on its side, the Scotchcoat will seep out.

Although outdoor antennas are designed to be waterproof, there are occasional reports of antennas that have design or material flaws that allow water to enter the antenna and degrade performance. Apply sealant around any antenna seam that appears to have less than a 100 percent waterproof factory seal.

Antennas frequently have a drain hole that is designed to face downward and to allow any moisture that condenses inside the antenna to drain out. Be especially careful *not* to seal this drain hole. Mount the antenna in a position that allows any drain hole to face downward. To prevent antenna failure due to water, restrict yourself to using only antennas that you have successfully tested outdoors over a period of time. After you have used an antenna in varying weather conditions, you will have first-hand knowledge about the antenna's reliability. You can stop using models that prove to be unreliable.

Attaching the Guy Wires

Any pushup mast with an antenna that extends more than 5 ft (1.5 m) above the top of the tripod (or other mast attachment point) should have at least one set of guy wires installed. The guy wires

- Keep the antenna from moving in the wind and causing the signal to fade
- Keep the wind from blowing the mast over and possibly causing damage or injury

Guy wires attach to the mast with guy wire rings that come with the mast. Guy wires attach to the building with anchor hooks arranged every 120 degrees around the mast. The distance from the mast base to each anchor hook should be a minimum of 80 percent of the height of the mast. For example, the anchor hooks for a 30-ft (9 m) mast should be at least 24 ft (7.3 m) from the base of the mast. Place one turnbuckle in each guy wire. The turnbuckle allows you to adjust the tension on each guy wire. A 30-ft pushup mast might need up to three sets of guy wires, depending on the extended height of the mast. Use the following guidelines to determine how many sets of guy wires your mast needs:

- If the extended height is 10 ft (3 m) to 13 ft (4 m), use one set of three guy wires attached to the mast 9 ft (2.7 m) above the base.
- If the extended height is 16 ft (5 m) to 20 ft (6 m), use one set of guy wires attached 10 ft (3 m) above the base and a second set attached 2 ft (61 cm) below the antenna.
- If the extended height is from 25 ft (7.6 m) to 30 ft (9 m), use one set of guy wires 10 ft (3 m) above the base, a second set at 20 ft (6 m), and a third set attached 2 ft (61 cm) below the antenna.

Precut the guy wires to the approximate length needed and attach all of them to the mast while the mast is still horizontal on the roof. Run the lower end of each guy wire loosely through its corresponding guy wire anchor. This way, the guy wire is already in place when it is time to fasten it permanently through the guy anchor and tighten the turnbuckle.

Raising the Antenna and Mast

Raising the antenna mast with the antenna already installed and the cable running down the mast can be a physical challenge.

WARNING   The only way to raise a 20 or 30-ft (6 - 9m) mast safely is by using at least a two-person crew. Do not attempt to raise a mast working alone.

Safety awareness must be everyone's highest priority in the installation crew. An antenna mast that falls on a person can cause a serious, painful, crippling injury. The following section describes how to raise a 30-ft (9 m), three-section pushup mast from 10 ft (3 m) up to the full height of 30 ft (9 m). Raise the mast and antenna by doing the following:

1 With the mast extended just 10 ft (3 m), both installers should raise the tripod and mast to the vertical position. Insert a screw through the third leg of the tripod and attach this screw into the wood base. Refer to the antenna alignment information in your site survey documentation and note the direction that the antenna needs to point. Rotate the mast until the antenna points in the correct direction; then fully tighten the tripod screws that hold the mast into the tripod. Now, the base and the tripod are supporting the mast in a vertical position.

2 One installer should place a 5-ft (1.5 m) or a 6-ft (2 m) stepladder alongside the mast. Position the ladder so that the person on the ladder can easily reach the 10-ft (3 m) point on the mast.

3 Attach and tighten the lower set of three guy wires. The mast is now firmly held in position by this set of guy wires. The site survey documentation might specify an elevation angle for the antenna, for example, up two degrees or down one degree. If needed, loosen the antenna-mounting hardware, adjust the antenna elevation angle, and retighten the hardware. The mast is now ready to be extended up to final height.

4 The installer on the top of the ladder pushes the mast up and secures the cable to the mast as he raises the mast. The other installer is at the bottom of the ladder and is the safety person who holds the ladder firmly in place throughout the mast-raising procedure.

NOTE   Remember: The person on the bottom needs to be wearing a hard hat in case a tool falls from above. The person on the ladder should be wearing gloves to protect his hands from possible injury by any sharp metal edges on the mast.

5 Double-check again and confirm that the antenna is pointing in the proper direction. The top section of the mast is pushed up first and the middle section of the mast is pushed up last. The person on the ladder pushes the top section of the mast up approximately 3 ft (1 m) at a time. Stop every 3 ft (1 m) by tightening the clamp between the top section and the second section and secure the cable to the mast using black zip-tie straps. As the mast is extended, keep the antenna pointed in the proper direction and keep the cable running down along the same side of the mast.

6 When the top section is fully extended, tighten the clamp that secures the top section to the middle section. Now, push the middle section up 3 ft (1 m) at a time, stopping to fasten the cable to the mast. When the mast is fully extended, tighten the clamp that secures the middle section to the bottom section.

7   Tighten the middle set and the upper set of guy wires. Adjust the guy wire turnbuckles while observing the mast from two different directions until the mast is vertical when observed from each direction. You can also use a level and place it against two sides of the mast to confirm that the mast is vertical. Cut off the excess guy wire and twist a short piece of guy wire in a figure-eight shape from end-to-end through each of the turnbuckles. These safety wires prevent the wind from loosening the turnbuckle and also help to keep the guy wire from separating completely if the turnbuckle should ever break.

8   After the entire installation has been completed, put the new system on the air. Ask one person to look at the signal strength reading while you loosen the mast hardware and rotate the mast and antenna back and forth. Rotate the antenna several times through the compass heading that you obtained from the site survey documentation. Leave the antenna pointed in the direction of the highest signal strength and tighten the mast hardware firmly.

TIP   It is easiest to peak the signal strength if you use a pair of cell phones or two-way radios to communicate between the person turning the antenna and the person watching the receive signal strength indicator.

CAUTION   If you do not feel confident and safe performing the mast/antenna procedure, have the antenna system installed by a professional antenna installation crew.

Running the Cabling

Running the cabling is one of the harder parts of installing a wireless system. It can sometimes be dusty, dirty, and even dangerous. You might be installing either coax cable or Category 5 Ethernet cable. Ethernet cable is easier to install because it is smaller and more flexible than coax.

You can install the cable from inside the building up to the antenna location or from the outside antenna location down to the equipment location. Neither installation direction (up or down) is better than the other. The actual route that the cable takes should have been determined at the time of the site survey, and that information should be supplied to you as part of the installation documentation. The following steps describe the process of installing the cable from the outside antenna down to the wireless equipment:

1   Unroll or unspool enough cable on the roof of the building to extend from the antenna down to the equipment location. The installation documentation should provide you with this information. Include approximately 20 ft (6 m) of extra cable. It is better to have too much cable and have to cut off the extra than to have too little cable and have to splice more on.

2   Run the cable before you install a connector on the far end of the cable. Install the connector as the last step after the cable is completely run. Refer to the installation documentation and run the cable along the described route. Run the cable and attach it as neatly as possible to the building. Along vertical walls, use a correctly sized cable staple hammered into the wall to hold the cable firmly in place. Using the correct staple (designed to fit the cable) is important to avoid flattening the cable. Avoid making kinks and sharp bends in coax because they will cause impedance "bumps" in the cable with increased signal loss. Use an electrician's snake and electrician's pulling lubricant if you need to pull the cable through electrical conduit.

3   Install the lightning arrestor at the location specified in the installation documentation. Ideally, the lightning arrestor should be installed at the point just before the cable enters the building. Waterproof the lightning arrestor connectors if the lightning arrestor is exposed to the weather. Connect the lightning arrestor to a good ground (see the following section).

4   Use a pre-existing entry hole to route the cable from the outside to the inside of the building, whenever possible. If you need to drill a hole through the building, drill the hole on a vertical surface, not on a horizontal surface. If you drill a hole through concrete, you will likely need to use a rotary hammer drill and a special concrete drill bit. These can often be rented at a tool rental shop. Be sure to use a drip loop and some silicone sealant to prevent water from entering the cable-entry hole.

Grounding and Lightning Protection

It is necessary to provide a good low-resistance, low-impedance ground connection for every antenna mast and every lightning arrestor. Why is it necessary to provide lightning protection? The typical lightning strike produces a peak current of approximately 18,000 Amps (18 kA). A lightning strike generates a voltage differential of approximately 243,000 volts (243 kV) across an unguyed tower and 108,000 volts (108 kV) across a guyed tower. As a lightning bolt passes through the air, it raises the temperature of the air to 60,000 degrees and causes the air to glow brighter than the surface of the sun. You must shunt as much of this energy as possible directly to the ground to minimize damage to the wireless equipment, to the building, and to any people who might be nearby.

Don't Worry—It's Only a Quarter of a Million Volts

Sermon Mode = ON

It is essential that you install a lightning protector (a lightning arrestor) on every wireless installation that you do. The risks from installing unprotected antenna systems are just too great. Even if you are located in an area that has little lighting, don't take a chance. Install lightning protection on every outdoor antenna system installation.

Sermon Mode = OFF

Types of Lightning Arrestors

You can install any or all of the following three types of lightning arrestors, depending on the configuration of the wireless equipment:

- **Coaxial arrestors that pass direct current (DC)**—Used where DC-powered equipment, such as mast-mounted amplifiers or frequency converters, is mounted near the antenna. DC power is carried on the center conductor of the coax cable.

- **Coaxial arrestors that do not pass DC**—Used where no equipment is near the antenna that needs DC power.

- **Category 5 arrestors that carry DC power over Ethernet (PoE)**—Used where the wireless equipment is located near the antenna or inside the antenna housing and receives power over the Category 5 Ethernet cable. This type of arrestor provides protection for all of the wire conductors—the Ethernet wires and the power wires.

Ground Connections

Finding a good ground connection point near the coax or Category 5 cable run is one of the most challenging parts of a wireless installation. The ground wire route and the ground connection point is another one of the tasks that should be performed during the site survey before the installation crew is dispatched. The following grounding information should prove useful to you during installation when you verify the site survey grounding information:

- **Grounding tower-mounted antenna systems**—Grounding a lightning arrestor for a tower-mounted antenna is relatively easy. First, the coax shield should be grounded both at the antenna and at the base of the tower using coax-grounding kits. The coax shield should also be grounded to the tower every 75 ft (23 m) using a coax grounding kit. (See Appendix B for vendor information.) There should be a grounded bulkhead panel at the point where the coax enters the equipment vault or the building. A lightning arrestor should be mounted on the bulkhead panel; this grounds the lightning arrestor. The bulkhead panel serves as a single-point ground system. Ground wires from all the equipment come together and connect to the ground system here.

- **Grounding commercial-building mast-mounted antenna systems**—Finding a good ground connection for a mast-mounted antenna system on the roof of a commercial building can be difficult. Both the mast and the lightning arrestor need to be grounded. Here are some single-point ground location options:

  — The structural steel framing of the building is the best lightning-protection ground.

  — A connection to the building's concrete-encased steel rebar also provides a good ground connection.

  — If a ground bus bar is already installed inside of a rooftop penthouse, it can be used as the ground connection point.

  — The least effective ground is a ground wire that runs over the edge of the roof and down to an 8-ft (2.5 m) ground rod in the earth.

CAUTION   Do *not* use electrical conduit for a ground connection. Building rooftops often have exposed conduit, but there is no guarantee that the conduit runs straight down to the building single-point ground system. Using conduit as a ground point might not provide protection against lightning injury and damage.

- **Grounding residence-mounted antenna systems**—Grounding an antenna system that is mounted on a residence usually requires that you drive a ground rod directly into the ground below the point where the lightning arrestor is installed as the cable enters the building. Sometimes, you might get lucky and be able to attach your ground wire to an existing ground rod where the electrical power distribution panel is grounded.

The required size and insulation color of your ground wire can vary from city to city (depending on your local building code); however, the minimum wire size is usually number 8. If you are in doubt, check with your local building department or a competent local electrician. You can usually find ground wire and ground-wire clamps of various sizes at large hardware stores.

Installing the Wireless Equipment

The site survey information should indicate where to install the wireless equipment. The equipment location should have the following characteristics:

- **Power**—Alternating current (AC) or, in a few cases, direct current (DC) power must be available. If operation of the equipment is important during commercial power outages, a source of backup power, such as an uninterruptible power system (UPS), should be available.

- **Space and accessibility**—There should be enough space both for the equipment and for service personnel to work on the equipment. The space should be locked so that the equipment is protected against unauthorized access.

- **Temperature**—The temperature of the equipment location should be controlled so that the temperature specifications of the equipment are not exceeded. Often, this requires that the equipment be mounted in a room with air conditioning for summer cooling and heating for winter warmth.

- **Dryness and cleanliness**—The equipment should be installed in an area that is free from exposure to moisture and free from dust and dirt.

- **Short cable run**—If coax is used, the equipment should be placed as close as possible to the antenna location. If Category 5 Ethernet cable is used, the length of the Category 5 cable should not exceed 300 ft (91 m).

- **Grounding**—A single-point ground system should be available or installable.

- **Seismic protection**—The equipment should be braced to prevent damage or injury in the event of an earthquake.

Testing Wireless Systems

The need to perform proper testing of a newly installed wireless system is frequently overlooked. Further, the time needed to perform this testing is often underestimated. The sections that follow describe why it is necessary to test wireless systems and what the proper test methods are to use.

Testing Point-to-Point Wireless Links

Always test each newly installed point-to-point wireless link by measuring the throughput, the fade margin, and the applications that the end user will use. The following sections describe these tests.

Measuring the Throughput

A wireless link that has been correctly installed should work immediately. It should be capable of delivering the full amount of data that it is rated to carry. The actual data throughput that the link delivers can be measured by transferring a large file and calculating the transfer speed.

TIP   You are measuring the speed of the wireless link, not the speed of the link and the speed of the Internet. To measure only the link speed, copy (download) a large file from a lightly loaded machine at your network operating center (NOC) to your laptop at the newly installed end user location. Then, upload the same file from your laptop to your NOC. You avoid going out on the Internet, so you avoid having variable Internet traffic levels change the results of your test.

For example, if a new wireless link requires 90 seconds to transfer a 10-megabyte (MB) file (with 8 bits per byte; the file contains 80,000,000 bits), the link speed is (80,000,000 bits divided by 90 seconds) 889 kilobits per second (kbps). If the same file transfer requires 125 seconds, the link speed is 640 kbps. Repeat the test several times; the results should be similar each time.

Some links might be configured for different uplink and downlink speeds, so be sure to test the throughput in each direction. Also, be sure that your test computers are fast enough to operate at the full link speed; otherwise, they might not be able to fill the link to capacity. In this case, you might be able to use two pairs of computers to transfer two files simultaneously. If using two computers on each end is not practical, do one file transfer and compare the indicated speed to the speeds that you have previously seen on well-operating links with the same amount of bandwidth.

Measuring the Fade Margin

Chapter 2, "Understanding Wireless Fundamentals," described fade margin, which is the amount of extra signal that a microwave link needs to overcome the fading that occurs normally. If the wireless equipment is *not* contained inside the antenna housing (a and b but not c in Figure 7-1), you can use a variable attenuator to measure the fade margin on the link. A variable attenuator does just what it sounds like: It adds an adjustable amount of attenuation (loss) into the signal path. The amount of loss can be adjusted, usually in 1 dB steps, from –1 dB up to approximately –70 dB. A normal length (less than 10 miles or 16 km) link usually needs at least 10 dB of fade margin to operate reliably. The higher the fade margin, the more reliable the link will be.

To measure the actual fade margin on a newly installed link, do the following:

1 Measure and record the throughput on the new link, as described in the previous section.

2 Insert a variable attenuator between the antenna and the wireless equipment. If the equipment is located inside, insert the variable attenuator at the bottom end of the coax. If the equipment is located outside, near the antenna, insert the attenuator in the coax between the equipment and the antenna.

3   Repeat the throughput test and add attenuation –1 dB at a time. Watch to see when the throughput starts to drop significantly. At that point, record the setting of the variable attenuator. The attenuator setting is equal to the fade margin of the wireless link.

4   To confirm that the fade margin reading is correct, reduce the attenuator by –1 dB (use 1 dB less attenuation—for example, reduce the attenuator from –11 dB to –10 dB) and repeat the throughput test. The throughput should go up again and return to the level before the attenuator was added.

5   Record the measured fade margin in your installation documentation.

Testing Applications over the Link

After you measure the throughput and record the fade margin, test one or two of the applications that the new wireless end user is going to use over the link. Many times, this application is web browsing. Select a few web pages and confirm that the link is working well as it downloads these web pages. After you verify that the applications are working, demonstrate the operation of the new wireless link to the end user.

Testing Point-to-Multipoint Wireless Links

Testing the performance of a point-to-multipoint wireless access point is similar to testing a point-to-point link except that you need to repeat the testing from a number of locations inside the access point coverage area.

Choose several points that are located in various parts of the coverage area. Some of these points should be at the far edge of the area, and some points should be close to the access point. When you have successfully verified that the access point is actually covering the proper area and that the throughput is correct (in both directions) at each end point, your testing is complete. Be sure to document the throughput and the fade margin for each point that you test.

Documenting the Test Results

Double-check to be sure that you have made a complete written record of the entire installation process as well as all the over-the-air link-testing results. When you return to your office, file the documentation so that it will be available if the link ever needs to be serviced in the future.

Review Questions

1   A site survey is normally performed immediately after a wireless installation is completed. True or false?

2 Anyone can install wireless antennas on radio towers as long as they are not afraid of heights. True or false?

3 At microwave frequencies, the signal loss in coax cable is relatively high. True or false?

4 A typical lightning strike produces a peak current of approximately how many amps?

5 Fading is normal for microwave signals. What term is used to describe the extra signal power that every microwave link needs to overcome this fading?

6 What should you do immediately after you test the throughput on a newly installed wireless link?

7 Name one advantage of standardizing on only a few customer premise equipment packages.

8 If your job responsibilities require you to work regularly in high-RF environments, you should use what piece of personal protective equipment?

CHAPTER 8

Solving Noise and Interference Problems

One challenge that you will eventually face when operating your outdoor license-free network is how to minimize the throughput-reducing effects of interference and noise. Although noise has many potential causes, there are also many techniques that you can use to minimize the impact of noise on your network. This chapter summarizes the following topics:

- The importance of understanding signal-to-noise ratio (SNR)
- How to maximize the desired signal strength
- How to minimize the noise from your own network
- How to minimize the noise from other networks
- How to minimize the noise from out-of-band transmitters
- How to monitor network performance and detect emerging noise problems
- How to use direction-finding techniques to pinpoint the location of noise sources

You need to become familiar with noise-reduction techniques before you need to use them. Noise problems can either develop slowly or they can appear suddenly. By becoming familiar with noise-reduction techniques now, you will know how to respond and what to do when a noise problem appears.

The noise-reduction techniques discussed in this chapter apply to all broadband wireless networks. It does not matter if you operate a direct-sequence spread spectrum (DSSS) network, a frequency-hopping spread spectrum (FHSS) network, a point-to-point wireless link, or some other type of broadband microwave network.

Understanding SNR

A strong signal alone is not enough for a broadband wireless receiver to work reliably. To work well, the level of the received signal must be consistently higher than the level of the received noise; in other words, the SNR must be high. A high SNR requires that both of the following conditions be met simultaneously:

- **The receiver must receive a signal that is at or above the receiver threshold level**—The threshold is the level where the receiver wakes up, detects that a signal is present, and begins to successfully decode the signal. Part A of Figure 8-1 uses a decibel (dB) scale to show the relationship of the receiver threshold to the level of the incoming signal.

- **The noise level at the receiver input must be lower than the desired incoming signal**—If the noise is high, the signal strength of the signal must be higher than the incoming noise level. Part B of Figure 8-1 shows the relationship between the receiver threshold, a high noise level, and two incoming signals. One incoming signal is lower than the noise level and will not be successfully decoded. The other signal is higher than the noise level and will be successfully decoded.

Figure 8-1   *Relationship Between Receiver Threshold, Signal Level, and Noise Level*

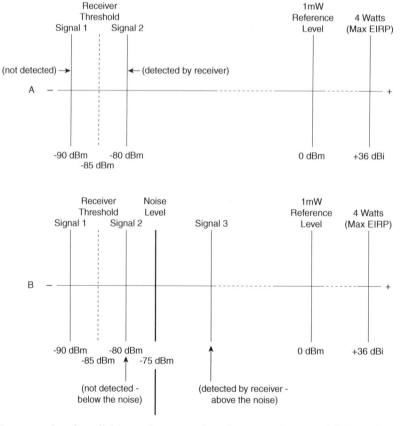

To summarize, for reliable receiver operation, there must be a good SNR at the receiver antenna input. The SNR allows the receiver to separate the signal from the noise. To design and operate a reliable wireless network, you need to be able to simultaneously maximize the desired signal level and to minimize the existing (and future) noise and interference level.

Maximizing the Signal Level

You have direct control over maximizing the signal strengths of received signals. The procedures for doing this have been discussed throughout this book and include the following:

- **Link budget**—Make sure that each link is designed with enough transmit power, receive sensitivity, fade margin, and antenna gain to overcome the free-space path loss and the coax loss.

- **Line-of-sight (LOS) paths**—Make sure that each wireless link has an LOS path with an unobstructed view from end to end.

- **Fresnel zone**—Make sure that each link has a clear Fresnel zone and that there is enough clearance above and between path obstacles to avoid additional signal loss.

- **Installation**—Make sure during installation that each antenna system is mounted securely, aligned correctly, and waterproofed completely.

When it comes to noise and interference, the situation is different. You have only indirect control over the noise level.

Minimizing the Noise and Interference Level

You do not have direct control over most noise and interference sources. Remember: Noise is defined as "everything other than the desired signal." Therefore, noise includes all the following:

- **Natural noise**—Atmospheric and galactic noise.

- **Manmade noise**—Noise that is present in the radio-frequency (RF) environment and that is picked up by your antenna. This includes noise from microwave ovens, cordless telephones, and indoor wireless LANs.

- **Receiver noise**—Noise generated inside the receiver circuitry.

- **Interference from other networks**—Interference caused by other signals in the same band coming from other nearby wireless networks.

- **Interference from your network**—Interference caused by signals coming from your own network. This interference occurs when you are using the same frequency more than once, using channels that do not have enough space between them, or selecting incorrect frequency-hopping sequences.

- **Interference from out-of-band signals**—Interference caused by strong, nearby signals outside of the frequency band that you are using.

It is important for you to use a combination of all the possible noise-reduction techniques to receive as little noise as possible and thereby maximize your SNR. This is true both during the initial system design as well as throughout the life of your network.

NOTE Noise levels in each area are different. In a city, noise levels are usually higher than in a rural area. The more people who live in an area, the more wireless devices are present, and the higher the noise level. If you are located in a rural area, do not automatically assume that there are no sources of noise. There is less noise than in a city, but it is likely that your network is not the only network in use. Use a spectrum analyzer or wireless site survey utility to look for other networks and sources of noise in your area.

Table 8-1 summarizes the noise-reduction techniques that you can use as you are designing your network. If you fail to design a noise-resistant network or if other noise sources appear after you deploy your network, you can use the solutions in the two right columns to reduce the impact that the noise has on your throughput.

Table 8-1 *Noise Sources and Solutions*

Source of Noise	Location of Original Noise Solution Description	Symptom	Solution (Before Beginning Wireless Service)	Solution (After Beginning Wireless Service)
Antenna directional patterns ignored. (Antenna pattern is too broad.)	Chapter 4, "Antenna Radiation Patterns" section.	Reduced throughput caused by picking up noise from unwanted directions.	Choose a more directional antenna for your access point (AP) with a coverage pattern that covers only the desired service area.	Research, design, purchase, install, and test a new, more directional antenna system.
High noise level from other transmitters near your AP location. These transmitters might be out-of-band (AM, FM, or TV broadcasting, paging, or two-way radio) or in-band (other networks in the same license-free band)	Chapter 4, "RF Site Survey" section; Chapter 5, "Cross Polarization" and "Sector Antenna Systems" sections.	Reduced throughput caused by picking up noise from nearby transmitters.	Perform an RF site survey using a spectrum analyzer.	Review Table 4-3 in Chapter 4. Then do one of the following: *For in-band noise:* Temporarily shut down all the transmitters on your network and use a spectrum analyzer to attempt to locate the source of interference. If the noise cannot be reduced, it might be necessary for you to move your AP to a new location. If you locate the interference source, reconfigure your antenna system polarization, directivity, or downtilt to reduce the noise. *For out-of-band noise:* Temporarily add a bandpass filter between the antenna and the radio to see if the throughput improves.

Table 8-1   *Noise Sources and Solutions (Continued)*

Source of Noise	Location of Original Noise Solution Description	Symptom	Solution (Before Beginning Wireless Service)	Solution (After Beginning Wireless Service)
Interference from another network that is on the same DSSS frequency channel.	Chapter 4 (Table 4-3).	Reduced throughput.	Choose a DSSS channel with as little use as possible, as determined by a spectrum analyzer.	Change DSSS channels; choose one with the least amount of use, as determined by a spectrum analyzer.
Interference from other networks using the same FHSS hopping sequence or using another hopping set.	Chapter 4 (Table 4-3).	Reduced throughput.	Coordinate your choice of hopping set and hopping sequence. Use the same hopping set as the other FHSS networks in your area but a different hopping sequence within that set.	Change your choice of hopping set and hopping sequence. Use the same hopping set as the other FHSS networks in your area but a different hopping sequence within that set.
Interference from another radio or from another AP in your network.	Chapter 5, "Isolating Antenna Systems" and "Sector Antenna Systems" sections.	Reduced throughput on both your APs.	Prepare a frequency plan. (See the "Minimizing Noise from Your DSSS Network" section following this table). Design your network to ensure adequate isolation between your antenna systems that operate on the same frequency. Use a combination of antenna directivity, cross polarization, antenna downtilting, vertical separation, horizontal separation, and obstruction isolation between your antennas.	Temporarily shut down one of your networks while you add isolation between your antenna systems by using a combination of the techniques listed at the left.

continues

Table 8-1 *Noise Sources and Solutions (Continued)*

Source of Noise	Location of Original Noise Solution Description	Symptom	Solution (Before Beginning Wireless Service)	Solution (After Beginning Wireless Service)
Wireless packet collisions between end users on your own network.	Chapter 6, "Access Point Feature Decisions" section.	Reduced throughput under moderate and heavy traffic levels.	Select equipment that is capable of polling end users rather than using the standard carrier sense multiple access with collision avoidance (CSMA/CA) protocol that allows hidden-node end users to collide with each other.	Upgrade both AP and user software to a version that provides end user polling. If this is not possible, install a bandwidth manager that can throttle (limit) each end user to a predetermined bandwidth level. If necessary, throttle end user upload speeds at a level less than their download speeds.
Multipath	Chapter 2, "Multipath" section; Chapter 5, "Polarization Selection Examples" and "Diversity Antenna System" sections. Chapter 6, "Multipath Resistance" section.	High error rates with reduced throughput.	Avoid placing wireless APs in reflection-prone locations. Use circularly polarized antennas whenever possible if you must operate in an area with reflective buildings, standing bodies of water, or large sections of concrete parking lots.	Move your APs to less reflective areas; temporarily substitute a circularly polarized antenna system on your AP and test to see if the throughput under load is improved.

Minimizing Noise from Your DSSS Network

After you successfully deploy your network, it is likely that the demand for service on your network will increase. This means that you will add more users to your existing AP and you might also add new APs. As you add APs, your risk of self-interference increases because the number of nonoverlapping channels that you can use in any geographical area is limited. For example, on the 2.4 GHz band in the United States, you can use a maximum of three nonoverlapping channels: channels 1, 6, and 11.

To eliminate self-interference between your AP sectors, make a frequency plan before you deploy your network. The frequency plan should show all of the following information:

- Location of each AP
- Geographic area covered by each AP sector
- Frequency used in each sector
- Antenna polarization used in each sector
- Equivalent isotropic radiated power (EIRP) used in each sector

If your plan uses more than three frequencies at the same AP location or if two or more of your AP sectors are within wireless range of each other, you need to reuse (share) one or more channels. To reuse channels, design your antenna systems so that there is at least 121 dB of isolation (wireless signal loss) between them. When you have this much isolation, the receiver in one sector can no longer hear the transmitter from the other sector. Now, you can use the same frequency on both sectors (or one sector and one wireless backhaul link) without causing self-interference.

Figure 8-2 provides an example of a frequency plan that requires one frequency to be reused.

Figure 8-2 *Example of a Frequency Plan*

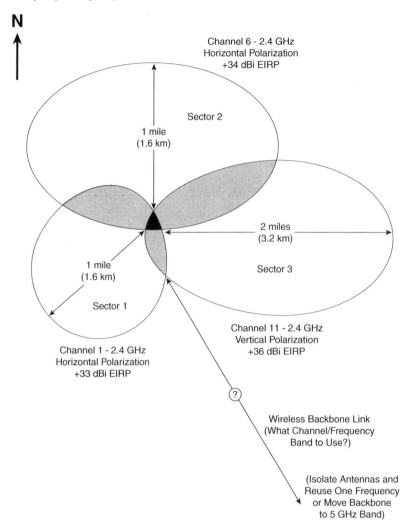

Figure 8-2 shows one AP with three point-to-multipoint sectors and one point-to-point wireless backbone link. This AP requires a total of four frequencies; however, at 2.4 GHz, there are only three non-overlapping frequencies (channels 1, 6, and 11). You can use either one of the following two solutions for this problem:

- **Antenna system isolation**—Isolate two of the antenna systems to allow the same frequency to be reused simultaneously for two different purposes; for example, one point-to-multipoint sector and the backhaul might be isolated and on the same frequency. Use the techniques summarized in the "Interference from another radio or from another AP in your network" row of Table 8-1. These techniques are described in more detail in the "Noise Reduction from Your Network" section of Chapter 5.

- **Different frequency bands**—Move one sector (or move the backbone link) to a different frequency band. For example, you could move the backbone link to the 5-GHz band. Now all three non-overlapping 2.4-GHz frequencies are available for use, one per sector, with no interference and no throughput loss from the backbone link.

Minimizing Noise from Your FHSS Network

If you operate a FHSS network, each sector has a lower throughput compared to a DSSS network; however, you can still deploy more sectors on the same tower or rooftop before you generate a significant level of self-interference. To minimize self-interference, do the following:

- Be sure to choose hopping sequences from the same hopping set for all sectors located in the same geographical area. For example, if you deploy six sectors on the same rooftop, the six different hopping sequences must be in the same hopping set. If another network is in the same area (your network or someone else's network), both your network and the other network should choose unique hopping sequences from the same hopping set.

- Avoid locating (collocating) more than 10 sectors on the same tower or rooftop or in the same geographical area where the sector antenna patterns can overlap.

Wow! 10,000 Sectors and No Self-Interference!

Some equipment vendors claim that up to 15 FHSS sectors can be collocated (placed on the same tower or rooftop) without significant self-interference. Personally, I will believe this claim when I actually see an FHSS system that can run fully loaded with traffic without a significant reduction in throughput (in other words, without self-interference). Until I see such a system, I would advise running no more than 10 collocated sectors unless you use effective antenna-isolation techniques. If you isolate some of the sector antennas completely from each other, you can run more collocated sectors without self-interference.

Minimizing Noise from Other Networks

The more people who live in a specific area, the more likely it is that there will be more than one broadband wireless network. The more networks, the more likely you are to experience noise from the other networks.

The best way to minimize noise from other networks is to do a wireless site survey before you commit to placing your AP in a specific location. If your AP is already in place and cannot be moved, you can use any or all of the techniques outlined in the "High noise level from other transmitters near your AP location" row of Table 8-1 to minimize your reception of signals from the other networks.

Minimizing Noise from Out-of-Band Transmitters

When your receiver is located close to high-power transmitters, the signals from those transmitters can overload (overpower) your receiver and act like noise to reduce your SNR. This effect is called de-*sensitization*, or *desense*. Out-of-band sources of desense can include AM, FM, paging, television broadcast, and terrestrial satellite radio transmitters. Performing a wireless site survey before selecting an AP location normally prevents desense problems from occurring; however, many times an AP location is chosen without performing a wireless site survey.

You can solve an out-of-band transmitter noise problem in two ways:

- **Move your access point**—Moving your AP to another location reduces the signal strength of the other transmitter at the input of your receiver and allows your receiver to operate at full sensitivity. Moving an AP that has already been placed in service can be difficult because end users are already connected to it.

- **Use a bandpass filter**—Placing a bandpass filter between your antenna and your wireless equipment attenuates all signals below and above the license-free band and allows your receiver to hear the incoming signals from your end users. The filter does not significantly attenuate signals within the license-free band.

Signal-to-Noise Variations over Time

Noise problems might occur at different times and noise might increase at different rates or last for different lengths of time. You need to be prepared to deal with all of the noise conditions mentioned in the following sections.

High Noise Level Before Installation

Noise levels might already be high before you begin to design and install your network. For example, other networks might already be operating in the same area. The high noise level from these networks will cause your SNR to be low. If a wireless site survey indicates a high noise level, you should find another location for your AP.

Slowly Increasing Noise Level

After you install your network, it is likely that the noise level will slowly increase over time. This increase occurs because more people will use more wireless devices as time goes on. The result will be that your SNR will decrease slowly over time. Be sure to monitor your network performance statistics. Be ready to redesign your network or your antenna systems to improve your SNR, if needed.

Suddenly Increasing Noise Level

Normally, noise increases slowly over a period of time; however, it is also possible for noise to increase suddenly. Noise that suddenly increases can be of the following two types:

- **Steady**—This is noise that increases suddenly and is present constantly or almost all the time. This noise is likely coming from a new network that has been deployed in the same general area as your network. This noise decreases your SNR and reduces your network throughput. It is important for you to locate the other network, contact the network operator, and ask that person to coordinate their frequency, antenna polarization, or antenna pattern with you. Most people understand the need to cooperate. Occasionally, you might meet someone who refuses to cooperate. In this case, you might need to redesign your antenna system to reject more of the noise from that system.

- **Intermittent**—This is noise that increases suddenly and that comes and goes. It might be present for only a few hours a day or a few weeks of the year. Temporary noise sources include network testing on other networks, military exercises using wireless equipment, cell phone traffic peaks, the operation of industrial equipment, and other sources, which might be difficult to identify. When this noise occurs, your network throughput slows down or stops. Patient, careful investigation with a spectrum analyzer can lead you to the source of this noise. After you identify the source, you might need to redesign your antenna system to reject more of the noise.

Using Direction-Finding Techniques to Locate Noise Sources

The following direction-finding tools and techniques allow you to find the location of a transmitter or other noise source that is interfering with your AP and reducing your network throughput.

Direction-Finding Tools

The following tools allow you to detect and locate interfering signals:

- **Spectrum analyzer**—A spectrum analyzer (SA) allows you to see other signals both inside and outside the frequency band that you are using. See Chapter 4, "Performing Site Surveys," for an explanation of how to use a spectrum analyzer and how to determine interference levels.

- **Directional antenna**—A directional antenna attached to the spectrum analyzer indicates the direction that an interfering signal is coming from as well as the signal polarization. A panel antenna with approximately 30 degrees of horizontal and vertical beamwidth is recommended.

- **Compass**—A compass allows you to read the direction that your directional antenna is pointing when the interference level is highest.

- **Map**—A map allows you to draw a line from the location where you take each of your spectrum analyzer readings to the location where the interfering signal is coming from.

- **Attenuator**—An attenuator (either a variable attenuator or a series of fixed attenuators) allows you to reduce the level of the incoming interference when you get close to it. Reducing this level prevents your spectrum analyzer from becoming overloaded and giving distorted readings.

Triangulation

Triangulation is a technique that allows you to pinpoint the location of the antenna that is connected to an interfering transmitter. Triangulation requires you to take a series of at least three directional readings from different locations. The spot where the readings cross is the location of the transmitter. Figure 8-3 shows an example of using triangulation to find the location of an interfering transmitter.

Figure 8-3   *Example of Triangulation*

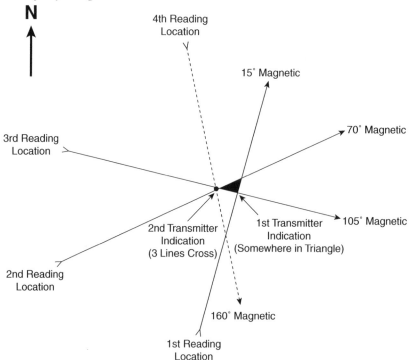

The triangulation steps are as follows:

Step 1   Identify the signal on the SA that you believe is causing the interference. Rotate your panel antenna to both the horizontal and the vertical polarization positions to determine the polarization of the signal.

NOTE   Review the radio frequency (RF) site survey principles in Chapter 4. Interference is relative, not absolute. There is no absolute indication that one particular transmitter is the only cause of the noise that you are receiving; it is possible that several, simultaneous noise sources exist. For this reason, it is good to practice direction finding before you use it to track down real interference.

Step 2   Use the directional antenna and the compass to determine the direction that the interfering signal appears to be coming from. Draw a line on the map that starts at your present location and extends in the compass direction of the interfering signal.

Step 3   Move to a different location (not on the first map line) a mile or two away. Take a second directional reading and draw another line on the map. The second line should start at your current location and extend in the direction of the interfering signal.

Step 4   Move to a third location, take a third reading, and draw a third line on the map. The three lines should either cross at one point or form a small triangle. If the lines cross at one point, go to that point. If the three lines form a triangle, move to a fourth location, take a reading, and draw a fourth line. Go to the location where at least three of the lines cross.

Step 5   As you get closer to the transmitter, the signal becomes stronger. Insert the attenuator(s) between your directional antenna and the spectrum analyzer to reduce the signal strength and prevent the spectrum analyzer from becoming overloaded.

Step 6   Finally, good eyesight is an asset when you are hunting a noise source. The better you are at spotting antennas visually, the easier it will be for you to quickly identify the exact rooftop or tower where the interfering transmitter's antenna system is located. Carry a pair of binoculars so that you can get a close-up look at the antennas that you locate.

Step 7   Confirm the polarization of the interfering signal and save an SA file showing the signal details. Record all the relevant additional information: the antenna system location and description, the signal strength, the polarization, and the network operator.

Monitoring Network Performance

You need to be familiar with all the noise-reduction techniques described in earlier chapters and summarized in this chapter so that you can respond immediately if noise problems do occur.

It is important for you to continually monitor your network performance so that you can detect SNR deterioration before it slows down your network and causes your end user's throughput to decrease. You can use a combination of the following techniques to detect SNR deterioration:

- **Monitoring SNR directly**—Some wireless equipment allows you to read signal strength, noise level, and SNR directly at each end user and at each AP location. Monitor and log or graph these SNR values each week. If you notice deterioration at one end user, the problem is probably at that location only. Perhaps the end user's antenna has turned in the wind or a neighbor has set up a new AP with an outdoor antenna. If you notice SNR deterioration at your AP, service to all users on that AP is slowed down. Perhaps water has gotten into your AP antenna or maybe another wireless network has started operating nearby or from the same tower that you are on.

- **Monitoring retransmission percentage**—If your equipment does not monitor SNR directly, you must monitor your network performance indirectly to detect problems. Most wireless equipment allows you to access management statistics that show the percentage of wireless packets that were retransmitted. The higher this percentage, the slower the network operates. A retransmit percentage of no more than 10 percent is desirable. Monitor and graph this information from each AP sector and each end user each week. If you see that this percentage is increasing over time, look for and correct the cause of the deterioration before your end users become unhappy with the slower network performance.

- **Monitoring ping latency**—If your equipment does not allow you to monitor SNR or packet retransmission percentage, you can monitor the average time needed for a large ping packet to be sent and returned over each link. Send a string of large (1400 byte) ping packets to each end user and note the pattern of the return times. If return times are consistently low (25 ms or less), the link is operating well. If return times are consistently high (50 ms and above), the link is operating poorly. If return times fluctuate between low values and high values, the link is experiencing problems that are causing performance to suffer. Locate and correct the source of the problem as soon as possible.

Regardless of the monitoring method that you use, keep a running record of the monitored information so that you can detect any deterioration over time.

Documenting Noise-Reduction Results

In addition to saving performance-monitoring information, it is important to document or log the results of all the noise-reduction activities that you perform. This documentation should include the date, the problem symptoms, the actions that you took or the network changes that you made, and the result of the actions or changes. This log will save you time performing future noise-reduction work because you can look back and quickly see the activities that have already been done.

Minimizing Interference to Licensed Wireless Systems

Just as other transmitters can create noise problems for you, your transmitters can create noise for other wireless operators, both license-free and licensed.

The licensed users in several parts of the license-free bands include amateur radio operators. Amateur radio operators perform many public service activities as well as advancing wireless knowledge through experimentation. Amateur operators use parts of the 900-MHz, 2.4-GHz, and 5-GHz bands for amateur television, satellite communications, moonbounce, and other weak-signal work.

Try to make personal contact with the amateurs in your area so that you can coordinate your use of these shared microwave bands with their use. This way, you can minimize any interference that you might cause them and they can minimize interference that they might cause you.

Review Questions

1 For reliable network operation, signal strength is more important than SNR. True or false?

2 A reliable wireless link needs a line-of-sight path and an unobstructed Fresnel zone. True or false?

3 Will the noise level always be low in a rural area?

4 How many nonoverlapping 2.4 GHz channels are available for use in the United States?

5 The consequence of a low SNR is reduced network throughput. True or false?

6 Reusing a DSSS frequency at the same AP location requires how many decibels of antenna isolation?

7 To avoid interference, collocated FHSS sectors should use different hopping sequences and different hopping sets. True or false?

8 When is the SNR highest at an AP?

9 When the percentage of retransmitted packets reaches 20 percent, you should start looking for the cause of the network slowdown. True or false?

10 Explain why it is necessary to write down the results of your noise-reduction efforts.

CHAPTER 9

Providing Broadband Wireless Internet Access

This entire book deals with issues that wireless Internet service providers (WISPs) need to address. This chapter in particular expands on some of these issues and introduces additional issues that you, as a wireless ISP, need to consider.

Planning for WISP Success

The success of any business depends to a large extent on the presence of a successful business plan. The business plan must correctly anticipate the profitable delivery of a needed service. In this case, the service is broadband wireless Internet access. The following sections help you understand some of the critical planning issues that your business plan must address.

Obtaining ISP and WISP Experience

What is a wireless ISP? It can resemble one of the following or some combination of the following two models.

Small and Simple WISP Model

A small, simple WISP can be nothing more than a wireless hotspot at the corner coffee shop or a community network that provides Internet access in a public park. The wireless range is limited to a few hundred feet in the case of the coffee shop or to a block or two in the case of the park. The WISP provides no additional services, such as e-mail accounts or domain hosting. The WISP only connects users to the Internet. The small WISP might charge an hourly or a daily fee for the wireless service, or in the case of the community network, the service might be provided at no charge.

If you plan to run a small WISP, you will not need a lot of traditional ISP knowledge. You *will* need to know enough to answer simple questions from customers, such as how to log in and how to configure Dynamic Host Configuration Protocol (DHCP). You will not need to know how to configure a core router or how to set up a domain name server. You can probably get the answers you need from the wired ISP to which your wireless access point (AP) is connected.

Large and Complex WISP Model

A large, complex WISP can provide wireless services in many cities covering hundreds of square miles. It might have dozens of wireless sectors and connect customers who are up to 20 miles away from a wireless AP. This WISP might also offer a full spectrum of wired ISP services including traditional dialup, digital subscriber line (DSL), Frame Relay, Integrated Services Digital Network (ISDN), and T1 access. It will offer e-mail, domain hosting, server farms, networking, and other advanced services.

If you plan to run a large and complex WISP, you must either have extensive ISP experience or you must hire people who have advanced ISP experience. You might also want to consider forming a partnership with an existing wired ISP; they provide the wired infrastructure and you provide the wireless infrastructure. Being successful as a large WISP requires having experienced ISP help.

To run a large, complex WISP, you also need extensive wireless experience. You can gain this experience either by educating yourself and then working with wireless on the job or by hiring employees who have substantial wireless experience. Either way, the more quickly you obtain this wireless experience, the more quickly your WISP will be successful.

Gaining Wireless Knowledge

If you plan to deploy outdoor wireless links, you need to understand the basic wireless principles that successful wireless network operation is based on.

The cost of 802.11b local-area network (LAN) equipment is continuing to decrease, and many new WISPs are using this equipment in outdoor wide-area network (WAN) deployments. You might believe that your wireless network deployment will be"plug and play," but nothing could be further from the truth. You must educate yourself about how wireless works and about how to deploy it successfully in an outdoor environment where there is noise and interference.

The wireless WISP world today is much larger than just 802.11b. Wireless WISPs have been around since about 1995—in other words, since long before 802.11b. Many WISPs have deployed and will continue to deploy non-802.11b equipment. Regardless of whether you have chosen to use 802.11b equipment or not, you need to be aware of these other equipment options. After your wireless signals leave the antenna, they will be sharing the "ether" with all the other signals in your area, 802.11b, non-802.11b, and other, non-WISP transmitters.

Following are some of the ways that you can gain the wireless knowledge that you need:

- **Read the advertising literature**—This is a good way to get an overall view of wireless principles, but be aware that this literature is designed to sell you equipment as well as to inform you. Always assume that there will be a few points that are either not mentioned or not completely accurate.

- **Join an e-mail list**—This is an excellent way to share your experience with others. You will learn and you will help others learn when you contribute to these lists. See Appendix B, "Wireless Hardware, Software, and Service Provider Organizations," for some of these lists.

- **Attend educational seminars**—Attending educational seminars is another good way to learn about wireless principles. Many times, these presentations give you a chance to ask questions. Keep in mind that most of these seminars are also designed to sell you equipment. This means that you have to focus on separating the educational material from the marketing material.

- **Visit existing WISPs**—This is one of the best ways to learn how real-world wireless equipment works. If you are fortunate enough to have an existing WISP nearby (one who doesn't see you as a competitive threat), visit it and observe its operation. Ask the WISP operators questions about the techniques that worked well for them. Ask them which of their initial expectations were met and which expectations needed to be changed.

- **Experiment with license-free wireless equipment**—If you are far enough along in your business planning to select one or two wireless equipment vendors, you can purchase a pair of radios and do your own testing and experimenting. If you have access to a pair of older radios, you can test with those. As you test the wireless equipment outdoors, you will feel your wireless understanding and knowledge grow.

- **Become a radio amateur**—If your interest in wireless is strong, you should consider obtaining your amateur radio license. Obtaining your entry-level license is easy and (in many countries) you no longer have to learn the Morse code. In many areas, amateur radio clubs teach free or low-cost licensing classes that run for a few weeks. At the end of the class, you take your licensing test and join the ranks of a select group of wireless experimenters. Then, you have the opportunity to experiment with licensed wireless equipment and vastly expand your wireless knowledge.

Serving Niche Markets

Broadband Internet access is advantageous to businesses, residences, and home office workers; however, wireless Internet access is not the best choice for all these potential customers. In many cities, low-cost broadband Internet access is already available in the form of digital subscriber line (DSL) service or broadband cable Internet service. Successful WISP business plans take this reality into account and focus on serving niche markets—those areas where broadband service does not already exist. It is difficult for a WISP to operate profitably while competing head to head with multimillion-dollar corporations such as the incumbent local telephone companies and the nationwide cable providers. A discussion of some of these niche markets follows:

- **Fixed business market**—Fast, reliable, wireless Internet access is valuable for many businesses. Businesses are willing to pay for value, but they expect prompt and efficient support from their ISP. Even when business customers have other broadband choices, WISPs that offer high-quality, fairly priced service can successfully compete for this business and make a profit.

- **Fixed residential market**—In cities where cable and DSL are available, customers in this market expect that price competition between the broadband carriers will provide them with fast service at low cost. This is not a good niche market for WISPs to compete in unless existing broadband service providers are not available. In that case, this is a good niche market where a WISP can supply service and price it to make a small profit.

- **Fixed SOHO market**—The small-office/home-office (SOHO) market is a cross between the business market and the residential market. If cable and DSL are not available, this is a good niche market where you can be profitable.

- **Portable market**—Portable wireless customers are nomadic. The customer first connects from one location (for example, a coffee shop) and then connects from another location (maybe an airport lounge), but he does not stay connected while traveling between the two locations. This is a difficult niche market to be profitable in. If you are interested in this market, see the discussion of wireless hotspots that appears later in this chapter.

- **Mobile market**—The mobile market, in which a customer connects and stays connected while driving or moving from AP to AP, is the most difficult market to be profitable in. Without pointing out all the reasons why profitability is difficult, you can look at the cell phone market that provides mobile voice connectivity. In spite of cell phone companies' large user base and billions of dollars of investment, most of them are losing money.

Differentiating Between Bandwidth and Throughput

This book differentiates between wireless throughput and wireless bandwidth. The throughput (data transfer speed) determines the experience that your customers have when using your network, not the theoretical bandwidth.

Your customers are not interested in paying for some theoretical bandwidth that they cannot perceive. They want to be charged for the throughput that they actually experience every time they load a new Web page or press the Enter key. Delivering throughput is the only thing that you can charge for. Because throughput is your only deliverable, you cannot afford to waste it. Plan to maximize, manage, and monitor your available wireless throughput.

Pricing Your Service Offerings

In the past, some WISP owners priced their services too low to make a profit in the hopes of quickly building up their installed base of customers and then selling their WISP at a big profit. In most cases, those owners ended up losing money, not making money.

Price your wireless services high enough so that you can make a profit. If low-cost carriers, such as telephone companies or cable companies, are already providing residential service in your area, you are probably better off looking for other niche markets to serve with wireless rather than trying to compete with these giants.

To operate most profitably with the throughput that you have available, you need to offer tiered levels of service. Customers pay for the throughput level they need today. When they need more throughput, you should charge them more for it.

Overselling Throughput

All ISPs—both wired and wireless—sell the same throughput to more than one customer. This overselling is possible because no ISP customer uses all his bandwidth (throughput) all the time. As a WISP, you will oversell (or share) your wireless throughput. If your customers ask if you are supplying dedicated or shared bandwidth, you can advise them that you are supplying shared bandwidth. You can also tell them that you manage your throughput carefully to be sure that the network is not overloaded and that they receive the throughput that they expect. You might even want to set up a test file on one of your servers that your customers can download to test their wireless throughput.

When you start wireless service on a new sector, it is best to use conservative overselling ratios, such as these:

- **Business customers**—A 6-to-1 ratio
- **SOHO customers**—An 8-to-1 ratio
- **Residential customers**—A 10-to-1 ratio

You can monitor your network performance, as described in the later section, "Determining Network Capacity," and adjust your overselling ratio upward when you see that your network performance is stable and reliable.

Committing to High-Reliability Service

Your customers will naturally wonder if their wireless service is going to be reliable. This concern stems from their experience with other wireless services such as cell phone services that occasionally drop their calls. When you first propose wireless service to customers, you need to be prepared to address these concerns. Then, you need to follow through on your promises by actually delivering reliable service.

Preplanning the Installation Process

Planning for a cost-effective installation process is critical to operating a profitable WISP. The installation process is important enough that you need to include it in your initial business plan. For more information, see the section "Deploying Stable Networks," later in this chapter.

Designing Reliable Networks

This entire book is about reliable wireless network design. This section reviews the most important wireless network design principles and provides some additional design techniques for you. The goal of successful network design is a stable, noise-resistant architecture that is easy to maintain and expand.

Selecting Low-Noise AP Locations

One of the most crucial decisions that affects your ability to deliver reliable throughput is your selection of low-noise locations for your APs. Please review the section "Access Point Vulnerability to Noise" in Chapter 4, "Performing Site Surveys," for the finer details.

Selecting low-noise AP locations requires more than just performing wireless site surveys. It is also important for you to think outside the box—to see beyond what looks like the obvious AP locations.

Avoiding Commonly Used High Spots

Try to avoid placing your APs on the highest mountain in the area or the tallest building downtown. These are the areas where many other transmitters are already clustered. If you locate your APs there, you expose your receivers to high noise levels. Unless you know how to protect your receivers against overload, they might be desensitized, have their signal-to-noise ratio (SNR) reduced, and be unable to receive very well.

My Building Is Taller Than Your Building!

Several times, I have seen WISPs proudly announce that they just obtained roof rights on the tallest building in town. Later, when they installed their APs, they experienced a short receiving range because of too much noise. Their pride in being on the tallest building in town did not translate into successful and profitable operation of their WISP.

Rather than locate on the highest building, it is better to use the second-highest or the third-highest building—whichever building *does not* have a lot of already-existing transmitters.

Your transmitting range will not be reduced much, but your receiving range will be noticeably improved.

The same principle (avoiding high-RF locations) holds true when you locate on a mountain. You do not need to be up on the top with all the FM, television, and two-way radio transmitters. Look for a site that is part way down on the side of the mountain. Your coverage area will be just as large; however, you will avoid receiving problems. The monthly site rental will probably also be lower.

To carry this principle further, you might not need to be on the mountain at all. Often, sites down in the foothills much closer to town will not only avoid receiver problems but will also increase the strength of the signal to and from your service area.

To summarize, do not blindly pick the highest location around. Pick the quietest available spot that is closest to your customers and just high enough to avoid line-of-sight (LOS) problems between you and your customers.

Avoiding Cell Sites

Locating your APs at cell sites presents three common problems:

- Receiver overloading (discussed earlier)
- In-band interference from 2.4-GHz and 5-GHz license-free T1 backhaul links used by the cell phone companies
- High site rent

You can avoid these problems by selecting your AP locations as far away as possible from cell sites.

Locating on the Periphery

Here is one more reason not to follow the herd and place your APs on the highest building in town. When your AP is near the center of your service area, all of your customers' antennas are going to be pointing toward the center of a circle. Their signals don't just stop when they reach your AP. Those signals keep going beyond the AP, and that means that they keep going toward your customers located on the other side of town. The collision potential is horrendous—basically, your customers are radiating toward each other. You can avoid this problem by placing your APs around the outside periphery of your coverage area. Now your customers are no longer radiating their signals toward each other and colliding with each other.

Planning for Emergencies

Fires, tornados, hurricanes, earthquakes, and other emergencies do happen. Think about the locations where you would need to place a temporary AP if something happened to an AP that you are using now. Which property owners would allow you to place a temporary AP on their property?

Planning for emergencies has another advantage. It can help you become aware of potential locations for new APs when you expand your network in the future.

Learning to Spell Decibels

If you drive a car, it is important for you to understand how many gallons (liters, litres) of fuel is in the fuel tank. The same goes when you use wireless; decibels (dBs) measure transmitter signal strength, receiver signal levels, antenna radiation patterns, interference levels, and so on. You need to understand how to use decibels and keep practicing until using them becomes easy.

In the two-way radio industry, there is an old joke that says, "It takes five years to learn how to spell dB." This means that it takes five years of practice before it becomes intuitively easy to work with decibels. This practice is needed because decibel measurement is not linear; it is logarithmic. Decibels are exponents, and they represent logarithmic power gains and losses.

Numbers that increase and decrease logarithmically get bigger (and smaller) much faster than normal. This is the same as wireless signal levels, which grow bigger and smaller much faster than normal (nonlogarithmic) numbers. Wireless signals become small quickly after they leave an antenna, and that is why logarithms are needed to represent their signal strength.

Table 9-1 shows how a simple one-number increase in the log of a number represents an increase of 10 times more than the previous value.

Table 9-1   *Examples of Log Values Increasing Logarithmically*

Number	Number of Times the Number Is Multiplied by Itself	Product (Total After Multiplying)	Log (Power of 10)
10	1 (10 to the first power)	10	1
10 * 10	2 (10 squared)	100	2
10 * 10 * 10	3 (10 cubed)	1000	3
10 * 10 * 10 * 10	4 (10 to the fourth power)	10,000	4

The first row of Table 9-1 says that 10 raised to the first power equals 10. The second row says that 10 raised to the second power (10 squared or 10×10) is 100. The exponent has changed from 1 to 2, but the product (the result of the multiplication) has changed from 10 to 100. That's a pretty big increase in the product when the exponent (the log) has only changed from a 1 to a 2. You can see that representing wireless power using a logarithmic notation (such as decibels) allows the easy representation of small amounts and large amounts of power. Decibels are covered in more detail in Chapter 2, "Understanding Wireless Fundamentals." It would be good for you to review the explanation in Chapter 2 and practice using decibel values as often as possible. To become good at wireless design, you need to be able to spell dB.

Using Licensed Backhauls

Remember that there are a limited number of license-free frequencies and that reusing these frequencies can be done; however, it is technically challenging and requires a lot of antenna isolation. If you run out of frequencies or if you need a high-throughput backbone link, consider using high-bandwidth licensed wireless equipment. The cost for a pair of licensed 18-GHz, 45-Mbps radios is not much more than the cost of high-bandwidth license-free equipment.

Licensed radios also enjoy protection from interference that license-free radios do not enjoy. Licensed radios are available in the 6-GHz, 11-GHz, 18-GHz, and 23-GHz ranges. The cost of obtaining a Federal Communications Commission (FCC) license is typically around $2000 per licensed link, and the license is good for 10 years. Except in the 23-GHz band, you can begin operation about 45 days after you start the FCC licensing procedure.

Deploying Stable Networks

Many important techniques contribute to the deployment of stable wireless networks. Most of these techniques were covered in earlier chapters; however, for those readers who opened the book directly to this chapter and have not yet read the earlier chapters, the sections that follow review these topics briefly.

Wireless Site Surveys

Perform a wireless site survey before you finalize the selection of a wireless AP location. The site survey confirms that the noise and interference are low enough to allow the AP to receive well. Please review the information in Chapter 4 that describes how to do a wireless site survey.

Standardizing Customer Premises Equipment (CPE)

Use only a few, standard combinations of customer premises equipment (CPE), cables, and antennas. This simplifies the installation process and minimizes inventory cost, as explained in Chapter 7, "Installing Outdoor Wireless Systems."

Avoiding Needless Equipment Mixing

Use a minimum of different brands of wireless APs and wireless cards. For example, a Brand A AP with a Brand B wireless card linking to a Brand C wireless card in a Brand D radio can be unreliable and difficult to maintain. Please (re)read the section "Compatibility Issues" in Chapter 6, "Evaluating and Selecting Wireless Equipment."

Meeting the Customer at the Ethernet

Most non-802.11b equipment connects to the customer's computer (or network) with an Ethernet interface. If you use 802.11b equipment in your wireless network, try to avoid the temptation to provide wireless service by just inserting a wireless card into your customer's computer. On the surface, this might appear to be the lowest-cost method of providing service; however, it might actually increase your costs and reduce your profits for the following reasons:

- **Long-term support costs**—After you open or insert a wireless card into a customer's computer, it is difficult to refuse to correct each problem that the customer experiences with that computer. For example, the customer might expect you to fix power supply failures and hard disk crashes. These problems, in most cases, are unrelated to the actual wireless card installation but, in the user's mind, the wireless card might be perceived as the cause of each problem. The cost of responding to and fixing these problems can result in a net loss for you.

- **Network management deficiencies**—The client software that goes with most wireless cards does not usually possess a full set of network management and monitoring capabilities. For example, you might not be able to remotely view signal strength or link performance statistics. In addition, you might not be able to perform remote throughput management tasks such as throttling throughput to that end user.

A better, more cost-effective approach than using wireless cards in customers' computers is interfacing with the customer's computer at the Ethernet level. You can provide wireless equipment that is external to the customer's computer and that connects via Ethernet to the customer's computer (or network). If the customer does not already have an Ethernet card installed, you can refer him to a company that provides computer-networking support.

Some WISPs have deployed wireless USB adapters (modified to accept an external antenna) in an attempt to provide low-cost CPE equipment and avoid opening the customer's computer. This approach works in some cases; however, sometimes USB/motherboard/software compatibility issues occur. In addition, some virtual private networking (VPN) features might not work with the USB adapter.

The price of wireless CPE that provides an Ethernet interface to customers' networks keeps decreasing. It is becoming more feasible to deploy such equipment. As a bonus, low-cost CPE equipment is available in a weatherproof housing and with power-over-Ethernet. Mounting such equipment outside, at the antenna, eliminates coax cable loss and increases link reliability.

Measuring Fade Margin

Use a standard throughput test and measure the fade margin for every newly installed end user. This confirms that the installation was done correctly and that service will be reliable. See Chapter 7 for details about measuring the fade margin.

Allowing AP Test Time

Do not assume that every new AP will perform perfectly when it is first turned on. Allow plenty of test time so that you can adjust, correct, and verify the performance of the new AP before you start using it to provide service. Chapter 7 covers the AP testing procedures.

Managing Network Throughput

Network throughput is your most important asset because that is what your customers pay you to deliver to them. The consequences of failing to manage throughput do not show up until your network becomes heavily loaded; then your network throughput deteriorates rapidly. If you are in the WISP business to make a profit, you need to manage your network's throughput; the next few sections help you perform this management function.

Minimizing Lost Throughput

The less network throughput that you lose, the more throughput remains for you to sell. Do your best to lose as little throughput as possible from the following causes:

- **Misunderstanding**—Do not confuse bandwidth (the raw data rate on a link) with throughput (the actual amount of data that the link carries). To avoid this misunderstanding, reread the section "Comparison Between Data Rate and Throughput (Including Simplex Versus Duplex Throughput)" in Chapter 6.

- **Wireless collisions**—Every collision between wireless users results in a loss of that time slot and a loss of throughput. You can minimize collisions by using software that polls your users. If your software does not include polling, the next-best thing you can do is fine-tune the RTS/CTS threshold to help minimize the packet collisions between users.

- **Interference and noise**—Every packet that needs to be repeated before it is successfully received causes lost time slots and lost throughput. The more you can reduce noise and interference in your network, the more throughput you can retain to sell to your customers.

Reusing Frequencies Successfully

Unless you are located in a small town, you need to reuse frequencies. Unless your antenna systems are completely isolated from each other, reusing frequencies causes you to lose throughput. The section "Benefiting from Antenna System Isolation" in Chapter 5, "Selecting Antenna Systems," explains how to isolate antennas so that you can reuse frequencies without losing throughput. The section "Minimizing Noise from Your DSSS Network" in Chapter 8, "Solving Noise and Interference Problems," provides an example of making a frequency reuse plan. Review these sections now so that you can successfully re-use frequencies and still obtain full throughput on each frequency.

Allocating Throughput Per Customer

In life, the same size of shoe doesn't fit all feet. In wireless networks, one size of throughput doesn't fit all wireless users. To manage your network throughput profitably, you need to sell customers only the amount of throughput that they need or want. Offer your customers a tiered service plan that allows them to buy only as much throughput as they need. Practice throughput management so that your customers get the throughput they pay for.

Some wireless equipment includes throughput management features such as the following:

- **Maximum rate throttling**—This feature allows you to set the maximum throughput that each customer will have, such as 128 kbps or 512 kbps, for example.

- **MIR/CIR**—This feature allows you to set both a maximum information rate (MIR) and a committed information rate (CIR) for each customer. The equipment always reserves at least the CIR for the customer; however, when the network isn't busy, the equipment allows the customer to obtain (up to) the MIR.

- **Asymmetrical throughput rates**—Some equipment allows you to assign throughput asymmetrically to each customer. In other words, you can set customers' bandwidth to be different depending on whether they are downloading or uploading. By configuring the upload speed to be slower than the download speed, you can serve more customers on your network.

If your wireless equipment does not already include these features, you can gain per-customer control by adding an external throughput control router. See Appendix B for vendor information.

Determining Network Capacity

You need to know how your network is performing and when your network reaches maximum capacity. The following tools and techniques can help you evaluate your network performance:

- **Ping latency**—Pinging across a wireless link with a string of 1400 byte packets is a real-time test that you can run to get a quick view of network performance. Interpreting these test results is described in the section "Monitoring Network Performance" in Chapter 8.

- **Retransmit percentage**—The percentage of packets that need to be retransmitted before they are successfully received is another meaningful indication of network performance. The section "Monitoring Network Performance" in Chapter 8 provides a detailed explanation.

- **MRTG**—Many WISPs use the Multi Router Traffic Grapher (MRTG) tool to monitor traffic levels and network traffic loading over time. Appendix B contains a link to more information about this tool.

Keeping Some Throughput in Reserve

Your network can provide up to a maximum throughput level; however, this level is affected by several factors that you cannot control. These uncontrollable factors include noise, interference, equipment deterioration, and the sudden appearance of nearby networks. It is important for you to keep some of your throughput unsold, in reserve, to provide a cushion of protection for your wireless customers. As you gain experience monitoring the performance of your network, you'll be able to estimate how much additional throughput you can sell. Always plan to leave some potential throughput unsold.

How Much Throughput Headroom Is Enough?

Based on my personal observations (and my play-it-safe nature), I would suggest that you leave 25 to 30 percent of your throughput unsold. It is more important to ensure your customers' satisfaction than to attempt to squeeze out every last penny of profit. Without a throughput reserve, all your customers will become instantly unhappy when another network suddenly appears and their throughput drops to zero.

Enhancing Network Security

As a wireless network operator, you want to do everything possible to help your customers feel comfortable using your network. Your customers want to be reassured that their data will remain confidential and that their network will not be attacked or hacked. The more information that you give your customers about your security procedures, the more comfortable they will feel.

There are many steps that you need to take to maintain and preserve the confidentiality and integrity of your customer's data. At the same time, you want to prevent unauthorized users from stealing service on your network.

First, as you already know, security is relative, not absolute. Although no network can be made 100 percent secure 100 percent of the time, every step you take reduces the likelihood of a security problem. Explain this to your customers and advise them of the security precautions that you have taken at each layer of your network. Here are some of those precautions:

- **Practice wired network security**—Secure your wired network. Stay up to date on known attacks directed at traditional wired IPSs and put countermeasures in place whenever necessary.

- **Use proprietary hardware and software**—Whenever possible, use proprietary wireless hardware and software. For every 100 people who have 802.11b hacking skills, there is less than one person who can hack non-802.11b wireless equipment.

- **Use unique network IDs**—Do not use the default network ID or extended service set ID (ESSID); use a unique ID. Recent surveys of wireless AP use show that about one half of all APs are using the default ID and are wide open to unauthorized users. Some newer operating systems, such as Windows XP, sniff the service set ID (SSID) or ESSID regardless of what you set it to. Even so, you should change your ESSID to something other than the default value.

- **Enable Wired Equivalent Privacy (WEP)**—Recently, published press reports have concentrated on the vulnerabilities of WEP; however, WEP capability does help improve security and should not be ignored. Surveys show only about 20 percent of APs have WEP enabled. If your APs have the capability to use WEP without a noticeable performance reduction, you should enable WEP.

- **Turn off beaconing**—If your network does not need to have beaconing enabled, turn it off. This prevents some network-scanning programs from sniffing the ESSID of the AP.

- **Use access control lists**—Use an access control list based on either MAC addresses or IP addresses. Sure, addresses can be spoofed, but remember: Each step that you take reduces the chances of hacking.

- **Implement 802.1x features**—Use these advanced security features whenever your AP or access controller supports them.

- **Enable all available security features**—Whether you are running an 802.11b network or a proprietary network, enable all the security features that your wireless equipment provides.

Advise those customers who need more security to run their own virtual private network, use firewalls with IPSec, or run a tunneling protocol.

Coexisting with Other Wireless Networks

In many cities, it is likely that there will be more than one WISP in town. The following sections provide some suggestions about working together with other WISPs so that everyone can benefit.

Cooperating with Competitors

You can cooperate with other WISPs in your area in many ways. Here are some ideas:

- **Split the market**—You provide service for the customers who you are most interested in, and you agree to let the other WISP provide service for the customers that it is most interested in.

- **Split the frequencies**—If your WISP and the other WISP both want to compete for the same customers, agree to use equipment that operates on different channels or on different bands. For example, the other WISP might operate on 2.4 GHz while you operate on 5.8 GHz.

- **Roaming agreements**—If your WISP and the other WISP are using similar equipment, you both might agree to allow your customers to roam between the two networks. This benefits your customers by widening the area where they can obtain service.

Interference from Other WISPs

If you discover an interference problem between your WISP and a competing WISP, it would be best if the two of you could meet and solve the problem between yourselves. You could agree to modify your frequencies, hopping patterns, or your coverage areas to minimize or eliminate the interference.

If you find that you have a WISP competitor who refuses to cooperate, your best course of action is probably to document the frequencies, power levels, and locations of the other WISP equipment and then make changes to your network to minimize the interference.

TIP	If possible, see if you can switch to the opposite antenna polarization, such as from vertical to horizontal. It might be inconvenient to change the polarization of your customer's antennas, but this is the simplest, lowest-cost way to minimize interference.

If you believe that the other WISP is operating with illegally high power, you can use a spectrum analyzer to determine the actual effective radiated power level. Then, try to schedule a meeting and diplomatically suggest that if he reduces his power down to the legal level, neither he nor you will have to waste time discussing the matter with the FCC.

If you believe that another WISP is intentionally interfering with you, you need to document that operation (again, with a spectrum analyzer) and then contact your lawyer to discuss the possibility of filing a civil lawsuit against the other WISP.

Interference with Amateur Radio Operations

The FCC licenses amateur radio operators; therefore, their operation has priority over license-free operation. Legally, you must not cause interference with amateur radio operation. Also, you must accept interference from amateur radio operation. In actual practice, it is pretty unusual to experience interference to or from amateurs because not many active amateurs operate on the 2.4-GHz and the 5-GHz bands. If an interference problem does occur, consider changing frequencies or reconfiguring your antenna system to eliminate the problem.

NOTE   You might want to consider getting an amateur radio license. It is a great way to experiment and learn a lot about wireless technology. It is also a good way to serve the public in times of emergency.

Living with the FCC

In the United States, the FCC is the government body that regulates all wireless communications, both license free and licensed. The next sections provide information that helps you to accomplish the following:

- Operate legally within the law
- Understand the FCC equipment certification process
- Respond to FCC inquiries
- Lobby the FCC

Observing FCC Power Limits

FCC regulations set maximum radiated power limits for license-free systems in the ISM and U-NII bands in the United States. These power limits are designed to minimize interference and maximize the number of people who can use the bands simultaneously.

There are thousands of times more users of license-free equipment than there are FCC personnel available to enforce the rules and regulations. It does not take many people running illegal high-power amplifiers to raise the interference level and make the bands unusable for everyone. To keep interference levels under control, license-free equipment must be tested along with the antenna system and certified to be operating within the FCC-specified power limits.

Most WISPs comply with the FCC rules and regulations. Unfortunately, a few WISPs are either not aware of the FCC power limitations or choose to ignore the rules. It is important for you to learn what the legal power limits are and to obey these limits. The alternative is to have the FCC tighten up its regulations or even to prohibit license-free operation completely.

NOTE   Tables 6-1, 6-2, and 6-3 in Chapter 6 list the FCC power limits in the United States, and
            Table 7-1 in Chapter 7 provides several examples of equivalent isotropic radiated power
            (EIRP) calculations.

If you are located outside the United States, it should be clear to you that observing the rules
and regulations of your country's licensing authority is a wise decision that helps you
enhance the stability of your network and allows you to continue to operate your network.
A few countries require user licensing in the 2.4-GHz band. If this is true in your country,
you should certainly obtain governmental approval before you deploy your network.

FCC Equipment Certification

The FCC requires that all license-free transmitting equipment be FCC certified. Certification means that a testing lab has verified that the equipment, the amplifier (if used), and
the antenna system have been tested together (as a complete system) and found to comply
with the FCC power and spectral purity requirements.

Most WISPs are curious and creative, and enjoy experimenting with various equipment and
antenna combinations to obtain the best equipment performance. To stay within both the
spirit and the letter of the law, you, as a WISP, need to do one of the following:

- Use equipment and antenna combinations that have already been sent to a certification
  lab by the vendor of the equipment.

- Use antenna systems that stay within the FCC power limits and that you have built in
  limited quantities (less than six units) for your own use.

- Use equipment and antenna combinations that you have sent to a certification lab and that
  have been successfully certified. This usually requires obtaining transmitter specifications
  from the manufacturer of the equipment and forwarding these specifications to the lab
  along with your antenna system.

- Submit the specifications for your new antenna systems to your wireless equipment
  manufacturer and request that the manufacturer apply for a "permissive change" to its
  existing equipment certification. The permissive change allows WISPs to use the new
  antenna system in place of the antenna system that the manufacturer originally
  certified with the equipment.

In the past, many WISPs ignored the equipment-certification step and used equipment that
met the spirit of the law but not the letter of the law. In other words, many WISPs used
equipment combinations that did not exceed the FCC power limits but that were not lab-
certified to be within the power limits. Recently, with the vastly increased use of the license-
free bands, the FCC began making unannounced visits to a few WISPs to confirm that they
were using only certified equipment and antenna combinations.

If you are operating with one or more non-lab-certified equipment and antenna combinations, you might want to spend the money and send samples of your equipment to a lab for certification. This step will probably feel burdensome and will cost you up to several thousand dollars per certification run, but it will also save you from legal embarrassment, costly equipment changeouts, and FCC fines.

NOTE   Do an Internet search on "FCC Part 15 Certification Lab" to locate a lab near you.

Responding to FCC Inquiries

Hopefully, you will never experience a personal visit from the FCC or receive a letter or other written correspondence from it. If you are ever visited, remember that the FCC has the right to inspect your equipment at any time, and you must allow it to perform this inspection. By operating a transmitter, even though it is license-free, you give the FCC the right to inspect your equipment and request (or order) you to make any changes necessary to comply with the communications law.

If you ever receive written correspondence from the FCC, you will be given a specific period of time to make an official reply. If you do not reply within the specified period of time, you might be fined and ordered to shut down your equipment. The wise WISP always replies appropriately and in a timely fashion to any and all FCC correspondence.

Lobbying the FCC

Although the FCC makes the communications rules, it is also open to considering new rules and modifying existing rules. Companies and individuals can petition, lobby, and comment on changes to the communications laws. These changes might be beneficial to the public as a whole, beneficial to some segment of the wireless industry, or perhaps beneficial to only one wireless company. The most successful lobbying efforts are ones that use the services of FCC-specialized, Washington-based (expensive) law firms. Small companies that want to petition or lobby for changes will probably be most successful by joining one of the existing wireless communications groups that has regular contact with FCC personnel. Appendix B lists several of these groups.

Anticipating Emerging Trends

You have probably heard it said that the only constant is change. Changes in the wireless industry occur practically every week. The sections that follow describe trends that can affect the ways you conduct your wireless business.

CPE Equipment Cost Reductions

More and more people are using wireless LAN equipment in their businesses and homes. As this market becomes larger, it continues to drive down the cost of 802.11b hardware. This hardware cost reduction, in turn, reduces the cost of 802.11b equipment that is usable by WISPs. You might want to keep up to date on this trend because soon CPE will be available in the under-$200 price range, including a built-in antenna and power-over-Ethernet (PoE) capability.

802.11 Creep

802.11b has been so successful that it has become the de facto broadband wireless standard, and 802.11b capabilities are appearing in a wider variety of devices. Soon, 802.11b (and follow-on 802.11a and 802.11g technology) will be as common as the remote control for your television set.

Multiband wireless chipsets will appear that allow 802.11b capabilities to be included in most consumer devices, such as personal computers, personal digital assistants (PDAs), printers, cell phones, video cameras, and so on. The pervasive presence of 802.11b, 802.11a, 802.11g, and Bluetooth technology will be a double-edged sword for WISPs—they will be both a blessing and a curse. On the one hand, you will have access to usable technology at lower prices that will allow you to deliver more creative wireless services to your customers. On the other hand, you will need to learn how to work around the higher levels of wireless noise, interference, and hacking that will be present.

802.11b and Cellular Service Integration

The rollout of broadband (3G) service by the cellular telephone carriers is proving to be extremely expensive, requiring the investment of billions of dollars. In comparison, the rollout of broadband 802.11b hotspot service is inexpensive.

The cellular telephone companies will, at the very least, seek to leverage this trend to lower their cost of providing broadband service. This will lead them to deploy new cell phone handsets that include 802.11b technology. When a caller is out of range of a 3G cell site, the phone will attempt to roam to an 802.11b hotspot.

Cellular carriers might also seek to dominate the hotspot market. Remember: Wired telephone service was a monopoly in the United States until recently. The monopoly-created incumbent local telephone companies today own and operate most of the cellular telephony companies in the United States. In the same way, it is not unreasonable for these same companies to attempt to gain control and dominate the wireless hotspot market.

Other Trends

This section mentions a few more emerging trends that you, as a progressive WISP, can keep your eye on.

Community Networks

More and more people, intrigued by the concepts of wireless networking and community service, are deploying community networks that provide free 802.11b wireless Internet access. You, as a WISP, must determine the role that you want to play in this emerging community networking movement.

Hot Spots

The hot spot concept of providing broadband wireless Internet access to the public in selected public locations (such as airports) and in selected business locations is growing rapidly. As a WISP, you might want to participate in some way in this business. Following are some ways in which you can participate:

- Provide backbone bandwidth wirelessly for the hotspots that are located within your wireless service area.

- Make agreements with local hotspot operators that allow your fixed wireless customers to connect at the hotspots when they are away from their fixed location.

- Place your own hotspots in high traffic locations. This allows you to provide additional connectivity for your current wireless customers and advertise your fixed wireless services to everyone who sees or uses your hotspots.

802.16 Standards

The Institute of Electrical and Electronics Engineers (IEEE) 802.16 Working Group on Broadband Wireless Access has developed standards that allow interoperability between wireless metropolitan-area network (MAN) equipment operating between 10 GHz and 66 GHz. Although this standard does not cover the current license-free bands, the 802.16a working group is currently working to expand the standard to the licensed and the license-free bands between 2 GHz and 11 GHz. In the next few years, this work might lead to greater interoperability between wireless WAN equipment.

Broadband Optical Equipment

Short-range broadband optical equipment is available now. Point-to-multipoint optical equipment is under development and beginning to become available. Instead of using microwave radio links, this optical equipment uses either lasers or light-emitting diodes (LEDs) to send and receive broadband information. In the future, this optical equipment might have a role to play as part of your wireless network.

Avoiding Black Holes

Black holes in the galaxy are invisible, collapsed star systems that have gravity levels so intense that they suck all nearby matter in. The broadband wireless world also has a few black holes. Wireless black holes are not quite as intense as black holes in the galaxy, but the principle is the same. You cannot see these black holes in advance, but they can suck all your money away. The following sections describe a few of these money traps to avoid.

NLOS Equipment Performance

Every wireless product is a non-line-of-sight (NLOS) product, yet no wireless product is a true NLOS product. If this statement sounds like a contradiction, please go back to Chapter 6 and read the section "Non Line-of-Sight Features."

Remember: The goal of this NLOS section is to prevent your money from being sucked into a black hole. There is still no magic bullet that can prevent a microwave signal from being attenuated (and diffracted and lost) when it strikes an obstacle. This attenuation means that the signal cannot travel far through a series of dense obstructions. Table 9-2 summarizes the conditions that affect link distances in an NLOS environment. Review this table and the paragraphs that follow it before you purchase NLOS equipment.

Table 9-2   *Factors That Affect NLOS Link Distances*

NLOS Factor	Best NLOS Condition
Effective radiated power (or equivalent isotropic radiated power)	The higher the effective radiated power (within FCC rules), the greater the NLOS distance.
Frequency	The lower the frequency, the greater the distance.
Multipath environment	The fewer the reflection points, the less the multipath and the greater the distance.
Modulation type	OFDM is believed by some to be better in a multipath environment.
Antenna directivity	The more directive the antenna, the greater the distance.
Throughput	The lower the throughput, the greater the distance.
Obstacle quantity	The fewer the obstacles, the greater the distance.
Obstacle spacing	The more space between obstacles, the greater the distance.
Link distances	The shorter the link distance, the greater the throughput.

Even when all the factors that combine to determine communications distance are optimized, the best NLOS system does not communicate far in a densely obstructed environment. For example, although an NLOS system might work when the LOS path is obstructed by a few trees, the system does not work when the signal has to pass through a densely wooded forest.

In conclusion, it is better to spend your time determining how you can obtain better LOS paths (higher CPE antennas, more APs covering shorter distances, and so on) than dreaming about all of those potential NLOS customers who are magically going to get reliable connectivity through miles and miles of dense trees.

Receiver Performance Near High-Power Transmitters

Another black hole to watch out for is poor receiver performance when an indoor LAN card is used outdoors on a site that has several nearby high-power transmitters. In this environment, without additional filtering, these cards are not likely to receive very far. Remember the following about low-cost wireless LAN cards: They are designed for use indoors with a built-in antenna in a low-power environment. They are not designed for use outdoors, with external antennas near multiple high-power transmitters.

If you plan to use low-cost LAN cards with outdoor antennas on AM, FM, or TV towers or on rooftops that have multiple cell phone and paging system transmitters, plan to use bandpass filters to attenuate the nearby high-power signals. Without external filtering to protect LAN cards from overload, you might never get them to receive properly on such sites.

Commercial Tower Companies

The behavior of large (nationwide) commercial tower companies can sometimes consume your money like a black hole. Occasionally, tower company management behaves in ways that require you to spend thousands of dollars in installation and maintenance fees that you never anticipated spending. For example, these companies can require that subsidiary installation companies (that they own) do all your tower work. These subsidiaries might charge you thousands of dollars to perform routine installation and maintenance work on your own tower-mounted antenna systems.

NOTE

The conversation might go something like this:

You: "I think my amplifier on the tower has failed. Can I go up and replace it?"

The subsidiaries: "Gosh, we're sorry to hear that your tower amplifier has failed, Mr. Brown. Only we can climb that tower safely, and we'll have to charge you $3000 to climb the tower and replace your amplifier. By the way, we're kind of busy right now, but we should be able to get back to you in about 20 days."

Beware of the black hole! Be sure that you will be allowed to use your own (properly trained, insured, and affordable) installation company before you sign a lease to place your equipment and antennas on a commercial tower site.

Changes to Government Licensing Regulations

A governmental agency or communications commission regulates the use of license-free frequencies in most countries. This commission has the power to either stimulate or inhibit the use of license-free wireless technology. If license-free wireless appears to be beneficial, it is likely that the government will encourage additional users. If license-free wireless appears to be detrimental, the government can reduce or even end the use of license-free equipment. Recently, in one country, the government prohibited new license-free use of the 2.4-GHz band. Many unlicensed users deployed illegal high-power amplifiers, and the interference levels became so high that the government finally stepped in and banned all new users. If you were a WISP in that country and suddenly you could not add new customers to your network, you would find yourself falling into a black hole.

Never abuse the license-free operating privileges that you currently enjoy. The best guarantee that you will continue to enjoy license-free operating privileges is to operate legally and ethically.

Review Questions

1   A WISP is an extension of a wired ISP. True or false?

2   WISPs have been around since about 1995. True or false?

3   The most profitable wireless markets are those where broadband DSL and cable Internet access are already available. True or false?

4   The mobile market where users stay connected while driving around is the easiest market to serve. True or false?

5   Customers pay you to deliver bandwidth, not throughput. True or false?

6   You can be successful in the wireless business even if you don't understand the meaning of decibels. True or false?

7   All 802.11b equipment brands work with all other 802.11b equipment brands with no problems. True or false?

8   Why do wireless collisions reduce throughput?

9   The higher the percentage of retransmitted packets, the lower the network throughput. True or false?

10   You should always sell all the throughput that your network is capable of delivering. True or false?

11   The best way to deal with a WISP competitor is to add an amplifier. True or false?

Wireless Standards Summary

This appendix provides a summary table of the 802.11 standards. It also includes related standards such as 802.1x and 802.16.

Table A-1 *Wireless Standards*

Standard	Description
802.1x	802.1x defines a new framework of authentication and encryption procedures that are designed to improve security. Some vendors have begun to incorporate proprietary adaptations of these features into their wireless equipment.
802.11	802.11 is the original wireless LAN standard. It specifies both direct sequence spread spectrum (DSSS) and frequency hopping spread spectrum (FHSS) modulation techniques. DSSS modulation is specified with raw data rates of 1 Mbps and 2 Mbps on 11 (in the U.S.) 22 MHz-wide channels at 2.4 GHz. FHSS modulation is specified with a raw data rate of 2 Mbps using any of 78 possible hopping sequences at 2.4 GHz.
802.11a	802.11a specifies orthogonal frequency division multiplexing (OFDM) in three 5 GHz subbands. These subbands are 5.150 MHz to 5.250 GHz (indoor use only), 5.250 to 5.350 GHz (indoor or outdoor use), and 5.725 to 5.825 (outdoor use). There are four 20-MHz channels per subband. 802.11a equipment must provide raw data rates of 6 Mbps, 12 Mbps, and 24 Mbps and might provide raw data rates of 9 Mbps, 18 Mbps, 36 Mbps, 48 Mbps, and 54 Mbps.
802.11b	802.11b adds a high-rate DSSS physical layer with both a 5 Mbps and an 11 Mbps raw data rate. 802.11b uses the same 11 channels as the original 802.11 standard.
802.11d	802.11d is an attempt to add features that allow 802.11 radios to operate legally in countries outside of North America and Europe.
802.11e	The proposed 802.11e standard adds quality of service (QoS) enhancements to 802.11a, 802.11b, and 802.11g.
802.11f	The proposed 801.11f standard is an attempt to specify an inter-access point protocol (IAPP) that would allow communication between access points made by different manufacturers.

continues

Table A-1 *Wireless Standards (Continued)*

Standard	Description
802.11g	802.11g is a standard that allows faster data rates (up to 54 Mbps) at 2.4 GHz. The 802.11g standard allows OFDM, packet binary convolution coding (PBCC) modulation, and 802.11b complementary code keying (CCK) modulation. The CCK modulation makes 802.11g backward-compatible with 802.11b.
802.11h	When adopted, the 802.11h standard will add dynamic frequency selection and transmitter power control to 802.11a. Dynamic frequency selection allows an access point to select the best frequency to use to minimize interference. Transmitter power control allows the transmit power to be adjusted to the minimum level needed to communicate with the most distant user.
802.11i	802.11i is an ongoing effort to define a new set of wireless security features that provide improved authentication and encryption. 802.11i will incorporate security features from the 802.1x standard.
802.15.1	802.15.1 is a wireless personal area networks (WPAN) standard that operates at 2.4 GHz and is based on the Bluetooth v1.1 specification. Bluetooth is designed for short-range personal communications between notebook computers, cell phones, and other handheld devices.
802.16	The 802.16 standard is designed to allow metropolitan-area network (MAN) equipment from different vendors to interoperate in the frequency range of 11 to 66 GHz.
802.16a	Work is progressing on 802.16a extensions to 802.16 that would cover both licensed and license-free equipment operating in the 2 to 10 GHz bands. This includes the current 2.4 GHz and 5 GHz license-free bands.

Wireless Hardware, Software, and Service Provider Organizations

This appendix contains a listing of organizations that provide wireless hardware, software, services, test equipment, books, training, peripherals, and industry information.

Wireless Hardware

The companies listed in Table B-1 design and manufacture wireless hardware that is designed for broadband wide-area networking. In addition to these, many smaller companies exist that either manufacture equipment or resell equipment that is manufactured by larger companies. These smaller companies are too numerous to list in this section.

Table B-1   *Wireless Hardware Companies*

Company	Website	Hardware Offered
Alvarion	www.alvarion.com	2.4-GHz and 5-GHz frequency-hopping spread spectrum (FHSS) and direct-sequence spread spectrum (FHSS) equipment.
Aperto	www.apertonetworks.com	5-GHz license-free (and 2.5-GHz and 3.5-GHz licensed) point-to-multipoint system.
Cirronet	www.cirronet.com	2.4-GHz and 5-GHz WISP equipment.
Cisco	www.cisco.com	Aironet 2.4-GHz access point and bridge hardware; upgradeable to 5 GHz.
Lucent/ Avaya/Agere	www.wavelan.com; www.orinocowireless.com	2.4-GHz access point hardware; upgradeable to 5 GHz. Proxim purchased this entire line of equipment in 2002.
Motorola	www.motorola.com/canopy/	5-GHz point-to-point and point-to-multipoint equipment.
Netnimble	www.netnimble.net	2.4-GHz products and peripherals
Nokia	www.nokia.com	Rooftop 2.4-GHz mesh network.

continues

Table B-1   *Wireless Hardware Companies (Continued)*

Company	Website	Hardware Offered
Proxim	www.proxim.com	Wide range of wireless LAN and WAN equipment.
Raylink	www.raylink.com	FHSS bridges and access points.
Redline	www.redlinecommunications.com	5-GHz bridge.
Smartbridges	www.smartbridges.com	2.4-GHz LAN and WAN products
Solectek	www.solectek.com	2.4-GHz point-to-point and point-to-multipoint equipment.
Teletronics	www.teletronics.com	Bridges, access points, and accessories.
Trango	www.trangobroadband.com	5-GHz point-to-point and point-to-multipoint equipment.
Waverider	www.waverider.com	See website for details.
Western Multiplex	www.proxim.com	5-GHz equipment. Proxim purchased Western Multiplex in 2001.
Wi-Lan	www.wilan.com	See website for details.
YDI	www.ydi.com	2.4-GHz and 5-GHz equipment and accessories.

Low-Cost 802.11b Access Point Hardware

This section lists a few of the many companies that manufacture low-cost 802.11b wireless LAN access points. These access points are designed for use in indoor wireless LANs; however, wireless Internet service providers (WISPs) often add external antennas and deploy these access points in outdoor WANs. These low-cost access points do not have the full software functionality that more expensive equipment (designed for WISP use) has. Operators of free public-access community networks frequently use these low-cost access points:

- D-Link (www.dlink.com)
- Linksys (www.linksys.com)
- Netgear (netgear.com)
- SMC (www.smc.com)

Wireless Hotspot Hardware

The following companies provide hardware, software, or services for use by wireless hotspot providers:

- Airpathwireless (www.airpathwireless.com)
- Bluesocket (www.bluesocket.com)

- Boingo (www.boingo.com)
- Café.com (www.café.com)
- Colubris Networks (www.colubris.com)
- Funk Software (funk.com)
- Hotspotzz (www.hotspotzz.com)
- iPass (www.ipass.com)
- Joltage (www.joltage.com)
- NetNearU (www.netnearu.com)
- NoCat (www.nocat.net)
- Nomadix (www.nomadix.com)
- Sputnik (www.sputnik.com)
- Reefedge (www.reefedge.com)
- Wayport (www.wayport.com)

Free Space Optical Hardware

The following companies develop or supply free space optical networking equipment that might be useful to WISPs:

- Fsona (www.fsona.com)
- Omnilux (www.omnilux.net)
- Plaintree (www.plaintree.com)

Security Hardware and Software

Table B-2 lists a few of the many companies that supply equipment designed to make networks, both wired and wireless, more secure.

Table B-2   *Security Hardware and Software Companies*

Company	Website	Product
Global Technology Associates	www.gta.com	Wired firewall and VPN products
Multitech	www.multitech.com	Access point plus security products
Securepoint Technologies	www.securepoint.com	Wired firewall and VPN products
Smoothwall	www.smoothwall.org/community/home	Open source firewall
Sonicwall	www.sonicwall.com	Wired firewall and VPN products

Antenna Systems

The following companies manufacture antenna systems that are useful for outdoor wireless WANs:

- Cushcraft (www.cushcraft.com)
- Gabriel (www.gabrielnet.com)
- Maxrad (www.maxrad.com)
- Mobile Mark (www.mobilemark.com)
- Pac Wireless (www.pacwireless.com)
- Radio Waves (www.radiowavesinc.com)
- Superpass (superpass.com)
- Tiltek (tiltek.com)

Coaxial Cable

Table B-3 lists some companies that manufacture low-loss coax cable often used by WISPs.

Table B-3 *Coax Cable Manufacturers for WISP Use*

Company	Website	Product
Andrew	www.andrew.com	Extensive selection of antennas, coax cable, and antenna system products
Belden	www.belden.com	Coax cable
Times Microwave	www.timesmicrowave.com	Coax cable and coax connector products that are popular among WISPs

Towers and Antenna Mounting Hardware

Table B-4 lists some companies that manufacture towers and accessories that are suitable for WISP use.

Table B-4 *Tower or Accessory Manufacturers for WISP Use*

Company	Website	Product
Heights Tower	www.HeightsTowers.com	Aluminum towers
Rohn	www.rohnnet.com	An extensive line of steel towers and antenna-mounting products
Trylon	trylon.com	Aluminum towers

Lightning-Protection Equipment

The following companies manufacture lighting-protection equipment designed to protect outdoor antenna systems:

- Citel (www.citelprotection.com)
- Hyperlink (www.hyperlinktech.com)
- Polyphaser (www.polyphaser.com)

Grounding Equipment

The following companies manufacture grounding hardware designed for low-impedance lightning-protection systems:

- Erico (www.erico.com)
- Polyphaser (www.polyphaser.com)

Test Equipment

A wide range of test hardware and software is available to WISPs. The majority of this equipment is designed for indoor wireless LAN use; however, some units might prove useful in the outdoor WAN environment. Table B-5 lists some of the major testing hardware and software for WISPs.

Table B-5   *WISP Testing Hardware or Software Companies*

Company	Website	Product
Airmagnet	www.airmagnet.com	Laptop and handheld-based wireless LAN analysis tools
AiroPeek	www.wildpackets.com	AiroPeek Wireless LAN analyzer
Avcom of Virginia	www.avcomofva.com	Spectrum analyzers
Berkeley Varitronics	bvsystems.com	A wide range of wireless LAN analysis tools
Ethereal	www.ethereal.com	A protocol analyzer that runs on Windows or UNIX
Kismet	www.kismetwireless.net	A software tool that locates access points
LP Technologies	www.lptechnologies.com	Spectrum analyzers
Netstumbler	www.netstumbler.com	A software tool that locates access points
Sniffer Technologies	www.sniffer.com	Wireless LAN analyzer

Peripheral Equipment Distributors

WISPs typically use a variety of peripheral equipment, such as cable, connectors, tools, and weather-sealing products. The following companies distribute a wide range of these products:

- Electro-Comm (www.electro-comm.com)
- Electro-Comm West (www.ecwest.com)
- Talley (www.talleycommunications.com)
- Tessco (www.tessco.com)

Wireless Software

The software listed by type in the following sections is useful for WISPs.

Access Point Software

Table B-6 lists some of the more commonly available software for wireless access points.

Table B-6   *Access Point Software*

Company	Website	Product
KarlNet	www.karlnet.com	Software that runs on access points and wireless clients that adds polling, bandwidth management, routing, packet aggregation, and other WISP features.
Mikrotik	www.mikrotik.com	Access point and router software with many features that are useful to wireless network operators.
Valemount Networks	www.station-server.com	StarOS access point and client software provides many WISP features.

Bandwidth Management Software

Managing wireless bandwidth is crucial for WISPs. The following companies provide bandwidth-management software. Several of these companies also supply optional hardware to run the software:

- Emerging Technologies (www.etinc.com)
- Packeteer (www.packeteer.com)
- Allot Communications (www.allot.com)

Wireless Link Planning Software

The following companies provide mapping software that helps you determine whether you have a line-of-sight path between two or more physical locations:

- EDX (www.edx.com)
- Microdem (www.usna.edu/Users/oceano/pguth/website/microdem.htm)
- Micropath (www.micropath.com)
- Pathloss (www.pathloss.com)
- Radio Mobile (www.cplus.org/rmw/english1.html)
- Topo (http://maps.nationalgeographic.com/topo)

Utility Software

Table B-7 lists some useful utilities for wireless networks.

Table B-7   *Wireless Utility Software*

Company	Website	Product
MRTG	http://people.ee.ethz.ch/~oetiker/webtools/mrtg/	Multi-router Traffic Grapher offers open source software that monitors network traffic levels.
Nagios	www.nagios.com	Nagios offers open source network monitoring software.
Qcheck	www.netiq.com/qcheck/howqcheckworks.asp	Qcheck offers software that performs throughput testing.

Site Survey Software

In the absence of a spectrum analyzer, the site survey utilities listed in Table B-8 are helpful to determine whether interference is present in a specific area. In addition to the following, most primary wireless LAN vendors provide free site survey software that operates with their hardware.

Table B-8   *Site Survey Software*

Company	Website	Product
Teletronics	www.teletronics.com	DSSS site survey utility that runs with the Teletronics 2 Mbps card and possibly the 11 Mbps card
Proxim	www.proxim.com	FHSS Site survey utility that runs with RangeLAN II cards

Services

The following organizations provide consulting and training services that are specifically designed for wireless security, wireless WANs, and WISPs.

Consulting

- The Final Mile (www.thefinalmile.net)
- Wireless InfoNet, Inc. (www.ask-wi.com)
- Wireless-Nets (www.wireless-nets.com)

Training

Table B-9 *Wireless Network Training Companies*

Company	Website	Type of Training Offered
Comtrain	comtrainusa.com	Tower-climbing training
Planet3 Wireless	www.cwne.com	Vendor-neutral wireless LAN training
Wireless InfoNet, Inc.	www.ask-wi.com	Vendor-neutral wireless ISP training
Wireless-Nets	www.wireless-nets.com	Wireless LAN training

Suggested Books for Further Reading

The following books provide information that is especially useful to designers of wireless WANs and WISPs:

- The *ARRL Handbook for Radio Amateurs* (published by the American Radio Relay League [www.arrl.org]). This book is a standard reference book in the wireless industry with more than 1000 pages of information.

- *ARRL UHF/Microwave Experimenter's Manual* (published by the American Radio Relay League [ARRL]). This book is a good microwave theory textbook.

- *802.11 Wireless Networks—The Definitive Guide* by Matthew Gast (published by O'Reilly and Associates). This is probably the all-around best 802.11 book in terms of providing practical 802.11 knowledge. It primarily covers indoor deployments, but some outdoor information is also included.

- *Microwave Radio Transmission Design Guide* by Trevor Manning (published by Artech House). This is an excellent microwave design book that explains microwave theory at the engineering level.

- *IEEE 802.11 Handbook—A Designer's Companion* by Bob O'Hara and Al Petrick (published by IEEE Press). This book provides a good engineering-level view of 802.11.

- *Broadband Fixed Wireless Networks* by Neil Reid (published by McGraw-Hill/ Osborne). This is a good reference book on many of the aspects of deploying wireless WANs, including licensed WANs.

- *Microwave Handbook* (published by the Radio Society of Great Britain [RSGB]). This is a three-volume set primarily intended for use by radio amateurs. The high quality of the theoretical information and the hands-on construction information make these books useful for anyone wanting to gain an in-depth understanding of microwave science and art.

- *Building Wireless Community Networks* by Rob Flickenger (published by O'Reilly and Associates). This book addresses many of the points that need to be considered by anyone who wants to deploy a community network based on 802.11b technology.

- *Lightning Protection and Grounding Solutions for Communication Sites* (published by PolyPhaser Corp.). This is an excellent book for anyone who wants to have an in-depth understanding of how to protect an outdoor wireless system from lightning.

- *Wireless LANs*, 2nd Edition by Jim Geier (published by Sams). The first edition of this book was one of the first wireless LAN books available. It provides a good description of 802.11 PHY and MAC-level operation as well as practical techniques that help you to deploy indoor wireless LANs.

Online Magazines

These are three of the online wireless news sources that publish articles of interest to outdoor broadband wireless and wireless hotspot service providers:

- Broadband Wireless Exchange (www.bbwexchange.com)
- Broadband Wireless Business (www.shorecliffcommunications.com/magazine/ index.asp)
- 802.11-Planet (www.802.11-planet.com)

WISP Industry Organizations

The following organizations address the particular needs of WISPs:

- Part-15.org (www.part-15.org)
- Wireless Communications Association International (WCAI) (www.wcai.com)
- Wireless Internet Service Providers Association (WISPA) (www.wispa.org)

E-Mail Lists

The following e-mail lists frequently contain information that is especially relevant to wireless service providers:

- Wireless ISP list (isp-wireless@isp-wireless.com)
- Usenet Wireless Internet Newsgroup (alt.internet.wireless)
- Wireless ISP equipment list (www.wisp-equipment.net)
- Wireless LANs discussion group (wirelesslans@yahoogroups.com)
- Broadband Wireless discussion group (broadbandwireless@yahoogroups.com)

FCC Rules and Regulations

You can find information about the FCC rules and regulations on the FCC website (www.fcc.gov).

Wireless Standards

You can obtain information on the various wireless standards from the following organizations:

- Bluetooth (www.bluetooth.com)
- IEEE (www.ieee.org)
- Wi-Fi (www.wi-fi.net)
- 802.16 (http://grouper.ieee.org/groups/802/16/)

Locating a WISP

You can locate a WISP at www.bbwexchange.com/wisps.

Community Networks and Wireless User Groups

For information about community networks and wireless user groups, use the following links:

- Los Angeles, CA (www.socalwug.org)
- New York City, NY (www.nycwireless.org)
- Portland, OR (www.personaltelco.net)

- San Francisco, CA (www.bawug.org)
- Seattle, WA (www.seattlewireless.net)
- Sebastopol, CA (www.nocat.net)
- St. Louis, MO (stlwireless.net)

The following two links take you to lists of community networks:

- www.toaster.net/wireless/community.html
- www.personaltelco.net/index.cgi/WirelessCommunities

Answers to Chapter Review Questions

Answers to Chapter 1 Review Questions

1 This book defines a broadband wireless connection as any wireless connection with a bandwidth of ____.

Answer: In this book, a broadband wireless connection is defined as a wireless connection with a bandwidth of 128 kbps or faster.

2 What year did the U.S. Government first require licenses for all transmitters?

Answer: The U.S. Government first required licenses for all transmitters in 1921.

3 What year did the FCC first allow broadband wireless equipment to be used without applying for a license?

Answer: The FCC first allowed broadband wireless equipment to be used without a license in 1985.

4 What does the process of modulation do?

Answer: Modulation is the process of adding information or "intelligence" to a wireless signal.

5 Name one way that a license-free broadband wireless WAN saves money.

Answer: Deploying a broadband wireless WAN saves money because no monthly bill must be paid to an outside communications carrier, such as the telephone company.

6 Why is the real world different for every wireless link?

Answer: The real world is different for every wireless link because terrain, interference, noise, and weather are different for every wireless link at any moment in time.

7 During antenna system installation, what safety practice helps protect workers on the ground from being injured by falling objects?

Answer: Injuries to workers on the ground from falling objects can be minimized if the workers wear a protective hard hat.

8 A fall from 18 inches can cripple a person for life. True or false?

Answer: True. A fall from as little as 18 inches can cripple a person for life.

9 If you need to work in front of a wireless antenna, what should you do first?

Answer: If you need to work in front of a wireless antenna, you should first turn off any wireless equipment that is connected to that antenna.

10 Every outdoor wireless antenna system should include a lightning arrestor. True or false?

Answer: True. Every outdoor wireless antenna system should include a lighting arrestor.

Answers to Chapter 2 Review Questions

1 How does the wavelength of a wireless signal change as the frequency of the signal increases?

Answer: As the frequency of a wireless signal increases, the wavelength of the signal becomes shorter.

2 When a 2.4-GHz signal encounters an obstruction, what happens?

Answer: When a 2.4-GHz signal encounters an obstruction, some of the signal is attenuated, some of the signal is reflected, and some of the signal diffracts around the obstruction.

3 Does ionospheric reflection occur at microwave frequencies?

Answer: Ionospheric reflection generally does not occur at microwave frequencies.

4 How is wireless power measured?

Answer: Wireless power is measured using decibel (dB) ratios compared to a recognized reference level, typically 1 mW (dBm).

5 In the abbreviation dBm, what does the "m" stand for?

Answer: In dBm, the "m" stands for 1 milliwatt, or one-thousandth of one watt.

6 If 1 Watt equals +30 dBm, then 2W equals how many dBm?

Answer: 2W equals +33 dBm.

7 The main lobe of a non-isotropic antenna radiates power in which direction?

A. In one horizontal direction

B. In two horizontal directions

C. Equally in all horizontal directions

D. Both A and C

Answer: D. The main lobe of a directional antenna radiates power in only one horizontal direction. The main lobe of an omnidirectional antenna radiates power in all horizontal directions.

8 If you can stand at one antenna and see the antenna at the other end of a wireless link, do you have a line-of-sight wireless path?

Answer: If you can see the other antenna *and* if you have a clear Fresnel zone, you have a line-of-sight wireless path. If you can see the other antenna but more than 60 percent of the Fresnel zone is obstructed, you do *not* have a clear wireless line-of-sight path, even though you might have an unobstructed optical LOS path. The obstructed Fresnel zone adds additional attenuation and the wireless performance is reduced.

9 Tripling the distance on an unobstructed wireless link requires increasing the power how many times?

Answer: Tripling the distance on an unobstructed wireless link requires a power increase of three squared, or nine times, assuming LOS paths.

Answers to Chapter 3 Review Questions

1 If you have one pair of backbone locations that need to be connected, which network architecture is the most appropriate?

Answer: Point-to-point architecture.

2 What type of antenna[md]omnidirectional or directional[md]does a point-to-point network normally use?

Answer: A point-to-point network normally uses a directional antenna.

3 When a microwave signal strikes an obstruction, what *always* happens to it?

Answer: The signal is always attenuated.

4 When a point-to-point network is expanded, what architecture is usually chosen? Why?

Answer: When a point-to-point network is expanded, normally point-to-multipoint architecture is used because it is cost effective for many users and it is easily expanded.

5 Why is SNR important in a wireless network?

Answer: SNR (signal-to-noise) ratio is important because high signal strength is not enough to ensure good receiver performance. The incoming signal must be stronger than any noise or interference that is present. For example, it is possible to have high signal strength and still have poor wireless performance if there is strong interference or a high noise level.

6 What network architectures use sectors?

Answer: Point-to-multipoint architecture and cellular architecture use sectors.

7 What are the consequences of selecting the wrong access point antenna system for a point-to-multipoint network?

Answer: Selecting the wrong antenna system in a point-to-multipoint network can result in poor network performance and the need for an antenna system redesign. An incorrect antenna selection can result in low signal levels or high noise levels. Either consequence requires that the antenna system be redesigned.

8 What architecture is used to allow frequency re-use while connecting several point-to-multipoint networks?

Answer: Cellular architecture is used to allow frequency re-use while connecting several point-to-multipoint networks.

9 What is the primary disadvantage of cellular architecture?

Answer: The primary disadvantage of cellular architecture is the careful frequency planning needed to minimize interference between sectors that use the same frequency.

10 What type of network architecture can be used if end users are located close together and have partially obstructed (non-LOS) paths between each other?

Answer: If end users are located close together and have partially obstructed paths, mesh architecture can sometimes be used.

11 What type of routing does a mesh network perform?

Answer: A mesh network performs dynamic routing.

Answers to Chapter 4 Review Questions

1 A physical site survey includes determining how to route cable from the wireless equipment to the antenna. True or false?

Answer: True.

2   Before you perform a physical site survey, you should know how high above the ground your antennas need to be mounted. True or false?

Answer: True.

3   If there is already wireless equipment operating on a building, you will first discover it during your RF site survey. True or false?

Answer: False. If there is already wireless equipment operating, you should discover it by asking about it during your initial meeting with building management.

4   Minimizing the distance between your wireless equipment and your antenna system is important. Why?

Answer: Minimizing the distance between your equipment and the antenna system is important when using coax cable because the longer the coax, the higher the signal loss and the smaller the wireless coverage range.

5   If power lines run near a roof edge, is it okay to mount your antenna near that roof edge? Why or why not?

Answer: If power lines run near a roof edge, it is not okay to mount an antenna system nearby. Antenna systems must be mounted far enough away so that it is impossible for them to fall or be blown into contact with power lines.

6   What is the biggest consequence from installing a wireless system in an area with a high noise level?

Answer: The biggest consequence of installing a system in a high noise level area is a reduction in network throughput.

7   If you have a wireless protocol analyzer, then you do not need a wireless spectrum analyzer. True or false?

Answer: False. A wireless protocol analyzer can supplement but not replace a spectrum analyzer. A spectrum analyzer is still needed to observe out-of-band and non-802.11b signals.

8   If the operation of license-free equipment causes interference to the operation of licensed amateur radio equipment, the operator of the license-free equipment is responsible for correcting the interference problem. True or false?

Answer: True.

9   The length of the spectrum analyzer sampling interval doesn't tell you anything about the level of RF interference in a particular area. True or false?

Answer: False. The more quickly that interfering signals are picked up, the higher the level of RF interference in a particular area.

10 In general, the higher the signal-to-noise ratio on a wireless link, the higher the wireless throughput. True or false?

Answer: True.

11 What part of a point-to-multipoint wireless network is the most vulnerable to a high noise level? Why?

Answer: The hub site access point receiver of a point-to-multipoint network is the most vulnerable to a high noise level. Noise reduces the signal-to-noise ratio, which reduces the size of the coverage area and the throughput of the network.

Answers to Chapter 5 Review Questions

1 When comparing light energy to wireless energy, a light bulb can be compared to what antenna element?

Answer: A light bulb can be prepared to the driven element of an antenna.

2 The orientation of an antenna's E-field determines what characteristic of the antenna's operation?

Answer: The orientation of an antenna's E-field determines the polarization of the antenna.

3 Relative to each other, the E-field of a vertically polarized antenna and the E-field of a horizontally polarized antenna are what?

Answer: The E-fields of a vertically polarized antenna and a horizontally polarized antenna are cross-polarized (at right angles) with respect to one another.

4 Omnidirectional antennas are available with either vertical or horizontal polarization. True or false?

Answer: True.

5 A diversity receiving system can automatically select the best signal from one of two antennas. True or false?

Answer: True.

6 When using a diversity system, the two antennas must always be the same type and point in the same direction. True or false?

Answer: True.

7 Anyone who deploys an outdoor license-free wireless system can provide reliable wireless service. True or false?

Answer: False. Only those people who learn wireless principles and apply those principles correctly can provide reliable wireless service.

8   A strong signal arriving at your receiver from another wireless network increases your network throughput. True or false?

Answer: False. A strong signal from another network reduces the throughput on your network.

9   How much is the typical cross-polarization isolation between a horizontally polarized and a vertically polarized antenna?

Answer: The typical cross-polarization isolation between a vertically polarized and a horizontally polarized antenna is 20 dB.

10   A sectorized antenna system does not allow you to serve more end users. True or false?

Answer: False. A sectorized antenna system does allow you to serve more end users.

11   In a sectorized antenna system, all the sector antennas should be identical. True or false?

Answer: False. In a sectorized antenna system, the sector antennas do not have to be identical. The horizontal beamwidth, vertical beamwidth, gain, and polarization of each sector antenna should be chosen to best meet the needs of that sector.

12   Sector antennas in a sectorized antenna system should always be mounted perfectly vertical. True or false?

Answer: False. Sector antennas should be mounted with a downtilt angle that maximizes sector coverage and reduces interference from outside the sector.

Answers to Chapter 6 Review Questions

1   Why is it important to visit an actual deployment site before you purchase wireless equipment?

Answer: It is important to visit actual deployment sites to learn about unpublished equipment interactions and unknown operational characteristics.

2   The electromagnetic waves that we call wireless exist at what layer of the seven-layer OSI reference model?

Answer: Electromagnetic waves exist at Layer 1, the physical layer.

3   How is a packet like a hamburger sandwich?

Answer: A packet is like a hamburger sandwich because the meat (the data payload) is sandwiched in the bun (packet management and control information).

4   Why does a wireless network need a big MAC?

Answer: A wireless network needs a big MAC layer because the MAC must deal successfully with management of all the invisible and unpredictable wireless-related issues.

5   Wireless bandwidth and wireless throughput are the same thing. True or false?

Answer: False. Wireless bandwidth and wireless throughput are not the same. Wireless throughput is always less than the specified wireless bandwidth.

6   The communications range under NLOS conditions is about the same as the communications range under LOS conditions. True or false?

Answer: False. The communications range under NLOS conditions is always less than the communications range under LOS conditions.

7   DSSS equipment hops from frequency to frequency. True or false?

Answer: False. DSSS equipment does not change frequency. FHSS equipment changes frequency.

8   Other things being equal, the higher the data rate, the shorter the communications distance. True or false?

Answer: True

9   If you start receiving interference from another network, the best thing to do is to get an amplifier. True or false?

Answer: False. When interference is high, an amplifier usually makes conditions worse. The best response is either to coordinate frequencies or to redesign your antenna system to minimize the effects of the interference.

10   Any 802.11b equipment works with any other 802.11b equipment. True or false?

Answer: False. Most 802.11b equipment works together; however, you can experience a number of incompatibilities if you fail to test thoroughly.

Answers to Chapter 7 Review Questions

1   A site survey is normally performed immediately after a wireless installation is completed. True or false?

Answer: False. A site survey is normally performed before installation.

2   Anyone can install wireless antennas on radio towers as long as they are not afraid of heights. True or false?

Answer: False. No one should install antennas on radio towers unless he has been properly and professionally trained to work on towers. The installer also needs to be equipped with the proper tools and be covered by the proper insurance.

3   At microwave frequencies, the signal loss in coax cable is relatively high. True or false?

Answer: True.

4 A typical lightning strike produces a peak current of approximately how many amps?

Answer: A typical lightning strike produces a peak current of approximately 18,000 amps.

5 Fading is normal for microwave signals. What term is used to describe the extra signal power that every microwave link needs to overcome this fading?

Answer: The term that describes the extra signal needed to overcome microwave fading is the fade margin.

6 What should you do immediately after you test the throughput on a newly installed wireless link?

Answer: After testing the throughput of a new wireless link, you should document the results.

7 Name one advantage of standardizing on only a few customer premise equipment packages.

Answer: Standardizing on only a few CPE packages lowers your inventory costs. In addition, it lowers your support costs.

8 If your job responsibilities require you to work regularly in high-RF environments, you should use what piece of personal protective equipment?

Answer: If your job responsibilities require you to work regularly in high-RF environments, you should use a personal RF monitor that provides an audible warning when RF levels exceed safety thresholds.

Answers to Chapter 8 Review Questions

1 For reliable network operation, signal strength is more important than SNR. True or false?

Answer: False. SNR is more important than signal strength.

2 A reliable wireless link needs a line-of-sight path and an unobstructed Fresnel zone. True or false?

Answer: True.

3 Will the noise level always be low in a rural area?

Answer: Not necessarily. Noise in a rural area might be low or it might be high.

4 How many nonoverlapping 2.4 GHz channels are available for use in the United States?

Answer: There are three nonoverlapping channels.

5 The consequence of a low SNR is reduced network throughput. True or false?

Answer: True.

6 Reusing a DSSS frequency at the same AP location requires how many decibels of antenna isolation?

Answer: Reusing the same frequency in the same location requires approximately 121 dB of antenna isolation.

7 To avoid interference, collocated FHSS sectors should use different hopping sequences and different hopping sets. True or false?

Answer: False. Collocated FHSS sectors should use different hopping sequences within the same hopping set.

8 When is the SNR highest at an AP?

Answer: The SNR is the highest just after the AP has been installed. As time passes, the noise level increases and the SNR goes down.

9 When the percentage of retransmitted packets reaches 20 percent, you should start looking for the cause of the network slowdown. True or false?

Answer: False. The network performance starts to slow down when the retransmit percentage goes above 10 percent. Start looking for the cause when the retransmit percentage goes above 10 percent.

10 Explain why it is necessary to write down the results of your noise-reduction efforts.

Answer: It is necessary to write down the results of your noise-reduction efforts so that you don't waste time repeating the same tests the next time a noise problem occurs.

Answers to Chapter 9 Review Questions

1 A WISP is an extension of a wired ISP. True or false?

True.

2 WISPs have been around since about 1995. True or false?

True.

3 The most profitable wireless markets are those where broadband DSL and cable Internet access are already available. True or false?

False. The most profitable wireless markets are those where DSL and cable Internet access are not available.

4 The mobile market where users stay connected while driving around is the easiest market to serve. True or false?

False. The mobile market is the hardest to serve.

5 Customers pay you to deliver bandwidth, not throughput. True or false?

False. Customers pay you to deliver throughput.

6 You can be successful in the wireless business even if you don't understand the meaning of decibels. True or false?

False. To be successful in the wireless business, you must understand how to work with decibels.

7 All 802.11b equipment brands work with all other 802.11b equipment brands with no problems. True or false?

False. Often, software incompatibilities result in equipment that does not work well together.

8 Why do wireless collisions reduce throughput?

Collisions reduce throughput because each collision wastes a time slot that could have carried useful traffic.

9 The higher the percentage of retransmitted packets, the lower the network throughput. True or false?

True.

10 You should always sell all the throughput that your network is capable of delivering. True or false?

False. You should leave some throughput unsold to be sure that your network does not crash if heavy interference suddenly develops.

11 The best way to deal with a WISP competitor is to add an amplifier. True or false?

False. The best way to deal with a WISP competitor is to meet with him and propose that you both cooperate and coordinate.

INDEX

Numerics

A

C

D

J-L

M

O

P

2614991

Made in the USA